THE EDGE OF PANIC

THE EDGE OF PANIC

MARILYN EDWARDS

Library of Congress Control Number:		2012919806
ISBN:	Softcover	978-1-4797-3741-3
	Ebook	978-1-4797-3742-0

This book was printed in the United States of America.

To order additional copies of this book, contact:
Xlibris Corporation
1-888-795-4274
www.Xlibris.com
Orders@Xlibris.com
121115

For Susie

Chapter One

Dawn Preston knew the graduation ceremony would accentuate the loss of two of her best friends, but she also knew to cancel accepting her diploma in person would break her mother's heart.

She tried to feel as she listened to the speeches, waiting with the class of '68—waiting to walk with earned pride to receive what they had spent countless hours studying for, striving ceaselessly for excellence, looking to the future with hope and anticipation, some with a dream in their hearts.

It had been fun, yes, right up until that late October night.

January 5, 1965

Fourteen-year-old Christi Temple shook the dice, and then tossed them onto the Monopoly board. She picked up her little silver car, haltingly skipped eight spaces, evading Mike's Boardwalk landing safely on 'Go'.

With a relieved sigh, she held out her hand for her big brother, Dave, to present her with two hundred dollars.

Lightening flashed and thunder sounded in the distance, the lights flickered, threatening to plunge them into darkness. Christi wouldn't mind, she loved to sleep during storms, except that it was past time for their parents to be home.

"Wonder what's keeping Mom and Dad," Christi said.

She watched Mike shake the dice in one hand, his eyes scanning the board. Hotels liberally sprinkled the properties with cash in short supply on both sides. This role of the dice could leave him a bankrupt loser.

"Well, you never know," Dave said his blue eyes alight with amusement. "Dad could call any minute and say they decided to spend another night."

"Yeah, right." Christi gave him a playfully peevish look.

He had stayed with them for the weekend while their parents were out of town. Dave knew they wouldn't miss her and Mike's birthday.

"Come on Mike, throw the dice!"

The distraction of this lengthy game of Monopoly would soon come to an end, hopefully, right now. Christi held her breath as Mike rolled the dice, then clapped her hands, bouncing in her chair when he landed his scruffy little doggie on Pennsylvania Avenue.

"Everyone loves a cheerful winner," Dave teased.

"Call me cheerful," Christi said delightedly.

She picked up her property card prepared to relieve Mike of everything he had bought since the start of the game. He moaned theatrically, she giggled, and unexpectedly, the doorbell chimed.

Wondering who would be arriving at their home at this late hour, Christi followed close behind her twin as he went to open the front door.

She gazed at the two young police officers standing on the porch. Her eyes zeroed in on the packages in the taller man's hands, one pink, the other blue, the traditional wrapping of her and Mike's birthday gifts.

As she glanced back at Dave, he stood and quickly approached them.

"What's this about?" he asked.

"I'm Officer Jamison." The one holding the packages introduced himself. "I'm sorry to inform you—there was an accident." He paused, emitting a weary sigh. "Your parents' car went over a cliff."

"Then we have to go to the hospital," Christi said anxiously. "They're in the hospital, right?" Looking at the packages, her eyes filled with tears.

"No." His expression held compassion. "We're sorry for your loss," he offered. "It might help to know—it was fast—they didn't suffer."

Christi stood indecisively trying to reject what he had said before she turned away from the sympathetic gazes of the officers.

Mike called out as she retreated down the carpeted hallway to her room, but she could not stop. If she stood there looking at the two nice officers with compassion all over their faces, she would have to believe them.

She threw herself onto the bed crying hard, racking sobs. Running had not let her escape the piercing truth, bitter reality washed over her in painful waves. They didn't suffer? How could he know they didn't suffer?

And what could he know about them to be sorry for their loss? Those were only words meant to comfort at a time when comfort could not be found.

"Chris—" Dave tapped on the door. She chose not to answer, and he knocked more incessantly, at last jiggling the knob. "Christi, open the door."

"Go away," she cried. "I want my daddy!"

"We need each other, Christine. You can't go through this alone."

The use of her full name drew her to reluctant obedience. She sat up slowly, shuffling unenthusiastically to the door, but when she unlocked it, Christi flung the door open throwing herself into his arms.

"Nothing has ever hurt this bad, Dave. Mom and Daddy aren't coming home." She looked up into soft blue eyes, the exact color of her daddy's.

"I know, baby. I know." He held her in his arms for a calming moment.

They walked into the living room where Mike sat on the sofa looking so forlorn it tore at her heart. They joined him there, Dave between them, one arm around her, the other around Mike.

She put her head on Dave's shoulder, feeling lost in despair.

"How could this happen?" Mike said, tears in his young voice. "I don't understand—why something like this would happen!"

"I don't know why, Mike," Dave said, hoarsely. "I can't think—I can't—"

Christi lifted her tear streaked face. Seeing tears shimmering in his blue eyes, she tore her gaze away from his sorrow.

"I wish I had the answers you need, but I don't—I don't understand," he said hoarsely. "They gave a lot and our loss is great, but they raised us to be strong—and we are."

"Is it all right to cry when you're strong?" Mike asked doubtfully, his eyes filled with barely irrepressible tears.

Dave reassured Mike, and then softly cleared his throat.

"I have to leave now—for a while," he said. "I have to go identify—to make legal identification—"

Christi felt a light shudder pass over his body and threw her arms around his neck giving him a tight hug. She wanted to hold him there, to never let him go, wanted to keep both her brothers safe in her sight.

"I'll be back as soon as I can," he said, gently disengaging her arms. "Do you want me to call someone to be with you?"

"We'll be okay," Mike said. "We have each other. We're okay."

"Are we okay Mike?" she asked after Dave left.

"Sure we are." He took a shuddering breath and tried to smile.

"We don't have any parents. We're alone."

"We're not alone. We have Dave."

"He's only twenty, Mike." Her voice trembled.

"Almost twenty-one, he won't let us down, believe me, okay?"

"Okay, I'll believe you," she agreed, without further doubt.

When Dave returned home he embraced them. He solemnly told them that it would be a closed coffin memorial service.

Neighbors brought food and condolences, but the many offers of support barely penetrated the desperate grief Christi felt.

Reverend Caldwell dropped by with seasoned words meant to comfort. Preston residents had been generous he said, presenting a check to Dave.

He told them donations were still forthcoming, assuring them that the memorial service and all other expenses would be covered.

Even that meant little to Christi. She had no comprehension of the costs, only that her mother would never tuck her into bed again, her dad would never kiss her forehead and tell her 'sweet dreams'.

She floundered helplessly, lost in memories, denial and acceptance, that she would never hear them laugh again, they would never go to the circus or a carnival; picnics, birthday parties, going to the beach, all the carefree, happy times—cut short.

The day of the funeral dawned overcast with misty rain. Christi felt forlorn and panicky, alone in a crowd of people.

She stared at the closed coffins amidst the lovely floral arrangements in the solemn funeral home lost in grief. Her parents were in those decorative boxes—she could only view her mother's delicate beauty, and the strong, handsome face of her dad, in the pictures displayed and within her heart.

At the cemetery, lightening flashed, thunder roiled across a gray and threatening sky. She and Mike approached their mother's coffin. They placed a rose on it, then on their father's. Her chest heaved as she struggled to keep from sobbing.

Mike reached for her hand holding tight, still, existence seemed a dreadful endeavor, livid with fear. Dave walked up behind them putting his arms around both their shoulders. The day remained dark and threatening, but she felt safe.

The next few days passed in a haze of sorrow. Christi didn't want to go back to school. She wanted to curl up in a miserable little ball and hide from the world. How could she face the carefree gaiety of the other students? How could she ever again? Her life would never be the same; there remained a vast emptiness that nothing could fill.

Dave gave them a week, indulgent of their grief, but on the following Monday, they returned to school. She began to function in this strange new existence without her parents.

With each waking day she felt pain, but as each day passed, it became easier to face the sunrise, laughter returned to her world.

"You've got a crush on Dawn," Christi sang the words with cheerful hilarity. She had caught him looking at Dawn Preston with puppy-dog eyes.

"Dawn's a conceited little snot," Mike replied, not one bit ruffled.

"Well, maybe so, but—you've got a crush on Dawn!"

"She's a Little Miss Priss." Mike could barely curb his laughter.

Dave interrupted their lighthearted bickering. "I have to talk to you."

Christi tossed her books on a chair. She looked at Mike, then back at Dave with an uncomfortable queasy feeling in her stomach. She sank onto the sofa next to Mike, watching Dave, fearfully expectant. He quietly told them that their home and anything of value was soon to be sold at auction.

"Mr. Harris, Dad's lawyer called this morning. He doesn't like it, but there's nothing he can do." Dave ran nervous fingers through his hair, a gesture Christi had noticed he used a lot lately. "Apparently there was a lot of debt, but Mr. Harris assured me this will take care of it."

"They're taking our home?"

"They're taking everything, Christi. Everything here of any value is no longer ours." He sighed helplessly. "I'm sorry, honey."

Christi viewed the room with renewed pain, each piece of furniture handpicked by her mother, not a room of furniture bought at a glance, but carefully selected for their home with time, effort, and love.

Her eyes rested on the intricately carved Cherry Wood Curio cabinet housing sparkling full-lead crystal statuettes and dainty hand painted figurines that could appear so real to an imaginative heart, exquisite visions of fantasy.

Cinderella danced with Prince Charming on a mirrored floor, Prince Philip knelt at the bed of Sleeping Beauty, ready to wake her with the magic kiss.

On another level, a mermaid lounged on a large rock protruding from the sea depths, and Merlin stood boldly before a hovering dragon. In another setting, a young maiden petted a unicorn beneath a shade tree and Pegasus reared proudly, wings spread, his legs up ready to take flight. How precious were these pieces?

The statuettes were expressions of her mother's love of fantasies and fairytales, but each enchanting one had monetary value. No other values mattered. Tears filled her eyes and trickled down her cheeks.

Everything would go to the highest bidder, be sold to strangers.

"There will be insurance money eventually, but for now, well, apparently they're questioning the accident. Mr. Harris said its pending investigation." Dave sighed wearily. "It's going to be tied up for a long time."

"What do you mean?" she asked, bewildered at this revelation.

"They're saying Dad did it." Mike stood up belligerently. "That he killed himself and Mom because his business was failing. That's it, isn't it?" he demanded. "That's what they're saying. Well, he didn't!"

Dave held Mike close, his anger subsiding into tears of frustration.

Christi joined in the embrace. She didn't know how they would make it, only that they would survive this difficult time together.

A week later they moved into an apartment on South Street. She brooded in the dumpy three-bedroom apartment and could only regard it as ugly and depressing.

The living room was large enough, but her bedroom was half the size of the one at home. There was only one deep sink in a kitchen/ dining room, featuring a large window, and a door that opened onto a fire escape, both presenting a splendid view of the apartment building across the alley.

Christi hated the apartment. She hated the noise from outside the grimy windows. She would never, *ever* consider this place home.

She wanted her pretty pink and white bedroom with soft pastel carpeting, the spacious backyard with trees and flowers and birds singing, but she wanted her mom and daddy more than anything. The loss of her childhood home brought on a fresh surge of grief from which to recover.

One evening, not long after moving into the Southside dump, as she regarded it, after a supper of leftover pizza and soda pop, Dave gazed somewhat despairingly at them from where he sat across the table.

Christi knew something else had gone terribly wrong. Dave walked listlessly to the ancient buffet, turned off the small radio abruptly silencing the Rolling Stones, then sat back down and softly cleared his throat.

"What is it?" Mike said.

"I don't know how to tell you this, kids—I've been trying to think of a way to tell you—there's just no easy way—"

"You're right," Mike said weakly. "There's never an easy way."

"Uncle Joe wants you, Mike. He's already filed for legal custody. He and Aunt Jenny want to adopt you."

Christi stared at the chipped white/yellow veneered tabletop. One part of her mind contemplated how she hated it while she slowly comprehended the soft-spoken words. She felt hysterical laughter growing like a bubble ready to burst and swallowed hard, a tear slid down her face. They wanted Mike, but of course they had no need of another girl.

"We knew it would come to this, didn't we? We knew I wouldn't be allowed to keep you forever, right?"

"What about Chris?" Mike's eyes flashed in her direction.

"Maybe I can keep Chris, if not, Social Services will find a good family."

Mike began slowly shaking his head.

"We can be reunited later—when you're older."

"No!" His chair tipped over as he pushed away from the table.

Christi started to follow, but Dave stopped her. "Give him a few minutes," he suggested. Then he sighed deeply bowing his head.

"David?" Christi looked at him feeling uneasy. She had never seen him so dispirited. "We've lost everything. Are we gonna lose each other, too?"

He raised his eyes, his expression changing. "We won't let it happen," he said with swift resolve. "I'll call Mr. Harris tomorrow."

Christi threw her arms around his neck giving him a big hug.

"Go get Mike," he said with a wide smile. "Let's talk!"

The next morning Dave called Mr. Harris's law office. He explained their situation to the receptionist.

"One moment, please."

"Hello, David," Mr. Harris said about five minutes later. "Julia briefed me. I understand you want to fight for legal custody of your siblings?"

"That's right."

"Okay," he said slowly. "I'll only need to see you one time before court. Stop by the office on Monday at nine a.m.—What your uncle is trying to do is naively cruel, David. I knew your parents, and I know they wouldn't want this. I'll be doing this pro bono, in memory of them."

"Thank you, sir."

Their day in court seemed encouraging enough, Mr. Harris had been convincing, but the weeks following dragged slowly by. The waiting had taken a toll on Christi's high spirits.

Mrs. Doro, a court appointed Social Worker, invaded their home and privacy at any given time, took notes as she watched their interaction, and discussed them with people in the apartment building.

Now that they had reached the end of those desperate weeks, everything she had kept bottled up inside suddenly erupted as she imagined the worst.

Christi stood outside the school waiting for Mike, crying and sniffling.

Dawn Preston glanced at her, started to walk on, but paused with a look of concern. "I recognize you—you're Christi Temple. I read about you in the human-interest section of the paper," she explained. "I'm sorry about what happened, it was—a tragedy. I'm Dawn, by the way."

Christi gave her a quizzical look. Dawn Preston, resident rich girl, cute, perky, and most popular, had actually spoken to her, and she wasn't simply 'Dawn, by the way', she was 'Dawn, by the way, *everybody* knows who I am.'

"You read the paper?" Christi asked dazedly.

"Mom says I have to broaden my academic social civic-science-something or other," she said elaborately. "But I think she mostly wants me to keep up on current events."

Dawn pulled a tissue from her purse. "It's pretty cool that your brother wants to keep you together. Here blow," she said tersely. "Now, chin up kiddo. It'll be all right. If he can't keep you—well, that's just unacceptable; don't even think such a deplorable thought. You'll win, *just know it.*"

"Right, no worries here." Christi blew her nose as discreetly as possible. She stuffed the tissue deep into her jeans pocket. "There would never have been a problem, if it wasn't for Uncle Joe. Does he really think Mike would be better off with him and Aunt Jenny, and their five bratty daughters? I can imagine *that*—Mike would go berserk."

They fell in step together, walking down Union Avenue.

"At least the waiting is done," she added. "We'll find out tomorrow."

"You're not very hopeful," Dawn said unhappily, looking bleakly at her tear-stained face.

"I'm scared to death." Christi sighed tiredly. "Mike says Mrs. Doro is on our side now, but I can't tell. She always looks the same to me."

"Give me a call and let me know how it goes, okay?" She wrote her number on a piece of scrap paper.

"Sure." Christi placed the slip of paper in her math book as Mike walked up to them.

They waved, going separate ways, Dawn turning onto Woodland Drive, she and Mike keeping straight on Union.

At court the next day, Mrs. Doro said the words that proved once more that Mike's perception could be trusted.

"It is my qualified recommendation that the minor children be left in the temporary custody of their brother, David Temple. I commend his devotion to their welfare and see no need to remove them from the home at this time."

Christi listened carefully as the judge explained how they would be living on a trial basis. Barring any incidents, they would return to court in one year and their case would be closed. The list of regulations didn't faze Christi, but she didn't like it much when the judge said they would be obligated to the standards of a court appointed social worker.

She noticed Dave seemed deep in thought on the drive home. Once they entered the apartment, he indicated the sofa.

"I need the two of you to sit and listen to what I have to say."

Christi and Mike obediently took a seat. He paced a couple of times before taking a stand, gazing at them in quiet contemplation, looking almost intimidating, regarding them, it seemed, somewhat unfavorably.

"You have to understand that I'm your guardian, guys, I can't be your babysitter." Dave walked a few more restless paces before he paused again to gaze at them with a look that had reverted to an expression of solemn concern. "If you have to go before the judge, it's all over for us."

He then proceeded to remind them of the things the judge had already made perfectly clear, words she didn't need to hear again.

"I will need serious cooperation from both of you," he finished.

Christi glanced at Mike for solace, but his face looked darkly sullen. She had never seen such a brooding expression on her twin.

"Yes, serious cooperation and strict obedience," Dave said apparently not quite finished. His tone held a touch of severity that seemed unwarranted, besides being so contrasting to his nature. "Unlike most kids, you can't make even one mistake."

Christi stared down at her clasped hands feeling mixed emotions. Dave had never been so uncompromising, and it wasn't fair, still she tried to rationalize it by acknowledging the grave responsibility of two teenagers.

"Now, I understand that you're young and want to have fun, but having fun is out of the question. Are we clear on that?"

When she looked back at him, his whole face spread into a smile. He reached down to gently tug one of her long, blonde braids.

"I'm kidding, all right! You've never been in trouble a day in your lives. Just go on being yourselves."

"David!" Christi shrieked. "You really had me goin'. Don't you ever do that again!"

Christi looked at Mike, he nodded, and they tackled him as he made a run for the door. In the midst of what should have been carefree fun with her brothers, during the revelry of a lighthearted wrestling match, she felt the weight of an uncertain year ahead, somewhere in the back of her mind an awareness of a degree of truth in Dave's pretentious speech.

Dave finally yelled 'uncle', then again he yelled 'uncle', and then he yelled 'pizza!'

"Pepperoni and mushrooms!"

"Hot peppers and jalapenos!"

"You got it, you little hellions."

They sat on the living room floor laughing. In that instant, the weight lifted, Christi knew somehow they'd make it.

Chapter Two

Christi sat by the soft glow of a table lamp trying to get through another chapter of *Mysterious Happenings.* The suspense thriller usually sparked her interest with every turn of the page, but it became increasingly difficult to concentrate as the large wall clock across the room ticked away the minutes while she waited impatiently for Mike's return out of the night.

She checked the time again, almost two a.m.

Street sounds drifted up to the second floor apartment. Some of the people in the building hung around out front half the night laughing and shouting with music blaring.

Car horns, squealing brakes and occasional police sirens were all part of living on the south side of Preston City, California.

Her friend, Dawn Preston didn't live very far away in terms of distance. Once she turned the corner off Union, onto Woodland Drive, only a moderately long walk remained, but it led to a different world. Dawn lived at the top of a gently sloping hill.

The serene neighborhood, the wide tree-lined sidewalks and quiet streets, was a wonderland to Christi. The homes on Woodland Drive were mansions surrounded by spacious lawns with beautiful landscaping, patios out back and fenced in pools.

She had given up trying to understand why Dawn had singled her out for a friendship. More than a year separated them in age, and they lived worlds apart in every other way—she heard someone enter the apartment, interrupting her thoughts. The door quietly closed, a floorboard squeaked. "Oops."

"Mike?"

She marked her page, placing the book on the end table as her brother, holding onto the doorframe for support, peeked around at her.

"Chris, why aren't you in bed?"

"I couldn't sleep. I was worried about you."

"You were worried about me?" He seemed bewildered at first by the simple statement, but then favored her with a lopsided grin. "Aw, that's sweet, but no need to worry about me, I'm fine."

"Easier said than not done," she admonished. "I feel the need."

"Easier said, than not done!" He chuckled. "That's cute."

"I'm not trying to be cute, Mike," she told him. "Can't you understand that this is important?"

"Now Chrissie—don't be so serious minded."

"You were out *late*. I was worried."

"Yeah, but—you my sweet little sixteen sister—worry so *easily*." He grinned at her staid look. "Now, you got-to ad-mit, in many in-sentences-in-senses—in men-y in-sten-sez—you do have a tenancy to—over-err-re-act."

Christi shook her head, scarcely able to keep a discontented expression, not wanting to encourage him with laughter at his antics.

"I don't think this is one of them," she managed.

He frowned, seeming to think hard on what she said. Then he wrinkled his nose and made a quick retreat, heading for the shelter of his bedroom.

She turned the lamp off before walking slowly to her room, troubled by a sense of foreboding that slipped away leaving an explicit, uneasy afterthought, *The Cobras*—a Southside gang that was too close to home.

Christi stared into the darkness unable to sleep. How could she expect Mike to understand? Sixteen-year-old boys did not want anyone worrying about them. She felt some concern for Dave, but not so much.

Their mother had been a romantic at heart. She and Mike were like her in many ways. Dave had their father's personality, a more assertive manner that she deeply appreciated. Christi knew if he had not been strong, that without those inherent characteristics, there would have been more unnecessary pain when their parents died. Thoughtless relatives wanted to adopt Mike. They would have been separated and placed miles apart.

Dave had served two years in the military immediately after graduating. He had been home for only a few months when they were orphaned.

An ache rose inside with the memory of that stormy January night when two police officers knocked on their door to tell them their parents, who were late returning from a business trip, would never arrive.

Their car had gone out of control, plunged over a steep cliff, down into a deep ravine killing them both instantly. The car had been totaled. Strangely enough, their gifts were undamaged. Weeks later, they were finally able to open the packages to discover a heart-shaped clock for her and a watch for Mike.

Tears gathered in her eyes with the painful memory, but subsided as her thoughts turned back to Dave and Mike, to the first year when the aftereffects of their parents' deaths had brought them even closer as they clung to each other for comfort and courage.

First, due to questionable circumstances regarding the insurance policy, they lost the home they grew up in and everything familiar. Then Dave had to fight a custody battle for Mike because their uncle wanted to adopt him.

After a six-week trial period, the social worker recommended a conditional term, and the judge ruled in their favor. He accepted that if they could meet the requirements set by the court, and the adequate environment set by the social worker, they would return to court in one year and their case would be closed.

Mrs. Dora stopped by quite frequently during that year, and they all pitched in to convince her she had made the right recommendation. They survived the challenging year, but their newfound freedom had brought on some extremely difficult conditions.

Dave had taken up with the Cobras, and John Burton, known troublemaker. She hated his relentless superior leer.

Dave didn't bring him around often, but when he was with John, he seemed remote, and when she asked about the pills she found in his pocket while sorting clothes, he told her, nonchalantly, that he would take care of his own laundry from now on. John was having an adverse effect on her big brother.

Christi finally drifted into a restless sleep. She woke up before dawn, turned over with sleepy determination, but awoke a second time at almost seven.

It seemed useless to even try to go back to sleep, but when she sat up, sufficient grogginess discouraged her getting out of bed. She fell gratefully back against her pillow drifting swiftly back into dreamland.

Christi opened her eyes. She glanced at the clock on her bedside table. Twelve-thirty! She never slept that late—but she felt wonderful for it.

Her thoughts preoccupied with various scenarios on how to approach Mike about her concerns, Christi took a quick shower, and then headed to the kitchen for coffee. After a while Mike came in. Straddling a chair, he sat with his arms folded on its back. He looked at her through mournful blue eyes.

"What did you want to talk to me about?" he finally asked.

After a moment, he tilted his head. "You're thinking way too long on this," he said with a tolerant sigh. "Lay it on me."

"Okay, I'm worried about you," she told him candidly. "You didn't used to stay out so late, and I never know where you are anymore."

She caught a glimpse of exasperation on his youthful face.

"I know what you're gonna say, but you're only sixteen, barely sixteen. That's just a day over fifteen as a matter of fact, happy birthday."

"Happy birthday yourself," he said with an easy smile. "Like I said, you don't have to worry about me. I don't miss school, still makin' those grades, right? Lighten up, Chris. You're sixteen—be sixteen, okay?"

"Be sixteen? You be sixteen." Christi pointed a finger, snatching it back when he grabbed for it. "You were drinking last night. You were drunk," she accused.

"You must be kidding. You are kidding? You're not—"

"Kidding? No, I'm not. This is my very serious expression."

"I wasn't drunk, I was teasing," he said, looking completely innocent.

She didn't intend to let him get away with his easy nonchalance.

"Are you getting involved with the Cobras?"

He met her eyes, tried to look remorseful, but gave up with a cute little quirk of his eyebrow. "I guess I should have told you." He came clean, much too casually, about his involvement with men like John Burton.

"I should have known," she said. "I did know!"

"You don't know what you think you know."

"Don't ever accuse me of not knowing what I think I know, when I know what I know—and I know—" As her words faltered into silence, he grinned mischievously.

"What do you know little sister?"

"How'd you do that?" she asked suspiciously. "I know one thing for sure, Jon Michael, you have no business hanging out with that bunch of delinquents. You do realize you're the only juvenile among them?"

"That's a sneaky way of calling me a juvenile delinquent, Sis. I am seriously wounded. Anyway, the guys aren't so bad."

"I doubt that."

"How can you doubt what you don't know?"

"There you go again! And delinquent is a mild word for them. Even you know that. John Burton is—"

"Is the exception," he interjected. "John and his lackeys *are* the exception," Mike stressed at her raised brow. "None of them have ever been arrested."

"Which proves they can evade the police?"

"Good one, Sis."

"And what about that other gang—the Monarchs?"

"I don't know what you've heard but there's no rivalry. They stay on their side of town and we stay on ours," he said with a dismissive shrug.

Leaving her wondering, Mike sauntered over to the refrigerator.

She couldn't believe his indifference. "I've heard about Billy Cole. You could get hurt or even killed."

"Nobody's gonna kill anybody," he assured her good-naturedly.

"That's encouraging."

"You are much too judgmental." Mike opened a soda, started to take a drink, but lowered the bottle with a speculative glance.

"I am not," she mumbled grudgingly.

"I like hanging out at the Basement," he stressed defensively. "It rocks—I meet girls there. Why don't you come down and check it out?" he suggested.

"Not likely."

"Why not?" he challenged with an artful lifting of one brow, which almost made her burst out laughing. "Scared it might take care of your silly notions?"

"My silly notions?" Christi narrowed her eyes, trying to give her teasing brother a distinctly demeaning look. It was difficult, he was such a cutup.

"Sorry to insult your notions," he said, eyes twinkling.

"That wouldn't change anything, anyway."

"Sure it will," he insisted. "You'll see what good little boys they are and ease your worried mind. So, what ya say?" He gently pinched her cheek. "You know, you want to."

"I don't know that I want to, but maybe later," she conceded, hardly able to repress a smile. "I have homework, and you do, too, if you would do it!"

"I can't be bothered with homework. I'm part genius, you know." He made a ridiculously silly face before heading out the door.

Christi sighed. She knew he did his homework during homeroom and study hall. He just breezed through it. It didn't seem fair that with so little effort, his grades remained excellent.

She gathered her books. Christi met Dawn at the prearranged time, on the corner where Woodland Drive turned onto Union. The two girls walked together toward the Preston City Public Library.

Everything about her friend impressed Christi, beginning with her dispassion to her name adorning various places in town, like the Preston City Public Library. Dawn's forefathers had founded their town. She and her mother were beyond rich. Dawn never said it, but everybody knew it.

The two girls were about as opposite as any two individuals could be. Dawn kept her auburn hair to a length just below her shoulders with bangs that nearly reached her emerald green eyes. A sprinkling of freckles across Dawn's nose gave her an endearing little girl look, when her face was free of make-up.

Christi wore her waist-length blonde hair parted in the middle, or sometimes in a high ponytail. Her violet blue eyes viewed the world from a clear, tanned complexion. At five foot-six, Christi acknowledged that her figure had not caught up with her height, while Dawn stood a petite five-four, with a shape that drew admiring glances.

On top of everything else Dawn had going for her, she had a disarming, natural sophistication. She also had a touch of the wild side, a reckless yearning that couldn't be camouflage with all the sophistication in the world.

"Mike's joined the Cobras," Christi confided. "I found out this morning, he's been hanging out at the Basement. First Dave and now Mike, I don't know what to do," she moaned theatrically. "It's making me crazy!"

"Has he joined the Cobras, or is he just hanging out at the Basement?" Dawn suggested. "Mike's a fun guy, but I think he's fairly levelheaded for a kid."

"What makes you think so? He's drinking, Dawn. *Drinking!* Sixteen years old, and he was tipsy last night. I hope it's only drinking." She had a horrible thought. "What if he gets the urge to experiment with drugs?"

Dawn gave a sympathetic sigh, but then her attitude changed.

"This is Mike, Chris," she said, as if that alone should dispel all her worries. "Level headed, remember? He won't do anything so ditzy. He probably likes hanging out at the Basement cause it's cool. You'll just have to trust him."

"I do. You're right—I hope. You probably are," she agreed tentatively.

Christi gave her a shrewd look. "Hey, you called him a kid. What's up with that? That means you called me a kid!"

"Oh that." She gestured indifferently. "Just an expression. I'm only a year older," Dawn said slowly. "And just between you and me, I think he's the coolest guy in school, most certainly the coolest sixteen year old."

"Really?" Christi tried to see it. "You drawing designs on my brother?"

"It's just a crush," Dawn said diffidently. "But I don't want anyone else to know," she added. "People would talk."

"Yes, it would definitely cause some controversy among our superiors and *your peers*." Christi struck a pose with one hand behind her head, the other on her hip, while coyly fluttering her eyelashes. She giggled, resuming walking. "You're one of the glowing debutantes, and he's just a poor boy."

"Don't call me that. I hate it."

"I was just kidding." Christi glanced at her friend, hardly able to stifle a laugh. "*Sor-ry*."

"You better be."

"Anyway, you don't act a bit snooty or arrogant for an uptown girl."

"Thanks for that, I think." Dawn gave her a mock warning look, and then they both laughed as she conceded to the tag of uptown girl with good humor.

Once in the library, they studiously did their homework with hardly a break for subdued idle chatter under the stern eye of Mrs. Jillian. Christi stifled a giggle as they received another warning glimpse from the librarian.

After two hours, with brief intervals of quizzing each other, interrupted by occasional boy-talk, Christi closed the dreaded history book.

"Well, I'm finished." She stacked her books. "You quizzed me well on that history test. I think I'll ace it."

"I'm sure you will." Dawn was fishing in her purse for something.

"I'm finished, too, but before we leave." She held out a small gift-wrapped box topped with a tiny pink bow. "Happy birthday."

"Oh, what's this?" Christi smiled happily.

She removed the adorable little bow before excitedly tearing the wrapping off to reveal a red velvet casing. She glanced at her friend, then back at the telltale jewelry box, waiting a few anticipating seconds before lifting the top to gaze at the gems within.

"Diamonds?" she murmured, staring in wonderment, overwhelmed by Dawn's generosity.

"Come on," Dawn said smiling happily. "They're not very big diamonds."

"Not very big? Dawn, they're beautiful."

Christi removed the simple earrings she had received with the piercing of her ears to replace them with the precious gift.

"You sparkle very nicely," Dawn complimented.

"Thank you, but I wish you wouldn't have."

"You really wish I wouldn't have?" She gave her a compact. "Have a look."

"No, I don't wish you wouldn't have," she admitted tilting her head slightly as she checked out her reflection. "Oh, they're gorgeous! I couldn't hope to get you anything to compare."

"Let me see, what could you get for the girl who has everything?" After a thoughtful moment her mouth curved in an impish grin. "How about a kiss from that handsome brother of yours?"

"Get real, Dawn—Dave's too old for you!"

"I was referring to Mike."

"The sixteen year old?" She looked baffled, a clearly over zealous expression of confusion.

"Sure, what's wrong with a little crush? Just don't tell him," she added.

"Then how do you expect to get a kiss?" she asked flabbergasted.

"I don't, did you think I was serious?"

"In a word, 'yes', and I'm very sure you'll get your kiss. But don't worry, I won't say a thing."

"You're gonna tell him!" Dawn charged, green eyes sparkling.

"I won't have to, not in so many words," Christi replied. "Mike has a way of knowing things, very intuitive, that brother of mine."

"Intuitive—how?"

"Well, he doesn't need tarot cards!"

"Interesting."

"It can be a pain."

Leaving the library, they walked unhurried to the corner of Union Avenue where Dawn turned left and Christi headed toward South Street.

As Christi prepared dinner, she envisioned her brother through Dawn's eyes. Boyishly handsome with wavy hair and vibrant blue eyes, his easygoing way and natural charm made a nice package—that nice package being topped off with a devil-may-care attitude that would remain appealing if not carried too far.

"Something smells great," Dave said entering the kitchen.

Christi glanced over her shoulder at her brothers.

"Our sister is the best little cook in town." Mike commented. "I remember when it wasn't so," he moaned. Opening the refrigerator, he took out a soda.

"Thank heaven for home economics."

"Aren't we lucky!" Dave agreed. He gave her a hug around her shoulders. "Nice earrings," he noticed. "Should bring a pretty penny at the pawnshop."

She smacked at him as he ducked and ran. "They're a present from Dawn," she told him laughingly as he retreated to the living room.

"Wow, those are real diamonds?" Mike came over for a close look. "What'd she get me?"

"Nothing," Christi said indignantly.

"A set of diamond cufflinks would have been appreciated," he pouted.

"The tee shirt king needs cufflinks?"

"So, what's the point?"

"Oh, go away."

He fingered the delectable diamond again. "Very lovely, you have a good friend, Chris."

Mike stepped over to the refrigerator. He took out tomatoes and lettuce and then began chopping them for a salad while Christi drained the potatoes.

"Do you remember when you had a crush on Dawn?" she asked curiously, slipping on oven mitts to remove the meatloaf.

"Oh, don't even start that again," Mike said with laughter. He gave her a curious glimpse. "What's this about?"

"Why does it have to be about anything? I just wondered," she said dismissively searching the refrigerator for butter. "How's that salad coming? Dinner's almost ready."

"Getting there." He dumped almost half a bottle of French dressing on the lettuce and tomatoes with a satisfied smile.

"Yeah, I guess you like a little salad with your dressing?" she teased.

He gave her a deeply puzzled look. "Doesn't everybody?"

Shortly after dinner, Trixi, Dave's girlfriend, came by with a birthday cake and a bag of balloons. They had a contest to see who could blow up the most balloons, which Mike won with Dave a close second, she came in third and Trixi last. They frolicked in the living room like a bunch of kids with the colorful balloons, flicking them up in the air, trying diligently to keep them from landing on the floor or furniture.

Pleasantly tired from play, they headed to the kitchen for coffee and cake. Dave sang a pitiful rendition of 'Happy Birthday' in an off-key tenor that had them all laughing and plugging their ears. Mike got out Neapolitan ice cream, topping each piece of cake with two scoops.

After they finished, she and Trixi cleared the table. The laughter and gaiety of the little birthday party had wound down. Trixi was about to head out.

She kissed Dave goodbye, then called them over, hugging both her and Mike. "Happy birthday, sweeties," she said, tearfully. "I love you guys!"

They returned the sentiment. Christi did love her. She could not remember when Trixi hadn't been a part of their lives.

The day was closing quickly. Melancholy slipped over Christi as she put her tennis shoes on preparing for the relatively long walk.

After the carefree celebration of their sixteenth birthday, the three of them visited a lonely cemetery at twilight.

Dave centered a lovely arrangement of flowers on the base of the double headstone with an engraved message that told any who ventured near, that Angelica Marie and David Lee Temple Sr. had been devoted and loving parents and they were missed.

Hand-in-hand, they gazed solemnly at the monument purchased with money Mr. Harris had secured from the estate. Misty eyed, she remembered how ungrateful she had been two years ago. At the time it had seemed insignificant; now she was thankful to have it in recognition of their love.

The pain lingered still. They had been taken from her world and her world would never be the same, but she could also feel the serenity of her emotions. Time had worked its healing magic to a degree.

After a while, they walked the long and winding road, retracing their steps through the immense cemetery to the exit gates.

"We hardly ever see each other," Dave remarked unexpectedly. "I enjoyed spending the day with you. We should do it more often, how about Sundays?"

Christi's spirit soared at his offhand suggestion. "That sounds wonderful!"

She looked at Mike for his response.

"It's cool," he said nodding, reflectively agreeable.

Feeling deeply content, she decided not to worry so much. Things had a way of working out.

Chapter Three

Billy Cole ambled casually, keeping stride with the girl he'd found sobbing in the alley near the corner of Devine and Nineteenth.

They crossed Twenty-Second Street, walking down a dimly lighted, almost deserted stretch of sidewalk that had never held any interest or fear for Billy, even though it ventured a serious degree into the south side.

She had asked him to walk her home in a broken, muffled voice. As they walked, he eventually began to wonder about the circumstances of her problem. The intensity of her crying had tapered to an occasional sniffle but she offered no explanation.

"How much further?" he said when he felt a disturbing sensation, the potential of dread with the realization that they had unwittingly passed South Street, entering into dangerous territory.

When she didn't say a word, and even picked up the pace a little, he glanced at her, contemplating the significance of long blond hair that partially concealed the lovely doll-like face.

His thoughts jumped to the carelessness of his actions, the candid idiocy of trusting a stranger, just as John Burton and Clyde Bauer stepped from within the shadows of a dark alley.

Billy looked sharply at the girl who had set him up. He wanted to remember every feature. He had been duped by her, lured into a trap much too easily.

With a quick, doleful glance, she ducked around John and ran down the alley, her footsteps echoing in the stillness of the night.

He recognized John and Clyde from the early days at Lewis Grade School. Being a half-breed Indian in a school of middle-class white kids had not been easy, and John had been the worst.

Now the cold fury of his eyes leveled on Billy.

"What's this about, John?" he said, cautiously surveying for a nonexistent escape route as Clyde moved stealthily behind him.

"I want to see you bleed," John said quietly, shoving Billy toward the alley.

"Then I want to see you bleed some more." He pushed him again, taunting, but still controlled. "Maybe they'll bury you on the reservation, half breed."

Billy clenched his fists wanting to pound John, but large hands fastened his arms, his muscled physique and physical strength rendered useless in the powerful grip of Clyde Bauer.

He saw Carl Howell, another of John's low-life flunkies cutting across the street. As he joined them, John stepped aside. Billy managed one good kick knocking Carl back. He lurched, almost freeing himself from Clyde's iron grip.

"Couldn't handle one-on-one, huh, John?"

John lit a cigarette, a lingering smirk conveying general unconcern with the insinuation of his cowardice.

Hate twisted Carl's face into a sneer. He rose up punching him hard in the gut. Billy folded, then was pulled up and held erect in Clyde's massive hands. Carl drew back to continue the assault.

At first the blows seemed aimed with precision to make the beating last, then the unrelenting onslaught grew more intense with hard, fast jabs, exacting extensive damage to his vulnerable face and body.

Billy saw John through bleary eyes, watching from a vantage point on the side, casually smoking. John glanced away for a moment, then back, tossed the cigarette and nodded to Carl, who delivered a powerful blow that sent blood spurting from his nostrils.

A distinct ringing echoed in his ears, liquid warmth filled his mouth pouring forth over his busted lower lip.

He felt consciousness slipping away. John's haughty gaze faded from view, shadows closed in but then subsided with bitter awareness. Billy sank to his knees; a kick flung him backward. Another boot connected with his side. He folded spasmodically and felt another well placed, merciless kick.

He heard their hollow, mocking laughter as they walked away.

Billy coughed and spit blood. He tried to push himself up but extraordinary weakness overwhelmed him as the world spun crazily, careening in turbulent motion. Darkness closed around him in swirling mystification, urging him to surrender, dragging him down, pulling him further into a deep and silent void.

* * *

House of the Rising Sun had just begun to play as Christi entered the unique atmosphere of the Basement, her brothers' second home. Her wary anticipation eased up a little, the Animals was one of her favorite groups.

She looked around curiously and had to admit it had an impressive ambiance, with glowing posters and mood lighting. An elaborate three-foot statue of a cobra sat on a shelf behind the bar illuminated by a light radiating somewhere beneath, eerily beautiful.

"I told you it was boss!" Mike said enthusiastically. "It's cool, right?"

Christi could hardly suppress a smile at his eagerness.

"I'll reserve my opinion, for now," she replied.

"Okay," he agreed. "Save your opinion. It rocks, though, so give it a couple hours, anyway. Help yourself to snacks," he said, taking off.

She watched his retreat, feeling deserted.

"There's cola in the fridge," he added over his shoulder. "If you need me, I'm around."

She crossed the room, took a Pepsi from the refrigerator behind the counter, and perched on one of the tall barstools.

"Hi, you must be Christi. I'm Karen Cable." The girl introduced herself with a tentative smile. "Mind if I join you?"

"I'd love some company." Christi indicated the stool next to her.

Karen mixed a drink before boosting herself onto the barstool. "How do you like our little hangout?" she asked absently stirring her drink.

"It's different," Christi said with a light shrug.

"In a good way? In a bad way?" she prompted.

"In a big way." Christi peered over her shoulder to view the clientele, young men with hair and beards of various lengths and styles. Some dressed with flair, like the fellow who wore bell-bottom jeans, a vest without a shirt and a hat just like the mad hatter in the Alice story. Others wore tie-dyed tees, cutoffs or frayed bells and were clean-shaven like Dave. They were trendy and with it, as were the girls, and they could dance! Maybe Mike was right.

Christi spotted Dave with Trixi. Feeling assured at her brother's presence, she turned back to Karen who held a match to the cigarette between her lips with trembling fingers.

She noticed the hardness of her expression but tried not to be obvious in her observance of this cute girl with short dark hair and pixie features.

Karen glanced nervously over her shoulder toward the entrance. The hard look softened, making her appear young and vulnerable.

"Are you all right?" Christi asked, concerned at Karen's anxiety.

"Not exactly." She took a long swallow of her drink.

Karen didn't say anything else for a while. She looked lost in thought, puffing incessantly on the cigarette and flipping ashes into a nearby ashtray, taking sips of her drink from time to time.

"I did something tonight that I might regret," she said at last.

"What happened?" Christi said uneasily.

"John used me to get Billy Cole into Cobra turf. I wore a wig and didn't say much, but I know he got at least one good look at my face, and I'm scared to death. He finds out who I am, he'll be after me when he's able."

"That doesn't make sense," Christi said confused and a little frightened. "I don't get it. That isn't keeping to our side! Mike said everyone kept to their own side."

"John's been waiting for a chance to pound the guy—I wish he'd have left me out of it."

"John? John Burton? Your John Burton's girlfriend?" she said surprised.

"You might say that."

She stubbed the cigarette.

"You don't sound very thrilled. Why don't you leave him?"

"You mean, just up and walk away?"

"Yeah, that's what I mean."

Karen laughed, but it ended on a hollow note. She carelessly downed the last of her drink. "You make it sound easy, honey . . . But you don't know John. I belong to him, and I can't go anywhere until he's through with me."

Christi watched closely as Karen mixed a fresh drink, thinking about what she had said, unable to comprehend belonging to anyone or being forced to do something against her better judgment or values.

"You couldn't understand," Karen said quietly, resuming her seat.

"No, I don't understand," Christi agreed, appalled at the thought. "Can you explain it? How can he own you?"

Karen sighed. "Never mind," she said dismissively with a wave of her small hand. "If you knew John, you might be able to see where I'm comin' from, but all the girls around here are dependent on one guy or another anyway, except for the ones who like to—"

Karen took time to strike a match. Christi watched as she touched the flame to the tip of another cigarette. She blew smoke, her mouth twisting a little in thought. "Never mind about them," she said with another immediate dismissal. "Anyway, it's just best to latch onto one guy. You're an exception, of course. They were told you'd be around and to leave you alone."

"I hadn't thought about it," Christi admitted. She sipped her cola feeling fortunate, but sorry for Karen.

"You always do what he tells you?" Christi asked, wondering.

"He's persuasive," she murmured.

"You could run away," she suggested again after more consideration. "Just get on a bus and take off."

Karen looked at her musingly, and Christi wondered what she was thinking.

"I wouldn't try it," John said from behind them.

Her heart thumped, John Burton had slipped up on them. How long had he been standing there? He slid his arms around Karen, pulling her close against him, his dark gaze on Christi.

"Get me a drink, babe," he said lazily.

When Karen left to do John's bidding, he took her place on the barstool giving Christi a heavy-lidded appraising look. When his leg brushed hers, she shifted uneasily, drawing instinctively away from him.

"Nice to see you've come out of hiding," he commented moving her hair aside, a familiar gesture expected of someone who cares for you.

She jerked her head slightly, a reflexive move, and didn't bother replying to his remark. Christi had no desire to encourage conversation, deciding quickly to end the disturbing encounter.

As she began to move away, John gripped her wrist. She gazed at him for a timeless moment. He was undoubtedly attractive, but the insolence in his brown eyes, the surly expression, left her cold and fearful.

A subtle change in his look acknowledged her unease and the pleasure he derived in it. Snatching her wrist away, she stood as Karen returned.

"Excuse me," Christi said. "It was nice meeting you, Karen," she added, walking deliberately away from his undesirable presence.

* * *

Billy heard his name from a distance, a voice calling through thick layers of darkness. He detected something emphatic and familiar in the voice begging him to wake up, but he resisted the urgings with no desire to relinquish the soft, web of comfort.

The voice kept interfering though, until a sudden coldness permeated his consciousness, uncomfortable and unacceptable.

He began to drift back into grateful oblivion but the urgings persisted almost frantic in their appeal, giving him the will to push through the dense fog that clouded his mind.

As awareness worked its way into his senses, Billy realized that Danny was beside him. He felt the hard surface of concrete beneath him, but his head rested on something soft and supportive.

With no idea of where he was or how he had gotten there, he felt in limbo, then the submerged pain surfaced and enveloped him—caught him in a relentless grip. He shivered convulsively.

"Stay with me, Billy."

Billy tried to apply pressure to Danny's hand, but the aching weakness was crushing. He couldn't tell that his hand moved at all or if he even noticed the feeble attempt.

"Are you with me?" Danny asked his voice urgent. "Can you hear me?"

Yes, he could hear him, but he couldn't move. His eyes refused to open and his mouth, his whole face, in spite of the pain, had an oddly numb feeling.

"Billy? Oh, *fuck*, who did this to you?"

He scrambled for an answer in the dark haze that clouded his thoughts. Had a car hit him? A hit and run? He wanted to tell Danny he'd be all right, but he wasn't so sure himself. His attempt to speak gave forth a painful moan when his lips wouldn't move to form words.

"The ambulance is coming, hold on."

Billy concentrated on breathing, sensitive of every shallow breath inhaled through his numb lips.

He fought a wave of dizziness that almost carried him away, being conscious meant being alive, but the temptation to let go crystallized with powerful intensity as breathing became more difficult, the effort almost too much to bear.

He heard a siren in the distance, directed his thoughts to the approaching ambulance, to the night sounds, to the insistent voice begging him to hold on and to the memory that suddenly emerged with vivid passion, *the memory of a longhaired girl that gave a solid foundation to a need for retribution.*

Chapter Four

Christi sighed in exasperation when she noticed John leaning casually against the wall in the somewhat narrow hallway that led back to the main area of the Basement. Devilishly handsome, anyone would have to be blind not to see it, but in her opinion, his arrogance and forward manner took away from his beautiful veneer, and the way he treated Karen had taken top of the list for why she disliked him.

She paused feeling nervous as he sauntered toward her, then stood, basically blocking her path. "Get out of my way, John," she told him, determined to not let him see her uneasiness.

"We need to talk," he said softly, moving closer.

"We have nothing to talk about."

"Oh, but we do," he insisted, his impudent look unnerving. "We need to get a few things straight."

"There is nothing—nothing at all to get straight except that you need to leave me alone." Strong, brave words, considering her pitiful, quivering stomach. She looked angrily at him when he continued to block her passage.

"You got it all wrong about me, baby," he said, his hand moving smoothly along her arm. "I could do you good."

"Keep your hands off me," she said evenly. "You don't have the first idea about relationships or how to treat others."

It took every effort to appear calm as her words brought a dark look to his face, but his fingers left her arm.

"I treat Karen the way she likes to be treated," he told her indifferently. "We have our fun; she's a good little slut."

"She's confused and afraid, and you've tried to drag her down to your level."

"My level?" he said unaffected. "And what is my level? You don't even know me." He began slowly closing in again, forcing her farther back into the hallway, pushing her against the wall as she tried once more to pass him.

"If you don't let me go, I'll scream."

"No one would hear you."

She looked hard at him, aggravated and frightened. With the jukebox blasting out front, no sound would carry above it from this isolated space.

"Dave or Mike could come back here anytime," she realized triumphantly. "How would you explain this?"

Her satisfaction didn't last. Several tense seconds passed with his quiet contemplation of her insecurities.

"I'll have you one day," he said assuredly.

"Don't kid yourself," Christi managed, in spite of her miserable diffidence.

He leaned close, she breathed in the spicy aftershave he wore, mingled with the faint odor of whiskey and cigarettes on his warm breath.

"I never was one to kid myself." He turned to walk casually away while she struggled with the anxiety created by his threat.

As weeks passed without incident, the threat lapsed into a distant corner of her mind. Even so, John worried her. That Dave accompanied the Cobras on bike runs far away from Preston concerned her, too.

Although rare, she missed him when he would be gone from Sunday night until to the next Saturday. It was cool that he trusted her and Mike, but she wondered what went on when he was under John's influence.

Christi began to feel more content about Mike's association with the Cobras, though. He didn't even own a motorcycle. He mostly just hung out at the Basement, like he said; lots of girls. She convinced herself that she wasn't rationalizing, Mike wasn't missing school and his grades weren't suffering.

She enjoyed hanging out at the club once in a while, too. The gang wasn't what she had at first imagined. With the exception of John, they treated her somewhat like a favored mascot.

After the initial unpleasant encounter, Christi never ventured down that dark corridor alone to chance another confrontation with John. Trixi Allen, Dave's girlfriend, usually accompanied her when she visited the ladies' lounge.

"John's drawing designs on you," Trixi said knowingly. She ran a brush through her long, silky hair. "It bothers you, I can tell."

Christi leaned against the sink feeling momentarily miserable. "I really don't get it," she grumbled. "He has Karen."

"He doesn't care about Karen."

"He doesn't care about anyone," Christi replied. "I can't understand how Dave can be so unaware."

"He isn't exactly unaware. He's just a little defensive, you know, about John. He's known him for a long time."

"Yes, and I still don't get it." Christi watched as Trixi reapplied red lipstick, which enhanced her dark beauty. "You're beautiful enough to be a model . . . Aren't you sort of wasting your life away here?"

Trixi smiled. "Thanks, sweetie, but I wouldn't have it any other way. I dig this place, so it's cool for now, and I love Dave, we go way back."

She said she loved Dave, but she said it rather casually. Christi knew there were many definitions of love and dismissed the expression as nominal.

"You knew John back then, didn't you? What was he like in school?" John was but a vague memory. Her being a child, he had not drawn her attention.

"I didn't go to public school. I went to Our Lady of Mercy, but since I spent time with Dave, yeah, I was around him quite a lot until they took him away."

"I didn't know you went to a Catholic school."

"For all the good it did," Trixi reflected with a faint smile. "I'm having too much fun, and the wrong outweighs the right, know what I mean?"

"Yeah, well, I think you're a pretty terrific person."

"Thank you." She smiled, almost shyly, and then her expression turned thoughtful. "John was kind of quiet and even timid in ways, as I remember."

"Quiet sounds like John," Christi said as they left the restroom. "But timid hardly describes the man we know."

"And he didn't have that arrogance." Trixi shrugged. "He's a paradox."

"This must be his evil twin."

Trixi laughed. "No, he's one and the same. I heard he made school days hell for Billy Cole."

As they stepped out of the corridor, Dave grabbed Trixi, swinging her around. Christi watched for a while as they stole the scene on the dance floor.

Eventually, she wandered back to the bar.

"Would you like some company?" Van Morrison settled casually on the barstool next to her.

Something about his eyes, something about *him* seemed oddly familiar, but Christi didn't actually know Van well, other than noticing he sat at Dave's table a lot. They'd only talked a couple times, his voice, low and smooth, emitting quiet confidence. She purposefully studied him over the weeks. He appeared to be a fairly speculative man, keenly observant. There were times, though, when he let loose and seemed almost carefree.

She happily consented for him to join her.

They moved to a table and chatted for a while about life in Preston, her struggle with school, her best friend and study buddy, Dawn.

Christi felt comfortable with him. She even told him about her parents dying in the car accident. He touched a part of her so intimately, warmed her heart with true affection, unusual, but strangely not disturbing.

"Where have you been all my life?" she asked with a grin.

He smiled at her as if she were a small child, not the reaction she wanted.

"You're such a cute little girl." He held her hand in his for a heart stopping moment. "Aren't you afraid of the big, bad wolf?"

Christi sighed wistfully. "Is that you?"

"No, sweetie, but they're around, unfortunately."

He adored this youthful beauty, so unaware of the captivating picture she displayed with silky, golden hair cascading around slender shoulders, tall and slim—she moved like a model or dancer. Her smooth skin glowed with pale-gold undertones, her features exquisitely feminine. Too innocent, he worried, unpretentiously oblivious of her beauty and perilously ignorant of the danger.

"Mind telling me what you're doing here?" he asked lightly. "You're too good for this, it doesn't suit you."

As she considered his comment, she thought how great it was to be sitting with someone so extremely boss. Van's dark, wavy hair hung to his shoulders, casually unruly, and he had a shadow of a beard, so completely *appealing*.

Her gaze lingered on his lean, muscled arms, then his chest. The pinstripe sport shirt, unbuttoned more than halfway down revealed strangely fascinating manly wisps of dark hair.

This being the first time she had noticed something like that on a guy left her feeling a bit self-conscious. As Christi leaned back and met his eyes again, she realized he was aware of her appraisal.

A blush warmed her face. "What's wrong with my being here?" she asked to cover her embarrassment. "No one bothers me."

"I've noticed John Burton giving you some hungry looks," he commented.

Christi stared into her cola, momentarily silenced as butterflies fluttered in her stomach. "Was I giving you a hungry look?" she asked, her cheeks blushing pink again.

He smiled fondly, putting her at ease. "No, you were giving me a curious look," he said kindly. "Want me to put the kibosh on John?" he suggested.

"Would you?" She grinned, relaxed in his presence.

"Anytime."

"No, I guess that's not necessary."

"You're sweet, Christi. Don't let this place drag you down."

"This place? No way, I only come here 'cause I'm madly in love with the tall, dark stranger who hangs out here a lot."

"Do tell—and who is this mysterious stranger?"

"That's a secret," she quipped. "But he's sophisticated, suave, and a most excellent hunk." Christi sighed exuberantly. "It's a drag, though, since he hardly knows I'm alive."

Van smiled at her dramatic flair.

"I'm sure you flatter him." His smile faded slowly. "But you're wrong, doll. He knows very well how alive you are, and he knows that someday the right guy will fall madly in love with you—considering your charming persona."

"Whoa! I have a charming persona?" she questioned with a dubious glance.

"You sure do! Why, that lucky guy will look into the most beautiful violet blue eyes I've ever seen and lose his heart in an instant."

"Can you assure me of that?"

"Yes, golden girl, I can—most confidently." He tilted his head slightly. "Would you like to dance?"

"I'd love to."

He led her onto the crowded floor where he took her in his arms as the melody surrounded them. She liked the feel of her hand in his, the way he held her not crushed against him and the delicious male scent of his cologne.

"This is my first slow dance," she confessed.

"I'm pleased to have the honor, and I would have never known, you're very graceful."

She felt his smooth lead made the dance about as easy as walking across the room, and told him so. Later when she was ready to leave, Van walked her home. They paused in front of her apartment building.

"I enjoyed tonight," he said. "I'd like to spend more time with you, Christi, but I'll be, regrettably, busy. Would you let me know if you need someone to put Burton in line? Really, sweetheart, it would be my pleasure to pound him."

"Thank you, but I'm hoping Dave can keep him straight."

He tilted her face up with an index finger beneath her chin. "You're too young for such worries."

He framed her face in his hands and kissed her gently on the forehead to the teasing whoops and wolf whistles of the night folk who lived in the apartment building and hung out on the cement steps at all hours.

Christi glanced in their direction, not offended.

Van smiled down at her, his hands resting lightly on her shoulders. Then his expression grew serious.

"You're so pretty," he said, with an actual touch of wonder.

Before she had a chance to respond to the compliment, he turned her with a deliberate little push in the direction of the stairs.

"Goodnight, little girl."

She glanced back. "Goodnight, Van."

Christi went straight to the bathroom to stare at her reflection in the mirror, to consider what Van had so kindly pointed out about her being a little girl. Lifting her hair, she thought, added two years to her appearance. Maybe a short haircut would give her sophistication? She let her hair down, realizing it wouldn't make that much difference. Regardless of style, the innocent wide-eyed look came shining through all the same.

Chapter Five

Christi sat cross-legged on the twin bed in the guest bedroom of Dawn's home, attentively regarding her friend who was lying on her back on the other, staring insipidly at the ceiling.

"Have you ever had a crush on an older guy?" she asked nonchalantly.

"What do you mean by older?"

"I would say he's about Dave's age. About twenty-two, I suppose."

"That sounds older enough to be interesting."

"Well, have you?" Christi persisted.

"I fell in love with a teacher once." Dawn rolled over on her side, supporting her head on her arm. "So, who is this mysterious older man?"

"Oh, just a guy who hangs out at the Basement," she told her trying to sound carefree about it and not hopelessly lovelorn. "He's a friend of Dave's, not a Cobra, though—but we seem somehow connected, ya know—there's just something about him. Know what I mean?"

"Yes, I know exactly what you mean. Does he know how you feel?"

"Are you kidding? I don't even know how I feel."

Dawn raised her perfectly arched brows.

"Okay, I'm head over heels for an older guy who probably knows how I feel, but I'm just a little girl to him."

"I'm your best friend; you have to tell me these things so that I can console you and say—it's probably for the best."

Sometimes her best friend could be too reasonable. "Let me hear you say that when you fall in love."

"I am in love," she replied airily. "I'm in love with Jerry."

"If you were in love with Jerry, you wouldn't want a kiss from Mike." Christi satisfactorily reminded her of the birthday request.

She sat up on the edge of the bed. "I wasn't serious!" she said feigning indignation, tossing her pretty red hair.

"I'm so sure! You were as serious as the night is long."

"The nights aren't very long in Preston . . . I wish you'd move in with me," Dawn said easily changing the subject. "I'd love to have you for a sister."

"I couldn't leave my brothers."

Not that the offer wasn't tempting. Christi ran her hand over the velvety texture of the rose-pink bedspread. She could have a room with soft lighting illuminating a pink and white décor, or any preferable color, an armoire and dressing table of cherry wood. She thought of her mother's curio cabinet.

"Chris?"

"Sorry," she said with a little apologetic grin. "What?"

"Have you had any problems with John Burton lately?"

"No, not much, but I stay out of his way."

"Be careful, okay?"

"Careful, how—" She splayed her hands. "I stay out of his way."

"I'm serious, living where you do—keep your eyes open."

Christi grinned at Dawn. She would seriously flip if she knew the hours she kept, sometimes getting home after midnight.

"Living where I do, I try."

"Want to cram some more for the English test? I'm here for you, kiddo."

"No, that's okay, if it's not in there it never will be. I've studied till my brain aches."

"Imagine, just one more month and we'll be free," Dawn said eagerly. "I am so ready for summer vacation."

"Weeks and weeks of fun in the sun without the worry of a pop quiz—or homework—or tests that I feel obligated to pass with flying colors."

"That's the spirit. You'll do great!" Dawn turned off the stereo. "I wonder if supper will be ready anytime soon, I'm hungry."

They headed downstairs.

"This is going to be the best summer ever!" Dawn said back on the subject of vacation. "Pool parties, sleepovers, bonfires at the beach—you'll get to know Carrie better. I love her, and you will, too. I can't wait 'til the fourth!"

Christi grinned at Dawn's enthusiasm about the Fourth of July celebration which she had already been invited to this year.

After their first meeting, two years ago, the day before the custody hearing, they had talked occasionally. Then they saw each other at the library and began doing their homework together, study sessions here or at the library. Dawn, being a junior, proved to be a good and willing tutor.

They had gotten closer this past year. As they became better acquainted, Christi discovered a fun-loving, gracious person; she cherished their friendship.

She had spent some time with Carrie and Dawn's other friends, but not a lot. She had a feeling that would change this summer. How would they feel about her? How would she feel about them? Would she be accepted, or would she have to deal with conceit due to exceptional wealth?

Christi repressed her doubts. It was difficult, being a loner at heart, except for Mike, she had one friend—Dawn. As a child, Mike had plenty of friends, but she didn't often mingle, and she hadn't changed much. When she was at the Basement, if she didn't sit with Dave, Trixi or Mike and occasionally Karen, when John wasn't around, she more or less kept to herself.

"I hope Ted hangs out with us," Dawn said, not sounding exactly hopeful.

"I hope for you that he does, too," Christi sympathized.

"I wish I knew what happened with him. He was always so much fun."

Dawn had voiced concern for Ted, Carrie's nineteen-year-old brother, more than once. She considered Ted for a contemplative moment. He was nice to look at, with sandy blond hair and solemn, smoky gray eyes. He seemed like a pleasant enough person, but she didn't know him very well, only what Dawn had told her, and now, that he had been drifting away from his friends for some reason, becoming, in Dawn's words, a pessimistic loner.

They entered the kitchen greeted by the savory aroma of roast beef blending with fresh baked bread. Tina had just finished whipping the potatoes and began dishing them into a fancy shallow bowl.

"Can we help with anything, Mom?"

"You can set the table while Christi and I finish dishing the food into serving bowls."

Christi grinned to herself, *serving bowls!* She always dished the food right onto the plates from the pot it was cooked in. It tasted the same, so why dirty a bunch of serving bowls?

After finishing a generous slice of homemade cherry pie alamode, Christi thanked her and complimented the cook with all sincerity on a delicious meal.

Tina smiled graciously.

"I guess it could be considered my hobby," she added unabashedly. "It's something I have always enjoyed."

"And something she does so well," Dawn agreed. "I wish I shared the passion, 'specially if it's truly the way to a man's heart."

"More pie, Christi?"

"No, thank you, Mrs. Preston, I couldn't eat another bite."

"You girls have fun with the kitchen," she teased leaving them to the chore.

Dawn loaded the dishwasher while Christi straightened up and wiped off the counter tops and stove. The small dining room, separated from the kitchen by a counter with comfortable stools, had a cozy atmosphere. They always had their meals here.

Christi had seen the formal dining room with the oak table that comfortably seated a party of twenty, draped with a delicate lace tablecloth. Dawn had told her that her father's mother had knitted it. Each piece connected one to another with a dainty little rose right in the center, the pattern so intricate, it must have taken forever, an heirloom to be cherished.

An antique buffet sat against one wall, a China cabinet displaying beautiful bone china and sparkling crystal dominated another. The magnificent chandelier over the table could be dimmed for a romantic glow or brightened to dazzling.

This room had a pendant light, also with a dimmer, not so glamorous, but it also had an antique buffet, and the sliding glass doors opened to a patio with comfortable lawn furniture, a barbeque, and a glorious view of a flower garden in the distance.

"I wish you would reconsider and spend the night," Dawn said.

"I spend Sundays with my brothers, the one time I can count on us all being together, so I like to be there in the morning."

"You're lucky to have brothers. Maybe Tina would adopt them, too."

"Now, there's a thought!" Christi said with a decisive nod.

Christi declined an offer from Dawn to drive her home. She enjoyed walking and never tired of the landscaping between Woodland Drive and Union.

Once home she straightened the apartment, took a shower, then read a couple chapters of her novel before going to bed.

Having had a good night's sleep, Christi woke up at about nine feeling great. When Mike joined her in the kitchen at nine thirty, they had a cup of coffee and chatted for a while listening to the little radio that sat in the window.

On Sunday, Dave usually got up between ten and eleven, so at about ten she put sausage in the frying pan and stirred up some pancake batter. The day began with lavish compliments on her cooking skills.

"You just want to keep me happy so I'll keep cooking," she accused.

"No way—your pancakes are light and fluffy," Mike said. "And the sausage is—well, it's done—clear through—no pink here!"

"And it's not burned," Dave added. "It's crispy on the outside, juicy and—"

"Okay—okay—fluffy pancakes, done sausage. I believe you!" she laughed.

They opted for a day at the beach, enjoyed vender hot dogs for a late snack, and arrived back home at about five. Christi poured iced tea; Dave set the timer for a quick game of Scrabble. One hour later, Mike won the word game. Christi shooed them out of the kitchen so she could wash the neglected breakfast dishes.

Donning rubber gloves, Christi listened to music from the radio as she washed, rinsed, and stacked the few dishes in the drainer before joining her brothers in the living room.

She plopped down on the sofa, happy with the day's events. Discounting the walks to school and back with Mike, she seldom saw him except for Sundays and her occasional visits to the Basement. She saw even less of Dave.

With her thoughts in that direction, Christi began to brood about Dave's close relationship with John Burton and wondered what could ever convince her brother to sever it.

She knew now that they had been close friends from kindergarten until John was fourteen, then for some reason, he had been sent away. Dave didn't say why, and she didn't ask, because she didn't care. She supposed that he'd been sent to DH or some institution, and only wished that he'd stayed gone.

"Cheer up, angel. It can't be all that bad." Dave tousled her hair, and she glanced up at him with a winning smile.

"I know one way you can cheer me up."

"Uh-oh, you're in for it now," Mike commented with a cautionary note.

"Nobody asked you." Christi tossed a pillow at his head.

He ducked, laughing, picked it up and threw it back.

"You name it," Dave agreed intercepting the pillow. "But no pillow fights. We'll end up with feathers all over the place."

"Okay," she conceded. "I want to learn how to dance."

He moaned, in what she hoped was mock-agony, feigning reluctance, but seeming most convincing.

"Your moves and your style. You don't really mind, do you, Dave?"

"Of course not," he smiled. "You have rhythm, you're a natural, but no matter what I teach you, you'll develop your own style, and that's important."

"Yes!" Christi agreed delightedly. "I like the idea of my own style!"

After moving the sofa back and the coffee table aside, the three of them danced around the living room, sometimes being silly, then Dave seriously teaching her steps and moves, before Mike, once more his usual hilarious self started dancing around her shaking his hips and laughing like a hyena.

Christi tried not to laugh. "David, make him stop!"

"Quit goofin'," Dave admonished. "I'm amazed you didn't teach our sister how to dance by now. This is some serious stuff; she has to learn the Pony."

"That's easy. I can teach her the Pony and the Swim!" Mike said.

"And just for fun, teach her the Bossa Nova. Now get down to it while I go for Trix. Back in a flash with Pizza and beer," he added heading out the door.

By the time the two showed up, she could do the Swim and Pony and had grown comfortable with the basics of the Bossa Nova. They demonstrated for Dave and Trixi the results of Mike's dance instruction.

"That's cool," Trixi said. "You got the moves, girl!"

"I do, don't I!" Christi said enthusiastically. "I can't believe it's so easy to learn these dances!"

"I said you're a natural." Dave opened a beer, offering it to Trixi.

"No, thanks, I'm taking penicillin—tonsillitis," she explained. "The worst is over, but I have to finish the prescription."

"Want a Pepsi?" Christi offered, lifting up her bottle of soda. "Plenty more where this came from!"

"Yes, thanks, I'd love it."

When Mike announced that it was after eleven, Christi dropped gracefully out of the Chinese Checker competition.

"Where'd the time go? I don't even feel sleepy."

"You will tomorrow, little grumble butt," Mike teased. "That's why I thought I'd let you know. The morning's gonna come early."

They exchanged goodnights and Christi went to brush her teeth, then straight to bed. She snuggled under the sheet feeling content. Spending a day with her brothers always gave a boost to her morale.

Leaving them would be out of the question, even though she loved Dawn like the sister she never had.

Her thoughts turned to Dave and Trixi. They seemed so right together. She wondered why Dave didn't simply marry Trixi, drop the Cobras, get a job and settle down to live happily ever after in a nice neighborhood. But maybe they were not in love. Maybe they just enjoyed each other's company, which was not enough to base a marriage on.

Christi felt herself drifting away, her thoughts settling as she succumbed to slumber. With astonishing suddenness, the alarm clock resounded in her ears. She reached for it with closed eyes, found the stem, pushed it in, and then fell instantly back into blissful sleep.

"Wake up sleepyhead," Mike said tugging at the sheet. He was *so* insistent. "Rise and shine, little miss up 'til midnight."

"Two minutes," she mumbled, covering her face with the pillow.

"You don't have two minutes!"

Mike yanked the sheet.

"Michael!" Christi looked at him resentfully rubbing the sleep from her eyes. "Why are you so mean to me?"

He laughed, and she smiled sleepily.

"Get ready for school, or you'll see mean."

"See how you are." Christi stretched, yawning loudly.

"You sound like a grizzly bear," Mike said laughingly. "Ten minutes, or we'll be late." He left the room, closing the door gently.

Wonderful, being compared to a grizzly bear first thing in the morning!

Doing a quick change from pajamas to a lavender mini-dress, she slipped into a pair of white flats, and then hurried into the bathroom to wash her face and brush her teeth and hair, forcing herself to move fast in spite of being groggy after the short, dreamless night.

Christi barely had time to finish in the bathroom before Mike was tapping on the door. "Right with you!" she yelled.

She viewed the shadows under her eyes. This morning was no fun at all. Mike knew her well enough to know she needed her sleep, but he had been enjoying the game. It was almost midnight before he realized it.

He stood waiting at the door, ready to leave as soon as she entered the living room. "Good morning, glory," he teased.

Christi gave an exaggerated pout. "It's not fair," she grumbled. "How you can go on so little sleep and still be all bright-eyed and cheerful!"

"I'm a speed freak—I thought that was common knowledge."

She gave him a quick glance and saw his amusement.

"Cute, Mike, real cute."

"So are you. Let's go."

She stopped short. "What? No coffee?"

"No time."

"Oh, Mike!"

"Just teasing!" He revealed the travel cup from behind his back. "Coffee with cream to go," he said giving her his most delightfully mischievous smile.

"You're the best," Christi said breathlessly, surprised and grateful. "How can you look so serious when you're kidding?"

"It's a gift," he said dryly, closing the door behind them as they quickly exited the apartment.

"Did I really sound like a grizzly bear?"

"Hell yeah, you sounded like a grizzly bear."

"I did not sound like a grizzly bear."

Chapter Six

Nancy Castell stood for a long indecisive moment in front of the imposing black door of a tavern simply called The Basement. She had never ventured so far down Broadway. This part of town had never entered her mind until she overheard an impetuous candy striper chatting with a friend in the cafeteria at Preston City General where Nancy worked as a front desk receptionist.

She had listened to the conversation without eavesdropping, the girl, Sally, talked loud enough to be almost annoying unless you *wanted* to hear her.

"The Basement is a tavern underneath one of the oldest apartment buildings in Preston City," the girl said in an excessively knowing voice. "It's located on Broadway and Price, if you're interested," she added flippantly.

"I've driven by there," the other girl said. "There's no sign of a nightclub."

"It's a nightspot, and it's easy to miss if you're not looking for it cause there's no sign, but I kid you not, my friend, it's a rocking place to go."

"So, you've been there?"

"Sure, I have," she insisted sipping on a milkshake.

Nancy wondered if Sally had even been to this place. She seemed awfully young, but the speculations appealed to a recent yearning for something—anything exciting to happen. 'A rocking place to go' might be daring and freeing, if she could find the nerve to live a bit reckless.

Nancy drew a deep breath. It sounded good at the time, but now she felt insecure about her impulsive behavior.

The Basement—located on a dirty corner of a dirty street—given lucid consideration, was distinctly undesirable. The streetlight overhead had blown and never been replaced, making the area dark and ominous. She began to wonder what had ever possessed her to come here, sending her plummeting courage into a final dive, urging her to follow rational instincts, forget about taking any crazy chances and retreat to the safety of home.

She started to turn when the door opened. A young man stepped out. He gave her an approving glance, and then smiled, holding the door open in an inviting gesture, not at all threatening.

Her apprehension slipped away. She stepped into the strangely fascinating room. The atmosphere enveloped her, vibrant-colored strobe lights blinked in beat with the music from a jukebox blasting a song about getting stoned.

A black light radiated onto the crowded dance floor bathing the writhing bodies in an eerie glow. Posters, iridescent and beautiful, shone from the walls, but one caught her attention, a king cobra with hypnotic eyes and exaggeratedly dangerous fangs.

Nancy recognized the symbol of the Cobra gang and fear crept into the night. She didn't know much about them, but she knew enough to realize she had no business being here.

John glimpsed the girl and swiveled further around on the barstool to observe her hesitant entrance into the room. He recognized quality and would bet she had never been inside a bar before. He detected her innocence, too, in spite of the enticing blouse tucked into a pair of snug-fitting jeans. This girl was courting danger and she was about to get her wish.

He elbowed Clyde, who had not noticed her, then watched intently as he ogled the girl, undisguised longing all over his ignorant face, sometimes lust could be amusing. Clyde was a moron, just shining on for the most part, but when given a nudge, he played happily.

John leaned back with his elbows on the bar.

"Looks good, doesn't it?" he said encouraging Clyde's interest. "Why not go for it?" John turned back to the bar downing a shot of whiskey. "Bring her over, but don't make a scene."

Nancy turned, ready to leave, but approached hesitantly when she saw a man leaning against the door watching her through half-closed eyes. He looked convincingly threatening, his tee shirt taunt against a muscled chest, his biceps powerful and imposing, his substantial frame significantly blocking the exit.

"Excuse me," she said through fear and desperation.

He looked at her insolently and didn't move except to shift his weight.

She turned away in fast growing panic to a scene that didn't afford any comfort. Her glance flashed from the dancers, to the jukebox, to the statue of a cobra behind the bar, nightlife this side of Broadway, a vivid nightmare of blaring music and flashing lights that had caught her so unsuspecting.

The air conditioning in the room suddenly seemed far too cold. Nancy shivered, glancing quickly around for another way out. She jumped when a hand seized her arm. Looking fearfully at the man who had blocked the exit, she tried to pull away. His grip tightened from uncomfortable to painful.

She fought the urge to resist, realizing that making a scene might not be wise. His look reflected a silent warning. He could easily knock her senseless with a single blow from the huge, rough hand. She felt helpless as a child in his grasp as he escorted her firmly to the bar.

Nancy sat tensely at the counter. The huge rough hand moved carelessly over her thigh. She felt someone playing with her hair, shifting it to one side, then lips on her neck pressing warm, moist kisses down to her shoulder.

Strong arms circled her midriff from behind. She pushed at the hands, but the big man gripped her wrist.

"Be nice, little girl."

Nancy stared straight ahead in dazed resignation, humiliation and terror fused, demanding every ounce of strength to remain calm in the midst of this revulsion. Her mind tried to grasp a feasible means of escape, but escape seemed absurdly impossible.

When she turned her head from one man, another held her face, his lips capturing hers for a long, vulgar kiss.

"Please," she whispered when he released her mouth. "I'm not supposed to be here. You don't understand." Senselessly, she longed for time to reverse, just a single half-hour.

"I understand." He pulled her blouse down over one shoulder, his teeth grazed her skin. "You're scared, I bet, but that's just 'cause you don't know us. Now, don't you worry, little girl, you'll get to know us real good."

He pressed a bottle against her lips tilting it upward. "Open your mouth," he gritted.

She gulped the liquid as it filled her mouth and throat. The strength of the liquor took her breath. She coughed, gasping for air, hearing sardonic laughter as they passed the bottle around.

A lighter flared, clicked shut, and then a choking, sickening smoke filled her nostrils. She had never experienced the stench, but she knew what it was.

As they passed it to one another, the smoke surrounded her, encircled her head, permeating her senses. She began to feel light and strange. Their laughter echoed hollowly within her mind.

"Please, let me go," she pleaded again.

"You've only begun to sample our hospitality, baby," a voice whispered from directly behind her.

"We're gonna take real good carra you, ain't we, John."

"We will," the quiet voice replied. "Let's take this party to the back room. Bring some booze."

"Come on, baby, party time."

Nancy stood on weak legs, walking obediently beside the man holding her arm, letting them believe she was resigned, feigning acceptance of her fate.

A dark corridor loomed ahead with stark realization that the 'back room' drew terrifyingly close as they ushered her along.

She scanned the faces of the people in the tavern. They all looked the same, laughing men, drinking and carousing, trashy looking women hanging onto or near them, no one giving any attention to what was about to happen—then she glimpsed a man sitting with someone quietly talking.

As they approached the two, Nancy gave a desperate lurch, scampering and stumbling; she fell to her knees at his feet.

"Please," she cried despairingly. "Help me."

Confusion clouded his handsome face until he took in the circumstances. Then, chillingly, the confusion slipped away, replaced by swift disregard.

Nancy held tighter to his leg as a strong hand gripped her shoulder.

"Please—" She pleaded again to the man who had been a glimmer of hope in the midst of darkness. "You can stop this." Her voice fell to a whimper. "How can you just sit here and let them hurt me?"

His expression revealed an implication of regret, but he turned away again with clearly no intention of interfering.

"I can't let them do it, Dave." The quietly confident voice gave her a renewed rush of hope.

The hand fell away from her shoulder. She looked up at the man named Dave. "She's your baby," he readily agreed. "But you know they won't let her go without a fight."

Nancy pressed her face against his leg, her eyes closed tight. She heard a chair scrape the floor. Still she waited, afraid to move.

"You might as well sit up here—if my girl comes in and sees you in this compromising position, she's liable to kick your little ass."

Nancy released his leg. She managed to stand with some grace, then after a fleeting glimpse around the room, sat across from him in the seat that had just been vacated.

"Where did they go?"

"They took it out back." He lifted his drink to her before downing it. "Could I get you something? It might be a while."

"You were going to let them have me," she said incredulously.

He shrugged dismissively, a slight movement of slender shoulders.

"You came here of your own accord."

"How could you rationalize what they were about to do?"

"Why should I have to rationalize anything?" he asked evenly.

"Those guys held back until you showed your indifference." Accusatory, she didn't try to hide her feelings.

"It's not that I'm indifferent," he said, but she couldn't tell by his face that he cared a bit. "Maybe I could have influenced John in this instance, maybe not. Fact is, little lady, you have no business being here."

Nancy shivered, feeling the sting of truth in his criticism.

"You're the leader of this street gang, aren't you?"

He watched her broodingly, his eyes still cool. "I'm nobody's leader, and we're not a street gang," he said finally. "We're a biker gang. Everyone keeps calling us a street gang." Dave sighed audibly. "Do you ever hear of us doing any damage on the streets of Preston?"

A biker gang? Like that would make her feel better? Nancy took a breath, shifted restlessly in the chair, but couldn't stop shivering.

"I'm afraid," she said defensively when he gave her a look of mild cynicism.

He left her sitting alone at the table, trembling and trying to assure herself that she was perfectly safe now.

"This should help you relax."

Nancy glanced up at Dave. He placed a tall, frosty glass filled with thick, pink liquid on the table in front of her before resuming his seat, setting a shot glass of amber liquid in front of him.

She took the straw between her lips, taking a delicious sip of the strawberry drink. His warm hand closed over her quivering fingers to steady her hand as she attempted to light a cigarette.

"Would you settle down?" he said reasonably.

"I can't. I'm frightened." She glanced uneasily around the crowded room.

"You said that before." He lit a cigarette, leaning back in his chair.

"Yes, but if they come back—if they leave him—"

"Van, his name is Van."

"If they leave him lying in that alley," she continued trying to keep her voice steady. "You'll let them take me to their little party room and who knows what they'll do to me!"

"I know," he responded. "I know, and so do you."

His eyes never wavered as she stared at him in amazement.

"What would keep me from going to the police?" she demanded.

"Oh—you wouldn't do that."

His expression didn't change, but his tone caused her heart to stop beating, or it felt like it. She took an uncertain breath and felt her heart pounding in her chest. The intimidation had touched her and she shivered again.

"You're not drinking," he said, his voice taking on a kinder quality as if there had been no threat at all. "Come on, live a little."

She drew a trembling breath. "You don't even care," she accused.

Dave leaned forward, his eyes burning into hers. Nancy couldn't pull away from the controlled antagonism in that look even though she wanted to. He started to comment, but apparently decided against it.

"This has happened before," she murmured finally breaking eye contact.

"I do what I can to protect the female population of Preston."

"Like what?"

"Like they don't take it on the street," he replied tightly. "I don't condone what they do, but I didn't invite you here. No one did."

She could not deny the painful truth of his words and closed her eyes for an instant wishing to grasp a reasonable defense for her idiocy.

"Why did you deny being their leader when you obviously are?"

His mouth twitched, a suggestion of annoyance, but he gave no reply.

"Maybe I shouldn't have said that," she apologized, quickly.

He leaned back in his chair looking at her intently. "Don't sweat it."

Nancy thought it might be a good time to have another sample of the sweet pink drink, when a boy approaching their table drew her attention. He did a rocking stroll, keeping beat to the pulsating music as he crossed the room.

He stood about five eight, not too tall, with a lanky frame, dressed in belled jeans and tie-dyed cutoff. His unruly hair curled from under a jean hat positioned haphazardly on his head

The young man pulled a chair out from the table and straddled it.

"I think Van and John musta had a disagreement of some sort," he said with a likable grin. "Van's doin' some major butt-kicking out back."

"Yeah, well, there was a disagreement, a major disagreement."

"Anyway, he told me to get the hell outta there." He shrugged; the same gesture she had seen Dave use. "So, I split. Who's the chick?"

Dave inclined his head slightly. "The disagreement—this is it."

"I'm Mike," he said with a wide smile. "You are—?"

"Nancy," she responded. "I'd rather not be known as 'the disagreement'."

Dave polished off the shot of whiskey he'd brought to the table earlier, regarding her with a casual look, his mouth tilting slightly, possibly offering complimentary reflections of the events going on outside?

Nancy tried to read something positive in his expression. She didn't want to think he felt so indifferent about what could have happened to her, but he did seem basically indifferent to it, also to the fact that Mike, whom she knew was nowhere near eighteen took a swallow from a mug of beer that she just noticed he had brought to the table with him.

* * *

Karen Cable watched discreetly from her seat at the far end of the bar, thinking that if Van had been here the night she wandered in things could have been different for her.

It had been raining that night, not a light drizzle, but a pouring down rain with loud rolling thunder and bolts of lightening that seemed too near as she huddled in a doorway.

She descended the stairs seeking shelter to wait out the storm. Van had not been here. Clyde had not been here that night, either. Carl and John had taken her to the back room.

The place had been packed, but no one cared as they took her away. The jukebox blasting, her screams wouldn't have disturbed them. Even if she could have been heard, nobody would have bothered with the welfare of a lone girl unfortunate enough to wander into their world.

After they left, Karen, trembling and crying, managed to dress. Crawling into a corner, she cried herself into an exhausted sleep. When she awakened surrounded by complete darkness, uncertain and frightened, she cried out.

The door opened. She squinted as a dim bulb lighted the room. After total darkness, even the faint light seemed intense. A man spoke, one of the men who had raped her only short hours ago.

"I've decided I want you to stay with me."

She stared at him unable to utter a word at his ludicrous request.

She folded her arms protectively across her chest, bewildered as she gazed at the man who had been so fierce earlier, confused by his attitude as he regarded her with a tender expression. He tilted his head to the left a bit and she was taken by his dark perfection.

"What's your name?" he asked pleasantly.

"Why would you want to know?" She still hugged herself, terrified.

He studied her long enough to see her dismay.

"You don't have anywhere to go, do you? You're a runaway."

She shook her head, no, not a runaway. She had been left here, abandoned, and San Francisco seemed so very far away.

"I won't let anyone else touch you—if you're with me."

With the implication punctuated by dark, penetrating eyes, she experienced, for the first time, the look she now knew so well. A cold knot formed in her stomach, she felt chilled deep inside, the cold dispersing throughout her body.

"You can't threaten me into living with you."

She learned, soon enough, John could do what he wanted. He touched her face, a deceptively tender gesture, and then gripped her wrist as she tried to move away from him. He pressed her back against the mattress, gently taking possession of her bruised mouth, kissing her tenderly.

The terror within her clashed against emotions gone out of control. She found her senses reeling in response to the soft caress of his lips. To her astonishment, she experienced another version of the man she had met earlier. He proved to be an ardent lover who could arouse passion with remarkable ease.

There were two sides, and she had known them both. His cruel abuse without remorse kept her fearful, but on occasion, with heart rending confusion, he became a different person, and she loved that person deeply.

She knew that he didn't love her though, and in spite of the love she felt for him, fear and hostility remained the greater emotions.

Karen looked enviously at the girl sitting opposite Dave.

Van pulled out a chair, taking a seat. "Hey Mike how about a drink, kid?"

Mike left, and Van turned warm eyes in her direction. "How ya doin'?"

"I'm all right now," Nancy said assuredly. "Thanks to you. Are you okay?"

His hand covered hers, warm and comforting. "Bruised knuckles, maybe?" He shrugged easily. "I'm good. I could have finished them off sooner, but I wanted to have some fun, and that damn Clyde's a mountain."

Noticing her drink, Van took a swallow. "Is this what I think it is?" he said with an inquisitive glance at Dave.

"What is it?" she asked.

"A sweet treat to calm your nerves," Dave replied. "From me to you, enjoy," he urged with a quick, trivial wink.

Nancy took a deep swallow, and then Van seized the glass.

"Not too fast," he cautioned.

"Well, what is it?" she asked, again.

"I'm not sure." Van took another swallow. "I can taste several ingredients, but there's something just a little mysterious in the flavor."

He looked at Dave curiously.

"It's called, screw you," Dave said flippantly.

"I know what it is," Mike confided, joining them and giving Van his drink. "What ya willing to pay?" he asked laughing and dodging out of the way when Dave made a playful lunge for him. "You got the mean green, I got the recipe."

Van slapped a twenty on the table and Mike grabbed it.

She watched them at play. Sitting here with them, the Basement seemed hardly threatening. The three seemed comfortable together. She felt they had an exceptionally close bond.

Dave and Mike were obviously brothers. They favored each other, had many of the same mannerisms, and Dave seemed as wonderfully good-natured as Mike now, but Van had helped her when Dave wouldn't.

She turned her wholehearted attention to her rescuer, gazing attentively at him, drinking in every aspect, every smile. Their eyes met.

"Are you okay?" he asked.

Seeing the amusement in his eyes, knowing she was already tipsy from the alcohol, she tried to suppress a giggle. "I'm great."

"Are you?"

"She's great," Dave verified, offering a tongue-in-cheek grin.

Van gave her a skeptical look tinged with humor. How she loved his expressions! But did she really, or were her perceptions due to the marvelous concoction Dave had prepared? Right now, it didn't seem to matter.

Music still blasted from the jukebox, the iridescent posters glimmered, people still danced with strobe lights pulsing, the cobra still sat majestically behind the bar glowing eerily from the lighting beneath, but the fear had evaporated, the atmosphere had changed.

"It's gone," Nancy said. She set the empty glass on the table with a regretful sigh. "Thanks, it was luscious."

"Another?" Dave offered.

"I don't want to carry her home," Van intervened before she could reply. "One is plenty."

"Yes," she agreed. "One is plenty enough."

The fear was gone, but the fact remained that she did not belong here. This could never be her domain.

"Have to go now," she said, trying to speak distinctly. She regarded Dave through sad eyes feeling disturbingly varied sentiments. "It would have been nice meeting you under other circumstances."

He tilted his head in compliance. "Goodnight—"

"Nancy," she reminded him.

"Take it easy, Nancy," he said with a viable grin.

Van escorted her out of the Basement with a gentle hold on her arm. She felt elated as they stepped out into the breezy California night.

"Thank you for coming to my rescue," Nancy said hoping her speech didn't slur. She certainly felt an amazing intoxication for only one drink.

"No thanks necessary."

"But you fought your friends over me."

"John Burton and his bitches are no friends of mind."

"No one else would have made a move to stop them."

"That's right," he said casually. "Now, where do you live?"

"4873 North Broadway, straight ahead all the way to the end."

"Did you drive?"

"No, I walked."

They continued strolling up the deserted street.

"Why did you go there, Nancy?" he finally asked.

"Because I wanted to meet you," she replied. Simply put, it made perfect sense to her.

"Me? You wanted to meet me?" Van on the other hand sounded stunned.

"Well, someone like you," she explained.

He let out a long audible breath. "No, you didn't," he said. "You think you wanted to meet someone like me. You don't, not really."

"How do you know?"

"Because I know you're a good girl, Nancy, trying to go astray for some reason, putting yourself in jeopardy . . ."

"I should have known better," she acknowledged with a light shiver. "What I did tonight could have been disastrous."

"You were reckless," he agreed. "What you did tonight could have ruined your life," he added quietly. "You won't find your prince in a place like that."

Nancy thought about what he said as they walked the remaining distance in silence. What he said was all true, but she had gone to the Basement with a purpose, she was tired of being considered a 'good girl' when she wasn't even sure the title fit her.

She found herself contemplating a night with him, wondering how he would react to such a bold enticement. She wondered, also, if she would have the nerve to ask him something so blatant—even though it was what she wanted, and even after drinking courage in the form of a mysterious pink beverage.

She stopped in front of the apartment building, still unresolved, thinking it might be best to simply appreciate being home and send him on his way.

"This is it." Nancy gazed up at him, drew a deep breath, and then took the plunge. "Would you like to come up for a nightcap?"

Van inclined his head in compliance. "If I could impose on your generosity to include a quick shower, I'd love to." A dark curl over one eye gave him an appearance of youth. "I worked up a sweat in the tussle."

When they stepped inside her cozy apartment, he glanced around. "Nice," he said approvingly.

"Thank you," Nancy replied happily.

The simple compliment warmed her. She laid no claim to being an interior decorator, but it had been fun picking out the swatches for the furniture, having the paint mixed to the right shades, then selecting the various wall coverings and drapes for the décor.

She had decorated in various shades of blue and green with oak accents, and country flair, intending to create a place of warmth and comfort.

Nancy gently cleared her throat. "The bathroom's that way." She indicated the hall to the left. "There are clean towels and washcloths."

"Thanks, Nancy, in the meantime, how about a shot of bourbon and a cold beer?"

"Ah—no beer," she said apologetically. "I do have bourbon, though."

"On the rocks then," he said agreeably.

Nancy watched his retreat—a man in her shower. Unbelievable!

She dimmed the lights, turned the stereo on low, and then went to the kitchen for ice. Nancy poured a wine glass almost full with Chardonnay and took an encouraging sip.

"I can do this," she whispered. "I can pour his drink. I can sip some wine while he has a shower. I don't have to do anything else if I don't want to."

In the midst of the different feelings erupting within her, she found herself experiencing some anxiety and more than a trace of doubt, but also a definite undercurrent of expectation and exuberance.

She tried to concentrate on the latter as she paused in the doorway.

Van emerged from the hallway, barefoot, carrying his shoes, wearing his jeans, his shirt unbuttoned.

He smiled sexily at her noticing the low lights and music. "Why don't you change into something a little more comfortable?" he suggested.

"Oh—well—" She felt tongue-tied. "Um—I—"

"It's okay, never mind." He sat down on the sofa. "Come here," he said.

She joined him, giving him the bourbon, taking another drink of wine.

"I want your promise to never go there again."

She sat beside him. "I assure you," she said fervently. "I have no intention of setting foot on the Southside again."

"Good girl," he said approvingly.

She leaned toward him. "But I don't want to be a good girl either."

He gave her a sensuous look that urged her further.

"I'm serious," she said, smiling, flirting. "I want to be a little bit naughty."

"So, you're interested in giving up the good girl status?"

He set his drink aside. "What if I say I'm interested in obliging your newest reckless endeavor?" He tugged at her sleeve. "What then?"

Nancy wished that she could just give in like she wanted to, but letting go did not come easy. "Could we get to know each other first?"

He looked at her uncertainly, easing casually away. She felt the distance.

"Why not?" she said delicately.

"A lot of reasons, little one; the big picture is more than you could imagine."

He slipped his hand around the back of her neck, drawing her face close for a lingering kiss. She felt a sweet wave of excitement but played it down.

"Could you tell me a little about yourself?" she insisted, thinking it couldn't be so much to ask considering he would be spending the night.

He unbuttoned the first button of her blouse, lowering his head to kiss the soft rise of her breast.

"Van, please."

He sighed. "I'm trying," he said, leaning back.

"You're not from around here. I know that much."

"Don't, Nancy."

"Why do you want to be so mysterious? Do you like to leave people wondering?" She found it difficult to accept his detached manner.

"I'm not trying to be mysterious," he said, impassively. "My life isn't open to inspection. Once I leave here, I want you to forget all about me."

He finally looked at her.

"Maybe you're right." Nancy felt mortified by the tears that gathered so quickly in her eyes. "The less I know, the easier I can forget."

She didn't understand such intense feelings or being captivated so quickly.

"Hey." He placed a finger under her chin, tilting her face up. "I'd better leave," he said, softly. "You're not the type for a one night stand."

Nancy blushed under the caress of his eyes, assailed by doubts all over again. He had seen her safely home, and he would leave if she agreed.

"I don't know exactly what I want, Van, but I don't want you to go. I'm not experienced with men, but I want to learn." She gripped his hand filled with unexpected eagerness. "I want you to teach me. I need to be a woman."

"You *are* a woman, a beautiful and sexy woman. How can you imagine you're not everything a man could want?" He ran his fingers through her hair. "There's someone for you, Nancy, but it's not me, it shouldn't be me."

"You don't understand. It's just that—I'm not sure. If you don't stay—I might not try again. I feel a little desperate," she confessed.

"You have to accept how it is with me, baby—desperation could lead to a lot of fun and games, but that's all it is. It's your decision."

He touched her face with the back of his hand, coming closer until his lips found hers, his hand moving easily behind her neck.

She accepted the caress of his lips on her mouth, hesitant at first, tenderly searching, deliberately tantalizing.

The tension drained from her body with his slow, drugging kisses. He eased her back on the sofa as his hands began to explore the supple curves of her body through her clothes.

Nancy exhaled a pleasurable sigh when he pushed her blouse open. She never dreamed a man's hands would feel so gentle and persuasive, but in spite of the desire, she felt uneasy.

His mouth covered hers again, parting her lips for a more intimate kiss.

He pressed kisses on her face, neck and shoulders, but when his lips brushed against her breast, she tensed. "Relax," he whispered.

The single word breathed against her skin brought on a barrage of memories. Nancy's first experience with a lover overwhelmed her, a voice, alluring in the dark. "Relax." Feather light hands, silky smooth, softly caressing.

While her parents slept, her cousin, who had come to live with them, seduced her in the night, introduced her to forbidden desires, a secret life.

They did not know; how could they have known their niece was a lesbian?

He finished removing her clothes slowly, planting kisses on bared skin. Gently his hand outlined the circle of her breast. "Let me taste you."

A moan slipped past her lips, his tongue tantalized her senses as he moved down, trailing little kisses. Desire welled within her, a deep yearning—unbidden memories, sweet anticipation, and delightfully familiar sensations.

His hands pressed her thighs open. Nancy almost cried out in explosive pleasure. She couldn't resist, she didn't try. Nancy embraced the rush, rode the wave of incredible enchantment as delicious spasms rocked her world.

He moved up her body, his mouth covered hers hungrily again. Taking her hand, he guided it to himself. "Touch me, Nancy," he whispered in a voice gone yearning and husky.

"I can't," she choked, withdrawing her hand with a light shiver.

"Are you a virgin?"

How could she answer? Such a simple question and yet so complicated.

"You're ready," he whispered. "What are you afraid of?"

Nancy shook her head unable to answer. She wanted his hard body beside hers—the comfort of his closeness, warm hands roaming intimately, intuitively seeking pleasure points—but ready for sex?

His experience at arousing sexual response could probably not be matched. She undeniably felt delightful sensations, an undefinable yearning, but could she let him claim her body in the way he would expect?

"You've enjoyed everything so far, haven't you," he said, his lips against her throat. "I can do more."

"Please, don't."

"I want you . . ." His hand slid across her smooth belly down to her thigh. "I could take you now," he said softly. "It would be so easy."

She trembled when his finger dipped into the warmth of her aroused body.

"Please don't—you don't understand."

"Then make me understand."

Her heart thumped uncomfortably. How could she make him understand that she felt completely terrified? What if it turned out that she didn't want a man? What if this is a terrible mistake?

He turned away from her emitting a disturbed sigh.

"Do you want to tell me why we can't have each other?"

"I don't think so."

"I think you'd better." He turned back.

"I'm afraid," she whispered. "I—I've never been with a man before."

"You said you want to." Van settled more comfortably beside her, traced a finger teasingly along her body. "I know you do, I can feel your desire, so yes, I need to know."

She swallowed with difficulty, knowing she had to explain. "I don't know how you'll feel about this, but I've had sexual experiences." The confession left her uncomfortable, bordering on humiliation. "But not with a man."

"So, you've had lesbian experiences . . ."

She flushed painfully. "When I was very young."

"What happened?" he asked gently.

"I've never talked to anyone about this. I don't know how to tell you."

"Take your time—something happened that has left you troubled and uncertain. It clearly needs discussing."

Nancy felt a terrible tenseness in her body, but knew he had insight that could not be denied, it had to be told. She sighed, releasing the tension, feeling surprisingly calm.

"My aunt's second husband was a cruel and abusive person," she began. "He *seemed* to be a wonderful, caring man who accepted her daughter as his own. He didn't appear to be a monster," she whispered. "They lived miles away—my parents never suspected. When we visited, Aunt Celia seemed happy, he seemed loving and attentive. She never mentioned any sort of problem."

Nancy stared straight ahead remembering the funeral and two coffins, one very small, too tiny to imagine.

"When she died giving birth to a stillborn son Alexandra was committed to his care." Nancy closed her eyes. "Her stepfather—raped her. He beat her, and he used her—and when he was through—"

A tear slid slowly down the side of her face.

"He just left her in the apartment to die."

Van gently brushed the tear away.

"She was found by the janitor, locked in a closet so near death he couldn't tell at first that she was even breathing. She couldn't ever remember being found."

Nancy took a shallow breath finding it difficult, now, to continue but knowing she had to. "I was fourteen when she came to live with us. She shared my room," Nancy said faintly. "It wasn't long before she was sharing my bed."

He began stroking her lightly, his hand moving warmly down the length of her body and back.

"It lasted for two years, until she graduated and moved to Florida."

There, it had all been told. That wasn't so bad. Nancy sighed and snuggled closer to him. "Now she wants me to join her."

"Do you think you're gay?"

"I don't know. I enjoyed being with her."

"She shouldn't have taken advantage of you. She was young and mixed up herself or it wouldn't have happened. You never told anyone?"

"I was afraid of the feelings—and ashamed at first. Then there came a time when I let go of the fear and shame, and simply accepted."

Nancy began to move her hand along his muscled body, her fingers playing at his chest hair, absorbing the texture of his skin, going slowly down.

He gripped her wrist halting the caress. "Is it me you want, Nancy?"

She pressed her lips to his shoulder, tasting him, breathing in the clean, subtly provocative scent of him. "I want to play your games."

"If we begin again, I won't stop," he whispered. "And I can't refuse if you come onto me, no matter how wrong this is. You better be very sure."

She ran her fingers through his dark, wavy hair and wanted to kiss him, an irrepressible urge, she touched her lips to his.

In spite of wanting him, her doubts escalated, threatening to spiral out of control. "Convince me," she said desperately.

His moan—a low, sensual sound as his mouth captured hers—gave her a feeling of deep satisfaction, igniting unexpected desire.

"I can't promise forever," he said quietly. "We only have tonight, but what's more important than this moment?"

His lips brushed over hers as he spoke, the sensation liquefying.

"You got me wanting you, baby, but more than that, you matter to me. I've never felt this before, not like this." The huskiness in his voice stimulated her senses.

"You're very persuasive," she murmured.

He moved away long enough to finish undressing, then his warm naked body covered hers.

Nancy tilted her head back, felt the warm caress of his lips against her neck, and arched toward him, desperately needing more. His electrifying touch had her moaning for release, impatient for him to possess her now willing body.

Van explored the soft, lithe body, spreading her legs a little wider. His eyes swept over her. She looked so seductive, so inviting. His gaze came to rest on her limpid eyes before he fervently claimed the remainder of her innocence.

After the initial stab of pain and pleasure, she experienced the feel of him inside her. This wonder absorbed her. She became a part of it, a part of him, lost in the firmness of his lips, the caress of his hands, the intoxicating smell of him. The sounds of his urgings freed in her a bursting of sensations, different and astonishing, flesh against flesh, a man and a woman making love.

Nancy ran her hands over his muscled shoulders, up into his hair and drew his face to hers in a renewed embrace, the kisses sweet and exciting. When his lips left hers, he nibbled at her earlobe, his breath warm against her skin.

She listened to idly sweet murmurings, taking them to heart, to hold forever.

His hands skimmed her thighs, and then gripped beneath them drawing her legs up. She felt burning desire like a ravenous craving, and tightened her legs around him, her body rising to meet his as she trembled with fiery vibrations, the pleasure pure and explosive.

He moaned her name, the affection sounding so *real,* tremors shook his body and she held on tight, her world filled with him and the incredible experience of the passion they shared, this experience of man and woman becoming one.

She exhaled a long sigh of contentment. He continued to move his hand over the contours of her body, his breathing gradually returning to normal.

"You are incredibly sensuous," he said. "I think you might have liked it," he added with a teasing lilt.

She blushed, turning her face against his shoulder. "You're wonderful," she said, her words muffled against his skin.

"So are you," he whispered.

Nancy closed her eyes savoring the words he spoke and the tenderness of his embrace. She felt drowsy, fully content, and almost drifted into a light sleep in his arms. She finally sat up, dreamily reaching for her clothes.

"Would you like another drink while I shower?" she suggested.

He snatched her blouse away, tossing it behind the sofa.

"I'd rather shower with you."

"Take a shower together?"

His laugh was deep, warm and rich. She realized this was the first time he had laughed in her presence. He had a certain captivating grin, appealing looks of amusement, smiling dark eyes, but his laughter was marvelous.

"Come on," he urged convincingly. "You'll enjoy it, I promise."

"I—can't," she protested.

"Ah, but your eyes say different." He began to pull her encouragingly off the sofa. "Fun and games, darlin'," he drawled playfully. "You're going to be more than a little naughty tonight."

* * *

Nancy awoke suddenly, turning to the loneliness of an empty bed. She suffered the emptiness of falling asleep in his arms, then awakening alone, but it didn't come unexpectedly.

He had not promised more than a night, living in the moment, experiencing remarkable, liberating sensations. Now she felt elated with the knowledge of her sexuality, free of the uncertainty that had been so imposing in her life.

His wonderful spell lingered still, the remnants of his appeal and mystifying charm. Nancy sighed as she remembered his words. Yes, she had been naughty, so naughty that it made her blush as she recalled the incredible lovemaking session during the shower that continued on into the bedroom.

She held tight to the memory of that passion and the sweetness of his goodnight kiss. A touch of sadness mingled with the happiness of her newfound freedom, but she refused to let it dim the sheer delight of this morning after.

He had told her that she must forget him, but she knew she would never forget him, those intense eyes, and the unbelievable fascination of his mouth. Nancy smiled to herself. She had a feeling that in spite of 'the big picture' he probably wouldn't forget her either.

She made a silent vow to never look back on this night with remorse, to ruin a night of passionate love and emotional revelation with feelings of regret for what might have been.

She had awakened too soon, but she located her terrycloth robe, and tying it around her, Nancy walked to the window opening the drapes to view a bright morning, mostly blue sky, with a few, scattered clouds.

It had rained during the night leaving the world clean and fresh. As sunlight beamed through the clouds, she reflected that her own little world was every bit as radiant and renewed as this clear day.

Drowsiness swept over her, the comfort of sleep beckoned. Nancy closed the drapes. Laying her robe at the foot of the bed, slipping naked between the sheets, she wished for dreams of her handsome stranger.

Chapter Seven

Christi locked the door to the apartment, breathing a sigh of relief to be inside. Sometimes the streets seemed safer than the halls of this building. She did not consider herself unduly edgy. They were dimly lit and radiated an air of animosity, even during the day.

"You're late."

She recognized the quietly imposing voice. Christi whirled to face John Burton. He stood in the doorway of the living room looking self-satisfied when she took an involuntary step backward.

"How did you get in here?" she demanded.

"Locked doors have never been a problem for me," he replied, leaning casually against the door frame, looking at her in a way that released the familiar sensation of fear she had felt when he cornered her at the Basement.

She took a deep breath hoping her voice wouldn't tremble. "I want you to get out of here, right now."

"Do you?" He took a step in her direction. "You know I've been watching you, baby. And you hang around the Basement a lot. You know how to move that sexy little body, too, making me want you."

She backed away from him and the unfair accusation.

"Do you get your kicks leading me on, knowing I can't have it?"

"What are you saying?"

He closed the distance between them, grabbing her by the arm.

"You're a flirt," he accused. "A common little tease."

"That's not true."

"Isn't it?" His gaze roved appraisingly over her body, down the full length of her slender frame.

She cringed inside feeling extremely uncomfortable. Her jean shorts dipped below her belly button, the matching midriff shirt left a lot of exposed skin. Should she be embarrassed in the clothes she wore, or ashamed of her body? No one had ever made her feel this way.

John's sullen gaze returned to her face. "You can deny it, baby, but you've been asking for it."

He held her face with one hand, pressing her against the wall, forcing her legs apart with his knee. His mouth came down hard on hers, a painful first kiss. She helplessly struggled to escape his expertly groping hands until her fear of him became the lesser emotion as a kind of rage took hold. She fought with a fury and strength she had been unaware of until now.

He backed off half-laughing at her defiance. "Easy, little champion," he said softly, his dark eyes dangerous. "Don't fight me. Don't make me hurt you."

"You'll have to hurt me." Christi edged along the wall, hoping to make a run for the kitchen, then out the back door to the fire escape.

John easily blocked the way. Slamming her hard against the wall, he kept her pinned with one strong arm, but rivaling his strength, eyes darker than night held her captive.

He popped the top of a tiny pill bottle, his stare penetrating.

One hand blocking air passage to her nose, she had to open her mouth to breathe. He forced the pills into her mouth, and then covered her nose and mouth compelling her to swallow.

She inhaled deeply when he took his hand away.

"Dave won't let you get away with this."

"Dave isn't going to know anything about it," he said evenly. "This is our private party. Yours . . . and mine . . . you won't tell anyone." He moistened his lips. "You're way too excitable, baby. You need to relax." He smiled easily. "You might decide you like my methods."

"How can you do this?" she pleaded, beginning to feel the effect of his drugs. Her vision blurred through tears of frustration, her numbing mind trying to conceive a way to reach him. "You're supposed to be his friend."

"I'm nobody's friend."

He loosened the knot in front of her blouse, pulling it free. When it fell open, he lowered his head kissing her neck, moving down to the slight rise of her small breasts.

He unfastened her shorts, tugging at the zipper.

"You say you're nobody's friend," she cried, feeling devastating fear and desperation, anger and helplessness. "But my brother considers you a friend, defends you, he cares about you—how can you be so cold? How can you rape your best friend's sister? Please, John, don't do this to me."

His gaze looked right through her, his eyes passionless.

She leaned against the wall feeling suddenly heavy, weak and oddly detached, a hazy feeling of indifference enveloped her. She realized the floor had disintegrated to leave her floating on a cloud.

Christi looked at him through half-closed eyes. Trying to focus took too much effort. She let her eyes drift shut. He said something, but the words were lost somewhere in a swirling void.

She heard a voice calling to her, pulling her up through the sinking emptiness. She did not want the intrusion, moaning a protest, she felt herself being raised to a standing position.

"Come on, golden girl, wake up."

Christi recognized Van's voice, gently urgent. He began walking her around the living room. "Pick up your feet," he commanded as she leaned heavily against him. "Come on, Christine, it's not an option."

"Oh, please," she mumbled, her eyes refusing to open.

She gasped in surprise, feeling an unwelcome cold washcloth bathing her face, awakening long enough to realize they were now in the bathroom.

"Christi, open your eyes! Or do you want to hit the showers?"

She heard his voice, that infuriatingly commanding tone, but it didn't matter, he sounded too far away to be very intimidating.

"Damn it," he muttered. "Okay, I don't want to take you to the hospital where they'll stick a needle in your arm and keep you twenty-four hours for observation, but I'm taking you to the hospital *if you don't wake up*. Christi!"

She sighed, barely hearing. Having her eyes closed felt so good. She meant to convey her feelings but the words simply drifted through her head.

"How about some tunes, then?" he suggested. He propelled her out of the bathroom, down the hall to the living room.

The sound blasted through her numb mind. Startled, her eyes snapped open wide, but only for a moment. He walked her around the room again, ignoring the intermittent pleading and complaining.

Finally, Christi opened her eyes feeling puzzled.

"Van—what happened?" she murmured.

"There you are," he said enthusiastically. "Let's get some coffee."

They walked into the kitchen where she sank onto a chair, still finding it difficult to stay awake, falling back into that warm blanket of comfort, her eyes closed to all things that might be painful, until the teakettle whistled.

"You're going to be alright," she heard him say. "This will help."

He measured two heaping teaspoons of coffee in a mug, poured in the boiling water, adding a couple of ice cubes to cool it.

"Getting you awake was imperative, but you were responsive, I knew I could revive you."

"What makes you think I'm revived?" she mumbled, but she was revived. She was beginning to remember. Christi covered her face with her hands unable to look at him.

"Christi . . . sweetie?" He moved her hands gently away from her face. Still holding her hands, he said, "Look at me."

She shook her head automatically, but then she took a breath. Christi lifted her face to his tender, concerned expression.

"Don't ever feel shame, Chris, what happened wasn't your fault. You have to understand that—he's a deceptive personality, and he plays mind games. Now drink the coffee," he urged. "It may seem a little strong at first."

She took a deep drink of the bitter brew and sighed wearily.

"You're right, this is horrible." She took another deep swallow.

She started to tremble. Christi set the cup carefully on the table.

"He accused me of leading him on, but I'm not a tease, Van—I never meant to be."

"Shhh . . . . I know." He reached over to replace a strand of hair that had fallen over her eye. "That's his strategy. He's convincing, but he's a liar."

Bowing her head in humiliation, shamed by the awareness of knowing how he had found her, Christi struggled not to break down. She felt shattered, self-conscious, thankful, but deeply embarrassed.

"Hey, what's this?" Van brushed a tear that slipped past her lashes with his thumb. He held her face gently. Christi finally raised soulful eyes to his.

"Everything's beginning to surface, isn't it?"

She nodded, unable to speak.

"Come here." He pulled her onto his lap. "Listen, sweetheart—you're a child, innocent as a baby to me . . . Or maybe a little sister," he suggested.

Christi cried on his shoulder while he rocked her like a little girl. She felt protected. She wanted to stay where she sat, to fall asleep in his arms, but as the tears subsided, Christi moved back to her own chair.

She took another long swallow of the strong, black coffee.

"He made me feel like it was my fault," she whispered.

"Of course he did." His troubled eyes searched her face. "I thought I already set you straight on that."

"You did," she said. "I'll try." Christi sighed sleepily, stifling a yawn. "Van, I have to go to bed. I can't stay awake any longer."

"Yes you can," he replied solemnly. "Finish your coffee."

"I don't want to—I want to sleep." But she drank obediently.

He grinned. "Now, go take a shower," he commanded.

"Van!" She whined a little for sympathy.

"You have to stay awake awhile longer," he said firmly. He lifted one eyelid, gazing closely at the pupil. "You're really stoned."

Christi shuffled grumpily into the bathroom. She removed the housecoat Van had tied around her.

In the shower, she stood under a tepid spray for several moments. As the shower revived her senses even more, she turned up the hot water and began to vigorously scrub her body, but she couldn't wash away the feeling of violation.

Back to the kitchen, with the housecoat wrapped around her, Van checked her pupils again.

"Am I going to live?" she said, with a sad little smile.

"A long healthy life," he replied, concern still reflecting in his dark eyes.

"Can I go to bed now?"

"Sweet dreams," he conceded.

Christi paused at the door. "Van, how did you know?"

"I had a discontented feeling, but I couldn't place it. Then it dawned on me—the way he disregarded you tonight seemed odd, more disturbing than his usual observance." He looked distant for a moment, but then his gaze came to rest on her questioning eyes. "When I get that feeling, I trust my instincts."

"Good you do," she murmured, noticing his still subdued scrutiny.

"Are you all right with this?"

"Not completely, but I will be."

"No guilt?" he insisted.

"I know you're right," she said agreeably.

"I'll stay until Mike or Dave gets home, and I'll have a locksmith install a dead bolt first thing," he promised. "Sleep tight."

"Thanks, Van, I love you for that—for everything."

Sleep had been immediate, deep and dreamless.

She kept her eyes closed, quietly pensive for several minutes after awakening. When she opened her eyes to shimmering sunlight, the events of the night before seemed foggy and surreal.

Christi sat up. "Dave!" She wanted her brother. "David!" Yelling hurt her head. John had drugged her, had come painfully close to raping her. Last night had been reality, not a nightmare.

She heard a light tap on the door before it opened. Dave entered and crossed the room to her bed.

"I'm sorry, angel." He cradled her in his arms. "Van told me what happened," he murmured. "I never imagined John would do something like this. It's unbelievable, but I promise it won't happen again."

"Are you sure?" She pulled back to look at him. "If it hadn't been for Van—you never took me serious when I told you John was coming onto me," she pointed out. "You thought it was harmless teasing. You shrugged it off."

"I said, I'm sorry, and I *can* assure you, he won't touch you again." He searched her face anxiously. "Are you all right?"

She shivered a little. "John's a user, Dave, why can't you see it?"

"Don't, Christi," he said softly but firmly, clearly considering the issue resolved. "He made a mistake."

"This was not a mistake," she told him. "How can you think it was a mistake? It was something he'd planned; he even accused me of leading him on, Dave." Christi waited briefly for a response, finally sighing unhappily. "Maybe I shouldn't come to the Basement anymore."

"Are you getting an attitude?" he said with a coaxing grin. "I am really sorry, but you have to let it go now."

Once more she sighed and shrugged. He seemed to accept the gesture as compliance, apparently oblivious to her disappointment.

Aware of his deep sincerity, she knew John was deceiving him, but there was no way to make him see it. She wasn't all right, not at all. She wanted him to hate John Burton for what he had done.

"Are you hungry?" he asked optimistically. "Mike's decided to try his hand at making an omelet. He's turning into a talented chief."

He left the room, closing the door behind him. Christi sat up on the edge of the bed. Uncertain doubts lingered still, but in her heart, she knew that she had never encouraged John's advances, did not even consider them flattering.

She wondered why Dave remained oblivious to John's evil nature. And she wondered how John could instill such a strong mental influence that made her have misgivings about her own character.

He was a talented manipulator all right, Van knew that.

Christi sat for a bleak moment longer, pouting wouldn't help; arguing wouldn't help. She decided to have breakfast, being with Mike might help.

Mike had a plate ready, complete with coffee and orange juice.

"Everything looks wonderful and smells great." She rewarded him with a sleepy smile. "Mike, you're becoming quite the chef!"

"Don't give him a big head," Dave teased. He finished his coffee. "Come on down to the Basement after while," he suggested. "Don't let John think he's scared you away."

"How can you dismiss what he did so easily?" She decided to try reasoning again. "He came into our home. He would have raped me."

"I'm telling you, Chris, you need to chill. He just got carried away—this one incident—"

"This one incident was too much!" she said intensely, interrupting him. "And you should know it, and the way he treats Karen—"

"How he treats Karen is not our business," he interposed firmly.

Christi realized her mistake in mentioning Karen. Why had she not expected the staid response? She sighed tiredly. His withdrawn expression closed the conversation again.

Nothing she said had changed his feelings and anything else would put him on the defensive. Dave headed out the back saying, 'later' over his shoulder. The screen door slammed.

Mike sat down opposite her. "They've been friends since kindergarten," he said. "Something happened that—"

"I don't really want to hear excuses." She raised her eyes to meet his.

"So something happened in John's life to screw him up, so what! Why should he take it out on me?" She picked at her food, struggling not to cry.

"He's psycho scum," Mike said ominously. "I'd like to kill him."

"Mike, don't, please! Talk like that just rattles me. I'll get over this."

"I'd just like to, that's all. Eat your breakfast," he said, gruffly.

"I will. Mike, I really will be all right."

"I know." He gave her an expectant glimpse. "You okay, then?"

Christi looked at him and had to grin. "Go on, get out of here."

"See you later." Mike paused at the door. "The dead bolt's been installed." He smiled, twisting it open and closed. "There's one on the kitchen door, too." He played at the lock a couple more times.

"If I were you, I'd take Dave's advice. Just put in an appearance, maybe an hour or so," he suggested, then with understanding. "Or maybe I wouldn't, if I was you, but I think you should."

She thought about what Dave and Mike had said as she washed the breakfast dishes. She decided to take their advice and just get it over with.

Christi stepped outside. She paused experiencing a compelling urge to turn right, to go visit Dawn and forget the whole unpleasant incident for a while, a day or two, maybe three or four.

She resisted the urge to procrastinate. Putting it off for a day or a week wouldn't change anything. It would only heighten her reserves.

The day was bright and breezy, the Basement dark and cool.

Christi headed toward the back table where Trixi and Dave sat. As she passed John, his eyes met hers with a steady gaze. He looked bruised, which gave her a moment's satisfaction, knowing Van had punched him a good one.

Then he winked at her, and she hurried past. Nothing had changed.

After sitting for about a half hour, talking, trying to act as if nothing had happened, she stood. "I'm gonna book," she said. "I'll catch you guys later. I'm kinda bummed."

She scooted the chair in, looking candidly at her big brother.

"I don't mean to make light of what he did," Dave said kindly. "But I can guarantee he'll tire of this little game."

"See ya later, kid," Trixi said with a sympathetic look.

Christi left them, feeling self-conscious and stiff in her walk with John watching her, doubting if she would ever feel comfortable in his presence.

John turned back to his drink after the door closed behind Christi.

"Why don't you leave her alone?" Karen said. "She's only sixteen. Why do you want to give her grief? She's a young girl who wants—"

"What?" He interrupted her, taking her arm in a tight grip. A thoughtful smile curved his mouth. "You jealous?" he suggested. "You wish you were sweet sixteen again?"

Karen knew better than to respond. She took a long drink of her gin and tonic, trying to ignore the implication.

He released her arm, giving her a casual glance. "I'm through with you, Karen," he said, with no infraction, typical of John. He swirled the liquid in his glass, downing the last of it. "I want you the hell out of my life."

Karen absorbed the softly spoken statement, slowly comprehending his words. He wanted her gone? Stunned beyond measure, she looked at his handsome face, completely void of expression, eyes that could hold such intense emotion looked eerily passionless and empty.

This man who had been her hope, her fear, hate and love for the past two years had calmly dismissed her. Living in dread that it might end this way did not make it less difficult to accept.

As he walked away without a backward glance, she began to fully acknowledge the certainty of his disregard.

"You're better off, you know."

"I know," she said bleakly.

Mike sat on the stool next to her.

"It still hurts, though. I didn't expect it to end like this, you know, without *any* warning."

In spite of all the doubts and fears or uncertainties that might have been, his callous words had taken the last bit of hope or any wishful expectations that there had even been a flicker of emotion in his heart for her.

"What will you do?"

"I have no idea." She finished her drink feeling completely forsaken.

Pushing the glass aside, she felt tears burn her eyes but blinked them away, hurt, yes, but angry, also. She didn't want to cry over the bastard.

Not now, not in front of Mike.

"He's put you down for too long, Karen."

"You don't know the half Mike." She fought for composure. "It was a destructive relationship based on fear and—I wanted out—I've wanted out." Karen sighed dejectedly. "But now that it's happened, I feel so alone."

"You're beautiful, you know." Dipping his head slightly, he said, "It won't be easy, no doubt you will feel alone at times, but don't sell yourself short. You have a lot to offer the right person. You'll make a connection."

He grinned when she gave him a wondering look.

"Are you sure you're only sixteen?" She tried to smile but knew it fell very short of portraying any sort of assurance.

"Is there a place for you to go? What about San Francisco?"

"I have a friend there." She gave him a speculative glance. She had just been thinking about Theresa. "I got in touch with her a while back . . . She said I'm always welcome . . . I could stay with her, if I could get there."

"A lot of people care about you, Karen. No one liked the way he treated you, but we couldn't interfere, you know how it is."

"Yeah, I found out how it is," she agreed.

He gave a light shrug, looking slightly uncomfortable. "What I'm saying is you don't have to worry about money for a bus ticket. I'll get it together."

He put some bills in her hand, wrapping her fingers around them.

"It's cab fare," he explained encouragingly. "Go pack. Meet me at the bus depot in two hours."

"Thanks Mike." She did smile then, and took a deep breath, setting free a good portion of the desolation at the prospect of a new start. "Will you tell Christi I said good-bye?"

"Sure."

Karen paused, looking somewhat bewildered. "Mike?"

"You don't have to say anything," he said thoughtfully. "Just get your act together, no more destructive relationships."

She hugged him close. "No more," she vowed. "Thank you."

He watched as she paused on her way out to speak to few of the guys and share farewell hugs with some of the girls hanging around.

Chapter Eight

Christi spooned instant coffee into her cup, poured boiling water from the teakettle about two thirds up, then added milk.

She sat down at the kitchen table, her thoughts turning to Karen. Mike had told her why she left so quickly. It would have been nice to say goodbye, but the consolation that she had escaped John Burton compensated for the swift departure. An unhappy twist, that John told her to leave—the only way out for Karen had been another form of abuse, his rejection.

From odds and ends of conversation, she picked up that Karen had been a lonely, frightened girl when she came here. Hopefully, John's treatment wouldn't leave her scarred for life. Mike said she vowed to stay away from destructive relationships.

Thoughts of John always brought to mind an uneasy awareness of his uncaring capabilities. She didn't go to the Basement often anymore, and when she did, she tried to ignore his presence.

Van had saved her—saved her—how could ever thank him?

Christi wondered, vaguely, about Van's showing up at the Basement and being accepted so readily by Dave, and her own attachment to him, even before the incident with John.

It didn't matter, though, he had been there, and he had been intuitive and attentive to her safety. It strengthened her affection, creating a deeper bond.

She decided to adopt him as a second big brother. He treated her as much like a little sister as Dave did. Christi realized, now, that it would have been a serious letdown if he had ever made an advance toward her.

She glanced at Mike as he entered the kitchen. Dave always slept until late noon except on Sunday.

"Good morning."

"Morning, Chris. Plans for today?" He turned the fire on under the teakettle.

"I'm going to a pool party at Dawn's."

"Sounds fun."

"You could come," she said, even though his 'sounds fun' seemed too nonchalant. "You would like the pool parties, Mike, lots of girls in bikinis."

"I'm sure it would be too much excitement for me," he teased. "With all those debutants prancing around, I might OD. Maybe another day, though. Don't give up," he grinned. "It could happen."

More teasing. "They're not all debutants," she informed him. "Scrambled eggs for breakfast?"

"No bacon?"

"We're fresh out."

"I think Dave better designate you to do the shopping."

"No thanks."

Christi made scrambled eggs and toast for her and Mike. She washed the few breakfast dishes so they wouldn't be waiting for her in the morning with whatever Mike and Dave might use. They weren't too big on cleanup, and she would probably crash at Dawn's house.

"I have something for you," Dawn said with a wide smile as soon as she opened the door. "Come on!"

Christi followed her through the entrance hall. "What is it?"

"A surprise!"

They headed up the wide marble staircase, and then advanced down the spacious hall to the bedroom. Christi noticed the plain white, unwrapped box on the bed right away.

"This is for you." Dawn practically pranced over to the bed. She handed the box to her, excitement lighting her green eyes.

"Dawn, another gift?" Just last month she had bought her the cutest flowing mini and sling back sandals to go with it.

"Just open it!"

Christi removed the lid. She knew the white bikini cost more than she would ever pay for two little pieces of material. "What's this for?"

"It's for wearing, silly," Dawn replied. "Do I have to have a reason to give my friend a present?"

Sometimes Dawn overwhelmed her with her gifts and giddy excitement.

"Yes—you're supposed to. How did you know my size?"

"I don't really—if it fits hooray!—if not—" Dawn shrugged. "Try it on!"

"Okay." She undressed quickly. The little white bikini did fit, perfectly.

"It fits, but there's not much of it, is there? I mean, it's so . . . it's um . . ."

"Tiny—revealing?"

"Both of those."

Christi turned to the full-length mirror and almost did a double take. She had noticed a difference in her body, of course, but the effect of this bikini was almost startling.

"You're a knock-out!" Dawn said smiling.

"Is that me? When did this happen?" she wondered aloud.

"Almost overnight."

She looked mature, with only a hint of the little girl Van had walked home from the Basement. She turned slightly for a different view.

"Wonder why I don't feel as grown up as I look?" she said, feeling her youth almost overwhelmingly.

"Grownup?" Dawn shuddered. "Don't use that word! You look like a life-sized Barbie doll is what *you* look like. You do," she insisted when Christi gave her a dubious glance.

"My swimsuit doesn't do this for me," Christi said, still dazed.

"So, trash it. This is the new you."

"Thank you, Dawn. I mean, thank you!"

"I knew you'd like it." Dawn tossed her a robe. "This goes with it."

"I thought a robe was supposed to cover you. This is so flimsy!"

"Yes, isn't it!" Dawn giggled. "It just makes it seem—what is the word I'm looking for—oh, yeah, more alluring. Now, let's go!"

The month of June passed as fleetingly as a dream. Besides the pool parties, they went to Mrs. Preston's beach house located several miles out of town every Friday. Several of Dawn's friends surfed and sometimes one or two of the guys would bring speed boats. There was water skiing and boat rides. Whatever they did, it was always a good time.

Christi enjoyed fantasizing, at times, that she lived in the mansion with the majestic circular stairway and crystal chandeliers, that these girls with the social graces really were her friends . . . just a fun little game she liked to play, knowing the offer to be Dawn's adopted sister still stood, but knowing also that she would not leave her brothers.

Some of the guys who came to Dawn's parties had started watching her with new interest, and there were requests to date, which she politely declined. It seemed okay to enjoy some harmless flirting but knew better than to take them seriously. These young men were headed for Harvard or somewhere similar and would never bring a Southside girl home to meet the family.

Christi left the Basement at ten o'clock. She walked the familiar street in the direction of home paying little attention as her mind wandered to the Fourth of July celebration planned for this weekend.

A bunch of kids were going out to Dawn's beach house on Saturday for an all-night bash, surfing and swimming, a bonfire at sunset, roasting hot dogs and marshmallows, dancing in the sand and a magnificent fireworks display.

Mike even said he'd be delighted to be there. Delighted—he could be so witty.

When two guys stepped out of the alley directly in front of her, Christi stopped short. She bolted and ran but was pounced on immediately. An arm circled her waist, a large hand clamped over her mouth. The assailant dragged her into the shadows of an alley.

"I don't want to hurt you," he said low in her ear. "Don't scream. Do you understand?"

Christi quit struggling, nodding agreement.

He cautiously uncovered her mouth. "I won't gag you, if you be quiet." Cooperation would be wise, she decided. These two were Monarchs, she knew it at a glance.

"Put your hands behind your back."

"Please, you don't have to tie me."

"Put your hands behind your back," he repeated mildly.

Tears sprang to her eyes, but she obeyed. He tied her hands securely, but not painfully tight.

The second man sauntered over to where they stood. His look reminded Christi much of the way John viewed her, but even more impudent.

"Cool it, Doug," his friend warned.

Ignoring him, Doug slid his hands down her back and over her hips. She realized the need to remain calm as he pulled her against him. She didn't want gagged. In spite of ignited hostility, Christi kept silently docile.

"I said, cool it." The other fellow pulled her aside.

He walked her over to some garbage cans where the smell of rotting food wafted in the air. An alley cat hissed making a quick retreat.

The man assisted her to sit on the brick surface and tied her feet. He looked briefly into her eyes.

"I'm sorry for your discomfort," he said, checking that his handiwork was secure. "This isn't my idea."

He left her to join Doug near the front of the alley. Christi wondered who had instigated this, and why. An obvious plan, they had chosen the street well, the darkest and least occupied on the walk home.

* * *

Billy's eyes narrowed as he watched John go down the steps to the Cobra's Basement hangout. He headed across the street, the Monarchs ambling close behind. Billy and Danny started down the steps followed by the others.

At first, no one noticed the place being infiltrated. When it became evident, everything grew quiet. The jukebox suddenly stilled as Monarchs positioned themselves throughout the room while Billy walked toward Dave's table.

Dave stood. "What the fuck are you doing here?"

Billy stepped closer. Then unexpectedly, the jukebox began to play. The beat of the record Running Bear blasted the area.

"I didn't even know that was still on there," a girl giggled nervously.

There were some mocking snickers going around, but Danny didn't find it amusing. He strode purposely to the jukebox, bracing himself to kick it. His booted foot did sufficient damage, then turning fast, his switchblade locking in place, Danny took an aggressive stance.

In the suddenly eerie stillness, Billy and Dave gazed at each other for the space of a heartbeat; then switchblades clicked throughout the room followed by an electrifying silence.

"Tell him to lose the knife," Dave warned through clenched teeth.

"Pocket the knife," Billy said calmly. He had no intention of making this a bloodbath. Swiftly in—punch John out—kick him a few times for the beating—quickly leave again and have some fun with the girl responsible.

Billy shifted his gaze toward his cousin who remained in his imposing position. With a tolerant sigh, the only indication of his displeasure, Danny closed the blade. The other Monarchs complied.

"Now tell your boys to put their toys away," Billy said evenly.

Dave tilted his head in agreement, and the Cobras closed their weapons.

"Now, why are you here?" Dave demanded.

"I want Burton. We can keep it between us."

"Not happening."

"I'll get him." Billy raised his head a little more.

Dave's eyes narrowed. "What's your bag, Billy Boy?"

"He tried to kill me. I don't die easy."

"You'd be dead if he tried to waste you," Dave said hotly. "You're a liar."

Murmurs rippled across the room, Billy turned a little, swung his fist and sent Dave sprawling backward. That started the free-for-all, with girls screaming and scampering, and Monarchs and Cobras going at each other as his eyes scanned the room searching for John Burton.

Billy looked at John sprawled out on the floor. He had taken him down too easily. Even though that had been his intention, the high of anticipation, the sudden victory, left him feeling somewhat disappointed. He gave John a hard kick and enjoyed the painful grunt so much that he did it again.

Billy turned slowly to walk away but angled back with a dark feeling of contempt, the temptation too great. He owed him more, at least one more.

Trixi and Mike dragged Dave through the hall to the back room.

She went into the lavatory, wet a paper towel, and then wiped it softly over his face and forehead. His eyelids fluttered. Dave struggled to sit up, but Trixi straddled him, pressing her hands against his shoulders.

"You're not going anywhere."

"Yes, I am—where's Mike?"

"Out the back. Van told him to beat it."

"Let me up."

"Billy knocked you out cold. You're not recovered yet."

"It was a lucky punch."

"It was still a good one."

She bent over, covering his lips with hers, felt him relax as his hands moved up to gently press her breasts.

"Isn't there enough back here to keep you occupied until things settle down out there?" she suggested playfully.

"Mmm . . . more than enough." Their bodies molded together as she stretched out his length. "You are a distraction." Dave squeezed her hips appreciatively, and then made a move reversing their position, holding her wrists over her head, he smiled down at her.

"Not fair!"

"You know I have to go." He kissed her again. "Are you gonna hang around 'til I'm through out there?"

She pretended to look indecisive. "I suppose."

"Then I'll be back," he promised. "With beer and pizza."

"Someday you'll solve the world crisis with beer and pizza," she said, smiling broadly. "Don't forget to duck!" she called.

Dave hesitated in the doorway. He looked around the room full of rowdy men searching for Billy, not seeing him; he jumped haphazardly into the brawl.

* * *

Christi tried shifting a bit to ease the ache in her arms. Unfortunately, the movement drew Doug's attention. He closed the distance, settling beside her, moving her hair aside, nibbling at her earlobe.

"I'm gonna do you, baby. I'm gonna do you good."

The threat horrified her but she didn't react. She didn't say a word, even when he pushed his hand roughly between her thighs.

"Damn you, Doug. Get the fuck away from her."

He reluctantly left her alone to rejoin his friend. Christi glanced warily in their direction, knowing now that she would fear the streets at night. Monarchs weren't even supposed to be on this side of town. Something had gone wrong.

She tensed in dreaded expectation as two more men turned into the alley. One of them leaned close.

"This isn't the girl," he said belligerently.

Christi thought for sure he was going to punch someone.

"Maybe it wasn't so much your fault, though," he conceded lifting a strand of golden hair. "Go on, get out of here," he ordered.

"She's a Cobra bitch," Doug objected. "What's the difference?"

"I meant beat it," he said squarely.

They left without further debate. He pulled a knife and after a brief showing of the sinister weapon, slit the ropes at her hands and feet.

As her heart resumed an almost normal beat, he helped her to stand.

"Sorry the guys shook you up," he said with a somewhat satirical glance. "Are you all right?"

"That Doug needs a muzzle," she said rubbing her wrists to hasten circulation. "And you did that on purpose. Were you trying to scare me with your stupid knife?—because you did."

"Hey, I'm the hero here," he said looking at her enigmatically. "You shouldn't be so discourteous."

She couldn't believe his audacity.

"What?" she fumed. "You want me to thank you? This was your doing!" Christi paused giving him an uneasy glance. "Who—are you?"

He studied her intently. "You're obviously quite all right," he decided.

Christi glared at him in the semi darkness.

"No, not quite all right," she replied crossly. "Okay, you can see I'm unharmed, but I was terrified."

"How about I walk you home?" he said amiably, completely ignoring her outburst. It left her feeling a little annoyed, for all the good it did.

A man on either side of her, they left the shadowed alley.

"I live at 442 South Street," she told him, still feeling irritated.

Christi stole a glance at the stranger clad in tee shirt, worn vest, jeans and motorcycle boots. Straight, dark, silken hair hung over his shoulders, almost halfway down his back.

She took a slow breath. Her contemplation continued. This guy had it all, tall, dark, and handsome. And muscles! She wondered, vaguely, when she had begun to notice and appreciate an attractive male physique.

A stranger, yes, dangerous—maybe, still her fear had begun abating with his unconcern. He didn't seem exactly friendly, but she didn't see him as a threat either. A simple escort home after what he had put her through, but why? He didn't seem obliged to offer an explanation for her being dragged into an alley, tied, manhandled and threatened.

"Do you belong to one of them?" he asked quietly.

She had an idea what he was referring to and didn't like it.

"What do you mean?" she said bristling again.

The irritating man gave her a sudden, significant glance.

"I have a brother who is a member of the Cobras," she said, impatiently. "I'm Christi Temple."

"I know who you are."

She looked at him sharply. "How do you know me?"

"Are you a Cobra girl?" he asked mildly.

"You have no right to ask me that."

"But are you a Cobra girl?" he persisted.

"No!" she snapped, exasperated that he could ask her, so placidly, if she was a 'Cobra girl'. "And I don't appreciate the insinuation, and if you really knew me, you wouldn't have to ask."

Christi took a long look at him, feeling a sudden chill in spite of the warm night. The thought occurred with renewed apprehension that it might not be wise to speak so rashly, and she softly cleared her throat.

"You're Billy Cole."

"It's about time. I was beginning to feel unpopular."

"I've heard of you."

He gave her a sidelong glance. "Do you believe everything you hear?"

"Should I?" she ventured.

"Doesn't matter, you will after tonight."

"Why? What happened?"

"We crashed the Basement."

Christi stopped. He took another step, turning to face her with a knowing look. "Don't even think about it."

"My brothers are back there!"

He smiled. "You want to rescue them?"

"This isn't amusing."

"They wouldn't want you there."

She glanced back over her shoulder, and then faced him again feeling torn, but he was right, it was no place for her. "Would you please let go of my arm?"

"It was a just little rumble," he told her, now appearing sympathetic to her distress. He released her arm, but his hand lingered, softly passing over her skin. "It didn't have to involve Dave, he chose it. I wanted Burton."

"Anything involves John Burton involves my brother."

"Unfortunately," he acknowledged. "I wanted you to hear my side."

"And why is that?"

"I don't know," he said softly. "It wasn't what I set out to do."

He came a bit closer, if he leaned down—his lips would almost touch hers.

"Let's go," he said, his voice still soft but abrupt.

As they resumed walking, Christi wondered, being caught up in the moment, how she would have reacted if he had chosen to close the distance and kiss her.

Then her mind began to wander. He had been after John Burton. Why had she been detained? The answer came, and the short-lived fascination died away.

Christi realized that they had grabbed her because of the incident several months ago when Karen had been forced to coax Billy into Cobra territory.

"You were after Karen Cable, weren't you?" He did not reply, so she took a calming breath and pressed on. "You will never have your revenge on Karen," she said with a hint of triumph. "She is safely away from all of you."

He glanced sideways, and Christi bit her lip, uncertain of her standing, considering again that being so carelessly impetuous in this man's company might provoke him.

"Did I make a bad first impression?" he asked with a wry smile.

The simple question almost made her laugh and left her feeling confused. After chancing another look at him all the fear and anger evaporated.

"It was John's fault," she said, fully relaxed for the first time since she had been snatched off the street. "He made her deceive you."

Billy put the matter aside with a casual dismissive gesture.

"By the way, on your other side is Danny Cole," he said mildly. "I'm sure he's feeling completely ignored."

"Pleased to meet you," Danny said as she gave him her attention.

"Hi, Danny." She liked his easy smile. "Quite the meeting place, huh?"

"Yep, alleys are the best, with the mellow ambiance and mood lighting—"

"And the aroma," she swooned. "So invigorating."

She and Danny shared a laugh, and then she glanced back at the leader of the Monarchs. Christi felt an undeniable attraction to Billy. She had felt it almost immediately, an intense feeling that she had tried to disregard. It could never be. There were too many wrong aspects to even contemplate a relationship with Billy Cole.

Christi laced her fingers together to keep from reaching for his hand, to wisely avoid touching him, wondering what it was about him that made her want to. She couldn't figure what had gotten into her.

As they walked on, she inevitably thought of how he had looked earlier when they had stood a breath away from a kiss. It made her easily imagine that he had felt the same strong attraction.

When they reached the apartment building, she and Billy stopped. Danny continued walking, stopping at length, to lean against a building to wait. His lighter blazed as he lit a cigarette.

"He's my cousin and my brother," Billy said, tilting his head in Danny's general direction. "He's my best friend, and now it seems he's determined to be my personal bodyguard."

"He's your cousin and your brother?"

"It's a story," he said insipidly. "Not all that heavy."

When he rested his hands lightly on her shoulders, she didn't feel the need to move away from the intimate contact.

"Tell me you won't go back there, Christi, to the Basement I mean." His thumb rubbed gently at her neck. "It's over by now, but there could be some guys hangin' out, you know?"

"I won't go back out tonight," she agreed.

"Then tell me you'll go out with me," he said easily with a fluent grin.

She stared transfixed into his startling blue eyes. Go out with him? He seemed so perfectly relaxed with the idea of them seeing each other. Didn't he realize the likely complications?

Christi was breathlessly conscious of Billy's hands still resting casually on her shoulders. He lowered his head toward her, his mouth so near, and he smelled so good. She closed her eyes but quickly opened them again, wondering why she had felt such an urge for him to take her in his arms and kiss her.

Feeling confused at the intensity of her emotions, she softly cleared her throat, taking a step away from the intoxication of Billy Cole.

"Christi, I don't want to let you go. It can't just end like this, can it?"

"Truthfully, I was wondering the same thing," she confessed, not shy to admit the quick attraction. "I thought you were obligated to see me safely home and that it would end here."

"I did," he said, moving in close again. "Feel obligated, but with that aside, I'd like to see you again, under better circumstances."

"I'd like that, too." He made it sound so easy.

"Will you meet me at the Blue Haze? Do you know where it is?"

Christi nodded. She had walked by the place. It had a reputation of harboring prostitutes and druggies.

"Six o'clock, tomorrow?" he suggested.

"I'll be there."

"Will you, really?" His hands slid smoothly down her arms stopping at her hands. "You won't disappoint me?"

"I'll be there."

He squeezed her hands gently, before leaving to join Danny. She watched them walk away, her heart beating rapidly with anticipation and a thrill of newly awakened excitement.

Looking up at the night sky, she viewed an array of stars, only one star seemed to be twinkling brighter than the others, a wishing star.

Christi closed her eyes. She made a wish before hurrying up the path to the apartment building and her beamingly captive audience that partied on the steps at night.

She blushed at their acknowledging attention, reticently smilingly as she quickly glided up the steps.

Chapter Nine

Christi knew her life would change dramatically if she allowed Billy to become involved in it. She couldn't even rationalize her thinking, accepting a date with Billy Cole had been *irrational.*

She knew there could be severe consequences—but something had passed between them, something dramatic, causing her to feel irrevocably out of control, but oddly undisturbed. Maybe a little uncomfortable, she relented, but the overall sensation of 'exciting in every way imaginable' neutralized the uneasiness of her reckless choice.

She went to bed, only to toss sleeplessly waiting for her brothers to come home. When they finally did enter the apartment, she breathed a sigh of relief as the tenseness that had her stomach tied in knots eased away. After a while, her emotions settled enough for her to fall asleep.

Christi awoke to the early light of dawn, moaned a drowsy protest, turned over on her right side and slept. When she opened her eyes a second time, glancing groggily at the clock, it was only a little after ten, but better than dawn's early light. Feeling somewhat rested, in spite of short sleep, Christi resigned herself to face a long, drawn out day.

After enjoying a cup of hot coffee, she took a tepid shower. Not quite fully revitalized, she sat drearily at the table sipping another cup, pondering the extensive time-on-hand.

Thinking breakfast might help, she made French toast and crispy fried bacon. Then, with the radio on a rock'n roll station, she busied herself cleaning the apartment, giving it more time than the usual once over.

Christi had just finished mopping the living room when Mike startled her.

"Spring cleaning?" he said, from the doorway. "But it's July already!"

"Not spring cleaning, just cleaning," she replied perkily. "You slept later than usual," she added casually. "What time did you get home?" She studied his face. No bruises.

"Didn't really pay attention; 'bout the usual." He peered at her intently.

"What are you looking at?" Christi asked trying not to sound defensive.

"You were looking at me first," he pointed out. "What's up, Chris?"

She headed toward the kitchen thinking about the laundry, the Fourth of July celebration, why does Dave sleep so late, thinking about anything and everything else.

"Coffee?" she suggested, hoping he wouldn't notice that she didn't answer his intuitive question.

"That's okay, I can get it."

"No, I don't mind. Breakfast?" she offered.

"I'll just have toast."

"It would be easy to fix you a decent breakfast, at least eggs—how about some French toast?" she suggested turning the burner on under the teakettle.

"We have bacon, too. Dave must have shopped, the cupboards are not bare."

"French toast and bacon does sound good," he agreed.

Taking what she needed from the refrigerator, she jumped right into fixing Mike's breakfast.

"You seem edgy," he noticed. "What's up with you this morning?"

"You keep saying that," she said cheerily. "Nothing's up. I'm just looking forward to tomorrow night. How about you?"

"Sure, it'll be good clean fun."

Happily, she had diverted him. The Fourth of July beach party offered an honest distraction since she couldn't confront him about last night without everything concerning last night being revealed.

"Are you bringing a date or going solo?"

"There's a girl. How 'bout you, Chris, is there a fella in your life yet?"

"No." Why had she asked that, drawing attention back to her? Christi returned his quick smile, but his look had a curious quality.

The kettle whistled. Mike measured coffee into a mug, added boiling water, milk and sugar. He took a seat at the table, appearing perfectly laid back, but as Christi dished up his breakfast, it was like she could tangibly feel his wondering. She hoped it was her guilt and overactive imagination.

"Thanks, Chris," he said when she set the plate in front of him.

"You're welcome . . . I have laundry, Mike, so I'm heading out as soon as I wring the mop and dump the water," she said quickly. "Catch ya later."

"Later, Chris," he agreed, sounding a little puzzled at her hasty retreat.

Christi felt bad rushing off, but she needed time away from him for now.

By the time she finished with her laundry, Mike had left. Sorry to be relieved that he wasn't there, Christi rationalized that once her feelings stabilized it would be easier to deal with his inquisitions, she *hoped.*

After hanging her blouses and putting her folded clothes away, she had a grilled cheese with a bowl of tomato soup. She washed the few dishes, tidied the kitchen, and then dialed Dawn. She wanted to get out of the apartment, besides needing someone to talk to.

Christi enjoyed the walk from South Street to Union—to Dawn's enchanting neighborhood with the changing scenery transforming slowly, until the final turn onto glorious, picturesque Woodland Drive.

There were other lovely areas, but the landscaping on Woodland Drive remained unsurpassed, the homes the most significant in Preston. Of them all, she considered Dawn's the most magnificent. It seemed a mile long walk along a circular drive to the carved steps.

The velvety lawn, trimmed shrubs, vibrant splashes of flowers, the lighted fountain; the mansion looked like a castle straight out of a fairy tale.

The huge front door opened to a spacious entrance hall that led to a massive living room. After all this time the crystal chandeliers, tapestries, glowing floors, glistening mirrors, Persian rugs, antique furniture, and precious heirlooms, still dazzled her.

Dawn opened the door right away when she rang the doorbell.

"Hi Chris. Want some iced tea?"

"Sounds great."

"So, what's up?" Dawn asked excitedly as they headed for the kitchen.

"Does something have to be up?" The aura of innocence didn't cut it.

"Doesn't have to be, but is," she replied pertly.

Christi smiled agreeably. "There is definitely something on my mind."

Dawn poured two glasses of iced tea. They went out back to the pool, took off their sandals to sit with their feet dangling in the cool water.

"So, tell me," she prompted eagerly.

"Okay, I'm not trying to be mysterious," Christi said. "It's just—I met a guy—a man—a fascinating man, but I have to warn you—our meeting was a little frightening."

Christi told Dawn about the incidents that led to meeting Billy and the intended date tonight.

"That's more than a little frightening," Dawn said anxiously. "Those guys holding you hostage must have been terrifying."

"It was, but don't flip over this, okay?"

"Hmm, why would I?" Dawn asked casually. "You just told me the dreaded confrontation between the Cobras and Monarchs finally happened."

"Thanks to John. He's such a psycho jerk. It worried me that the Monarchs invaded the Basement, but I guess it didn't amount to more than a brawl. I don't think anyone was seriously injured."

"Glad to hear that," Dawn murmured agreeably. "Now tell me about this wonder man you met that walked you home. Oh, that's right," she said as if just enlightened. "You don't know anything about Billy Cole, except that he's the leader of the Monarchs!"

"Don't you believe in fate, Dawn?" Christi asked buoyantly. "He's not a bad person, and he has—I don't know, the most magnetic personality."

"Magnetic?" Dawn raised her eyebrows with an inquisitive glance. "Are you like steel, then?"

Christi laughed. "No, I just mean he's—" Christi sighed at a loss for words. How could she express this too wonderful for words feeling?

"All that fascination." Dawn tilted her head giving her an indulgent smile. "Okay, fate can sometimes be good," she said pleasantly. "How old is this Billy guy?"

"Early twenties, I'd say. He's not a kid."

"You're going out with a man, and you've never even been out on a date. There could be some conflict," she pointed out, swirling her feet distractedly in the pool. "What if he wants you to go all the way?"

"Oh, I hadn't thought of that."

"Well, you better, 'cause I bet he has."

"You really think so? We just met."

"Oh, you are too naïve!" she chided. "Who is he, Christi? Think about it for a minute."

"I've done nothing but think about it, Dawn. You don't have to worry."

"Okay," she conceded looking somewhat skeptical.

"You don't think I could handle it," Christi prompted.

"Do you?" Dawn leaned closer. "Do you, really?"

"Have you and Jerry, you know—have you gone all the way?"

"Well, yeah, but that doesn't mean you should."

"So you don't think I should."

"I didn't say that. Should I say that?"

"You were thinking it."

"You're my friend, and I don't want to see you hurt."

"Well," Christi hesitated. "What's with you today, Dawn? You're not usually so level-headed."

"You don't think he might be out for what he can get?"

"No, what I do think is, he's someone special."

"You met him once, in a dark alley, in a frightening situation, and you think he's special?" Dawn sighed wearily. "Did you even stop to consider what he would have done to Karen—or you if he hadn't realized?"

"There you go again," she admonished, wagging a finger playfully, not wanting to consider any such thing. "Just be happy for me, okay?"

"Sorry, okay," she smiled resignedly. "Here is me, being happy for you. I just don't want you to do something you'll be sorry for," she said.

"Don't worry, I'm not going to," she murmured, but the look on Dawn's face reflected concern that there would be no resisting Billy Cole.

"Are you sorry?"

Dawn shrugged restlessly. "I don't know, maybe sometimes. Come on, let's go to my room, I have the new Beatles album."

Christi sat down at the vanity while Dawn walked over to the stereo.

"Do you believe in love at first sight?" she asked dreamily.

"Are you, by any hopeful chance, on birth control?"

"No. Do you think I look eighteen?" Christi asked with considerable skepticism. "I think I'd die if he knew I'm just sixteen."

"Then avoid phrases, such as 'I think I'd die'," Dawn advised coming up behind her. "And avoid giggling—I mean, don't laugh at every little thing he says . . . With the right application of makeup, I think you'll pass . . . Your hair needs layered. I'll see if Margie's available; my treat," she said quickly. She met her eyes in the mirror and smiled. "Don't get pregnant, okay kiddo?"

While Dawn phoned the stylist, Christi considered the way Dawn slipped the 'don't get pregnant' comment into the end of the conversation. She was concerned for her, and Christi appreciated her caring.

"Margie can work you in at four-thirty," Dawn said rejoining her. "In the meantime, I'll give you a makeup lesson."

The right application of makeup did make all the difference, looking at herself after Margie had finished clipping and styling, Christi felt confident, more mature, and she thought she looked at least eighteen.

Dawn pulled the dark blue Cadillac to the curb in front of the Blue Haze Tavern at ten 'til six.

She didn't try to conceal her distaste. "Why would he ask you to come to a place like this? Maybe I should wait with you," Dawn offered, her lovely green eyes emanating concern.

"I'll be fine," Christi said. "This place isn't so bad, I hope," she added with another wary glance at the dreary front entrance of the slovenly tavern. "He should be here in just a few—thanks for everything, and don't worry."

Christi exited the car, closing the door with a last positive smile at her friend, before she turned to walk as quickly and assertively as possible, into the seedy establishment. She drew some curious stares from some men at the counter. Even the bartender gave her the once over with ogling eyes.

She slid into the first booth to wait, feeling edgy in the dour atmosphere. Drug addicts, dealers, prostitutes, the Blue Haze had it all.

Before the waitress even had time to offer service, Billy slid in the booth beside her. Seeing him again, she accepted that her first observation had not been exaggerated in her mind. He did look almost too good to be true, with deeply tanned skin, the bluest eyes she had ever seen, and lustrous dark hair that hung straight over his muscled shoulders.

Once again, she found herself taken by his attractive, male physique. She wondered what it would be like to dance with him, feel the strength of his arms holding her.

"Hey, girl, good to see you." Billy placed an arm casually around her shoulders, turning slightly inward, a smile tipped the corners of his mouth. "Lookin' foxy, baby," he said, his gaze making an unhurried glide over her body, then back to her face.

"Hi, Billy." Christi smiled her greeting, trying to appear laidback, with his deliciously masculine cologne awakening senses that she had not even been aware of. She hoped her face didn't reveal the dazed feeling he evoked.

"Christi? Are you okay? Nobody bothered you?" He looked quickly around, then back at her.

"No, I'm all right," she said, amazed that the words had emerged from her dry throat. "I've only been here a few minutes."

"You don't look so all right," he observed with a slight frown. "You look uptight, baby. This place was a bad idea."

"I am a little nervous being here," she said, grabbing a reasonable excuse for her 'uptight' look.

Christi moistened her lips wishing for a cola but willing to settle for a glass of cool water. She looked toward the bar where Danny was being served a draft beer in a large mug.

"It's okay, it was only a place to meet anyway. I'll be right back."

Billy left her, going over to the bar. He spoke briefly to Danny, returning in less than a minute. "Ready?" he asked, not bothering to sit back down.

"Where are we going?"

"Anywhere is better than here, right?"

"A good point." She followed him outside.

"You ever hear of Kelly's Place?"

"No, I haven't."

"You'll never be able to say that again," he smiled.

Billy straddled one of the impressive motorcycles parked at the curb and handed her a helmet.

"Here, let me help you," he said, noticing her problem adjusting it. He secured the strap for a snug fit. "Hop on, and hold on tight," he instructed.

Christi deftly straddled on behind him, her arms circling his waist.

He rewed the cycle, skillfully taking control of the big machine. He pulled away from the curb heading down the middle of the empty street.

Several city blocks further into the west side, he pulled into a parking lot dominated mostly by other motorcycles.

Billy held the door, and she entered the tavern called Kelly's Place. Christi felt conspicuous here, too, almost expecting the room to go silent upon their entry, but it didn't.

The laughter and talking continued. Several couples were on the large dance floor, dancing to rock 'n roll music blasting from a jukebox.

There were few empty stools at the bar, and many of the booths that lined the right were occupied. Her eyes scanned the huge room.

She noticed a large dining area in the back on the left, with small tables and softly lit atmosphere. Very appealing, but no one was taking advantage of the intimate setting.

Two couples were engaged in a game of pool in the far back, near a hallway that indicated access to the restrooms.

Kelly's Place had its charm. The lighting animated her idealistic nature, but it wasn't nearly as decked out as the Basement, more like a basic bar. The room emitted a lively, friendly ambiance, and the crowd seemed no different than the rowdy bunch at the Basement.

With his arm around her waist, he guided her past the jukebox to a booth midway of the large room, making introductions along the way. Everyone greeted Billy with enthusiasm and her with good-natured acceptance, except for one person.

"Maybe you can tell this is where I usually hang out," he said giving her a kind of shy, appealing grin.

"I did get the impression you're not a stranger here," she replied. "Nice crowd, are they all Monarchs?"

"Yeah, we're exclusive on weekends."

As she slid into the booth, Christi wondered about the girl who had approached Billy and stopped so abruptly upon noticing her by his side.

Billy had made a simple introduction, without regard that the woman he introduced as Susan had a blatant look of pure hostility during the brief encounter.

A cute, perky little barmaid, dressed in go-go boots, red miniskirt and white pullover came to take their order. She soon returned with a shot of whiskey and a beer for Billy, and the Pepsi Christi had requested.

"I almost didn't show tonight," he said without looking at her.

Christi's heart skipped a beat, and then resumed, thumping dully in her chest. He had almost stood her up? Her first date and he had almost stood her up? It would have been devastating to be left waiting at that dumpy bar.

"I wouldn't have left you stranded," he said apparently attentive to her feeling of shock. "I considered sending Danny to take you back home. You realize it could be complicated—a relationship, I mean."

A *relationship?* She hadn't actually expected him to mention a relationship. His fingers beat a little crescendo on the table before he wrapped them around his beer can.

"If you want to go home, I'll take you now and we can forget about it," he offered quietly. "I don't want to, but you know how things are."

He finally looked at her, an inquisitive, sort of hopeful expression.

As their eyes met, the jukebox playing, people dancing, the whole place rocking became an insignificant blur. She hadn't expected him to look at her like that, like everything in his life depended on her decision.

Christi thought about what he said. She didn't want to go home, but she could never let her brothers know. The idea of deception didn't appeal to her moralities, but she made her decision.

"I don't think I could forget you so easily," she told him honestly.

"No, me either. Are you still in school?"

She nodded vaguely, hoping he wouldn't pursue that line of thought. She didn't know if she could outright lie to him about her age.

"I graduated Central four years ago. No one expected it, 'cause I went a little wild for awhile, go figure, right?" He grinned wryly and downed the shot followed by a swallow of beer.

Dave graduated four years ago, she had been twelve.

"You must have been about fourteen. That was the year Dave graduated."

He thinks I'm eighteen. Now is the time to set him straight, to be forthright and honest. Christi took a sip of cola as the moment passed.

"Ever wonder how a half breed Indian came to be living in Preston City?"

"No, I hadn't thought about it."

"My father was full blooded Cherokee," he said. "My mother was upper middle class. Somehow, they met and fell in love." He took a long swallow of beer. "No one ever approved of the union," he said motioning for the barmaid. "She disgraced the whole family, they said. All I know, he was found dead in an alley, beaten to death."

The waitress discreetly set a shot glass of whiskey on the table.

Christi listened solemnly as Billy told her of complications of his birth, that his mother died from those complications, and that he felt his aunt blamed him to a certain extent.

He looked at her briefly as he spoke, small glances from time-to-time with sad, troubled eyes. Even though she wanted him to be happy again, Christi was glad he was comfortable discussing his personal life.

"I was adopted by my mother's sister and her husband," he explained. "Danny was six months old."

A frown passed fleetingly over his handsome face.

"I don't know why they adopted me, really," he commented, seeming puzzled that his mother's family had taken him in. "They never treated me like family. I was never allowed to forget I'm half breed, not at home or in school."

He traced his finger around the rim of the miniature glass. It seemed a habitual gesture when he drifted into contemplation.

"I tried not to let it bother me that I was treated different, but I was a kid, you know, and stuff like that bothers kids. I could never understand why some people wanted me to feel shame about who I am. They didn't convince me to be ashamed, what they did was instigate a lot of hostility. I've worked through most of it, though, with Danny's help."

He downed the second shot in a smooth motion.

"We're blood brothers," he said on a lighter note.

"So you're brothers twice," she grinned. "You must have a close bond."

"Yes we're close. As close as two brothers can be, I guess." He smiled briefly. "It was his idea. We did it the summer we were fourteen. I went to visit my father's people that summer, learned some ways, and felt good about it, but I didn't fit in there either.

"It might be some people's opinion that I have a chip on my shoulder, and it could be true—since I was old enough to do for myself, I never asked for anything and haven't given much, but Danny—Danny's always been a big brother. He kept at me. I don't know how this happened." Billy indicated the room full of people as the waitress served him another shot glass of whiskey and a fresh beer.

Completely taken by his openness, Christi hung on every word. She could understand some pessimism, considering all he had been through, recalling what Trixi had said about John making school days a miserable experience.

"These people care about you," she told him. "Don't you think that's a possibility?"

"Yeah, I know, they must." His looked at her thoughtfully. "I don't quite understand what's happening here. There are people I've known for years who don't know as much about my life as you do already."

"I'm glad you were able to confide in me."

"You're not just someone to confide in. I want it to be so much more than that." He reached for her hand. "Do you care about me, Christi?"

She looked into his compelling blue eyes, then at his hand holding hers—thinking about the question of caring, once again feeling the burden of youth—every bit as young as her sixteen years.

Christi wanted to affirm his confidence in her, but wondered if she could even find words to express how much she was beginning to care.

She hesitated, wondering if she should admit it, afraid to open her mouth because she might admit it. As Danny slid into the booth across from them, she gracefully avoided the question.

"Are you getting to know each other?" Danny said.

"She knows everything there is to know about me, but here is a woman of mystery." Billy put his arm around her.

"What do you want to know?" she asked flippantly.

"Are you seeing anyone?"

"There's no one special," she said with a smile.

"I'm glad to hear that, in fact, that's all I need to know." He pulled her closer. "I think I'll keep her."

She could hear teasing laughter in his voice, but the possessive gesture brought on a sudden feeling of shyness as he gazed into her eyes. Then he glanced at his cousin.

"Can I keep her, Danny?"

"Yeah, I think she's a keeper," Danny replied, with a grin. His smile widened, when she blushed with his casual approval.

Their friendly laughter surrounded her, a comforting sensation. She settled back, enjoying the feel of Billy's arm around her. Being here felt right, Dawn must have been mistaken.

When Christi excused herself to go to the rest room, she didn't think anything of it as someone entered directly behind her. It seemed strange that the lock clicked, though, the large lavatory had several stalls.

Christi turned. The petulant, dark-eyed girl Billy had introduced as Susan gave her an antagonistic look without any preliminaries.

"Why didn't you stay on your own side?" she demanded angrily. "You're a Cobra girl, what are you doing here?"

Christi gazed at Susan, momentarily speechless. She looked experienced in the ways of the world, a raw—wild beauty.

This woman seemed so different from her that she felt deflated.

"I'm not a Cobra girl," she finally managed. "I'm not a part of that gang."

"And you are not a part of this one, leave Billy alone."

"What's this about?" Christi asked keeping a steady voice.

"Don't play innocent." Susan's eyes conveyed a simmering fury within her. "You know very well what I'm talking about," she gritted.

In all honestly, Christi knew she was feigning ignorance. This girl had been involved, probably intimately, with Billy.

"If you knew how we met—" she began, but fell silent as another swift shadow of anger swept across Susan's face.

"I know how you met. Not that it matters. I also know his intentions, everyone here does. He just wants to have some fun with you, little girl," she said, the angry frown still settled in her features.

Susan paused briefly after the cutting remark watching closely for a reaction before lifting her head haughtily. "Billy's had other girls; he always comes back to me."

"What are you saying?" Christi murmured pretending to not understand.

A smirk crossed her face. "I can accept that sometimes he likes variety."

"How can you accept him being with other girls?" Christi said, with a reflexively skeptical glimpse. "I could never accept that if he was mine."

"You naïve, self-righteous little bitch, he'll never be yours. I know what he wants from you," she reiterated, her voice thick with contempt, her fists clenched at her sides in an unmistakable threat of violence. "And when he's through, he'll toss you aside like yesterday's trash."

"If you're so sure of that, why are you harassing me?"

"Harassing you?" Her lip curled in a facsimile of a smile showing straight, white teeth. "If you think you're being harassed, just wait. Don't imagine that I'll stand by and let you have him."

Christi stood lost for words, staring at the dangerous young woman confronting her. Lush dark hair fell in soft careless waves around graceful shoulders, and if not for the intimidating expression, her wide brown eyes could easily portray innocence—deceiving innocence.

"You had better accept that he's mine," she said, her hand resting on the doorknob. "You're no more than a simple diversion." The menacing woman opened the door. She walked out, closing it with a loud slam.

Christi sank down on a straight-backed armchair positioned in front of a counter and sink. She felt weak, almost tearful after the aggressive run-in. Absorbed in her struggle to suppress the threatening tears, she flinched when a hand touched her shoulder.

"Are you all right, honey?"

Christi looked up at the girl who had spoken.

"You're crying," she said, with concern.

"I'm all right now, thank you." Christi failed miserably at bravado.

"I take it Sue's been giving you a hard time," she said kindly.

The sympathy weakened her further, Christi's eyes, already brimming, overflowed. She wiped angrily at the betraying tears.

"My names Vicki," the young woman introduced herself. She gave Christi a tissue, and then leaned against the counter.

"Thank you."

Vicki spread her hands with a glimmer of understanding.

"If you want to hang with the big girls, sweetie, you have to act like a big girl." She tipped her head with another caring look. "I was afraid something like this might happen."

Christi swallowed hard, finding it difficult to speak.

"That's right, honey, swallow those tears. He needs you out there."

It took a minute to regain her composer, but when she had calmed enough to respond, her voice did not waiver.

"I didn't mean to cry. I didn't cry in front of her," Christi added, in her own defense. "She's a vindictive person, isn't she?"

"Vindictive?" Vicki seemed to consider the potently descriptive word. "I would say she can be, and possessive of Billy, even though she has no right."

Vickie opened her purse removing a compact.

"Here, powder your nose."

"Thanks," Christi mumbled, accepting her offer. Trying to amend the damage of her sniffling, she determined to not let this Susan person ruin the evening, whatever her relationship to Billy.

"Sue can be a genuine bitch, but don't let her get to you like that. She's been after Billy for a long time."

"She talked like she had him."

"Well, she did once, sort of."

"Sort of?" Christi said, confused.

Vicki shrugged indifferently. "It was never really a big thing between them, even though she made it out to be, and since he caught her necking with Doug in a back booth, it's been off and on, mostly off."

Satisfied with the touch-up, her face hardly revealed the effects of her crying, Christi closed the compact, giving it back to Vickie.

"She had Billy and was messing around with Doug? Too bad," she said unable to subdue an ironic smile. "Doug is—kind of slimy, isn't he?"

"Slimy fits."

Christi went into one of the stalls.

"I'll bet she's trying to make time during your absence," Vicki said through the door. "But don't let her scare you away, honey."

"Thanks, I won't. I don't scare too easy." She heard the outer door open and close as Vickie left.

Thinking about what Vicki said, reflecting on her brave words, Christi washed and dried her hands, anxious to be with Billy but still uneasy. It felt as if all eyes were on her as she reentered the barroom.

Christi struggled to maintain self-control when she noticed Susan sitting beside Billy, very near, in fact, with their heads bent intimately close in a private conversation.

Bringing to mind Dawn's coaching to keep a refined air regardless of possibly uncomfortable circumstances, she forced herself to walk across the room with a dignified, graceful movement, even though she felt a powerful urge to rush over and snatch the scheming girl out of her booth.

As she drew near, Billy glanced up, meeting her eyes. He quietly said something to Susan, who then stood, giving Christi a willfully hateful glance before walking away, hips swaying in the tight shorts that revealed enough to be enticing but not exactly vulgar.

"Did I interrupt something?" she asked, concealing the extent of her jealousy that he had been smiling into Susan's eyes, only moments ago.

"I would never consider you an interruption," Billy replied, standing for her to slide into the booth.

"Maybe I was an interruption to her, though," Christi persisted. She resumed her seat, hoping the inquiry still appeared casual. "She seemed perfectly comfortable with you. Is she someone special?"

"Just one of girls," he said easily. "Why do you ask?"

She opened her mouth to tell him exactly why, but asked for a drink instead, a screwdriver, she told him confidently when he asked what kind.

It was the only drink she could think of, and Dawn said that it tasted good.

Billy gave her a long look, and then motioned for the waitress.

The decision to ask for a drink instead of obsessing about his hopefully ex-girlfriend surprised her, but it would be too awkward to change her mind.

Since she had the drink, Christi took a tentative sip, deciding to forget about the unpleasant incident in the restroom. Susan being so obviously jealous and hostile should be proof enough that she feared their relationship.

When a wistfully, romantic love song began to play, Billy led her onto the dance floor, his strong arms going easily, possessively, around her waist.

She rested her hands on his shoulders, and he drew her even closer. Moving her hands under his lustrous hair, Christi rested her head against his chest as they moved effortlessly to the music.

The dance was everything she had imagined, and when he kissed her after the dance, his lips firm, but tender, it was more than she had imagined.

His kiss singing through her veins, he walked her back to their table. With some unease, she wondered if this delirious feeling was signature of her youth. Maybe not, maybe the feelings would be the same if she were eighteen or even twenty-one.

As they talked and danced, laughed and shared another kiss, she thought nothing would be different. A few years wouldn't make any difference at all.

Christi studied him discreetly as time passed. She could see his father in his masculine physique and dark hair, and maybe that wondrous smile that gave her such warm feelings.

But she could see his mother in those remarkably blue eyes. She could see in him the woman who fell into forbidden love and followed her heart.

Chapter Ten

Christi left Kelly's Place feeling light as air, and free as a bird suddenly let loose from a cage.

Billy didn't take her home. She wondered if she had even expected that he would, not altogether surprised, when he pulled his cycle to the curb in front of an apartment building on the corner of Park Ave.

They walked hand in hand into the three-story brick building. When he put his arms around her, pausing for a kiss in the dark stairwell, she denied the apprehension in the far reaches of her mind that suggested this had been the intended destination.

Once inside his apartment, he lit candles. Christi settled on the worn sofa. Reminiscent of her own apartment, Billy's place was neat, but dreary.

He turned the stereo on low, the overhead light off, transforming the room to a romantic setting in the soft glow of the candlelight.

"Do you like red wine?"

She had never tasted wine, but readily agreed to his choice. A warning voice whispered in the recesses of her mind, but she refused to be intimidated by her usual sensible self. It wasn't easy, though, to embrace new feelings and this strange innovative excitement. Christi watched by the soft glow as he poured two long stemmed glasses almost to the brim.

"You're uptight," he said offering her one of the delicate glasses.

She accepted willingly, drinking deeply of the wine hoping it would ease the tension Billy obviously noticed.

"You're not afraid of me, are you, Chris?"

"No, why would I be?" She took another swallow almost emptying the glass. It tasted fruity, the alcohol hardly detectable.

"But you're afraid of something." Billy smoothed her hair, placing a wayward strand behind one ear. His eyes searched her face. "Are you having second thoughts about me?" he asked solemnly. "Do you want to go home?"

"So you can go back to Susan?"

Christi wished she could take the words back. She wondered what had given her the nerve to voice a question that so empathically announced the jealousy she felt for the other woman in his life.

"I want to be with you—if I wanted Susie, she'd be here."

He smiled suddenly, running his hand softly through her hair.

"Are you afraid of this?" Billy drew her close, touching his lips to hers, caressing her mouth in a slow kiss that took her breath away.

He pulled back a moment, staring deep into her eyes. "You have the most amazing eyes," he whispered. "I've never met anyone so lovely."

Billy took the remainder of her wine, setting it on the coffee table.

He ran his fingers smoothly through her hair to the back of her neck, brushing his lips across her forehead, her temple, then slowly down her cheek, before pressing his mouth to hers, again, his tongue teasing her lips.

With a light touch, one hand slipped inside the neckline of her middy blouse to caress the soft rise of her breast while he continued his expert exploration of her mouth.

She felt weak as a kitten when he eventually drew away.

"You like that, don't you?" he murmured. She felt his warm breath on her shoulder, then the heady sensation of his lips against her neck.

Christi struggled with uncertainty as he slid his hand beneath her blouse, and around to nimbly unhook her bra giving him easy access to touch. Gently his hand outlined the circle of her breast. Her body responded with waves of pleasure, but the intimacy of his hands, the thrill of arousal, these amazing sensations created unease.

"Have some more wine," he suggested, refilling her glass. He poured a shot of whiskey from a bottle that sat nearby. Giving her a questioning look, he took a marijuana cigarette from a narrow canister on the coffee table.

"Do you get high?" Billy lit the joint drawing deeply. He held his breath for several seconds before offering it to her as he exhaled.

"No, thank you." She watched him smoke with curious speculation.

He noticed her observance. "Here," he urged. "Let's get high together, baby, there's nothing like it . . . I promise." Billy had put it on a clip. "Here you go . . . it's mellow, baby," he said dreamily.

Christi accepted as he reached it toward her a second time. She didn't like the smell, or the way it made her lungs feel. She didn't care much for it at all, but they shared the one, and then he lit another.

"I feel so strange and light, and—"

"Stoned?" he suggested with a smile that set her pulse throbbing.

"That must be it," she agreed with soft laughter.

Taking a last sip of the sweet wine, she set the glass down. She leaned her head back listening to the music drift softly through her consciousness.

He moved her hair aside. The sensation of his lips against her neck, nuzzling sensually, exhilarated the desire pulsing through her body. Christi ran her fingers through his hair, carefree and impulsive.

"I want to make love with you," Billy said softly, his husky voice close to her ear, persuasively stimulating desire.

Christi moistened her lips unable to speak, to approve or oppose.

He dropped gentle kisses on her closed eyes, her lips and neck.

"Do you want what I want?" he urged, convincingly. "Do you?"

"Yes," she sighed, fighting conflicting emotions. "But I don't know if we should—"

"Yes, you do," he whispered. "You know we should."

Billy pushed her blouse over one shoulder, his lips brushing her skin. He gently eased her down onto the sofa, slipping her sandals off, and then unsnapping her jeans. She raised her hips slightly for easier removal.

He pulled her panties and jeans down her long, slim legs tossing them on the floor. He placed feathery kisses on her calves, moving slowly up to her thighs, then to her flat stomach, flicking his tongue lightly into her belly button. Billy traveled leisurely down between her legs introducing her to stimulating sensations both wonderful and overwhelming to her newly aroused body.

With an unsteady breath, Billy moved away unsnapping his jeans.

Christi watched him undress. She had never seen a naked man, not even a picture. Gazing in wonder, she felt both fascination and fear.

He lowered himself over her, pressing her legs further open. She felt his erection and a moment of panic, before he claimed her body in an irreversible instant, capturing the soft cry that escaped her lips with his warm, firm mouth on hers.

Billy buried his face against the softness of her neck, motionless; he held her, their hearts beating as one. He began to move, slowly at first.

She moaned elatedly, and he let himself go, his body moving faster but ever sensitive of her needs. Carried away by the intensity of his passion, she gave herself to pleasure she had never expected for the first experience.

Disregarding anything she had ever heard of 'the first time', Christi ran her hands over his hard body feeling the muscles ripple beneath her caressing fingers. She held tighter as his enthralling moan filled her senses.

Before she fully realized that the moment of ecstasy was over, the warmth of his body left hers with inexplicable swiftness. She felt suddenly cold and tense, unnerved because she had expected him to hold her, to whisper words of love, if not words of love, at least words of caring.

Confused by his unexpected departure, she watched him pull on his jeans. As time ticked by, anxiety replaced the confusion.

He did not look at her, but sat on the edge of the sofa, his eyes fixed on the floor at an area midway between the sofa and door while she tried to focus on a reason for the bewildering distance between them.

She touched his shoulder with uncertain inhibition. Billy jerked slightly, snatched from his reverie, he turned on her with a dark, piercing anger.

"Why did you come here with me?" he demanded. "How old are you?"

"I'm eighteen." Christi flinched as he raised his brows, his disbelief obvious in the all-pervading glare.

"Okay," she gulped. "Okay, I'm sixteen. What difference does it make?"

"What difference?" Billy's expression changed to a malicious look, which she felt was inappropriate and unfair.

Christi wished she had a place to hide or at least a sheet to cover with—some protection from his intimidation. Experiencing painful humiliation, she drew her legs up, wrapping her arms around them. She gazed at him through tearful eyes feeling stripped and violated.

"You weren't so interested in my age before," she muttered insolently.

"You had every opportunity to tell me you were only sixteen."

Christi shivered and swallowed despair. That, unfortunately, was true. It added to her frustration a distinct obligatory feeling of guilt, but she had no intention of giving him the satisfaction of agreeing with his suddenly proper attitude. The man sitting here rebuking her did not in any way resemble the one who had held and caressed, and whispered sweet words of persuasion.

"Would it have mattered?" she demanded feeling completely exasperated. "Why are you acting so suddenly righteous? You knew very well that I was a virgin before you—before—"

She faltered, silenced by his menacing expression.

"A sixteen year old girl should not be alone in a man's apartment drinking wine and acting like she knows the score."

"Is that how it seemed to you?" she asked wonderingly. "You didn't mean anything you said, did you?"

"Oh, my God, you're a baby."

"You thought I was playing hard to get?"

"You weren't so hard to get, you know," he said, looking straight at her with no compassion.

The insensitivity of his reply took her off guard for an instant.

"You led me to believe I was special to you," she accused, her embarrassment turning to anger again, furious at his demeaning attitude.

It felt better than the emptiness.

"And you led me to believe you were old enough to consent."

"You did that on purpose to take advantage of me."

"Take advantage of you?" He gave her another scathing look. "You knew why I brought you here. You can't deny that even if you are a child."

"I'm not a child," she fumed.

She reached for her jeans wanting to get dressed, but as she stood to pull them on, the room spun. Christi sank back on the sofa, the dizziness receded.

"When you said make love—you didn't mean it. Why did you even use that word?" She paused, drew a short breath, and felt amazed that she could even attempt to pluck any defiance against him from her dulled senses.

"You didn't want me for more than a one night stand," she said, her voice now resigned. "Is that the making of a man? Is that what it's all about?"

Why had she come here with him? It seemed so ugly now.

"You said I'm a baby, and I admit that I was too easily misled, but for your information, you don't have to feel one bit of obligation to me, Billy Cole, not that you would," she added, he was so unmistakably a jerk.

Deep silence permeated the room. She waited patiently, hopefully, for some response, but it became evident that he did not intend to reply. She had not misjudged him, he felt no commitment.

When she looked at him, her heart constricted with a renewed ache. Christi located her blouse. The extreme dizziness passed, but she still felt light headed as she finished dressing.

"I shouldn't have expected more."

Threatening tears choked her, but she strode to the window. Standing with her back to him determined not to cry, Christi stared morosely into the darkness of a Westside night that had turned formidable and very painful.

He came up behind her.

"I hadn't planned on a one night stand with you," he said quietly. "Or maybe I did, I don't even know now." He turned her around to face him, his expression surprisingly tender. "Did I hurt you?"

"More than you'll ever know, if you even care."

He closed his eyes briefly, and when he opened them, his gaze held remorse. "I'm sorry, okay?"

She looked steadily at him, waiting, as he seemed to be waiting for her to reply. Could he possibly want her to accept his glib apology? Somehow it didn't seem like enough. His eyes searched her face, she remained stubbornly silent. He finally ran a hand through his hair giving her a tolerant look.

"Listen, it may have been wrong to persuade you with wine and drugs to do something you wouldn't have," he said in a grudging voice. "But you wanted me to, didn't you?"

She tensed again. "Are you apologizing or accusing?"

"I was rude," he admitted. "I was obnoxious and harsh," he added softly. She accepted the comfort of his arms as he embraced her. "I'm sorry I upset you. Yes, I care. Of course I do."

He held her face gently, pressed his lips to hers, effectively erasing every perceived fear with the sweet tenderness of his kiss. Christi sighed, feeling an unexpected surge of excitement. Her eager response to the touch of his lips shocked her senses.

She wanted to let herself go, to thrill again to the lovemaking of this man she knew so well and yet did not know at all. Her desire for him, the tangible love, effectively dispelled the mean things he had said.

"You're so responsive," he murmured, his lips against her neck. "It's thrilling for me, too, Chris; this feeling is new to me."

"But I need to know it's real."

"How can I convince you?" He pulled away. "Do you have to go home tonight?"

She nodded.

"I want to make love to you one more time before I send you home," he said holding her hands. "Come into my bedroom?"

She bit her lip gently. "Can I have a shower first?"

His approving smile sent her pulses racing. "Can I wash your back?"

Christi felt herself blush at the suggestion.

"You're not going shy on me now, are you?"

"Maybe a little," she admitted.

"Okay, you can have a private shower. Meet me in the bedroom very soon." His lips brushed hers. "I may become impatient."

Before she stepped under the shower, Christi wrapped her hair in a towel to keep it out of the way. She washed, rinsed and dried quickly, feeling a little impatient herself. She took the towel from her hair, letting it cascade over her shoulders and breasts.

Billy had his shorts on, sitting with his back against the headboard, legs crossed casually at the ankles. His eyes opened a little wider when he saw her standing naked in the bedroom doorway.

She walked slowly toward him, enjoying the way he looked at her.

He kissed her hand, turned her hand over to place a stimulating kiss on her palm, teasing her with a touch of his warm tongue, trailing to her wrist, then the inside of her arm at the elbow, before pulling her down on the bed.

"I meant everything I said to you about love," he murmured.

She absorbed the whispered words of adoration, the special words that mean so much once you have given your heart away.

His skilled caress imprisoned her in a web of growing arousal and exhilarating feelings that she never wanted to escape. He took her a second time, teaching, giving—sharing, leading to higher levels of ecstasy. Her response matched his, for every touch, she complied. This is what it means to belong to someone, she realized, this is what love should be.

She held tight to him, feeling the inexplicable delight he could release in her. When tremors shook his body, when he moaned her name and whispered, 'I love you', she sighed with serene happiness.

Christi remained in his arms enjoying the comfort of her body snuggled against him. She sat up, though, and left his bed when she began to feel drowsy with the desire to drift into a contented sleep.

When she finished in the bathroom after freshening up, Billy had come into the living room dressed only in jeans.

He smiled warmly at her. "Hey, baby," he said dreamily. "I'll get Danny to take you home. He lives right across the hall."

She sat beside him.

"I'm blitzed, baby," he explained with a little crooked smile. "Been doin' shots all day, and it's hitting hard right now. If it was just me, I wouldn't care, but I don't want to risk your pretty neck."

He paused, caressing her neck.

"You really have to go?" The huskiness in his voice made her wish she could stay with him, make love again, and then fall asleep in his arms.

"I have to," she said on a sigh. "I should have been home by now."

"Okay, I'll let you go—reluctantly."

She waited, fidgeting nervously as Billy went for Danny. Christi stood when he reentered the apartment.

"Danny's waiting," he told her.

She joined him by the door wanting to say something, to let him know—what? What could she let him know that he didn't know already by her response to him, that he couldn't read in her eyes filled with hope and dreams? With all of this in her heart, she felt sadly inept to express her feelings as they stood facing each other.

Billy passed his thumb over her full lower lip. "You have the prettiest pout," he said with a grin. Running his fingers through her hair, one hand going to the back of her neck, Billy drew her face to his in a deep kiss.

She experienced the now familiar ripple of excitement at the touch of his firm mouth. When they parted, his hand on her shoulder again, she felt him caress her neck with his thumb.

"Can I see you tomorrow?"

"I want to—but I have previous plans. If I tried to cancel, it would create too much suspicion, and I can't see you Sunday." Christi sighed longingly. She wanted to be with him. "I spend Sundays with my brothers."

"Okay, then, call me Monday? I'm in the book."

"I'll call," she said, her arms still around his neck, her fingers in his hair.

"I'll be impatiently waiting."

She looked up into brilliant blue eyes, being overtaken by a curious lost feeling, a vulnerable, almost childlike reliance. His expression stilled and grew serious. His arms encircled her, one hand at the small of her back, he pressed her closer.

For the passing of a few seconds, the world dropped out from under her. She knew if he let go now, she would be falling forever. Billy released her from the strange sensation as he bent his head touching his lips to hers.

"Good-bye, Christi."

She whispered "good-bye" wondering at the sound of finality in the words. Christi had felt comfort in his embrace, comfort and refuge, but when the door closed, she felt at odds, it seemed somehow conclusive.

She joined Danny. They began a silent walk down the hall. Once outside, standing on the curb beside his Harley, there still seemed to be a loss of communication. He quietly helped secure the helmet for the ride.

When they reached her apartment building, she quickly dismounted the motorcycle. "Thanks," she said, handing over the helmet.

"Christi?"

She had turned to walk away. She turned back attentively. He hesitated, staring at the ground. Perhaps it was simply her uneasiness, but when he looked down and then slowly raised his head, cold fear encased her heart.

"Whatever happens, Chris, with you and Billy? You have to understand him."

"What do you mean?" She studied his handsome face, his expression gentle and contemplative.

"He's liable to hurt you without meaning to. I don't know, I could be talking out of turn."

"You're scaring me, Danny," she murmured, past the rising dread.

"That isn't my intention," he said quickly. "I don't mean to, but you're different, Chris, from anyone I've met in a long time—you're so unaware," he added, busily attaching the helmet to his cycle.

"You mean naïve?"

"No," he said, his soft brown eyes meeting hers. "I mean, I don't know, maybe, but don't ever change, baby love, just become aware of the dangers. Stay as sweet as you are now, but don't let anyone walk all over you, either."

He revved the cycle, and then took off, leaving her to speculate exactly what he had meant.

Had this been the reason for his quiet contemplation? It sounded to her like Danny was warning her about Billy. Christi wondered if tonight had been the biggest mistake of her life.

Feeling troubled, she hurried up the walk. Christi spoke to the clientele gathered outside the building before entering the dimly lit hall that led to the dark, narrow stairwell.

About halfway up, a shuffling sounded behind her. Christi rushed up the remaining stairs, heart pounding, and blood throbbing in her temples. She somehow managed to fit the key in the lock in spite of her shaking hands.

Once inside she slammed the door, hastily turning the deadbolt. Breathing heavily from anxiety more than her sprint up the stairs, she leaned against the door wondering if the time would ever come when she would feel safe.

Her chest still heaving, she stepped away from the door when someone began knocking. She turned to stare tensely at the door wondering who it could be at this hour. After another brief crescendo of impatient rapping, followed by much louder pounding, she heard Mike's welcome voice.

"Christi! Christi! WAKE UP!"

"Mike!" She opened the door quickly. "You'll wake the whole apartment building!"

"I left with Dave and forgot my key," he explained. "Haven't you been to bed?" He looked at her curiously.

"Weren't you behind me on the stairs?"

"No," he frowned. "What were you doing out this time of night?"

"There was someone behind me on the stairs."

"You're paranoid."

"I am not."

"No, seriously, I didn't see anyone."

"You got here right after I did."

They walked into the kitchen.

"Why were you out so late?" he persisted. "It's the middle of the night. It's past the middle of the night, even."

"I had a date." She ignored his inquisitive look.

"You had a date and stayed out 'til now?" He sounded surprised and concerned. To be expected, but still, she ignored the concerned part.

"So, you're always out." She avoided looking directly at him. "Are you hungry?" she asked, hoping to change the subject.

Christi opened the refrigerator to peer inside in search of easy to fix leftovers.

"How about a roast beef sandwich?" she offered enthusiastically.

"Sure, thanks. Who's the guy, Chris?"

She gave him a long-suffering look.

"Nobody you know."

Christi busied herself with making the sandwiches.

He sat at the kitchen table without further comment. Still, she felt his disappointment, worse than that; she felt disapproval for the first time in his quiet contemplation.

"I hope you didn't do something you'll be sorry for."

The words cut like a knife, the sadness in his voice. She poured them each a glass of iced tea, gave him his sandwich and drink, then sat across from him. Christi wondered if he knew, or if he was only speculating.

He looked at her steadily for several long seconds.

"Mike, please get out of my head."

"You've never kept anything from me before."

"And you've always understood."

"Okay," he said with a tolerant grin. "You're my little sister and I worry, that's all."

Christi couldn't finish her sandwich. She felt nauseous and headachy as she took a shower. The awareness of the loss of innocence settled over her with a deep sense of sadness. In one hopelessly impulsive night with Billy Cole, she had abandoned forever the child of yesterday.

John entered her thoughts just before she slept—how he had touched her when she still mirrored the innocence of a child. She never wanted to see him again. There would be no more going to the Basement, no more subjecting herself to his wanton looks and penetrating brown eyes.

Christi fell out of bed and awoke with a start. She took a couple of deep breaths relieved to be awake. John Burton had invaded her dream and turned it into a nightmare.

She sat for a while, leaning against the bed, afraid to go back to sleep. It had been horrible enough to toss her to the floor, but the dream receded as minutes ticked by.

She walked into the living room, stirrings of dread churning her emotions. With a heavy heart, she sank onto a chair near the window to look out at the streets that had been her home for the past two years. The streets that teamed with so much life and gaiety were quiet now, deserted, as the sun's first rays penetrated the darkness.

Christi's heart fluttered as she reminisced her impetus night with Billy. She could still feel his caress, his kiss, unfortunately accompanied by unpleasant piercings of doubt.

She grew drowsy and decided to go back to bed, hoping not to dream. Christi closed her eyes, trying to focus on the promising things Billy had said, the assurance of his love, but Danny's parting words kept interfering.

She awoke feeling restless, and reluctant to face Mike, but he was sitting at the table when she entered the kitchen.

"Coffee water's hot," he said. "It should boil quickly."

"Thanks." Christi turned the fire on under the teakettle.

"I know what happened, Chris," he said. "Sorry."

"Mike, I wish you would quit that!" she said, with possibly undue agitation. "I can't have any secrets. It isn't fair!"

"Don't be mad at me," he shot back, all but reprimanding. "I didn't do it on purpose. Okay?"

"I suppose."

"If Dave finds out—"

"Mike, please, just don't." A dull ache lodged inside her as she thought of Billy and the night. "You can lecture me another day. I know, what, if Dave finds out. He won't."

"How can you be so sure?"

"He doesn't pay enough attention." She spoke without bitterness.

"Christi—"

The kettle whistled. She poured boiling water into her coffee mug, and then irately reached for the coffee she had forgotten to measure into it.

"I love you, Chrissie—I wouldn't see you hurt for nothing."

Tears welled in her eyes. "I'll be all right." She sat across from him trying ineffectually to maintain her emotions.

"Are you still looking forward to the beach party?" he said with gentle understanding.

"Oh, sure I am—hot dogs, marshmallows." Christi burst into tears suddenly remembering Dawn's cautionary words.

"Yep, you're gonna be fine," Mike said going over to the rickety buffet for the box of tissues that sat on it.

"Thank you." She dried her eyes. "I don't suppose I have to tell you how I feel," she said on a sigh.

"You're experiencing growing pains, too soon." He kissed the top of her blond head. "I wish you would have talked to me." Mike began to firmly massage her shoulders, relieving some tension.

"I appreciate your care, Mike, but I couldn't talk to you about Billy."

His hands left her shoulders. "Billy? Billy Cole? My God, Chris, what were you thinking? Dave will kill him dead."

"I thought you knew."

"I knew what, I didn't know who. He's a man—" Mike pointed out in useless exasperation. "I thought you'd gotten carried away with a guy your own age, and that would have been bad enough. The jerk seduced you."

"Mike, stop it!"

"Are you gonna cry again? I'm sorry, Chris. Don't cry, okay?"

Christi took a deep, trembling breath. "Let's just never talk about it again. It's between us, okay? Dave doesn't need to know."

He sighed distractedly. "Okay," he agreed.

Christi told Dawn everything, not avoiding her apprehension or the fact that she hadn't used protection. She urgently needed her friend's support and Dawn didn't let her down. She wasn't judgmental and didn't even hint at 'I told you so'. Confiding in Dawn helped her feelings considerably.

Monday, after school Christi dialed Billy's number. She listened to the relentless ringing for much longer than necessary before hanging up.

"You were a fool," she whispered. She did not attempt to hold back tears of hurt and anger. He was expecting this call and just ignoring her.

Such a humiliating, deflating feeling overwhelmed her that she wanted to hide from Dawn, Mike, anyone who might know her shame. She gazed at the phone with a deep ache inside, the memory of a night of love gone sullied and repulsive. Christi made a solemn vow to never call him again.

Chapter Eleven

Christi stared moodily at the calendar with the black magic marker poised in hand. Having berated herself quite sufficiently, she resolutely drew a large X over day eighteen of July, time to accept that she had been used, to forgive herself for being so gullible, to chalk the reckless night with Billy Cole up as a painful and extreme learning experience.

It was time to get on with being sixteen again, to move forward, to have fun, to somehow forget the man she had so foolishly trusted.

She looked around the messy living room wishing she had cleaned earlier instead of languishing in the dispirited grip of the last of her self-pity.

It had to be done, but she decided it could wait until after a shower. Christi heard the phone ringing as she came out of the shower, grabbed her terrycloth robe and made a run for it, snatching the receiver to her ear.

"Hello?"

"Hi, Chris, I almost gave up. What took you so long?"

"I just got out of the shower, Dawn, what's up?"

"Carrie's spending the night and I thought the three of us could have a jammie party."

"It's still a little early for that, isn't it?"

"No, a little late, actually, I'm almost eighteen, we have to hurry."

"Silly girl, you'll never be too old for pajama parties."

"I thought we'd have a movie fest, you know? Pig out on popcorn and chocolate chip ice cream."

"I need to do some laundry, and the living room is a total wreck."

"Never do today what you can put off until tomorrow," she said most seriously, although she had the adage in reverse. "Can it wait?"

Christi glanced wincingly around once more. "It's waited for long enough, but your philosophy sounds good. Okay, the laundry can wait, but I have to clean up in here, shouldn't take more than a half hour or so."

"Want me to pick you up?" she offered.

"No, I like the walk. See you soon."

Christi hung up feeling an honest touch of happiness for the first time since that foolish, distressing night. In the half hour she allotted herself, Christi decided the room looked presentable. After penning a quick note to let her brothers know where to reach her, she hurried downstairs.

She started to open the outside door, when John stepped out of the shadowed hallway on the left quickly pressing the door firmly shut.

"It's been a long time," he said sounding deceivingly good-natured. "Look at you—all grown up."

"What are you doing here," she said, tensing at his touch.

"I've been waiting for you," he responded, running his hand softly along her arm. "Where have you been keeping yourself?"

Christi recoiled from the unwanted touch.

"Don't be difficult," he said sounding annoyed. "You knew it would come to this, you had to know."

She looked around nervously. Carl stood near, leaning against the door that led to the hall where the first floor apartments were located. His gaze moved slowly down her body, then up with a knowing look that sickened her.

John pressed closer, crowding her into a corner.

"You're scared, aren't you," he whispered.

"Of course, I'm afraid," she choked. "But you'd better let me go . . ." Her words ended on a sob as he clamped his arms around her.

He tightened the hold crushing her against his chest. Christi felt his rapid heartbeat and hot, heavy breath with the familiar faint smell of whiskey.

"You won't get away with this," she said desperately. "Dave won't let you—get away with this." She bucked in his arms, frantic for release.

He shoved her inside the basement door forcefully, half carrying her down the stairs where he released her twisting body. She ran across the room to the back door, turning the knob, pushing hard against the solid door.

Christi closed her eyes against the frustration. He had known, of course, that it would not open. She felt his presence behind her and whirled around, maneuvered from between him and the wall to stand facing him.

"Please, John, you don't really want to do this."

"Oh, but I do, I really want to do this."

His fingers brushed her cheek, and she jerked away with a choking sob. His eyes narrowed, danger reflected in the depths of darkness.

She moved backward, slowly at first, then turned and ran back across the room. Christi twisted on the doorknob at the top of the stairs, unable to accept the obvious, both exists were secured.

"You can run," Carl said from the other side of the door. "But you can't get away." His taunting laughter filled her head. "No interruptions this time, Christi girl. He's got ya, now."

She sank to the floor with a low moan. John's footsteps sounded on the stairs. Plastering herself into the corner, Christi pleaded with him, but he callously took hold of her, one arm firmly around her waist, dragging her back down the stairs struggling in his arms. When he abruptly released her, she took a step back, and then felt the sting of his hand across her face.

"I'm tired of playing," he said fiercely. John wound one hand in her hair gripping her throat with the other. "Why do you want me to hurt you?"

As his face lost all expression, she stared, fascinated, unable to drag her eyes away from the emptiness of his.

"Don't fight me," he said softly, in an oddly gentle tone. "Stay very still."

Every part of her screamed to oppose his touch, but she stood terrified, fists clenched at her sides, willing herself to remain prone and silent.

His eyes slowly focused on her again, the sardonic smirk reappeared.

"You can deceive yourself, little girl, but I know what you want."

He pulled her tight against him and she felt the hardness of his twisted excitement. John reached behind to pull the string, releasing her halter.

"No, Christi," he warned with a slight shake of his head. Gripping her wrists, he moved her arms. His dark eyes lowered. She stood before him, defenseless and humiliated, filled with an insurmountable hate.

"You are a beauty," he breathed.

"Damn you, John! You have no right to look at me." Her voice broke, choked with tears. "I'm not beautiful to you. I'm nothing to you except something to be used and hurt. Do what you intend to, and get it over with."

"Oh, I will," he whispered. "You can pretend to be something you're not, but what you are is an uppity little bitch that has to be forced."

"I hate you, John."

"Tell yourself what you need to hear," he quietly replied. He took a step back, his look seductive and provoking. "You can finish undressing for me."

She stood rigid, confused and unable to move.

"Do you understand this is not a request?" His knife appeared, then the lethal, gleaming blade. "Do it."

Keeping her eyes on the weapon, she stepped out of her sandals, and then unsnapped her jean shorts. Shivering in despair, she slid them down.

Using one leg to trip her, John held and lowered her onto the cement floor. Staring hard into her eyes, he took her body with a quick, painful thrust.

Christi turned her head aside peering across the empty space, before the knife he had discarded took her attention. As he began to move with firm deliberate action, she gazed, transfixed, at the blade.

He raked his hands roughly over her vulnerable body, his movement becoming wild and forceful, his fingers digging into her flesh, grasping and pulling, forcing her to move with him.

She endured the punishment, concentrated on the pain. Her stomach cramped, heaved, and constricted again. Dizziness almost overcame her as a suffocating sensation tightened her throat. She thought she would pass out, wished for the mercy of oblivion, but it didn't happen.

He continued mercilessly using her, pounding relentlessly. Christi embraced the pain escaping the insufferable degradation.

His groans amplified filling her consciousness, until at last, with several hard thrusts and deepest penetration, he shuddered in violent orgasm. John collapsed on top of her breathing heavily for several long seconds.

She stretched a little further for the knife, so close now, almost within reach. Her fingers groped for the weapon, then wrapped firmly around the handle, in the same instant, his hand clamped around her wrist.

With a quick twist, the knife slipped from her hand.

His breathing still ragged, John seized the knife touching the blade to her neck. Held in the grip of terror, gazing into savage eyes, she felt the point pierce her skin. Christi closed her eyes against the panic, afraid to even breathe—afraid she would die here in this dank basement.

"Billy can have you now," he whispered. "It was a thrill, but I won't bother you again."

The words, penetrating her numb senses, made her realize in some way this had been an act of vengeance.

He eased his body from hers and then stood gazing down at her as he meticulously straightened his clothes. He shook his hair back, running his fingers through it, such casual gestures, not at all the likeness of a man who had just shattered a young girl's world.

"You know Dave would kill me," he said softly. "Even if you went to the police, Van or Dave—I'd never make it to trial. Unless you want to see someone in prison for killing the likes of me, just accept that it happened and let it go." He tossed her clothes at her. "Get dressed."

Shivering with cold, revulsion, and the miserable truth of his taunting, Christi managed to pull her clothes on. She stood on trembling legs. John had gone, but his scent lingered around and on her, his aftershave, his cologne, and the clean smell of soap. Why couldn't he smell of stale perspiration and vomit? Why couldn't he portray the monster that he was?

Still fighting nausea and dizziness, she sat on the basement steps, resting her head in her hands, waiting for it to pass.

After a few minutes, she made her way upstairs to the apartment, closed and locked the door, and stood for another moment wondering what it was she had to do before recalling that Dawn would be expecting her.

Christi went to the phone and dialed.

Her friend's cheerful voice came on the line. "Preston residence."

"Dawn, I—" She covered the mouthpiece with her hand, struggling again with her emotions.

"Chris, is that you? Christi, are you there?"

She could hear the panic in Dawn's voice. "I'm here . . ." she managed. "I'm sorry . . ." Christi muffled a sob. "I can't make it tonight."

"What's wrong? Are you crying? You sound strange."

"I can't talk now."

She replaced the receiver. Dizzy and weak, Christi staggered into the bathroom. She turned the shower on to stand under the punishing spray, scrubbing her body in a useless attempt to erase the feel of him.

With a towel around her head, she stood naked before the full-length mirror, examining the bruises around her breasts and thighs through a mist of tears. She knew they would fade within a few weeks, the scrapes on her hips and back were painful but not deep.

She ached all over, but would, no doubt, heal without physical scars.

She checked her neck; it didn't even need a band aide. He had terrified her with the knife, but the wound was merely superficial. Where he had slapped her left only a slight bruise, it wouldn't be difficult to conceal from her brothers with careful application of make-up.

Christi tied her bathrobe miserably around herself. She shuffled in a gloomy daze into the living room where she huddled on the sofa.

Slowly becoming aware of someone knocking on the door, she walked cautiously to the hallway. "Who is it?"

"It's Dawn, let me in."

Christi removed the chain, and then twisted the dead bolt to open the door.

"I had to see you," she explained anxiously. "You sounded desperate. Are you all right?"

"No, I'm not all right." Her eyes filled with tears that threatened to spill over again. "John was waiting for me downstairs. He raped me, Dawn . . ."

"Oh, my God," she whispered. Dawn quickly closed and locked the door. Turning to Christi, she held her in a close embrace. "Did you see a doctor—no, of course not—you need to see a doctor. Did you call the police?"

"The police?" she murmured with dull perception. Then with realization, "No, I didn't call the police. I don't think you understand, Dawn."

"What's to understand, Chris?" Her friend's expression held compassion but determination. "He tried to rape you before and you let it go," she pointed out. "He needs arrested! You have to report what he did to you."

"I can't," she said frantically. "You have to understand, Dawn, please!"

"Okay, if you won't report it to the authorities, at least tell Dave," she asserted. "Let him deal with John Burton."

Christi began to shake. Dawn's eyes opened wide.

"Chris—Christi, stop it!" she pleaded. "Christi, you're scaring me!"

Taking deep breaths, she fought rising hysteria. "I can't tell Dave. I don't want him to go to prison for what John did. Dave loves John as a friend, something he doesn't deserve, but Dave would kill him for this."

"It's all right," she assured her. "I understand, okay? You don't have to tell anyone." Dawn touched her cheek. "He hit you."

"I tried to fight him at first, but then he became so furious. He found out about Billy," she said, a tremor in her fragile voice. "I think that must be why he was so enraged."

She relived the rape in that instant, a brief but almost overwhelming sensation, the pain, the humiliation, the horror of it. Dawn put a comforting arm around her as they walked toward the living room.

"Why couldn't he be as repulsive as his actions?" Christi said, her voice trembling, a mere whisper as she struggled to speak without breaking down again. "He smelled clean and fresh, and—" She inhaled a jerking breath. "I had the smell of him all over me when I came up here."

Christi sighed despairingly as she recalled his accusation. "He said, I wanted him to," she choked. "He always accused me of leading him on."

She chewed on her lower lip, feeling a rush of misery with the realization.

"He took me so easily—" Christi shivered with the awareness. "I just let him have his way with me."

Dawn frowned, a deeply concerned look. "You can't mean that," she said gently. "There was no way, Chris, he might have—Chris, he might have killed you if you continued to fight. You have to understand that you didn't cause this, and there was nothing you could say or do to stop him. Can you understand that?"

"I know you're right. In my mind, I know, but I don't know what to do with these feelings." A fresh torrent of tears cascaded down her face, senseless, useless tears that could not drown the shame.

"Christi . . . oh, God, Chris, I don't know what to say to convince you—you can't blame yourself. You are not guilty of anything." She touched her arm, tears shimmering in her emerald eyes. Christi stared into those glistening eyes trying to comprehend what she meant.

"I can't stand for you to blame yourself for this atrocity." Dawn took her hand and held it. "Talk to me, Chris, tell me again—remember what you've told me about John Burton."

"He's frightening . . . He is extremely capable of—of—mental influence." Christi sighed, swallowing a choking sensation, reaching for tissues from the box that sat on an end table. "But he's always portrayed an intense calm. He's unstable, Dawn. It's like—on the outside he's quiet, but inside he's ready to explode. He'd never shown his rage. I never realized he was so volatile. And he had a knife! Dawn, I was so terrified."

Dawn's green eyes held deep concern and something—illusive. She looked down at her hands deep in thought, about what, Christi could not imagine, unless she was having second thoughts.

Taking a trembling breath, she gripped her arm. "You can't tell anyone, Dawn, please. I couldn't bear to lose a brother. I have to put this behind me, and no one else can know."

"Of course, I won't tell anyone if you don't want me to, but John had such an obsession for you, Chris."

"He was obsessed, yes, but I have to believe he'll leave me alone, now. He said as much." She drew her arms around herself remembering the scathing words. "He wanted to have his way with me, now he finally has."

Dawn considered Christi's rationalization. She could be right. It was entirely possible now that he had brutalized Christi that he would leave her alone. Still it seemed risky and too unfair—what if he raped another girl? What if he turned on Christi again?

"Stay with me until Dave and Mike come," she whispered. "I don't want to be alone."

Tears clung to her long eyelashes, her violet eyes looked huge and still frightened, filled with pain. Dawn knew she would abide by her wishes and keep quiet. Right or wrong, it was Christi's decision.

"Of course, I'll stay," she said. "I could never leave you like this. Let's have some tea," Dawn suggested. "Would you like some tea? It might be relaxing."

"Yes, I'm sure it will be," Christi agreed, inhaling a trembling breath. "But I have to comb my hair or it'll be a tangled mess." She laughed shorty, a small nervous sound, then removed the towel, her long blonde hair falling down around her shoulders.

"I see what you mean," Dawn agreed. "Want me to comb it for you? Here, you sit on the floor, and I'll sit on the sofa and comb your hair."

"Thanks Dawn, that sounds great. It's been a long time since anyone's combed my hair."

Dawn combed and braided Christi's hair.

"You should be a hairdresser . . . You have a nice touch."

Then Christi realized she had just told a millionaire heiress that she should be a hairdresser. She really was about to go off the deep end!

"Thanks," Dawn said, smiling. "Now you sit here and relax. I'll fix our tea. I might have to yell if I can't find the tea and sugar, okay?"

"Okay," Christi agreed with a smile that almost felt normal.

Chapter Twelve

As Christi sipped the warm tea, as minutes ticked by, she grew calmer. They talked until after midnight, the intimidations of John Burton dominating the conversation. The danger he posed with mind games and convincing edge, his extreme mesmerizing impact, had dimmed in the wake of the violent attack. Having talked it out, Christi looked exhausted.

Dawn persuaded her to go to bed shortly after midnight. She went to sleep right away, but tossed restlessly. Dawn sat in a chair by her bed, dozing off and on, until she heard Dave and Mike enter the apartment.

Leaving the bedroom, she viewed the small, unpleasant apartment with avid disdain. It distressed Dawn that her friend lived in a tenement dump.

Dawn could not understand why Christi should live like this when she could live in luxury as an adopted sister. She would have been safe from harm's way on Woodland Drive.

Dawn felt frustrated beyond measure with that single thought as she entered the living room and faced the two brothers. Before she had a chance to say hello, Mike swept her into his arms.

"Well, if it isn't the sweetheart of Central High!" He tipped her backward kissing her right on the lips.

Hanging suspended in his arms, her birthday kiss request came to mind, but it was being delivered three months early.

"What are you doing here?" Dave asked when she was back on her feet.

Dawn stood recovering her poise, thinking about what just happened. Mike had never been shy, but that kiss had been—amazing—came to mind. She had felt a definite thrill in his arms and it startled her. She swallowed with effort and met Mike's eyes briefly.

Oh, yes, the question. Why did the question take her by surprise? Of course, he would wonder about her being in their apartment.

"Christi was going to come over to my house, but she called and said she wasn't feeling well." Dawn gently bit her lip realizing her mistake in being caught off guard but what explanation could there be?

The excuse sounded lame, but what excuse would even be plausible for her being here? Weariness enveloped her as she tried to think.

"I came over to stay with her until someone came home."

"Is it serious?" Dave looked toward her door.

"A sore throat, slight fever." Dawn nervously moistened her lips. "I wouldn't disturb her. She was feeling better—much better before she went to sleep. I have to go now."

She hoped to make a quick retreat but Mike halted her in midstride.

"Wait, Dawn, I'll walk you home."

"I drove."

"Then I'll ride with you and walk back."

"That's *really* not necessary."

"I insist," he pressured gently, taking hold of her arm.

"Well, if you insist," she complied half-heartedly, as he accompanied her toward the door.

Dawn remained quiet on the drive. Every comment that came to mind seemed inappropriate. Not that it mattered, when she glanced obliquely toward him, she noticed Mike gazing fixedly out the side window lost in thoughts of his own.

"What happened?" he said finally, when she drove between the brick pillars into her driveway. "You were hiding something; I could see it."

She pressed the brake. "What do you mean?" she asked shifting into park.

"I mean, I have to know what happened."

Dawn turned off the ignition. She stared straight ahead with definite misgivings, unable to figure a way to avoid his inquisitions, unable to find the words to tell him, especially since Christi had been adamant that it be kept between them. What kind of friend would she be?

"It might be easier if you say it without thinking too much," he suggested.

"Chris didn't want—"

"Tell me, now." His voice had an edge she had never heard before.

Dawn ran a hand through her hair. "Mike—"

She felt tears gather in her eyes. He knew something terrible had happened to his sister. She had to tell him.

"John was waiting for her downstairs at the apartment," she said in a small, choking voice. "He took her to the basement, and he—"

"He raped her."

Dawn looked at him quickly. "Don't go crazy," she pleaded.

Mike bent his head. He sat for a long time before moving, and when he did, he looked out the window away from her. His fingers curled around the door handle.

"I'll kill him. I'll get a gun—I'll blow his fucking head off."

"Mike, no!" Dawn grabbed his arm. "You can't do that," she pleaded.

"I can't let him get away with this," he said with sedate calm.

"He already got away with it," she said frantically holding tight to his arm, taut under her fingers. "It happened, you can't change that it happened."

Dawn drew a calming breath.

"If you kill John, you'll go to prison," she said evenly. "This is why she didn't want you to know. There's nothing you can do to take it away."

"I know I can't, but I'll feel better," he said stolidly.

"It won't help Chris—Mike, you don't want to go to prison," she said, seeking desperately to reach him. Dawn feared his capabilities in his serene determination. "It would hurt her more than she is already."

She felt his arm flex again, and then relax.

"I wanted to call the police Mike, but she seemed certain that you or Dave would take matters into your own hands—or some guy named Van. That's where her thoughts were. And John said something that convinced her he would stay out of her life now."

She swallowed thickly remembering exactly what Christi had told her.

"How can I just forget about it?"

"You have to deal with it," she said softly. "She loves you and David more than anything in this world."

"Damn it, Sommer!" He hit the door with his fist, and then sat in brooding silence.

Sommer? she wondered. None of her friends were aware of her first name. It was a well-kept secret, Sommer Dawn—she couldn't help feeling a bit embarrassed even though the name held special meaning to her mother.

Born on a late October night, she asked Tina why she had been given the unusual name. As it happened, Sommer was her grandmother's name on her mother's side and Dawn was her grandmother on her father's side, and so she had been christened Sommer Dawn Preston with no say in the matter.

Mike opened the car door. Dawn followed anxiously when he climbed out. She could tell he was still seething.

"Promise, Mike," she persisted, brushing other thoughts aside. "Promise you won't do something irrational. You cannot retaliate on this."

They stood silent in the moonlight. Mike finally broke the silence.

"How is she—" His voice cracked. He let out a resigned sigh that sounded miserably dispirited.

Dawn reached out to him. He pulled her close, holding her in a tight embrace, burying his face in her hair. She sensed his struggle with intense emotions. Her head resting against his chest, she felt his heart pounding and noticed with dazed awareness the affection she felt for her friend's brother.

Confused by the passionate feeling, she pulled away.

"She was physically bruised, but—" Dawn cleared her throat. "What she's going through emotionally, I can't imagine, but she'll be all right, Mike. She had calmed down by the time she went to bed." She looked deep into his grief-stricken blue eyes, momentarily lost for words.

"I'll make an appointment with my doctor for her to have a physical, to make sure—you know—that everything's okay."

"Thank you, Dawn." He brushed his fingers lightly through her hair.

"I'm glad I can help," she said quietly. "I want to do all I can to help her through this. You might not know it, Mike, but she's like a sister to me."

"No—I do know," he murmured. "I'll go now." He kissed her forehead.

"Don't worry, I won't—retaliate."

Mike appreciated Dawn, but he felt unaccustomed rage as he began the walk home. He felt sick and empty inside with impotent hate. He needed someone to hold onto, to keep him from sinking. He needed Carla.

Since they had met on the night of his sixteenth birthday, she had been there for him in every way. In many ways, he considered her a friend. When he needed to talk, she listened.

Seventeen years his senior, she had been turned onto the streets at the tender age of thirteen, but she had not been a street girl for a very long time.

He crossed the intersection, taking long strides in the direction of 4873 North Broadway. Mike felt the long, brisk walk lessoning the fury, and calming his jagged nerves. Still, he felt restless.

He needed to see her, but he paused in front of the impressive apartment building having second thoughts about coming here unexpectedly.

He leaned against a lamppost gazing at the massive structure. 4873 was not actually anyone's address. It covered four full blocks with apartments all around, and had entrances on all sides. Front and side balconies overlooked a huge courtyard with brilliant flower gardens, wide walking paths, shade trees, and benches for relaxing, basically a private park. A stone fountain sat in the midst of the square with gleaming gold fish swimming lazily around in it.

Balconies in back overlooked a humongous pool, lighted to comply with nighttime preference, you could almost always find a party going on out by the pool.

Mike lit a cigarette. He took his time with the smoke, mulling over being here without calling first. Deciding to take his chances, he started across the street, casually tossing the cigarette.

After a brief wait, she buzzed him in. He took the elevator up to the sixth floor pondering the wait, figuring she wasn't alone. Carla opened the door in the sheerest nothing of a red negligee. Her softly tousled hair suggestively enhanced her seductive beauty.

"I had to see you," he said, looking into magnificent brown eyes that always seemed to appear mysteriously pensive. "I hope it's all right."

She gazed at him with those beautiful eyes for a few wondering seconds.

"It's all right." Carla drew him inside the luxury apartment, touched her fingertips to her lips and then his. "Fix yourself a drink."

She made a swift retreat. Mike sighed as he paused in the archway of the spacious living room. Music from the entertainment center on the right housing a television and stereo/tape player surrounded him, emitting from a sound system of hidden speakers all around the room.

His eyes skimmed the attractive area. Carla had exquisite taste in art and stylish furnishings, but he had been immediately captivated by the seventy-five gallon lighted aquarium in the back where there lived an exotic, bubbly undersea world, a diversity of tropical marine life, miniature sunken ships, lost treasure, skeletal remains of pirates, hats still intact.

Mike slipped his shoes off before stepping onto the plush blue carpet. He walked to the bar, a gleaming black counter with matching cushioned stools, going directly to the back where a built in compact refrigerator held ice and soda. Bottles of various spirits and an assortment of mixes lined two shelves.

He took his drink over to the sofa. As he tried to relax, his thoughts wandered back over the past months. Carla had been a 'gift' to him from the gang on his sixteenth birthday.

Dave had been kept in the dark about their birthday surprise, and he'd never told him that his buddies arranged for his little brother to be seduced by a call girl, but in his opinion, it was the best present ever!

He had been mesmerized by the intrigue, the mystery, and the undisclosed promises in the depths of her brown eyes. Only she took it much further than a night of expected sex. In fact, sex as expected did not happen that night. Nearly a month passed before *that* magic moment, but the initial night had been amazing enough.

He experienced his first everything with her, his first drink, first meaningful kiss and first intimate touch.

That night, he learned the *art* of kissing, soft gentle kisses, tantalizing seductive kisses, deeply passionate and persuasive kisses. He had been an adept student enthusiastic to learn.

Carla took the time to teach him how to take his time, to entice, and persuade, the valuable knowledge that anything worth having was worth the wait. It had been lovely torture as she seduced him very slowly, and he became knowledgeable in the many ways to please a woman.

Mike returned to the present as he finished the drink. He felt a little strange, slightly agitated, never having been here when she was entertaining a client. He mixed another scotch, lit a cigarette and tried again to relax, recognizing the neglect he felt, knowing that he shouldn't even be here.

She had made it understood from the beginning that her business required specific dates for their time together. *Apparently some clients stopped by on their way to work in the morning.* Crushing his cigarette in an artfully crafted ash tray, he leaned back, momentarily closing his tired eyes.

A call girl, he knew, was nothing more than a high-class prostitute, but it didn't matter. She gave him the attention he craved, when he needed to talk, to hold her or to make love, and he gave her the real affection that no client could. Her chosen profession didn't matter to him, what people would say if they knew didn't matter either.

Mike heard a door close and let out a relieved sigh. Waiting had been difficult. He would never, again, barge in on her unannounced.

When she joined him fresh out of the shower, draped in a towel with damp, blonde tendrils of hair framing her face, everything dimmed in the haze of desire. He pulled her down beside him. The towel fell away and his hands slid across her silken skin. Mike felt like he was in possession of pure pleasure.

"Let's get you out of those clothes," she whispered, beginning to unbutton his shirt. "I seem to be underdressed."

"I want to kiss you first." He stood, enthusiastically pulling her to her feet. "Every underdressed inch of you."

They made their way to the royal blue playpen couch positioned in a corner flanked by mirrors on each side and tumbled onto the cushioned sofa. His yearning enhanced by her naked reflection, he crushed her against him, losing himself in the sensation of her exotic smell, her touch, her taste.

After desires had been fulfilled, Mike held her in his arms. They clung to each other, needing the incomparable closeness they shared.

"Mike?"

"Did I hurt you?" He rose above her looking into her sleepy eyes.

"No, but—" She hesitated.

"What? Was it too fast? Were you—?"

"Mike, you were wonderful, okay?"

She brushed his hair back from his forehead, smiling up at him.

"You just seemed, I don't know, a little desperate, like you were trying to—" She shrugged helplessly.

"Consume you?" Mike sighed, turning over on his back.

"Something like that." Carla snuggled closer, laying her head on his shoulder.

"I was desperate," he said. "Something happened that's left me feeling more desperate than I ever have in my life."

As he spilled his heart, she listened quietly. He felt relieved to let it out, his insurmountable hate of John, John's obsession of his sister and his inability to protect her or even avenge what happened.

He cherished Carla, that he could let tears fall unashamed in her presence, also her serene thoughtfulness and compassion, that he could tell her anything weighing on his mind without concern.

She didn't offer advice, possible or improbable solutions, she listened with quiet understanding and acceptance. Sometimes he just needed that.

When he kissed her good-bye and headed home, he left the woman behind, his thoughts dominated by the girl he had held earlier. With his arms around Dawn, she had been vulnerable to his perception. He had felt deep emotions radiate from her those few minutes in the driveway.

He had suspicions in the past, but now he knew, even though she did a fantastic job of repressing it, she cared about him more than mere friendship. She cared more than she wanted to admit, even to herself.

Chapter Thirteen

When school started in September, Christi determined to put the past behind her and look to the future. July would undeniably leave scars, but time had a way of healing wounded emotions. She hoped to eventually escape the overall horror of it—that the reality would fade to an indistinct shadow.

"I need to ask you something kinda personal," Mike said on the walk home from school the second week of October. "Is that okay?"

"You can ask me anything."

He looked a little bewildered. "Since when are you taking birth control?"

The personal nature of the question didn't surprise her since they openly discussed anything, but she laughed happily at the unexpected revelation that he could be unsure about something in her life.

He threw her a shrewd look. "You got a boyfriend stowed away somewhere?"

"No, I don't have a boyfriend."

"Then why the pills?" He sounded troubled.

"I wanted to be on birth control, for when I *do* have a boyfriend."

"But you don't, you're sure?"

She chuckled. "I would know."

"You don't have anyone in mind?" he asked apprehensively.

"If you're worried about Billy, you don't have to. And it will probably be a long time before there's anyone. Dawn took me to her doctor for a physical, you know, after what happened." Christi drew a deep breath, her voice faltered. "I didn't really want to talk about it."

"No, I understand. You must really miss having a mother sometimes," he sympathized. "It has to be hard for you."

"Dawn will do," she said, feeling a stab of unexpected grief. She gave him a playful shove to lighten the mood. "Of course I miss having a mother but no more than you. I *knew* you were a mama's boy," she teased.

"Yeah, I miss her, too," he acknowledged.

The nostalgic undertone brought tears to her eyes.

"I miss Daddy. Dave looks a lot like him, doesn't he?"

"Except Dad was bigger." Then he grinned. "I knew you were a daddy's girl," he drawled. With another playful shove the solemn moment slipped away.

"Well, since you obviously don't know everything about me all the time," she said speculatively. "How does that e.s.p. stuff work?"

"Haven't given it much thought . . . I pick up on what's fundamental, I guess," he said with a casual shrug. "A lot could depend on your . . . e.s.p. stuff?" Mike gave her a puzzled look. "Where'd that come from?"

"Well, whatever it is. A lot could depend on what?"

"Your mood."

"That's nice to know," she said dryly. "What should my mood be?"

"Oh, I don't know . . . sometimes if you've got a lot going on, things can get sort of muddled."

"Well alright," she said enthusiastically. "Good to know you're not as all-knowing as I had imagined. I deserve some secrets."

"Yes, you do, and I don't mean to invade your privacy," he said grimly.

"You big faker—are you going to the Halloween party this year?"

"Ah, yes, the great October social event of Central High School."

She giggled at his imitation of W.C. Fields.

"Well, are you?"

"I don't know." He kicked at a stone with the toe of his shoe. "I might put in an appearance, but I can't dig a high school dance party for very long."

"I know what you mean, it seemed so cool before," she said offhand. "Do you think we're growing up too fast, Mike?"

"Maybe, but we were put in that position. We can't change what's happened. Can't change the fact that I'd like to kill John Burton," he added ominously. "Or that I'd like to put a hurt on Billy Cole, *real* bad."

"Mike, you're sounding a little bit sinister. Stop that."

He favored her with his infectious grin. She smiled and shook her head. "You're impossible," she reprimanded, lovingly.

"Better?"

"Yes, thanks. Anyway, you're helping decorate the gym, so you might as well attend the party. How did that happen, by the way?"

"Dawn cornered me, flattered me, complimented my style, and without all that, it's nearly impossible to say no to that girl."

"Yeah, she's like that," Christi agreed.

"But here's the question, little sister, how would she know anything about my 'style'?"

"I think maybe someone told her that you helped deck out the Basement and how great it is down there."

He gave her a sidelong suspicious glance.

"Okay it was me."

His face brightened. "Thank you, I think."

"Oh you know any reason to spend time with Dawn is better than none," she said, then grinned mischievously. "You know it's true. You've got a crush on Dawn," she sang.

"Hey! Stop that!"

They shared laughter but Christi felt very sure there was some truth to the taunting little melody. Only Mike knew Dawn had a boyfriend, and Christi suspected that Mike didn't especially like seeing the two of them together.

* * *

Dawn hung the phone up. She walked back to the table where the assorted Halloween decorations, after being taken out of boxes, lay scattered in general disarray.

She felt like Mike should be here by now. It was almost one o'clock. He had said one o'clock. She had tried calling last night for his assurance that he would show up. He wasn't home. It seemed he never was. Dawn surveyed the mess, knowing that if he didn't get here it would be a disaster.

Would Mike Temple, with his dubious interests and too mature lifestyle, remember that she had recruited him, and that he had agreed to oversee a school dance decorating committee?

As she thought of the crew coming, Carrie crossed her mind. They had gotten closer these past two years. She was glad their childhood friendship had been restored. In many ways, she had Jerry to thank for that.

For some reason he didn't care for the little circle of friends that had been a part of her life before they began dating. Hanging out with them would have caused too much tension.

Unfortunately, a couple of the girls were more than a little uppity. They wouldn't hang with Carrie and some of her other friends, except at certain parties. Before she turned thirteen, they had gravitated to their own little clique for the most part.

Those young-teen years had been fun, and it had been difficult to give up her girlhood friends, but she had known Carrie all her life, too. When she had been tight with the others, she and Carrie drifted apart, but Ted had stayed close, and now he had drifted away from all of them.

Dawn saw Carrie with Paul, Jerry's brother, approaching and waved. Carrie smiled, reminding her of Ted, who favored his sister with the same easy smile and mild ways.

Ted had been head of the decorating committee last year, here with the rest of them cutting-up and having a blast, getting it together for Halloween night. This year, he declined. He kept drifting further away, and she didn't know how to draw him back.

"Dawn?" Carrie gave her a quizzical look. "You were somewhere else entirely."

"Yes, I was thinking about Ted."

"I wish he would be up front with me. I can't believe a word he says, anymore." Her mouth tensed for just an instant. "It's like he tells me what I want to hear and does what he pleases. He keeps his distance."

She sounded bewildered and Dawn understood, aware of the bond they had shared, more than brother and sister; they had been best friends growing up.

Paul put his arm around Carrie's waist. "I hate to see you so down."

"I can't help it. He said he's through with drugs, but I have my doubts."

"Yeah, I know what you're saying," Paul sympathized. "He's not his usual self. What do you think, Dawn?"

"He hasn't been his usual self for a while now," Dawn agreed.

"Paul, will you talk to him?" Carrie pleaded.

"What makes you think he'd talk to me?"

"You're a guy, maybe it's a guy thing."

"Okay, I will." Paul put his arms around her, looking directly into her eyes. "But only if you promise to relax and have a good time."

"I'll take you up on that," Carrie agreed with a serene smile.

Dawn's attention was suddenly averted to the person who sidled up and draped an arm casually around her shoulders.

"I think we should get started on the decorating or we'll be here all day," Mike said.

"It's about time!" She gave him a wide, forgiving smile. "I'm glad you're here—I've been trying to call you forever. Hey, Chris, did you tell this brother of yours how frantic I was?"

"Yes, I did that," Christi replied.

"You doubted my reliability?"

"I was concerned when I couldn't reach you," she admitted.

"I'm seriously wounded." He gave her a deliberate crestfallen gaze. "Didn't I tell you I'd be here at one? You tryin' to give me a bad rep—or what?"

He quirked an eyebrow and she smiled indulgently, amused at his cute expressions. Seemed the guy could melt her heart any day of the week. She recognized the attraction, his amusing appeal. Maybe it's time to take a step back, she thought, but she didn't want to.

"I told you he's seldom home, Dawn," Christi interjected. "This guy's a perpetual roadrunner, but dependable no less."

"Well, I'm glad, okay? And you're right, it's not quite one. It's just that, well, you're so good at this sort of thing, I guess. Christi said so."

"Well, then, if Christi said so, it must be. But I'm good at everything I do, Dawn. It's my nature—and I keep my word."

"Don't take it so hard, I'm earnestly sorry that I doubted you reliability," she humbly apologized. "It won't happen again."

"Shake on it?"

He offered her his hand, which she accepted, but instead of a playful handshake, he held her hand gazing into her eyes with a compellingly sweet look of expectation. Before she could forget where they were, he favored her with that quick flirty wink.

Dawn remembered the kiss in his apartment, feeling unsure of what had passed between them. Just as she began to doubt being able to stay afloat in the sea of swirling emotions, he gave her that spontaneous flash of a smile that indicated his harmlessly teasing conduct, turning his attention to the assortment of decorations.

With abstract wonder if she would ever be able to take him seriously, she thankfully snagged the needed lifeline in his impish grin.

Mike assigned four groups of four teens and set them to each task, with her, Paul and Carrie in his assemblage.

"Let's get these monsters out of the way, first," he suggested.

"Okay, where should we set Frankenstein and Dracula?" Paul asked.

"Frankie can stand by the front door—to welcome all the hideous creatures of the night," Mike replied.

"Dracula can stand over by that door congenially directing the formerly mentioned hideous creatures to the restroom down the hall," Dawn suggested.

"Yes, he's shockingly congenial," Mike agreed.

He took Frankenstein by the head, she got his feet, Paul and Carrie went the opposite way with Dracula. They were tall and cumbersome, but easily handled by two.

"What about the witch?" Dawn asked as they met again after positioning each perspective monster.

"Over by the refreshment table inviting people to a glass of punch, aka 'witches brew'." Mike recommended. "She will be a perfectly wicked hostess."

As they carried her over to the table, Dawn's mind wandered. Ted, Paul and Jerry, their freshman year in Woodshop, had made these wooden replicas of Dracula, Frankenstein, and a wicked looking witch.

The three were in the same grade because Ted had failed a year. Naturally the memory of that Halloween drew worrisome thoughts back to Ted. Why did he pull away? Why did he lose interest in things that used to matter?

Dawn glanced around the room to divert her mind from distant thoughts. It didn't help—she could picture Ted there with them, now.

Some of the teens were busy twisting black and orange streamers, others were applying wall decorations, while the fourth group, which included Christi, were hanging plastic skeletons and witches.

Mike intervened and soon had her laughing and chatting, abandoning tender memories. They stretched rubbery plastic spider webs with large plastic spiders attached in various areas, also soft, synthetic cobwebs with big and little spiders woven in and out to achieve the desired creepy effect.

She worked cheerfully at his side filling orange and black balloons with helium and tying them in clusters.

With the last jack-o-lantern placed, the kids of the decorating committee stood in the middle of the room satisfactorily admiring their accomplishment.

"Get the overhead lights," Dawn said. "Let's see how it looks with spooky mood lighting."

Mike went to the sidewall to pull the switch.

"What a scary looking place this is," Mike said in a good imitation of Peter Lori. "Now it's out for pizza!"

"That sounds like a great idea," Dawn agreed. "My treat. Art's Pizza?" she suggested. Everyone enthusiastically approved, and then began filing out.

"I thought you had a boyfriend," Mike commented linking arms with her. "That's okay, I'll keep you company. Where's good ole Jerry, anyhow?"

"His mother isn't well," she said, experiencing a touch of guilt for being glad to have this time with Mike. "Guess it's his turn to keep her company."

"Yeah, well, he don't know what he's missing."

His arm moved easily around her waist. Dawn marveled at how right and how good it felt to be close to him like this. She didn't even try analyzing the feeling, she just accepted it.

"I wanted to tell you, I'm sorry I missed your birthday party," he said.

"Me, too."

"I mean it. I won't miss another party you invite me to, okay?"

She glanced sideways at him. "Why didn't you come?"

"I'll tell you someday."

Curiosity itched inside for an answer, but she didn't press him. "I'll hold you to it," she said eloquently.

They quickened their step to catch up with the others.

Chapter Fourteen

As the annual Halloween Dance Party swung into the third hour, the teens of Central High filled the gymnasium with gaiety and electrifying excitement.

Carrie grinned as she watched wolf-men dancing with witches, vampires stalking fairytale characters and zombies paired with ghosts, dancing to the pulsing beat of Rioters, the local rock 'n roll band. Others stood on the side talking, sipping punch, nibbling snacks or just horsing around.

She noticed Ted leaning against the wall near the south exit.

"Is anything wrong?" she asked, walking up to him, observing his solemn expression. "You okay?"

"Everything's cool," he said, without looking at her.

"Is it, really?" she pressed. "You seem a little down to me. You should have brought a date, you seem so alone."

"And that's the way I want it, Carrie Ann. Did that thought ever occur to you?" He softened the rejection with a lopsided grin.

She looked into his eyes easily detecting that he was on something, what drug she could not surmise.

"You're stoned," she whispered, hating the accusatory tone of her voice. "Ted, you told me you quit using—you promised."

She felt deep disappointment at his most recent deception.

"Get off my case, Carrie," he said shifting his dreamy gaze across the crowded room pretty much ignoring her. "Go play, have fun, dance. Just get off my case."

Tears misted her eyes, her feelings easily hurt by her brother. The rude indifference, the uncaring attitude was painful enough, but it hurt more to see the damage he inflicted upon himself and be helpless to stop it.

Dawn came up to them. "Is everything okay?" she asked. Carrie shook her head, looking troubled, but Ted grinned wryly.

"It's all boss," he replied dreamily. "Your little Halloween party's far out Dawny. Hey, you look adorable Little Blue Fairy," he added.

"Extremely adorable," Mike echoed as he joined them. "Are you blue, Dawn? A Blue Dawn is sad to contemplate, so if you are, feel free to call."

He winked, nearly imperceptibly before his eyes scanned the crowd.

"Tell Chris I took off, okay. Catch ya later, babe." He gave Dawn another quick wink before ambling toward the exit.

"Mike winked at you," Carrie said grinning expressively. "Twice."

"Oh, he always does," Dawn said with a flippant air. "It's just his way."

"I think he was flirting with you," Carrie insisted with a mischievous look. "He's kinda cute, don't ya think?"

Dawn watched his retreat. He was very 'kinda cute'. "I happen to be dating your boyfriend's brother—don't encourage me!"

"Hope he doesn't get in trouble. No one's supposed to leave the dance 'til it's over at midnight," Carrie said.

"I don't think rules apply much to Mike," Dawn replied thoughtfully. "Maybe the really important ones."

Paul and Jerry joined them, twin vampires, extraordinaire.

"So, here you are!" Paul took Carrie's hand. "Come on, let's dance."

Jerry pulled Dawn possessively close.

"I wondered where you disappeared to."

"Oh, we're just hangin' out here with our sullen little wallflower."

"Well, come and hang out with me," he said pulling Dawn toward the dance floor while Paul waited for Carrie.

"Ted?" Carrie gave her brother an inquiring glance reluctant to leave him standing alone on the sideline.

"Go on," he urged. "I'm okay—I'm more than okay."

Paul led her away. She forgot about her brother for a while as they danced, laughed and talked and stole kisses when chaperones weren't paying attention. The next time she looked back, Ted was lost to her searching eyes.

His disappearing act left her shaken.

"Remember me?" Paul teased.

Carrie smiled faintly, resigning her attention to her date.

At midnight as everyone prepared to leave, Carrie made her way to the refreshment table, anxiously searching the faces of the students milling around. Most had gone to the locker rooms and changed into street clothes.

"Mrs. Preston, have you seen Ted?"

"No, I haven't seen him since before the costume contest, but that's not surprising—there's quite a crowd here tonight."

"I've looked everywhere; no one's seen him for a while. He's not here, Mrs. Preston."

"Don't panic just yet, Carrie," she soothed. "He could be home right now, for all we know. Maybe he looked and couldn't find you, like I said, quite a crowd."

Being a professional and adept at retaining composure in emergencies, Dawn's mother seemed calm, but Carrie could sense subdued alarm. No one was supposed to leave until the dance ended. In spite of recent behavior, Ted wouldn't have, not without telling her. He knew how she worried for him.

"Paul, what's wrong?" Mrs. Preston took hold of Paul's arm as he rushed up to them. He seemed stunned and unsettled as he focused on Mrs. Preston.

"It's Ted," he said dazedly.

"Did something happen?" Her voice sounded loud in the sudden silence.

Carrie stared at Mrs. Preston, then at Paul with wide, frightened eyes.

"I think—he's dead." Tears choked his voice. "I was helping Carrie look for him, and I—I found him."

Carrie watched his expressive face, so many emotions; concern, hurt, despair and total helplessness. There had been no misunderstanding.

Realization swept over her in a flood of misery.

The anxious speculations of her friends began in low tenor but picked up pace with mounting intensity. She staggered with a shock of overwhelming dizziness before everything around her grew hazy.

Paul embraced Carrie as she fainted.

Bob Kaley, the social studies teacher rushed to his aid, lifted and carried her to an exercise mat near the wall where he gently laid her down.

"She'll come out of this pretty quickly," he consoled. He stood and glanced around. "Has anyone called the police?"

"I did," Dawn said. She knelt beside her friend.

Carrie moaned softly, her eyes fluttering open. Given a few minutes she recovered considerably, then, accompanied by her mother, Dawn walked with Carrie, Paul and Jerry to the teacher's lounge to wait for her parents.

* * *

Christi walked slowly along the quiet streets, pondering the night that began with jubilance and festivities only to end with the shocking incident of a student dead of a drug overdose. Ted Harrison, Carrie's brother, Dawn's friend, using the worst drug imaginable, had paid the ultimate price.

It had not been formally announced but the whispers spread like a wave over the gymnasium, Ted overdosed on heroin. Fortunately, Carrie had already been escorted out of the room.

They were not detained long, after giving names and phone numbers to officers taking the information, they were released to go home.

Walking toward Market Street, she heard a distant thin wail of a siren wafting over the stillness of the recently desolate October night.

The unmistakable revving of a motorcycle drawing closer made her unwitting think of Billy Cole. At first he had been an almost constant pain, now thoughts of him, though not as frequent, were still painful. She clung to the adage that time heals, but sometimes it takes a little more time.

When the motorcycle pulled to the curb, she glanced around to see Billy, one foot placed on the street for balance, dark hair blowing gently in the breeze, his presence even more innately masculine than memory served.

Christi ignored the instinct to run fast and far, away from his unsettling presence. She raised her chin in what she hoped to be a cool stare.

"What are you doing here?" she demanded, making her voice hard to hide the rush of feelings she was experiencing at the sight of him.

He ignored the question and asked one of his own.

"What happened at the school?"

"A student died," she said, frustration throwing her off balance. "Something to do with drugs."

"I'm sorry to hear that." He glanced briefly over his shoulder before directing his look back to her. "I was hoping—I have to talk to you."

"We don't have anything to talk about," she said edgily.

"How can you say that?"

"How can I?" Once more, Christi hoped her caustic tone would hide the mixed emotions she felt other than wonder at his absolute ignorance. "How can you imagine we have anything to discuss?" she said impatiently. "Would you go away, please?"

Christi resumed walking. She didn't want to talk to him. It hurt just to look at him. She hadn't expected to see him again. After putting him out of her mind for the most part anyway, he had to show up and open wounds that had not quite healed even yet.

"You have to listen to me!" he insisted.

"I don't have to do anything!" She determinedly did not look back, almost taken by the beseeching quality in his voice. Christi picked up her pace. The sound of the motor died, and then Billy caught up with her walking alongside.

"Why won't you talk to me?" he said, as if she were being irrational.

She whirled to face him. "Why won't you leave me alone?"

"I tried to leave you alone, baby, it didn't work. I can't let you walk out of my life again," he said huskily. "I tried to forget—"

"Try a little harder," Christi interrupted, her temper flaring at his resilience. "It's only been four months."

Anger surmounted the pain in her heart. "And don't call me baby, I'm not your baby. I'm nothing to you. A one night stand, that's all I was to you."

"No, it isn't like that." He held her shoulders. "Please, let me explain."

"Take your hands of me," she said heatedly. "I don't want to hear your lies or lame excuses."

Billy released her immediately. He appeared somewhat flustered by her demand as he pushed his hands deeply into his pockets leaning back on his heels staring at her like a dejected little boy.

A cruiser pulled to the curb. "Is there a problem here?"

"No problem," Christi said.

"It's past curfew." His voice, while not severely stern, held a distinct reprimand. "Call it a night and get home where you belong."

He drove on. She watched the taillights turn the corner.

Christi looked back at Billy and decided to be done with it. Facing him was not getting any easier.

"I didn't walk out of your life," she reminded him in an effort to summon more anger. "Did you listen to the phone ring the day I called? You were the one who rejected me." Christi took a deep calming breath unable to contend with him any longer. "I want you to get out of here," she said with quiet firmness. "And don't ever bother me again."

"Five minutes," he said. She noticed he almost reached for her again but thought better of it. "Give me five minutes of your life."

A protest caught in her throat as their eyes met, but she nodded. She had wanted, after all, to give him her whole life.

"Have you been seeing anyone?" he asked. "I wouldn't ask, but—"

"Don't flatter yourself," she interposed. "I haven't been pining over you."

"You haven't? I've been doing some pining." He gave her a hopeful glimpse, which changed to downcast at her expedient look. "Sorry I asked."

"You should be sorry. You should be more than sorry."

"I deserve that—but I am sorry, Chris. And I meant everything I said to you. You have to believe me. I meant it when I said for you to call me."

She gazed at him, her eyes steady and clear in spite of the mounting pain deep in her chest. She would hate herself for crying now.

"Before you left that night, just before you walked out the door, when you looked up into my eyes—it felt like I was falling into you, somehow. I was losing myself and it scared the *hell* out of me. I didn't know what to do with those feelings. I didn't expect it to happen. I—damn it, Christi, don't look at me that way, like you don't believe a word I'm saying."

"Maybe I do believe you," she murmured. "Maybe that's worse."

"What do you mean?"

"You're explanation makes no sense at all," she flared. "You want to turn this around like it's my fault."

The repressed hurt began to surface. She hid it by narrowing her eyes at him, determined to see this through without losing composure.

"I'm the one who's offended here. I'm the one who was humiliated, and your time is up." She turned her back on him determined to walk away.

"I wasn't entirely honest with you."

She hesitated.

"I sensed your youth, and I wanted it."

Christi turned to look at him feeling incredulous wonder.

"I figured you were a virgin." He stroked his thumb gently down her face. "I wanted that, too, and since I'm going all out honest, it didn't hurt that you were Dave Temple's little sister."

She gazed at him beginning to grasp the bitter reality. Christi felt shame at being so naïve.

"I led you every step of the way. I sensed your fascination; your starry-eyed nature just gave you away."

What was he saying? Their every moment together was a farce? His eyes searched hers, and she wondered what he expected to find.

"You're not helping your case," she managed, her throat tightening.

"When you ordered the drink, I knew it was because you were upset. You only played into my hands. It was pretty obvious you'd never drunk before, but I didn't care. I had one thing on my mind."

Her mouth almost dropped open. She felt dazed at his admission. Christi realized that had been her essential accusation, but hearing him confess it as truth was horrible.

"I wonder if you can imagine how that makes me feel."

He moistened his lips and glanced down, then raised his eyes to hers.

"It doesn't do much for my feelings either."

Her gaze clouded with tears, the struggle with her emotions becoming increasingly difficult. She didn't trust herself to speak. It took all her effort just to maintain control.

"Afterward, I lashed out at you because I was angry with myself for taking advantage of you. Don't forget, I was drunk and stoned, too. Maybe it didn't show, but I was."

"That is no excuse," she choked. "You weren't drunk and stoned when you made your little plan."

"I didn't mean to hurt you."

"You didn't care if you hurt me or not."

Christi swallowed hard, barely able to keep the tears at bay, needing to be away from him, recalling Susan Shaffer's haughty look, her harsh words. He had done exactly what that woman said he would. She had experienced extreme degradation, exactly like something used and discarded.

Billy had made her feel those horrible emotions.

"I realize there is no excusing what I did, but I need you to understand how bad I feel and how sorry."

"I'm glad you're sorry." She turned away.

"Christi, wait! Can we start over as friends?"

She stopped again, letting out a disturbed sigh, his words creating mass confusion. There was no doubt in her mind that she still had deep feelings for Billy, but how could she risk chancing anything with him?

Christi turned to face him. "How can I ever trust you?"

"It won't happen too soon, I don't suppose. I have something for you," he said with a note of excitement. "Please accept it as a token of friendship, an extremely profound friendship."

His beguiling tone and pensive look widened the crack in a wall that had not been built strong enough to withstand this onslaught. Christi took the little box he offered and opened it.

Her pulse quickened as her eyes took in the delicate elegance of an exquisite sapphire and diamond ring setting in a bed of silk.

She snapped the box shut, holding it out to him.

"I can't accept this," she said, surprised that he would expect her to take possession of such an expensive gift.

"If you don't, it goes down the sewer," he threatened. "I'm serious."

"You wouldn't do that," she challenged nervously, to some extent fearful that he actually would.

"Try me—no, don't try me," he said with a hesitant laugh.

Christi rubbed her forefinger thoughtfully over the velveteen covering, wondering about the ring and the things he had said. She knew if she hadn't wanted this benevolence she wouldn't have hesitated.

"I need some time," she said slowly.

"Will you keep the ring?"

"For now."

"Will you call me?"

"I don't know when, but I will call."

His hands resting on her shoulders, he lovingly caressed her neck with his thumb, an achingly familiar memory.

"Promise me."

"I will." She drew away. "I have to go home now."

"Can I take you?"

"No, I'll walk."

He took a breath, looked as if he was going to say more but thought better of it. Christi gazed into his eyes for a lingering moment before turning away, the tug of her heart warning enough not to subject herself to his presence any longer. Her arms around the man she had given herself to with childlike trust would not be a sound basis for rational thinking.

Walking toward Market Street, she heard the cycle rev up, and then fade into the night. Slowly approaching the area of nightlife and neon lights, with the high-spirited, animated laughter of the nocturnal, she took surprising comfort in the familiar surroundings that she never had before.

Once home, Christi went straight to her room. She felt empty inside. While her eyes remained dry, the need to cry left an ache deep in her chest.

Although she hadn't known Ted personally, her heart went out to Carrie, his parents and close acquaintances. Dawn, like a sister to her, had lost a longtime friend. She knew from experience that recovering after the loss of a loved one takes a long and painful season.

Christi went to bed with the hope of avoiding unpleasant thoughts in slumber, but tossed restlessly. Wide awake with anxiety, she gave up on sleep, deciding that a glass of warm chocolate might sooth her nerves.

She shuffled unhappily into the kitchen.

"How was the party?" Mike asked.

Christi closed the refrigerator, turning to her brother fretfully.

"Ted Harrison died tonight."

His eyes widened in understandable shock. "How?"

"Heroin, he shot up and overdosed."

"Ted didn't do smack," he said indisputably. "He hated needles. Even if it was the poison of choice for Teddy, he would have sniffed it."

"Maybe he decided to advance the high."

"Believe me, he didn't. Not like that."

"I don't understand." She looked at him with a feeling of dread.

"He was selling, Chris, speed, downs, pot . . . cocaine." He shook his head, sighing gloomily. "I tried to warn him."

"I could have guessed," she admitted. "I've seen him at the Basement. Why else would he be there?"

"Except to deal," Mike confirmed. "And he was dealing major, everything except heroin. It's easier to get into than out of, is my understanding."

"Mike, what are you saying?"

He shrugged uneasily. "If you want out—if you know too much—"

"You don't think it was an accident, do you," she realized. "You're saying he was murdered." A sudden disturbing thought brought her up short. "Do you know who did it?"

"No, I don't."

She felt immense relief. She didn't want Mike at risk.

Christi poured a cup of milk into a small pot to heat as she contemplated Mike's revelation. Dawn and Ted had practically grown up together, but something had sure gone wrong. He had kept secrets. Dawn couldn't have been aware of his association with drug pushers.

The milk began to simmer.

"'Night Chris, I'm gonna crash. You should, too," he advised glancing back. "You look tired."

"I will, soon," she said taking a glass from the cupboard.

Christi absently stirred chocolate into her warm milk. She drank the chocolate milk, sipping slowly, her mind wandering as she thought about what Mike had said. So many questions needed answers.

She tossed restlessly in bed, falling asleep in the early morning hours to awaken a mere six hours later. Sleep had been deep and dreamless bliss.

She closed her eyes wishing to forget last night's tragedy awhile longer, to postpone the reality that Ted Harrison had been murdered. Mike wouldn't have given such a serious insinuation if he wasn't certain.

Christi kept her eyes closed but her mind remained active. She finally gave up on further sleep, dragging her miserable self out of bed.

In the kitchen, she put water on the gas range to heat for coffee.

"You don't look like you feel so good," Mike observed as he joined her.

"I don't feel so good," she acknowledged. "I feel terrible about Ted."

"Yeah, me too."

Christi glanced in his direction. She noticed the little boy look of tousled hair and dreamy eyes. Her brother—how she loved him! She could not even contemplate losing Mike or Dave.

"The water's about to boil, want coffee?"

"Yeah, great." He sat at the table.

"How well did you know Ted?" she asked.

"Didn't really. I knew him well enough to know he had problems. He was selling to support his habit, that's all. He thought I needed a contact, 'cause I hang out where I do, you know, a lot of people assume I'm into drugs."

"That's not exactly an unfair assumption, is it?"

"No, it doesn't bother me much, but yeah it's an unfair assumption."

He added sugar to the cup of coffee she set in front of him, stirring absently, swirling the spoon with a look of distant speculation.

"He didn't try to entice me into using, though. He wasn't a pusher, Chris, not the hard stuff."

"That's good to know." She looked fondly at her brother. She had not missed the struggle of emotions in his expression as he told her Ted thought he needed a contact for drugs.

"I can't even imagine losing you or Dave," she sighed. "I didn't know Ted, really, but I'm pretty well acquainted with Carrie. I can't imagine what she's going through, or Dawn for that matter, they were close."

"I know, friends since preschool."

"Dawn's been worried about him," Christi told Mike. "He disassociated himself from longtime friends," she said with a tinge of exasperation. "Why would a kid with his background go so wrong?"

"For the thrill, little sister, always for a thrill."

"Mike, this scares me."

"I don't want you to be afraid, little sister, is there anything I can do?"

A teasing smile lit his face, and she gave him an impulsive hug.

"Well, you can quit rubbing it in that you're ten minutes my senior," she offered. "And you're right, Mike, people thinking you use drugs is a wrong and unfair assumption."

"Unfair but inevitable," he remarked with an easy shrug.

"Mike, I feel like I've been sixteen forever," she said, her mood going melancholy again. "Everything seems out of control."

"With all the changes you've gone through this past year, I'm not surprised. And murder is enough to make anyone feel out of control—but take heart," he said, inspiring a tentative smile. "You're almost seventeen, after all. Hard to imagine, isn't it? One more year, we're of age."

"Of age to what? Graduate—out of school—on the street."

"You're in a sour mood," Dave said as he joined them. "I heard that remark, little glum one." He gave her a speculative look. "Sweeten up, sweetie. You won't be on any street in this town."

He walked to the stove, setting the teakettle on to boil.

"You're up early," she said, pleased.

"I could go back to bed," he hedged.

"No way, you know I love it when you join us for breakfast."

"Anyway, you're both going to college. That's what the insurance money is for." He sat across from her. "Why are you so dreary this morning?"

He gave Mike a quizzical look, also. "The two of you look bummed to the max. I thought you went to a party last night. What's up?"

"Ted Harrison died last night," she told him. "It was drug related. He died of an overdose of heroin, Dave, and Mike says he didn't use heroin."

The teakettle whistled. Dave gave her a sympathetic hug on his way to the stove. "I'm sorry about your friend—I can't imagine what happened, unless Teddy graduated to big time," he suggested. "If you don't know what you're doin' overdosing can happen easy enough."

Mike had been adamant that he did not use needles, but she kept silent with a glance at Mike who shook his head in negative affirmation.

Christi experienced an upsetting mixture of anxiety and love for her big brother, the reckless one who could be a little too wild for conventionality, a bit rakish too, and still a genuinely caring individual.

He had enlisted in the army right out of high school. She understood that he planned to make a career in the armed forces but something happened, an experience he had never elaborated on, that changed his mind.

She gave him an admiring glance. Christi was proud of her brother and would always feel that pride, even though when he came home after two years of active duty, a new lifestyle had emerged.

She wondered if the death of their parents had propelled him into it. She also wondered what might have been if they had lived.

Christi struggled through the grief stricken moment. Their parents were gone, no use contemplating. She immediately decided to try to loosen up for now, toss off anxieties and discontent, to enjoy breakfast with her brothers and to make the rest of their morning exchange as pleasant as possible.

After Dave and Mike left, she went to her room. Christi opened the little box Billy had given her.

Her eyes grew misty as she viewed the delicate ring of gems. With grim reluctance, she acknowledged that seeing Billy had inadvertently brought John Burton back into painful focus.

There were still times when going down the stairs of the apartment building brought feelings of unease, and she had never gone back into the basement to do laundry. The half block walk to a public Laundromat was preferable to the stark reminder of what he'd put her through with a casual comment about accepting what happened. She would never forget those words, as if her rape had been no more than a minor interference in her life.

Returning her thoughts to here and now, Christi removed the ring from the silken case. It fit perfectly on her third finger, left hand.

She held her hand out admiring the sparkling jewels with pensive, wishful reflections, but her mind clouded with doubts and suspicions when it came to trusting Billy. Where did he get it? How had he come by such a quality piece of jewelry?

Christi removed the ring without further contemplation, returning it to its bed of silk, placing it in the drawer of her nightstand where it would be out of sight, out of mind.

She retrieved the small key that had been tossed thoughtlessly in the drawer, a drawer that had never been used for anything significant, but one with a lock. Christi locked the ring within, and then set the reading lamp on top of the key.

Chapter Fifteen

Dawn had never been to a funeral service. She had survived eighteen years without losing a loved one. The service tore at her emotions, the sorrow almost overwhelming.

A local church choir sang the mournful melody of "Precious Memories" and other appropriate heart piercing hymns, seemingly to bring the reality of loss into painful focus.

A Saturday service, Ted had been gone for only a week. The autopsy hadn't interfered with a timely funeral.

The huge church was filled to capacity. Dawn had known the turnout would be commendable. All the kids from Central High attended, together with concerned parents and numerous neighborhood acquaintances.

The vast majority went home after the service. Dawn, with a few close friends, accompanied the family to the cemetery.

Dawn felt deep despair, standing across from the shattered family, in view of their pain, Carrie and Mrs. Harrison sobbing brokenly, and little six-year-old Timmy clinging to his mother's leg sniveling pitifully.

Mr. Harrison picked up his son. Timmy rested his head on his dad's broad shoulder. She turned to Jerry, her eyes overflowing. He put an arm comfortingly around her shoulders.

It was time to leave. Dawn hugged Carrie. "I love you—I'll call you."

"I'm going to be with her," Paul said. "Don't worry."

Dawn turned away before more tears could fall and walked toward the car with Jerry, her sorrow a huge, painful knot inside. She didn't feel like sharing, she wanted to walk, to remember, to wonder how it had come to this.

"I want to walk home, okay? I need some time. I'll call you later."

"Sure." He squeezed her hand gently.

As she strolled slowly through the quiet neighborhood, her mind wandered back over the past couple of years. She couldn't pinpoint exactly when Ted began drifting away and could hardly accept that he had been using heroin, but it was more difficult to accept his death, that he was gone from her life forever. It seemed unreal. She thought a funeral was supposed to give closure. She didn't feel closure. She felt despondence.

Heroin—how could he? How could he take chances with such an addictive and destructive drug? It destroyed lives and shattered dreams.

She wondered, but of course there was no answer.

With Ted being considered a 'troubled teenager', suicide had been deliberated but proven inconclusive. The coroner's inquest determined death by accidental overdose, a common outcome with use of the dangerous drug.

Not the sort of story anyone wanted to make headlines, but it did, and it hurt to read it, to hear it on the news. It hurt his family and his friends. Their neighborhood, a small town within itself had suffered a powerful loss.

The dusty, tree-lined streets were strangely desolate, as if everyone was in mourning. They probably were. He had sauntered up to these houses from age two to twelve yelling 'trick or treat' right along with the rest of them.

Many people in the community knew and loved Ted. Had he even been aware of the love?

A squirrel crossed the sidewalk in front of her, scurried up the trunk of a large tree, and chattered noisily from an overhead limb. Distracted for an instant, she almost smiled, but then a large gray cloud passed over the sun.

The day had been unusually cool, now the air felt cold against her bare arms. She quickened her pace to hasten the moderately long walk from the cemetery to home, last stop on Woodland Drive, commonly called 'the Castle' by her friends, where she lived with her mother.

Dawn felt proud of her lone parent, a gentle but strong woman who lost her husband in an automobile accident shortly before the birth of her baby.

Given their wealth and possible pitfalls, raising a baby alone, who is privy to every luxury in life, and somehow preventing her from turning into an insufferably spoiled child—Dawn felt Tina fully deserving of admiration—from infant to marginally normal teenager, she had been taught true values.

Dawn had perfect understanding that some things money can't buy.

Her thoughts turned suddenly and arbitrarily to her absent father. She'd visited his grave and read the headstone of James Paul Preston, 'gone but not forgotten'. At times she experienced random feelings of loss for the father she had never known. Her mother had told her what a kind and caring man he had been, how he was looking forward to the baby, and that he would have been a wonderful father. Pictures of him seemed to reflect that description.

Dawn leaned on the doorframe watching her mother move with easy expertise in the kitchen. Good smells filled the air, baked chicken with Tina's special stuffing, and spiced apples from a pie cooling on the counter were unquestionably luscious, but what usually served to awaken her appetite almost made her ill with memories. Ted had loved Tina's homemade apple pie, especially still warm and served alamode.

Tina turned around, her eyes filled with concern. She had been to the funeral but did not accompany them to the cemetery.

Dawn blinked away the sting of tears, and even managed a faint smile. "I'll set the table," she said going to the cupboard for plates.

"You'll need an extra setting. Bob's coming to dinner."

Bob Kaley, the ninth grade Social Studies teacher had been dating her mother for about five months. They went out occasionally, but spent time right here at home, too.

She wondered, almost hoping not, if the relationship was serious. She wondered also about her possibly self-serving attitude. They seemed well suited in some ways, but something about Bob rubbed her wrong, and bottom line, she could not imagine him as her mother's husband.

Dawn picked at her food, pushed it around on the plate, took a bite and almost gagged. She took a sip of water, her glance reverting to Bob's hand as he removed a ring from his shirt pocket.

"Take a look at this," he said, handing it over to her. "Unusual, isn't it?"

She looked closely at the jeweled ring. "Yes, I suppose."

"I found it in the parking lot Halloween night."

Something about the ring seemed almost sinister. She gave it back.

"It's a beautiful ring, an expensive piece of jewelry," he said. "Someone must have lost it. It seems whoever lost it would want it back."

"I suppose."

"Would you have any idea who might own an unusual ring of this style?"

"No." Dawn felt numb with distraction. "May I be excused, Tina?"

"Of course," she consented gently. "But you should eat something."

"I can't." Dawn could hardly speak past the tightness in her throat.

"We're all saddened by this tragedy—" Bob began.

"Yes, we are. Excuse me." She pushed away from the table.

In the confines of her room, Dawn fell across the bed to stare at the ceiling and wonder about the ring; a tiny coiled version of a cobra.

She turned on her side, closed her eyes, and began drifting into a dream. Walking through her serene neighborhood, she felt calmness and tranquility.

Suddenly a king cobra loomed in front of her, swaying and hypnotic, pinning her with its mesmerizing movement until it transformed into a tall skeletal phantom, grinning crazily, eerily within a swirling mist.

She pushed herself through the darkness, sitting up with a gasp, escaping the terrifying nightmare.

A wave of apprehension swept through her as she recalled a cobra being part of the horrid dream. With further consideration, the cobra ring itself didn't strike her as something evil, but she had seen it Halloween night.

It must have been associating the ring with the night Ted died that made it appear malevolent. A man in a phantom mask with a long black cape had bumped into her that night and pushed rudely away.

He had been wearing the ring—that ring should have been given to the police. It could be an important piece of evidence. Dawn took the troubling thought with her as she headed to the kitchen for a cup of herbal tea.

She felt extremely tense, realizing without undue surprise that she was thinking of Ted's death in terms of being a murder. The phone rang, and she jumped, before quickly snatching it.

Her heart pounded in her chest as she experienced an odd sensation sometimes called premonition. "Hello, Carrie," she said, expectantly.

"Dawn," Carrie said. "How did you know it was me?"

"Sorta just knew, you want me to come over, right?"

"I've called Jerry. He'll meet you on the way."

Disregarding her tea, Dawn walked through the living room. Whatever Carrie wanted to talk to them about, it would be disturbing, she felt in her heart that it was something relating to Ted's death.

"I'm going out for a while," she said, pausing at the doorway of the foyer.

Her mother looked over from the sofa where she sat talking to Bob. The two of them together bothered her for some reason. They didn't seem to fit, like two pieces of a puzzle being forced into place.

Her mother's quiet beauty, soft brown hair, gentle blue eyes, slim, and delicate body coordinated nicely with Bob's tall, dark, and handsome—very handsome, actually—she had almost developed a crush on him when he first started teaching at Central, but something about him set her on edge.

"Who was that on the phone?"

Her mother's voice interrupted her contemplation of the twosome.

"It was Carrie," she replied with an uneasy feeling.

"Where are you going?" she asked, then. "You're still upset, and it's getting late."

"It's okay, I'm meeting Jerry," she said, a rather vague but acceptable explanation. "I'm all right, Mom."

Her eyes met Bob's as if drawn by a magnet. Dawn gazed into the midnight blue darkness wondering exactly what his expression meant.

She finally summoned the strength to pull away, looking once more at her mother who still appeared concerned.

"I won't be long," she promised hastily.

When she closed the front door, Dawn leaned against it, feeling like she had made the great escape. She had thankfully avoided lying to her mother by simply telling her she was meeting Jerry. Tina trusted him implicitly.

She had never outright lied to her mother, and she almost did, because she didn't want Bod to know where she was going. She had not even wanted him to know it had been Carrie on the line—but why not? Why this sudden, huge feeling of mistrust?

Because he was the man in the hall that night!

The words echoed within the deep recesses of her mind. Dawn shook her head as they resounded very clearly. Bob Kaley? The thought was more than ridiculous, a caring teacher and oft times acting school counselor, Bob would do anything for the kids at Central.

The cynical inner voice cut through her thoughts again—a caring teacher? A man who has only been here one short year?

Dawn sighed, restlessly. The idea put forth could not easily be discarded, but she had to ignore it for now. Why should Bob having possession of a ring rouse suspicion anyway? He had shown her the ring, deliberately brought it to her attention. The answer came—withholding evidence, the ring should have been given to the police. Dawn wondered if that was reason enough for suspicion. That one wrong thing in that one instance didn't necessarily make him bad. Maybe irresponsible or unwise, but he didn't strike her as either.

She began to walk, thinking hard, trying to remember if she had seen the ring before that night. It seemed somehow familiar, but maybe the creepy circumstance made the damn thing so memorable.

Dawn dismissed the ring as her thoughts turned once more to the look Bob had given her. A probing gaze, almost hostile, and Tina had been unaware of the exchange, but had his look really been hostile? It seemed too far-fetched to even speculate Bob being a threat.

Sometimes a look of sorrow can be misconstrued, she rationalized; his grief may have been reflected as a threat by her feeling of mistrust.

Still deep in contemplation, Dawn walked quickly along the path through a grove of trees they'd discovered as kids, was a shortcut from Woodland Drive to Church Street. She wanted the confusing feelings of uncertainty toward a person who had never given any reason for distrust to go away. Dawn wished she could somehow quit analyzing.

Coming out of the shortcut, Dawn turned toward Carrie's house. When someone grabbed her from behind, she shrieked before realizing the culprit.

"Jerry! You scared me!"

"You should have expected me to be here," he said laughingly. "You were a thousand miles away."

"According to you I always am," she replied. "So don't sneak up on me."

"I didn't mean to, okay? Can I help it if your head's in the clouds a lot?"

He gave her an affectionate squeeze. "What were you pondering so deeply?"

"Nothing, really. Do you know why Carrie wanted us over?" she asked, skimming his question, wanting to avoid planting suspicion in the minds of others when it could be way out of line.

"She didn't say," Jerry replied. "She sounded kind of desperate, though."

"I noticed that, too."

They turned onto the cement walk that led to Carrie's front door. Her friend opened the door immediately, Paul stood nearby. They must have been waiting for them.

The sadness in Carrie's eyes drew Dawn to immediately embrace her. She hoped to convey the love she felt and the sorrow for her loss.

"I'm glad you guys could come," Carrie said, her voice trembling only slightly. She was holding up. How hard it must be, Dawn thought painfully. "Let's go upstairs." Carrie led them directly to her room.

"I called you here because there's something I have to share with you." Walking over to her desk, she opened the top drawer, rummaged around, closed it and opened another. Carrie pushed it shut slowly.

"It isn't here," she said in amazement. "I can't believe—it's gone."

"What are you talking about?" Paul caught Dawn's eyes with a cautious glance in her direction. "What's gone?"

"I found Ted's journal. It was sort of like a diary."

When she turned, Dawn noticed how tired she looked, dark shadows hollowed her eyes, and her shoulders had slumped in defeat at discovering the journal missing.

"His life was being threatened."

"Why would you think his life was being threatened?" Paul objected. "And why didn't you talk to me about this? Ted was—he was paranoid as hell, you know that."

"I don't know any such thing! I'm telling you!" Carrie paused to take a deep breath and continued. "He was involved with some men who were dealing in drugs," she said. "He smoked pot and took uppers. Paul, you knew that, didn't you? And he took downs, I don't know, maybe even cocaine," she added miserably. "I had reason for suspicion. He told me he wasn't going to use drugs anymore, but he did. He was high at the dance."

A look of sudden, bleak despair took her expression.

"It's my fault! Oh, God, it's my fault he's dead. I should have done something. I don't know what happened, but somebody—"

"Carrie, don't," Paul said abruptly but with compassion. "You are not to blame." He went to her, but she turned away.

"No, I have to tell you. He was dealing drugs, okay? But he wanted out. It was in the journal, he didn't want to be a pusher—he refused to deal heroin. If he was paranoid, he had reason."

She looked at the three of them with tearful eyes, but her voice did not waver. "He didn't deal in heroin, and he didn't use it."

"You should go to the police with that information," Dawn said. "You'd better let them know about the journal."

"That's a bad idea," Paul quickly disagreed.

Dawn looked at him, completely bewildered.

"She doesn't have the journal now," he pointed out.

"She doesn't have it, but she read it!"

"There's no proof that it was even there in the first place," Paul said decidedly, taking Carrie in a fond embrace.

Dawn looked to Jerry for support but he averted his eyes.

"I don't know," he murmured.

"What are you going to do?" Dawn felt somewhat invasive, but had to ask. She still felt that Carrie should notify the authorities.

"She's going to put this behind her," Paul intervened. "It won't be easy, but I don't want anything to happen to her."

"Don't worry about me, Paul. I'm no heroine." Carrie pulled away from him. She walked to the window, standing with her back to them.

"He mentioned a guy named Van Morrison. I don't know how involved he was with him, but he wrote in the journal that he's a pusher on the Southside."

Carrie's voice cracked, she lost all composure. "There's nothing I can do," she moaned. "I know he was murdered, but I don't know who did it."

Paul put his arms around her again, and this time she accepted the comfort, turning her face against his shoulder sobbing with renewed grief.

"It isn't your fault, sweetheart," he said softly. "We all tried to help him." He continued to whisper soothing sounds of comfort.

"Let's go, Jerry." Dawn spoke softly not wanting to intrude. "They need some private time and I need to get home."

They slipped quietly away, closing the bedroom door silently, going through the familiar hallway, down the stairs and out the front door into the early evening coolness. The breeze felt soothing on her warm face.

As they began walking Dawn dealt with the knowledge that what Carrie told them confirmed her suspicions. Ted had not died of an accidental overdose. There was no doubt in her mind now that the person in the mask who bumped into her that night had murdered Ted.

"Knowing he was murdered makes it worse," Dawn said reaching for Jerry's hand, holding tight to the familiar. "It was awful, but knowing he was murdered makes it, I don't know, horrifying."

"We don't know he was murdered," he said, sort of echoing Paul. "But I've heard of that Van character. He's from New York, and not a person to mess with. He could be a threat to our town, you know, and if Ted was associated with him, who knows, maybe he was murdered."

Dawn decided not to tell Jerry about the man in the hall, not yet. She wasn't going to mention that her best friend knew Van Morrison, either.

It had to have been at least a year ago that he came to Preston.

That night, Dawn sat alone in the darkness of her room feeling almost positive that her estimation was right. In the comfort of the window seat, she stared out at the night, contemplating the knowledge that Van Morrison had been here for about the same amount of time as Bob. It seemed noteworthy. Were the two somehow linked or was it coincidence?

She looked up at the countless stars in the sky, realizing her own insignificance in a mass universe, wondering if she would ever figure out how something could be comforting and disheartening at the same time.

As she thought of the two men, Dawn felt more certain that Bob was not the wonderful person everyone thought he was. She couldn't get it out of her mind that he and Van Morrison had arrived in Preston almost simultaneously.

Ironically, it seemed natural as she thought of one, now, to think of the other, which made no sense. Van Morrison was a disreputable drug pusher, Bob Kaley a creditable social studies teacher.

She considered how opposite they seemed, and still wondered if the two had any connection. What a conjecture! Dawn sighed, restlessly. She felt a little unsettled, but not necessarily surprised that a minuscule coincidence had been enough to ignite more suspicion.

It's not exactly minuscule, she thought defensively. With a last wistful look at the starlit sky, she made a mental note to ask Christi about Van Morrison. Christi had met him at the Basement, and Dawn had a suspicion the guy she had fallen 'in love' with was one and the same.

Maybe she would have some information to give her a handle on the guy. He hadn't been mentioned much in conversation, but enough that Dawn knew they were close, their acquaintance meant a lot to Christi.

The previous week, school had been cancelled for the students to have time to come to terms with what happened. Counselors were available if anyone wanted to talk.

She knew it would be good therapy for many, but Dawn felt no need to share her grief with strangers.

Chapter Sixteen

Soft music from the clock radio on the nightstand urged Dawn gently into wakefulness. She moaned resentfully at the disturbance turning over on her back to stare at the abstract swirling design of her ceiling. Remnants of the recurring dream she had been experiencing came explicitly to mind.

This miserably unpleasant dream had invaded her subconscious four times since Ted's funeral. The man who collided with her in the hall as she walked back to the gym appeared in the dream, shrouded by mist, starkly evil.

At the party, rejoining the festivities, she thought little of him.

Dawn had all but forgotten the man who bumped into her in the hall that night until experiencing the nightmare on Saturday, featuring a ginormous cobra, immediately after Bob Kaley showed her a quite elegant cobra ring he claimed to have found in the parking lot. That man had been wearing the cobra ring, and that man was haunting her dreams.

The mask obscured his face, his clothes were basic dark and nondescript, to a great extent concealed by the long black cape, but the ring had been clearly obvious. She could not shake the feeling that it could very possibly be an important piece of evidence.

She wondered if she should talk to Bob about it, but then the doubts she harbored about him resurfaced.

The loss of her friend washed unexpectedly over her again. Dawn closed her eyes against the pain. She had talked to Carrie last night. She wouldn't be in school this week. Carrie needed more time, bereavement time.

Dawn wondered what another week would do. Could she learn to cope within this week—to enter the doors he had entered, to walk the halls he had walked—without him? Would the world ever be the same without him in it?

Death . . . she turned it over in her mind, thinking of her dad, Christi's folks, and now Ted. So uncaring—it snatched people out of the world with unexpected swiftness. No time to say the things you meant to say, no time even, for good-bye. You're left floundering helpless in a sea of pain and sometimes remorse.

Dawn picked up the photo album she had taken out last night and opened it. Her mind wandered back over the years of a happy childhood as she slowly turned the pages that illustrated her life as it merged with Ted's.

Her fifth birthday, a group picture, she, Carrie and Ted seemed to stand out in the crowd of kids. Then at age seven, covered in mud, after Ted pushed her into a puddle, she ran home to tell her mother. Tina had grabbed the camera, laughingly snapping a picture.

Still, he had been required to make a formal apology, which he did, begrudgingly, shuffling from one foot to the other, looking down at his shoes as he mumbled, 'sorry, didn't mean to'.

She turned the page and smiled through tears, passing a finger gently over his face. He stood amidst a pack of kids at her tenth birthday party, dressed in a suit and tie, reflecting his extreme displeasure in the dour expression on his young face.

It had been a turning point in their relationship as they both grumbled at the required formal attire. Up until that year, she had loved the frilly dresses, but sometime during the year, she had turned tomboyish.

So, they became best buddies, they climbed trees together, went fishing and swimming, practically inseparable. He had given her a first kiss on her fourteenth birthday, the night they ventured into forbidden temptations.

That night, hours after her birthday party, she snuck him and a few close friends into her room. He brought Vodka; she supplied the orange juice. They all drank it and became deathly sick, suffering in silence to avoid severer consequences from their parents. *No more of that, thank you.*

Time passed in a flurry of activities until her fifteenth birthday when he kissed her tenderly and asked her to go steady. Dawn didn't have words to express her surprise—she had never considered Ted in that light.

When she could not return the affection, he held her as she cried tears of remorse that she had been so cruelly blind to his emotions.

She had already begun dating Jerry, and besides, she loved Ted like a brother. Due to his caring, warmth and resiliency, it had not affected their relationship. They hung out together, best buddies again and remained as close right up until he began slipping away from his loved ones and she couldn't hold on any better than anyone else.

Her mother's voice came over the intercom asking if she was awake.

"Yes, Mom, be right down."

Dawn could hardly concentrate during morning classes. When the lunch bell rang, she met up with Christi and they walked into the cafeteria together.

Once seated with their trays, Dawn took a cautious glance around. They were fairly isolated from the other kids. Still the conversation would have to be low key.

"Christi," she said quietly. "What can you tell me about Van Morrison?"

Christi gave her a puzzled glance. "What did you want to know?"

She lowered her voice even more. "You won't like hearing this, but he might be a drug pusher."

"No, I don't like hearing it, and it's the most ridiculous thing I've ever heard. Why would you say that?" Christi demanded in hushed tones.

Dawn sighed unhappily. "It might not be ridiculous, Chris. Ted was keeping a journal. Van's name was in that journal," she said halfheartedly. "Carrie read part of it, but then it was stolen. Ted had written that Van Morrison is a Southside pusher. Can you tell me anything about him?"

She watched Christi's face as it took on a look of clear disbelief, and something Dawn had never seen, an almost guarded demeanor as she pulled slightly, probably unconsciously, away from her.

"There's not much to tell," she hedged.

Dawn wondered if her friend was being purposely evasive, it had never been her nature to be reticent.

"How well do you know him?" she asked, saddened that he was someone Christi obviously cared for. "Do you know what kind of person he really is?"

"He's always been wonderful to me," she said after deep contemplation. "There's nothing to tell," she reiterated. "I can't see him being a drug pusher either. Remember when I fell 'in love' with an older guy? Van is the guy I had a crush on—remember? Now he's, I don't know. I guess he's my hero," she said with a wistful little smile.

"Yes, I remember," Dawn said feeling miserable. Lowering her voice a bit more, Dawn confided the threats to Ted in the missing journal, and how sure Carrie felt that her brother's death was no accident.

"Mike basically said that—the same thing," Christi responded, her voice also a mere whisper. "He told me Ted didn't use heroin."

Christi picked at her lunch and finally pushed her plate aside.

Dawn glanced around. No one seemed to be paying undue attention. She didn't feel like they were being watched, just a peculiar sensation that they were discussing something better left alone.

"I wonder if anyone else has any suspicions," Christi speculated.

"I doubt it. It's old news, now. Seems like, I don't know, a cover up."

The first bell rang, signaling the end of their lunch period. They sat a few minutes waiting for the majority of the students to file out into the hall.

"Don't say anything to anyone," Dawn cautioned.

"I won't, but what does Van have to do with any of this?" Christi said, as they stood. "Even if he is a pusher, which I have serious doubts, what would that have to do with Ted's murder?"

"Maybe nothing, but he might know something. You seem to have high regard for him, but you can't deny the facts," Dawn said realistically.

"I have extremely high regard for him," Christi confirmed as they began walking toward the hall. "Maybe those aren't facts, maybe it's a mistake."

"A man bumped into me that night. I haven't told anyone else, but if I could connect the unique ring he was wearing with someone, it might give the police a suspect, at least something to encourage investigation."

"What kind of ring was the man wearing?"

"It was a tiny replica of a king cobra," Dawn said. "Kind of strange, different but beautiful, rubies set in gold."

"A cobra ring, huh?" Christi glanced around the almost empty hallway. "We'd better hurry or we'll be late for class."

As Mike and Christi walked home from school that day, Dawn's words dominated her thoughts. ' . . . a tiny replica of a king cobra . . .' She knew of one.

It so happened, Dave came home for supper that evening. Christi usually enjoyed the rare times he did, but this evening she had disturbing thoughts.

After clearing the table, she poured a glass of juice, and then resumed her seat across from him. Dave lit a cigarette. Christi wondered what to say, she had never felt alienated from her brother before, it was genuinely painful.

He left her, returning immediately with an ashtray.

"Okay," he said slowly. "I don't have Mike's perception, but I'd be blind not to know something's bothering you, Chris. What's on your mind?"

She had wanted to discuss a few things since Ted's death, but had been reluctant. Since Dawn had told her about the ring, the only one of its kind, she wanted some answers, now.

Christi opened her mouth but couldn't bring herself to come right out and ask about the insignia ring that her brother had worn for more than a year.

"Do you know anything about Ted Harrison's death?"

He didn't seem unduly surprised by the abrupt question. He looked steadily into her eyes, beguiling and dear, her sweet brother. Innocent, too, this was inconceivable. How could she suspect him of anything so wrong?

"Should I?" he asked blithely.

"Do you?"

"Why would I know anything about Ted's death?"

"Someone said he was involved with people dealing drugs, serious, dangerous drugs, like heroin."

"I don't know. I can't say he was pusher, but I can't say he wasn't. I know he never brought heroin to the Basement. I know that much," he offered. "Not a good enough answer?" he asked gauging her expression.

"I just thought maybe you would know more."

"Why would I know anything?" he said again, crushing his cigarette.

Christi stared sadly at his slender hand where the ring had been. She could feel him watching her. She didn't think he intended to be evasive.

"He was a friend of yours, wasn't he?"

"What makes you think so?"

"Stop that!" she snapped impatiently. "I've seen him at the Basement."

He gave her a puzzled look. "Of course, he was an acquaintance."

"He was selling drugs," she said dejectedly.

Dave shrugged his shoulder indifferently. "I figured you knew. He sold a little hash, uppers, and downs, coke, enough to support his habit."

"What habit?"

"I don't *know* what habit. I just know that's why he dealt."

Dave swallowed the last of his coffee, and then glanced at his watch.

"Pressed for time?" she inquired, with some irony.

"In a way." Dave gave her a sympathetic glance. "I am sorry about Ted Harrison," he said pushing away from the table. "Now, any more questions?"

"Where's your ring?"

"I lost it."

"Where?"

"If I knew where, it wouldn't be lost then, would it?"

"Dave, don't tease."

"I got wiped out one night, when I woke up the ring was gone."

"Did you report it to the police?"

His eyebrows raised a fraction in surprise, and then he looked faintly amused. "Oh, yeah! Right, Sis."

"It's not such a stupid question."

"No, I didn't."

"When did this happen?"

"I don't even know." He kissed the top of her head before leaving. "You're such a serious little girl."

Christi glanced up as Dave walked out. Mike stood in the doorway, leaning against the frame looking at her, his expression unbelievably sad.

"Do you honestly suspect our brother?" he said clearly skeptical, and maybe a little annoyed. "Then why didn't you just ask him?"

"How could I?"

"It wasn't Dave."

"Are you absolutely certain?"

"I don't know who it was, but I know who it wasn't," he insisted. "And it sure as hell wasn't Dave."

"Your love for him isn't coloring your perception?"

"No, it doesn't work that way."

"Then how does it work, Mike? Who was wearing his ring?"

"I don't know, and I don't want to, Chris, and I don't want you getting into this, understand?"

"Don't worry, Mike. I'm not much on sleuthing."

"Chris—if I was around the person, I'd probably know. That's how it works," he told her with a rueful grin.

"I'm glad you don't know," Christi said honestly.

She retreated to her bedroom to sit staring morosely out the window at the deserted public playground across the street. It seemed desolate and lonely.

Neon lights flashed on either side of it, Town Tavern and Tony's Bar and Grill. They both did fairly decent business. Once in a while the police were called to break up a fight or take someone to jail.

Her mind continued to wander; someone was pushing drugs in Preston City. What other answer could there be to the availability? Drugs had never been so plentiful as nowadays.

There used to be an occasional addict, but the drug-related crime rate had shot way up the past year, with no reasoning of the people who seemed obliged to stick a needle in their arm once it became readily attainable.

The north side had escaped the effects until now. What a rude awakening that a young man who had never been in any serious trouble was using and selling drugs.

She wondered about the cover-up. Who in Preston would have that much influence? Trained authorities conducting the investigation must have been aware that the heroin had been forcibly injected, an autopsy had been performed, but foul play had not been mentioned. As Dawn so prevalently pointed out, there wasn't even the suggestion of an investigation.

The most serious wonder of all though, would trouble her until she had the answer—who had been wearing Dave's ring that night? Because she sensed with dreaded conviction that whoever had been wearing his ring had taken Ted Harrison's life.

Chapter Seventeen

Carrie ignored the ringing phone. Being restless with broken sleep, it had awakened her from a much-needed nap. She had no desire to talk to anyone, anyway. She pulled a pillow over her face, but her mother called up the stairs, "Carrie, pick up the extension!"

She obeyed reluctantly, thinking it might be another well-meaning friend wanting to draw her out of the shell she had determined to hide in, but she had told her mother not to pass through calls from friends. She didn't want drawn out of her shell, she wanted to withdraw further into it.

"Carrie Harrison." She identified herself in a bland, disinterested voice.

"Good day, Miss Harrison." The crisp businesslike tone rang irritatingly cheerful. "I'm calling from Society Bank to inform you that Mr. Theodore Harrison left the contents of a safe deposit box in your name . . . Since you have not inquired about it since his—demise." She heard the woman sigh, as if she wanted to say something else but decided not to. "We felt you should be notified at this time. I am sorry for your loss," she added.

Everybody is, Carrie thought.

"Thank you." She hung up, glancing at the clock on her nightstand, still plenty of time to have a cup of tea and get to the bank before it closed.

Carrie wondered as she washed her face and combed her hair, what Ted would have possibly left for her. Her mind whirled with the question as her misgivings and hope increased.

Maybe he had left a backup journal! Her emotions conflicted, fear because of Paul's warnings versus hope, she wanted Ted's killer to rot in jail.

Carrie began the walk to downtown Main Street, a twenty-five minute stroll from Church Street, where she had lived all her life.

She liked the central location, easily assessable walking distance to Dawn's house, to Main Street, to school, and to the Candy Store on Union Avenue where the gang used to hang out.

Other thoughts came to an abrupt halt as a searing pain pierced her heart. Vivid memories of time spent at the corner store with Ted, Dawn, Paul, and Jerry suddenly filled her senses.

The intense ache gradually diminished leaving her feeling drained and tired. The usually exhilarating walk seemed a burden.

She waited insipidly in line, at the bank, to retrieve the key and discontinue the safety deposit box Ted had rented.

Once home, she opened the inconspicuous padded manila envelope to discover a small audio reel of tape in a plastic container.

Inhaling deeply to calm her quickening heartbeat, Carrie finally picked up and opened the plastic holder, placing the tape carefully in the recorder Ted had received on his fourteenth birthday.

When she pressed 'play', the familiar voice she had never expected to hear again sparked renewed grief. "Carrie, I know you have questions, and you deserve answers. I have answers, but first I need to talk to you."

After a short pause he continued. "I don't want you to miss me too much, Carrie Ann. You tried to help me. This isn't your fault, but I know you'll blame yourself. Please don't. I'm the one who let you down. I didn't mean to—I just really messed up. And I am so sorry."

Tears slid from her eyes as he began to explain his addition.

"I started taking pills for the high, for the feeling of being able to do anything. I didn't believe what I'd heard about drugs. I knew I could handle it, but I was misled . . . I see now it was inevitable. I took uppers, smoked pot, dropped some acid, and was eventually convinced to try cocaine, easily convinced, though, and no way to support my developing habit." She heard a choking cough followed by another pause.

"The addiction happened so amazingly fast . . . and I was given opportunity. Being a dealer didn't seem so bad to me. I thought what I was doing wasn't so wrong. It was like, if they didn't get it from me—they'd get it somewhere else. Don't judge me too harshly, Carrie . . . the desperation was unbelievable, when the high at times gave way to depression, and I needed more of it—"

His voice broke. Seconds passed. "I'm sorry. I'm so very sorry for the way I treated you, but I was in the process of making changes."

She waited through another very long pause.

"I was trying . . . at least I can honestly tell you that . . . I'm making this tape . . . because if you're listening to it, well, it was my fault, Carrie, that I trusted the wrong person."

She clicked off the recorder experiencing the racking pain of loss until sleep gradually laid claim to her from physical and emotional exhaustion, a momentary escape from the world of reality she no longer wanted to face.

A soft knock on the door awakened her.

"Dinner is ready," her mother said. "Please don't keep us waiting."

"In a minute, Mom," she answered sitting up, swinging her legs over the edge of the bed.

Carrie stared solemnly at the innocently silent tape player. She reached over to press the button, but hesitated. She did not want to hear anymore of what he had to say—not yet.

What if he revealed the murderer? Conflicting emotions tore at her as she remembered Paul's warnings.

It could possibly hold the means of bringing her brother's killer to justice, but would it put her own life in jeopardy? Tears clouded her eyes, and she closed them tight, forcing the pain back inside.

Carrie paused at the dining room door.

Gazing at her family seated at the table waiting for her brought on another wave of agony. It would be easier to stay in her room and sleep, at least when sleep came to her, but her parents insisted that she join the family for meals. She felt a deep, pitiless ache as her eyes shifted to the empty space where Ted should have been.

Carrie walked slowly to the table, took her seat across from where her brother used to sit, bowing her head as her father said grace.

After a feeble attempt to choke down a few bites, she pushed the plate aside. "May I be excused?"

Her mother gave her a disapproving glance. "Carrie, you have to eat. You may not be excused until you eat some dinner."

"Sorry, I don't have an appetite." She wanted only to escape.

"You've lost a lot of weight," her father said, concern softening his voice. "Starving yourself won't change what happened."

"Nothing will change that now, will it?" She blamed herself and it hurt too much. She needed to direct the pain somewhere else.

"How could you let it go on until it came to this?" Carrie demanded. "Why didn't you make him stop? You were his parents for God's sake—You had authority! Why didn't you help him when there was time," she wept bitterly. "You closed your eyes—you didn't want to see."

Carrie pushed away from the table not even caring that her chair tipped over, just needing to go back upstairs, to be alone again.

She slammed the door to her room, and then threw herself on the bed feeling miserable and guilty. Why did she do that? She didn't like causing her parents grief, but the outbursts happened rashly, followed by remorse.

They had talked to him, they had even threatened him, but living in denial they accepted his word that he had quit. If he hadn't been using those drugs, he wouldn't have been involved with whoever had taken his life. They hadn't done anything and neither did she, and now Ted was gone forever.

It wasn't fair that he was dead. It wasn't fair, and she couldn't accept it. But they had buried a child, their first-born son. The loss was certainly not hers alone, but it seemed she carried the burden alone, she felt the blame, a deep and painful gnawing within her heart.

Thanksgiving Day had introduced the beginning of unrelenting sorrow as the Christmas season approached. The weeks before Christmas had been a time of sharing childhood memories. Even last year had been wonderful.

He had taken the time to spend with his family. They watched the ever-favorite children's Christmas shows while stringing popcorn for the tree.

Decorating the tree—her eyes grew misty with the memory. It was a family party, listening to wonderful age-old carols as their dad strung the tree with lights. She and Ted would hang the homemade decorations created by the two of them as children, working side-by-side in the living room with crayons, construction paper, ribbons and glitter. When they were finished, their mother carefully added the ornately beautiful glass ornaments.

They had taken turns placing the tinseled star atop the tree, until at age ten; he relinquished the privilege to her. When Timmy turned four, Carrie gave him the honor of adorning the star. Giggling as their dad lifted him up in the air, Timmy carefully positioned it. Love and laughter abounded in their home.

On Christmas morning, she knew there would be a special gift, a gift with a large candy cane tied on top with a big red ribbon. He had only been a little boy when he started the tradition. Since there would be no more candy canes, there would be no stringing popcorn, no decorating a Christmas tree, not for her. She determined that it would be just another day and hoped it would go by without any reminders that it was even December twenty-fifth.

On Christmas day when the doorbell rang, she opened it to see Dawn standing there with a smile, bearing gifts. Carrie felt more than a little remorseful for her neglect of the season.

"Come in," she said, with a contrite smile, accepting the gifts held out to her. She put them on a nearby table. "I didn't expect anyone."

"Well, I wasn't going to call and have you dismiss me," Dawn replied.

"Is that what I've been doing?"

"Yes, simply put. I should have come sooner," Dawn said unhappily.

"I shouldn't have let the time slip by while you declined all invitations. You're my friend and I feel that I've let you down, but you should have known I couldn't let this day go by without coming to see you."

"You could have, but I'm glad you didn't." Carrie hung the light suede jacket in the hall closet. "And you've never let me down, Dawn, please don't ever think that."

They drifted toward the living room. "I didn't do any shopping this year. I'm sorry. I couldn't get into the spirit of things."

"I know, I couldn't even get you over to my house for eggnog, and you know Mom makes the best!"

"I'm sorry; I've been bombarded with too many memories, just too much."

"You needed to be with your friends."

"I would have dragged you down to my depths of despair," she disagreed.

Dawn placed a hand on her arm. "I understand that you felt that way, but it's time to come back. You can't retreat from the world forever."

Her little brother ran past them with one of the toys he had received that morning, a toy airplane that he could give marvelous sound effects to.

He had cried, he had mourned, but now he seemed so unaffected.

Carrie sighed with instant exasperation. "Let's go to my room," she suggested. "My nerves are shot these days. I feel like screaming at every little thing."

"Okay, but wait . . . Timmy!" Dawn called cheerfully.

The little boy paused in his play looking quizzically in her direction.

"On the hall table—the big one with Santa and Reindeer is for you."

His smile warmed her heart.

"Thanks, Dawny," he said, scurrying toward the hall as she and Carrie started up the carpeted stairs.

"Since Ted's death, I can't seem to take an interest in anything. I've even neglected Paul," she confided.

"I'm aware," Dawn replied meaningfully. "He's so alone, Carrie."

"I'm surprised he hasn't dumped me by now."

"He loves you, Carrie. You must not know how special you are to him. I'm sorry about Ted, and I can't even imagine what you must feel, but I loved him, too," she said gently. "I know you blame yourself. I blamed myself for a while, but it wasn't me or you—" Dawn's voice trembled, her avid green eyes shimmering with tears.

"It's hard, I know, but I had to accept, and you have to accept that Ted did this to himself."

"I've heard that, and it's said with love—and it must be true, but it's so difficult to understand."

"I know," Dawn said softly with a glimpse of compassion.

"I don't know if I can accept it," she said, her voice wavering. "He's dead, but I feel dead on the inside."

"You're mourning, and you will mourn for a long time, but Carrie, you have friends who love you, and we need you," Dawn asserted, entirely too reasonably. "I have to tell you, Carrie, you're not honoring his memory with those paralyzing feelings of gloom."

"Dawn, I don't know if I can—"

"Yes, you can," she interjected. "It's been too long already. You have to come back to us. Now, tell me you'll come to my New Year's Eve Party."

Carrie recognized her please don't disappoint me tone along with that sweet pout that inspired compliance.

"I can't make any promises."

"Oh, yes, you can," she insisted. "I lost Ted . . . I don't want to lose you, too. You need to be there . . . Come on, it'll do you good."

"Dawn, it still hurts so badly."

"I know," she said with compassion. "But you have to come to my New Year's Eve party, Carrie. Please, please, *please*!"

Carrie gave her friend a wry smile, feeling a touch of happiness. Her determination would not be diminished. She would not leave her alone unless she agreed to join in the festivities on New Year's Eve.

She wanted to be with her friends again. Even at school in class, in the lunchroom, in the halls, she felt so alone, not joining in conversation, just being there, but Carrie didn't know if she was worthy of having fun.

To accept his undoing as his fault seemed like betrayal to his memory.

"I didn't know what he was going through." Carrie took a shaky breath. "I didn't know the extent of his addiction," she said through tears.

Dawn put her arms around her, and as they held each other, Carrie felt her tears, at last, were healing.

Chapter Eighteen

Christi watched the merrily flickering lights of the Christmas tree as she reminisced the past month. The holidays had been wonderful. In spite of the grief so many suffered over Ted Harrison's death, there had been gaiety and warmth in Dawn's home.

She and Mike spent Christmas Eve with Dawn and Jerry, Dawn's mother and Bob Kaley. She wouldn't be surprised if Jerry didn't punch Mike one of these days. He had caught Dawn under the mistletoe and given her a more than friendly kiss. Jerry seemed to take it in stride, though, knowing they were all friends, but Christi had suspicions of Mike's underlying motives.

On Christmas Day, while listening to Christmas Chorals one last time, she and Trixi had prepared roast turkey with all the trimmings. Christi smiled to herself. Trixi was fun to have around, and she had helped with set up, the tedious peeling of potatoes, stirring and clean up duty, while she laughingly admitted to not being much of a cook.

Dave had even joined them, helping in the preparation of fresh baked clover rolls. What a mess that had been!

The New Year's Eve Bash at Dawn's house this weekend would wind the season up right. Dawn told her that Carrie would be there. She had been keeping to herself far too much since Ted's death.

The ringing phone interrupted her thoughts. "Hello?"

Christi waited. No one answered her greeting, but the silence was not absolute. Someone was there. "Hello?" she inquired, cautiously.

After another pause, she hung up. It rang again almost instantly. She listened to the insistent ringing, nerves on edge, finally lifting the receiver.

"Temple residence," she said impersonally.

"I don't know quite what to say to you, Chris."

Recognizing Billy's voice, Christi gripped the phone tighter.

"Why didn't you call me—is this payback?" he asked quietly. "Is that what this is about?"

No, she didn't know what it was about, but she had never called him. She had wanted to—and many times lifted the phone just to put it back—and days would pass before she could try again.

She suffered an inexplicable form of paralysis when it came to getting in touch with Billy, helpless against it—days, weeks—two months had gone by, and now, here he was accusing her of payback. How could he know she would never be capable of such a thing?

"I promised myself that I would wait for your call—Chris, are you there?"

"Yes." Christi cleared her throat softly. "Yes, I'm here."

"We might have had something. I ruined it, I know, and I accept that, but you should have, at least, called me."

"I tried, Billy, I really did," she said quickly. "And you can't think that of me, what you called payback? I wouldn't do that."

"Maybe not consciously."

"Billy—" She spoke his name helplessly, searching her mind that had gone numb, deserting her at a most inopportune time, for something to say to him.

"I won't bother you again."

The sadness in his voice twisted her heart as the phone clicked softly in her ear. Christi closed her eyes, reliving their meeting in the alley, the walk home, that undeniable attraction they felt toward each other.

She longingly recalled how he caressed her neck with his thumb, such a gentle, probably subconscious motion, and the dance, the way he held her in his arms so tenderly possessive. If she never saw him again, she would never forget the first loving kiss that had ever touched her lips, before or sense.

Tears welled in her eyes, spilling down her face as she remembered their last moment at his apartment. Their eyes had locked for a crucial instant. She had felt it, too, the feeling he so aptly described as losing himself, the emotion had affected her deeply. Why hadn't she told him? Maybe that was what falling in love felt like.

Christi brushed her tears aside, then rifled through the phone book for Danny's number. She dialed through misty eyes.

"This is Christi," she said when he answered. "Remember me?"

"Sure I do, you're very memorable. How are you?"

"I'm okay." She felt incredibly sad, wondering why she hadn't called Billy. Why didn't she now? For some reason, she felt a need to speak to this cousin of his who was so close to him. "Danny, I need to talk to you, but not on the phone. Will you meet me at the Sugar Shack?

"Oh, I wouldn't go there." She heard laughter in his voice. "It's an unsavory place, you know."

"Unsavory?" She couldn't understand. "The Sugar Shack?"

"Cavities," he explained.

"Oh, right," she said, with a soft laugh in spite of her aching heart.

"How about, I pick you up in about ten minutes?"

"I'll be out front."

She went to the bathroom, rinsed her face and ran a brush through her hair, securing it at the nape of her neck with a large clasp.

Christi retrieved the little velveteen jewelry box from the drawer in her bedroom before going downstairs to wait for Danny.

Within a few minutes, he pulled over to the curb on his Harley.

"Is Kelly's Place all right?" he asked as she put on the helmet he gave her.

"Sure."

"Here, let me help you with that."

He adjusted the helmet, and then she climbed on behind him.

Although she had only been there once, the memories of that night settled over her as she entered the tavern. She marveled at the contrast, though. That Friday night there had been a marvelous crowd, with music blasting a loud pulsing beat.

This evening there were only a few men and one couple at the bar.

Danny chose a booth midway and slid in. She sat across from him, thankful for the jukebox playing not too loud, but effectively distractive.

The waitress, looking weary and bored, took their order. She brought their sodas and Christi took a sip of the fizzy liquid. Extremely thirsty, she took another grateful swallow of the refreshing drink.

She gazed absorbedly at the cubes of ice floating in the fluid, wondering what to say. She hadn't called Billy, and she had promised.

When Christi glanced at Danny, he tipped his head slightly with an expectant, somewhat amused expression. She offered a diffident smile as he waited patiently for her to speak. Christi felt entirely comfortable in his presence but at a loss for words to explain her feelings.

She placed the ring on the table in front of her.

"Billy called me earlier, well, just before I called you," she began. "I was supposed to get in touch with him."

"He told me. You're a cold-hearted woman, Christine Temple."

"I broke a promise."

His smile faded, replaced by concern, as a tear slid down her face. Danny moved quickly to her side of the booth.

"Now, don't do that," he said with an arm around her shoulder. "I was just playin'. I'm sorry . . . I didn't mean to be insensitive."

"No, it's me, but I'm all right, now," she assured him determined to be strong. She didn't want pity, but some understanding couldn't hurt.

"You sure?" His eyebrow raised a fraction in doubtful inquisition. "Can I go over there and you won't cry?"

Christi smiled reassuringly. "I'm fine, really."

He resumed his seat. "Billy didn't mean to hurt you. Remember, I touched on that the night I took you home."

"I remember," she admitted. "But I don't know what to do. I'm being torn because I have feelings for Billy—I think I love him, Danny, but I'm afraid of him, too."

"He was hurt once," Danny told her. "It took him a long time to get over it, and there's some stuff you might need to hear about. He was pretty fucked up, excuse my French."

"Was it Sue who hurt him so badly?"

"No, it happened in school." He gave her a searching look. "The idea of Sue still bothers you?"

"Well, yeah, I guess," she acknowledged feeling flustered.

"Don't let her concern you," he said dismissively. "Sue was later, and what they had doesn't count for much."

Hearing that bit of information eased her tension to some extent.

"He was about your age. And that's mostly why he was almost as afraid to trust as you are now," he explained. "I'm sure he'll tell you about it sometime," he said absently, his attention diverting to the little velvet box on the table.

"What ya got there?" He picked up the ring case.

"Billy gave it to me."

He opened it, viewed the ring, closed and placed it back in front of her.

"Do you know anything about this?"

"Yeah, I do," he said with a thoughtful look. "But I'll let Billy tell you."

Her heart skipped a double beat as Billy slid into the booth beside her. She took a breath as it resumed beating, a hard throbbing in her chest.

Somehow it came as little surprise that he had shown up here, just seeing him had prompted the excessive response, this was not good. Christi realized she had built no immunity.

"I'll leave the two of you alone." Danny stood, offering an appealing smile and almost imperceptible wink. "The time will come for answers Chris, and about this—sorry, he twisted my arm." He turned and left them.

Christi looked at her hands, amazed that they appeared so remarkably steady, considering the excitement and panic she felt as Danny walked away.

"I've been thinking about you," Billy said. "I've done nothing but think about you." He sighed deeply. "It's like my life has been on hold—" He gave her a probing look. "Like hell," he added. "My life has been on hold."

"It was your own doing."

"Don't get mad at me again, you hot tempered little sweetie."

She glanced at him, then back to her remarkably steady hands that now gripped the cola glass. How could he know his warm voice had gone straight to her heart with a persistent push to get in? His comforting hand moved tenderly to and lingered at the back of her neck.

"Look at me?"

She did, and her heart took a perilous leap when her eyes met his, just as she feared it would, the same as it had on Halloween night.

"When you called Danny, I knew there might be a chance. I hoped—" A pensive look passed over his face, and her eyes fell away from his steady gaze to stare into the amber liquid of her cola.

"Christi?"

When she felt the soft brushing of his fingers against her cheek, her heart fluttered painfully. "Don't, Billy." She raised her eyes to meet his again.

"You have to give in. You can't stay mad at me," he said solemnly. "I've paid penance. I really have."

"How have you paid penance?"

"Sack cloth and ashes?"

"That's not enough." Christi looked at him with amused wonder, unable to deny the joy of being with him, even though her trust had been shattered.

"This is going to take some time," he accepted with a tolerant sigh. "I can see it in your eyes."

"I'm not so starry-eyed, now?"

"Oh, there are still stars," he said lovingly with a disarming smile.

The distrust coursed through her, chilling her with reserve as she recalled how easily she had been led by his irresistible charming way. It made her wonder, restlessly, what else he could see in her eyes.

The waitress brought his drink. He took a swallow, then set it down and looked back at her.

Billy held her hand, caressing her fingers. "I know I'm asking a lot." He paused, distracted. "You're not wearing the ring."

"No—I wanted to—" she stammered. "I was going to—but I didn't know where it came from."

"It came from me." Taking her hand again, he slipped the exquisite piece of jewelry from its case onto her finger. "Perfect fit."

He smiled into her eyes, leaning a bit closer, disrupting her equilibrium.

"It belonged to my mother," he said softly.

"But you were going to throw it away. You said—"

"I was hoping so desperately that you would accept it." His eyes brimmed with tenderness and passion, and she knew he had captured her again.

"I had determined that if you didn't take it, no one else would have it—ever. I felt that if you did accept the ring, there might be a chance for us."

"I don't understand feelings like that."

Christi understood the feelings, all right. Intense feelings were very much a part of her, but she wanted to hear more as he gazed into her eyes.

"Do you understand that I love you?"

"How can you profess your love so easily?"

"Believe me, baby, this isn't easy." He leaned even closer. "Is it all right if I call you baby?" he murmured.

"If you mean it," she replied softly, still hesitant.

"I mean it, I've been there, and it's time to stop being afraid of love."

Her head swirled with doubts, hope and fear, and a big surge of sudden, unexpected elation. She wondered that her body didn't float right out of the booth. It felt so light and airy that gravity surly couldn't hold her.

The man Christi knew she would never forget—who would always be a part of her, even if she never saw him again, had spoken the most beautiful words in the world—but her heart still bore the bruise of his rejection.

"What I feel for you is real, Chris, but it takes a lot to develop a relationship, and we started out all wrong."

She felt defenseless as his captivating blue eyes searched her face.

"How do we make it right?"

"We have to get to know each other first."

She watched him moisten his lower lip as he looked at her, and he swallowed, casting his eyes away for a second.

"I made a promise," he said. She started to ask what he meant, but he placed a gentle finger to her mouth. "It would help if you didn't have such a pretty pout."

She pressed her lips together and his face relaxed into a smile. She smiled back, happy to have eased his mood.

"If you tell me your dreams, I'll tell you mine. We'll share our hopes, and our fears. Do you have any of those?" he asked, the warmth of his smile drawing her closer.

"Yeah, I'd say, I do."

"I have lots of that kind of stuff," he admitted. "And you're the only one I want to share it with. You're the one I want to share my life with."

He took her hand. "You don't have to profess your love, just yet. I can wait. I have to earn your trust."

That will take a long season, she thought, the trust part, but professing her love? She wanted to do that now. She ached with wanting to.

His gaze held hers again. "It's going to take time, I know, and a lot of communication, but I will."

"How can we be friends?" she whispered his lips so near she could hardly stand the hesitation. He smiled and kissed her gently.

"I can't answer that with words, but I can show you, you'll see. It won't be easy, but it will be worth it. By the way, what are you doing New Year's Eve?" He bent his head toward her. "Will you do it with me?"

"I would love to," she replied. "But a party at Dawn's house might be boring to your expectations."

"My expectations are going to be watching the light shine in your eyes," he told her. "Anywhere is fine as long as I'm with you."

She glanced down at the ring he had placed on her hand. The months of sadness would never be forgotten, but maybe they had grown during those months, maybe they had learned more about what love could mean to them.

When Mike got home that night, Christi told him that she had been with Billy earlier that evening. She told him about seeing him Halloween night, her promise and inability to call him, and about Billy finally calling her.

She tried to assure Mike with what Billy had said about them starting over as friends and getting to know each other, but affirmed that the decision to resume a relationship with Billy was not in question.

Mike listened carefully without interruption. Christi couldn't read an expression as she waited anxiously for his reply, urgently hoping for his approval. Then a frown formed between his eyes, and she watched his bright eyes darken to cobalt blue.

"He's not for you, Christine. I'm sorry, but I can't condone a relationship with him. He's—"

When his voice faltered, seemingly at a loss for words, she hastily grabbed the moment of uncertainty.

"Please try to accept my decision—try to understand."

"I understand more than you know. He's too worldly, okay?"

"Mike, this isn't like you—to be so judgmental."

"I know what he is."

"Do you, really?" She looked at him expectantly.

"Okay, really, I don't, but I know gangs, and I don't want him dragging you into that."

"I won't be a part of the gang, Mike. Not anymore than I'm a part of the Cobras. We'll be apart from them."

"Even so—I know what he put you through." Anger lit his eyes, now, giving them a startling glow. "I know what he did to you."

"He wants us to make a new start. Don't you think he deserves another chance? I believe he's sincere, Mike. Look." She held her hand out to display the ring on her finger.

He stood up from where he sat on the sofa, walking over by her chair. "Very nice," he acknowledged.

"Mike, I need your support," she entreated hopefully.

"Do I think he deserves another chance?" he said quietly. "I don't."

Christi didn't think his voice held a severe ring of finality. Still, she couldn't quell an edge of panic at her brother's rejection.

"It was his mothers, and he gave it to me," she informed him bleakly. "Does that count for something?"

"It's up to you," he said, grudgingly, resuming his seat.

"I called Dawn earlier," she said, hoping he would get past his reluctance. They had never butted heads on anything very seriously, and this was the single most important aspect of her life. "He's going to be at the party. Is that all right with you?"

"You saw him Halloween night," he mused. "How'd you keep something so major from me?"

"I had a lot of other stuff to think about, I guess. Is it all right, New Year's Eve?" Christi gave him a most appealing look, drawing from every sentimental fiber of her being. He finally smiled.

"What about Dave?" he said reluctantly.

"Dave can't know," she said quickly. "There's animosity between them."

"Yeah, ya might say that," he agreed. "Well, if it matters, it's all right—the New Year's Eve party. I'll still go with you."

"It matters! Of course, it matters," she said, giving him a hug. "I couldn't handle it if you weren't on my side."

"I'm always on your side, little sister."

Christi went to bed feeling that a burden had been lifted. Mike had finally, tentatively accepted her decision, regardless of her determination, his approval had a significant effect to her peace of mind.

She tossed restlessly and then stared into the darkness, her peace of mind slipping considerably as Mike's first objections began seeping into her consciousness, creating doubts.

What was she letting herself in for? Billy was still the leader of the Monarchs. That hadn't changed. Had he even meant the things he said?

She tried to imagine the love in his eyes, to recall the promises and the sincerity in his husky voice. Why was it so easy in his presence and so difficult only a few hours later?

The sense of apprehension increased, sleep an elusive hope as her thoughts rushed on to an uncertain future. John Burton remained a menacing shadow in her world, and given the fair assumption that Dave would never accept Billy Cole, where could their relationship go from here?

She needed some reassurance, big time. Christi sat up on the edge of the bed. Slipping into her house shoes, she padded quietly into the living room.

Billy's phone number had been imprinted forever in her memory. After hastily dialing, she listened to the ringing with an unwelcome feeling of wariness, unhappily remembering the last time she had called him.

The phone rang four times before a sleepy voice responded.

"Hello?"

"Billy . . . it's Chris."

"Hey, baby."

His drowsy voice emanated a warm, soft sweetness.

"Did I wake you?"

"You did, but it's okay."

"I need to talk to you."

"It sounds serious," he said, thoughtfully. "Did you get scared?"

"Yes," she admitted.

"Is it because of me?"

"And Dave, too," she confirmed. "You know what you said—about the difficulties?"

"You got to thinking about that?"

"Yeah, I guess I did."

"You don't like keeping secrets, do you?"

"I don't like it, but I understand the necessity. I have to ask you something, and please be honest."

"I will."

"How would you feel if I didn't want to go to Kelly's Place anymore?"

"We don't have to go there," he said without contemplation. "There are places to go and things to do without Kelly's Place. You're all in the world that matters to me. I meant what I said about trust and love."

"I want to believe you, but you're still who you are, Billy—leader of a gang." She sighed distractedly. "I'm not asking you to give that up, even if you could, but I don't know how we're going to deal with the complications in our future—if we even have one," she added softly.

She waited for assurance, wondering in the long silence.

"We can have a future," he finally said. "I don't know what brought that on, but whatever it takes, I'll do my part. We can make this work, I promise you."

"It was something Mike said," she told him. "He's being a bit cautious about accepting our involvement."

"I can't blame him. I almost blew it, Christi. I realize that it was a close call baby—losing you would be no good at all. You know." He laughed softly. "I'm supposed to be the adult here, but swear to God, I feel like a kid right now."

Surprised at his frank and honest feelings of unease, the revelation gave her a warm and gentle sentiment toward him as he conveyed his confusion.

Christi noticed the darkness giving way to the light of a new day as they said goodnight. She hung up with a sleepy smile.

They had talked through the night, of everything and nothing, important issues and incidental fun stuff, discussing her fears, and his.

He told her about the girl in school that Danny had mentioned. They had dated for almost a year, but her parents' had only tolerated Billy, thinking she would 'come to her senses'. When it became evident that the relationship wouldn't burn out, they had forbidden her to see him.

She told him about the loss of her parents, and how she felt about Dave's reinstated friendship with John Burton, and how close she was to her twin.

They discussed the uncertain future she had been contemplating, with the validation that they would walk it together. That he consoled her without simplifying what she was experiencing gave her confidence in their newly forming relationship.

He had begun to weave within her heart an extensive portion of the trust he wanted to gain back.

Spending the night with Billy on the phone had not changed the condition of their lives, uneasy circumstances remained, but she felt a peaceful repose.

Chapter Nineteen

Dawn opened the door for Christi and Mike with a wide smile. "Thanks guys! I don't know what I'd do without you. I'm so glad you're here to help get ready for the onslaught!"

"Wouldn't have it any other way," Mike said casually. "This is my favorite place to party, you know."

"It's the first time you've been here, Mike," Dawn said, bemused.

"Oh really?" He gave her an approving glance taking special notice of the slit up the side of her dress. "This is the place where alcohol flows freely, right?" he asked coolly.

"There is no alcohol."

"Well that's not my fault. If you'd told me, I could a brought some—"

"Christi—?"

"Don't ask," she said hopelessly. "It's Mike—the level-headed one."

"Seriously, kiddo, your New Year bashes are the best."

"You've never been to one of my New Year's Eve 'bashes', Mike."

"I hope I'm not at the wrong address—this is the place where they, like, pass drugs around in candy dishes, isn't it?"

"I know you're not serious."

He smiled sweetly, still admiring the gown.

"Who's not serious, sweetheart?"

"Mike, are you high?" she asked breezily.

"Half the time," he said with a cocky grin. "What's the point?"

"Christi! Help!"

"He's high on life," Christi said. "Mike, be good."

"I'm always good." He sidled closer to Dawn.

"Is he ever serious?" Dawn asked.

"Rarely—I think I'd worry."

"Okay, I'll be good. I mean, seriously!" He slid his arm casually around her waist. "I'm just here to admire you in that knock-out gown. It is quite the evocative fashion statement and you are quite the—"

"Unhand her, this instant!" Christi came to her rescue.

Mike gave her the cutest look of disappointment she had ever seen.

"I think we'd better set up the table, don't you, Dawn?" Christi dragged her away from Mike. "Do you think Carrie will show?"

"I'm sure she will. Paul's picking her up."

"He loves to torment you," Christi laughed when they were out of earshot.

"More so than usual!" Dawn agreed. "And he's never been so good at it."

Dawn returned to the main room with a platter of assorted cheeses and calm continence. She placed the elegant serving dish on the coffee table near a bowl of mixed nuts.

"Mike, would you get the punch bowl?" Dawn asked. "It's in the fridge."

Christi helped spread a gala tablecloth on the long utility table set up for refreshments, Mike placed the punch bowl in the center, and they set out a variety of tiny sandwiches, assorted chips and dips, homemade candies and a specialty cake Tina had baked and decorated. It looked festive and delicious.

Dawn went to the mirror to check her hair and make-up, considering Mike's comment. Was the floor length, white gown she wore suggestive? Sure the soft material clung stylishly to her curves, toga style, off one shoulder, with a daring slit up the length of her thigh, but evocative? Where did he come up with that word?

The gown showed hardly any cleavage. Dawn thought it had a certain subtlety; besides, she liked the trendy gold rope belt cinched at her waist.

Mike came up behind her, obviously ready for more mischief. He slipped his arms around her waist nuzzling her neck.

"Very nice," he said. "Mmm, you smell luscious," he complimented.

"Am I a dessert?" she quipped.

"Good enough to eat," he replied in a voice much too seductive for an almost seventeen year old. He pulled her gently against him.

Dawn laughed with delight catching the twinkle in his ever teasing blue eyes. He certainly loved to play with fire.

"You've conned everyone into thinking you're such a nice guy, Michael, but you're a regular hellion, aren't you."

"I don't con, sweetie. I offer no apologies and feel no shame. I am what I am, half male—half party an-nim-al." He growled softly, clamping his mouth down over her shoulder. Dawn squealed, and Christi doubled over with laughter as the doorbell chimed interrupting their antics.

"Behave yourself!" Dawn chided, laughingly giving him a light shove toward the sofa before quickly composing herself to open the door.

She greeted Billy and Danny with recognition from Christi's vivid description, then Jerry, Paul and Carrie who arrived right behind them.

Some other friends arrived. Mike dimmed the lights, and yelled, "Party—let's rock 'n roll!" He put on his first pick, a fast paced Rolling Stones number that had everyone dancing to the beat.

The hours slipped quickly by. With the New Year just moments away, Dawn looked at Mike, her head puzzling with unanswered questions. When he suddenly glanced up, she smiled at him not minding at all that he caught her gazing. She had noticed him corner Billy earlier and they had an in-depth conversation.

No one interfered during the time they were engrossed but she made a mental note to find out later what the little tête-à-tête had been about.

Afterward Billy returned to Christi's side, and the rest of the evening passed with dancing, fun and laughter. Dawn appreciated that Mike had agreed to play D.J. With him in charge of music and entertainment, they rocked the night away. Back to his usual rollicking self, he kept everyone entertained.

Mike had come alone, and she didn't question that he didn't bring a date. He requested a dance with her, late in the evening.

As the countdown to 1968 began, she recalled the dance. He had held her in his arms, an innocent embrace, nothing daring or inappropriate, but her pulse quickened with the touch of his hand. His simple nearness kindled feelings that she decided to repent of later.

Momentarily squelching any thought of the boy who was there with her, Dawn enjoyed the dance much more than she should have, lost in the lyrics. The slow ballad, a song of unrequited love, left her feeling nostalgic.

They toasted the New Year with pink champagne and some exchanged kisses, just a friendly meeting of the lips to express 'Happy New Year!'

When Mike took Dawn in his arms to claim her mouth in a deeply passionate kiss, his effect on her senses rivaled the champagne.

He had caught her unprepared, as usual, especially when he held her hands, looked into her eyes and kissed her once more very softly, then whispered 'Happy New Year' before walking away leaving her feeling dazed and a little confused.

"Dawn?—Dawn—earth to Dawn!"

Yanked out of her reverie, Dawn responded with a smile. She felt only slight contrition, the kiss, though not innocent, meant nothing at all. Mike and his flirtatious ways! He was quite the Casanova.

"Jerry—"

"Am I entitled to a New Year's kiss? Really, I should have been first."

"You are first," she smiled, hiding any reservations. "He's just quick."

Jerry put his arms around her and drew her close against him. She gave all the assurance she could into this important first kiss of the New Year with the boy she loved, repressing emotions that wanted to rise within her for the boy who had walked out the door.

"We're leaving now," Carrie said.

Dawn hugged them both, and then escorted them to the door, happy for the distraction, that she didn't have to gaze into Jerry's eyes with what, right now, might not be appropriate reflections.

She gave Carrie another hug and smiled fondly. "I'm so glad you came. I'll call you tomorrow and we can talk."

They were the first to leave as the party wound down, except for Mike. She knew some of her friends would hang out. They'd watch horror flicks, some snoozing, some wide awake, until about the break of dawn, and then go upstairs for pancakes or French toast and sausage breakfast, courtesy of Tina Preston's Kitchen.

Then the girls would go upstairs, the boys back downstairs, and they'd sleep most of the day away.

* * *

Paul and Carrie declined when the waitress stopped by to offer more coffee and apologize for the extensive wait.

"We'll have more with breakfast," he said pleasantly.

The popular dining hall of the Rendezvous Club, famous for their steaks, seafood and French cuisine had packed with couples out for an after midnight banquet.

Carrie did not mind waiting to be served. She was occupied enjoying their time together. It had been too long since they shared an evening of simple fun. Her own fault, but they were together again and it felt great.

"You're very quiet," Paul commented, his voice taking on a sad note as the waitress left. "That's to be expected, I guess, considering—but where are you, Carrie? I'm trying to understand, but I want you now, for tonight, at least."

She gave him a quick, reassuring kiss. "Would you believe me if I told you, I'm right here with you?" A thoughtful smile curved her mouth. "I was thinking of us, how selfish and unfair I've been to our relationship. So, there you have it, I admit, I've been all wrapped up in my own misery."

"You were going through some grief," he said, with a tender look. "You were really thinking of me?"

"Yes." Carrie held his hand, their fingers entwined.

"I was beginning to feel like you were out of my life forever."

"I'm glad you waited for me. I was afraid you might find someone else."

He lifted her hand touching it to his lips. "There could never be anyone else for me, Carrie," he told her, his voice husky with emotion.

The waitress approached the table, unavoidably interrupting their intimacy. She took their order for steak and eggs and hurried on her way.

"Why did you push me away?" Paul asked.

"I don't know. I was lost for a while. I didn't feel like I deserved to have friends or fun. I didn't even feel like I deserved to live with Ted gone."

"It wasn't anything you did or didn't do," he told her. "He was on a road to destruction."

A road to destruction—he did it to himself—you are not responsible.

She'd heard it all, more than she cared to hear, even if it was true, but it was time to heal, to let go. She took a quivering breath.

"We've talked enough about it, haven't we," he said considerately.

"Yes, I believe so, but I have to say one more thing." Carrie paused for a moment. "Paul, I am recovering. It's not easy—but I have a life, I have a love, and I have friends who love me, and now I can accept that I deserve my life, my love and my friends," she said with a sense of conviction.

"Welcome back, Carrie," he said with a warm smile.

When the waitress brought their meal, and more coffee, they ate in comfortable silence, then lingered a while longer as the popular restaurant began to clear of customers. Finally, he motioned for the waitress.

"No, thank you, just the check," he said when she offered more coffee.

Carrie felt serene as they left the restaurant, not exactly happy, but better than she had been in a very long time.

When Paul parked in front of her house, he leaned over to kiss her, his hand a light caress on the back of her neck. "I'll call you," he said.

"I'll accept," she promised.

Carrie turned to get out of the car, but he grabbed her hand.

"Wait—I love you, Carrie."

She let him pull her close, their lips met instinctively, fervently.

"I don't want to let you go," he whispered. "Tonight was wonderful."

"It was perfect," she murmured between kisses.

"I just might keep you out here all night," he teased.

"How about if you do?" she agreed. "I feel safe with you."

Carrie realized her mistake as soon as the words were out.

"What do you mean?" He sat back from her, his eyes searching hers in the dim lighting.

"I didn't mean anything. It was just—I was joking. I don't know—I'm not sure exactly what I meant," she said, with a short, nervous laugh.

"You're stumbling Carrie, you meant something, or you wouldn't have said it."

"Okay, I just—I suppose I have some kind of phobia. I feel like I'm being watched, maybe even followed. It's nothing—really. I'm sure it will stop eventually."

"It doesn't sound like nothing to me!"

She flinched a bit at the force of his reply.

His voice softened. "Why would you feel paranoid?" he asked gently. "Carrie, is there something you're not telling me?"

"I don't know what you're talking about," she answered, but could not look directly into his caring eyes.

"Have you learned anything else about Ted's death?" he prompted.

"You mean his murder?" she blurted carelessly.

Carrie hesitated, torn by conflicting emotions, longing to tell Paul about the tape Ted had left her, the damning evidence that she hoped would be on it, but she couldn't tell him about the tape until she knew exactly what was on it, if she could even get up the nerve to listen to it. Finally she met his eyes.

"I didn't mean to ruin this moment," she whispered. Her arms circled his neck. "I promise you, I don't know anything. Please, just love me."

"You know, I do, Carrie." He returned her urgent hug before pulling gently away. Paul held her hand, the clutch almost as desperate as his words. "Talk to me. Please, Carrie."

"Paul, please don't," she pleaded. "What matters most is getting our relationship back. I've missed you in my life."

"I've missed you too, but honey, you don't know these people."

"What people are you talking about, Paul?" she asked with quizzical wonder. "Do you know who they are?"

"I don't know who they are—I just know what I've heard."

"I'd better go inside, now."

Paul sighed, apparently resigned. He exited the car and circled around to open the car door for her. She held his hand as they walked to her front door. He kissed her goodnight, holding her close, his mouth lovingly tender.

"Come over tomorrow and I'll fix brunch," she whispered.

"Sounds good. I'll call first."

He kissed her again, reluctant to go. "Dream of me?"

"Always." She opened the door. "See you tomorrow."

Carrie shut and locked the door as he turned away. She proceeded up the stairs humming softly. When she opened the door to her bedroom, she stared in shock at the disarray of her personal belongings.

Drawers were opened, the contents thrown and scattered over the floor, pillows and stuffed animals ripped apart, the insides torn out. Whoever did the search had been thorough, and left the room in shambles.

Carrie closed the door. In the next instant, an arm circled her from behind; a hand pressing tightly over her mouth muffling a startled cry.

"Don't scream," he gritted. "If you want to live, you'd better be still."

Carrie nodded to show understanding, acceptance of the situation.

"What do you want?" she said when he released her.

"The tape. I want the tape your big brother left for you."

She turned to face him. A nylon pulled tightly over his face, distorted his features, an effective disguise.

"I don't know anything about a tape," she said hastily.

A strong hand closed around her throat. "Don't play dumb."

Her hands came up trying useless to release the tight grip of his large hand that abruptly cut off her breath. Feeling pressure and dizziness, blackness closing in, she fought reflexively, growing weaker, until he released the grip.

"The tape," he growled.

"Okay," she choked. "I had it, but I destroyed it."

He looked at her menacingly. "A lie could get you wasted," he gritted, his face twisting under the nylon, giving him an even more sinister, fear evoking appearance. "Wasted like your brother."

"I don't have it!" she cried, her voice raspy. Pain over the loss of her brother ripped through her again. Carrie swallowed painfully. "I was afraid and smashed it to pieces."

He pulled her closer. She viewed his distorted features at close range, almost gagging on the foul, heavy smell of stale cigarettes. His fingers tightened painfully on her arms.

"I wanted that damn tape, but if you destroyed it, you might be allowed to live—if you're lying to me, you're one dead bitch."

He released her with a forceful shove that sent her reeling backward, and then left quickly, nimbly scampering out through the open window.

A shudder passed over her body as she watched his confident departure, realizing her defenselessness. Taking an unsteady breath, she told herself she was safe now, he wouldn't come back, he would never invade her world again, but she didn't feel entirely reassured—because he *had* invaded her world, ransacked her room, rifled through all of her personal belongings and in the process destroyed several cherished treasures.

Carrie walked uncertainly to the window through which he had exited feeling a terrible sense of bitterness, staring out into the night at the familiar landscape of her backyard, a secure haven of love her father had created for his children.

A sturdy fence had kept them from venturing out into the streets when they were little. She had always felt protected, but now a frightening man out of the night—from another life—had left her feeling exposed and vulnerable.

She had been right about the tape. Hopeful but apprehensive, she had hidden it carefully under a loose floorboard, covered by carpet with her desk placed precisely on the indentations. It must certainly have incriminating evidence, and now, she had a difficult decision to make.

Chapter Twenty

They left the beach party behind, Danny with his current girl and some other guys and gals. Christi could hear the rock music in the distance as she and Billy walked along the shoreline holding hands.

A hazy April night, it would probably rain later, but the misty darkness felt comforting, like a soft, warm security blanket.

They paused to share a kiss. He drew her closer.

"Want to go for a moonlight swim?"

"A quick moonlight swim? The ocean's still a little cool."

"A quickie moonlight swim, then I'll warm you up," he smiled.

He took her hand, already dressed in swimwear, they raced into the ocean. Billy swam far ahead of her. The water actually felt good, still a little cool but not uncomfortable.

He swam swiftly back. His arms encircled her, then his lips touched hers in a sweet, teasing caress.

Christi sighed as he swam away again. These past months they had been together more than apart. It had been an extended dream come true since that evening at Kelly's place when he vowed his love.

He took her for rides in the mountains on his motorcycle, parties on the beach—like tonight—boat rides, picnics, cookouts, a perpetual spin of events, and when she was with him on a school night, he always got her home by ten.

True to his word, he never asked her to go back to Kelly's Place. Some evenings were simply spent in his apartment as he helped her with homework, or to study for a test so her grades wouldn't drop, and afterward they'd watch a little TV.

Billy kept strong in his commitment, although more than friendly, they shared no more than passionate kisses and occasional caresses to express their love.

She felt him under the water, moving up her legs, further up her body, at last emerging from the water. As their lips met, she clung to him, loving him with her whole being. Sometimes the intensity of the affection she felt scared her because she didn't want to be hurt again, but he had won this love, a love he had proven, a love he vowed to cherish forever.

They waded out of the water heading toward the bonfire in the distance.

Tonight Billy had asked her to leave with him. He wanted to make a fresh start somewhere, away from the Cobras, away from the Monarchs. Christi wanted that, too, more than anything, but the decision to leave her brothers would be the most painful experience of growing up.

She didn't feel capable of making that decision tonight, or any time soon. Billy understood. He had not pressured her for an immediate answer.

* * *

The two men sat in the dark van, quietly listening to the recorded voice of Ted Harrison telling his sister things that should never have been revealed.

"He was right." Carl Howell lit a cigarette with shaky hands, easy to tell he would need a fix soon. "She had the tape, and now she listened to it. So, what now? You gonna waste her?"

"Hell, yeah! She's good as dead."

"Wait, something's happening. She's making a phone call."

"Preston residence."

"Dawn, this is Carrie, did I wake you?"

"No, is something wrong? It's after midnight."

"I have a tape, Dawn. It explains a lot. Do you know what I mean?"

"I have an idea," she said cautiously.

"Can I come over?"

"You know, you can, anytime."

"Dawn," she said solemnly. "This is better than the journal."

"Okay, come on over. Did you call Paul and Jerry?"

"No . . . I'll be there in a few."

"This couldn't be easier." He opened the van door. "Drive with the lights out," he instructed. "Circle around and pick me up on Woodland Drive, at the clearing with that park bench and fancy light."

He left the van. Trotting less than a half block to Carrie Harrison's house. He hid behind a large tree waiting.

She had been under twenty-four-hour surveillance since she'd gotten the tape. He didn't know or care who else kept the vigil, just glad that she had chosen his watch to break down and take the fatal step.

The surveillance gig had paid big bucks, and since he would be the one getting the tape and silencing the girl, he'd get a fat bonus for a job well done, enough bread to take off outta here if he decided to.

Carrie came out of her house, closed and locked the door, then hurried down the walkway turning toward Union Avenue. He followed close, but far enough behind to duck quickly out of sight if she started getting nervous and happened to glance back over her shoulder.

She turned to walk along a wide path that led through a grove of trees. He figured this must be a short cut over to Woodland Drive. It couldn't have been easier if he planned it.

Carrie walked quickly. She turned onto the path that led straight from Church Street to Woodland Drive. Once she got through here, Dawn's house was less than a block away.

She held the tape within the pocket of her light jacket.

Keeping the fast pace, Carrie contemplated calling some law enforcement agency out of Preston. The Preston PD could not be trusted and who knew how far reaching the corruption might be?

She was anxious to get this evidence to someone in authority that could be trusted. She ached with wanting to, but in some dark corner of her mind, she wished that she hadn't even listened to the tape.

Carrie could hardly believe it, even in Ted's own words, and after she heard it, she knew there was no way she could pretend to be unaware of the damning information.

She cried out, startled as someone gripped her shoulders. He pushed her roughly up against a tree, skimming his hands over her in a searching procedure.

Wrenching out of his careless hold, she raced with long strides over the well-worn path, terror driving her toward the light beyond the small forest of trees. Just as she reached the clearing, he pounced on her, dragging her back into the shadows.

He cursed softly slamming her hard against the coarse bark of a huge tree, drew his fist and slugged her. Stunned by the solid blow, Carrie stood in a dazed stupor as he roughly removed the jacket, and then tossed it aside.

"What do you want now?" she whispered, beginning to recover from the shock of almost being knocked out. "You have the tape, take it and go."

"It isn't enough, now, is it you stupid bitch."

She recognized the voice. The impact of his intimidating threat on New Year's Eve settled over her with the stark realization that she would not be allowed to live. "No, please. I won't tell," she promised, quickly.

Tears welled within her eyes. "I swear—I won't. No one would believe me anyway. Please." She could think of nothing else to say, except to promise again in hopeless appeal. "I won't tell anyone."

"Shhh." He pressed his hand tight against her mouth.

It happened so fast, she could hardly comprehend being stabbed. Carrie sucked in her breath, he had struck a second time then ambled away, leaving her leaning weakly against the tree.

Retrieving the tape from her jacket where he had thrown it a few feet away, he walked casually toward the street whistling softly. A hauntingly familiar melody drifted back to her on the quiet breeze.

Carrie whimpered, crying feebly in the aftermath of violence.

Pressing both hands against the wounds, feeling the warmth flowing through her fingers, she moaned despairingly.

She took a faltering step before her legs collapsed. Dropping to her knees, and then facedown onto the cool grass that grew alongside the path, Carrie pulled forward, gradually advancing toward the light of the clearing.

It began to drizzle, a gentle but chilling mist. Drawing another ragged breath, exhaling on a tremulous sigh, she finally let herself relax, accepting that she did not have strength to go further.

Carrie felt a startling coldness. She knew with every beat of her heart, blood pumped steadily through the fatal wounds, no one could get to her in time to save her ebbing life.

With her last breath, a dismal sense of loss merged with a burning hope that her death would not be in vain, that somehow, someone would discover the truth.

* * *

Dawn shivered more from nervousness than the coolness of the air as a light rain fell from the dark sky. She quickened her pace. Too much time had passed already, Carrie should have arrived at her house by now, and she wasn't even in sight.

When she saw a man climb into the passenger side of a dark van parked down the street, and then speed away, she felt disturbing apprehension, more than a sensation—Dawn knew there was something seriously wrong.

She ran to where she had seen him board the vehicle looking around uncertainly. The familiar park bench and charming replica of an antique lamplight made her wonder if all this panic had been unwarranted. The area had a serene, calming effect.

She knew something had to be wrong, though, because Carrie didn't show up. If she'd changed her mind about coming over, she would have called.

Feeling troubled, Dawn walked anxiously toward the trees. From the glow of the quaint light, she spotted Carrie near the edge of the clearing.

Dawn began trembling as she approached the quiet form.

She touched her fingers to the carotid artery, no pulse. Stifling a sob, she turned her over onto her back. Carrie's eyes stared lifelessly into oblivion; still, she began CPR working frantically, breathing, pumping—breathing—pumping.

Useless, it was useless, her life was gone. The glaring acceptance sent her reeling back away from her friend's body.

She fled the scene, half-blinded by tears, running home and stumbling into the house. Dawn closed and locked the door.

She stood, leaning weakly against the door, breathing much too rapidly, helplessly out of control, wanting desperately to reject the appalling reality of what her eyes had seen, what her hands had touched, but the awful truth could not be evaded. *Carrie is dead, I have to call the police—the police have to be notified—because my friend is dead. I tried to save her, I tried, but the blood, there was so much blood!* She stared at the blood on her hands on the verge of hysteria. The panic rose within her threatening to take over and break her down into a sobbing child.

Dawn slammed her head hard against the door, achieving the desired effect, an almost pacifying, numbing misery that let her focus on her responsibility.

The calm she felt in the wake of her previous hysteria seemed bizarre, but she accepted the respite. She washed her hands, refusing to cry, closing her eyes and heart to the blood swirling down the bathroom sink drain.

Dawn phoned the Preston City Police Department. After giving the pertinent, devastating information, she was told a patrol car would soon be dispatched to her residence.

When Officer Jarred arrived, she invited him in, walked him through the entrance hall into the living room, and offered him to sit, indicating the sofa.

He stood with hat in hand, his whole stance conveying compassion. "I'm sorry for your loss," he said. "I know how hard this must be for you."

Officer Jarred had known the teenagers of Preston since they were kids. For the most part, he and his partner patrolled the streets, and warned them home after curfew.

"Do you know why she was out tonight?" he inquired gently.

"She was coming over here. She had a tape, evidence of—proof of Ted's murder—that he *was* murdered. Maybe even the name of his killer."

"What are you talking about?" he asked, puzzled. "What did she say?"

"Nothing very specific," she admitted.

"I don't understand."

"We suspected that Ted didn't accidentally overdose, that he didn't even use heroin. He had important information in a journal, but it was stolen."

"There was never any mention of a journal."

"She never reported it to the police, Paul convinced her not to."

Dawn drew a trembling breath, her composer slowly crumbling. "He was selling drugs, Officer Jarred, he was in deep trouble."

She sighed distractedly. "Carrie had a tape. She said that it was better than the journal. She had that tape with her, and I know she was murdered for it. They can't ignore the fact that Ted was murdered now, can they, Officer Jarred? Shouldn't there be a homicide detective here?"

"There was no tape, Dawn."

"Of course not! Whoever killed her would have taken it." Dawn paused to take a calming breath. "I just told you, it was evidence concerning Ted's murder. And now Carrie was murdered for it."

"You keep saying Ted was murdered, but you said she didn't tell you anything," he reminded her.

"No," she faltered. "But she didn't have to tell me."

"There are indications that it was a rape attempt," he told her calmly.

"I don't understand. I told you that Carrie was bringing evidence of a murder, and suddenly a rapist shows up to kill her? It wasn't a rape attempt. Carrie was murdered for the tape."

Dawn wondered how many times she had said that to the deaf ears of Officer Jarred.

"You know it, too," she said with certainty.

"Your friends are dead, and I understand you want to make some kind of sense of it, but you have to think about it realistically."

Realizing the futility of the conversation, Dawn refused to say more. No amount of talk would make a difference. Why should it be any different with Carrie? Ted's death had been ruled an accidental overdose, hers would be considered a random act of violence or worse.

Officer Jarred took her arm with gentle authority. "You'd better sit down, Dawn, you look a little pale."

Dawn's heart beat hard in her chest. She wanted this man out of her sight, she wanted to scream at him to get out of her house, but he was authority, so she politely pulled away from his touch.

"I want you to leave now," she said briskly, but staidly courteous.

"You mentioned a van—can you describe it?" His voice seemed detached, almost automated. "And you saw a man. Can you describe him?"

"It was dark, the van. I couldn't see the license plate. The man was tall, around six feet, thin—white, I think. It was at a distance." She looked at his passive face. "Please, just go."

Dawn left him standing before losing the ability to remain civil. How could she have considered him an ally? Hopelessness closed around her as she fled up the stairs. Dawn knew she would be dead too, if Carrie had revealed the discovered evidence on the damn tape that she had died for.

The reality that Carrie was gone came crashing down on her again and she pounded her bed in frustration. Sorrow took a stronghold and painful sobs racked her body, giving vent to pent-up emotions.

She sat up on the edge of her bed, taking the time she needed to recover from the force of the grief-stricken reaction.

Dawn took a deep, unsteady breath. Walking over to the window, she looked up at the night sky. The rain had stopped but threatening clouds obliterated the stars. As a cloud drifted lazily past the moon, she accepted another big dose of responsibility. She had to tell Paul.

She went into the bathroom to splash cool water on her face before making the call. It was the first time she noticed the blood on her clothes. Dawn stripped the bloody clothes off stuffing them into a plastic trash bag.

Refusing to succumb to tears again, she showered quickly and thoroughly.

After drying and hurriedly dressing in lounging pajamas, she dialed Jerry's number. After the third ring, he answered with a mumbled greeting.

"Jerry—it's Dawn."

He yawned drowsily. "It's awful late, Dawn."

"I have to talk to you and Paul—tonight," she said, her voice trembling. "Could you come over right away?"

"Are you crying?" His tone took on a sharp contrast to the grogginess of a moment ago. "What's wrong? What is it? Dawn—"

"Please, don't ask." Her fingers gripped the phone tight. "Just get here."

"Dawn, tell me what's going on!"

"Jerry, please—I can't." She placed the phone back in the receiver, knowing he and Paul would be there as quickly as possible.

Telling Paul was one of the hardest things Dawn had ever done. He sat in stunned silence, a mixture of pain and disbelief on his face.

It hurt to witness his sorrow. He moaned softly folding over in his chair.

"Carrie discovered the person responsible for her brother's death?"

Dawn could hear disbelief clearly evident. "She did, Paul."

"I don't understand—why didn't she listen to me?"

"Because she couldn't settle for not knowing, and I won't settle either. I intend to find out who killed her—and Ted," she said determinedly. "I'm going to get to the bottom of this if—"

"If it's the last thing you ever do?" Paul interrupted fiercely. He sat up, sighing bleakly, but recovering himself. "Even if it really *is* the last thing you ever do, even if it kills you?"

"Think about it, Dawn," Jerry advised. "Consider what you're saying. If you should stumble onto the person responsible or any evidence concerning the crimes, you would probably be killed. Dawn, I can't even grasp that she's gone yet, and you're thinking of investigating her murder?"

"Give it up, Dawn," Paul advised, tears still lingering in his sad brown eyes. "Hasn't there been enough death in our town?"

Jerry put his arms around her, placing her head gently on his chest. It was comforting and right now she needed comfort.

They seemed passively tolerant of their friends' deaths, and that probably would not change. Dawn had no doubt of Paul's deep love for Carrie, or that Jerry had cherished her as a friend, the significant difference was that she could not accept Carrie's death in quiet defeat.

"You should tell your mother," Paul said abruptly.

"I'll wait 'til morning to tell Tina," Dawn said shakily. Her mother slept way in the back, where nothing short of a bomb dropping would disturb her.

"You can stay here as long as you like," she added. "Let's go downstairs, I'll fix us some hot chocolate and we can talk."

With Jerry's arm around her and Paul trailing behind, they left her room.

* * *

Dawn held tightly to Jerry's hand as they entered the solemn atmosphere of the Florence and Young Funeral Home. She stopped at the open double doors of the display room staring at the back wall where a lonely white coffin sat in the midst of colorful blossoming flowers, mostly roses in various stages of bloom. Dawn felt dark despair as she reluctantly walked forward.

Carrie looked like a doll lying in a silk showcase, light brown curls softly framed her face, dressed in peach silk and chiffon, in what would have been her senior prom gown, a deceivingly peaceful aura surrounded her.

The last moments of her life had been anything but peaceful, they must have been terrifying. Dawn repressed the dreadful thought, she couldn't bear it. She finally turned forlornly away from the semblance of her lost friend.

Jerry stayed with her for a long while, but she could tell when he began to feel uncomfortable, fidgeting and glancing warily around.

"I understand if you want to leave," she told him as they sat close to each other in the vestibule. "I want to stay with the family awhile longer, but it's okay if you go."

"Really? You sure?"

She gently squeezed his hand. "I'm sure. Just call me tomorrow, okay?"

"First thing," he promised.

When Dawn left the funeral home, she felt ready to drop. It had been emotionally exhausting, but she had managed to pull herself together enough to support Carrie's mother throughout the visitation hours, greeting an array of friends who stopped by to pay their respects, besides many relatives of Carrie's from out of town that she had never met.

She tossed and turned that night thinking about what Mrs. Harrison had told her. They would be making arrangements after the funeral to move away.

They did not want to go on living in Preston City. There was nothing here for them anymore except painful memories and fear.

Dawn finally drifted into a restless sleep, her dreams invaded by a man wearing a hideous mask, an ornate cobra ring and flashing a deadly knife.

Chapter Twenty-One

The graduation march began. Dawn fell in line with the other graduating students with practiced grace. They had prepared for this moment, to Dawn rehearsals had been a simple necessity as surely as walking down this aisle.

The future should be anticipated with lively expectation, especially today, instead, during the walk down the long aisle, Dawn thought back of Carrie's plans to be a nurse, how many would have benefited from her gentleness and empathy! Carrie should have been here, right beside her, Teddy also.

In the lobby and outside Central High, she posed for pictures with friends, hoping her smile appeared convincing. It felt pasted on as Tina snapped away, not oblivious to her pain, but determined to have memories of the day.

Tina snapped some final shots of her and Jerry, and then Bob took the camera for some pictures of her with her mother. The photo shoot was over.

Dawn didn't feel up to a rowdy celebration. Most of the graduating class was headed out to the beach for an all-night bash, including Jerry.

When she declined, Jerry grudgingly accepted her refusal. A little upset that he still wanted to go, as if he couldn't understand her deep sadness, she passively hid her disappointment that he could so easily move on.

Dawn was glad she had invited Mike and Christi to join them in the semi-casual dinner celebration at the Castle Supper Club.

After dropping Christi and Mike at their apartment, on the way home, Tina quietly told Bob that she felt a need to spend the rest of the evening with Dawn alone.

She quickly left the two adults to say goodnight and had changed into lounging pajamas by the time her mother came in. They enjoyed The Ed Sullivan Show along with two scoops of strawberry ice cream.

When the variety show ended, Tina suggested herbal tea.

Sitting at the counter, feeling listless, Dawn felt Tina's worried gaze.

She had tried to reflect a sincere optimism at celebrating graduation, but did not have the heart to offer valid enthusiasm.

"I've waited for you to mention it, Dawn, but since you didn't, have you decided which college you'll be attending?"

"No, I haven't given it much thought," she confessed. "With everything that's happened, college doesn't seem to matter."

"It's still soon, but it should matter," Tina said straightforwardly.

"I can't even think right now, about college or my future—but I will, I promise. I don't mean to be a bummer."

The kettle whistled. "You're not—you can't help it if you feel bad," Tina said, pouring boiling water into cups she had readied with teabags.

"I think I'm just really beat. I'll feel better tomorrow, right? Thanks, Mom." She accepted the cup. Absently lifting the teabag in and out of it, Dawn wondered when she might actually feel better.

"It might take a lot of tomorrows," Tina said with compassion. "I wish there was a way to console you, but it takes time to heal."

"I'll be fine, but I am exhausted."

Sipping the mint tea, contemplating what Tina said, Dawn readily agreed, a lot of tomorrows, yes, quite a few.

"Do you have any idea of what your major might be?"

"None, major—or minor."

Her mother sighed. "I know, honey, that you and Carrie were planning on attending college together. She was one of your best friends, and no time has passed to amount to anything when it comes to getting on with your life after losing a friend, but Dawn, you have other friends, Christi and Mike, for example—Jerry, he cares a lot." Tina's eyes looked misty as she spoke. "You have to consider what you said to Carrie. Remember?"

"I remember." Dawn thought for a moment. "I'll probably go to Cal State—close to home. Sound good?" She gave her mother a hug, having finished her tea.

"If that's your choice," she said agreeably.

"It's where I would have gone with Carrie."

"Cal State's fine."

"Thanks ma!" Dawn drawled, attempting a light humor.

Dawn felt saddened as she prepared for bed. She didn't even want to think about college without her friend. She and Carrie had made their plans, happily intending to be off campus roommates.

She didn't want to think about how different life would be if Carrie was still here, useless despairing thoughts, but even so, it all came back now in a rush of sorrow.

Dawn willed herself to the present with determination, once more turning speculations to Van Morrison. She needed to talk to Christi about him.

She sat up reaching for the phone before remembering that Christi was still in school. Dawn relaxed back on the bed. She would call tomorrow after school and request to pick her up, regardless of her insistence that she loved to walk. Christi could spend the night and go to school from here.

With that decided, she turned over on her side hoping for peaceful sleep.

At nine-thirty Dawn awoke feeling well rested, surprised that she had slept the night through without the intrusion that had plagued her dreams quite often since Ted's death.

The day dragged on from a cup of hot tea, to forcing herself through her morning routine, to idle contemplation. She wondered what Christi's reaction would be to her inquiries. She seemed devoted, earnestly fond of the man.

Would this affection color her view of him? Even so, Dawn rationalized, they were best friends, and no Van Morrison could change that.

Dawn called Christi at four; of course, she would come over, and yes she would spend the night. She even consented to being 'chaperoned'.

"What's this about?" Christi asked again for the umpteenth time, as she hung the dress she had brought for school tomorrow in the closet, and again Dawn insisted on waiting until later.

"You brought your swimsuit, right?"

"I never visit your house without it."

"Great! We have at least an hour out by the pool before we need to shower and get ready for supper."

In the pool house, Christi tried again to convince her to tell her what she was doing here on a school night. Dawn told her again, very patiently, but firmly, "There's something I want to discuss with you—later."

"Oh, that's just not fair."

"Last one in is a longhaired blonde!" Dawn shouted running to the pool.

As they helped with the final preparations of supper, they chattered excessively, girlishly, about anything and everything.

Dawn felt almost normal. She had pushed dismal thoughts aside for today to enjoy her friend's company with the added bonus of noticing how pleased Tina was with her markedly brighter attitude. Even so, she could hardly contain herself as they finished the evening meal.

"Okay, it's later, tell me what this is about," Christi insisted as Tina left and they began to clear the table.

"After cleanup," Dawn replied, suppressing her eagerness. "We have to sit down for this. It's pretty important to me, and I want to relax and discuss what's on my mind without thinking about anything else."

"I've been thinking about it ever since you called."

"Sorry to be so mysterious. I can hardly wait myself," Dawn said truthfully. "Let's just finish the kitchen, okay? It won't take long."

They hurried through the task and then headed for the bedroom. Dawn put on a stack of records, a mixture of the Beatles, Stones and Animals before finally confiding to Christi her intentions of investigating Van Morrison, reminding her of Ted's mention of him in the mysteriously missing journal.

Christi looked at her with concern.

"Dawn, don't do this, please! Don't go there," she said emphatically. "You can't mess with Van, Dawn. I trust him, but—"

She caught on Christi's faltering voice. "Do you? Do you really?"

"I do," she vowed, solemnly.

"Then help me," she pleaded. Dawn took a deep, calming breath, drawing strength from her decision. Tears had a time and place, not here and not now. "Please, Chris," she said with purpose. "I'm depending on you. He's the only link I have to Ted and Carrie."

Christi gave her a brooding look. "You were just waiting for graduation."

"Maybe I was," she readily admitted. "I told Jerry and Paul that I couldn't let it go. Jerry said that once I got past the initial grief that I could forget it, but it's still the same."

"It's only been a month, give yourself time."

"Maybe if it had ended with Ted, but Carrie—" Dawn almost choked. She paused to regain composure, looking at Christi expectantly. "Their killer is still out there."

Christi met her look with a wide-eyed worried gaze. "It wasn't Van."

"Nothing ventured, nothing gained—I'll be glad if it wasn't Van."

"I'm telling you now, that Van is no killer," she said grudgingly.

"Okay," Dawn said patiently.

Christi looked far away for a moment.

"Oh, all right," she decided. "But I don't like it, Dawn, and you better be careful. You'll be going places you have no business just to find out for yourself that Van wasn't involved."

"I'll be careful, but I need to know where he spends his time."

"I think he still goes to the Basement occasionally—" she said slowly. "I haven't been there for a long time—what am I saying?" She slapped her hand against her forehead. "You can't go there! Promise me, okay? You don't need any run-ins with John Burton."

"Okay, I promise."

"You mean it!" she said forcefully.

"I promise!" she said just as forcefully. "I sure don't want to see him!"

Christi seemed satisfied and resumed her thoughtfulness.

"There is one place—the Blue Haze, remember where you took me to meet Billy that time? I guess, everything considered, that's your best bet," she said with another anxious look. "Though I wouldn't recommend going there either. That place is grotey."

"I have to go somewhere, Chris, if I'm going to meet him, I have to venture out."

"I suppose. Why can't I just introduce you?"

"I'm afraid that wouldn't work," she replied impishly. "I have to pretend to want drugs. What do you recommend I ask for?"

"Yeah, like you could pull that off." A ghost of a smile crossed her lovely face. She shook her head, mystified. "This does concern me."

"Well, don't," Dawn leaned toward her. "Tell me about his friends. Does he seem mysterious to you?"

"I hadn't thought about him being mysterious." Christi bit her lip thoughtfully. "He and Dave were close, but he's basically a loner."

"How about girlfriends?"

"There must be someone, but I've never seen him with anyone, ever." She paused musingly, looking somewhat puzzled. "You know, now that I think about it, I suppose he is a bit mysterious," Christi conceded. "But not in a bad way. He's a private person."

"Well, Ted had mentioned him, and Jerry said he's from New York, and—"

"And what?" Christi demanded managing not to sound irritated.

"He arrived in town at about the same time as Mr. Kaley."

"What does Mr. Kaley have to do with this?"

"I don't trust him, but I don't want to think about him right now."

"Well, you're wrong about Van, Dawn. You'll see."

Christi's obviously partial feelings toward Van left little room for criticism, much less outright accusations.

Throughout the conversations and cautions rendered, she remained adamant about her opinion of Van Morrison. He had surely won her over—heart and soul.

When Tina peeked in to say goodnight, Dawn glanced at the clock. Ten-thirty seemed early, but Christi had school tomorrow.

Dawn turned off the stereo, meticulously replacing each album in its respective holder.

They pulled back the bedspreads folding them neatly at the bottom of their beds. Christi climbed into bed, Dawn turned out the lights.

"I'm leaving with Billy."

As Dawn slipped between the sheets, she didn't comment on the almost whispered disclosure. She didn't want to believe what her ears had heard.

"Did you hear me?"

"Yes," she said hastily. "But I—I can't believe it."

"We're leaving next month."

"Why, Christi?" Dawn asked as the realization began to fully sink in that her friend was running away, still not wanting to believe it.

"He wanted to leave in April, but I convinced him to wait until school let out for summer vacation."

"That's just two weeks away . . . Christi, this is huge. What about school, you would graduate next year. What about Mike?" she said anxiously.

"It wasn't an easy decision, and I need your support like you need mine."

"But you're running away," Dawn moaned.

"Could you at least be happy for me?" she murmured dejectedly.

Dawn's heart constricted. Leaving her brothers must be tearing her apart.

"Of course, I am. I'm happy for you, I guess, but I'm having a tough time with this. You must love Billy! I mean, really love him!"

"Yes, I do—don't you love Jerry?"

"I love him, but I think it's about over between us. I mean, with school being out, and so much is going to be happening in my life—"

"Then you don't really, truly love him."

Dawn knew Christi was right. Her 'love' for Jerry had never been an everlasting love. At one time, she thought it was, or maybe deep inside, she had known it would never be more than a high school romance.

"Did you and Billy ever make love again?"

"No, I would have told you."

Dawn sat up, turning on her bedside lamp. "What about the Monarchs?"

"He's through with all that now, and I'm glad." Christi turned over on her side hugging the pillow. "We're going to be married."

"But you're underage."

"There are places—you know."

"Oh." Dawn turned off the lamp. "Christi Cole," she reflected mulling it over. "Has a nice ring to it, I guess."

"You guess?"

"No, it does, I'm just, befuddled."

"Befuddled? What kinda word is that!" Christi demanded.

"It means puzzled."

"I know what it means," she said grumpily.

"I'm sorry."

"Are you?"

"I am—about the teasing. I really was just teasing, you know, with the befuddled remark. I couldn't be happier for you, Christi, honest, I am truly." But she would miss her. "Christi Cole sounds wonderful. It must be amazing to be so much in love."

"You can't just up and say you're befuddled!"

Dawn giggled.

"Hey, that sounded great," Christi said warmly.

"It felt good," Dawn acknowledged.

Dawn stared into the darkness thinking about the seriousness of what Christi was about to do. Billy seemed like a great guy, but she didn't know him that well, and her friend would be going far away with that man.

"Can you tell me what it's like to be so completely in love?" Dawn asked reflectively.

"It's indescribable, my friend, and you'll know what I mean when it happens to you."

"Yeah? Well, too bad it's so indescribable that I won't be able to tell anyone," she said with a hint of laughter.

"I'm glad we had tonight," Christi said quietly.

Dawn turned over feeling sudden dismay, weighed down again with the painful reality that Christi was leaving.

"Will you come back home someday?"

"I won't stay gone from Preston forever," she promised.

Christi opened her eyes in the darkness. The dream had been vivid—and disturbing enough that she knew with a certainty that she had to tell Van, to warn him of Dawn's suspicions.

Then as dreams sometimes do, it began quickly to disperse, and with it, the apparent urgency of betraying her friend.

How could she? How could she trust Dawn to Van's care, when in fact, she knew so little about him? Sure, she would trust him with her own life, but could she trust him with Dawn's?"

Chapter Twenty-Two

Van entered the Blue Haze Tavern striding purposely to the far end of the bar. The brawny bartender set his regular beer and shot in front of him. He downed the whiskey, followed by a swallow of beer.

The restless feeling about the drop dead gorgeous girl who had started showing up outside this particular habitat had become a serious concern.

She made no attempt to be inconspicuous. She had been quite bold, in fact. It could only mean trouble. He decided to check out the who and why of the foxy little chick in those sexy, short shorts and get some answers.

A light touch interrupted his troubled thoughts and he turned. "Christi." He greeted her with mild surprise, and then took a quick survey around the bar. "What are you doing in here?"

"I have to talk to you."

He noticed a note of desperation in her voice that set him on edge. He could think of only one person who had ever brought her to such distraction.

"I'm gonna kill that SOB and be done with it," he muttered before taking another swallow of beer.

"What? No," she hastily assured him. "This has nothing to do with John. Can we go to your place? Do you have time?"

"Just this once," he grinned and started to stand.

"No, you can't leave with me," she said quickly. "I'll go out the back and you meet me there."

"Okay—here." He gave her the key to his apartment.

Christi left through the back exit. He remained long enough to finish his beer, wondering about this urgent meeting, relatively certain that it concerned his unknown admirer.

When he stepped outside, Van noticed the girl across the street leaning casually against a lamppost. The young woman was very brave, extremely naïve or just plain stupid. As he walked on, he decided that maybe she had a big dose of dangerously naïve bravado, and was entirely too reckless.

"Thanks, Van," Christi said, when she opened the door for him. "I'm sorry to intrude like that."

"Not a problem. What's up?" He sat relaxed on the black leather love seat while Christi began to pace in obvious agitation.

"Hey, girl!" he said finally. She looked toward him, and he quirked his forefinger. "Come here."

Christi complied and sat beside him, her hands folded on her lap.

"Now, let me speculate," he said with an easy smile. "There's only one reason for you to entice me here, Christine Temple, you naughty girl. I might have known you planned to seduce me!" He draped an arm over her shoulder. "You could a just asked."

His attempt to lighten the mood worked. Her face relaxed into a smile, the appealing dimple in her left cheek making its usual appearance.

"Now, you wanted to talk?"

The studious look once more dominating her sweet expression, Christi tilted her head slanting a close look at him. He wondered what she read in his expression as her eyes searched for reassurance of his integrity.

"I don't even know where to begin."

"Is this about the cute little redhead?" he ventured. "Stands about five, four, with a—" He drew an hourglass in the air, following with a low whistle.

"Yes." Christi flashed a grin, but reverted back to her frustration fairly quickly. "She inquired about you last week."

"About me?—concerning, what?"

"I'm only telling you this because I love you, and I trust you." She sounded hesitant.

"Talk to me, Christi." He touched her hand.

"She thinks you were involved in some way with Ted, and then Carrie's murder, Van. Carrie found Ted's journal after he died but then it was stolen. She had a chance to read some of it before it was stolen, though. Your name was in that journal, Van, *your name.*"

He tried to keep his expression impassive because of her close attention.

"I think I need a beer," he said to get away from her probing gaze.

His compassion toward Christi made him feel exposed, like she could see through to his darkest secrets; that she might, at any given time, start telling him his business and ask him what the hell he thought he was doing.

"So, tell me more," he said directly upon reentering the living room. He gave her a Pepsi.

"Thanks," she said. "Okay, she's suspicious of Mr. Kaley, and she's suspicious of you because you arrived in town at about the same time, and—the journal." Christi sighed with discontent. "I'm worried, Van, promise me that you won't let anything happen to her."

"I have a problem with promises, Christi."

They were just words. Promises meant little. Promises could only be as meaningful as the promise keepers. He wondered about the worst that could happen. Christi's friend was important to Christi, but—

"What's wrong with making a promise, Van?" she chided, interrupting not so pleasant contemplations. "I need some assurance."

"To the best of my ability," he agreed reluctantly. "But between you and me, not another word about anyone being murdered, you got it?"

"Got it." Christi gave him another mournful look. "I'm depending on you to protect her."

"I will . . . I will if I can." He offered an encouraging glimpse, which she rewarded with an engaging smile.

Van sighed, leaning back. This had turned into a merry little fix. Christi had made him say what she wanted to hear. Now he would be responsible. How could he have agreed to protect this girl when she had already ventured in too deep with her dangerous imaginings? How had she become suspicious of Bob Kaley?

He glanced at Christi feeling a gentle tug of regret.

She looked down for a long, thoughtful moment before raising her eyes to meet his. "She's the best friend I ever had, Van, tell me I did the right thing, and mean it." Her eyes fell away again.

"You did the right thing," he affirmed. "Look at me." He felt a painfully impulsive need to assure her. It bothered him that she was so apprehensive of him. "I mean it, okay? By the way, does *she* have a name?"

"Oh." Christi's look turned into a cute expression of perplexity, and they exchanged a candid look of amusement. "Dawn Preston."

"Of Preston City Heritage," he murmured knowingly. "She was your study buddy?" He recalled the night Christi confided her feelings to him, as they became better acquainted. That night seemed so long ago.

"She's an amazing person, Van."

"I know of her." He suppressed a weary sigh wondering how much of a problem this girl would be with her snooping. Given her wealth, she could easily have him investigated, but what would she do with her findings?

Maybe he could get to know her, gain her trust, divert her—

"I'm leaving with Billy."

The soft-spoken words caught his full attention.

"Oh, Christi, I am not hearing this," he objected without thinking.

"Van, please don't make me apologize."

"Well no, we couldn't have that."

"You've been a good friend—more than a friend, Van."

"I don't mean to seem over-protective, Chris, but is this something you've considered carefully?"

Christi raised her head, her violet eyes, so trusting, filled with passionate devotion. "I love him, Van."

"Do you have to run away?"

"We have to—we have to get away. I wish you could have met him."

"Maybe someday I will." Van rested concerned eyes on her young face, knowing how easy it is to make wrong choices. "When are you leaving?"

"Next Friday."

He gave her a tender look—if only he had words to keep her in Preston—

But of course there was no such influence. "Does Dave know about this?"

"No, Mike can tell him later."

"He's going to be very hurt. You know that, don't you?"

"Oh, I know." Her eyes filled with tears, but she held strong. "Please, Van, don't make it any harder on me than it is already."

"Okay, sunshine, long as you're sure."

He gave her a winsome smile, trying to keep the weariness out of his expression, knowing there was no way to change her mind.

"I better take off," Christi said standing.

"I'll drive you home."

"No. She may have followed you. I can't take a chance on her seeing us. It would put a rift in our friendship if she discovered I broke her confidence."

"Then I'll walk with you. We can leave out the back."

They left the building, via the fire escape. Turning out of the alley, they walked along the familiar streets together one last time.

On the way, he questioned her about Dawn Preston. He needed to learn everything Christi knew about her, anything she could tell him about Ted and Carrie's deaths regarding exactly why Dawn felt Ted had been murdered and more about why the girl would suspect him of any involvement.

"I feel torn Van," she confided when they reached the apartment building. "It's like I betrayed my sister. I don't even know if I'm worthy to be called her friend," she said unsteadily.

"You didn't betray her," he said quietly. "Don't assume that you did, Chris. Don't regret what you did, either. Dawn Preston's fortunate to have you, you're the best friend she could hope for."

He leaned down pressing a kiss on her forehead.

She swallowed thickly, her throat tight. Christi felt a weight of incredible sadness as he left, so miserable that she wanted to break down and cry.

She spoke to the very familiar step dwellers on her way up the stairs to the lobby.

Tatty runners lined the steps leading to the second floor apartment. The not unpleasant aroma of tenant's suppers lingered in the hallway. Everything struck a sad note, now. Still the same old apartment building, but the comfort of familiarity could not be denied.

"Is that you, Chris?"

Christi went into the kitchen where Mike sat munching a sandwich of leftover roast beef piled high with meat, cheese, lettuce and tomato.

"You're home early."

"Don't rub it in—now that you have a nightlife," he said deadpan, making her grin in spite of it all.

"Mike, I have to ask you something, and I need you to tell me the truth."

"I would never lie to you," he said, sobering for real.

"I know." Christi sighed unhappily, feeling bad for phrasing it that way.

"What's the problem?"

"I need you to tell me if there's anything about Van that I don't know."

He studied her thoughtfully before taking a deliberate bite of his sandwich. As he chewed, she gazed at him with questioning eyes.

There could only be one reason for his hesitation, no explanation except that what she heard was true.

He finally swallowed, pushing the sandwich aside.

"What do you mean by anything?" he asked with a concerned glimpse.

"I mean anything. Don't try to protect me."

"Van didn't want you to know," he said gently. "And you didn't want to know either. I'm not even sure you want to know now."

"Don't tell me he's a pusher, Mike. Please don't tell me that."

"See? I knew it—"

"No, it's alright, Mike," she said, terribly hurt by the certainty. "I had hoped that he wasn't—but I had to know. What do you perceive of him, Mike? Is he a bad person?"

"No, I mean, he doesn't seem to be." He gave her question considerable thought. "I don't know, really. He's puzzling for sure." Mike shrugged in helpless resignation. "I know there's a lot of anger."

"Did he have anything to do with Ted and Carrie's deaths?"

"I already told you I don't know who killed Ted, and I don't know about Carrie either, but when I'm around him—I don't know, there's something." He sighed regretfully. "Sorry, Chris, I'm in the dark about the connection. Van is a closed and complicated person and I haven't seen him lately."

She gave her brother a hug. "I guess he would have to be."

What else was there to say? If Mike didn't know, then yes, Van must be closed and complicated, and what he did know worried her.

Pusher. The very word was repulsive. She still found it improbable, so difficult to believe that of him.

In spite of everything, she needed to believe Van was a caring person, even knowing the awful truth, the abject knowledge that he was a pusher and the danger he could pose regardless of personality.

She couldn't believe he would intentionally manipulate her, the way he looked at her with genuine caring in his eyes.

Christi hoped beyond measure that she hadn't been misled into trusting him. She couldn't quite erase his guarded expression. What disturbed her most, though, was the promise he had tried to avoid.

She firmly closed her mind to any further dismal thoughts concerning Van. He had made the vow; she determined to trust that he would be true to his word.

The stolen journal had planted suspicions, but now she renewed her devotion to him, refusing to believe he had anything to do with Ted and Carrie Harrisons' deaths, or that he would mislead her or cause any harm to come to Dawn.

Christi drifted into an uneasy sleep knowing that Dawn would take any risk to avenge the death of a friend. Even though she insisted that she did not want revenge, but justice for Carrie, Christi saw danger in the depths of her green eyes that she had never seen before.

This troubled her, because Dawn could be deceiving herself.

Chapter Twenty-Three

Mike raised his hand to knock on Christi's partially opened bedroom door but let it fall back to his side, almost overcome by sorrow. He paused, taking time to curb the intense sensation, and then knocked.

"Come on in, Mike."

"How's it goin'?"

She glanced over. "Almost done."

He entered the room with an unusual downcast feeling. He leaned against the wall watching her pack, the unfamiliar emotion, although not exactly unexpected, bothered him. He would never accept being without his sister.

"So, you're determined to go away with this guy, huh?"

"Mike, try to understand . . . I love him."

"I know you do," he said quietly. "And he loves you, but this doesn't seem like the right way."

"It's the only way, Mike. I'll let you know as soon as we're settled," she promised, closing the suitcase.

"Here's fifty bucks. It'll help with gas and food." He tucked it into her jeans pocket.

"I'll miss you." She hugged him. "I'll keep in touch. Okay? I'll call frequently. Mike . . . I'll be relieved to get away from here. You know I've never gotten over what happened."

He wiped a tear gently from her face feeling a surge of overwhelming tenderness for his twin who seemed so much younger.

"Call tomorrow . . . call collect."

"I will."

"I have to go now." He hugged her tight, not wanting to let go. He kissed her temple, closing his eyes, appreciating the closeness they had always known. "I have to go."

"I understand," she said, tears in her voice.

He left the building to walk aimlessly along the gray colorless streets. Everything looked so bland to his eyes, now. It would be lonely with Christi gone, and Dave—Dave would be hurt and angry.

He would place the blame solely on Billy for taking her away, but it wasn't entirely Billy's fault. Mike had felt it coming a long time before she told him. It had taken a while for her to finally make the decision. Christi wasn't impetuous, but it had been her choice. Getting away from it all, while eloping with the guy she loved, was too much to resist forever.

He felt bad for Dave, but he felt worse for himself.

By the time Mike noticed John, Carl and Clyde it was too late to avoid a confrontation. They stepped out to block his path.

"I won't keep you long," John said. "There's something I have to know, then you can be on your merry way."

"Drop dead, Burton."

"Mike, I don't really want to hurt you, but I don't really care either."

"I don't have anything to say to you. So, you might as well let me be 'on my merry way'." Mike tried to push past, but Clyde grabbed his arm easily restraining him.

"You haven't been entirely honest with me," John said, his voice taking on a quiet forbearing quality.

"I haven't been anything with you," Mike replied, hostility rippling through him at John's overbearing act of tolerance.

"Want to take some time to discuss it?"

"Fuck you, John. You don't want to discuss anything—you just want to prove what a badass you are."

John accepted his badass remark with an indifferent, blatant smirk. Mike jerked angrily, and Clyde's grip tightened. He didn't attempt any further resistance as they began walking with him in tow.

They turned down the next alley, and about midway Clyde slammed him against a building near a garbage can overflowing with the nauseating smell of various foods permeating in the California heat.

A tabby cat hissed at their unexpected presence, shy of humans and fast as lightening, she surrendered her unsafe territory followed in speedy succession by two black and several multi colored kittens.

The alley cats found refuge escaping down cement steps that led to the basement of a South Street diner.

"So, Christi has herself a half-breed boyfriend," John said in a shrewdly, conversational tone. "You should have told me."

"I don't know where you're goin' with this or where you're comin' from Burton, but why would I tell you anything concerning Chris?"

"You must know how I feel about your little sister," he insisted with an ironic grin. "Did she tell you about the party we had in the basement?"

Mike struggled against the strong grip that held him, feeling like a rag doll in Clyde's massive hands.

John chuckled softly. "What? Did she say it wasn't good for her?"

"Go to hell."

John stepped aside and Carl moved in. For the pleasure of telling John to go to hell, he took a sharp punch in the gut. John casually lit a cigarette. "So, is it true that Christi is planning a little trip out of town?"

"You have nothing to do with my sister or her life," he said with hard emphasis. "Maybe you don't hear well, I said, go to hell, Burton."

As soon as the words were out, Carl's fist connected with his face. He knew this could prove to be brutal, but they would pay eventually, he knew that, too.

* * *

Christi stood gasping in dismay. Carl had just entered the living room with Mike in tow, Mike's battered face bloody and bruised. She ran toward him, but John caught her in his arms.

"It took some persuasion, but Mike finally told me you planned on leaving without saying goodbye." He smiled wryly, his mocking grin making her hate him more than she ever had before, most especially for what he did to Mike.

"I know you're meeting Billy, you just have to tell me when and where."

Less than a minute passed before John looked toward Mike folded over on the sofa. "I have little patience. Tell me where you're going to meet him."

Carl jerked Mike's head back, his other hand clenched in a tight fist.

"Leave him alone," she cried. "I'll tell you."

Mike couldn't stand anymore. She couldn't bear to see him hurt even if he could stand it.

When Carl released him, he fell over on the sofa moaning in agony.

"Now you're being reasonable." The grip on her arm tightened. "Give it up, baby-doll."

"You are such a coward John Burton," she said, hoarsely.

"Don't come up with too many cute remarks, Christi." He bent her hand at the wrist, and she gasped at the sudden pain. "Now, tell me—without the opinionated comments, where you plan on meeting that bastard half-breed."

"I can't," Christi said miserably. "Please . . ."

He released her hand. "You have no choice."

She looked at him through tear filled eyes, but his cool vibes remained intact. Her emotions had no affect. He seemed beyond any reach, he always had. She took a trembling breath. "You can't seriously expect me to—"

"Christi, I am deadly serious."

She floundered in agonizing uncertainty. If she gave Billy up to John, he might kill him. Then she looked at Mike, his pain-wracked body vulnerable to Carl's attack. "He's picking me up here at six," she whispered.

"So, it's close time. Why don't we meet him at his place instead?"

He propelled her out the door. "Carl," he said over his shoulder. "Have Mike call Billy. Tell him Chris is on the way."

John had gotten a vehicle somewhere. He opened the back door of a maroon Chevy. "Get in."

Clyde sat in the driver's seat.

"How did you know?" she said as he slid in beside her.

"His ex-girlfriend," he replied indifferently. "She told me about you and Billy last year, too, when you first got together. That's what prompted our little party in the basement," he informed her, his face impassive as ever with the occasional hint of an arrogant grin. "I couldn't take the thought of him having you without getting a taste."

The information came as little surprise, but Christi felt sickened. She had recognized that Susan was a spiteful person, but had not expected her malice would ever hurt Billy.

"Have you ever loved anyone, John? Why do you have so much hate?"

"Can it, girl," he said without a glance. "I know you love the guy, but I don't want to hear it."

When they arrived at the apartment building, he pushed her through the doorway into the hall. "If you say anything to indicate that you didn't bring us willingly, Chris, I'll kill him just for kicks."

She led him up the wooden stairs, praying for a miracle, for some of the gang to be there, for something, anything to prevent what was about to happen. Billy was alone in the apartment.

With Clyde being a large man and having the advantage of surprise, he didn't stand a chance. Christi backed against the wall as Clyde pounded him.

"That's enough," John said.

Clyde held him firmly in place, a mountain of a man who could not be budged. Billy looked at her. "Are you all right, Chris? Has he hurt you?"

John moved directly in front of her. Christi forced her eyes to meet his triumphant gaze. He had control, and he knew it.

He put his arms around her, sort of smiled, and then pressed his lips firmly on hers. Their eyes remained open, staying locked for the duration of the so-called kiss.

When he broke the embrace, he continued to gaze into her eyes. "She set you up, little man," he said casually. "Don't you know when you been had?"

"What's going on?" Billy demanded. "Christi, say something!"

"You should have known better." He continued the taunting. "Did you forget who she is? Dave Temple's little sister."

John turned to look at Billy, disregarding her for the moment.

"I know who she is," Billy muttered, wiping blood from the corner of his mouth. He looked hard at her, the face of the man she loved turned dark and angry. She lost all hope that John's tactics would not deceive him.

Christi averted her gaze, unwilling to see reflected in Billy's eyes what he thought of her now.

John had achieved his purpose with his casual innuendo, his blatant lies, with every well-placed action, all a convincing strategy.

"Take him out." John turned his attention to Christi as they left through the back door that led to the alley. "Billy Boy would gladly have killed you with his bare hands." John Burton, her bane and tormentor, tilted her face up with one finger placed beneath her chin. "You did real good, baby," he said, patting her face in mock affection.

She turned away, but he gripped her chin forcing her to look at him.

"I won't be long," he said impassively. "Don't try to run. I can find you."

He walked out. Christi collapsed on the sofa venting pent up emotions in a flood of tears. She had watched their love disintegrate before her very eyes, and John would return, he did not make idle threats—on that intolerable thought, her tears abated with fierce determination that she would not just sit here waiting for him.

Christi rummaged in an old desk drawer for pen and paper. She knew of a safe location, and Danny had been there several times. Thankful that he lived across the hall, she scribbled a hurried note to Billy's cousin and slid it under his door before rushing out into the street.

She ran to a cab cruising slowly by, digging in her jeans for the money Mike had given her. After giving the cabby directions to Dawn's beachfront property, Christi leaned back in her seat. Her stomach twisted with anxiety for her brother—and for Billy.

She disregarded her first despairing thoughts. Billy's furious look had only been a reflection of John's deception, but what would Clyde do to him under John's direction?

The beating that had led to the night they met had been near fatal. Would John finish him this time? She felt an abrupt rush of anxiety, and prayed again, that there would be some sort of intervention.

Unable to deal with hopelessly negative aspects, Christi crowded the defeating images to the farthest corners of her mind.

When they reached the destination, she paid the driver, and then hurried down the gentle slope that led to a golden beach. She kicked off her shoes to walk barefoot through the warm sand.

Christi glimpsed upward at dark gray clouds moving in to block a blue sky, but at least they had a shimmer of the proverbial silver lining—suddenly the sun streamed through, sunbeams filtering down like a promising beacon.

The air smelled fresh and sort of fishy. She loved the smell of the ocean, the sound of the waves breaking on the shore, the beauty that nature supplied free of charge to any who chose to walk along the seashore day or night.

Dark clouds passed over the sun, and a chilly breeze whipped up along with the darkening atmosphere. A light shiver passed over her as cool misty rain began to fall. She quickened her pace toward Dawn's beach house.

Christi turned on the stereo trying to relax, but the music only gave a backdrop to the racing images in her mind as her thoughts kept jumping. How serious were Mike's injuries? Did he need to go to the emergency room? Was there internal bleeding or anything else life threatening? Knowing John's callousness, concern for Billy's life left her weak with anguish, reflecting on how they had been so close to getting away. She could not erase the hurt and anger on Billy's face, the emotional turmoil. How could it have come to this?

The minutes ticked by remarkably slow. She walked aimlessly around the room, sat down on the sofa, and then stood to pace restlessly. An hour crept by. What would Dave do when he found out about this, because now he surely would! He would be angry, and saddened, and hate Billy even more.

She sat back down, dozed without meaning to, then snapped awake, her thoughts racing first to her injured brother and then to how disappointed Dave would be when he found out she had been running away! Then to Billy again, she needed to know he was all right, Danny would know, and she would know too, as soon as he arrived.

The door opened. Christi sat up, a flood of relief washed over her when she saw Billy enter the room, but her relief turned to dread as she recognized anger burning in his eyes. He crossed the room quickly, his large hands gripping her upper arms, Billy pulled her roughly up.

"You're hurting me," she said faintly, dazed by his action.

"You don't know the meaning of the word," he gritted.

"Billy, please tell me what happened."

His hands felt like iron clamps tightening, his fingers digging into her flesh. Christi didn't struggle, knowing it would only incite anger.

"How did you get away from John?"

"Surprised?" he asked heatedly.

He raised his hand and struck her abruptly, a stinging backhanded blow across her face that sent her reeling backward onto the sofa. She stared at him, stunned and frightened.

Gripping the front of her blouse, he hauled her up, dragging her savagely against him. Christi pushed ineffectually against his wide chest, held tight, immobile, and infuriatingly helpless, he took her mouth with harsh intensity.

He released her suddenly, stepping away with a contemptuous look.

Tears found their way slowly down her cheeks as she realized the irony of Billy safe in her sight, so near she could touch him, but sadly inaccessible.

Her eyes riveted in astonishment to the swift appearance of his knife as the blade clicked into place, intimidating and terrifying.

"The thought of you being with him is enough to make me want to kill you." His voice trembled with emotion.

"I would never betray you!"

He pressed the tip of the blade to her skin right where the pulse beat in her throat. Christi felt pressure and held her breath, staring into wide, blazing eyes as endless seconds ticked by, afraid that anything she might say could antagonize him.

In many ways, it did not seem real, but she made herself accept the cold reality of a steel blade at her throat, in the hands of a man she couldn't recognize.

When he tossed the knife aside, Christi felt intense relief, even though his eyes still held a disturbing shimmer.

"All this time," he said, his voice distant. "You made me believe in love again, but it was just a dirty little game."

Christi opened her mouth to deny the accusation but something in his wild sapphire eyes silenced her. She stood speechless with no defense against his extreme anger, because in his mind there was no defense. His fingers dug into her arms again, callously painful.

"You lying, whoring slut!"

The words slammed her, shocking beyond measure.

Billy shoved her back on the sofa. He strode decisively across the room, leaving with a resounding slam of the door.

She huddled where he left her, arms wrapped around her legs. A feeling of sadness settled all around. What had happened here? Why had he been so completely unresponsive? What made him so unyielding?

She had never seen such fury in him, had not realized the possibility of him ever hitting her. Bombarded with ceaseless questions, aching with an inner pain, Christi drifted in exhausted but restless sleep.

The door opened. Christi awoke instantly; tense in expectation of more undue anger from the man she had thought loved her. When she saw Danny, she sat up, relieved and thankful. He sat next to her releasing a tired sigh.

Tilting her face up, he examined the damage, concern emanating in his gentle look. "Did Billy do this?" Danny caressed her arm where Billy had gripped so tight that bruises were beginning to form there also.

She nodded. "Will he hate me forever?"

Danny looked into her eyes affectionately. "Billy doesn't hate you." He gave her shoulder a gentle, reassuring squeeze. "He loves you, Chris, of that much, I am certain."

His assurance didn't quite dispel her doubts. She couldn't get over the wild-eyed anger, the hateful words. The actual threat he had posed.

"Tomorrow when the two of you have a chance to talk this out, everything will be resolved," he said with unrelenting confidence. "It was only luck that Susan told one of the guys she thought Billy might be in trouble, and they'd better look for him. I wonder how she knew."

"It had nothing to do with luck," Christi said heatedly. "Susan told John we were leaving."

Danny looked genuinely bewildered. "I knew she had a thing for Billy, but I had no idea she was capable of something like that."

"I had an idea," Christi replied, her tone conveying the newly developed derisive feelings for Susan Shaffer. "That's cunning, isn't it, telling John about us, then tipping the Monarchs?"

She heard Danny's disturbed sigh and hoped she had dispelled any feelings of friendship he might have had toward Susan Shaffer as disillusion.

"Come on," he said, seeming to have recovered from the surprising news, consequentially dismissing Susan. "Let's go see Mike. He'll be worried if I don't get you home."

She sat straight up. "Carl was with Mike when we left," she said, in a rush of panic. "Do you think he's all right? He was hurt so bad! What if—"

"It's all right," he interrupted smoothing her hair away from her flushed face. "Mike is alone now, and he seems to be okay. After reading your note, I stopped by to tell him that I was on my way to pick you up."

She breathed a sigh of relief. "Thank you."

"Come on." Danny started to stand, but she stopped him with a hand on his arm.

"No, wait." She sighed again bombarded with mixed feelings, wanting to go to Mike but needing some time.

"Could you tell him for me that I'm all right?" she asked eagerly. "I just need to think about what happened and try to make sense of it."

"You can't make sense of it, baby love, Billy wasn't himself tonight."

Noticing a concerned tone in his voice, she glanced at him uneasily.

"He did some drugs, really dangerous drugs, Christi."

"That's why he seemed like a different person."

"Believe me, he was. Josh told me—" Danny shook his head wearily. "He hasn't done this since he met you."

"Then, I'm hopeful that tomorrow will bring a new perspective."

"You bet it will, now let's go."

"No, Danny, I want to stay the night, anyway. I don't really want to go back to the apartment right now." She managed a quick, tentative smile. "Could you pick me up in the morning, say about ten? Is that too early?"

"Not at all, I doubt I'll sleep tonight, anyway, but why, Chris?"

She gave him another timid smile. "I need to be alone for awhile," she offered. "Would you tell Mike? He'll understand; he knows me so well."

"I'll tell him."

"Thanks, Danny."

"Get some rest, okay?"

She could see reluctance in his eyes, but he left.

Christi lay down on the sofa letting her body relax even though her mind wandered over the day's events. Why had Billy resorted to the use of drugs?

Would tomorrow bring a new perspective? She wanted to believe so, but she wondered what effect his actions might have on their relationship, if their love would suffer or if she could easily forgive. How would she feel to face him after he had treated her so cruelly?

Emotional fatigue settled heavily on her with the grim contemplations, and she fell asleep almost immediately.

When the door opened, she sat up groggily.

John and Carl entered the room and she stood, feeling a bit disoriented.

"You just went a little pale," John goaded. "Problem, Christi?"

She looked past him at Carl, feeling sudden fear, wanting to run, knowing there was no place to run, no escaping the menace of John Burton.

"I don't believe you!" she fumed as anger infused her fear. "How can you be so flippant?"

"What is it you don't believe, Christi?" he asked on the dangerous edge of anger that she knew so well. "Are you really surprised that I found your little hideaway? I told you not to run."

"Why don't you leave me alone?"

"I have plans for you," he said, taking a slow step. "A life you never imagined in your wildest dreams."

Christi shivered, feeling a rise of terror with John's intimidating threat. Remembering Billy's discarded knife, she swooped down, grabbed the switchblade and brandished it in front of her, boldly facing him.

"You have plans for me? You can forget them. I have had it! I'm through being afraid of you."

"You're not afraid of me?" He took another step.

"Stay where you are or I will kill you. John, I swear I will."

He took another step, his expression fathomless.

"I know you'd like to, but you can't." His eyes never wavered. "There's no doubt in my mind that you would if you could," he said feigning sorrow, drawing ever closer. "But a knife is a slow weapon, Chris, even when you know how to use it, and baby, you don't know the first thing about knives."

Overwhelmed by the torment he had put her through the past year, filled with angry humiliation at Billy's treatment of her, and that was John's doing, she felt capable of murder. The rage ran deep. Killing John Burton in self-defense would not bother her in the least.

Christi tried to connect her brain with the weapon in her hand and what to do to counteract his stealthy approach.

She felt frozen in time, unable to even react to his final advance as he took her to the floor in a swift move, her wrist clamped firmly in his grasp.

"I think I liked you more when you were afraid of me," he murmured.

The knife dropped from her helpless fingers.

"Could you at *least* tell me why you're so hell-bent on destroying my life?" she demanded.

"It's nothing personal. It's just that you're so damn convenient."

"Convenient? You're a liar." Christi stopped struggling. "Why do you hate me, John?"

"I don't—you hate me, remember?"

"Will you please get off me?"

"No, I think I like it right here."

He pushed her arms above her head, kissing her lips fervently.

"If I had time, I'd rape your little ass right now," he whispered.

Christi didn't respond, afraid of what might provoke him. She didn't whimper or flinch as he pressed his body against hers. She despised him silently.

After several terrifying seconds, John glanced over his shoulder.

"We don't have all night."

Carl came around the sofa. "It's ready."

Christi saw the needle. John tightened his grip on her as Carl secured a thick band around her arm. Then John took the needle. Carl held her struggling hard, but ineffectually. She went limp as the needle pierced her skin. John slowly pushed the syringe, sending the drug she feared more than any other, the one she had always considered most deadly coursing swiftly through her blood stream.

John looked into her eyes. He waited . . . giving it time . . .

Christi looked at him, feeling the effect of the narcotic.

With a vague hint of satisfaction, he released her.

"Get up," he said softly.

She turned on her side, wanting to escape the desirable result of the shot.

John took her by the arm, pulling her up.

"Where are you taking me?" she demanded, ending on a note of dwindling enthusiasm, realizing that maybe she didn't want to know.

"You don't have to concern yourself about that," he told her, firmly grasping her arm, helping her to remain erect as they walked the stretch of beach. "See, I know what it takes to make you feel good, then you get a little more until you get used to it, then a little more until, soon enough, you won't be concerned about much at all, except how to accommodate your addiction."

The rain had not lasted, the breeze felt cool and comforting. The clouds had dispersed, leaving the night luminous with stars and moonlight.

What a beautiful night, Christi thought listlessly—for such a hideous nightmare.

Chapter Twenty-Four

Dawn walked quickly, anxious to reach her destination. She had passed through various nightlife districts on the way here, some bright and lively, some darker and not so rousing. This area had an ominous quality, a tangible insidious aura, very different in the dark.

Turning the next corner, Dawn came to an abrupt stop, feeling somewhat confronted. As she viewed the entrance of the Blue Haze Tavern at midnight, she experienced a sensation of fascination and mild wonder.

Something about it seemed mysteriously inviting, it made her edgy.

Dawn took a prolonged moment to summon her determination and push aside the unexpected apprehension, before entering the heavy atmosphere, quickly but avidly, scanning the bar-crowd.

A paunchy bartender gave her a curious look as he set a beer down in front of a tough-looking straggly man who cast a glance her way.

She glimpsed a couple in a booth making out like they were in a private room, and another couple on a greasy looking wooden dance floor doing a slow grind to the music of an old jukebox.

As her eyes further adjusted to the lighting, she spotted Van at the counter in back of the long room. When someone gave a low wolf whistle and vulgar remarks reached her ears, she saw him glance her way, then turn back to his drink, unperturbed.

Dawn ignored her surroundings, walking purposefully toward Van Morrison, when suddenly a man reached out, grabbed her with strong hands pulling her close to his foul-smelling body. She pushed away, surprised and angry at the intrusion of the common stranger.

"Let me—go!" She twisted in his grasp, trying not to gag at the smell of sour beer, and overwhelming body odor. Her resistance met with mocking snickers as he easily retained her.

Bending one arm behind her back, he held her face with a large hand kissing her slovenly, forcing her lips open as she gagged and struggled, maneuvering enough to manage a hard kick to the shin, hoping to escape.

His hold didn't loosen. He released her mouth to trail a wet line along her neck and shoulder, applying pressure to her arm.

"Do that again, I'll break it, bitch." He pulled her tighter, his free hand squeezing her hip.

She pushed ineffectively against the wide, firm chest feeling a mixture of anger and deep humiliation, along with the pain, wondering about this strange place where a man could molest her and act like he had every right to—this couldn't be Preston City—not her town.

A few men approached them. Her heartbeat quickened in stark fear as her mind registered the significance of their actions. They were isolating her, men from the bar forming a semicircle around them, so he could force her toward the booths in a darker area in the back.

Shocked by the extent of their depravity, Dawn looked at them leering at her, pressing closer. She swallowed the plea that rose in her throat, biting down hard on her lower lip experiencing deep misery, resisting the urge to beg for mercy, trying to maintain any bit of dignity that remained.

"She's with me."

The quiet but dominant voice came from behind them. When the vulgar man glanced irritably around, his hold let up enough that she managed to tear herself away. He grumbled menacingly, glaring with glazed hostile eyes.

"It's your choice," Van said mildly, casting him an unconcerned look.

After a tense moment, the crass low-life stranger turned reluctantly away, cursing under his breath. He ambled back to the bar followed by the others.

Van held her wrist firmly, pulling her along behind him, away from the curious eyes in the barroom to the sidewalk out front where he released her.

She looked at him, afraid to trust herself to speak, diffident but also livid, knowing he could have prevented what happened from the beginning.

Dawn wiped her mouth with the back of her hand. A light shudder passed over her body. She didn't try to talk at first, knowing she would stammer in her frustration, she took a breath, struggling to regain composure.

"That man was—he was—" Another shiver passed over her. "He was—"

"Hideous?" Van suggested blandly.

"Yes, hideous! Why did you allow that to happen?" she demanded dragging her hand across her lips again.

"It was fun to watch." His voice, low and sensual sent an unwelcome ripple of awareness through her, but she summoned enough resentment to give him a look of pure hostility for his callous remark.

"I can't think of a word to describe your vulgarity."

"What?" he said, with no attempt to conceal his vague amusement at her expense. "Don't I even get a thank you for saving your little posterior?"

"You're despicable."

"I see you came up with a word to describe my vulgarity," he said coolly.

"You don't have to be so mean. I had to talk to you."

"You're a silly little girl for walking into a place like that half-dressed, or even walking in there at all, what were you thinking?"

"I wasn't thinking very clearly, I guess."

"And I can't sympathize with such a reckless act." He took hold of her arm again. "Over here."

She could have shrugged off his hand, but followed compliantly. He led her into the alley, pressing her gently against the building. He looked her over unhurriedly, his dark gaze moving down her body and then up like a velvet touch, lingering on her lips.

Dawn's heart thumped painfully. She felt completely uncomfortable under his scrutiny and still annoyed that he had allowed what happened to her in that bar of his—his hangout. What right did he have? Who did he think he was, anyway?

He raised his eyes from the leisure assessment, to meet hers. She looked steadfastly at him even though she felt completely intimidated, on display. She had never experienced such a vulnerability to anyone in her life.

"Do you like what you see, Mr. Morrison?"

Her voice wavered as the total helplessness of her position settled in. Standing outside a dirty bar in a filthy neighborhood, longing for the sweet, clean smell of Woodland Drive, the attempt at sarcasm failed miserably.

His hands on her shoulders, he bent toward her. Dawn felt helpless to avoid what she knew was about to happen, she wasn't at all sure that she wanted to avoid it. He kissed her, a surprisingly gentle touching of his lips that left her feeling off balance as his hands slid down her arms, moving in an easy motion to her waist.

"I like it," he said with casual approval.

Dawn stood transfixed, unprepared for the warm feeling the simple kiss had evoked. She wanted to be angry, knew that she should counter his suave remark. Instead a warm confusion infused her, she felt infuriatingly timid, and way too mindful of his hands moving up and down the bare skin between her shorts and halter.

She could tell he enjoyed the underlying confusion, vulnerability, and the ripple of emotions passing over her. She didn't like it but determined not to comment. Words meant to ridicule him would probably serve to enhance her sensitivity anyway.

"So, what is it you want, then?" he finally inquired.

His voice came to her smooth, almost lazy, his gratification unmistakable.

"I want some pills," she said raising her head. "Uppers or speed—prescription speed," she added, hopelessly aware that she did not sound the least bit streetwise.

"You do," he commented with a hint of reservation.

"Yes, I do. Is that so unusual?"

"I don't know, Dawn." His hands slipped up her arms bringing her closer as he spoke her name with such intimacy. Then he held her face gently in his hand. The firmness of this kiss sent a shock wave through her entire body.

A lost and frightened feeling tightened her throat with emotion.

"You're being way too presumptuous," she managed.

"Maybe, but you're a strong temptation."

He gave her a long, thoughtful look, then led her out of the alley to a silver Corvette parked at the curb. When he opened the door, Dawn gazed at the beauty of it, breathed deeply of the rich smell. New cars were nil, of course, but this car left her breathless.

"What's wrong?" he said, as she hesitated.

"Aren't you afraid I'll get your car dirty?"

"Get in the car, kid," he said dispassionately.

Dawn obeyed without further comment, but when he climbed in the driver's seat, she gave him a cold stare. "Don't call me kid."

"Then don't act like one. Does your mother know you're out?" he added.

"What do you know about my mother?" she snapped hiding her uneasiness.

He turned the ignition key, pulled away from the curb, then accelerated. She grasped the dash for support, suppressing an urge to tell him to slow down.

"I'm surprised you made it to the bar without getting raped in an alley." His disregard of her question left her vaguely annoyed, but when he glanced at her again, the look expressly admiring, Dawn felt something different, an unwelcome something that she shouldn't feel at all.

"Isn't it past curfew?" he goaded.

Annoyed again, she wondered why he chose to provoke her.

"What do you care?" she retorted. "I'm almost nineteen."

"Old enough to make your own mistakes?"

"Old enough to do what I want to."

"Oh? Can I do what I want to?"

"I have the impression that you do," she replied still feeling indignant.

"So, when's your birthday—almost nineteen?"

"Why do you want to know?"

He grinned and accelerated.

Dawn looked out the window . . . wondering . . . He had kissed her, twice, nothing to him, maybe, but he had certainly stirred something within her.

Chancing a quick glance, she realized that he posed a threat she had not even thought to consider. In spite of his self-satisfying attitude, the man personified appeal. While contemplating the will it would take to resist the magnetism of Van Morrison, she still had to wonder if he would eliminate her should a higher authority deem it necessary.

Dawn almost moaned aloud, but tampered the dread with conscious effort, drawing comfort in the knowledge that Christi thought so much of Van. She trusted him explicitly.

The ride didn't last long. They sped out of the insidious neighborhood to familiar streets, soon zipping past the tall pillars into the drive and around to the front door of her home, coming to an incredibly smooth stop.

"I took the liberty of finding out where you live," he explained to her quizzical expression. "A princess in a castle, no less."

She didn't thank him. His comment left her cold. She opened the car door, but turned back inquisitively when he gently took hold of her arm.

He softly kissed her, a teasing brush of his lips. She found herself helpless to pull away and wondered at his captivating affect, his ability to quickly break down barriers she had thought were secure.

"I'll be here tomorrow at six," he murmured, his mouth still close.

"What makes you so sure I'll go out with you?"

"What makes you so sure I want you to?" he countered. "Speed—right?"

"Well, because of—because—" Dawn had no answer. The request for drugs had slipped her mind.

He grinned at her in a way that tugged at her resisting heart. "Because I've taken certain liberties?" He quirked an eyebrow, very cute.

She exited the car wanting simply to be away from him.

"Dawn?"

She turned curiously. He had opened the window.

"I want you to."

"You do?"

"Will you?"

"Maybe."

"Yes or no?"

"Depends."

"This is not a trick question."

"You're sure?"

"Yes, Dawn, I want to take you dancing."

"Okay, then."

"Six o'clock." Shifting his pretty silver car into gear, Van rounded the drive, roaring like a lion onto the quiet streets of Woodland Drive.

She smiled to herself. The first step of her plan had been almost too easy. Well, not too easy, she amended, the man at the bar had been deplorable, but once in Van's company, getting the date had been—too easy.

Dawn began to consider that he knew her name without introductions, had asked if her mother knew she was out, and he knew where she lived. Just how much did he know? Did he know that she didn't even use drugs? He probably knew her birth date, too.

How could she have been so blind? That he had obviously been watching her as closely as she had been watching him had eluded her in the wake of distress after the bar experience, that he knew so very much about her came as a disturbing surprise, and that she seemed so pliable in his hands had its own disturbing aspects.

Chapter Twenty-Five

Mike didn't want to move. After a shower, he fell asleep on the sofa, and the pain settled deep and silent. Another loud rapping on the door followed by a booming announcement that it was the Preston City Police made the decision unavoidable.

He sat up slowly, moving carefully, he walked unsteadily to the hallway.

Mike opened the door, wearily leaning on it, examining the faces of the two officers, his gaze resting on Officer Jamison. He knew with dizzying foreboding that something had happened to Christi.

"What happened?" he said faintly.

"Mike, I'm sorry, but we have some bad news," Jamison said. "Your sister's been in a serious accident . . ."

He stared at the officers, his hand gripping the doorknob.

"We'll take you to the hospital."

Mike noticed Officer Jarred candidly observing his bruised face and painful stance. "You need medical attention . . . Who did this to you, son?"

"I'm okay."

"You are clearly not okay."

He glanced at his watch, nearly two a.m. "I'm all right," he insisted. "Give me a minute."

He went into the living room where he wrote a quick note for Dave in case he came home.

"Two boys heading out for some night fishing found her," Jamison told him as they started down the stairs.

"How is my sister?"

"We don't know. The doctors should have some information soon," he offered half-heartedly. "It seems she fell or was pushed from a speeding car and rolled over an embankment."

At the hospital, a doctor talked to Mike while the police stood by.

"Christi is unconscious and it doesn't look good," Dr. Hamilton told him. "If those boys hadn't found her, she would have been dead by morning."

"Do you know anything about this?" Officer Jamison asked.

"John Burton's responsible, along with Clyde Bauer and Carl Howell."

Officer Jarred wrote the names. "We'll put out an APB."

"Good luck with that," he murmured as Jarred walked away.

"Are they the ones who hurt you?" Officer Jamison asked gently, for the first time acknowledging Mike's bruised face.

"Yes. They forced me to bring them to my sister." Mike blinked away tears that stung his eyes. He felt hopelessly responsible.

An intense looking middle-aged man in scrubs approached. "You must be Michael," he said cordially. "Christine's twin brother?"

Mike turned his attention from Officer Jamison. "Yes, I'm Mike."

"I'm Dr. Kline," he introduced himself before looking around curiously. "We need her guardian. He should be here. Where *is* he?"

Mike didn't miss the emphasis. He felt defensive, but defenseless. "I'm not sure. How is Christi?"

"Your sister isn't regaining consciousness," he said directly, then with a look of belated compassion. "There are internal injuries, also. She needs immediate surgery. Can you locate David?"

"I—I have a couple of numbers I could call."

"Write the numbers down." He gave Mike a prescription pad and pen.

"If he's not home by now, he's either at Corey's Supper Club or at Van's." Mike wrote the numbers. He returned the pad and pen to Dr. Kline.

"Okay, young man, while we attempt to reach your brother—" The doctor wrote on the pad he had given to Mike. "I want you to take this to x-ray."

"I'm all right," Mike insisted.

"Is that so? Does this hurt?" The doctor touched with enough pressure where he stood holding his aching side to bring the pain into sharp focus.

Mike couldn't avoid grimacing. "Not—much."

"What I suspected." He tore off the sheet. "Go now," Dr. Kline said firmly, leaving no room for compromise.

Dave paused uncertainly in the vestibule of Preston General. He noticed a closed gift shop to his left, and on the right a cafeteria, also obviously closed for the night.

He looked up front to the main lobby, where a few people sat reading magazines, while others stared at an all-night station on the television. None of them appeared very anxious.

Dave felt anxious and conspicuous as hell as he walked to the counter where a sign read 'information'. The receptionist looked up inquisitively before recognition flickered deep within her clear brown eyes.

He recognized her, also, as the girl who had come to the Basement that long ago night. Van had not hesitated to move to her defense against John Burton and his psycho buddies, while he sat idly by, not caring enough, justifying their actions with the simple fact that she had carelessly entered in—the wrong place at the wrong time.

Nancy Castell. He committed to memory the name on her ID.

"My sister was brought here—she was in an accident."

"Name, please?"

"Christine Temple," he replied feeling agitated and restless.

Nancy Castell presented an understanding smile. "You're David Temple, of course. It's good you're here . . . I've been expecting you. Come with me, please." She stood, walking briskly around her desk.

"What happened?" he asked feeling desperation.

"I'm sorry, I don't know any specifics," she said gently, leading him toward the elevators.

"What can you tell me?" Dave had a dreaded feeling of dependency, lost and frightened as a six year old abandoned in a huge, unfamiliar facility.

"They need you to sign papers for admittance and surgery immediately," she explained, turning right. "I'm sorry, I don't know the details of her condition," she added with an apologetic glance. "I'm sure a doctor will speak with you soon."

They reached the admitting office where she deposited him leaving unobtrusively.

"Thank you." The calm of his voice belied his emotions. He felt ready to sink into depths of despair as she walked away.

They hurried him efficiently through the signing of the necessary papers. It was Christi's life—*imperative that you get here.* What had happened?

Finished with admittance, he was told to go to the second floor.

Dave glanced around indecisively before noticing an open door up the hall. He walked indolently toward the waiting room, wondering how much time he would have to spend here, to walk these hollow halls with a mixture of acutely pungent smells and the palpable sensation of fear in the air.

Hospitals reminded him of sickness and death. He took a deep breath to refocus—recovery, hospitals can be places of recovery—not necessarily death. Not death at all—healing. *Hospitals are healing institutions.*

Dave took a seat in one of the semi comfortable chairs. He lit a cigarette, blowing smoke sullenly into the air.

His mind wandered uncomfortably back over the past year and a half. He felt an urge to put his hands around John Burton's throat and squeeze. The desire hit with such intensity that his hands convulsed.

John was responsible, he knew it, but if he had listened to his sister a long time ago this may never have happened, so he felt a degree of responsibility by being involved with John in the first place.

"Excuse me."

His thoughts interrupted by a gentle voice, Dave looked up at the familiar receptionist. "I asked to be relieved," she explained. "I thought you might like some coffee."

"That's thoughtful of you," he said, distractedly accepting the cup.

"It's not hospital coffee," she said, with a friendly, appealing smile. "We have a coffee maker in our lounge. It's fresh."

Her hands fluttered for a moment before she clasped them in front of her.

"I'm sorry about your sister," she murmured.

"She'll be all right." He struggled, hearing the panic in his own voice.

"We have excellent staff," she told him confidently.

A dangerously obstinate sensation assailed him, excellent staff? Right, except nothing was right about here. It was all wrong, unreal, an outlandish mistake. Dave took a breath—he needed to shake off the hostile feeling.

After a brief hesitation, in the stillness of the room, he heard a soft sigh.

"I'd better get back to my station."

"Wait," he said as she turned to leave. "Thanks for the coffee."

"It's okay—you already thanked me," she smiled.

"No, Nancy, wait."

She turned back, a flowing pivot, elegant as a ballerina. He took a moment to appreciate her slender beauty and graceful movement.

"Nancy, would it be all right if I call and talk to you sometime?" He looked around feeling a sense of confusion, stifled by the cold, impersonal atmosphere. "There's a lot I need to say but this is not the time or place."

"Sure, call me," she said agreeably. "I'm listed."

A doctor stepped in as she walked out. "Are you David Temple?"

He stood. "Yes."

"No, please sit. I'm Dr. Hamilton, the twin's general practitioner," he introduced himself. "Though you're probably unaware of me, I haven't seen them for a while."

Dave looked bleakly at the doctor. It hadn't been spoken as an accusation but it made him feel incompetent as hell, but he had been incompetent as a guardian to his brother and sister. He saw it plainly, now, painfully evident.

"Mike will join you soon. He has some contusions about his ribs and face. He'll be sore, but nothing is broken."

"What happened to Mike?" he asked, confused.

"Your brother was beat up, but he'll mend quickly," Dr. Hamilton assured him, dismissing Mike's contusions. "Your sister's condition, however, is severe. She was prepped for surgery before you arrived, so there should be some news soon. Our most serious concern is that she never regained consciousness. She's been diagnosed as being in a coma."

"A coma?" A coma! He didn't know much about comas, but the word sent fear spiraling through him. It sounded terrifying. "How bad is it?"

"The longer she is under, of course, the more serious it becomes," he explained. "I have to caution about the severity, but I don't want you to despair, most coma patients recover quickly . . . and intact."

"Intact," Dave repeated the word inanely. "When can I see her?"

"You will be notified as soon as she comes out of surgery. You can see her then. In the meantime, try to be optimistic."

Yeah, right. Dave sighed tiredly. "I wasn't ever told what happened."

"Christi jumped or was pushed from a speeding vehicle headed out of Preston in the direction of San Gabriel . . . David, did your sister use drugs?"

"No," he said vehemently, scoffing at the mention of his sister and drugs in the same sentence.

"We found a needle mark in the bend of her left arm."

"Damn, John Burton," he muttered heatedly.

Mike entered the room, beaten, young, looking incredibly vulnerable. Dave felt anger and anguish. Hatred stirred within him.

"Your brother can fill you in," Dr. Hamilton concluded. He left them, the door closing softly behind him.

"So, Mike, tell me, what exactly happened?"

Mike told him the whole story, from Christi's meeting Billy right up to their intentions of running away and John's intrusion on their plans.

Dave couldn't feel anything but grief that Christi had not confided in him about Billy. He had given her no reason to come to him, or to trust him.

"I have to find Danny, or Billy," Mike said. "I tried to call, but no one's home. He needs to know about this."

Dave nodded, Christi and Billy—that would take some getting use to—if she lived, if she recovered unscathed from the incident that had brought them here tonight, Billy would be a part of his life.

His nerves unexpectedly propelled him out of his chair, Dave strode to the window feeling too many emotions, topmost being his own helplessness.

"I'm afraid, Dave," Mike said shakily. "I'm really scared."

Dave turned away from the window. He surveyed his brother grimly, his desolate blue eyes shimmering with unshed tears, his face bruised from the beating he had taken at the hands of John Burton.

"I'm afraid too, Mike," he admitted aching to reach out to him, wanting to give him the assurance he needed, but hopelessly inept to the task.

"I know," Mike said expressly understanding. "And it's okay."

Dave smiled wryly. "Go on, then. Hurry back."

When Mike left, Dave resumed his seat, leaning back and stretching his long legs, crossing them at the ankles. He closed his eyes hoping to relieve the tension that had started to express itself as a throbbing headache.

Christi and Billy together, it explained her growing absence in his life these past months. That absence bothered him now. They had grown apart.

How had it happened? Christmas had been amazing. After the New Year—that's when she began drifting away.

Did she have any idea that he had been breaking connections with the gang? He hadn't realized it at the time, but John making that move on her had affected him. What had happened to their Sundays together? They had dwindled to a few hours here and there. He thought her interests had averted to kids her own age, obviously not.

He and Trixi had gone separate ways, with farewell tears and a distinct ache in his heart. Childhood sweethearts, they had walked the tender years together, and together they had experienced a time of fierce passion with the Cobras—naively believing it would never end, but of course, it did.

Dave opened his eyes as Mike entered the room. Not asleep, not awake, he felt more than weary. Mike handed him a cup of coffee.

"It isn't good, is it?" he said.

"She's still in surgery—" Dave opened his coffee. "Did you find Billy?" he asked as Mike sank into a chair next to him.

"No, but I found Danny. He's looking for him, now."

Mike shivered. It wasn't cold in the room. Dave wanted to say encouraging words, but he felt hopeless. Right now *he* needed a shoulder and Mike wasn't strong enough. He refused to burden him with his despair.

"She's going to be all right, Mike. Our sister is strong. We're strong—remember that." Dave wished he could feel as sure as his spoken words.

"I will, Dave. I'll always remember."

"You better." He placed his hand around the back of Mike's tense neck, massaging heartily and grinning encouragingly. "It's true." Dave felt Mike relax. Withdrawing his hand, he leaned back in the chair trying to believe.

* * *

Danny entered the dank tavern, immediately assaulted by the stench of stale beer and stagnant smoke and the distinct possibility that someone had been sick in one of the side booths. He recognized the lone figure sitting all the way in the back of the dreary bar.

Danny leaned against the counter. "Could you have picked a better dump?" he asked with mild disdain. "This place reeks."

"Hey, Danny Boy," Billy said, his words slurred and inaptly jovial. "D'ya wanna drink? Come'n join the party!"

Danny sighed, wishing there was an easy way to break it to him about Chris, but really, there wasn't. "Christi's been in an accident, Billy."

He waited a moment for some reaction. "Did you hear me? Christi's been in an accident."

"Go 'way. Just leave—leave me alone."

Danny raked his fingers anxiously through his hair. "Am I getting through to you, here?" he asked with deep frustration. "She needs you."

"No she don't," he said grudgingly. "You go be with her."

"What's up with you?" Danny demanded. "What's your problem, man?"

"Not a problem. Simple fact, you're in love with 'er. You always were." Billy turned back to his drink. "Go for it, Danny. You'll be better for her than I'd ever be."

"Billy, stop it!" he seethed. "You have to sober up."

"I don't have to do nothin'."

"Okay, what if I do love her? What if I have since the night we met her? What difference does it make," he said forcefully, jerking Billy around to face him, gripping the front of his shirt in a tight bunch. "Why would you offer her up to me? She's your girl and you know it."

"You gonna hit me now?" Billy asked mildly.

Danny looked at his hands, slowly relinquishing the aggressive hold.

"Christi didn't cross you," he said, evenly. "Susan told Burton that the two of you were leaving together."

"I know that," he said vaguely. "Not about Susie, but I knew Christi wouldn't—I knew, once I took the time to think—"

"You're not the first person to jump to a wrong conclusion," he offered consolingly. "You won't be the last. Let's just get the hell outta here."

Danny wondered what was on Billy's mind as he sat in staid silence. He pushed the rock glass with the remainder of his drink aside, taking a shallow breath, releasing it in a painful sigh.

"I can't face Christi. I can't, not after what I did."

"Billy, she'll forgive you—"

He rested his elbows on the bar, supporting his weary head in his hands. "Before I came here," he choked. "I was with Susan."

"What do you mean? You were with—oh." The realization slowly penetrated. He had never imagined something like that, but Billy had probably beaten himself up over it already. He was hurting. The betrayal of his love had to be a heavy burden.

Danny placed a comforting hand on Billy's shoulder, dreading having to tell him the severity of her condition. "Christi's hurt bad . . . She's in a coma."

Billy raised his head. Their eyes met. "How? What happened?"

Danny told him what little he knew.

"I did that to her," he said bleakly.

"It isn't entirely your fault," Danny said quickly, wanting to shoulder a part of the blame, to make it easier if he could, but also feeling responsible. "I was with her after you. I shouldn't have left her alone."

Billy closed his eyes, swaying precariously on the barstool.

"Are you all right?" Danny asked, steadying him.

"I better go home and clean up. I been here since I left Chris. I mean—after—you know what I mean." His eyes drifted closed again, practically asleep on his feet.

"You do look like hell," Danny observed. "Maybe you should get some rest. We can go to the hospital later."

Billy stood, leaning against him for support.

"The room is spinning," he said, his voice a mere whisper.

"Maybe you better sit back down for a minute," Danny suggested. "You haven't eaten in a while, I'll bet—or slept."

"Oh, well, yeah, not for a day or two—"

Once again, Billy passed into unconsciousness and then came back.

The bartender phoned a taxi for them, and the cabby pulled up in front of the bar within minutes. Danny helped him out to the cab where he promptly slept. At home he half carried him up the stairs.

When Billy fell onto the sofa fully clothed, Danny took his shoes off, so he would be more comfortable. He didn't even mumble.

Danny went to the bedroom for a sheet that he draped over him.

Billy looked so young and defenseless. His face relaxed from the worry of the world, he reminded him more of the sixteen-year-old boy who almost died when he tumbled his motorcycle—young and innocent, yes, but way too knowledgeable.

He shouldn't be surprised that Billy knew how he felt about Chris, knowing how he felt about almost anything had been a knack for him since they were kids. Of course Billy knew, but he had never, and would never act on it. Billy knew that, too.

Danny sat down in a nearby chair. He lit a cigarette, refusing to consider the possibility of Christi dying. Disregarding his own feelings, Billy would be lost without her. His own love had always been secondary, but it was too real to disregard any longer.

* * *

Dave and Mike stood as a doctor entered the room. He introduced himself as Dr. Kline. Mike had already met him.

"Please, please, sit," he said congenially. "Your sister is being set up to monitor. The surgery went well, internal damage was minimal—barring complications—" Drawing out the word until it was almost a question, he paused before going on. "She's young and resilient, no broken bones, a moderate concussion induced a coma, but she should have awakened."

Dave closed his eyes briefly. Yes, the coma. Once more the doctor explained the circumstances, ending with the advice to remain optimistic.

Right now he couldn't even contemplate the aspect of optimism.

"Do you think the drugs caused it?"

He shook his head. "We did a work up right away, it appears the drugs in her system were just enough to induce a mild rush sensation, to more or less introduce her to the drug." Dr. Kline paused a minute for more questions. "Okay then . . . Soon a nurse will be here to show you to her room."

Minutes after Dr. Kline left, the nurse showed up. She escorted them to Christi's room, and then quietly slipped away. Dave approached the bed with more regrets than he cared to contemplate.

A purple bruise showed below her right eye and a small cut above her lip. He tried to make sense of it as he waited for her eyes to open. She looked fragile, pallid, but only asleep—an IV for fluids, and a heart monitor—nothing indicated such a critical condition.

He glanced at Mike. His young brother looked beaten down. Dave felt the weight of this incomparable tragedy, unable to cope himself, completely unprepared to withstand this sorrow, how could he guide Mike through it?

Dave put a comforting arm around him and drew comfort himself.

"We'll get through this," he said determinedly. "We all will."

"I know."

Seconds ticked by forming long minutes. An hour passed as her heart continued a slow, steady beat on the screen.

Dave gazed at Mike with concerned scrutiny. He looked done in, bewildered and frightened. "You go home and get some rest," he said firmly. "I'll stay with Christi."

"I doubt if I could rest."

"There's no point in both of us staying," Dave insisted. "Go home, try to sleep. Come back in a few hours."

Mike stood. He approached the bed feeling the sense of loss.

"Come back to us, Chris. We need you." He swallowed thickly. "I need you—there's a lot to accomplish here, you know, like getting married and having kids. You gotta make me an uncle—I'm not gonna let you go, Chris, I can't."

He took her hand between his, gazing at her, wanting to feel a trace of light, reaching for a slender thread of hope. He sighed forlornly. She was gone from him, he felt nothing, only a lonely emptiness deep inside as his once vibrant sister lay close to death.

As Mike left the hospital, his emotions turned to hostility and depression. He didn't want to go home. He didn't want to be alone. His thoughts turned naturally to Carla. She had always welcomed him when he needed her. Mike needed to be with her now. His considerations didn't reach any further than that one simple fact.

She opened the door with tousled hair and a sleepy smile that quickly dissolved as she noticed his injuries.

"What happened to your face?"

"It's a long story," he said with a tentative grin.

"I've got time," she replied.

"Ah, maybe not so long—Clyde beat me up—I could sure use a drink."

Mike crossed over to the sofa where he relaxed with his head back, eyes closed. He felt weary but not so hostile, now.

He had taken another pain pill. It was working its magic. He felt his mind relaxing to the effect, the pain being buried, hidden away where he couldn't find it.

"Here's your drink," she said.

Carla sat beside him, within stroking distance, tucking one leg beneath her. She gave him a thoughtful look, a teasing grin. Mike wondered what was behind the expression as he downed half the Scotch and coke.

"There seems to be something missing," he remarked frowning into the glass. "Scotch and coke minus the scotch."

Her melodious laughter rang out. Mike caught the reason behind the look.

"I'm not giving you alcohol," she said sweetly. "You're on drugs."

"Yeah, and I don't mind sayin' they're damn good drugs, too." He smiled affably at her. "Guess you're right," he admitted feeling dazed.

Mike looked into her brown eyes, sleepy, dreamy, sexy eyes.

"Thank you for taking care of me, Carla . . . You are amazing, baby."

He traced his finger down the gentle curve of her heart shaped face thinking there could be no one more beautiful in the entire world.

"You are . . . extraordinarily . . . extraordinary," he mused.

"You are on drugs," she said, laughing mildly.

"Extraordinarily . . . beautiful." He planted kisses on her face, neck and shoulder. "And if I may say so, extraordinarily—sensual."

"Oh, you may certainly say so."

The rich fragrance of her exotic scented perfume filled his senses, drawing him closer.

Carla's vibrant smile faded as their eyes met. He traced his fingertip across her lower lip. Running his fingers through her hair, he kissed her fervently, his tongue exploring the familiar velvet warmth of her mouth.

Mike trailed kisses along her bare shoulder, leisurely caressing her seductive body so teasingly assessable through the flimsy material of the negligee. She arched gracefully pressing against his hand.

"Come on, baby," she whispered huskily. She grasped his hand pulling him gently, leading him into the bedroom where she helped him undress.

"Lay down, Mike. Take it easy."

He watched Carla slip the gown over her head bringing into clearer view the shapely beauty of her naked body. Mike reached for her as she lowered herself on the bed next to him, but she shook her head with a seductive smile, pushing him gently backward.

"I said, 'take it easy'."

He relaxed back letting her take the lead, her warm mouth incredibly exciting, creating purely delicious sensations. After a while they made love, not wild and unrestrained, it was slow and easy, tender passion.

"I was afraid I wouldn't be able to make it with those drugs in my system," he said caressing her back. "See, you are amazing."

"No, you're amazing."

She rested in his embrace for a while. She seemed awfully quiet. Then he heard a soft sigh, and she rose up to press her sweet lips to his.

Mike felt something alarming—terribly sad in the touch.

"Carla?" He breathed her name, rising on one elbow to look into her brown eyes surprisingly bright with tears.

"I want you to know, Mike," she said softly. "I want you to understand that what we had—right or wrong, meant more to me than you'll ever know, and what I have to say doesn't come easy."

She left the bed, almost rushing across the room to the window. Pulling the curtain back she viewed the fading night. He wondered why she had become melancholy and what she had to say that didn't come easy.

Most of all, he wondered bleakly why she was talking in the past tense.

"You're the only person in Preston that I've loved, Mike," she said without turning. "I guess you know that."

"I know—I don't know what I would have done without you, Carla."

"There would have been someone for you if I hadn't taken your time," she said in a choked voice. "Someone you could have related to better than me."

"No one could compare," he said feeling a sudden desperation. "You're good for me, Carla. I love you too, you know I do. There's no one—"

"Mike, don't say it." Having composed herself, she turned from the window. "I'm going back to Iowa."

He stared at her baffled. "Don't hit me with this, baby," he whispered.

"Listen to me," she said with painful aspiration. "You've been good for me, too, but this is my last day here, Mike. My life is going nowhere; really, your visits are all I have."

Carla looked at him, love shining in her eyes. "You're a handsome young man. One of these days you'll meet some cute, little teeny-bopper who would put an end to even this."

"It won't happen, baby," he promised wanting more than anything for her to say she would not leave him, would never in a million years leave him.

She walked back to the bed. "You say that now, but you're young."

Carla pressed the palm of her hand gently to his face when he looked up at her. "I want a home, a husband and children."

She sat on the edge of the bed, gently brushing his hair back from his forehead. Tears gathered in her eyes, and he automatically took her into a comforting embrace. She needed comforting, yes, but he needed to hold her, somehow convince her not to go, not to put an end to this relationship that had taken him from boy to man.

This had taken him by surprise, and it was just wrong. Then he realized the trauma of the beating, his sister's accident, or the drugs for pain, any of that could have affected his perception.

"You're not ready for what I want." She smiled fondly. "You're young, wild and free, Mike and that's how it should be. Even if you wanted to tie yourself to me, you'd wonder what you missed—eventually you would."

Mike sighed unhappily, recognizing the wisdom in her words.

He stroked her leg reviewing in his mind the history of her life, a badly neglected child, abused by her stepfather; she ran away from home at the tender age of thirteen, ending up here, tired and broke.

A smooth pimp had picked her up right at the bus station, took her in, won her trust, used her for a while, but eventually put her to work on the darker side of Preston.

She had gotten pregnant, went through a botched-up abortion that nearly cost her life. She worked for no more than a meager living, turning over the majority of her earnings to her abusive pimp, enduring sadists who got their kicks in ways Mike didn't care to contemplate, until the night she met an affectionate older man, Barry Anderson.

Barry had been enchanted with the child, the haunted eyes, and the still sweet expression. He took her off the streets a week before her sixteenth birthday, setting her up in this luxury apartment—Carla became a high-class call girl. *Kindly old pervert,* Mike reflected, but he put an end to the cruelty.

The abusive pimp mysteriously disappeared never to be seen again.

When Barry died of cancer seven years ago, Carla had been left with a wealth of clientele if she wanted to continue working at the oldest profession, or since Barry had no family, he had left her a small fortune; she could well afford to retire. Apparently she was ready to get out of it.

"I got in touch with my aunt in Iowa," she broke into his thoughts. "My mother divorced Mel, and remarried my dad. They want me to come home," she told him smiling through her tears. "I have a twenty year old sister who wants to meet me. I have a family. I need you to understand, Mike."

He knew she was fighting her every instinct in leaving and decided not to make it more difficult. For Carla's sake, he would accept the finality, the end of this brief and passionate love affair.

"You'll find happiness with your family in Iowa," he said, hoping to offer some assurance. "And you'll meet someone to love, I just know it. You'll have a good life," he added, with only a trace of sadness.

"I can't help feeling sorry for myself, though. I don't want to let you go."

He moved a strand of curly blond hair behind her ear. "Would you have left without saying good-bye?" he whispered. "If I hadn't come by this morning, would you have gone away?"

"No," she assured him quickly. "I had decided to wait for you to come see me again. I couldn't bear the thought of you coming to an empty apartment."

"I'm happy for that." He sighed, feeling undeniably sad. "I love you, Carla, I do. I know I'm young, and I understand your reasoning, but don't ever underestimate what you meant to me."

"Sometimes I think I shouldn't have," she murmured. "I feel like—"

"Shhh." He touched her lips with his finger, traced it down her dimpled chin. "Every boy should learn from his own little professional."

He ran his fingers up through her tousled curls and kissed her, enjoying the soft sweet lips for a moment, then looked into her sad, sparkling eyes.

"No more tears, sweetheart, and no regrets . . . except that I can't keep you, my little plaything." He felt whimsical as he regarded her exquisite beauty.

"Did I do you well, baby?" he whispered. "Am I a good lover?"

"A good lover?" Carla gave him a sultry look of desire, pressing him back on the bed. "I taught you well," she said with a sweet smile.

He listened to her soft musical laughter, treasuring the moment, the remnants of a dream that was over. They had played lover's games, enjoyed romantic nights, shared a diversity of sweet emotions, but in all honesty he had known they were not meant to walk through this world together.

Chapter Twenty-Six

As she waited for Jerry, Dawn tried to think of the right words to tell him about her plans to associate with Van Morrison, to discover if he was in any way responsible for the death of their friends, most especially, Carrie.

She decided against telling him exactly how they met. That wouldn't go over well. Dawn knew he would be concerned for her safety and upset, but he would have to accept her decision even though he wouldn't like it.

When Jerry arrived, he followed her to the kitchen where she poured them both a tall glass of iced tea before they settled in the living room.

Since she had decided to omit the gory details of the bar scene, and she had already told him she had something serious to discuss, Dawn kept it short and to the point. First she reminded him about Van Morrison being in Ted's journal; that drew a shrug, but he looked at her like she was crazy when she told him that she had arranged to meet him, finishing with a brief explanation of her intentions.

"You can't be serious," Jerry said in a satirical tone she had never heard before. "Surly you won't follow through with this ludicrous plan."

"My plan is not ludicrous. Jerry, this is important to me." When she noticed a dangerous glint in his intense brown eyes, she pulled reflexively away. "I was hoping you'd understand," she murmured.

"Understand? I understand that you do not seem to have matured since you were fourteen years old, that you do not have full comprehension of the severity of this situation, or you think you're somehow protected from this man because he's attracted to you."

"No, I don't. How can you say that?"

"What were your real objectives for meeting him?" he demanded. "You're not even considering the danger of what you're doing."

His response surprised her, she had expected he would be upset but not like this. He paced back and forth in front of where she sat on the sofa, watching him wearily. Jerry's young, handsome face had gone dark with anger. She found his antagonism disturbing. Her breathing increased, and she felt a terrible tenseness in her body, uncomfortable and unacceptable.

Dawn took a couple of deep breaths determined to gain control of her emotions. If this kept on, she would not have a prayer of standing up to him, something that she had never actually done during their relationship.

"You know what he is," Jerry said stopping to look down at her. "—what you suspect him of doing, but is it actually getting through to you?"

Dawn shifted restlessly under his uncompromising gaze.

"I don't understand your attitude—" she began.

"I won't let you do it," he said decisively, interrupting her, but at least he finally sat down. "You cannot go through with this—this is insanity!"

"This is not insanity." Tears stung her eyes, but she blinked them away, lifting her chin determinedly, if not defiantly. "And you can't stop me."

"No, you're right—I can't save you from yourself or Morrison. I can only, with all sincerity, hope you live to regret it."

"Yeah," she muttered, reticently. "Me, too."

"I seriously don't want you to get hurt," he said solemnly.

"I can take care of myself."

She needed to appear confident, but last night had been harrowing, not something easily forgotten.

His demeanor changed again. "Oh, can you?" he challenged. "Can you, really Dawn? You're an impetuous, immature kid playing a dangerous game. What really attracted you to Van Morrison?"

"I was 'attracted' to him because he was in the journal, because he—"

His hand closed around her arm with considerable pressure. She winced looking at his hand, the grip he had on her. Jerry had never touched her in such a way. "Because he's a little bit dangerous?" he suggested. "Morrison is not a person to play games with."

“I am not an immature kid playing games. Let go of my arm, Jerry!”

She jerked away from him as the hold loosened, then his voice softened.

“Why do you feel like this is something you have to do?”

“I just do,” she stated stubbornly, realizing she had no genuine answer.

Dawn wondered what would be accomplished by her efforts. How could he possibly understand when she could not fully grasp the reasoning herself?

He leaned back on the sofa drawing her close. She closed her eyes resting her head on his shoulder, taking comfort in his embrace.

“You don’t really want to do this, Dawn,” he said, stroking her arm as he spoke quietly. “Seems to me you’re compelled, maybe even obsessed.”

He continued in his persuasive voice until she felt herself being lured away from her conviction. This was not what she intended. She wanted him to offer support, not dissuasion.

“No, Jerry.” Dawn sat up straight, wondering why she thought he might have been comforting her because he cared.

He regarded her with dark eyes, a derisive expression that left her shivering. She swallowed convulsively, her mind spinning bewilderedly, surprised at the affects he had drawn out of her.

“I think you’d better leave, now.” She wrapped her arms around herself. “I need to be alone for a while.”

“How long, Dawn?” he demanded. “How long do you need to be alone?”

“I don’t know.”

“How long will your little venture take?”

“I don’t know that either,” she said honestly wishing he wouldn’t take such a hateful stand. She didn’t want to remember him this way.

“You don’t know how long it will take or even why you’re doing this? Do you think maybe you have a little infatuation going on for Morrison?”

“Please stop,” she said softly. “I’m doing it for Carrie.”

“You’re doing it for your own satisfaction,” he said tightly. “You should at least admit the truth.”

“I’m through trying to explain myself to you.” She straightened herself with dignity. “This ends now.”

“It’s okay, do what you want, because you’re going to anyway, regardless of how I feel about it.” He sighed, and with that soft breath, Dawn realized he had lost composure, too, and had just recovered.

She gave him a quick instinctive kiss. "I'll call," she promised. "I wish you could be on my side. I might need someone—"

"I can't," he interrupted softly. "I can't. Let's just go with that. Call me when you're done with this absurdity."

She walked with him to the door, opened it for him to exit, careful not to touch. She felt alienated from her high school sweetheart. Dawn felt bad, but it was his choice.

"I'm worried about you, Dawn." His voice held a grave note.

"Is that all it is?"

"Take care."

Jerry walked home hoarding dark feelings, agitated with the conflict of despair and hostility that Dawn had provoked. She reminded him of a spoiled little girl who had to have her way. As naïve as she could be at times, and as trusting, she would do exactly as she intended, regardless of his opinion.

Charged with loneliness and anger, he thought of her with Van Morrison, deeply resentful of the man she would be spending her time with. She would probably imagine herself in love with the tall, dark stranger.

She thought she could take care of herself. He knew much better than that. Dawn had always been an innocent in many ways, a child at heart, trusting, but with an adventurous spirit.

She was gone from him, he felt it, and more than saddening him, and it did sadden him, it left him infuriated.

Dawn was supposed to be his, he had their life planned, and if it hadn't been for her friend's death she would have never ventured from his side, in spite of Mike Temple and his constant flirtations with her. That would have passed inevitably.

There could be no good outcome of her actions. Even if she came back eventually, her defiance made him feel like things would never be the same.

* * *

Dawn agonized about what to wear for half the day. She finally chose a chic black mini with gold metallic designs woven through the material. Her gold sling-back pumps were perfect with it.

She sat down at the vanity to look over her assortment of makeup. Using sponges and brushes, she applied just enough to look 'unmade', but more perfect. This she did with an expert hand, having started experimenting with make-up at the tender age of twelve.

Tina had pictures of her first attempts. Dawn smiled at the memories of her little, clown face.

She wore a vintage gold rope necklace borrowed from her mother, a gold link bracelet and dangling gold earrings. After brushing her hair, and pinning it up with wispy tendrils framing her face, she took a close critique of her appearance. Ready as she'd ever be, at least she looked her age.

As Dawn entered the living room, Tina set aside the book she was reading and smiled her approval. "My, you look all grown-up."

"I was thinking the same thing," Dawn agreed. "When I wear make-up and something other than cut-offs." She leaned back in the recliner with an indulgent sigh prepared for the inevitable question.

"Special date with Jerry?"

"No, not Jerry."

"I thought you and Jerry were serious."

Dawn heard obvious disappointment in the speculation. Tina had always liked Jerry. She had known this wouldn't come easy.

"Jerry and I have an understanding." She felt bad saying it. "It doesn't mean we won't be friends," she added. "We just want some freedom."

"Jerry approves of this arrangement?" Her brows furrowed doubtfully.

"I . . . well . . ." Dawn glanced at her watch as a horn sounded out front.

"Where are his manners?" Tina asked, warily, clearly displeased.

"Yeah, um—good point. Maybe you can meet him next time."

"Next time? Why not now?"

"Because, Mom."

"Okay then, when I can I expect you?"

"Expect me? Mom, you expected me nineteen years ago. I'm here, now." Dawn looked hopefully at her mother. She didn't seem amused.

"How late will you be?"

Demanding—her mother? Dawn sighed at this sudden intervention, but she could not have Tina upset. It would be too much to bear right now.

"I don't know," she said with an engaging smile. "Do I have a curfew?"

"It's not like you're with someone familiar."

She gave Tina a quick kiss on the cheek. "I'm raised, already. It's a done deal. I won't do anything wrong," she consoled, then hurried out the door.

"Where to?" he asked, when she settled in the car. Then he did a double take, his dark eyes observably admiring the length of exposed thigh. "You look incredibly enticing. Are you doing that on purpose?"

"You said something about dancing, Van," she said pointedly, avoiding the comment that thrilled her more than she cared to contemplate. "Do you like to dance?" she inquired as they sped into the street.

"Yes, I would love to put my arms around your body—and hold your body close to my body."

"On the dance floor," she clarified.

He looked at her, his expression slightly incredulous.

"Or any floor, Dawn."

"You're incorrigible, I wouldn't have thought it."

He flashed a sensuous look, his mouth tilting up in a come-on grin that was a little flustering.

"Where to?"

"The Cactus Flower?" she suggested recovering from that look. "Do you have to drive so fast?"

"I thought you liked speed."

"You thought I liked speed," she murmured reflectively. "Good one."

"What, you don't?"

She did not comment, but gave him a not so quick once over, noting his informal style. Dark wavy hair hung casually over the collar of a light blue shirt open half way down, black slacks, and black shoes or ankle boots, nothing at all extraordinary, but way too alluring.

"I think you're beautiful," she said, completely veering off the subject.

He glanced sideways. "Why doesn't it surprise me that you said that?"

"I suppose I should have said handsome?"

"I've been told a lot of things, but that was a first."

"I didn't mean you're not masculine."

"I know, Dawn. I hope you're hungry," he said, pulling into the parking lot of the popular supper club. "Are you?"

"Yes. I hope you can get in without a tie and jacket, this place has standards, you know."

"High standards and a dress code, but they don't have valet parking."

Van circled the car to open the door for her. "Are you in the mood for sea food? How about lobster?" he suggested.

"I've never tried it." He took her hand as she exited the car.

"Are you a poor little rich girl?" he inquired quirking an eyebrow.

"Excuse me?" She flashed him a hostile glance hoping to communicate how absurd it seemed that he would ask such a thing. She had heard the expression, not in a good sense, and found it offensive.

It didn't have the effect she wanted. An easy smile played at the corners of his mouth until he finally gave a short, almost apologetic laugh.

"I can't imagine . . ."

"No, I bet you can't," she muttered. "So, I've never eaten lobster, what's the big deal? Don't get on my case, Van. I can't help being rich."

"You are just a touch defensive about that, aren't you, sweetie? Being rich? And you wear it very nicely."

"Didn't say I don't like it, and you're not exactly a poor boy, and don't call me sweetie—if you don't mean it."

"You were born with a silver spoon in your mouth, sweetie."

"Are you trying to antagonize me?" she asked pleasantly. "You seem to have accepted the silver spoon without any quirks, my friend."

"Yes, I have," he said with easy candor. "And don't call me friend, if you don't mean it," he added.

From the trunk of his car, Van retrieved a black tie. After buttoning his shirt, he knotted the tie quickly and expertly. As she wondered how much practice it took to be able to do that, he shrugged into a blazer that looked tailored—he looked wonderful.

"Are you trying to impress me?" she said ignoring his quip about not calling him 'friend'. "And if you are, don't mention caviar or clams."

"No caviar or clams, just plain ole Ship 'n Shore." He flashed a grin that made her quiver just a little. "So, have you sampled filet mignon?"

"Of course, I have." She had always enjoyed steaks on the grill, or *burgers* or *hot dogs.*

"You don't eat out a lot, do you?"

"Not often, most usually on special occasions."

"I suppose anything can become monotonous eventually."

"What are you implying?"

"Nothing, not a thing, Dawn, calm down."

"It seemed to me, you were implying something."

"You are way too suspicious."

"I am not—if anything I'm too trusting."

He draped an arm casually around her shoulders as they neared the entrance. She glanced up at him feeling much too comfortable.

"If it feels good, do it," he said with a gleam in his eyes and a quick little wink that seemed somehow familiar. "So, you're trusting, are you?"

She gave him a targeted look.

"I wasn't," he insisted and laughed softly.

"You weren't?"

"Not a thing," Van assured her as that same easy smile played at the corners of his too sexy mouth.

She tried to erase the risky thought with abstract notions. It didn't work. When they entered the dining area of the Cactus Flower, she walked with him to a reserved table. Dawn received an assuming but admiring look from her escort.

She gave him a faint smile for his knowing persona, a light flicker of acknowledgement to being a favored child of society, thinking, I would love to have met you under different circumstances, *way different circumstances.*

As they enjoyed the meal, she had to admit her preference of lobster over fish and filet mignon over any other red meat. She decided not to voice her opinion, though, Van was quite smug enough.

Van agreed with Dawn to pass on dessert, so they left the restaurant, walking through a narrow hall into the Supper Club's Lounge.

It opened into a huge room with a bar, curving on each end, spanning the length of the room, and a large area with small round tables, romantically lit by artificial candlelight that served couples, while closer to the bandstand several tables qualified for larger parties.

Their waitress for the evening greeted her with friendly familiarity. "Dawn, hello! Table for two?" she suggested with a smile.

Dawn returned her smile. "Yes, please."

Jane escorted them to one of the small reserved tables in the back. Van held a chair for her.

She decided on white wine. He ordered a whiskey sour. Dawn couldn't help noticing that as the pert cocktail waitress walked away Van watched her for some distance across the room.

"I like it here," he said, approving of her choice.

"You've been here?"

"You consider me a typical rogue, don't you?"

"Actually, Van, I don't think there's anything typical about you. Classic would be more like it."

He gave her a direct look, a somewhat disconcerting look, but she smiled to cover her uncertainties.

"There's nothing typical about you either." He leaned closer. "Were you ever going to tell me your mother owns this nightclub?"

"Maybe not. Does it matter?"

"Have you ever been to New York during the Christmas season or Paris in the spring?" he asked.

"I don't want to go to Paris in the spring."

"I could change your mind about that . . . Been to the Bahamas?" he asked arrogantly suave.

"No." She felt defensive. She *sounded* defensive. "I've been to Disneyland more than once," she offered. "And to the Beatles concert—best seats available, and my mother took me to see Elvis. I have an authentic—"

"Do you own a car, Dawn?" He stopped her rush of words.

"You probably already know that I don't."

"You're right. You have a fortune at your fingertips and you don't even own a car."

"We have several cars I can use at anytime."

"Are you afraid of what you're worth?" he challenged. "You could have a chauffeur-driven limousine."

"I could," she complied.

"I have to wonder about this." He lifted the delicate wrist that sported a diamond watch.

"A gift from my mother and all my clothes are tailor made."

"And the gold, Dawn?"

"The necklace is an heirloom." Tilting her head to one side, she gave him a rueful look. "Are you trying to depress or simply annoy me?"

"None of the above, maybe I'm just trying to gauge you. Do you mind?"

"Incredibly."

"Would you like to dance or shoot darts at me with your eyes?"

"I would rather dance," she replied softly.

He led her onto the dance floor where he held her close. She breathed in the brisk masculine scent of him, turning only a little weak in the knees.

Gazing up at Van Morrison, a handsome man, a sense of humor, friendly, irritating, inescapably captivating, she tried without success to picture him with a knife pressed against Carrie's heart.

The killer in the night had no face. He would always be a remote and obscure form climbing hurriedly into a vehicle.

Van's personality being altogether different from what she had imagined, made it too easy to believe that he had not committed any mortal crime. He didn't even look like a pusher! But what did a pusher look like?

The way he held her with tender confidence when they danced, and gazed willingly into her eyes while they enjoyed inconsequential conversation, created an inconceivable feeling of comfort, causing confusion and piercing doubts.

Dawn drew a deep breath when their eyes met again over the candlelit table. She wanted him to be absolved of any responsibility for her friends' deaths. Through blurred rationalization, not exact clarity, just an unsettling undertone, something seemed to whisper that if he was involved—she didn't even want to know. With the wavering contemplations, disturbing feelings of guilt began to filter into her consciousness.

"You look tired," he observed.

"I'm not," she protested.

"Do you want to go somewhere quiet?" The touch of his hand on hers felt warm and comforting. Too warm, too comforting.

"Yes, I'd like that, but give me a few minutes."

Dawn walked to the back of the room escaping to the ladies' lounge where she leaned against the wall suffering an odd sense of betrayal to Carrie and to herself as well. The fact that she was attracted to Van made her feel a deep sadness and unreasonably disloyal.

Then she told herself that being attracted to him could be an advantage. To enjoy being with him made it easier to deceive him, an ugly word, but sadly appropriate. Amazingly, these thoughts incited a sense of peace to accompany the pain, rather easing her frazzled emotions.

Dawn straightened her shoulders, blinking a few times to discourage the unwelcome tears. She paced the length of the room determined to get a glow on, to be what he expected.

As for fear, she didn't fear losing her life nearly as much as she feared losing her heart. His appeal was devastating. Van infused her with an unusual yearning, most definitely fear provoking. She determined right then and there that he would not dissuade her any further with his savoir-faire.

Dawn left the lavatory, walking toward the front of the room where he stood waiting by the outside door. As she approached, their eyes met. She smiled a very real and true, not one bit deceiving smile.

Dawn hoped she wasn't lost, but she felt a little lost.

They entered the cozy atmosphere of the smaller lounge where the soft tones of a piano were a welcome relief from the blasting of the previous band. Dawn had never been to the Déjà vu Club.

"Better?" he asked after they were seated comfortably in a back booth.

"It is," she smiled.

"We can do this often. I'd like to get to know you."

"Why?" she asked simply.

He knew her, so very much about her. She knew very little about him, and what she did know wasn't good. So, why did she feel good in his company?

"Because you're different, Dawn Preston," he said lightly, lifting his glass, drawing her gratefully from her wonderings. "I will certainly enjoy your acquaintance."

"Friendship?" Somehow, she had not imagined being friends with Van. Still, she lifted her glass to join him in the toast. "You know, Van, in some ways it seems that I've known you for a very long time. I can't understand why you have such an effect on me."

"It's lust," he said mildly. He inclined his head in her direction, winked and smiled slow. "Don't look so serious."

"You jumped very smoothly from friendship to lust."

"There's a thin line," he replied. He leaned back in his chair giving her a sleepy-eyed seductive look.

Damn his savoir-faire.

Where had all those suspicions come from, Dawn wondered despairingly, accepting that her perspective had become lost somewhere in the way his eyes crinkled when he smiled, the sound of his laughter, and the way he released the pins that held her hair, letting it fall freely to her shoulders.

It had been easy to place the blame before she met him. Now it seemed too incredible to imagine. Dawn wondered if she could be manipulated so easily. An abrupt notion of being a gullible child caused stirrings of doubt and anxiety.

"Van, I have to level with you."

"Confession is good for the soul."

"You know I don't use drugs."

Dawn met his eyes, his steady gaze.

"Not the illegal variety," he answered good-naturedly.

"I'm sorry, I lied to you."

"It doesn't matter." He offered a forgiving grin.

Dawn returned his smile but with a certain unease. "Yes, it does matter. For all I know, maybe that's why you felt like you needed to 'gauge' me, but I'm not—I'm not like that."

"I can tell that you're not," he replied.

Since he knew so much about her, the probability that he knew Carrie Harrison had been one of her best friends could not be ignored. Even so, they had gone to the same school, were the same age, in the same grade. What reason could there be for him to think she suspected him of anything?

She stared dejectedly into her glass of wine, knowing he had every reason to think she suspected him of everything.

Van tilted her face up with an index finger beneath her chin.

"Don't look down like that," he advised. "It makes you look defeated. Do you feel defeated, Dawn?"

"No, just tired," she lied again, wondering if she would become that type.

When Van took her home, she went straight to her room. Preparing for bed with conflicting emotions, a part of her remained in defense of Van, while a distant voice echoed deep within her mind with disturbing questions, making her feel like succumbing to tears of despair. With everything going on in her life, she didn't wonder that tears were always so near the surface.

Not only did she feel ill equipped to undertake the task she had rushed headlong into, she didn't want to anymore. Too late, Dawn realized, she was in too deep, she was already feeling the pull of a downward spiral she would have to struggle to escape, if she even wanted to.

Dawn decided to make it easy on herself and call their lawyer, to let the investigation of Van Morrison be distant and appropriately professional.

Deep in thought as she always seemed to be these days, Dawn didn't notice, at first, when Bob's blue Cadillac pulled to the curb and stopped.

She paused when he lightly pressed the horn.

"Where you headed?" The question seemed affable, but she gave him a dubious look. "I just want to talk to you," he said reasonably.

She was on her way to a local store where they bought little incidentals. Technically Smith's Store, also the Corner Store, or the Candy Store. It had a soda bar in back where all the kids in junior high used to hang out.

Those were the days of easy delight, with the Beatles on the jukebox, the Dave Clark Five, the Rolling Stones and others, all new and different.

Don't look back, it hurts too much. Dawn focused her attention on Bob Kaley. In her opinion, he had no business stopping her on the street. Bob remained infinitely low on her easy-trust list.

"Can we talk?" he prompted.

Dawn didn't think they had anything to talk about. He was her mother's acquaintance, possibly boyfriend, the thought depressed her, but she would accept it. She did not, however, feel a need to talk to him at all.

"Are you afraid of me?" he asked with a slightly incredulous glance.

"I'm not afraid of you. Why would you think that?"

"Then get in," he said amiably, by no means an order. Still she hesitated.

"You're dating Van Morrison, aren't you," he said.

"I don't think that's your concern."

"He's not the best person for you to be hanging out with. What happened between you and Jerry?"

Dawn gave him an apathetic look, hoping to convey an indifference she did not feel. "Again, I don't think that's any of your concern."

"Maybe not."

She considered his mild response. Why did he have to be so agreeable?

"I didn't mean to be rude," Dawn said, feeling contrition.

"Then let's go for a drive," he suggested. "This is hardly the place to discuss anything."

"I still can't imagine what we have to talk about," she restated settling in the car.

Bob put the car in gear with no reply. Glancing at him, Dawn noticed his face looked a little drawn, strange, he appeared somewhat tense. Good, she felt a little tense herself. Dawn didn't want him, now or ever, to take any interest in her affairs, which in her estimation had nothing to do with him.

These thoughts kept her preoccupied since she couldn't think of a thing to say to Bob Kaley. Silence ensued as they left the city limits.

"Has Van said anything to you about his associates?" Bob's voice had taken on a resigned note.

The sudden question startled her. "What do you mean?"

"Have you accomplished anything in your association with him? Has he given you any inkling of his dealings or a hint of what he is capable of?"

When he glanced at her it seemed to be with shrewd calculation in his dark blue eyes. "Do you think he killed Carrie Harrison?"

"I don't know what you're talking about," she said, recoiling further.

"You know very well what I'm talking about, young lady," he said impatiently. "Van Morrison has a reputation in this town, Jerry's a decent kid. You would do well to reestablish a relationship with him."

Young lady? "You would do well not to speak to me in that tone," she countered feeling more than a little impatience of her own. "I don't even know why I'm talking to you."

He pulled to the side of the road.

"You know, Dawn. Deep inside, you know I'm right."

"Sorry, Bob, it's way over my head. I like Van, that's all. I don't actually know him very well yet." She stared straight ahead feeling perturbed. "Take me home, now?" she said stolidly.

"Do you resent my dating your mother?"

"Where did that come from? What does that have to do with anything?"

"It seems you can barely conceal your hostility."

"I'm going through some stuff, okay?" she said trying not to sound too irritable. "I'm still working through the grief of losing my best friend. Your dating my mother is the least of my concerns."

"Okay, then. I have to tell you what I've found out in my investigation."

"What investigation?" She straightened in her seat, interested.

"When I showed you the ring, the cobra ring, I saw how upset you were."

Dawn waited. She didn't care to offer any information or to be flippant, only to get this conversation over with.

"I did some checking and found out it belonged to David Temple."

She felt the shock, made a quick recovery, but knew he had noticed.

"Why were you upset about the ring, Dawn? You never told me," he said passively. "Is there something significant?"

If he had been the man she bumped into that night, he would know she was lying if she glibly dismissed the cobra ring as unimportant. If not, then it wouldn't matter one way or another. Still feeling at a loss as to why she was so suspicious of Bob Kaley, she told him, "The man who killed Ted was wearing that ring."

"So, you do believe Ted Harrison was murdered?"

That had slipped out. Dawn sighed irritably. "Don't you? You said you're investigating, why else would you?"

"You're right, and the one piece of evidence points to David Temple."

Dawn gave it a long moment to let him think she actually considered what he said, that his words might have some validity.

"So, you're essentially saying that Dave killed Ted."

She didn't believe it, not for a minute.

"It's not beyond the realm of possibility," Bob said with maddening calm. "Could you accept it if the evidence indicated that he did murder Ted?"

She felt defensive, bordering on angry, but realized that it might be best to not make this a confrontation. Resuming her relaxed position, Dawn sighed delicately and only then realized how tense the exchange had been.

"Where is the ring now?"

"I turned it over to the police," he said indifferently. "But since there is no investigation at this time, it's sitting safely in an evidence locker. I'm not concerned about the ring. I'm concerned about you, Dawn."

"In what way?"

"That you airily disregard the evidence of David Temple being Ted's killer," he said pointedly. "And your infatuation with Van Morrison."

"Excuse me?" She shot him a hostile glance. "That was over the line."

He held up a hand. "I'm sorry, Dawn, I didn't mean to offend you. Forgive me, but it's difficult to view things credibly when your emotions are involved. I would like you out of this whole messy business. There are some very influential people in town, Van could confide information that could be potentially dangerous to you, and Dave Temple might be a danger, also."

"Why would Van confide in me?"

"He's attracted to you, it could lead to careless words."

"Regardless of what you think I know, I don't know what you're talking about, Bob. I lost two very dear friends and that's all. I'm not playing detective or investigative reporter."

Part of the statement had been true.

"Then why are you seeing that man?"

She bristled at his disapproving tone. Bob had no right trying to exact authority over her in any way, but she kept poised in spite of his prying.

"I'm dating him because he's fascinating, he's sophisticated and, well, I haven't met anyone quite as charming."

"You haven't met anyone quite as dangerous." He studied her with that vaguely shrewd expression that she thought she would grow to hate. "Is there anything I can say to convince you to discontinue the relationship?"

"I think you've said enough," she answered unhappily.

Bob started the car. He made a U-turn, heading back toward Preston with no further discussion. Dawn sat quietly trying to digest what he had said.

If she took Bob's word, he implicated Dave, put him right in the middle of it, presenting him as Ted's killer. She didn't know Dave personally, but she knew Christi and Mike. It seemed absurd. She simple couldn't see it.

"You can drop me off at home," she said when they were back in town, completely forgetting what she had been going to the store after. "I'll think about what you've said."

"That's all I ask."

Once in her room, she did think about it. She couldn't think of anything else. There was no denying that Van was a drug pusher. There had never been any doubt. How could she imagine anything good in his character? So he was handsome, his mouth was enticing, his slow sexy smile could send her into a daydream, and his arms around her felt amazing, that had nothing to do with character, that was, as he so aptly put it, only lust.

Oh, the man made her swoon. How she hated the attraction! It made her deny what should have been obvious.

She had always felt confident in her instincts of people. It was difficult with Van though, as Bob had cleverly pointed out, because her emotions were involved.

Dawn buried her face in the bed pillow as she considered Bob implicating Dave. It came to mind, now, why the cobra ring had been familiar. Dave had been wearing it the one time she met him.

Was the ring unique, or were there others like it? Had it been specially made, or did every member of the gang own one? She could not imagine him a murderer, and why hadn't Christi confided in her about the ring?

She felt certain that Christi would not have just let it slide. She probably talked to Dave about it, or maybe Mike, with his unique insight.

Dawn felt uncomfortable that Bob had been telling the truth about that.

She couldn't help taking it personal about Dave Temple, being close to Christi and Mike, but personal feelings aside, something still wasn't right, sort of like, once again, trying to force two pieces of a puzzle together that didn't fit. Bob was the odd piece of a puzzle, she decided.

Not quite ready to give up the fascination of Van Morrison, Dawn decided to continue dating him. She wanted to spend time with him, whatever the consequences. Since she had known from the beginning that he was a risky venture, nothing had actually changed.

So what harm could come of it, a broken heart, maybe, a devastated life?

Dawn stood. She walked to the window thinking about what Bob had said, influential people, what a subterfuge, besides being old news. Two teenagers were dead, murdered. An accidental overdose, a rape attempt gone awry—She knew better, but there had never been an official investigation.

Dawn wondered in an abstract sense if she had misjudged Bob.

Christi told her that Dave and Van had become quick friends. Christi had been taken completely by him—not to mention herself.

Dawn felt pressed in on all sides, subtly entertaining what Bob had said, creating minuscule doubts about Dave Temple, while she still harbored a lack of trust for Mr. Bob Kaley, newest pillar of the community.

Her thoughts went in circles as they sometimes did during times of oppression. She desperately needed someone to talk to but could not even call Jerry or Paul. She knew very well either one of them would tell her to simply put it behind her, accept what happened. Get on with her life.

She continued to gaze out the window at the blue sky and green acres. Their property covered a vast amount of land with an impressive brick fence bordering beautifully manicured lawns, marvelous flower gardens with bursts of red, orange yellow and lavender varieties—wide walking paths through lovely orchards and glades with ponds suitable for swimming and sunning.

Heading left from the house, a well-worn path led to a large pond, rock gardens, lush shrubbery and a lovely orange grove.

Dawn viewed the forest of trees to the right, a thick woodsy area with another walking path, and further into it, a second pond in a wide area completely secluded.

Of course the magnificent landscaping required consistent professional care, but she requested that area be off-limits to gardeners until six p.m.

That spot had been a favorite for swimming and sunbathing.

She and Carla, Jill, Stephanie, Becky, and Carla's little cousin Judy had thoroughly enjoyed the privacy the summer of sixty-four with skinny dipping and lying unimpeded in the sun for an even tan.

That summer had been a blast, no tan lines when they wore sleeveless! Sometimes she missed the friends she had quit associating with after she started dating Jerry. Maybe someday they could have a reunion.

It would be nice just to talk to Stephanie. She let the wishful thought slip away, returning to the present. It would be nice to talk to Stephanie, but they hadn't been in touch for so long, now might not be the right time.

It hurt to be alone in this, and Dawn felt more alone than she could ever remember feeling. The one-time gaiety of her existence, the parties, fun and friends of even her recent past seemed a distant memory.

Chapter Twenty-Seven

Billy opened his eyes. He glanced at his watch, eight-thirty. He had fallen asleep in the waiting room, drifted into a dreamless sleep of exhaustion that had lasted a full hour.

He sat for a minute, just staring dazedly. Finally coming out of the unthinking reverie, he poured a cup of coffee from the tall urn. He ate half a doughnut with a few deep swallows of coffee before going to Christi's room.

Mike stood as he entered. He admired Mike, even though weeks had passed while they watched her losing the battle against darkness, a light of hope still glimmered within his eyes. He seemed to be holding onto faith of his sister's recovery remarkably well. They all were. It was all they had.

"You ought to go home, Billy," he said with concern. "You've been here almost sixteen hours."

"I had a nap. I want to stay with her awhile longer."

He sighed tiredly. "A nap sounds good. I'll be in the waiting room." Mike held his sister's hand for a moment, and then turned away.

Billy walked to the bed. When the door closed, he sat in the chair beside her, taking her slender hand in his. Her skin was so pale, her golden tan a thing of the past. Her beauty still radiated, pale, flawless beauty, but she had lost weight, a dangerous amount of weight, the doctor said.

"Wake up, Chris," he whispered. "You have to wake up now." Tears filled his eyes. He sighed, gently caressing her fingers. "I'll never forgive myself," he told her. "I want you to know that. I need you to come back to me," he said painfully. "You can't just leave me like this. You changed my life. You are my life, Chris, I can't lose you now."

Her eyes remained closed, the delicate hand limp in his own.

"I'm sorry, Christi, so sorry. Come on, baby, don't punish me this way. I didn't mean it. I'll make up for all the bad things that ever happened to you—if I just get another chance." Billy closed his eyes. He had never been one to pray, didn't know for sure if he even believed, but he prayed now, he prayed silently and fervently for Christi's life, for a full recovery. Tears burned in his eyes, and he prayed.

* * *

Dave sat across from Nancy Castell in the relaxed atmosphere of Lindsey's Bar. A pianist in the back played the sweet tune of an old familiar love song. It seemed appropriate.

They had been here several times during the past five weeks. Dave wondered if he deserved to have someone like her care about him. He hadn't really talked much about important things, and now he felt a need to.

As he admired her gentle and exquisite beauty, the quiet strength that he had leaned on more than intended, he couldn't find words to tell Nancy how he felt about her when he felt so worthless.

"I don't know what you're doing here with me," Dave said, feeling a bit unnerved about who she was, who he was, their different circumstances, and how completely opposite their lives had been.

He ran his finger around the rim of his glass feeling debased, ashamed of the past couple years of his life, regretting the circumstances in which they had met and feeling frightened, in many ways, about his yearnings for her.

"I'm no good for a girl like you," he murmured, wanting her to deny the simple fact even though he felt it with his whole being.

"Are you very sure about that?" she asked softly.

"I'm not, not really. I'm not sure of anything anymore," he said, in a rush of hopelessness. "I thought I could handle John. I've known him since we were kids. I knew his circumstances, but I didn't know how bad he was broken. I thought if he had a friend, I thought I could help."

He glanced at her feeling uncomfortable with hindsight. "I couldn't even handle myself, much less someone else."

"It isn't your fault that he was evil," she said positively.

He lowered his gaze again. "I neglected Chris and Mike."

"The interaction I've seen between you and Mike, it hardly seems you've neglected him."

As their eyes met, she offered a faint smile.

"Why, Nancy?" he asked with quiet despair. "Why should Chris have to suffer for my stupidity?"

"Quit putting yourself down, Dave. You tried to help someone who was beyond help. It's a good quality."

"I know you mean well, but I made some wrong choices. I could have put a down payment on a house, or bought a lot to have one built. She needed to be in this environment, not the south side."

He felt painfully dismayed that he could see so clearly now, when it might be too late.

"We lost everything when our folks died. I thought it was in their best interest when the insurance money came through to think of their future," he explained. "Instead of replacing what was lost to us, I invested the majority of it for Mike and Christi, for college or whatever they might need later on. I wanted them to have security, but I should have lived for the present."

"Dave, you're an amazing man."

"Now Christi might die—" He took a deep breath to compose himself. Even though he felt comfortable in her presence, he did not want to cry, to expose his vulnerability to such an extent. "What—what did you say?"

"I said, you're amazing. You made some wrong decisions; we all do at times, but don't punish yourself with useless regrets. That won't help Christi or Mike . . . and the security part was a good idea," she added.

Nancy reached over to hold his hand, a reassuring gesture she often extended. Her small hand in his felt right. Everything about her felt right. Nancy seemed to him to be sweet perfection, her loving kindness, her compassion, the understanding in those crystalline brown eyes.

Dave threw some bills on the table to cover the check and a tip.

"Come on, let's get out of here."

They left Lindsey's.

"You ready for another motor cycle ride?" He straddled the Harley.

"You better believe it. I'm seriously considering getting myself one of these!" She took the helmet he offered and strapped it securely. "Let's go," she said eagerly climbing on behind him.

They arrived shortly at her apartment building. He drove around the building into the ample parking lot.

"Think you can tell me a little more about how great I am? I think I like that," he said as they entered the courtyard.

"Okay, for one thing, you were in the process of change," she reminded him. "Blaming yourself, sometimes you don't remember the positive." She smiled cheerfully. "You have to consider that. Just keep your perspective clear, all right? Don't let what's happened cloud it."

"I *was* in the process of change," he accepted. "You know exactly what to say to make me feel better. Every time I'm near you, I want to get closer."

He framed her face in his hands and kissed her, then held her close, the warmth of her slim body rousing desire, but not just sexual desire, a desire for emotional stability that he hadn't expected.

"I've never felt like this before," he confided.

"You've never felt like what, Dave?"

He sighed. "Like I've found a place where I really belong."

"You're sure?"

He grinned. "Very sure. I need you, Nancy." Admitting his need to a woman was a strange sensation, but instead of uncertainty, he felt a sense of security in her arms. "I've never really needed anyone before, what I'm not so sure about is if I'm worthy of someone like—"

She put a finger against his lips. "Want to go upstairs and make love?" She smiled shyly, a pink flush coloring her cheeks.

"It's what I've wanted to do forever."

Her mouth curved into a delightful smile. "You should have asked."

He looked into her eyes, he saw hope and the promise of a future reflected within. He felt amazed at the prospect.

"Do you really want someone like me?" he ventured.

"You're the person I wanted to meet that night," she told him, still holding his gaze. "Where were you, Dave, when I was being terrorized?"

He drew her hand to his mouth, pressing his lips against her fingers.

"I was about as dazed and confused as a man can be," he said softly. "Let's go upstairs."

The phone was ringing when they reached her door. Since the hospital had her number on file, she hurried to answer it in case it was about Christi.

"Hello—? Yes, Dave Temple is here." She glanced at him briefly, concern etched in her lovely face.

Hope and fear clashed within his chest. "The hospital?"

She gave him an understanding glance but held her index finger up to indicate she needed a moment to finish listening. "Okay, I will . . ." She glanced again at him. "Yes, I'm sure he'll be there right away."

Nancy replaced the receiver. She turned to face him smiling radiantly, her eyes glowing. "Christi's regained consciousness."

They began to laugh. He picked her up, swinging her around. Still laughing heartily, Dave set her down. "I have to go to the hospital."

He held her close in his arms, his hands caressing her back, his face buried in the sweet fragrance of her hair. "Do you want to come?"

"I don't want to intrude just yet, enjoy some time alone with your sister and brother. You should tell them what you told me," she suggested.

He swallowed thickly. "I will."

As the realization sank deeper, relief flooded his system. He felt almost weak with it. "Can I stop by later? We have so much to talk about."

"I'll be waiting."

Nancy walked to the door with him. She looked up into his eyes with an expression that he imagined could be love. He held her in a brief tight embrace feeling an instant's flash of amazement.

"I can't begin to thank you, Nancy, for helping me through this."

"Don't—" Drawing in a slow, steady breath, she sighed with a smile of pure pleasure. "I'm glad I could be here for you."

"I won't be long," he promised. "We have a lot to talk about—I'm repeating myself, right?"

He started to turn, still feeling the wonder of a new beginning.

"Is it possible to make up for lost time?"

"It must be, I hear that expression a lot," she said laughter in her voice. "But even if it isn't possible, we can try."

"And we have from now on, don't we."

"Yes, we do."

He headed for the hospital with a newly awakened sense of life, so much had bordered on Christi's recovery. Everything else would fall into place.

Since he had been viewing the world through clear eyes, it seemed more beautiful than it had ever been. This had not been an easy time, but managing to stay away from drugs throughout the nightmare meant something.

It had taken effort and a strong determination. The temptation had been great to just let go—get high and feel free, but he didn't, and since he had been phasing out of the Cobras, there would be no gang complications to interfere in their life.

He would make up to his sister what she had missed. He decided to start by buying a lot on Fairview Boulevard, hire a contactor to build a house, and together they would make it a home.

These thoughts mingled with whimsical dreams of his newfound love.

Chapter Twenty-Eight

Dawn sat on the front steps of her house waiting for Van Morrison, alias drug pusher, heart-breaker, playboy, sweet and funny, wonderful . . . warm . . . charming . . . mystifying . . .

Her thoughts filtered back to the night she'd met him. From that first night her emotions seemed to rule, stirring confusion by a lack of fear.

She had found out a few things she would rather not have known, but at least she could feel gratified that regardless of his unprincipled activities, at least there wasn't a killer lurking beneath the charm.

Their family lawyer's PI friend had investigated and disclosed that he had been involved in other dubious business the night Carrie died.

There were still blank areas though, answers that she might never find.

The now familiar silver Corvette came into view, rounding the driveway. She stood as it came to a smooth stop. Dawn walked toward the car, too conscious of his eyes—his intensely charismatic, dangerous eyes.

Now she could accept that Jerry's estimation had been right in many ways.

"Would you mind telling me how you got started in the drug business?" she asked bluntly as they drove around the circular drive.

"I mind," he said pleasantly.

He didn't give her the courtesy of a glance. Leaving Woodland Drive, he accelerated, keeping his eyes on the road as they sped past Union Avenue.

"Are you involved with Bob Kaley?" she persisted.

"Bob Kaley? I don't know any Bob Kaley." His brown eyes flickered briefly toward her. "Is he a friend of yours?"

"Hardly, he arrived in town at about the same time you did."

"You jump to conclusions with extremely pallid reasons," he said mildly.

No reaction concerning Bob Kaley. He seemed polished at that particular practice. Did it come natural, not conveying his feelings?

"How did you happen to come by Preston?"

A smile played at the corner of his mouth. "You have a nice town here, not exactly a city, but with an abundance of nightlife."

He reached over, to casually squeeze her thigh. She felt warm where his hand touched her. Dawn shifted uneasily.

"Where do you spend so much of your time, Van," she asked, her voice softening, knowing the answer but wanting to hear him either lie or confess.

"It's not open for discussion, sweetie. Don't concern yourself about my associates, real or imagined," he said, conveying, she thought, an obliquely subtle warning. "And don't concern yourself with what I do or don't."

He grinned, too cute, the subtle warning if it had been there at all disintegrated with his easygoing expression.

"I have a right to know something about you," she pouted.

"I have a right to know something about you, too."

"You know everything there is to know about me."

"Not everything." He turned left at the next corner.

"Where are we going?" Dawn turned her head looking forlornly toward where they should be driving.

"We're going to my apartment," he said, without hesitation.

"What if I don't want to go to your apartment?" she objected, feeling more than a slight thrill, which concerned her deeply. "Don't I have a say in this?"

"No, Dawn, you don't, not this time." He still had that easy smile going as he glanced her way. "This is my choice."

Dawn stared out the window as she considered that this was not an impulsive decision even though it seemed spontaneous. She knew enough about Van Morrison to know he made plans. She wondered what else he might have planned. What if he wanted to make love? Warning signals tried to flash but they were ineffectual flickers, and way too late.

He turned on the lights as they entered the south side apartment, swiftly adjusting the dimmer making them soft. The cozy room felt comfortably cool, with a faint scent of spice. Dawn looked around, taking it all in. She had not known what to expect, but certainly not this.

"Feel free," Van commented, noticing her inspection of his premises.

Plush red carpeting covered the floor and heavy drapes drawn across the windows served to eliminate the not so pleasant view.

It was a perfectly nice room, Dawn thought, the woodwork looked natural and gleaming. The coffee and end tables were oak wood, or quality veneer, and the black leather loveseat and chair appeared soft and luxurious.

He had no television, but the elaborate stereo system that he turned on before walking over to a small corner bar had great sound.

"Nice place ya got here," she drawled with a grin.

"I'm glad it passed," he said musingly.

The romantic atmosphere of the apartment enveloped her as easy listening music flowed softly from the stereo speakers. She paused to view a large picture of a ship on a stormy sea that hung above the love seat.

The drawing seemed symbolic to her, a tiny vessel at the mercy of the angry waters. Dawn looked closely, visualizing demons in the bludgeoning waves threatening to drag the defenseless boat under. The demons were real, but they seemed illusionary.

Dawn strolled over to another wall, a large, framed penciled drawing, presented a grinning skull, a transparent pipe with smoke curling from it, and a horned skull with hollow eyes that appeared to be laughing at her like the phantom of her nightmare. Devoid of color, gray and white swirls of smoke depicted illusionary demons—there were demons in the smoke.

"My brother's work," he commented noticing her interest. "He wanted to be an artist."

"The drawings—they're beautiful, but a little on the dark side, aren't they?" Dawn glanced at him curiously. His voice had sounded incredibly sad. He actually had a little boy lost look.

"What happened?" she asked. She had never seen this side of him, this almost vulnerable impression.

"Someone came into his life and changed his way of thinking." With a light shrug, he cast aside the melancholy disposition. "Would you like a drink?"

"I'll have a screwdriver . . ." Dawn took a stool at the bar. "Van?"

He glanced at her, then back to the task.

"Would you like to talk about it?"

"Talk about what?" he said, seemingly without a clue.

"Okay." She let it slide, taking another appreciative look around the room. "I didn't expect such a lovely apartment on the south side." Dawn accepted the drink. "It's like a whole 'nother world in here."

"It is a whole 'nother world." He smiled warmly. "You're such a kid."

"I guess I am," she confessed. "And many would consider me, in a polite term, 'pampered', used to getting my own way and pouting when I don't."

"It seems to me, you did comparatively well, considering that you're the only child of one indulgent parent and filthy rich."

"Compared to what?" she asked with a fleeting smile.

"Your smile . . ." he speculated. "Anyone would believe it's cultivated—that you went to charm school, but you're a natural."

"A natural what?"

"It's a compliment! See, you are suspicious. You have charisma, Dawn, a catching personality."

"I'm all that?"

He ambled over to the love seat. "All that and more. You're beautiful, and it's not just skin deep with you."

"You don't consider me a snob?"

"No, Dawn. Come here. Come on," he urged when she gave him a long look. "I don't bite—not hard, anyway."

"Somehow that's not reassuring," she said walking toward him.

When she sat down, he took her drink. He set it on the table, his mood shifting gears again. He looked at her, his expression reflective.

"I've meant to ask you . . ." His lips brushed hers and then covered her mouth with hungry persuasion. She closed her eyes being consumed with a sweet desire as he ran one hand up through her hair.

Dawn returned his passionate kiss with reckless abandon, but jumped as if an electrical current passed through her when he touched her breast.

"No, Van, the answer is . . . no!"

"That wasn't what I had in mind," he said raggedly.

"No? What did you have in mind, Van?"

Van lifted his glass to down the rest of his drink.

He bit at his lip thoughtfully as he looked at her. Dawn glanced away feeling uncomfortable, then raised her chin to stare resolutely back at him.

He moved closer. "What do you want with me, Dawn?"

If that was the intended question, what could she say to him?

"Do you want to know me? Is that what you want?"

She could not pull her eyes away from his dark questioning gaze.

"I know you've been checking up on me. I know that you know what I am, but you don't know me, do you."

She swallowed hard. "I think—I might."

"No, Dawn, you don't know the half."

She regarded his avid expression, not his usual smooth style. Dawn took a deep swallow of her drink trying to ease the tightness in her throat.

"Will you take me home?"

"Now?"

"Please."

"Do you have a problem being here with me?"

"In your apartment, yes, maybe I do."

"Why did you come here?" he whispered.

"Not for this."

"Are you sure?"

She started to stand, but he grabbed her hand pulling her back on the love seat, shifting positions, his body above hers. Dawn didn't struggle as he held her, staring into her eyes for a long, searching moment.

"Your feelings are driving you wild."

Van seemed fully aware of her emotions, and he was right, she felt her will merging with his. He settled beside her. His lips against her neck sent deep responsive sensations swirling in a compellingly warm glow, smothering the danger of allowing him to subject her to his persuasion.

She moaned softly in unspoken surrender wanting very much to give in, to know his love . . . *love*? She tried, but couldn't justify the word in her mind.

This wasn't love. He was a gorgeous man who led a secret life. Who was he with when he wasn't with her? She felt no more than a mere conquest.

"No, Van."

"You can't mean that," he whispered. With deft hands, he freed three buttons of her blouse. Pushing it aside, his lips skimmed her shoulder.

"Let yourself go, baby, you want to."

His thumb brushed her breast, tantalizing.

"You live pretty much in the fast lane, don't you, Van," she said, desperately groping for a way out of this weak and crucial moment.

"Pretty much."

"But I don't—this isn't me, it's not fair for you to put me in this compromising position."

"Compromising?" He grinned sexily. His lips brushed hers lightly. She felt the warmth of his breath, teasing her senses. "This is what you want, Dawn," he insisted, seductively urgent. His lips, so near hers, demanded positive responses. "You were safe in your world, why did you venture out?—admit it, you decided to try the fast lane and you were enticed by it."

He pulled her closer pressing his mouth firmly to hers, deepening the kiss as her lips parted beneath his. He released her mouth, trailing kisses to her vulnerable throat. With his lips and tongue playing at her neck, her thoughts scattered in useless turmoil.

She struggled for strength but he had stolen her resistance and left her floundering, searching for something to hold onto but there was only him.

"You're afraid, but you want it." His voice had gone throaty, filled with yearning, too persuasive. "You stepped out of your world, Dawn, into mine."

He suddenly released her and broke off with an apology.

Dawn hastily straightened her blouse. She tried to button it with shaky fingers. He helped her with the last button and then strode to the bar.

"I shouldn't have said that, I'm sorry. None of this is your fault."

Huskiness lingered in his tone, desire still softened his expression.

He poured himself a shot of whiskey. In a fresh glass he poured vodka over ice and added orange juice.

Dawn struggled with the uncertainty he had ignited. Had it been her decision? Yes, maybe, but she had valid reasons.

When he finally looked in her direction his eyes were filled with a curious deep longing, an emotion she had not anticipated.

"I didn't expect it to come to this, our relationship was supposed to be superficial . . ." Van met her eyes looking genuinely remorseful. "Oh, God, what am I saying?" He sat beside her on the sofa. "I didn't mean that."

Dawn accepted the drink he offered.

"What did you mean?" She set her drink down hard on the coffee table, her eyes narrowing because she feared that had been exactly what he meant.

"Don't look at me that way, Dawn," he said softly.

"How should I regard you? What do you expect of me?"

He held the shot glass in his hands staring morosely into the amber liquid as if to find some magic words within to erase the hurtful remark.

"I don't know, Dawn. I'm not sure what I expect of you, anymore than I know what you expect of me." His voice sounded distant and troubled.

He tilted his head, looking at her uncertainly. "But it isn't expedient, as you may well suppose . . . for me to become involved with anyone. You can be hurt. I don't want to be the one to hurt you."

Held in a gaze that she could not break, she wondered what he might be referring to. There were so many possibilities.

He broke eye contact, looking back at the shot glass. "There's something I want you to know. It isn't that I—"

Interrupted by the ringing phone, he tossed back the shot.

Dawn watched intent flicker and disperse from his eyes. Sensing an instant withdrawal as he went to answer the phone, she swallowed her disappointment. He had been about to reveal a part of himself to her.

Now, leaning back on the sofa, she gloomily accepted that the crucial moment had come and gone.

Van replaced the receiver. "I hope you don't mind, a friend of mine, Dave Temple is stopping by." He glanced at his watch. "Be about ten minutes."

"I should go." Dawn started to stand.

"You know I wouldn't let you walk home from here."

Van dropped down beside her. He ran a careless hand through his mussed hair. "His sister was in an accident. She regained consciousness yesterday. There's something he wants to discuss."

Dawn felt revived. Her whole being had filled with waiting at the mention of Dave Temple. Now she felt the tension ease from her body as fast as it had gripped her. Good news, thank heaven.

Mike had called immediately to let her know what happened. She had not gone to the hospital. She couldn't, she had tried, but felt paralyzed at the prospect, and had settled for talking often with Mike concerning Christi's progress. Dawn glanced at Van. He had fallen into silent contemplation.

She felt neglected and a little restless knowing that whatever he had been about to tell her had been dispelled. He had no intention of confiding now. He might as well have been a thousand miles away.

She settled back, not even bothering to mask her discontent. Leaving him alone with his thoughts, whatever they might be, she dealt with mixed feelings of hurt and trepidation, wanting to reach out to him, but fearing rejection.

It seemed like the longest ten minutes of her life as they waited.

When Van opened the door for Dave, he proceeded directly to the bar.

"I get my hands on John Burton, he's dead," Dave said with a certain calm deliberation that belied the spoken words.

Dave poured whiskey into a shot glass. He drank it down, then refilling the glass; he carried it with him to a nearby chair.

Dawn watched him warily, contemplating the significance of a ring, and his association with Van, then forced her eyes away, not wanting to stare.

In the span of silence that followed, she remembered a time, not so very long ago, when Preston City was the safest place to live. Then drugs became more than a troubling issue, Cobras and Monarchs were practically household words and Christi lived in constant dread of John Burton.

Van Morrison and Bob Kaley invaded their town, and death walked stealthily through the halls of their school, out onto their quiet streets.

Her eyes were drawn again to the serious, angry face of Dave Temple, possibly cold-blooded killer, then to Van Morrison, drug pusher. She felt a frantic need to get away—she had to escape, but there was no way out.

"Who's she?"

She heard Dave ask Van about her, but at a distance. Her breath seemed to have solidified in her throat, and her heart struggled within her chest.

As she wondered what was happening to her, the panicky infringement began to fade—intense but temporary, Dawn took a deep calming breath.

Dave was looking directly at her. Since the pressure dispersed, she could meet his probing blue eyes, purposely veiling any recognition. He gave no sign of awareness either, but she felt certain that he really did not remember the night she was in the apartment with Christi when he and Mike came home.

"She's cool," Van said unaware of the struggle she had just experienced. "Want to tell me what happened?"

Dawn glanced at Van. He leaned forward, concerned eyes on his friend. A close bond existed. A friendship had developed within one short year.

"I could leave . . ." she faltered.

Van touched her arm. "You know how I feel about that. Please, stay."

She settled back in compliance, still feeling invasive. Dawn listened attentively with mounting tension as Dave filled Van in on what had transpired that led to Christi's accident. He glanced her way occasionally, but directed most of his attention to Van.

She began to nibble at a well-manicured nail. Mike had given her a brief account of everything, but had not mentioned a word about being beat up.

Van reached to remove her finger from her mouth, his warm hand gave hers a gentle squeeze. Appreciative of the kind gesture, she glanced at him, surprised that he had been observing her reaction with no apparent indication of interest.

Dawn folded her hands in her lap, trying to relax. Nail biting was something she had not done before.

Dave leaned back in his chair after finishing the account that had led to his ultimate hatred of John Burton and polished off the shot of whiskey.

"Chris almost died to escape Burton, and he'll die for what he did. I treated that man like a brother, and I'll take him out without blinking an eye."

"Leave Burton to me," Van countered quietly. "Mike and Christi need you, I'll deal with him."

"He doesn't deserve to live," Dave said vehemently.

"I know that better than anyone."

Dawn wondered why Van felt that way. He had not attempted to disguise his distinctly hostile feelings toward John Burton. He probably had tender feelings toward Christi, too, she decided, certainly, he would feel protective.

The men talked quietly. Van had a good effect on Dave. Dawn watched his notable relaxation, admiring Van's influence.

When Van drove her home, when he put his arms around her in the moonlight, when he kissed her warmly and promised to call, she felt lost in confusion. She wondered if it might be time to bring it all to a halt.

Relating to the little boat in the painting on Van's wall, she felt in too deep, the waves of her complex emotions threatening to pull her under.

Dawn awoke the next morning with eager anticipation to see Christi. She sped through her morning routine, and then joined her mother for a hasty cup of coffee as she filled her in on Christi's recovery.

Dawn bought roses at the gift shop. She waited impatiently for the elevator to take her up to room 411. Her friend had, at last, awakened from a dreadful sleep! She felt exuberant with thanksgiving but still anxious as she peeked around the door.

The bed had been rolled up to a relaxed sitting position, her eyes were closed. Dawn carried the vase of roses over and placed them on the table.

Christi's eyelashes fluttered, her remarkable violet eyes opened sleepily.

"I just found out last night." Dawn gave her a contrite smile. "I would have been here sooner."

"I slept all day yesterday, anyway, and most of this morning." Christi sighed with a wistful look. "I didn't get far, did I?"

Dawn struggled with tears. Christi's voice sounded too fragile, her skin unbelievably pale, her usually slim body now notably thin.

"Can I give you a hug?"

"Sure, I won't break."

"Well, you look very breakable." Dawn gave her a close hug. "You mean so much to me, Chris. I don't think I could take losing another friend."

"You very nearly did."

"Dave told Van the whole story. I was there."

"So, you arranged a meeting with Van, and it sounds like you're spending time with him?"

"Yes, we've spent some time together, and I've learned some things I would rather not have known." She gave Christi an exaggerated sullen look. "Why didn't you warn me?"

"I tried, didn't I try?"

"On the contrary, there's a lot you neglected. I'm practically swooning over the guy."

"He is kind of irresistible."

"You were right about Van, Chris." Dawn felt wonderful passing on this tidbit of news. "He's into a lot, but he had nothing to do with Ted or Carrie."

"That means more than you know."

Dawn pulled a chair over to the bed. She sat on the edge of it leaning forward a bit. "I still don't know what happened that you ended up in here."

"John thought I was submissive once I was in the car," she said shakily. "I grabbed the opportunity to jump out."

Her large eyes filled with tears and she started to tremble. Dawn put a warm hand on Christi's, so cool and fragile.

"I shouldn't have asked," she apologized. "I already thought it had been due to a daring escape." Dawn searched to change the subject. "So," she asked brightly. "When do you get out of here?"

“Dr. Hamilton says to relax and enjoy my vacation.”

Then a soft smile lit her eyes. “Dave and Billy are like that.” She held up her hand with her fingers crossed to signify closeness. “I was amazed.”

“Well, they have you in common, now,” Dawn smiled.

She noticed Christi’s struggle to stay awake.

“Well—” Dawn glanced at her watch. “I’m going to leave now so you can get some rest, you look exhausted. I’ll be back soon,” she promised.

“I want you to be careful,” Christi urged suddenly. “Please don’t take any unnecessary chances.”

“I haven’t yet, I don’t suppose I will.” Christi seemed to relax with the assurance.

Danny came in as Dawn left.

“What a nice surprise,” she said before noticing his solemn expression. “What’s wrong?”

“I’m leaving, Christi.” He took her hand. “I know this is going to be hard for you to understand. I don’t even know how to say it.”

“What are you talking about?” She looked at him bewildered.

“This isn’t easy, Chris. It’s not fair to you or Billy—or me either. It’s not something I chose.” He sighed dispiritedly. “I thought about just leaving and never letting you know—”

“What are you saying?” she demanded, not understanding why he would suddenly be leaving Preston and why he would even imagine leaving without letting anyone know. What was he thinking?

“I’m saying I love you.” He raised his eyes to meet hers. “Billy knows. I guess he knew all the time.”

“Danny, I still don’t understand.”

“I guess there’s no understanding. It just happened. I’m sorry, Chris. I tried to bury my feelings, to bury them so deep that I could forget and he would never imagine.”

Christi felt stunned. She had in no way suspected. He had never given her reason to believe his feelings were anything other than friendship.

“Do you have to leave, Danny?” she whispered. “Where will you go?”

“Away from here,” he said simply. “There’s no other alternative.”

Except to be away from me, she thought sadly.

“Is this the only way?”

“Please, Christi . . .”

“I’m so sorry.” A tear slid down her face.

"This isn't your fault." He wiped the single tear away with his thumb. "Please don't cry, baby love, not now, not ever."

Christi swallowed hard. "This is—difficult," she managed.

"Don't cry for me, Chris. Be happy."

Danny gently cradled her face in his hand.

As she wondered sadly at her insensitivity, he pressed his lips to hers in a gentle kiss, both innocent and confusing, because it made her feel connected in a way she only wanted to feel toward Billy, and because it meant good-bye.

Christi felt extreme disturbance at the ache he had created within her.

Mike entered, as Danny exited.

He sat on the edge of her bed. "It gonna be okay, Christi," he murmured.

"I'm not so sure."

Tears gathered in her eyes, then streaked her face. Danny was gone from their lives and who knew when they would see him again.

"Is it possible to be in love with two people at the same time?"

Mike took a tissue and gently dried her tears.

"Billy and Danny?" He tossed the tissue in the wastebasket as she waited for what he had to say. "You're in love with Billy—you care for Danny—what you're feeling is compassion."

She inhaled a slightly tremulous breath. "Really?"

Mike shifted from the bed to a nearby chair. "How would you feel if Danny met a wonderful girl and fell in love with her?"

"I'd be happy for him."

"How would you feel though, if Billy met a wonderful girl and fell in love with her?"

Christi managed a weak smile. "I get your drift."

"Now you can go to sleep." He tucked the cover around her slim body. "Danny will find his own love and his own happiness someday."

Chapter Twenty-Nine

Dawn filled a tall crystal goblet with crushed ice, and then poured iced tea over it, almost to the brim. In her room, she turned the stereo on to stare bleakly out the window, the pulsing music of rock 'n roll keeping beat to a turmoil of rampant thoughts drifting through her mind, always returning to one vital question, where would she find the words to say goodbye to Van?

She took a deep drink of iced tea. Crunching on some ice, Dawn tried to focus on the immediate future, but her mind fluttered away in anxiety with no resolving answers, certainly nothing agreeable with the feelings of her heart.

She had already accepted the sad truth that she didn't want to let him go, had realized for a while now that she wanted to hold on tight.

He was fun and exciting. The Fourth of July celebration had never been as wonderful, the fireworks bursting in the night sky had never been so amazing. In a crowded room or sitting in his car talking, listening to a rocking band or a table for two in a cozy bar.

Her thoughts were filled with him, at night before going to bed, first thing upon waking in the morning. The man dominated her aspirations.

Dawn refused to admit that she had fallen in love with him, just thinking it created a flood of discontent.

What kind of life would it be? Eventually he would be caught and she would be left alone to suffer the degradation. Or, if he did not return her love, she would be left alone anyway.

Obviously a no win situation, unless he loved her in return and loved her enough to want to escape the destructive life he had chosen. She suffered a dull ache of desire with the ideal imaginings, because she refused to give in to wishful thinking. He had never given any indication that he wanted out of that life, and she could not live in such an existence, even though she did love him. Dawn sighed, there; she had admitted her love, now what?

They had spent so much time, so many wonderful hours in each other's company. How could he not return her love, how could he not give up the life that generated such destruction to so many people? She sat erect as she saw Bob Kaley's car coming around the drive.

The cobra ring question came to mind now. Bob and her mother would be spending the evening at the Cactus flower, opportunity beckoned to search his apartment, so why not?

Why not? Christi's serious concern came to mind, *don't take chances.*

The idea of searching Bob's apartment had never occurred to her before. Why now? The answer came, not necessarily the answer she wanted, but it came nonetheless.

She needed to know before she could get on with any sort of life at all, before she could break up with Van, before she could enroll in college, before she could go to the cemetery to say goodbye to Ted and Carrie, mourn their deaths and let go.

If she didn't take the chance she would never know. She had to find out his involvement, or to settle her doubts. Bob Kaley, being such an important part of her life, made it increasingly difficult to cope with the lack of trust.

Tina tapped and then opened the door. "I'll be leaving soon," she said.

"Okay, Mom, I guess you're allowed," Dawn said brightly. "Don't have too much fun—be home before midnight."

Her mother came over to where she sat, arms circling, big hug.

"I love you, kitten."

"I love you, too, Mom."

Tina left. She wondered how long they would be downstairs before heading out to dinner and dancing. She needed to go now before she lost her nerve. The queasy feeling in the pit of her stomach, a mildly nauseous sensation reminding her of the all too considerable risk of being caught, wouldn't diminish with time.

So she would have to leave through the window, it was closer anyway. Going out a side gate would eliminate the long walk around the drive.

She hastily climbed out the bedroom window to a nearby tree, dropping from a low hanging branch to the ground.

She paused for a moment in wistful memories of the advantages the limb had provided. If her mother had known the secrets of this tree and a young girl, the easy access it provided in and out, she might have cut it away years ago—but times had been simple then, lighthearted and carefree. Those happy days were gone forever.

The hurt cut so deep she wondered morosely if she would ever be happy again. Dawn shivered at the dispiriting thought, turning firmly away from melancholy feelings and leaving her secure world behind.

She ran for a while, then alternately walked and ran the distance to Jerry's house on Fairview. He had been the magic act at many kiddy parties and on through his young teen years. Besides the usual parlor tricks, Jerry had demonstrated an extraordinary ability to pick locks. Unless secured by a dead bolt he could get her inside, if he would.

Please be home, she thought, her finger pressing the doorbell twice, then again. Fortunately, he opened the door; sadly he gave her a questioning, nearly unfriendly look. She'd hoped he would be over it by now.

"Jerry, I need your help," she gasped. Her heart pounding furiously, she leaned against the doorframe for support.

His expression turned to concern. "Dawn, what's wrong?"

"No—" She held a hand up at his troubled look. "I'm okay, I just—I need you—you have to—break into—Bob's apartment for me."

At last, she managed a deep breath.

"Bob's apartment? Bob Kaley?"

"Yes, please, hurry."

He continued to eye her dubiously. "I thought something was seriously wrong, and apparently—I'm right. Dawn, you have lost it. You're crazy, okay? You want me to break into Bob's apartment?"

She sighed despairingly. He had every reason to feel that way. The gravity of the situation could not be denied.

"I'm not crazy, okay? I have my reasons."

Breathing a little easier now, she tried to drag him through the doorway.

He finally let her pull him out onto the porch.

"You want me to break into Mr. Kaley's apartment—you have to tell me your reasons."

"I don't have time to explain," she said, pleadingly. "Please, just do this for me." *Before I lose my nerve.*

"It's been weeks, Dawn, the whole freakin' summer."

"I know, but you didn't call me either."

He opened the passenger side of his powder blue Camaro. "Get in the car, will you, please? I don't feel like running four blocks. I don't know why I'm going along with you on this when . . . Wait a minute." He looked over at her, his expression taut and decisive.

"You have to give me an explanation if you expect my help. Did it occur to you that I could be arrested for breaking and entering?"

Dawn sighed resignedly. "Okay Jerry, but you won't like it."

"Well, I couldn't like it any less than I do right now," he countered.

"I don't know about that—Bob Kaley might be involved with everything that went down. I haven't trusted him since the day of Ted's funeral."

"Why not?" he said doggedly. "Why don't you trust him?"

"He showed me a ring that he said he found in the parking lot the night Ted was murdered. He said the ring belonged to Dave Temple."

Jerry shook his head, looking puzzled.

"And?"

"A man bumped into me at the dance that night. The man was wearing a mask and that ring. Since Christi is my friend, I know he expected me to recognize the ring, to purposely plant suspicion in my mind about Dave Temple, but the suspicion fell on him."

"Yeah, and you never told me about that. It didn't seem important?"

"I'm sorry, Jerry. I really am. But I know Christi, and I know Mike—"

"This doesn't mean you know Dave Temple."

"You're right, and I need to get into Bob's apartment to see if I can find anything. Maybe if I don't—" She shrugged helplessly.

"You'll quit this crazy charade?" he suggested. "Forget being an amateur detective, and forget Van Morrison? Maybe come back down to earth and back to me where you belong?"

"I don't know. I just know I need your help."

He started the car. "And I need to know when you're going to be through with this," he said pulling away from the curb much too quickly.

"I don't know, Jerry." Dawn felt bad. He was angry, but he was hurt too, and she knew her feelings would never be the same.

"If you found someone else I'd understand," she murmured. "We haven't been together, you know, so I'd have to understand."

"Yeah, guess you'd have to since you've been seen all over town with that New York City tuff. You've fallen for that Morrison guy, haven't you?"

"I don't know how I feel about anything," she replied, evasively.

"Have you slept with him?" he demanded pulling along side the curb a short distance from the apartment building where Bob lived.

"No!" she snapped exiting the car. She almost had to run to keep up with his furious pace.

"This is not happening," he muttered when they reached the front door.

"Jerry, please, all you have to do is open the door and get out of here."

She looked around nervously in the well-lighted vestibule. They hurried up the carpeted stairs. Jerry easily slipped the lock. The door was equipped with a deadbolt, but it wasn't engaged.

"Take care," he said softly.

"Thanks pal." She kissed him impetuously.

As Dawn closed the door behind her, a menacing growl reminded her of Bob's Doberman. Unaware of Prince's location or what room would be her sanctuary, she made a mad dash, turning the knob on the first door she came to. The door opened and she fell inside slamming it shut.

Safely behind the closed door, she took a deep, calming breath. As his threatening rumble reverberated on the other side, she let her gaze wander around what appeared to be a master bedroom. The soft illumination of a bedside lamp didn't afford much light.

Not wanting to risk turning on the overhead, she rummaged in the top drawer of the nightstand for a flashlight. Locating a flashlight, she pushed the on/off switch. It emitted a suitable glow to light the way.

Dawn searched the bedroom quickly and efficiently, and found nothing. She swallowed the guilt of invading another person's privacy, thinking it might be a good idea to split—out the window—down the fire escape.

Scanning the room one last time, she noticed an obscure door. It opened to a small, narrow closet with one high shelf at the top.

She dragged a chair over from the desk for better access. Pushing some clutter out of the way, directing the beam of light toward the back of the closet, she noticed a garment box. She pulled it out, and then climbed down.

Setting the box on the chair, Dawn removed the lid. Inhaling a soft gasp of air she gazed at the contents. Had she expected to find a phantom mask, a black cape and a jeweled cobra ring?

She continued to stare, completely absorbed with the undeniable evidence within. Resting atop a carelessly folded cape was the significant cobra ring, and the phantom mask of her nightmares, but why had he kept evidence that could easily have been disposed of? The answer was too easy.

He had tried to turn her suspicions to Dave Temple. It stood to reason that Bob intended to eventually frame him for the murder of Ted Harrison, so obvious—but why? Ted's murder had already been ruled a suicide.

The nonsensical realization came at the same instant that the missing piece of the puzzle fell into place, the eyes behind the mask had been midnight dark, Dave's were lighter, like the sky on a cloudless day.

The discovery hit with shocking force, even as it occurred to her that down deep she had thought he might be innocent, even wanted him to be innocent. This would hurt Tina terribly. No, she had not wanted Bob to be guilty of any crime, but she couldn't help her feelings, and had simply wanted to put it to rest once and for all, but now, what she wanted more than anything was to be out of that apartment.

Dawn tensed at the slamming of a door and the voices of men talking.

Prince gave two sharp barks outside the door. She heard Bob commending him, almost envisioning him petting that hateful Doberman on his sleek head.

She stood frozen as the bedroom door opened. Bob Kaley, Van Morrison and Paul Jenson entered in. It seemed that time stood still as her eyes rested on Paul. Recovering from the shock, her eyes darted toward the window wondering what the chance would be. None, she knew, her chance was an absolute zero.

"You naïve little girl," Bob said pitilessly. "How could you have imagined that you could gain access to my apartment without my knowing it?"

A shadow of annoyance crossed his face. "I knew you were suspicious, but I'd hoped to divert your curiosity to David Temple."

She took an involuntary step backward. "You thought I was an idiot, and I had hoped you weren't such a hypocrite," she seethed. "How can you be such a twofaced, evil man—destroying the lives of young people?"

"Being a teacher simply didn't pay enough," he replied complacently.

She could see derision in his eyes. He was exactly what she had thought of him. Somehow, that didn't help her feelings as he sighed with irritation.

"Ah well, even though I don't appreciate my evening being interrupted, I can, at least, get this messy business out of the way."

His lips twisted into an ironic smile. "You've made it too easy, breaking and entering, an unlawful act, and that's why I have a guard dog . . ."

The Doberman sat dutifully beside him.

Her eyes widened as she realized Bob's intent. She stared transfixed at Prince waiting patiently at his master's feet. Prince, harmless and deceivingly docile could turn vicious as he had been when he made a lunge for her and then growled menacingly behind the door where she had found refuge.

Her hand fluttered to her throat and she tore her eyes away from the animal. "I don't want to die." Dawn could not be certain if she had spoken the words aloud or if they had drifted through her numb mind.

"I'm not real concerned with what you want," Bob said, detached now, since he'd obviously made his decision.

Van walked toward her.

"She's mine, Bob," he said evenly. "I've invested too much time."

He gripped her upper arm with one hand, the other around her shoulders, the hold firm but not painful.

She held her breath as Bob Kaley looked indecisively at the two of them.

"All right," he said dismissively. "Take her. Have your fun. Just make sure you dispose of her properly."

She did not bother to struggle with no means of escape. Besides, any fate now seemed preferable to being ripped apart by that animal.

"Oh, you were right about Ted," Bob added, as a cruel afterthought. "I injected the lethal dose of heroin, thought you might like to know."

She gazed at him with true loathing. "I already knew." Dawn drew a shallow breath. "What about Carrie?"

"I had it done," he said indifferently.

He wasn't going to tell her. She would never know. Dawn looked at the boy who had been a friend, who stood on the sideline looking sad, a hopeless misery that he could not hide.

"Paul?"

"I'm so sorry." His troubled voice mumbled the useless heartfelt apology.

"You let them kill Carrie?"

"I didn't know," Paul said in quiet desperation. "I couldn't have saved her, even if I'd known, not any more than I can save you."

"Did you love her?"

He turned away. "I love her," he whispered.

Dawn felt the betrayal of one of her best friends. "Does Jerry know?"

"Jerry has nothing in this."

The comfort in knowing Jerry had been sincere was short-lived.

"I'll try to help Tina get over the grief of losing her only child," Bob goaded. "I think she might warm up to my condolences."

"My mother's principles will stand up to you any day of the week," she told him scornfully. "You don't stand half a chance."

Sudden anger lit his eyes. "You don't know how badly I wanted to slap your smug little face that day in the car," he said, his voice low but hostile. "I decided then and there that you didn't have long to live."

He looked at Van. "Get her out of here."

Dawn wilted in Van's arms offering no resistance as he propelled her out the bedroom door to the hallway, rushing on out of Bob's apartment to the lobby, down the stairs and out into the warm night. He flung open the car door dumping her unceremoniously onto the car seat.

Tears spilled silently down her face, dripped off her nose and over her lips and chin. She wiped uselessly at the flood of tears, unable to compose herself, her breath catching as she tried to breathe.

Her misery running deep and painful, she cried quietly on her side of the car as he drove in staid silence

He didn't even bother to glance in her direction. Terrible regrets assailed her but it was much too late for that. She struggled to grasp a shred of dignity, the decision to not beg settled deep inside engaging a sense of peace, to nullify the ache of knowing her life on earth would soon be no more.

Dawn's attempt to wipe the tears with her hands wasn't working very well. She drew a breath that seemed steadier now than before.

"What—are you—g-going—to do—with me?" she stammered.

"Haven't you figured that out by now?" He glanced at her, an odd mixture of derision and sympathy in the quick look. "You're pretty damn smart about figuring things out, aren't you?"

Dawn didn't answer. She wrapped her arms around herself shivering.

"Are you cold?" His voice softened.

He touched her arm with a warm hand. Van turned the air conditioner down. "There's Kleenex in the glove box."

She looked at him quickly, hopefully, but he had dismissed her, his gaze steady on the road again. She took some tissues to wipe her face and hands, then discreetly blew her nose, composing herself further.

They drove on in silence except for the radio he had turned on low as they raced through the night, the wheels of the speeding Corvette distancing them from Preston City. Dawn decided to break the silence.

"I didn't expect it to come to this," she said weakly.

"What did you expect?" His response held a note of impatience. "You were looking for a murderer, Dawn, you found one."

"I don't understand your attitude. I don't understand how you can be so indifferent now when you were so—" She left the statement unfinished feeling humiliated and rejected.

"What was I Dawn?" he said with a touch of exasperation. "Why would my attitude surprise you? You know what I am."

"Will it be painless?" she whispered.

"What do you want, Dawn?" he said, his voice dark and angry. "You want a nice little death?" He slammed his hands hard against the steering wheel. "How can it be painless?" he demanded. "You're thinking about it now, and it hurts, doesn't it."

"Yes, it hurts." She stared arbitrarily at the stars in the night sky wondering at his emotion, hoping he could control the speeding car.

"You were wrong, Dawn," he said abruptly accelerating even more.

"Maybe I was wrong for—would you please slow down just a little?"

"Scared you'll die in car wreck?" he asked with a touch of irony, but he obligingly let up on the gas.

She drew a deep breath after another intermittent silence.

"Okay, I was wrong," she accepted. "But I don't deserve to die for it."

"Neither did Carrie."

His words cut deep, she moaned feeling intense sorrow. Unexpected sobs shook her body, almost as painful as the night she'd found her.

She grabbed more tissues. Drying her eyes, blowing her nose, again, Dawn determined to stop this pathetic crying, to somehow restrain this useless, remorseful ache.

"An overdose of heroin, a stabbing, or a bullet in the back of the head," he said cruelly. "Dead is still dead."

"I don't want to die," she whispered. "I can't believe Paul is involved with drug pushers and murderers! I've known him since I was a child, from the time I can remember, I remember him!"

"Paul is another Ted. He'll be dead before this whole thing is over if something doesn't happen fast. The kid has no cool."

"Ted was not like Paul. Maybe Paul didn't expect anyone to get hurt, but Ted was nothing like him," she insisted. "I have to believe that. Paul fooled me, and so did you, but I was right about Dave."

"You were right about Dave," he conceded. "He's always been set against heroin. When I first met him, he was doing a lot of drugs, sort of neglected Chris and Mike, but he's getting his life straightened out now."

"I knew he couldn't have killed Ted." She took a breath, feeling calmer, Van's comment about Dave somehow reassuring. "I was right about Bob Kaley, too," Dawn added icily. "I could never pinpoint it, but—he always seemed thuggish in a smooth way."

"Bob wants Dave Temple out of the way. He's too influential. Do you know there was only one heroin addict in the Cobra gang?"

"No, I don't know much about them," she murmured. "I only know what Christi told me."

That seemed to end the conversation. Dawn fixed her gaze on Van and studied his features, once more wondering at her sense of security. She felt no apprehension now. It had gone, evaporated into the night along with her hopeless tears. When he continued to ignore her, she turned her head to stare pensively into the night.

Chapter Thirty

Dawn began wondering about the strange conversation, analyzing his tone, the compassion oddly conflicting with what he represented.

Reviewing the things he had said, his express regret, the kindness he had shown, gave Dawn a glimmer of light in the darkness, hope that she wasn't on her way to be murdered.

She had distinctly heard remorse over Carrie and Ted's deaths, even vaguely for Paul, considering the path he had chosen. She considered the pride in his voice when he spoke of Dave Temple being a good influence.

Drawing on faith that she wasn't mistaken, her emotions shifted from anguish to relief so fast, she felt dizzy. The dizziness receded quickly, leaving her with simple blessed relief.

She didn't say anything at first, she let her body relax, let the awareness and calm infuse her. After several minutes, she took a long breath, feeling so elated with the comprehension that she could hold it no longer.

"You're not a pusher," Dawn said fluently.

Van gave her an arbitrary glance, and then almost grinned.

"You're not a pusher, no way! This is so cool," she said, feeling giddy now with sheer joy, unable to contain her jubilant animation. "You're in vice! Oh, my God! You're a narcotics cop!"

"Cool, Dawn? You could have died, you little minx." He gave her a wary glance. "Easy sweetie, I think you went from low to high, way too fast."

"I'm calm," she disagreed. "I'm calm already, can't you tell? But you should have let me know once we were out of Bob's apartment," Dawn said, disturbed that she had been allowed to think death was imminent.

"I should have made you suffer more than you did," he replied bluntly.

"Whatever possessed you to go there in the first place?" he demanded. "And believe me no answer is good enough. If he had decided to kill you it would have blown everything straight to hell."

She accepted the verbal chastisement in humble silence.

"Carrie and Ted would have died in vain. I would have had Bob, but he's the lesser evil, believe it or not."

"That is hard to believe."

"I might never have gotten another chance for them."

"I guess I should be sorry, but it turned out all right, didn't it!"

Van shook his head in apparent wonder at her simplicity.

"You know what would have happened if I hadn't been with Bob," he told her meaningfully.

"I don't care to think about it."

"Think about it," he advised.

Dawn looked at him with brief consternation.

"I'm not even going to try to explain. You wouldn't understand—so what happens now?" she asked, not surprised at his glimpse of astonishment.

"You're not one bit sorry for what you did," he challenged revealing a degree of exasperation. "You have no regret for taking your life in your own hands."

"What?" she said, defensively. "You can't leave me just wondering about this. I need some answers. I mean, I'm thinking Ted was murdered because he knew too much and maybe wanted out."

"He refused to deal smack and he was getting pressure, and yes, he did want out. I found out after—he'd planned to turn state's evidence."

"He must have revealed too much information to Carrie. He must have told her—" Dawn's voice broke, the rest of the sentence wedged in her throat.

She didn't try to finish what she was saying as the memory of finding Carrie tore at her heart with recurrent grief for a second time that night.

"I'm sorry about your friend. I couldn't save either one of those kids. Unfortunately, I didn't know Bob was gonna take them out any more than Paul did." Van sighed heavily. "He kept it close to the vest."

"So, what does happen now?" she asked softly.

"There are four men that I've been after since the onset of my career, four men who have stayed out of sight for three years."

Van's tone and expression of contempt didn't surprise her. He obviously had a serious abhorrence for anyone associated with drug distribution.

"They'll be right there in Little Sin City—just long enough for me to make the biggest drug bust of my career."

Then his voice softened.

"Actually, I'm not very far into my career," he confessed. "But I've put a few hoods away, took out a couple major honchos. I've been under cover for a while now on this one. It took some time to get everything into play." He gave her a quick look. "I thought about getting you out of it in the beginning. Maybe I should have."

"There's still something I don't know," she said, forcing the words through the lump in her throat. "Who killed Carrie?"

"John Burton—I'll get him when I'm through in Preston."

"What do you mean, you'll get him? You mean you'll arrest him?"

"What else would I mean?" he asked casually.

Van hated John Burton, but so did she. The man who tormented Christi for so long had also killed her best friend. Why would it surprise her? He was that kind of monster, the kind who would do anything.

"Then let me get him, Van!" Dawn felt a mixture of emotions, anger, yes, but also a surge of excitement, a pure adrenaline rush. She realized she had grabbed his arm and released it immediately when he looked over at her.

She wanted John Burton, she wanted to be the one to bring him in, and she knew Van Morrison could help her make that happen.

"Forget it."

His response didn't faze her. She hadn't expected him to readily agree.

"You almost succeeded in getting yourself killed once," he reminded her. "I'm not letting you take a chance like that." He gave her a quick glimpse, his voice firm. "I mean it, Dawn. There's no reason."

"I have my reasons."

"You want to retaliate . . . . not a reason, and not a good idea."

"If you don't let me, I'll do it on my own."

"I'm beginning to think you have suicidal tendencies."

"I'll go after him with or without your help."

"You can't do that. You don't know where he is."

"I have resources," she said with easy defiance.

He stared at her for many long seconds before giving his attention back to the road.

"Just to be on the safe side, I'll have Mark keep an eye on you."

"Mark?"

"Mark Winston, my contact. I'll drop you off at his place before I go back to Preston. He won't mind babysitting, considering the circumstances."

"Babysitting?—I'm not a child! How can you be so unreasonable?" she demanded, her newfound confidence taking a dive.

"Me unreasonable? Dawn, you don't know what you're asking. You don't know what he is capable of."

"I know what he's capable of," she informed him. "Christi told me about John Burton, I'm willing to take my chances."

"You're too willing to take chances, but I'm not willing to let you. I'll put you under lock and key if I have to."

"You don't understand."

"Damn right, I don't."

His tone gave her a start. She wasn't real used to emotional Van, yet. Taking a moment to gather her strength and reserve, she tried to slow down.

"Will you please just consider it?" she asked reasonably. Dawn could not believe how well she was holding up, keeping her cool in the face of wanting to explode.

"Not happening."

"You can't tell me what to do!"

"Oh, yes, I can." His words held finality that she would not accept, but her misgivings increased by the minute, as she couldn't think of a way to convey how adamantly she felt about this.

"You don't have the right," she finally managed. "You couldn't possibly understand how I feel. I want this more than anything."

"Why, Dawn?"

Tears almost choked her, but she had to be strong.

"He killed Carrie!" she replied scathingly, refusing to portray weakness. Her temper, having flared hot, quickly diminished.

Dawn inhaled a deep, steadying breath. "He took her out of my life, and he had *no* right."

"You know what you thought I was," he said, imposingly calm. "He is that, and more. He has no conscious, no remorse; no real grasp of what is even right or wrong." His voice hardened. "He's a fuckin' psycho, sociopath and doesn't give a damn. He—" Van took a breath reinstating self-control. "You simply don't comprehend, Dawn. You can't comprehend, because your emotions are in turmoil."

"I can't argue with that, but I'm not taking this lightly. I'll be vigilant," she said solemnly. "I won't take anything for granted, I promise—Van." She touched his arm gently. "I have every confidence that I can do this."

"You're not getting the picture." He stayed quiet for a long interval, determinedly disregarding her again.

"You take chances every day," she said, unable to withstand the silence any longer. "Why can't I do this one thing that's so important to me?"

"You're teasing death, Dawn. This is my job. You're a pampered little girl who doesn't know the first *thing* about taking care of herself. Didn't you learn anything in Bob's apartment?"

She remained silent at the reprimand. That had been the most terrifying experience she ever wanted to live through, but it didn't change her mind.

"I can still see the look of terror in your eyes when you thought you were going to die." He expelled his breath in a deep sigh.

She heard a yielding quality that sparked hope.

"I won't take unnecessary chances like I did by going to Bob's apartment."

"You want revenge," he said, doggedly.

"It's not revenge. It's justice."

"He'll get justice," he replied with quiet emphasis.

"You couldn't possibly know I feel," she flared.

"I know exactly how you feel."

His remark puzzled her. She waited, but he left it at that. Dawn thought better of asking him to explain, calmly letting the quiet miles pass behind them until she began to feel rejected, like he had fully dismissed her request.

"Van?"

"You have to give me some assurances," he said quietly.

"I will, anything," she vowed, feeling relieved and oddly elated.

"Don't back him into a corner, and don't argue with him. Believe me, you don't want to—do you understand?"

"I understand."

"Don't give him an ultimatum—don't challenge him in any way."

"No challenge, I promise."

"All right," he relented, still sounding uncertain. "I'll give you this . . . But I'll have to think on it."

Dawn sighed happily, pleased with his consent, but then she gripped his arm again. “What about my mother?” she said worriedly recalling Bob’s innuendo. “Can you let her know I’m all right?”

“How can I tell her that?” he said with another deep sigh that held a depth of feeling. “Even if you weren’t going into a world of danger—I’m sorry, but she can’t know until it’s over.”

They drove in silence again.

“We’re almost to Anaheim,” he said, wearily. “I’ll get you settled in a motel for the night, and get with you in the morning about arrangements.”

“I want you to stay with me.”

Van kept his eyes on the road while she wondered at his silence.

“Did you hear what I said, Van?” Dawn felt an unwelcome dose of insecurity, punctuated by his silence. “I want you to stay with me tonight.”

“I heard.”

Her emotions for him had been mass confusion from the beginning, the doubt, the love, the anxiety of believing he was a vile criminal while her inner most feelings could not imagine it. Now that she knew the truth, she felt both excited and apprehensive, but she needed to know.

“All the time you spent with me, Van, was it—was that part of your job?”

Van pulled the car to the side of the road. He stared for a moment at the road ahead. “No,” he said turning toward her. “My interest was too damn personal. I can admit that now. I shouldn’t have let it happen.”

“I’m glad it did.”

“I have nothing to offer you, sweetheart, not what a girl like you needs, anyway.” A distinct sadness punctuated his voice.

“Pretty sure you have quite a lot,” she disagreed.

“I can see it in your eyes, Dawn—those emerald jewels tell it all.”

“I still want you to stay with me.”

“Are you sure about this? Your emotions are—”

“In turmoil, I know. But there’s no confusion here.”

Van shifted into drive. They passed some roadside hotels before he spotted a Holiday Inn. He parked in front of the motel office.

Van sat with his head bent in quiet contemplation.

“I’m sorry for what you went through Dawn, but I couldn’t stop it. If I’d told you, I would have had to move you out of town immediately, and that would have been difficult with the complication of Bob’s involvement with your mother.”

"She would have thought I was dead. That would have been cruel."

"Maybe I should have put you both in witness protection. Maybe I was wrong for not getting you out of town," he admitted. "If anything had happened to you, I don't know what I might have done."

"You almost told me something significant. You were about to when Dave called and interrupted you."

"That was a weak moment."

"I was having a weak moment, too," she said softly.

"I wanted you to know, I wasn't evil."

His sincerity touched her. Dawn realized, she had never thought he was, not from the beginning.

Suddenly his sensuous mouth curved in a teasing grin. "I could have corrupted you that night," he said. "I knew you were being torn, though. I didn't want you to do something you'd regret."

"You would have loved for me to do something I would have regretted," she objected, remembering the night.

"I did, but I didn't," he said with a lazily seductive look. "You seem so damn innocent, but you're wild at the same time."

"You're right on one count, Van—pretty sure I was past resisting that night—but I've never been wild."

"It's there, you're cultured, but I can feel it, the untamed yearning."

He leaned over his lips brushing hers gently.

She closed her eyes savoring the intimate moment. He cared. Dawn knew he cared about her, she could see it in his eyes, too.

When Van went to register, she leaned her head back. Dawn found herself swathed with unwanted thoughts of John Burton. She drew her arms around herself, feeling cold to the bone with apprehension.

Van was right, she knew it, and she still perversely convinced him to let her go after John because of—what some would consider a budding obsession.

It wasn't obsession, it was more, and it was more than revenge, it was above retaliation. Dawn wasn't sure exactly how to label what she felt, maybe a conviction of sorts.

The unbidden thought that Carrie would never have expected her to take such a risk gave her renewed determination. It didn't matter if her reasons were evasive, if she was a tad obsessive—John Burton would pay for what he did, the sooner the better.

Dawn sat up watching for Van, glad that he was coming out of the office.

"Our room is on the other side," he said when he was back in the driver's seat. He glanced toward her, their eyes met. "Are you sure, Dawn?"

"No second thoughts, I promise."

He didn't say more, he just looked at her with that heart-tugging grin and started the car. He parked in the designated spot. She was hardly aware that he exited the car before he was opening the door for her.

Dawn felt transported as he took her hand accompanying her to the rented motel room—she had heard the expression *'walking on air'*. But she'd never thought it was an actual feeling or that she would experience the sensation of such overwhelming happiness.

Feeling shy as the door closed behind them, but eager to know the love of this man, she put her arms around him in a tight embrace.

His hands came up to cover her breasts with mild pressure. She moaned softly as the gentle massage erupted a flooding of desire.

Dawn caressed his muscled arms, moved to his chest, wandered down, hesitant at first, then with more daring. She touched his body intimately, pressing her hand against the hardness of his mounting excitement, enjoying that she was responsible. Now that she was free to express her affections, Dawn ached with that wild yearning he had mentioned.

When he lifted her in his arms to carry her to the bed, the awareness of future heartache couldn't override the longing for him or the hope that maybe she would be special, that he would want to keep her for his own.

They helped each other undress. She felt sexually alive for the first time under the influence of his touch, her temptation intensifying now that she could fully express her desire.

"I'm not responsible for what I do," she murmured, running her hands over his chest, gently, playfully pulling at the chest hairs. "I'm under the influence of Van Morrison."

He kissed the tip of her nose. "You're zany," he smiled.

"The word is intoxicated," she replied.

"You sort of knocked me off my feet, too, you know that, baby?"

Her response matched his arousal as she experienced what she had only fantasized. When his body finally claimed hers, after the uninhibited kissing and touching and the remarkable introductions to sweet desires, she knew irrepressible joy, just having him possess her in this sharing of love.

She moved with him in total abandon of any hang-ups she ever had. He gave her such pleasure she thought she would scream. Biting his shoulder to keep the scream inside, Dawn soared to an awesome, shuddering ecstasy—then floated mildly back to the reality of a simple motel room from the height of glowing passion. The awareness of her love for him settled deep.

"You are wild, baby."

She let her legs drop languidly from around him. He kissed her once more before he sat up.

"I want a shower, how about you?" She sat up pulling the sheet around her. Dawn smiled at his pleased looked, then moved into his arms.

"You're a dangerous little girl," he whispered into her hair. "I could spend—some time with you . . ."

His lips touched her shoulder. She sighed with wistful aspiration, his hesitation giving her the impression that he wanted to voice a commitment but something held him back. His lifestyle, his job? No doubt, he already had a commitment.

"When I thought you were a pusher, I was afraid of falling in love with you," she confided. In her mind, she whispered, 'Now I have fallen in love with you. What am I to do?'

"About love, Dawn."

She placed a finger over his lips. "Please—don't say anything."

"I don't want to hurt you," he said, uncertainly. "You're vulnerable—"

"Pretty sure I said don't say anything," she laughed weakly. "I'm not vulnerable, not really. I don't expect words of love, or promises that you can't keep."

No, she didn't expect words of love, but she sure wanted them.

"I want you to love me tonight," she said urgently.

"I want that, too," he said softly, caressing her back.

"Okay, let's do it." She threw her arms around him, kissing him eagerly feeling exhilarating happiness that for them the night had only begun.

Dawn felt free with Van in a way she could never have imagined. Her slightly shy demeanor clashing with her eager to please in any way possible performance, created a night of enchanting passion.

She snuggled in the arms of the man she loved, closing her eyes as the sun began to rise over the city.

Chapter Thirty-One

Dawn opened her eyes feeling an odd sense of desertion. Realizing she was alone in the double bed, she sat up, immediately spotting a note on the pillow beside her. Sweet memories of the night drifting through her mind, she read the assurance that Van would be back soon.

Going into the bathroom, she found all the necessary toiletries for a shower and smiled at his thoughtfulness.

Dawn stepped under a tepid spray turning slowly. She let the water revive her, before lathering luxuriously with one of the miniature, delicately scented soaps he had chosen.

After the thoroughly enjoyable shower, she combed and fluffed her auburn hair, feeling a bit miffed because she had no makeup. Clean and fresh-faced, wrapped precariously in a plush, royal blue bath towel, she sat on the bed waiting for Van.

Troublesome doubts began to invade her consciousness, the undeniable risk that she would soon face, taking front and center. Dawn didn't want to dwell on impending dangers, useless worries that served no purpose.

Luckily she didn't have long to dwell.

"I have coffee and doughnuts," he said upon entering. "Or would you rather go out to breakfast?" He eyed the towel.

"Coffee is fine."

"You're good to go, Dawn—I've taken care of everything."

She loved the way he couldn't take his eyes off her but pretended not to notice. "When will I be leaving?"

"You're not on any time schedule, but I have to be back in Preston today."

"Why do you have to get back today?"

"Bob might get suspicious." His gaze settled on her, his eyes burning with sudden desire. He drew in his breath. "You're doing that on purpose, aren't you—sitting there looking all sweet and sexy."

"Maybe . . ."

He took her coffee, setting it on the nightstand.

"Why didn't you wake me?"

"I thought about it, but I probably wouldn't have been out of here yet." He tugged at the towel. "I'll always remember you that way."

She moved into his arms knowing he would effectively turn off the world with the intense hunger of his kisses, the rousing pleasure of his hands, the feel of his long, lean body sheltering her.

As he held her close in the elation of the climax of their love—even at that ultimate moment—she sensed a quiet desperation.

"Mmm," he moaned burying his face against her neck.

He stayed in that position, just being close to her as she ran her fingers slowly through his thick dark hair. Finally, he forced himself to move. He turned over on his back staring at the ceiling.

When Van sat up to light a cigarette, she noticed an elusive look in his eyes as he glanced her way. Dawn recognized his feelings weren't quite in sync with hers, even though existence had become a perilous venture for them both.

In a little while he would be driving back to an indeterminate destination, but his concern had nothing to do with Preston. He was worried for her life.

She had her own misgivings, vague traces of uncertainty trying to push their way through again, disturbing questions about her motives. It took effort but she managed to push those doubts aside again, convincing herself that her reasons were valid and had nothing to do with revenge.

Dawn reached for her clothes.

"There's a driver's license in your purse identifying you as Cynthia Marie Kaley, Bob's daughter. That should put the fear of God in him—"

He sighed, momentarily distracted as Dawn pulled her jeans up, zipped, and then snapped them.

He drew her close burying his face against her neck. "Get dressed you little nymph."

"What if John calls to check it out?" she murmured enjoying the nuzzling.

"Don't worry; Burton won't be able to get in touch with him."

"Does Bob have a daughter?" She slipped her arms through the bra straps, turning for him to fasten it.

"He did," Van confirmed. "How did you manage this before me?" he teased, working with the hooks.

"Well, it's just that you're so good at this sort of thing."

"Oh, is that it? I think I'm more adept at getting it off than getting it on."

"Oh yeah? I think you get it on pretty good."

He kissed her shoulder. "Hmmm, we'll pick up this conversation later."

Dawn located her pale green shell.

"Bob had a daughter—she died six years ago in an auto accident. If you have any doubts, baby, you can reconsider."

"Reconsider is not in my vocabulary," she said pulling the garment over her head.

"I didn't think so. Okay, I sketched your route on a makeshift map. It's in the side pocket of your purse. By the way, I bought you a horrendously expensive, handbag." He went to the closet to retrieve it. "You like it?"

"Pertinent," she murmured approvingly of the black leather midsized purse with a long shoulder strap.

"There's a ladies' wallet, plenty of cash, the driver's license identifying you as Cynthia Kaley. There's also a keychain with the keys to a silver Impala and this room." He lit a cigarette. "I think I've covered it all. You'll have to stop on the way and buy purse things. I wasn't sure what to get."

Dawn walked to the window, peeking around the drape to look at the new car parked out front. "Is silver your favorite color?"

"Oh, yeah—Mark's number is in the nightstand drawer, by the way."

"So, I'll be getting in touch with your contact," she said vaguely, strolling back over to sit cross-legged on the bed watching him dress.

He pulled his jeans on, standing to snap them. She admired his lean, muscled body, and he noticed, his face relaxing with a hint of a smile.

"Mark will call me," he said reaching for his shirt. "If you manage to get Burton here, get him a room. Mark can take it from there . . . I don't like this," he muttered sitting on the edge of the bed to put on his shoes.

"I know. I know I don't have to like it." He sighed, heavily and she heard the uneasiness. "Okay. It won't take long to get there, a couple hours to San Diageo, about four hours the other side of the border. You'll find him easy enough. There's only one tavern in town."

She heard weariness in his voice again. Dawn wished he wasn't so troubled. "I know you don't think I should do this," she said quietly.

"It doesn't matter what I think. The problem is; I'm afraid you don't. You're such a little girl," he said tenderly. "John is—cunning and harsh."

"You can't worry about me," she said desperately. "You have business to take care of."

"I want you to think when you're with him, Dawn," he cautioned. "Don't let him fake you out."

He gripped her shoulders. "Do you understand? Don't voice doubt or uncertainty of any sort. One bit of hesitation and he'll have you—and he'll hurt you." He pulled her close in a tight embrace. "I have to go. I'll see you when you get back."

She walked with him to the door, lifted her face expectantly for his kiss. Van's lips touched hers like a whisper, the gentlest kiss she'd ever tasted.

"You be careful," he said softly. Then reclaiming her lips, he crushed her to him. She clung to him, never wanting to let go.

When he released her mouth, he kept his arms around her.

"I mean it, Dawn," he said raggedly.

"I will," she whispered. "You too."

Dawn leaned languidly against the doorframe watching his casual stride as he walked to his car. Once inside, the Corvette roared to life. Van would be back in Preston, soon, to face whatever dangers awaited in her hometown.

She turned to take a last look at the suddenly lonely room. Last night it had been a place of passion and romance. Now it was only an insignificant room with a bed, television and dresser.

Dawn opened her forgotten coffee. It was barely warm, but drinkable. Anxious to be on her way, she decided to take it with her.

She carried the overnight bag out to the car. He had supplied a huge thermos of cold water. All she needed was makeup, a few essentials and clothes for the trip, which she purchased at a local shop.

She'd only had about five hour sleep, and noticed her eyes growing heavy little more than an hour on the road. Dawn pulled into a rest area for coffee. Sipping the strong brew, she reviewed the map.

With less than fifty miles to the border, then seventy more before the route turned off the main road, then a straight shot of a hundred miles or so to the little town—with steady driving, she would be there easily before dusk.

She downed her coffee, made use of the rest stop facility, and then with the radio blasting, resumed driving to the beat of her favorite rock and roll.

After a brief inspection by border patrol, on the road again, she struggled with rising apprehension. A short while ago, if anyone had predicted her life taking this turn, she would have thought it an unlikely fantasy, exciting and terrifying, not something that could actually happen.

Aware of the need to be in control of her emotions, she turned her thoughts to devising a story for John, preparing for the perilous encounter.

Dawn arrived in record time. She parked in front of the only hotel, located on the dirt main street, before sunset as anticipated. There wasn't another car in sight. The only people she saw were a couple of men sitting out in front of a General Store.

She carried her luggage inside, setting it down in front of the counter.

Dawn paid for the night, signing in as Cynthia Kaley. The smiling, big-bellied clerk carried her suitcase and overnight bag to a room on the second floor of the two-story hotel.

"I have a large thermos of water, could you bring it up for me?" She tipped him generously for his trouble.

"Se, Senorita, gracias Senorita."

He returned immediately with the water and more broad smiles. He set the container on a side table.

"Thank you." Dawn locked the door behind him.

Emotionally and physically exhausted, she undressed immediately.

After slipping a lightweight gown over her head, she turned around and found the bathroom. It was so small, she didn't feel comfortable closing the door, and she had never been claustrophobic. Talk about a bed and bath!

Dawn replaced the worn and dingy sheets with the new set she had purchased, before falling into bed.

She wiped away a sweat drop that trickled down her forehead with the corner of her sheet. An ancient, tinny fan positioned in the window supplied only a warm breeze that barely wafted against her face while a gnawing in her stomach reminded her of the doughnuts she had neglected to eat.

Discomfort abounded, but in spite of that—in what seemed the passing of an instant—lively music filtering its way into her dreams awakened her.

She moaned pulling a pillow over her head to no avail.

The music persisted, lively and invigorating. Dawn sat up swinging her legs languidly over the side of the bed. To help revive her and because she felt parched, she poured a tall glass of water, drinking it down thirstily.

Removing her gown, she haphazardly tossed it at the trashcan on her way to the closet sized bathroom.

She brushed her teeth, took a quick, cool shower, and after thoroughly drying, before sweat started dripping again, sprayed liberally with Secret antiperspirant deodorant. She sprinkled on body powder. Mmm, it smelled faintly of her favorite scent of musk, another one of Van's purchases.

Dawn applied a bit more make-up than usual, hoping to look age appropriate.

She brushed her hair, noticing the bangs seemed to make her look so young. She hadn't thought that before, but now—she brushed them back away from her face. They were long enough to stay softly to the side.

Dawn stared at her reflection in the slightly distorted bathroom mirror, anxiously nibbling her lip. Since it gave her the appearance of about a twelve-year-old child, she determined not to do that again.

Dressed in hip hugger jeans with a soft white tee shirt tucked in, she slipped a wide black belt through the loops of her jeans, hoping to appear casual, but sophisticated and confident, not young and inexperienced in life.

Taking slow calming breaths, Dawn steadied her emotions. Trusting her weak legs not wobble, she felt as ready as she'd ever be.

She slipped a jean vest over her tee shirt, pulled on tan ankle boots and then headed downstairs. Standing out on the wooden walkway, Dawn took in a view that made it easy to imagine restless young cowboys riding into town with whooping shouts and rowdy moods, heading into the tavern for a wild night of fun and brawling.

It looked like a scene from a western movie, complete with an old man in sombrero and poncho moseying slowly down the dusty road with his donkey clomping along behind. She wondered idly where his destination might be, which brought to mind her own destination.

Dawn turned to the music that beckoned through the swinging doors. She spotted John sitting in the back at the counter his eyes on a woman doing a lively dance to the music of Mexican guitars.

She recognized him from Christi's description, an exceptionally handsome man, strikingly handsome, in fact. He looked so normal, but Dawn knew how dangerous and unstable he could be.

She walked right up to him. "Excuse me, Mr. Burton," she said clearly, her voice unwavering.

He didn't even glance her way. She felt vague uneasiness, the way he disregarded her presence.

"You are John Burton, from Preston City?"

"Who wants to know," he said casually, his eyes still on the woman.

His voice affected her, subtly unnerving—soft and smooth as honey flowing, but with a still ominous quality. She remembered with vivid clarity Christi telling her about that distinction.

"I know who you are."

His expression didn't change at first, but when he turned dark eyes in her direction, a glimmer of awareness lit within the depths of his gaze.

He lowered his head, his look not exactly dangerous, but chancy.

"How do you happen to know me, when I don't know you? Sit down," he indicated the stool beside him. "Tell me a little about yourself."

Fearing he might hear her heart beating, but determined, nonetheless, she slipped onto the bar stool next to him. "I'm Cynthia Kaley." She introduced herself, offering her cutest beguiling grin.

"Is that so?" he replied, apparently indifferent to her name and charms.

"I'm here to make you a business proposition, John," she said eloquently. "Does the name Christi Temple mean anything to you?"

Dawn had been uncertain of what to expect, but *something*. His utterly impassive air was unpleasantly intimidating.

"She's dead," he said, his voice flat and dismissive. He took a long swallow from the drink sitting in front of him.

"She is alive and well and living in Preston."

"Who is Christi Temple to you?"

His attention, now that she had it, was highly unnerving. He had a distant and strange air about him. Afraid and not knowing what to expect, she imagined the worst, that this was the weird John, Christi had described.

Dawn repressed an anxious shiver, thinking maybe he was acting a little peculiar because of the unexpected news about Christi.

He placed a hand on her shoulder, almost comforting. Gazing into her eyes with a perfectly bland expression, his hand slid smoothly down her arm, clamping her wrist, uncomfortable but not worth flinching over.

"You enjoy causing pain?"

"Not especially." He unhurriedly released her. "Alright, Miss Cynthia Kaley," he said with a satirical glimpse. "This is no place to talk business. We should go somewhere private."

He left her sitting.

Dawn watched his retreat feeling frustrated, and indecisive.

She carelessly picked up the drink he had left, downing the contents with a shudder. This is not the time to start thinking about consequences.

She hurried after him. If his eerie, freaky self only lasted for that little length of time, she could cope.

He entered the hotel, Dawn caught up with him, following him upstairs.

She walked a few feet into a grungy, efficiency apartment. This room had a sofa and chair, all the comforts of home, she thought dryly.

When she turned, John was leaning against the door, giving her a musing look that she did not wish to further consider, since she was alone and defenseless with him, in a motel room.

She didn't shy away though, she met his steady gaze.

"Okay—let's discuss what we came here for," Dawn suggested, hoping her voice sounded stronger and more confident than it did to her own ears.

"Discuss what?"

"Christi Temple."

Dawn heard the faltering quality. She cleared her throat, realizing that her strategic meeting was not going well. He would have picked up on the edgy hesitation, a point in his favor.

"Why should I want her? I have you now."

A slow smile surfaced as he took out a slim black knife, pressing the release button instantaneously. The glistening blade held her focus. Her throat tightened, pressure filled her chest, but she finally shifted her gaze away from the blade to look at his self-satisfied face.

"Do you want to get out of your clothes, or do you want me to help you?"

Think of what Van said, think! She knew she was on the edge. She had to snap out of it or lose control.

"You boys and your toys," Dawn said reclaiming her calm. "John, you surprise me! You seem intelligent, and you're an exceptionally good-looking man. Why would you force yourself on a woman?"

"I've wondered myself before."

She could almost think he was serious except for the little smirk.

"I suppose it could be classified as a perverted desire. Doesn't it have something to do with violence?"

"I thought you were bright enough," she said summoning her strength, acting faintly derisive. "Don't you care if you live or die?"

"Oh, I care about that. Why do you ask?"

"Bob Kaley is my father, you idiot, and I'm his pride and joy, his only child," she said, her eyes never wavering. "He's an influential person, as you may well know. How do you think I found you?"

Hoping the name calling wasn't too much of a push, she waited. If she only took into account his expression, the revelation didn't seem to faze him, but he pocketed the knife.

"What if I believe you? What's the deal, here?" John looked her over head to toe, his dark gaze returning to her face. "You didn't answer my question. How do you know Christi?"

"That's unimportant. I want Christi Temple out of the way."

He studied her intently for a few seconds with observant eyes.

"I'll decide what's unimportant. How long have you lived in Preston?"

"Long enough to meet Billy Cole, and long enough to know about your somewhat fixated involvement with Christi."

"So what's your bag?"

"I want Billy, and he's too hung up on her."

"You don't care if she gets hurt?"

"I won't be dwelling on it."

"You look far too innocent to be so lethal."

"Looks can be deceiving. I get what I want." Confident and defiant—but as seconds passed, she felt herself coming unraveled under his quiet stare.

"You would be well compensated for your efforts," she told him feeling a need to break the silence.

What was he thinking? Why didn't he say something?

"You can let me know tomorrow," she suggested, wanting to be out from under his scrutiny.

"Two o'clock," he said agreeably.

Dawn walked to the door, but he lounged against it unmoving. She met his eyes, penetrating and incisive; he seemed to reach into her thoughts.

The few acting lessons she had indulged in with her friends in junior high had gotten her through so far. She softened her expression to project a calm exterior, hoping John could not detect that she felt striped, her emotions exposed, under his keen observance.

John leaned forward, his voice low and softly mocking. "You might act all grown up, but you are a terrified little girl."

He moved out of the way continuing to watch in waiting silence.

She clenched her hands at her sides, angry and afraid. "I'm not afraid of you," she said in a clear, positive tone, then stepped quickly into the hallway before he could make another unsettling comment.

She knew his intimidating statement had been meant to leave her trembling in fear of his explicit observation. Getting the last word in seemed somehow necessary, giving her the sensation, on a somewhat broad spectrum, of being not so out of control.

Using Bob Kaley's name had been an inspiration, the best insurance in this frightening situation. Suddenly it seemed more important to get out of here alive than taking John back to Preston City.

All she had to do was hop in her little Impala and drive away, leaving this nothing town behind in a cloud of dust. That was all she had to do—but the thought left her feeling empty and unsatisfied. Leaving here without giving it her best shot was not an option.

Dawn opened the door of her room to discover a small boy wearing a large sombrero sitting in a wicket chair. He smiled at her, and she spontaneously felt obligated to smile in return.

"Well, hello there." What a *cutie,* she thought, before subduing her smile, wondering at her slight response to finding him looking quite comfortable in her room. But his smile was contagious, and he was so little in that huge hat.

"Okay, Mr. Sombrero." Dawn tried to regard him more seriously. "Who are you and why are you here?"

"Senorita, I am Enrique." He stood, sweeping the sombrero off in an elegant gesture.

"What are you doing in my room, little man? Isn't it past your bedtime? And is it okay if I call you Ricky? Enrique seems so—I don't know, big."

"Si, Senorita—call me Ricky." He laughed heartily. "You ask plenty questions," he commented with that bright smile

"And that reminds me, why *are* you here?"

"I see you with Senor Burton."

"Yeah, well, don't hold that against me. What do you know about John?"

"Senor Burton is bad hombre," he told her gravely. "Why do you come to see?"

She leaned toward him, lowering her voice. "John committed a serious crime. I came to take him back to California."

"You are bounty hunter?" His big, brown eyes widened in surprise.

"Shhh! No." Dawn had to smile again. This boy did have a way about him. "It's a long story."

"Is a sad story," he observed. "I see your eyes hurt."

"You are perceptive." She sighed feeling suddenly empty and drained. "Yeah, you might say my eyes hurt when I remember."

"Then I will not ask," he promised solemnly. "I do not wish to bring you sorrow. Forgive me for sad memoria."

Dawn's heart melted. "It's not your fault. It's difficult to avoid memories, really, when they're the reason for your actions . . . You're an okay guy, Ricky. I like you."

"Then I will be your amigo." The wide, captivating smile lit up his face again. "I have mucho amigos," he informed her, with an affirming nod.

"Well, you can never have too many, right?" He made her feel like smiling, and she enjoyed the feeling tremendously. "Thank you, Ricky," Dawn said happily. "I would be honored to join your list of many amigos."

He looked pleased with her acceptance. "Si bueno," he said happily. "Hasta manana, Senorita."

"Goodnight," she called after him.

Completely captivated by the precocious little boy, she wondered why he had singled her out to be his 'amigo', but then sighed tiredly, supposing that he could observe quite easily that she needed a friend.

Dawn took another thin gown out of her suitcase. The tiny bathroom had a shower stall, sink and commode. The water was little more than a trickle but the second shower felt almost as good as the first. She made it another quick one, though, preparing for bed with minimum effort.

The day had taken a toll in spite of the nap. It had not been nearly long enough to revitalize her after the long drive.

She felt an oddly slight hunger, knowing she should be ravenous, considering that she had not eaten in over twenty-four hours.

Her focus had been on meeting John. Now she felt too physically and emotionally exhausted to go in search of sustenance.

Tomorrow will be here soon enough, she thought drowsily. Lying down on the surprisingly comfortable bed, Dawn drifted off to the music still pulsating from the tavern below.

Chapter Thirty-Two

Nancy waited anxiously, wondering what Dave would say after he hung up the phone. Earlier in the evening he had been worried about Van.

"Van still isn't answering," he said uneasily. "I have to go."

"Dave, please don't," Nancy begged.

His lips brushed against hers, finally settling in a long, sweet kiss. He caressed the bare skin of her back and shoulders. They had just made love, and now he was about to leave her to venture into a night of imminent danger.

He released her, smiling softly, understanding reflecting in his blue eyes.

"Isn't there anything I can say that will convince you to stay?"

"You're pretty darn convincing, lovey, but not in this case."

"Dave, I love you." She brushed the dark tendrils of hair that always curled over his forehead. "I'm afraid for you."

"I'll be fine." He cupped her face in his hands, kissing her again tenderly. "I love you, too."

She gave him a long woeful look as reached for his jeans.

Nancy leaned back against the pillow watching him dress. He was concerned for his friend, it was wrong to try to stop him. Still, that detail didn't help her feelings as she reluctantly pulled a short terrycloth robe over her nude body to walk with him to the door.

"Hurry back," she whispered putting her arms up around his neck.

"I won't be gone long," he promised.

Their lips met for a lingering kiss as he slipped his hands inside the robe. She pressed closer burying her face against his throat, inhaling the masculine scent that was distinctly David Temple.

"It might be a few hours, so get some sleep."

"A few hours is long," she protested.

"You know how fast time passes when you're dreaming," he said softly. He brushed his lips over hers, light, and promisingly teasing. "I'll be back here before you know it."

* * *

Billy had just been drifting to sleep when a sudden pounding on the door caused him to jump about two feet off the sofa. He warily opened the door not knowing if he should be worried.

"Hey, Dave, come in." Billy yawned elaborately as he opened the door a bit wider before turning back to the sofa. "Is everything okay?"

"Yes and no, Christi's fine, but there's something else. Bad timing, I take it," Dave apologized. "Were you sleeping?"

"About half, what's up?" He noticed Dave's agitation as he lit a cigarette, then looked around for an ashtray. Billy put an ashtray in front of him waiting expectantly, sensing an uneasy something in the air.

"Do you know Van Morrison?"

The suddenly uneasy feeling accelerated to tense. "The pusher?"

"He's not a pusher—he's a nark," Dave confided. "I had a feeling about him all the time," he added with a distinct ring of pride.

Billy felt mass confusion. "Excuse me," he said with an arbitrary glance. "Do you want me to like, kick his ass or somethin'?"

"This is serious," Dave said solemnly. "He was going to make a drug bust tomorrow night, but I think something's wrong. I can't find him anywhere."

"Yeah, well what's it to us?" Billy couldn't help feeling a bit cynical. Sure he was off drugs now—"Narks aren't my favorite people, Dave."

"You don't know him like I do," he interrupted. "Van's solid, Billy. He's helped Christi more than you could imagine. He's been tight with us."

Billy cast his eyes down, Dave's words sinking in. It was true. He had never known Van Morrison enough to give him any consideration at all. Now he felt mixed emotions, but trust in a nark, regardless, he could not fathom.

"Come on," Dave coaxed. "I know it seems odd but I know what I'm talking about. Listen to me, Billy," he said forcefully, obviously noting his discontent. "Van isn't just any nark on the block. He's a narcotics cop. Pushers are killers, and I liked Van when I thought he was a fuckin' pusher."

"Okay, so he's a nice guy. The best way to help is stay out of his way."

"I thought I could count on you." Dave's voice had dropped a perceptibly disappointed note. "But if that's how you feel, I can dig it." He spoke the words amiably, stood, and then left, closing the door softly behind him.

Apparently his advice to stay out of Van's way didn't carry any weight. Billy sighed audibly, his heart beating heavy in his chest. Many thoughts raced through his head as he sat in the complete stillness of the apartment.

Everything had been on solid ground, now it felt shaky, but he couldn't just sit here. Billy ran into the hall after him.

"Hey, Dave, wait up!"

He stopped abruptly, smiling self-consciously. Dave was standing right outside the door leaning against the wall with his arms crossed waiting. They headed out of the apartment building together, taking long strides as Dave filled him in.

"There're some men in town, Billy, drug lords—big time, bad news. The meeting with Bob Kaley and Van was supposed to be at the Bailey Mansion tomorrow night. I have a hunch, and it isn't good."

Billy remembered the old Bailey Mansion from way back. It had been deserted for years, rumored to be haunted, of course. As kids, they had used it on Halloween for an 'authentic' haunted house.

They had partied in it as teenagers. It had been a fun place. If Dave's feelings were right, it would not be fun tonight.

"He's been after these particular men for a long time, deep undercover for over two years." Pride rang strong in his voice. "Gotta admire the man."

"Yeah, maybe *you* do," he said, confused. "I don't get why he let you in on it, though. What's up with that?"

"It wasn't something he meant to do—Paul Jenson was damn near the breaking point after what happened to Carrie," Dave explained. "When he thought Dawn was dead, too, Paul fell apart. He came to me and spilled his guts. I was ready to take Van out, or die tryin'."

Dave shrugged casually, and then grinned.

"So, Van didn't have a choice, he had to tell you, but isn't it dangerous for others to know he's a nark?"

"Well, yeah—but after tomorrow night he would have been done here, but something's happened. I don't know what, but nothing good."

"Do you think he'd want us butting in?"

Billy had his own opinion about this, and it wasn't good either. He searched for words to discourage Dave, but with another glance at his set, determined face, figured it was a useless expectation.

"It's personal, too. I take it kind of personal when someone plans to frame me for murder. That was Bob's intention. I don't know why I involved you, though," Dave speculated. "This isn't really your concern."

"Yes, it is," Billy said good-naturedly. "You thought I was someone you could count on . . . Besides, do you think Chris would ever speak to me again if I let you do this crazy stunt on your own?"

"Ah, probably not," he said agreeably.

Dave lit a cigarette. They continued in silence, departing the west side, entering a less occupied, quiet area, finally ascending the gently sloping hill, ducking behind some shrubs, moving stealthily but quickly upward.

A full moon and sky full of stars offered enough lighting while plenty of tall shrubbery in the area provided a swath of shadows. Drawing close to the house, keeping well in the shadows, Billy began to get nervous.

"Lights are on. Someone's there for sure."

"Okay—they set it up a night early."

"So what do we do?" Billy wondered aloud as seconds ticked by. "I'm almost sure that was an unmarked cop car down there," Billy told him feeling more uncomfortable about the situation. "They're up here somewhere."

"Something's wrong about that," Dave said.

"I wonder—stay here, I'll be back."

"Billy—"

Billy put a hand up at Dave's cautious tone. "It's okay, I'll be careful."

He ran in a crouch to the house, then moved cautiously around the side and peeked through a window. He took it all in at a glance, and then dropped to the ground, Van, three men in suits and four brawny henchmen.

He saw them a few feet away, lying side by side. Billy felt certain that they were undercover cops. Van's back up? Upon inspection, he discovered they had been shot in the head.

"Oh, shit." He backed quickly away.

Billy looked for a sickening moment at the blood on his hands. He wiped them through the grass to get most of it off before hurrying back where Dave waited crouched behind some shrubbery.

"They're dead," he told him. "Four dead cops for Christ sake. They were discovered, taken by surprise, disarmed, and executed."

"They were his—they must have been his back up—son of a bitch!" Dave gazed steadily at the house. "Van's in there."

"Yes, I saw him. I'll go radio for help. Wait for me." Dave seemed ready to pounce. "Don't go in alone."

"Hurry! We don't know how much time he has left."

Billy went to summon assistance thinking how lucky for Van that Dave had decided to get involved. So far Van was unhurt, but for how long? They were already suspicious. Discovering cops on the scene couldn't have helped.

He wondered if Van knew the cops were dead. Well, if he didn't, he had to know something was wrong by now, and he had looked calm. Come what may, he felt the man would keep his cool. If his cover wasn't blown, he surely wouldn't try to take them out alone! Billy had never seen death until tonight. He didn't want to see any more.

He made it to the car, radioed for help, and then headed back up the hill with serious misgiving about interfering in police work. He tried to think a way out of this confusion. Narcotics cops, drug lords, undercover crap—

He didn't want any part of it.

Billy sidled up to Dave. "They're on the way," he said. "It shouldn't take long. Why don't we get the hell outta here?" He looked around uneasily.

"I bet it won't be too soon for Van," Dave reflected. "How many?"

"Three suits and four big body guards." Billy told him. "This isn't our scene, buddy, let's split."

"I'm not leaving."

He noticed Dave's anxiety again and urged him to be cool. He watched the lighted window feeling out of control, like he stood on the edge of a high cliff about to topple over.

Time passed at a snail's pace as he wondered what he would do if Dave decided to barge in. The officers arrived bringing an extent of relief.

Officer Jarred ordered the two of them to get out of there. Billy started to move, but Dave stayed him with a hand on his arm. He looked at the officer deadpan, without comment.

"You don't need to be here," Jarred insisted. "We can handle things. We have back-up coming."

"There are seven of them," Billy said looking toward the house. "Maybe you should wait."

"They'll be right behind us."

Billy looked behind him as the officers moved in. He didn't see anyone.

"It's goin' down," Dave said. "Come on!"

Against all better judgment, but knowing he could not stop Dave, Billy stayed close. Whatever the reasons, Dave felt they had to follow through, and there was no way he would let him go it alone.

The reaction to their entering was rapid gunfire. Officer Jarred, riddled with bullets, managed to take out one of the men who got him as he went down. More shots rang out. Officer Jamison was hit, probably dead.

Desperation moved him, Billy jump-kicked the guard, sending him reeling. The big man regained his footing, coming back up with his gun.

He was ready. The second kick sent the gun flying out of his hands, but the guy was right back at him. Billy punched him a few times, dodging the slower man pretty easily. He felt a searing pain in his arm—but the mountain of a man was on him again before he had time to consider it.

Billy pounded him with blows, dodging and punching—the man was weakening, almost out on his feet, when suddenly someone shot him.

Billy knew the guy was shot, but apparently he didn't—he still wanted to fight. "Don't you know you're dead?" Billy said, punching him one last time—he went down. Billy wasn't sure if it was from the gunshot wound or the fact that he was about to drop anyway.

With a sweeping glimpse he saw everyone was down.

In the sudden quiet, he realized it was over. Then he saw a man making a mad dash for the door from behind a chair. Dave tackled him, turned him around, and took a punch—knocked off balance by a flailing fist.

Watching the last of the traumatic interaction, Billy felt a sense of urgency. It happened inconceivably fast, a gun in the man's hand as Dave straightened; Van uselessly pulling the trigger of the gun he had retrieved.

In that same instant Billy flung his knife. It spanned the room and met its mark with precision.

The man's eyes went wide in astonishment, an ultimate look of disbelief. The gun dropped from his hand before he collapsed to the floor.

With a relieved sigh, Billy realized it really was over. It had happened quicker than it felt. From the time they came in until now had been minutes, the longest minutes of his life. His eyes scanned the bodies around the room.

No one stood except the three of them, but with an observant look, he saw Dave leaning weakly against the wall, holding his stomach.

"Dave's been hit!" Billy yelled as Dave sank to the floor.

Van reached him first, lifting his head, cradling him on his arm, smoothing the dark, unruly hair back from his face, feeling helpless with instinctive knowledge that the wound was fatal.

"Ah—Van." He grimaced in obvious pain. Van felt the tight clutch of his hand. "It wasn't—supposed to happen—ah, fuck—"

Then it seemed the pain let up, a brief smile softened his features.

"I saw Kaley—go down," he said.

"He did, and the rest. We got them all."

"Van—" His eyes fluttered shut. Van looked at the hand holding his as the grip loosened.

"I'm with you, Dave. I'm here—Dave, I couldn't have done it without you."

He tried to say something but it seemed like the words stuck in his throat.

"Don't try to talk," Billy said despairingly seeing a trickling of blood at the edge of Dave's mouth. "Hold on."

His eyes focused on Billy. "Take care—of Chris." A strangled cough ended on a soft moan.

An expression of pain clouded his face.

"Van, I think I know why—" He grinned faintly, drew a short breath and tried to say more but his voice faded. Van leaned closer.

"Tell Nancy—" Dave's grip tightened, then fell loose as the light left his blue eyes in a fleeting instant.

Van sat silent for a reflective moment . . . Feeling deep sadness at the loss of this young man, he gently closed Dave's eyes, and then lowered his head carefully to the floor.

He wondered if he would ever forget that if he hadn't shot that useless guard, he could have saved him, a gun is faster than a knife.

"Let's get the hell out of here."

He strode over to Kaley's body, and retrieved Billy's knife, wiping it on the dead man's shirt. Billy still sat in stunned anguish on the floor near Dave.

"It's time to go," Van said, reaching him the knife.

"We can't just leave him here like this."

"Take this—we have to go. Dave is dead—he's dead, Billy." Van took his arm. "Are you with me?"

He looked at him through dazed eyes, and then drew a sharp breath. Billy headed for the door, pocketing the knife without looking back. Van kept his stride. As they left the grounds, he heard sirens in the distance.

"Oh, man," Billy choked, his voice rough with emotion. "I feel like running. I feel like fucking running. I never saw anyone die like that," he said fiercely.

Van could hear desperation in Billy's voice while he struggled to rein in his own emotions. Why had they been there?

"How do I tell them? How can I?" Billy moaned helplessly. "I can't do it. I can't—it's too much."

Van felt his own raging emotions, swayed by the impact this would have on the twins' lives. He easily understood Billy's need to run. The last thing he wanted was to face Mike and Chris with the devastating consequences of a drug bust gone awry.

There were too many questions without answers.

"I'll be with you. This isn't something you have to go through alone."

He put a comforting hand on Billy's shoulder. Van felt him flinch.

"What's wrong?" he said. Then he noticed the dark blotch on his shirt. "You're bleeding."

"It's just a flesh wound."

"It still has to be cleaned and dressed," Van said vaguely, distracted with facing the twins. "Infection could set in. I'll get you to the hospital and make sure they get you in fast. Don't worry, you won't have to answer any questions, but I have a few calls to make, and I'll get Mike. He's probably home."

* * *

Van paused under a streetlight. He wondered if he could ever erase the scene in the hospital room. Mike and Christi clinging to each other, Billy wanting to comfort them, his eyes reflecting the helplessness he felt—that anyone feels when faced with the greatest loss.

He lit a cigarette, taking a deep draw, delaying for a time the inevitable encounter. He glanced up at the lighted window. He had to be the one to tell Nancy. Dave's last request had been to tell her something significant, but it had died with him. Nancy would never hear what he wanted her to know.

He remembered the day Dave told him about his and Nancy's budding relationship, how happy he had been.

Van sighed heavily, it was time. He tossed the cigarette aside before entering the apartment building. Nancy opened the door to his knock. She glanced behind him quickly.

"Van, I wasn't expecting you," she said in a low, reserved voice.

"May I come in?"

"Of course." She opened the door a bit wider inviting him inside.

"Let's sit down," he suggested.

"Dave sent you, didn't he?" she asked softly. "Something happened and he couldn't come. He wouldn't want me to worry."

Van captured her cold hands in his as her expression wavered.

"I know where he went. He told me, but he should have been here by now." Her voice cracked.

"I'm sorry, Nancy," he said gently.

"Dave isn't coming back to me, is he?"

He offered the comfort of his arms around her. She sobbed brokenly against his shoulder. Crying could be a good thing. He hoped it was good that she could let it out. He wondered illogically if it hurt more to ache silently without the tears.

"It doesn't seem possible," she whispered. "He was just with me. How can he be gone forever? He said he wouldn't be gone long. He said to sleep for a while and he'd be back."

"Here, you'd better sit down." Van led her to the sofa.

"What happened?"

Her eyes were swimming in tears. It tore him up to see her like this. His attitude of self-command and studied relaxation deserted him.

"Bob had a gun, Dave went for him."

It sounded so damn heartless, cold as he reviewed it in his mind. Bob Kaley shot and fatally wounded David Temple, and who cares; his sister, his brother, his girl, maybe a few others.

For the most part, the people in this town would never realize what he had done for them. People would read about it and enjoy weeks of gossip about the 'gang member'.

For many reasons, notwithstanding Billy's presence at the scene, he couldn't divulge the reason for Dave's being there. All they would know is he was a Cobra. They wouldn't know about the hero within the bad boy.

"They're dead, too," he told her, hoping she might draw some comfort in the disclosure. "Every one of the lousy bastards that had anything to do with Dave's death, they're all dead."

He took some tissue from a box on the end table and wiped her tears.

"I begged him not to go," she said tremulously before wrenching sobs overtook her again. He held her, helpless to ease the suffering.

He played idly with the softness of her hair as her crying diminished. She rested her head on his chest. Van sighed wearily, feeling deep despair.

"It wasn't supposed to go down this way."

"What do you mean?"

"Tomorrow night—it would have been a whole different scenario. We would have bombarded that place."

Van couldn't make sense of it. If Bob didn't trust him, why have the meet at all? It couldn't have been Bob. Something else had gone wrong, and he wouldn't rest until he found out what.

They sat silently for a long time.

"I miss him," she finally whispered. "I miss him already."

"I know," he said compassionately. "I miss him, too—we got acquainted this past year," he told her. "I was fortunate to know him. I'm glad I took the opportunity to spend some time with him."

She lifted her face and he looked into the saddest eyes. He fell silent. Words meant to comfort can sound empty in the midst of grief.

"I have to go now. Can I take you somewhere, to your parent's house?"

"No, I want to stay here."

"You shouldn't be alone."

"No, I'll be alright."

She walked with him to the door, remembering after he left that she had not asked about Dave's brother and sister. Walking back through the empty apartment, Nancy sighed despondently. They would have been her brother and sister-in-law, but now, well, they didn't need her in their lives.

She sat alone in the darkness feeling the grief, the emptiness, and the complete senselessness of it all.

It didn't seem possible. She could hardly make herself believe that in a sudden instant, everything was gone—his life, his love, their life together . . .

Nancy wrapped her arms around herself. She had found love. In this world that could be so cold and foreboding, they had shared a warm and wonderful affection.

Enveloped in sorrow throughout the night, in the silent loneliness of her apartment, she gazed out the window at the lightening sky. Nancy watched the stars begin to fade as the night gave way to a gray dawn. It would be hard not to think about what might have been. It would be impossible.

Chapter Thirty-Three

Dawn glanced at her watch as the minute hand slipped past the twelve. One minute after two o'clock. She rapped gently on John's door.

He opened it, giving her access. "Come in, Miss Kaley."

She walked a few feet into the room. "Have you thought about my proposition?" She turned to face him.

John had closed the door and was leaning against it with his arms crossed. Dawn forced herself to stand firm, to not take another step back or flinch at his expression—his mouth with the know it all smirk and the way his eyes leveled on her like fire and ice. She almost shivered under his gaze.

"Tell me some more about Billy Cole," he said emanating a menacing quality that made her uneasy.

"What is it you want to know?"

"How you met him might be a good start. Why you would want him might be a better one." His look held a hint of suspicion.

"You could at least offer me a drink," she said airily, buying some time.

"Won't you have a seat Miss Kaley?" he suggested.

"You can call me Cynthia."

He indicated the threadbare sofa, but she chose a high back wooden chair, sitting gingerly upon it, uncomfortable physically and almost falling apart emotionally.

"Okay, so I met Billy at one of Dawn Preston's beach bashes. Her parties are renowned, you know—It was lust at first sight for me, but for some reason he had taken up with the likes of Christi Temple." Just a touch of disdain, not too thick, he would notice overkill.

"Mmm-hmm . . . And what would you want with 'the likes of' Billy Cole?" he said with a deliberate wink, handing her a shot glass of whiskey.

She held the little glass carefully.

"Have you seen him?" she asked, letting her voice go a little breathless. She answered her own question. "Of course you have . . . He's a beautiful male specimen. Besides," she pouted. "I just want to play with him."

Dawn took a tiny sip of the nasty whiskey. Fighting a gag reflex, she set the glass down on a rickety end table.

"Anyway—I met him at the party . . . He was there with her." Dawn shifted in her chair, crossing her legs, leaning forward. "I stood half a chance when she was in a coma. I heard all about how you tried to breeze out of town with her, by the way."

A dark look clouded John's face, reminding her of his twisted feelings for Christi. Dawn decided not to press it.

"What is it about Billy Cole?" he murmured vaguely.

Dawn chose to ignore the low key remark.

"Anyway, I seemed to be making headway, playing sympathetic and all." She sighed dramatically. "Then she recovered, and he was right back at her."

"That's a cute story. I enjoyed it." His dark eyes studied her face.

Keeping her features deceptively composed, she took a short breath and moistened her lips wishing for a swallow of her precious water. With the realization that it wasn't going well, Dawn stood, adjusting her purse more comfortably on her shoulder. "This seems to be a waste of time," she said resolutely. "Since you haven't made a decision, I'll check with you later."

"No, no I don't think so."

His tone caused disturbing quakes in her already faltering serenity. She bit her lip gently, too late recalling the youthfulness it conveyed, the doubt it would reveal to John, and the warning Van had so carefully explained.

She straightened herself with dignity to give him a derisive 'low-life' sweep of her eyes.

"You present yourself well," he told her knowingly. "But I did some checking. Kaley's daughter is older than you, stands five-six, weighs in at about a hundred and fifty, with blond hair and baby blues—wears glasses this thick." He held his thumb and forefinger up to indicate almost an inch.

He pushed away from the wall giving her a half-smile, evocative look.

"You're busted," he said softly. "Little Miss not-so-clever. You aren't going anywhere."

Dawn moistened her lips again. She couldn't keep from averting her eyes, afraid they would reflect the stark fear that held her in a paralyzing grip.

He walked forward stopping in front of her. His hands moved slowly up her arms to rest on her shoulders. It became difficult to breathe as he wound a hand in her hair, tugging her head back.

The lethal calmness in his intelligent eyes sent a shiver of dread over her defenseless body. She was dead. Here and now, in this small hotel room, in a dusty, insignificant, little nothing town.

She searched for a sign of mercy; she saw a glimpse of triumph, an almost imperceptible flicker.

Dawn raised her chin with a calm that amazed her. "My father is going to *kill you.*"

His expression stayed observant, but he slowly released her keeping eye contact. Not averting her eyes, being as daring as possible, she nonetheless took a step back. Any distance would help her weakening composure.

"Do you have identification, Little Miss Kaley?"

She started to reach into the purse, but he took it, rummaged through it, removed the wallet, and then carefully viewed the fake ID. He gave her a quick glance, and a blatant grin, before giving the purse back.

Dawn draped it casually over her shoulder once more, amazed that she did not tremble visibly. Her insides felt like jell-o.

"So I lied," he said dismissively. "I'm not going back with you."

Instead of letting her mouth drop open in dismay, she managed, barely, to keep her poise. Dawn knew better than to question his decision, had been warned that it wouldn't be safe to push or argue, but it took more effort to keep her emotions in check than she had even imagined possessing.

"I know better than to step a foot in Preston. You came a long way for nothing."

She gazed at him restraining every instinct not to challenge. She opened her mouth to speak, closed it again, and swallowed the retort that came instantly to mind, the defiant insult that she could almost taste along with the disappointment, hiding it all with an appearance of indifference.

"Your loss," she said casually.

Van would have been very proud, but she had risked her life for nothing.

"You gonna split today or what?"

"Why do you ask?"

"I thought maybe we could have a drink," he grinned, with an appealingly expectant glimpse, so different she almost fell through the floor.

"I'd like that," she agreed, thinking there might be a slim possibility of getting him back to Preston. "Sure, I'll join you for a night on the town."

"Eight o'clock, then, at Miguel's."

"Eight o'clock," she readily agreed with the warmest smile she could fake.

Dawn left the room, pausing outside his door to catch her breath. She had been panic stricken. He had sounded so sure of himself, had looked so confidant—except for that one disturbingly brief moment.

If he had known she was not Bob Kaley's daughter he would have had no need to feel victorious when he took hold of her. He almost had her. Almost? He had her—she had nothing to lose by calling his bluff.

Back in her room, she found Enrique waiting.

"Buenos dias, Senorita," he said, his enthusiastic self. Then with a worried expression, "You have problema?"

"John isn't going back to California with me," she said, throwing her purse on the bed. Dawn poured a glass of water.

"My plan fell through, stupid—useless plan. Unless I can think of something—"

Dawn bit her lip feeling deflated, resigned, the hope she had briefly felt in his room disintegrated. It had been a bad idea. Preston City was a venture he would never risk.

"He made it perfectly clear. John's not going back to Preston."

"You no go back without him!"

She smiled in spite of herself at his thickly accented speech.

Dawn walked to the window, the sense of defeat and disappointment a deep churning sensation that felt almost nauseating.

"I don't want to, but I don't know what else I can do. I can't exactly twist his arm. Van told me not to challenge him, not to push. If he's made up his mind not to go back to Preston—I don't know. I just don't know how I can convince him." Dawn sighed feeling helpless. "We're meeting tonight for drinks at Miguel's. Maybe if he has more than a few drinks, he'll change his mind."

She had her doubts, though. It would take total inebriation to head him in that direction.

"You will meet with Senor Burton at Miguel's for drinking?"

She turned at the excitement in his voice.

"Well, yeah, it's the only place, Ricky."

"Que bueno," he declared heading for the door. "Miguel is me amigo."

"Well, of *course* he is," she said astutely. "But what are you getting at? I'm not sure about que bueno—something good?" she said once again hopeful, happy for his enthusiasm but otherwise confused.

"Si Senorita. What is it you say—twist his arm?" Enrique nodded with a knowing twinkle in his eyes. "Could be we do the twist for you."

"Do the twist for me?" she said, smothering a smile as she inadvertently thought of Chubby Checker. "Where are you going?"

"To see Miguel, pronto. You like tortilla?"

"Yes, I would, thank you. I haven't eaten since I don't know when."

"I will bring tortilla," he promised before heading out the door.

"I would like some coffee if it isn't too much trouble," she called.

Dawn left the window overlooking a deserted and dusty street to stretch out on the bed. What was the little guy up to? She drifted into a half sleep as fleeting, indistinct dreams passed through her mind, disturbing images that slipped away when her eyes opened to gaze at a worn ceiling with a big brown spot spreading out of one corner.

She turned her face to the side for the dubious benefit of the warm breeze provided by the timeworn, clicking fan.

"Come on, Ricky, I'm starving!"

Dawn sat up, ready to go downstairs to find a tortilla for herself when he tapped lightly before entering the room.

With elaborate gestures, animation, and enthusiasm that kept her amused while she ate, he told her about the simple plan to thwart John Burton.

The town wanted rid of him, his threatening presence wasn't appreciated. They had to tread carefully where he was concerned, and he had committed at least one rape, the dancer at Miguel's. Ricky sobered as he told her Maria was his unwillingly 'novia'.

"John is a horrible man."

"Se, he is bad hombre."

After she met with him as agreed, the bartender would take it from there.

"Your drink, Senorita, is weak. Senor Burton is drinking *mucho* rotgut. At ten o'clock, Miguel will give him a knock-out."

"Knock-out?"

"Si, knock-out, to knock him out. You no understand lights out?" he exclaimed. Dawn laughed at his gesturing.

"Yes, I understand lights out. Sorry, I was somewhere else, I guess, but I'm here now." She took a sip of coffee. Dawn set it aside, smiling again at his quizzical expression. "I meant that I wasn't paying attention. I should have been, and now I am."

"He will be lights out for all night," Ricky said, confidently.

"You seem very certain of that," she said uneasily.

"Se, you take him back to United States of America and collect bounty." Ricky threw his head back and let out a great peal of laughter.

Dawn joined in his merriment. She couldn't help herself, she burst out laughing and it felt wonderful.

"You are mucho bonito," he said. "Even in your eyes sonriso!"

"Thanks to you," she said, tousling his dark hair. "You've helped me in so many ways since I've been here."

"I am mucho contento, Senorita."

"All I can say is thank you—well, gracias," she said sincerely.

Ricky gave her one of his brightest smiles before heading for the door. "Hasta la vista. Is time for siesta."

"Already? I haven't even finished my coffee."

Apparently that didn't matter to Ricky. He was out the door.

Dawn walked over to the small bed. She felt much too excited to sleep, first stark fear that she had been busted, then the distress of John refusing to go back, now the possibility that she might not be going back to California empty-handed—with the ever present possibility that something could go wrong, there were no guarantees.

Lying in the oppressive heat of the small hotel room, she turned her thoughts to Preston City and Van. She wondered if the drug bust had gone down—had it been a success? Were Bob and the others in jail awaiting trial?

Worrisome questions tumbled around in her mind. It troubled her not knowing, but it was also a temporary diversion from John Burton.

A knock on the door awakened her from what had been a decidedly sound nap. Dawn glanced at her watch, forcing her sleepy eyes to focus.

"Who is it?" she asked, groggily.

"Is your amigo, Senorita!"

Dawn dragged her tired body out of bed. "You make me go to sleep, then you wake me up," she grumbled opening the door for him. "Another hour would have been appreciated."

"Buenos tardes, Senorita" he smiled. "Is time un café?"

He held a cup of coffee out to her with a big smile.

"You know me too well, Ricky. Okay, I forgive you."

Dawn sat in the wicker chair by the window. Ricky sat cross-legged on the floor. She opened her steaming coffee taking a little sip.

The man in a sombrero walking down the middle of the road leading a small burro caught her attention again. Dawn wondered idly how many times a day he took that walk and where he might be going.

She fell in love with the quaintness of this little town that did not even have a location on a map, except the one Van made for her.

They talked of little incidentals as she drank her coffee before going to Miguel's for dinner.

Miguel's place served as the only restaurant as well as the only tavern in town. Ricky ordered their dinner. She enjoyed the homemade vegetable soup, slices of beef, and salad tremendously.

"Miguel is an excellent cook," Dawn said. The beef had been melt-in-your-mouth tender with a unique marinade, juicy and flavorful. She picked up an orange as Enrique laughed out loud.

"Miguel is no cook! His Senoria," he explained, still laughing.

"Is that very funny?" she asked, tossing him an orange. "Let's go for a walk while we eat these, okay?"

He reached for his sombrero. "Is mucho funny," he agreed, still chuckling as they left the bar.

Dawn fell silent on their walk through the dusty town. Thinking about his plan, it seemed way too simple.

"You fear Senor Burton mucho," Enrique said thoughtfully.

"Yes, I'm afraid of him."

"Miguel is to trust," he said confidently. "Nothing is going wrong."

"Hmmm, I want to believe that." Dawn took a tremulous breath. "John Burton is a man to be feared."

"Se, Senorita," he nodded solemnly.

She put her arm around his shoulder. "When my friend died—when she was murdered—I knew I had to find out who did it, but then it wasn't enough, even knowing he would be caught and punished. I insisted on being a part of bringing him to justice. It seemed right at the time."

He looked up at her, sympathy in his big brown eyes.

"Now I have doubts, I don't feel convinced that I'm doing the right thing," she admitted. "What motivated my need to bring him in? I thought it was inspired by good intentions, now I'm not so sure.

I don't want to feel like I have vengeance in my heart. I don't want to be that person."

"You have mucho sorrow." He wrapped his little hand around hers. "Come, I want to show you."

He led her to a nearby chapel. Ricky smiled encouragingly, releasing her hand. Dawn walked slowly into the small sanctuary. She approached the humble alter, feeling a sense of wellbeing as she knelt to pray.

Tears fell from her eyes to her folded hands. The solace that surrounded her in this temple offered an inner peace she had not known for a while.

She left feeling comforted. Enrique was waiting by the door when she stepped out into the sunshine.

Dawn entered the bar about ten minutes after John did that evening. He watched her approach, and then stood to greet her. Strange, she surmised, what the prestige of being Bob Kaley's daughter could accomplish.

"I'm glad you decided to come," he said sincerely. "I thought maybe you'd change your mind."

She returned his smile. "Not a chance."

They sat in a dim corner of the bar, getting to know each other in a way she would have rather not. John didn't attempt to molest her intimately, but he did touch—he touched in a caring way that belied his persona.

When he caressed her arm, her hand, her neck, the tenderness left her bewildered. He seemed to be sincere, but even so, it did not change the danger of his character. She determined not to be caught off guard by his benevolence.

He talked about his life, sharing personal revelations, things she did not want to know. From the time he could remember, he had been an abused child with only vague recollections of his mother.

She died before his fourth birthday. With no one to stand between him and the cruelty of a sick mind, he suffered horribly at the hands of Samuel Burton. Being beaten, locked in a dark closet or tied to a bed for hours at a time, were his first distinct memories.

His father eventually remarried, but hope for a normal life had been brief.

"She was one perverted bitch," he said with an ironic smile.

Things had gone from bad to worse for John, sexually molested by his stepmother as well as physically abused by his drunkard father, he ran away, only to be returned for more torture.

"I botched a suicide on my fourteenth birthday and they—" John laughed softly. "They hit the ground running. Since I was underage, I was put in a home for boys—and since I was incorrigible, truant from school, running away so many times, it was a home for *bad* boys—I lived in that luxury 'til I was eighteen." He picked up his drink, took a swallow, and shrugged dismissively. "When I got out, talk on the street was my Dad went to New York—I went lookin' for him, I meant to kill him, but I never found him."

Experiencing his painful past and capability of tenderness made it difficult to remember the contained violence within him. She did not want to feel compassion for this man, and he didn't seem to expect it. He discussed that time of his life as casually as any everyday event.

Dawn swallowed the rest of her whiskey-flavored cola when she actually had the urge for a double shot straight up. She had never had a double shot straight up, but it sounded good to ease her inexplicable guilt complex.

"I don't know what to make of you." His words came slow as he spoke in an alcoholic daze. He picked up a lock of her hair, tugging it gently.

"There's something in your eyes—something—" Taking her chin in his fingers, his lips lingered close, then closer, caressing her mouth more than kissing it, she felt oddly fascinated with the gentle persuasion of the touch.

Happily the bartender came over, a much needed interruption. He nodded as he set the fresh drinks on the table, removing the empty glasses.

John lifted the glass ready to take a swallow. Dawn knew when he got a nice big gulp of this drink it would have a far greater effect than the already obvious intoxication.

He gave her a sleepy-eyed look. Some of his drink sloshed out as he haphazardly lifted the glass.

"Careful," she cautioned. He gave her another foggy glance.

"A toast, John," she said lifting her glass. To what? Her mind raced, but drew a blank. Finishing projects? Believing in your convictions? If her life depended on it, she could not think of one feasible thing on earth to toast.

"What 'r we toastin'?" he said, his hand wavering.

"To us, John," she said quickly.

Tipping the glass to his lips, he drank it down, every bit of it.

"Strange how I feel about you." His voice sounded listless. "Maybe if I met you before," he said distantly. "If I could a cared before—"

"And if you had, would you have murdered Carrie Harrison?"

He looked at her sharply as she scrambled away from the table wondering why she had even said that, to ease her guilt, maybe, being immensely sorry for the misery he had endured as a child.

"Who're you?" He managed to get to his feet and take a step forward. John raised a hand to his forehead, staggering another step.

He murmured something incoherent, and then a brief look of wonder at the betrayal passed over his features. She would rather not have seen that dismal expression before he fell at her feet.

She followed the bartender and Miguel as they carried him out. Enrique sat on the banister of the porch still wearing the huge sombrero he had not been without since she met him. She stood beside him feeling distressed as they shoved John into the backseat, but then she figured she didn't have to exactly worry about him being comfortable.

Miguel went into the bar, but Dawn touched the bartender's arm to retain him. She looked up into his calm dark eyes and weathered face. They were rid of the man who had invaded their peaceful town and brought disarray.

"Will he be all right?" she asked.

"Si Senorita," the man said with assurance. "Buena suerte."

He entered the tavern leaving her and Ricky to say goodbye.

"Adios," Enrique said. "Buena suerte, me amigo."

"Adios, and gracias," she said with a wide, genuinely happy smile.

Enrique had helped her earlier bring down what she was taking back with her, now Dawn hugged him fondly. "I'm glad you came into my life," she said sincerely. "I couldn't have done it without you."

"Si, Senorita!" He smiled brightly, his brown eyes glowing.

Dawn walked down the few steps to her car. She climbed in feeling a little downhearted.

She adjusted her rearview mirror, watching as Ricky hopped off the banister. Her last look was a small figure in a huge hat waving goodbye.

She began the journey home, painfully aware of John Burton's presence. Her heart broke for the suffering of a little boy, and she knew he had only revealed a part of that suffering. Dawn shuddered at the thought of explicit details that were locked inside his mind.

Life had dealt him a painful hand. But life dealt a lot of people painful circumstances. Still, her resolve to do what she could for him became the prominent ease to her aching conscious.

She told herself also, that he should have sought professional help long ago instead of letting bitterness and hatred take control of his life to the point of needing to be a dominant and cruel person, reminding herself that he would have raped her or worse in his motel room, if she hadn't caught that telltale glimmer of victory.

As these thoughts crossed her mind, Dawn realized exactly what she had done. Van had been right; she had felt bitterness, and even hate. Instead of letting time heal, she held to the pain, permitting a need for revenge to take control of her actions. She acknowledged the valuable lesson learned, and the price. John Burton would hate her.

Chapter Thirty-Four

Dawn reached Anaheim in record time. The required check at the border proved brief and perfunctory. She sped through the night, stopping once at a Texaco to fill up the Impala, almost afraid to go into the restroom thinking he would be gone when she came out.

On the road again, she had one thought, reaching her destination as quickly as possible.

When Dawn pulled into her parking space at the motel, she left the motor running, the air conditioner on low, and exited the car without a glimpse in the back seat.

She dialed the number Van had left in the nightstand drawer. A pleasant voice identified himself as Mark Winston.

"Hello, Mark, it's Dawn. I'm back," she said excitedly.

"I was expecting your call, Dawn," he said, warmth emanating from his voice. "I was hoping for your call," he added. "Are you at the Holiday Inn?"

"Yes." Sounded like he hadn't actually expected her call, she thought. "Were you worried about me?"

"Worried? You might say that. Is he in any way suspicious of what's going on?"

"No." She automatically glanced through the motel window at the car.

"I'll notify Van that you're here and safe, and I'll be there soon."

The phone clicked softly as he hung up. Dawn did some stretches to relieve tired muscles. Logically she knew it hadn't been necessary to drive straight through with only one stop, but she hadn't been comfortable with John in the backseat. It felt good to be inside, away from his presence.

From the third car that turned into the parking lot, a tall man exited, came to the door and identified himself. When she opened the door for him, he came inside taking her hand, immediately easing her tension.

"I'm pleased to meet you, Dawn," he said with a melt your heart smile. "Very pleased to meet you."

"Thanks, I'm pleased to meet you, too."

Again, it sounded like he hadn't actually expected to meet her. Had Van left Mark with the impression that she would not make it back from Mexico?

She had to admit it had been a dubious and dangerous venture, but she had made it just fine, thank you, and thanks to Enrique.

She gazed at Mark, sort of awestruck, deciding that he, like Van, could be described as decidedly gorgeous, with long, wavy, luxurious hair any girl would strive to attain, and the bluest eyes she had ever seen, reminiscent of a boy she knew. It seemed so long since she'd seen him. Her thoughts turned momentarily to Preston, and to Mike.

"Dawn?"

"Sorry," she smiled. "I was just thinking, lost in thought, as they say. He's in the car."

She walked out to the Impala with Mark.

"Good thing Van didn't get you a two-seater sports car," he commented eyeing John sprawled out in the back. "Looks like he'll be out of it for a while. How did you manage that?"

"With a little help from a friend and his amigo," she said blithely. Dawn explained quickly about Enrique and Miguel.

"Well, sweetheart, make yourself comfortable. I'll have him taken in then join you 'til Van gets here. Do you need anything?"

"Now that you mention it, I'm starving. I think I could eat a horse, but I'll settle for something greasy with the works, crispy and salty, double thick and chocolaty, oh—and cheesy with extra pickles."

"I know just the place to get exactly what you need," he said with a grin.

"Okay, thanks!" She retrieved her luggage from the trunk.

Dawn took a shower, then towel-dried and fluffed her hair. Dressed in the little pink baby doll pajamas she had bought earlier with Van in mind, she applied a light touch of makeup.

When Mark came in with her cheeseburger, large fries and shake, she sat cross-legged on the bed and spread her feast out before her.

"How do you feel?" he asked settling onto a comfortable looking chair.

"Happy to be back," she said between chews. "Extremely, excruciatingly happy, I never want to leave California again."

"You've been through quite an experience," he said, obviously concerned.

"Yes, but, I know it's over—" Dawn paused to chew and swallow. "And I haven't been left with any adverse effects."

"Really?" he questioned. "None at all?"

She munched for a minute. "Well, maybe just a little," she confessed. Dawn took a sip of the shake. "Mmm, this food is delicious."

"Greasy spoon delight," he replied with that cute, self-assured grin. Mark surveyed her kindly. "How are you, really?" he asked.

She paused to contemplate the probing question.

"I'll be all right, Mark. I've been living on the edge of panic for so long, I was almost getting used to it, but it's over now. There's a lot of pain to work through, but that's life, right? Life happens and sometimes it's painful, but I don't want to go investigating any more murders, or chasing any more bad guys," she added, then popped a French fry in her mouth.

"Our superiors are fit to be tied. Van still has them to contend with."

"Will he be in trouble? He won't be, will he? How'd they know anyway?" she demanded.

"They know everything, but no, he won't be in trouble—not much." He chuckled as if recalling an earlier incident.

"It was my choice, after all," she said solemnly.

"No, seriously, don't sweat it. I'm sure he isn't."

Dawn finished her meal, stood and stretched. She put the containers, wrapping paper and napkins in the bag, tossing it all in the trash container.

"There's been a lot of sorrow this past year," she said slowly.

Dawn resumed her place on the bed. "I felt bad for Ted. I grieved for him, truly, but my biggest regret is Carrie." She sighed tiredly. "I lost a childhood friend who was innocent of any wrong, and I will never fully understand. She was a mixed up kid, so afraid, trying to cope with so much. None of us thought we could trust the police."

"Ted was a sad casualty," he agreed, regret clearly etched on his handsome face. "Carrie, too, no one expected her to get caught in the middle, or you either, for that matter," he added. "Unfortunately, there was police corruption in Preston. They've been apprehended."

"Yeah, it seemed pretty obvious with Ted's and Carrie's murders being disregarded. We didn't know who we could trust. I was a mixed up kid myself," she acknowledged, only to Mark. "If Van hadn't been with Bob when he caught me in his apartment, I would be dead, too. I didn't stop to think, which is what Van accused me of. It's true," she admitted, ruefully.

"You're still a kid," Mark said affectionately.

Tilting her head to one side, Dawn gave him a wry grin. "I hear that a lot," she told him. "But I think I've matured a little. If I had it to do over—"

She wondered, if she had it to do over—if she had known John's story would it have made a difference to her way of thinking, her determination to be the one to bring him in—if she had it to do over? That might be something to reflect on later, right now her brain felt too tired.

"Earth to Dawn . . ." Mark snapped his fingers drawing her away from the contemplation. "Dawn?" he said questioningly.

"Sorry." She inhaled, releasing the breath in a weary sigh. "One thing I have no doubt about," she said reflectively. "When he convinced me that he knew I wasn't Cynthia Kaley—? At that precise moment, when I thought I was gonna die, I wished I had never gone to Mexico. My convictions just—vanished, and I wished I'd never laid eyes on John Burton. But it turned out alright—I remembered what Van told me, plus John had a tell."

Mark looked at her closely. "You look exhausted, Dawn, why don't you take a nap? A catnap would do you a world of good."

"I could," she agreed. "I'm tired."

Dawn slipped under the sheet and fell immediately to sleep.

* * *

Van let his mind wander as he sped through the night, trying to out distance thoughts of those who had lost their lives. It would take a long time to find the answers to why his backup had been fingered and why two of the kingpins supposed to be there were not.

He concentrated, instead on the lives that had been saved, the several heroin addicts who were in rehab, and most especially on the girl waiting for him right this very minute. Dawn had accomplished what she set out to do.

It occurred to him now, quite harshly, that he had not been at all certain that she would, and even though he was completely unorthodox, he still wondered what had possessed him to let a civilian take such an unnecessary risk. He could have refused, maybe should have, but he rationalized that she was alive and happy, and that meant a lot.

Dawn had been determined to go after Burton, up front and personal, she would not have been at all happy if he had not let her. She had begun her little venture because Carrie Harrison meant a lot to her, Ted, too, she had been determined to see it through, who was he to stop her?

He would have to tell her about Dave Temple, a tragedy, completely unexpected. Dave should not have been there. Billy told him about his concern and determination, but the unsung hero had so much to give, so many reasons to live, so much more in this life he could have accomplished.

Van's thoughts drifted back in time to the night he had been told that his sixteen-year-old brother had died of an overdose of heroin, news that changed the direction of his life, he turned from his calling, to another. He turned to the streets; setting his sights on those he considered essentially the blame.

He pitied users, boys like Ted. Users were victims thinking they had it all under control—addicts were victims who knew they had no control of their shattered lives. In his experience, users ultimately became addicts.

Corruption in the police department had led to the death of six officers. Dark anger infused him. The cops on Bob's payroll had been caught and would stand trial but that didn't bring anyone back, did it. They would be convicted and serve time, but not enough. It would never be enough.

He could understand Dawn's need for revenge, a feeling he lived with and would hold close until the resolution, if there could ever be resolution for him. If it never ended, if the anguish never completely dispersed, if he could not find closure, at least he had taken out most of the men responsible for his brother's death and then some.

He had made a name for himself, acquired quite a reputation in the past four years, with offers of promotion regardless of his deviating, sometimes, vaguely unscrupulous ways. He wasn't exactly a rogue, but he did have a tendency to not take prisoners.

He acknowledged without qualms that he had to veer just a little to the left once in awhile. He didn't want to lose himself, his identity, his zest for life. It made existence bearable in the battle against evil; men like Bob Kaley who thrived on the continuing abuse of drugs.

Van thought of the girls he had left behind, girls like Dawn, but none affected him quite like her, with Dawn, he had stumbled. What he said to her that night was true. Their relationship should have been superficial.

Mark sat up, wide-awake, as soon as the door opened.

"Van," he said, instantly alert. "Good to see you."

"Good to see you, Mark. Thanks for keeping an eye on my girl."

Dawn, his little sleeping beauty sat up in bed looking momentarily confused. "Van, you're here!"

"I'm here," he said, giving her an approving look. "And so are you. We made it, baby."

"Take care, Dawn. Van, see you tomorrow—today—whenever."

"Thanks again, Mark," Dawn called. "For the greasy spoon delight."

He grinned, waving a farewell salute.

Alone with Van, Dawn found herself mesmerized. She could not take her eyes off him.

"We got them all," he told her.

"I was wondering if you did."

He walked over to the bed gazing at her with admiration glowing in those warm brown eyes. "I'm proud of you."

"But I didn't do it for recognition," she murmured. "I'm glad it's over."

"I know you didn't do it for recognition, I know it was much more personal. But it sounds like there might be just a touch of regret?"

"More than a touch," she admitted softly, beginning to unbutton his shirt, longing to be in his arms, to know his fiery passion, to be his desire.

She could not understand the intensity of the love that had taken her so quickly and so completely, only that it felt real—real, true and amazing.

"Dawn." He spoke her name and she could hear regret. "If I could give you tomorrow, I would. When I look in your eyes, sweetheart—"

She put a finger over his lips to still the words.

"Please don't say it. I don't want to know."

Dawn released his belt buckle, unsnapped and pulled the zipper down on his jeans. "You're ready," she whispered. "You want me."

"I want you," he said huskily, slipping the gown off her shoulders. It slid to the floor, and then he slowly pulled the sheer pink negligée up her body.

Dawn experienced a deep rush of pleasure watching him finish undressing. He joined her on the bed, their naked bodies coming together.

The caress of his lips on her mouth and along her body set her aflame with yearning desire. No longer shy in the arms of her lover, she caressed his muscled body with soft and firm strokes of her hands and then her lips and tongue, tasting him, loving him, giving and taking exquisite pleasure.

Heartache blended with enchantment as he possessed her eager body, because she knew he could never be hers. Still she held tight to the man of her dreams, to the wonder of his love, and to a secret hope.

From the heights of passion, she floated gently, contentedly back to earth.

Dawn fell asleep in his arms. She awoke to his touch in the early morning light, to the bittersweet embrace of his love, knowing their time together neared completion, that this might be her last chance to hold him.

She snuggled against him after they made love a second time.

It didn't seem reasonable that this would be their last loving encounter, when the first had been such short while ago. Van exemplified all she wanted in life. It seemed too unfair that they couldn't be together. He held her until she felt drowsy, drifting into a dream.

"Dawn, it's time to wake up," he whispered, breathing warmly against her neck, nuzzling affectionately.

"Already?" She stretched lazily.

"You're too sexy," he moaned, turning over on his back. "I could stay here all day making love to you."

"Now, there's a thought." She turned over on her side, rubbing his muscled chest provocatively. "Care to pursue it?"

He turned back to her with a sigh of unmistakable desire, touching his lips to her bare shoulder. "You know I want to," he whispered. "But there's not enough time in a day, you know, places to go and things to do." Van turned toward her. "You're a distraction with perfectly wonderful delay tactics."

"The place is here, the time is now, and the thing to do is make love."

"You are such a sweet little sex maniac," he chided, taking her in his arms. "Now what can I do for you?"

The pain in her heart merged with the delight of passion as she felt herself being absorbed in this brief space of time and tangled emotions. Her world had been filled with him. Now her world would be empty without him.

* * *

Dawn and Van lingered over coffee after brunch at the motel restaurant.

She explained briefly about John's abusive childhood. "John could have been a normal person with a normal life. He suffered in his youth—he was created Van. He was turned into what he is," she concluded. "Maybe with therapy he could be rehabilitated."

After a long silence, he lit a cigarette never looking at her. "I wouldn't count on it," he said, finally. "Sounds like his scars run too deep."

"Van?" A flicker of apprehension coursed through her.

"Look at it this way," he said, his voice still cold and exact. "With you he gets justice. With me he would have gotten judgment."

"I didn't have any feeling for John except fear and hate, either—" she began but he cut her off.

"I don't have any fear of Burton."

He wasn't even aware that she flinched at the force of his seething reply.

"Not personally," he clarified. "He's psycho scum. He isn't worth a minute, not one minute of your compassion."

Van took a deep breath, reached over and held her hand, a comforting touch, soothing his scathing words. His eyes met hers, the tension melted, his voice softened. "Don't forget the extent of his crimes, and what he would do to you if he had the opportunity."

"I know, but I thought counseling might help him," she said, trying to temper his sentiment. "That maybe he could be mentally competent again."

"He's not incompetent," Van said emphatically.

The hardness permeated in his voice in an instant, and the coldness in his eyes as a frown set into his features made her wonder all the more about his venomous feelings. Considering the adverse affect it had on him, she decided not to pursue any further discussion of John Burton. Besides, what he said was true. John wasn't mentally incompetent. He was an angry young man, a rapist and a murderer.

Dawn pushed the remainder of her coffee aside. "What do you suppose will happen with Paul?" she said, unable to conceal her distress. "Do you think he'll have to serve time in prison?"

"It's his first offense. He shouldn't get hard time, but you never know. He was on the road to being a full-fledged pusher. His lawyer will plea bargain, at any rate. Don't worry so over the bad boys, Dawn."

"You're right, I know, and I'm very proud of you, and thankful that you came to our town and cleaned it up." She tilted her head giving him a long look wanting to memorize every feature.

"Yeah." He lowered his eyes. "Dawn, there's something I have to tell you," he said quietly.

Dawn wondered about his solemn expression and saddened tone. She knew it was something she didn't want to hear, but knew also that it was something that would affect her.

"What happened?"

"Dave Temple was killed the night of the drug bust," he said softly.

Her thoughts raced immediately to her friends in Preston as she recalled the love of the small family. "How is Chris?—and Mike?" She ran nervous fingers through her hair. "This is unimaginable. When will it end?"

"It's ended, Dawn, believe me. As for Mike and Chris, they have each other, and they have Billy, but—it was rough."

"What happened?" she said fretfully. "Why was he there?"

"Billy told me—" His voice was thick and unsteady, his eyes suspiciously bright. He slowly shook his head as if he could hardly believe the reasoning.

"He said he took it real personal that Bob was planning to frame him for Ted's murder, but I know he was worried about me—I don't know what would have happened if they hadn't shown up."

Van took a light, shuddering breath. She recalled her wonder of the closeness that had developed between the two of them in such a short while.

"They arrived in Preston a night early," he went on, quickly recovering. "They were suspicious. Bob had cops on the payroll, something tipped 'em off. What little backup I had was spotted. They were killed and I was disarmed. I might have made it out alive." He bit his lip gently, tipped his cup looking at the remains of his creamy coffee as if he might find an answer there. "I'm fairly sure I had them convinced that I didn't know anything about the cops casing the place."

He pushed his cup aside.

"There was a thug standing in a position that gave me access to his gun if I was fast enough and my timing was right. I might have been able to take 'em. I might have tried, anyway."

Dawn shivered with the thought of how close he had come to losing his life. If he had tried, on his own to grab a gun, he would have probably been shot down. She held his warm hand in hers caressing his fingers, loving him with all her being.

"It would have been next to impossible for me to let them walk out that door knowing they could be lost for years. They were leaving state that same night, not Kaley, but the others, and with Kaley going down, hard telling when they would have surfaced again."

"None of this should have happened," Dawn said sadly, thinking of the night Officer Jarred came to her house, the night Carrie died. "Was Officer Jarred a dirty cop?"

"No, he was one of the good guys, Jamison, too. They died helping me, Dawn. The corruption was higher up."

Another contemplative moment, then Van gently squeezed her hand.

"We have to go now. I'm meeting Mark in a half hour."

"But how will I get home . . . I don't have a car here."

"Mmm . . . I forgot to mention, the Impala is my gift to you." He gently cleared his throat. "It's my way of saying forgive me for not telling you immediately that you were safe with me that night. I was wrong for—I don't know, trying to teach you some sort of lesson."

"This isn't necessary."

"I insist. It's already in your name. Now you own a car, Dawn Preston."

"I don't understand. How can you just give me a car?"

"Oh, remember when I gave you the impression that I wasn't born with the proverbial silver spoon?" He grinned eloquently.

"Okay then—I accept."

They held hands walking out to the car. Their lips touched longingly in their last moments together. He stroked her face gently with the back of his hand, the look in his eyes pure melancholy.

She put her arms around his neck, and he pulled her in close, holding her tight. Not a word, just one last kiss, painfully sweet, before she climbed into the car. He closed the door, taking a step back.

Dawn began the drive to Preston, viewing the world through a mist of tears, knowing she would always love him. They had shared a summer, three painful, terrifyingly beautiful months.

In the midst of the pain of losing her friends, Christi's horrid near-death experience, her fear of him being a drug pusher, in spite of it all, she had not been able to resist falling in love with the charismatic Van Morrison.

The end of August had brought the end of a summer romance. She knew her love couldn't be considered any more than that. A summer romance was all it had ever been, hard to face, but regretfully true.

Now came the consequence of her battered heart, but even though it hurt, she would always cherish the memories. He had made time to share with her, given her his every spare moment.

Her thoughts turned to Preston City. The confidence of a town had been badly shaken. They had suffered loss, and they had lost innocence. A late October night had changed her life and the lives of those close to her forever.

A part of her had died, a part of Christi and Mike, too.

Time would heal the wounds, but there would always be scars. They had survived the turbulence of the past year, but something carefree was gone, and she wondered if it could ever be replaced.

Chapter Thirty-Five

The ringing phone drew Christi out of a drowsy state. She reached for the receiver. "Hello." Sitting up in bed, she pressed the bed remote to adjust to a more comfortable position.

"Hello, Miss Christine Temple?"

"Yes."

"This is Debra Wade calling on behalf of Robertson Construction Company. I'm sorry to disturb you." The crisp, clear all business voice paused briefly. "The contract needs finalized before construction can begin at 622 Fairview Boulevard."

"Yes, I know."

"Mr. Robertson told me to get verification, but since you and your brother are under the age of consent, it isn't possible for either one of you to sign the necessary papers."

"That won't be a problem. Send the papers to our lawyer, Christopher Harris, the Law Offices of Harris and Prescott."

"Thank you, I'll take care of it right away."

Christi hung up. She reclined against the pillow, still finding it difficult to accept the knowledge of her brother's death.

She had not cried since the first night, when she lost control and had to be sedated. She woke up later feeling numb with denial. There were no tears then, just lonely emptiness, because she had not seen Dave in a while.

It seemed like he would walk into the room any minute, and when he didn't the empty feeling kept growing with nothing to fill it.

Due to her weakened condition she could not attend the funeral. Yes, she understood, but not being there made it even more difficult to believe.

In the days that followed, she couldn't stop thinking about him, his warm eyes the color of a clear blue sky, his laughing teasing ways, and when she felt grumpy, the way he tousled her hair telling her to cheer up that it would be okay, always convincing her that somehow it would.

Now it could never be okay again. It didn't seem possible, but in her heart, she knew the truth of it. She had no choice but to accept that truth—face that truth. The woman on the phone pronounced him dead yet again.

Dave wouldn't be here for her anymore, a trusted man in the community had murdered her brother, a man who had infiltrated their town and caused catastrophe they had never known before.

As the finality of his absence became certain, emptiness became an intense sorrow that felt like something squeezing her heart until she thought it would burst inside her chest.

Her thoughts turned to Mike and the pain washed over her in a renewed sense of loss with the recollection of his tears, his shaking body as he held her during the severity of the first grief. As the ache became an irrepressible force from within, she cried hard, wrenching sobs muffled into her pillow.

* * *

Christi felt disoriented, for the space of a heartbeat forgot that Dave was gone. Then the crushing realism, she had cried herself to sleep. She would never see her beloved brother again.

Billy stood when she opened her eyes. "You were restless," he said worriedly. He poured ice water from a plastic pitcher refilling her glass.

"Mmm, thank you." She took a deep swallow of the cold water.

"How are you, baby? You've been crying?"

"I just had a pretty rough time of it," she admitted. "How long have you been here?"

"About an hour. I should have been here with you."

"You can't be with me all the time."

"I need to be with you," he insisted gently. "When you need me, I need to be here for you." His arms encircled her, strong, comforting arms holding her in solid protection.

She relaxed her head against his chest, resting in his embrace.

* * *

Christi sat up when Dr. Hamilton entered the room making his morning rounds. He stood by her bed, hands clasped in front of him.

"How would you like to go home tomorrow?"

Christi smiled. "You wouldn't tease me?"

"You've gained enough weight that I'm satisfied you'll keep progressing." He looked into her eyes again with his little light. "No headaches—"

"No headaches," she confirmed. "No dizzy, either. I'm fine."

"I concur. The only feasible reason for keeping you any longer is that I do so enjoy our morning escapades."

"Thank you, doctor," she replied coyly fluttering her lashes.

"Now see, I'm going to have to keep you forever," he said with a brief smile. He picked up her chart, flipping through a couple of pages. "I want to offer my condolences again, Christine, for the loss of your brother. You may wonder why you're being released so soon after his funeral when you were not allowed to attend."

She took a trembling breath, bewildering tears flooded her eyes. The thought had crossed her mind.

"You were too fragile . . . Not just your body, but your emotions. You had gained some weight, but lost a lot in the aftermath of the tragedy. You may not realize it, young lady, but you came close to having a breakdown."

"No, I didn't realize."

"That is why, with all due consideration, I had to keep you in my protective custody for a while." He grinned kindly. "But you've regained enough weight to go home, and you've done extremely well with your physical therapy, enough that you can continue as an outpatient. If you promise me that you will, I can sign your release."

Her tears had evaporated. "I promise."

Dr. Hamilton sighed. "You are doing extremely well physically." He closed her chart, returning it to the slot. His expression held concern. "If you need counseling, Christine, Dr. Lloyd comes highly recommended."

"If I do, I'll call him," she agreed. "But I think I'll be all right."

"You know, I believe you will, too," he agreed assuredly. "I'll see you in the morning."

She fell asleep easily that night with the prescribed sleeping pill, but her restless mind brought her out before dawn to sit by the window of the lonely room as the joy of going home mingled with despair, miserably tempered by the void in her world. She wondered when the feeling of desolation would go away. It felt like it would be a part of her life forever.

In one of the last conversations they had, Dave had expressed regret for not being a better brother. He was a wonderful brother, and she told him so, then he joking said, yeah, he'd been a wonderful brother, but a piss poor guardian, and they had laughed, and hugged, and things had been great.

Filled with deep sorrow, she looked up at the starlit sky noticing a specifically bright twinkling star that she had always considered a 'wishing star'. It didn't impress her now, she would never wish on a star again. Makes no difference who you are, they lie.

Christi wanted to believe. She hated being assailed with this terrible awareness of bitterness. It wouldn't last forever, the desolation and the despairing emptiness would surely pass.

Time would be a friend. Time would make it better. Dave had even said that. Her eyelids grew heavy. Christi knew she needed sleep, sitting here stressing wouldn't do her any good.

Slipping between the sheets, she drifted into an immediate sound sleep. She woke up when the nurse came in to take her vitals, with few words, quickly and efficiently, hurrying on, leaving Christi staring at the ceiling until the Candy Striper arrived with breakfast.

Dr. Hamilton stopped by for one last morning visit on his rounds. Among other things, he talked to her again about grief counseling.

"You'll be given a schedule for outpatient therapy when you leave." He looked her chart over one last time. "I hadn't expected to be discharging you for maybe another two weeks, so, behave yourself when you go home, no wild parties for at least a month or so," he cautioned playfully.

"I promise to follow all instructions, doctor, especially the part about having a wild party next month."

He chuckled good-naturedly. "You do that, and call my office," he reminded her.

Christi was escorted in a wheel chair to the waiting vehicle, released from the Rehabilitation Center of Preston General, immediately after lunch.

She took a seat on the passenger side and waved at the nurse's aide who wished her the best as they said goodbye. Billy gave her a quick kiss before turning the key in the ignition. Mike sat in the back seat.

Preoccupied with thoughts of how it would feel to walk back into the world where she had lived with their brother—without him in it—almost caused her to miss the wrong turn Billy made.

"Where are we going?" she asked, wondering how he had missed the turn.

"I'm taking you home—to your apartment."

"But you're going the wrong way."

"No, I'm not. I know the way very well. I've spent a lot of time there."

"What's going on?" She glanced back at Mike.

"He does know the way," Mike agreed. "I do, too, actually, very well."

"I'm taking you to your new apartment," Billy finally told her. "I think you'll like it." He parked at the curb of 1600 Belleview Avenue, came around, assisted her out of the car and then whisked her up in his arms.

With Mike going before them opening doors, Billy carried her into the vestibule, up the stairs, into a first floor apartment.

He set her gently on the sofa, arranging plump cushions around her.

"I could learn to like this," she said positively.

"Do you need anything?"

"How long do I get this VIP treatment? Is it a forever thing?"

Billy removed her shoes. "This is just for today, after that, you're on your own, babe."

"Oh, let me absorb what's happening here," she said with a contented sigh.

"I hope you like the furniture. Mike helped me pick it out."

"Oh, I do! It's perfect."

"Mike was helpful, but I designed the bedroom myself." He took her hand. "I would like to think of it as our bedroom, Chris, will you marry me?"

She stared into his brilliant blue eyes unable to say a word. Her mind flashed back to that night in the alley when he leaned over studying her face, solemn and threatening when their eyes met for the first time.

"Wait—let me do this right." He knelt in front of her on one knee. "Since you came into my life, I haven't been the same. Ask anyone."

Billy kissed her hand. He opened a blue velvet jewelry box. "Will you be my wife?"

She entwined her fingers through his. "Was it just a year ago we met?" she said in wonder.

"One year, one month and twenty-nine days, more or less, but who's counting, right?"

"So, you've decided you won't miss the excitement of the street life?"

"I will never miss my former life." He kissed her hand again. "Christi, I swear I'll make it up to you, everything that I can fix, I'll fix it."

"You have, already."

His eyes held a look of anticipation. "I applied for a job with Robertson Construction, and they hired me," he snapped his fingers. "On the spot."

"So, you're a working man now," she said hesitantly.

"Don't take it so hard! It had to happen sometime." He removed the engagement ring from the jewelry box. "Now, my love, will you marry me?"

She gave him a radiant smile. "I love you, Billy. Yes, I will!"

He slipped the ring on her finger and they kissed.

"I congratulate you, little sister, and you, my friend," Mike said with a smile. "I'm leaving now."

"Mike, be careful!" Her voice caught, the words just slipped out.

He tipped his head. "I'll be home for supper," he promised.

Christi sighed as Mike headed out the door. She held her hand out to admire the diamond. "It's so beautiful, but it had to cost—I can't imagine."

She turned questioning eyes on him.

"I sold my motorcycle . . . Shhh." He placed his finger quickly over her lips. "Don't say a word. I'll buy another one someday."

His face came close to hers, and then their lips touched gently, temptingly. She closed her eyes, savoring the kiss as his mouth finally claimed hers.

"Mmm, I've missed that, something about kissing in the hospital, it just isn't the same."

"I agree, my love, hospital kissing is mediocre at best."

He chuckled softly. "How do you feel?"

"A little sad," she admitted. "A little happy, too."

"Love me?"

"You know I do."

"Want to see the bedroom?" he asked, bright blue eyes sparkling with eagerness.

She started to stand.

"No, allow me." He lifted her effortlessly, and she squealed with delight.

"I love that sound!" he said earnestly, holding her even closer as they headed out of the room.

"Billy, we could get lost in that bed!" Her arms tightened around his neck. "It's gigantic!"

"Yeah, we can play hide 'n seek." He lowered her onto it.

She viewed the room, noting the quality of the furniture. The dresser, chest of drawers, armoire and bedside tables were mahogany. The large pillows she reclined on had satin cases atop a velvety blue bedspread.

"Oh, my God—this room is so gorgeous! You must have gone in deep."

"I had to have two cosigners, but it's okay. I'm going to make it my mission in life to give you everything you deserve," he vowed.

"It's a little scary—the being in debt part."

"It had to happen, we needed a car and we needed the furniture." He smiled reassuringly. "I don't want you to worry about anything. This is what we're moving into our new home, baby, and I wanted the best I could get."

He looked down for a moment, and then lifted his eyes. "I'll never do drugs again, Christi. I promise you, not any kind of drug, not even pot."

She thought he must still feel guilty about what happened at the beach house. Even given her unconditional forgiveness, he had yet to forgive himself.

When his expression turned to a new, kind of concentrating aspect, she smiled hesitantly.

"What is it?"

"You asked if I would miss the excitement of the streets, and I won't, but what about you, Chris. Your life wasn't exactly boring." His look turned seductive, affecting her deeply, desire for Billy blazed unexpectedly swift. "Now that I'm not a mystery, revving my Harley around town and sporting a Monarch symbol, will I still excite you?"

"Excite me, yes—I want a life with you, not some leader of a gang."

Billy leaned back gazing absorbedly into her eyes.

"I've been around enough to know you're the one I want to spend my life with, Christi. You were so young and innocent, you still are." He sighed pensively. "Are you going to grow up and leave me, baby?"

They were lying close on the bed. She snuggled in his warm possession for a long, quiet moment wondering at his unusual question.

"Are you serious?" Christi lifted her face looking into his eyes. "I'll love you forever."

The touch of his lips, the urgency of his kiss, ignited a spark that set a quick flame. Christi pressed closer, molding her body to his. She needed more than passionate kisses and caresses, she desperately wanted his love.

"We'd better find a minister soon," he said between kisses. "Or I won't be able to keep the promise I made."

"What promise was that?" she asked, beginning to unbutton his shirt.

"That I wouldn't touch you again until you're Mrs. William Cole." He covered her breast with one hand, and she smacked at him playfully.

"You are touching me—keep your hands to yourself!" The tantalizingly light caress had sent her passion rising.

"I didn't mean no caresses or kissing. I need to cop a feel once in a while," he pouted, idly stroking her thigh.

"Where is a justice of the peace?" Christi said, breathlessly. "We'd better get married soon or I guarantee you won't keep your promise!"

She sat up suddenly. "Billy—I—I just thought of something. I *am* only seventeen. Can we even get married?"

"I've already talked to Mr. Harris." Billy said, quickly erasing her fears. "He assured me he could take care of the legal aspects."

* * *

Mike watched his sister's face as she spoke her vows, so sweet, so serious, so perfectly radiant. Then he glanced at Billy, totally absorbed with the soon to be Mrs. Cole, his love evident in his attentive gaze.

After the wedding there was a reception in the church dining hall. Mike left early. He stayed long enough to see Christi and Billy enjoy smearing cake in each other's faces for more pictures, to join them in a piece of the magnificent four tier cake served with coffee, and to have one dance with Dawn to a romantic melody performed by Rioters the local band.

He rode his motorcycle back to the apartment where they were meeting with a few of Billy's friends who hadn't actually wanted to attend a wedding.

It had been Dave's bike, and he had the leather vest, the switchblade, and of course, the Cobra ring Van had returned to him. All he had of his big brother except for the memories and a few pictures.

"Thank you for convincing me to having a church wedding," Christi said, her eyes shining.

Except for Dawn, everyone had gone, the little get together ending with congratulations all around. Mike knew Chris and Billy were aching to be alone, and that Dawn would soon leave, then he would split, but for now he was thoroughly enjoying her presence, the way she moved, her graceful gestures, her delightful laughter.

"I had not even imagined the spiritual aspects of a traditional wedding, how touching it would be." Christi sighed avidly, her violet eyes dreamy. "The flowers were gorgeous, and the pictures, I can't wait to see them! It was so amazing. It's something I will remember the rest of my life."

"And it's something I'll be paying for the rest of my life," Billy added with a teasing note, not exactly jovial but good-natured.

"I thought you knew that was my wedding gift to you and Christi," Dawn said, sounding puzzled. "You can't refuse a gift," she added merrily.

"I'll reimburse you for our wedding, Dawn, it's not negotiable."

"I won't let you pay me back, if you even try, I'll be insulted."

Mike exchanged an amused look with Christi as they listened to the debate.

"It was my idea, you know—" Dawn said firmly. "I insisted, if you remember."

"And I agreed, only because you were able to pull it off so quickly, which, thank you, by the way. We'll talk about it later."

He lifted the half full pitcher off the coffee table. "More punch, ladies?" Billy refilled their glasses. "It'll make your toes tingle. I know—I spiked it myself."

"We won't talk about it later," Dawn mumbled, more to herself than Billy.

Mike couldn't dispel a grin. Billy might think so, but he wouldn't be paying for that wedding.

He exchanged a quizzical glance with Billy when they heard someone knock on the door.

"Expecting someone?" he asked.

"No, you Christi?"

"No."

"Okay." Billy headed toward the door. "It better not be a salesman."

After a murmured conversation, he closed the door. Billy walked back to where Christi sat, giving her a somewhat contemplative look.

"Who was it?" she asked uneasily.

"It's—Susan," he said guardedly. "She wants to talk to you."

She looked surprised, then irate. "I can't believe she would have the nerve to show up on my wedding day."

"Why don't you talk to her, Chris?" Billy urged thinking he was being reasonable. "She's sorry. She's really upset—Chris, she's crying."

"If she's sorry for what she did, fine—if she's even sincere."

Christi bit her lip, uncertainty rippling in her eyes, but then she raised her chin decisively. "I can't do it, Billy. I sensed her malice from the first time we met. You might be able to forgive her, but I can't. You know it was her fault—"

Christi broke off abruptly, her eyes lowering to stare at her tightly clenched hands.

Mike watched his sister's face closely.

"Try to understand." Her gaze lifted, her pretty face determinedly set. "But even if you can't, I have to insist that you accept my decision. I want her away from me, and please tell her never to come here again."

"It's okay, baby—I understand."

Mike glanced briefly at Dawn, and then looked back at Christi.

He felt her renewed pain, instigated by this woman's planned intrusion. No, Billy didn't understand, he couldn't possibly understand. Billy knew it was Susan's fault, yes, he knew everything that was Susan's fault except for the one thing that his sister was too ashamed to even tell him.

Billy did not know that Susan had ignited a rage in John Burton that he had taken out on Christi. The hostility and his own rage fully restored, Mike felt an intense, ominous reaction. A sickening lurch in his stomach, followed by dead calm, left him motivated to a dark purpose.

"I hate to break up the party, but I need some air."

He heard Christi call his name as he exited the door but could no more turn around than he could stop breathing. Whatever she had meant to Billy, however she had felt about him, this girl's love had not instigated her actions.

"Mike!"

He stopped abruptly when he heard Dawn's urgent cry. Aware of his clenched fists, he watched Susan retreat further up the street.

He relaxed his hands when he felt Dawn touch his arm. He turned to face her. "Dawn." Mike gripped her hands tightly.

"You left in a hurry," she said, her eyes searching his.

"Let's walk."

He knew Dawn practically had to run to keep up with him, but he needed the speed to hopefully get rid of the hostile feelings.

They headed in the opposite direction that Susan had taken, eventually turning onto the grounds of Fairview Park.

Mike slowed his clipped pace to a stroll as they entered the scenic area.

He paused under a large tree feeling the intensity still with him. The distant laughter of children and the happy prattle of families picnicking on the expanse of grass became an unwelcome drone in his aching head.

Mike leaned against the tree, concentrating on getting his emotions under control. The moment of calm had passed followed by an almost inexplicable eruption of violence. With the adrenaline pounding through his veins—like it or not, it would take a few minutes to regain composer.

Dawn touched the furrow between his closed eyes. He had all but forgotten the girl with him. Mike opened his eyes, placed his hands on her shoulders, sighing weakly.

He bent his head to hers.

"I wanted to make her suffer the way Chris did," he confessed. "I wanted to take her somewhere and give her a dose of hurt and shame."

He leaned back against the tree again, still angry, but calmer, and sorry for the expression on Dawn's face.

"Any idea where to go for a good stiff shot of scotch?"

He massaged her shoulders a bit, feeling the tension relax beneath his nimble fingers.

"I happen to know a place that has the best in town," she smiled. "It's called my place."

"Far out, babe." He took her hand as they began to walk, sensing the friendship they shared, knowing instinctively that Dawn was comfortable with him holding her hand.

They left the park headed in the direction of 1800 Woodland Drive.

Mike sat on the sofa in the den while she went to the bar to mix their drinks. When she joined him, he took a long swallow of the scotch and soda feeling the warmth. The long walk had calmed him, the drink helped more.

"I couldn't help the feeling," he told her unashamed.

"I understand."

"No, I don't think you do."

"Do you want to talk about it?"

He gazed at her, thoughtfully measuring her reaction scale, deciding it would be best not to share. Dawn did not think him capable of any sort of violence, and he could see how the idea affected her, the distress reflected in her green eyes as she studied him. That distress didn't settle well.

"I don't blame you for your feelings, whatever they are. What Susan did was immoral, and even if she's sorry now, it doesn't make it all right."

She gave him a momentary doleful look. "A time to forget isn't it," she added bleakly.

"Yeah, we've been through changes," he agreed recalling his sixteenth birthday. It seemed a lifetime ago.

"I don't think anything will ever be the same."

"No, not quite the same."

"You're back in school, aren't you?"

"Yep, I can tough it out this year."

"Are you going to be valedictorian?"

He pretended to puzzle over the question for a moment, then as if enlightened. "Oh—I get it," he said laughingly.

"Mike?"

"Sorry, thought you were joking. I mean, I could if I wanted to," he said casually. "I can do anything I want to, so I'll graduate in May, piece a cake."

"I'd like to be there."

He glanced sideways in surprise. "I thought you knew you have a standing invitation to every minor or major event in my life."

"Are you going to college?"

"Probably, some business management courses, stuff like that."

"How about Christi?"

"She's interested in being a wife and mother," he conveyed, acceptingly. "I suppose a GED will be the extent of her formal education."

"Hmmm." Dawn considered her decision. "We hadn't discussed it."

He took a swallow of his drink, cupping the glass in his hands, giving Dawn an inquisitive glimpse. "How about you, Dawn?"

"Yes, college. I feel a little disillusioned about going, but I'll get over it. I want to go, really. I just—I don't know." She felt at a loss for words.

"You fell in love with Van," he said conclusively, rewarded for his observance by a winsome smile and undeniable stars reflecting in her emerald eyes. "You are aware that Van will never love anyone, right?"

"Pretty much aware of that," she agreed with the sweet musing look he found so captivating.

"You're special, Sommer. Don't ever forget." He took her hand, leaning in close to kiss her softly on the lips. "It's just something you might need on a dark and lonely night."

"Thank you."

"I should thank you. I do appreciate what you did for me . . . and the drink."

"I didn't do anything," she protested, standing with him.

"Oh, but you did," he assured her. "You saved me from myself."

He paused at the door, his hands resting on her shoulders. Gazing into his eyes, she felt a connection, incredibly tangible and at the same time elusive.

"If you ever need a friend, I'll be there for you."

She watched him walk away and could not understand her loneliness or why it felt so right when he called her Sommer.

Chapter Thirty-Six

Dawn enrolled in college with little enthusiasm. She accepted the logic that attending college lent a positive aspect in a bleakly futile existence, it pleased her mother, and a little extra education never hurt anyone.

The final plus, it kept her busy, even though she had no chosen career, or even an iota of what she hoped to accomplish in an obscure future.

Life moved on in a monotonous tone without clear focus. Intellectually, she realized the waste of it, but to her battered heart, it seemed better not to rock the emotional boat, to simply drift, time being, safely afloat on still waters. She knew though, if Van happened to get in touch it would rock her boat all over again.

After their parting in August, he had shown up at her house a week before Christmas and whisked her off to New York for the holidays. They had stayed at the Plaza Hotel for two full weeks.

She experienced the wonder of Christmas in New York, window-shopping, glorious lights and decorations, and riding in a horse drawn buggy as he showed her his world.

They built a snowman in Central Park on Christmas Day, and were present for the dropping of the ball ringing in the New Year of 1969. The festivities were amazing with high-spirited and electrifying excitement.

She went into a daydream of sharing that life with him, and of springtime in Paris. The second day of spring break, he showed up with two tickets and a smile she could never refuse.

Like a vivid dream come true, they jetted to Paris for a wondrously wild and romantic two-week retreat. April in Paris, where he wined and dined and swept her off her feet again, another experience to cherish, a taste, a sample of love that could never be.

Christmas came and went without the appearance of her elusive lover. Every car in the drive, every chime of the doorbell sent her heart racing, but she celebrated Christmas with her mother, Mike, Christi and Billy.

New Year's Eve, she went out with Christi, Billy and Mike to usher in the New Year of 1970 at the Castle Lounge. It was all high spirited fun. She did not let useless yearnings for Van ruin her holidays.

Dawn realized her coffee had grown cold without even having a sip.

She dumped it, her thoughts drifting in another direction. Jerry attended Cal State, also. She poured a fresh cup reflectively. She rarely saw him and never socially. His current girlfriend seemed possessive of his time. Dawn's feelings had developed into an abiding friendship that she hoped he shared.

She would always cherish her 'first love'.

Dawn opened the morning paper to read as she enjoyed her coffee. Her eyes scanned the page taking in the important features.

Being a speed-reader had helped tremendously in school, not to mention when it came to reading the paper, something her mother had instilled in her from the tender age of twelve. Now an instinctive value, she never missed being informed of local and world events, although sometimes news could be depressing.

She set her cup down and backtracked to reread the column. No, this had to be wrong. It wasn't possible! But the words jumped out at her in bold black lettering. John Burton had escaped from the institution where he had been placed. Dawn read the article for a third time trying to absorb the undeniable and dreadful fact.

How could they have let this happen? He had been placed in a high security criminal facility. How could they have let him escape?

She did not have to testify at the trial of John Burton, everything she knew being hearsay and inconsequential, but she had offered to testify in his behalf and the defense had put her on the stand.

She had not thought much about John since then, but it had not mattered to him that she was there to try to convey sympathy to his case. She recalled his bridled fury as he promised to kill her, one day, somehow, some way.

The spectators became deathly quiet to hear what he had to say in the immediate aftermath of her testimony. Then everyone started talking at once.

The judge pounding his gavel, demanding order in his court, had little effect on the excited crowd. No one listened to the judge's irate command, and John said no more, because shouting was not his manner.

He looked at her with those fire and ice eyes, his dark gaze pinning her as the judge continued to pound his gavel threatening to clear the courtroom. She needed desperately to get out of his sight. Dawn wished she had stayed completely away from the trial and the man who harbored such livid hatred.

She read on to discover he had been transferred from the criminal facility to a minimal security prison. Anxiety spurted through her, even though she lived in a mediocre present with no hope of forgetting the past or Van Morrison, she did not want to die for the benefit of John Burton's satisfaction.

Her mind raced in defense of her simple and boring existence. Life, at a stalemate today, could bring a brighter day tomorrow. She might one day contribute something to the world—some one day in the distant future.

Would there ever come a time, Dawn wondered, when she could accept an actual life after Van? Not just existing on the hope of seeing him again? Dazed as she felt at this development, it still remained too difficult to accept that she never would.

Dawn tried to be optimistic as she demanded her thoughts to abandon Van and concentrate on the present. John would have to be careful. It would not be rational for him to bother with her. Still feeling vague apprehension, she picked up her coffee cup, viewing the cold creamy liquid distastefully.

She dumped the old, poured a fresh cup, added milk and resumed her seat at the small round table as Trixi came into the kitchen wearing cute little baby-doll pajamas, her favorite mode of dress until sometime afternoon.

Trixi made a beeline to the counter, opening the overhead shelf for a mug.

"Mmm, that first cup is always the best," she commented exaggeratedly appreciative. "What's up?" she said taking a seat across from her. "You look sorta like you saw a ghost."

"I—almost feel that way."

"Sounds heavy," Trixi mused. "Go ahead, lay it on me."

"Okay, it is." Dawn shifted uncomfortably. She hadn't talked about this in a while. "In 1968 a friend of mine—was murdered, first her brother, Ted, and then Carrie. Carrie Harrison, did you hear about it?"

"I heard about it," Trixi nodded.

"I wanted to find out who did it, so I arranged to meet Van Morrison. Did you know about the drug bust in Preston?" she asked inquisitively.

"Yeah, I was sorry to hear about Dave. Did you know him, too?"

Dawn nodded, she could tell Dave's death had an effect on Trixi, but didn't have any idea of how she was acquainted to him.

"Christi is one of my best friends," Dawn said. "I hardly knew Dave, but Mike is a good friend also."

"Dave and I grew up together," Trixi said, on a wistful sigh.

Clearly, the memory touched her.

"We dated all through high school. Chris and Mike were good kids. I felt bad for them, they were very close." Trixi's eyes took on a soft, dreamy glow. "I still miss him. I've never met a guy quite like him. I doubt if I ever will. We were wild and crazy in a way that—" She sighed. "Well, let's just say, I guess there wasn't anything we didn't try. It was a different era," she added reflectively.

"You were wild and crazy? I can't see that." Dawn smiled. "And honey, it's practically the same era—this is only 1970—what decade are you in?"

Trixi grinned diffidently. "Well, it *was* a different era—for me, anyway."

"You must have been acquainted with John Burton, then, remember him?"

"Who could forget—hey, I know who you are now!" she exclaimed gleefully. "You're the girl! You brought in the infamous John Burton."

Trixi abruptly sobered at her expression. "You've never mentioned this before. Did something happen?"

"Something happened." She handed the paper to Trixi.

"A trustee? Limited supervision?" Trixi looked up from the news article. "Unbelievable."

"He killed a girl." Dawn's eyes misted as she thought of Carrie. "How could he have pulled it off?"

"He's amazing in his psychotic way. I would venture that he convinced his psychotherapist that he was a changed man." She gave the paper back and took a sip of coffee. "You're probably the last thing on his mind, right now."

"That's what I was telling myself," Dawn said eagerly.

"He'll probably try to get as far away from California as possible."

"Do you think?"

"Knowing John?" Trixi shrugged indecisively.

"He should never have been allowed to be a trustee," Dawn muttered indignantly. "His offence was a lifetime sentence."

"Right, solitary confinement would have made more sense."

"He threatened me with a vengeance, Trixi, I can't see him letting go."

Dawn felt edgy again and made a conscious effort to relax.

"Yeah, they made a major blunder. Maybe you should go to the police," Trixi suggested. "Tell them you want protection until they get him."

Dawn sighed, staring into her coffee. "I wish I knew where Van is. He would know what to do."

"I worry about you, Dawn."

"It's done already. Can I get a little sympathy, please?"

"You still harbor the notion of him making the scene for another wild week—or two—and he could—it isn't unfeasible—" Trixi gave her a broad wink. "But in case not, would it help if we have a pity party?"

"No!" She stomped to the sink to dump the remainder of her cold coffee. "You won't even let me mourn a lost love. You're barbaric."

"Anyway, while you're grieving for Van, this barbarian will be in the living room, I can't tolerate sitting here watching your heart break."

Dawn giggled, slipped rubber gloves on her hands and drained the water that last night's dishes had been soaking in. She turned on the faucets adding dish liquid, thinking contentedly of her roommate.

Trixi was passionate in her distaste for anything to do with the kitchen cleanup, but she was a superb cook. That lady's cooking could compete with her mother's, but she'd never tell Tina.

Dawn had met Trixi last year when she put an ad in the paper for a roommate. She needed the company, Trixi wanted someone to help share expenses so there would always be money left over for extras, like clothes, clothes, and more clothes.

In conversation during the interview, Trixi told her candidly that she had decided to take cooking classes, qualifying her to prepare delicious and nutritious meals. Aside from being an immediately likable person, that bit of information had finalized Dawn's decision.

Trixi worked as a Cocktail Waitress in a high-class supper club. At five feet, ten and built like a centerfold model, with exquisite dark beauty, Trixi chose to remain mostly a homebody, dating on occasion but keeping it light.

She hardly appeared the type to be 'wild and crazy'. Her relationship with Dave Temple came as a surprise. She had an outgoing, even sparkling personality, but wild and crazy? Apparently, Trixi had changed a lot.

Jerry came to mind again, as he often did. Dawn thought fondly of their high school romance, back in time, earlier than the tragedy, but unfortunately, if she let herself dwell too long, memories of those days, as wonderful as they were before her senior year, inevitably brought on painful memories and useless questions.

Dawn finished with the dishes, leaving them to air dry. She wiped the counters and stove before joining Trixi in the living room.

"So, have you decided on your plans for the weekend?" Trixi asked.

"I don't know." Dawn picked up the black velvet throw pillow dropping onto the chair, tucking one leg beneath her. "I might go home. How about you? Are you finally going to accept a date with Bobby?"

"I'm giving it some serious thought. He's kinda cute." Trixi wrinkled her nose in a habitually endearing fashion. "Or I might just curl up with a good book."

"A good book on Valentine's Day?" Dawn shook her head pityingly.

"I've decided—I'm going home for the weekend."

"Who you going home to see?" Trixi asked slyly.

"I'll probably sit in my room and dream about Van," she admitted. "Or I might go out for a not so romantic dinner."

"Oh, rain on Mike's parade, why don't you." Trixi stood and stretched. "Do you need the bathroom?"

"No, why would you say that—about Mike, I mean."

"Well, now that I know 'Mike' is Mike Temple, I think you're ignoring a good thing. Little things you've said about when you visit makes me have some wondering thoughts." Trixi shrugged dispassionately. "I could be wrong."

"Way wrong," Dawn assured her. "Mike's fun and flirty, but we're friends. We've been friends for a long time."

"I said I could be wrong, right?"

"See you Monday, you wild and crazy party animal. I'm practically out the door."

"And I'm practically in the shower."

"Hey—if you decide to give Bobby a whirl, persuade him to come over for supper on Monday, 'kay? You know the way to a man's heart is through his stomach, or so they say."

"Yeah, I've heard that, too, but I don't want anyone's heart, honey. I'm too afraid of having my own cut out and handed back."

"I know the feeling." Dawn sighed loud and dramatically. "Maybe we should have a duo pity party," she suggested.

Trixi laughingly pushed her toward the door. "You're joking, right? I'm not waiting around for no-body!"

"Well then, have a good time!"

"Always do, sweetie. You do the same. See you Sunday!"

Dawn picked up her purse and snatched her car keys from the hook where they hung by the door.

Chapter Thirty-Seven

Dawn struggled out of a dream to the continuous ringing of the phone. She reached groggily for the receiver, but drew her hand back, still in a fog of interrupted sleep, but reluctant to answer.

She stared at her pink princess telephone, listening to the relentless ring. The grogginess lifted, her mind alert and suddenly wary, she felt terrified with the probability of the unknown caller.

"Hello?" she whispered.

"Happy Valentine's Day, sweetheart." He spoke softly, his voice low and smooth, deceivingly pleasant. "I know you were expecting my call. I would never disappoint you."

She nervously moistened her lips. Dawn swallowed dryly, her throat so tight that she could hardly speak. "John—I can't say I'm surprised that you called," she finally managed. "I can imagine how you feel—"

"You could never imagine," he interrupted. "Not in your worst nightmare."

"John, please listen to me."

"No, I don't think so. You listen to me, and listen very carefully. I can't stop thinking about that night in the bar when you were so willing to let me kiss and touch you. I can't stop thinking about the softness of your skin and the taste of you, and the way you—" He didn't finish.

"John, I didn't mean—"

"To lead me on? Sure you did."

"That wasn't what I was going to say."

"Personally, I don't give a damn, what I want is basically to finish what we started, Dawn, and then, well, there are other possibilities. I have to think on it, but your death seems imminent."

Her fingers tightened around the receiver. "John, you don't mean that."

"Oh, I mean it, baby," he said. "You don't know how bad I mean it."

He paused for a drawn-out moment of pressure. "I have a friend of yours with me, Dawn. I want you, but if you're not available, she'll be an enjoyable surrogate."

"What are you saying? I don't understand."

"I have Trixi Allen. Is that clear enough for you?"

"Why did you involve her, John? She's no part of this."

"Too bad, I sent for you, but you weren't there."

"Is she all right? You haven't—"

"I said, I want you," he interrupted.

"Please, don't hurt her."

"She means nothing to me," he reiterated. "I won't touch her if you follow my instructions."

She sat in the dark, in tense anticipation, gripping the receiver, weighing the innuendo and threats of violence conveyed in a disconcerting and gentle voice—the volatile calm of John Burton.

"Dawn?"

He broke into her thoughts and she gripped the phone tighter.

"In the morning, tell your mother you've decided to drop out of college for awhile. Think on it tonight, make it convincing."

She swallowed, again with difficulty. "It won't work."

"You make it work, Dawn."

She marveled at the condoling and encouraging tone.

"Where are you coming from, John?" she pleaded, her voice still a whisper. "How can you imagine that you can get away with this? You are so obviously full of bitterness and hate that your judgment is blinded."

"Don't talk."

Dawn drew a deep, trembling breath in an effort to calm herself but her heart pounded painfully. She wanted to say more and the unspoken words traveled through her mind with the speed of light.

"Carl will be waiting at the corner of Market and Union at seven."

She tried to focus as her mind swooned.

"You'll recognize Trixi's car. Be on time. If you're not here by the time I feel you should be I might decide that something went wrong, or I might get tired of waiting. Your friend is dependant on you, Dawn."

She waited in numb silence as once again he let long seconds pass.

"Bring your savings account book and proper identification, of course," he instructed. "If anyone follows, you're dead, both of you."

She sat in stunned despair after hearing a soft click. Finally she unsteadily hung up the phone.

Dawn curled on her side, hoping desperately for the respite of sleep.

Tossing and turning, drifting from one nightmare into another, sickened by the struggle within her, she awoke from another fitful nap at four a.m., grudgingly accepting the uselessness of remaining in bed.

Thankful for the sleep she had gotten before John called, she climbed out of bed, making her way unsteadily to the adjoining bath to rinse her face in hopes of reviving.

She walked downstairs dazedly, measured coffee and water, and then headed upstairs, automatically breezing through her basic morning routine while it brewed. Dawn took a little more care with her make-up, hoping to effectively remedy the damages of a restless night. When she surveyed the results, telltale signs of tears and sleeplessness were hardly noticeable.

Knowing the coffee would be ready, she headed downstairs. She suddenly thought of Trixi 'that first cup is always best!' Dawn felt like crying.

She poured a mug of coffee, wandered down to the basement, leaning against the doorframe of the party room, her head filled with nostalgia. Her thoughts traveled back through the years recalling good times to be treasured forever.

Precious memories had been made in this popular room. She visualized the early days of the Beatles and Rolling Stones—the Animals, DC5 and so many others.

She could not deny that a lot had been taken for granted here, but being the richest girl in town had occasional but serious drawbacks, in spite of all the parties, fun, and games.

There were times when she sensed vague resentment, when she could not detect sincerity, and times when it became difficult to decipher pretense from genuine friendship in a world where she lived in commonplace luxury.

Fortunately, she had been blessed with a mother who taught her deep enriching values that had nothing to do with money. Money could not buy friends or love. Real friends, true love—were relationships money should never influence—could never be allowed to touch.

Dawn turned slowly retracing her steps. Five-thirty by the wall clock in the kitchen. The minutes ticked by remarkably fast as her stupefied brain tried to function, tried to consider another option.

She could go to the police. Maybe they could get the location from the person waiting to pick her up, but all the while, Trixi's life would be at risk.

"Good morning early bird," her mother said from the doorway. "What are you doing up at this hour! You're usually my little sleepy head."

"There is a reason," she said softly.

"The coffee smells great."

"I'll get you a cup." Dawn went to the counter. "How was your date? Did you have fun?"

"I had fun," she said, hesitant, almost reluctantly. "Jake's a decent guy, far as I can tell. But then, how can I trust my judgment after Bob Kaley? Let me tell you, it's not easy after you trust someone and discover in the end, he was the opposite of the man he portrayed."

"Don't let that paralyze you, Mom, okay?"

"Oh, just because he was vile and disgusting? I'm dealing. Now, what's up with you this morning?"

Dawn knew what she had to do. More devastation, how could she do this? She took a deep breath, trying to summon her acting abilities.

"Mom, I don't want you to be upset, but I've decided to drop out of college for awhile." Dawn knew she sounded convincing, reflecting an air of lighthearted gaiety without appearing overly zealous, even though she did feel slight hysteria.

"You're dropping out of college?"

Dawn set a cup of steaming coffee in front of her mother along with some cinnamon rolls.

"For a while," she emphasized. "I just want some time out to travel, Mom. I haven't traveled much, you know, and Van sparked my interest. I'd love to see him again, too, and you never know, maybe I'll run into him in New York." Now that's optimistic, Dawn thought.

"Is that what this is about?" Tina said, obviously concerned. "I don't believe this is a good decision, Dawn. I thought you had accepted that he was out of your life."

"I could never accept that, Mom. But really, that's not all this is about."

"When do you plan to leave?"

"This morning, soon actually."

"This isn't something you should do on the spur of the moment," she protested. "You can't just up and go without thinking things through."

Dawn could hear the tears in her mother's voice, see the brightness of her blue eyes, the struggle not to cry. She felt the strongest urge to tell her everything, to ask for any advice she might have to offer, but advice in this case could lead to Trixi's death. Her mother, although compassionate, would not think of the other victim in this instance.

"I love to do things on the spur of the moment," she said softly. "You know that. But it so happens, I've been considering it for a while now."

"You never gave me a hint."

"Well, our plans were moved up a bit. I'm going with Trixi, by the way. I should leave. I'm meeting her downtown, and we're going out to breakfast."

Dawn forged a relaxed and natural expression.

"You do know John Burton escaped from that institution where he was incarcerated?" The concern in her mother's expression washed over her. "Do you think this is a good time?"

Dawn cleared her throat softly. "Yes, I know about that, and really, this is the best time. In fact, it influenced our decision," she said wanting to dissuade any further opposition. "I'm hoping they'll find him before we get back in a few months."

She gave her mother an encouraging smile, a perfectly happy smile. Glancing up at the wall clock again, knowing it was time to go, she stood.

"I love you, kitten." The bewildered look in Tina's eyes cut deep into her aching heart as she said good-bye to her mother.

"I love you, too." She gave her a tight hug. "This isn't forever," she reminded her. "I won't stay gone too long."

Tina walked her to the door.

"Call me."

"I will, and please don't worry, we're gonna have tons of fun." Dawn draped her purse over her shoulder, and then picked up the overnight case.

"And I'll be careful," she added, because she knew Tina would worry.

In spite of her very real terror, the threat of John Burton's intention to kill her blended with hope that he would not. How else could she walk out of the house and head in the direction of Central High School?

Turning off Woodland Drive, Dawn walked slowly up Union Avenue, covering the distance far too quickly, at any rate. She came to the grocery store where purchases were made when they ran out of something during the week, saw Mr. Smith preparing to open and waved.

She had been trusted, at the age of seven, to look both ways when crossing a street. A 'big girl' now, she had skipped most of the way on her first trip alone to the corner store.

Commonly called the Candy Store, she stopped by with Carrie most days on their way home from school when they were kids.

As young teens, the soda shop in back had been the place to be on Saturday night—dancing to rock'n roll blasting from the old jukebox, eating greasy French fries and sipping double thick chocolate shakes through an impossibly thin straw.

The memory made her long for the days and friends that were gone forever.

Dawn saw Trixi's car where John said it would be. A raunchy man, who looked completely out of place in the familiar little red sports car, sat in the driver's seat watching her approach with leveled eyes.

Dawn opened the door, settling morosely on the passenger side, staring absently out the window.

"Why are you doing this?" she finally asked.

"Money," he muttered in an unpleasant growl.

"If you help me, I can offer you far more than John is," she told him fearfully, but eager to gain his assist.

He snorted a short, humorless laugh, a horrible guffaw. Dawn looked at him warily accepting that he was clearly unhinged.

"I'll be sure to tell John about your generous bid."

"I can make it worth your while to help me," she said uneasily. "You won't be doing anything illegal. It could be considered a reward."

His square jaw tensed, and then he spoke with his raspy snarl. "You don't get it, do you? John ain't someone you cross and live to tell about it."

"When they get him back, he won't escape again," she said hopefully. "They underestimated him. That won't happen a second time."

"Forget it," he gritted giving her a warning glimpse.

"I need your help. You're my only hope."

"You don't got no hope, lady."

Dawn could not understand her inability to penetrate this man's reasoning. He appeared dimwitted and terrorized by John, but the offer could be easily understood, money for nothing and freedom.

"Why won't you help me!" she demanded. "Don't you know John is insane?"

He reached over and struck her hard in the face. The blow took her by surprise. She covered the place with her hand looking at him through frightened eyes, shrinking further away, huddling against the car door.

She kept silent for the remainder of the long drive.

He eventually turned onto a deserted road, passing a couple of places falling to ruin. Their destination turned out to be a big, old-fashioned house that appeared to have been abandoned for a long time.

A perfect location, no one lived for miles around. He hurried her up the steps onto a large front porch.

John opened the door. She stood still as he embraced her, turned her face away so that a soft kiss touched her forehead near the temple. He led her into the house where she glanced around the sparsely furnished living room.

"That's a nasty bruise. What happened, Carl?"

"She wanted me to cross you, so I hit her. I didn't mean to, but she wouldn't shut-up," he added defensively.

"Is that so?" His dark eyes held hers captive.

She glanced around tensely. "Where's Trixi?"

John gave her a long speculative look. "Resting," he said with a faint smile. "She had a rough night. You can see her if you want to."

He walked her over to a closed door, opened it and Dawn entered a large, dismal room. A dark covering hung over the window blocking the sun. The whole of it was lighted by a low wattage bulb, in a lamp without a shade at the far side of the room.

Trixi was lying on the bed, her face turned to the wall. Dawn approached hesitantly. She gently touched her shoulder. "Trixi?"

She turned, gradually. Dawn covered her mouth horrified, tears sprang to her eyes. Trixi's face, the exquisitely fragile, beautiful face of her friend had been battered. Filled with despair, she took in the damages, her busted and bruised mouth, another grossly huge bruise across her swollen, possibly broken nose, and both eyes blackened, the left one swollen almost shut.

"Trixi, I'm sorry," she whispered. "I'm so sorry."

"This isn't your fault. Oh, God, Dawn, we're not getting out of here alive. I wish you hadn't come here."

John's hand circled Dawn's arm. He pulled her away from the bed, back into the living room. She jerked away from the light hold he had on her, facing him, breathless with rage.

"You told me she wouldn't be touched!"

"I said I wouldn't. And I haven't touched her."

"My friend is suffering—you lied to me!"

"Lying isn't my greatest sin." He walked over to the mantle. "I've been giving some consideration about what to do with you, Dawn. I've decided to introduce you to something that will be quite terrifying at first, but soothing in many ways."

He held up a needle, and she took two steps back. Strong hands gripped her upper arms and she automatically responded with a struggle. "I want to hurt you," he said in her ear, his raspy voice igniting fear as his fingers dug into her arms. "Give John a reason to let me."

"I wouldn't fight it," John advised. "Carl can be crude; do you want a demonstration of his abilities?"

"John, p-please, don't—don't do this. I d-don't want that—that n-needle in my . . . my arm—John."

She could see her stammering pleas were adding to his pleasure and clamped her mouth shut.

"One day soon, you'll beg for it. You are going to live for the needle, baby," he promised. "I might even decide not to kill you, maybe just settle for making your life a living hell."

Dawn stood motionless as Carl tied a think, rubber band around her arm. Eyes closed, she felt the stinging sensation of the needle piercing her skin.

"See, it hardly hurt. I'm good at this," he said amiably. "Now, I'll fix you a drink. Any preference? There's whiskey, and then there's, whiskey."

She could hardly believe her ears. He sounded as though they were casual friends ready to enjoy a sociable evening. At the same time she felt an unwelcome desirable feeling—it was startling—it was terrifying.

"I don't want a drink."

"You're wrong, Dawn, you do want a drink. I am going to enjoy controlling your life, and you will want what I choose to give you."

"I despise you, John," she said with loathing. "You can inject your drug into me, and you can threaten me, but the day will never come when I submit to your will. You will not control me."

He slapped her across the face, the violence sending her to her knees. He pulled her back to a standing position by her hair.

"I could kill you very easily. Don't push me."

"All right, John, it's your party." She took a trembling breath, her face burning. "I'll have your drink."

"I could hear you breathing on the phone," he said, his fingers slowly loosening their grip in her hair. "I thought about that while I was waiting for you . . . the way your breath sounded."

Dawn swallowed convulsively.

He gripped the waistband of her jeans, pulling her closer.

"Are you afraid of me?"

She drew a breath. "Yes, John," she conceded. "I am."

When he released her, she walked over to the sofa dropping onto it, waiting uneasily for his next move. Dawn looked at the front door as Carl trailed behind him into another room.

Left alone, she wanted to run away, open the door and take off in either direction, but she had traveled that road and there had not been another vehicle on it, besides, nothing had changed since she received his call, Trixi was here, and now he had her, too, the reality of it terrified her.

He returned, and she grudgingly accepted her drink, whiskey over ice.

Dawn stood as Carl headed toward the door on the other side of the room, John's hand clamped tightly around her wrist.

"Don't let him hurt her anymore," she pleaded. "Please, John, for the love of God. You promised me—you promised." She fought the urge to break down sobbing. Poor Trixi, it wasn't fair! She hadn't even known Trixi when she went to Mexico, and if she had been in the apartment, Trixi wouldn't even be here now. "You have me! Do what you want to me," she choked feeling anger that she dare not reveal, and despair that she couldn't hide.

"Carl, ease up on the girl."

"Listen, you said—"

"Let me put it this way, she's not a punching bag. Take it easy on the girl."

Dawn saw the hostility in the look Carl gave him, but as he turned away without comment, John didn't seem to notice.

"He won't hit her again."

"How can you be sure?" She searched his face for any sign of mockery, another play of words, another hidden lie.

"Because he does what I say."

Dawn wondered at his arrogance when Carl was obviously unstable. He seemed as volatile as John, just not as intelligent.

After a while, a deep feeling of calm infused her. She decided there must be a way, somehow, to get through to John, to bypass the hate and bitterness.

She took tiny sips of the whiskey, until becoming accustomed to the taste.

It wasn't so bad.

"She was always above him," he said abruptly. "Having her here like this must have gone to his head."

"What do you mean?"

"He used to watch her at the Basement when she was with Dave. He lusted after that girl almost as much as he lusted for smack."

"And he has to abuse her—because he wanted her before?"

"Some guys get off on that."

"And you don't?"

"Not so much, I have other methods."

He turned her face to his, claiming her mouth in the surprisingly gentle kiss reminiscent of the night in Mexico. As his firm mouth moved over hers, she experienced an eager response to the touch of his lips. The shock of wanting him reverberated through her body.

Raising his head, gazing into her eyes, he smiled slowly.

"You're a hot-blooded little bitch, aren't you?"

Dawn sighed tiredly. She crossed her arms staring straight ahead.

"I did what I could to help you."

"You were the one who put me in that place."

"No, John," she protested cautiously. "You put yourself there. They would have sent someone after you."

"Someone else wouldn't have fooled me so completely . . . It would have been better than what you did."

"I'm sorry." She swallowed with difficulty, unable to understand this onslaught of emotions.

"You will be."

"You don't have any feelings, do you?"

He looked at her, a coolly appraising stare. "Oh yeah, baby. I have feelings." He lifted his glass. "A toast, Dawn," he said, his eyes penetrating. "To us."

Dawn bit her lip glancing away. She had been close to him—maybe closer than anyone had ever been—and she had hurt him more than he would ever let her know.

"Lift your glass, Dawn, join me in the toast."

She picked up the glass.

"Now drink." He clicked his glass to hers, watching closely as she forced herself to swallow the whiskey, which actually went down rather smoothly.

"Are you hungry?"

"No, but I have to use the bathroom."

"Come with me."

She followed him obediently up some bare wooden stairs to the second floor landing where he stopped at the first door they came to.

Dawn closed the door of the large grimy bathroom. She smelled the odor of mildew, and rusty stains marred the sink, commode and the clawfoot tub, but at least the plumbing worked. A roll of toilet paper sat on the tank.

When she came out, he took her across the hall into another gloomy room with an old four-poster bed and a nightstand with a gaudy lamp on it.

He tied her hands to the top bedposts, her feet to the bottom. The ropes were tight and cutting but she turned her face to the wall without a word.

She heard him walk away.

Hours passed as she drifted in and out of fitful sleep. Dawn struggled within herself to not call for him to untie her. Whatever he decided to do would have to be endured; begging would enhance his pleasure, adding to her degradation. Darkness finally came and sound sleep accompanied it.

He awakened her sometime later. He released her left arm, tied the band around it, and then administered another shot of heroin.

"You'll get to like," he promised with a cocky grin.

John released the other arm. He gently examined her wrists.

"You're very tender, your skin is so soft," he said lightly massaging the marks the ropes had made. He tied the ropes again, securely but not as tight.

She refused to look at him. John left her again, alone in the night.

Dawn opened her eyes, frightened by the unfamiliar and dreadful room, uncertain for a fleeting instant of where she was before the realization washed over her in a wave of agonizing misery.

She gazed out at a misty dawn through a grimy window, the brightest stars faded as light penetrated the darkness. A soft glow outlined some wafting clouds and streaks of red and orange shot out across the gray sky.

Eventually, she had to turn away from the window to be met with the emptiness of the large room and the discomfort of her position.

In spite of the warmth of the room, she shivered. How nice it would be to curl up under a soft pastel sheet in her bed at home! But not her room now—the room with the canopy-bed and princess décor, the pink and white room she moved into when she outgrew the bed in the nursery, her only clear memory of being four. She had felt like a little princess. Her mother always made her feel precious. *Oh, Tina, I'm so sorry!* Tears filled her eyes but she blinked them away determinedly. Time passed in tortured minutes.

Dawn watched the door, anxiously waiting for it to open.

Her stomach began to pain for the need of food. Surrendering to tears of frustration would have been a relief as the discomfort increased. When John finally came in, he gave her another injection. Released of the bonds, she sat on the edge of the bed filled with misery, until the misery disintegrated leaving her marveling and still terrified.

He sat beside her. "How did you sleep last night?"

Dawn looked at him with deep contempt. The question did not require an answer. It was absurd. She watched guardedly as he took her hand in his lightly caressing her fingers.

"Answer me," he said softly. She knew the dangerous inflection in his voice. His grip tightened as she tried to withdraw her hand.

"I had a wonderful night—I have to go to the bathroom."

He nodded in compliance, allowing her the luxury of her hand back. She rushed across the hall thankful that he had not hurt her.

She relieved herself and then washed her hands. After washing her face and brushing her teeth, she felt even better, but was despairingly aware that the drug in her system induced new and improved feelings.

"Let's go have some breakfast," John suggested when she stepped out into the hall. "I bet you're hungry."

She looked at him in wonder at his amiable tone. He clearly was psychopathic. What did he actually feel? Or did he feel anything at all?

Trixi was preparing breakfast. Dawn joined her friend at the stove while John took a seat at the table. Trixi's eyes were glazed. She looked pitiful and lethargic, but busied herself at what she did well.

Dawn pretended to be a puppet, a puppet could avoid being concerned about what might be happening to its body, because being made of wood, it could not be harmed, and it must not need food because her hunger had diminished.

She stood gazing out the window after helping Trixi serve breakfast—accepting the reality of her blood, flesh and bone existence—accepting the reality that her human body, being subjected to a dangerous and addictive drug felt oddly sensational, which brought on a host of conflicting emotions.

"We need money," Carl grumbled crossly. "Our whole stash is short, and smack, man. I don't know why you want to waste it on her."

Dawn turned from the window to see him glaring at her.

"Don't look at me. I didn't ask for it."

"You will, baby, you will." John leaned back, his gaze piercing. "I need you to close your savings—you do have savings, don't you?"

"Well, yes, I do. You know, I do." Dawn looked at him listlessly. "They won't let me close it."

"The bank here is an affiliate of the one in Preston," he went on as if he hadn't heard. "So it won't be a problem. Carl is going to drive you to town, and you're going to close out your account."

"You must be crazy if you think . . ." The words caught in her throat as he stood abruptly, his chair tipping over with the motion.

She took a step back as he approached. Standing in front of her, he gripped her wrist, very deliberately twisting her arm behind her back.

"Don't ever make that mistake again."

"They won't give it to me," she whispered.

He tightened his grip, cruelly increasing the pressure.

"Look at me, Dawn."

She tipped her head up obediently, meeting his avid gaze.

"You'd better convince them."

"I'll try." Dawn clenched her teeth against the pain. If he intended her to suffer, she decided, staring into dark fathomless eyes, he could determine the extent without the benefit of her pleading.

He released her, suddenly. John sauntered back to the table, casually righted the chair resuming his place, reverting to his remarkably controlled self. But it was there, the bridled anger below the surface.

"Why don't you call her mother and get our money?" Carl muttered. "We could do the girls, split this scene and travel to the other side of the world."

Do the girls? Massaging her aching arm, Dawn looked at Carl. Was he talking about killing them? Her eyes shifted nervously to John as he casually lit a cigarette.

"Never second guess me, Carl," he said softly, blowing smoke toward Trixi. "With the money in her account, we might not have to contact her mother and make it messy with threats of violence."

"Oh, yeah? How much bread you got, lady?"

"A lot," Dawn said dryly.

They walked into the living room. Carl ushered Trixi to her room, locked her in, then walked on outside without a word, leaving the door open.

"If you care about your friend, don't try anything."

She looked at John convinced that something horrible would happen to Trixi if she left her here. Why would he even suggest such a threat? He had her under his thumb, wasn't that enough?

John placed a detaining hand on her shoulder as she started to go out the door. He looked down at her through dark, threatening eyes.

"Trixi's depending on you."

She nodded, unable to say a word.

Then he smiled that slow, deceptively appealing smile that she had started to hate. "Don't look so terrified. She's safe in my care if you cooperate. Just remember you're on drugs, and they're very effective."

Mr. Maxwell, the bank's president, did not prove to be an easy man to get along with when it came to the parting of cash. Not that she was surprised when he balked on closing the saving's account, considering it unacceptable to withdraw that amount of money.

Although she had three forms of identification, he had his secretary call the Preston Branch. He spoke quietly into the receiver. She couldn't hear what he said before passing the phone to her.

"Mr. Regis wishes to speak with you," he said, quite primly.

Dawn took the phone. Mr. Regis had been their banker for years and recognized her voice, but conveyed his anxiety about the decision to close her savings. Fear that he would not permit it began to creep up her spine.

Dawn had known that trying to close the account would be a useless venture, but try to tell John Burton that. What would he do if she couldn't get the money he demanded?

She talked calmly, masking her inner turmoil, as she worried for Trixi and what John's reaction would be. Mr. Maxwell listened on the side with undisguised approval that her banker was also giving her a difficult time.

Finally, Mr. Regis suggested 200,000.

"Okay," she relented, speaking amiably. "Two hundred thousand is a nice, even number." Dawn understood the necessity of respect.

But I shouldn't have to beg for my own money, she thought furiously.

Mr. Regis still expressed concern with her having 200,000 cash on hand. He had agreed to give her a goodly amount of cash, so he needed some lecture time. She listened distractedly while hoping the lesser amount of money would appease John. His speech wasn't long, but it seemed lengthy as she bit back the urge to demand her money.

She knew better than to risk a show of impatience. If the bank insisted, there could be a lengthy waiting period for the amount of cash she needed. Besides, he might call her mother who would never approve without talking to her about it.

"Thank you, Mr. Regis." Dawn replace the phone as Mr. Maxwell looked on suspiciously. "Mr. Regis agreed to 200,000."

He looked skeptically at the phone. She knew he was itching to call him back, but didn't want to seem irrational to his associate. He eyed her doubtfully, and then started giving her some more grief about taking so much money in cash, finally stepping on her last nerve.

"You have no idea of my worth," she said coolly, a bit haughtily, all the while feeling ready to snap, strung to the limit.

Dawn forced herself to remain composed, not wanting to blow it now. At least she would have something to offer.

She found it hard to accept that Mr. Maxwell had her best interest in mind while wondering what John's reaction would be with the compromise she had been forced to make.

Still, she managed to keep calm, to assure him that she was not alone, that she would be perfectly safe with this amount of cash-on-hand. Completion of the transaction took a long enough time that she once again began to feel the icy speculation that something could go wrong.

The nervous tension didn't ease from her neck and shoulders until she exited the bank with the money in an inconspicuous black briefcase, finally in her possession. Still, she had to face John with the lesser amount.

Upon arriving back at the old mansion, John told her that of course, he hadn't expected her to be able to close out the account. Dawn bridled her own anger, knowing he had only wanted to make her squirm.

Chapter Thirty-Eight

Dawn turned her face away as John tied her hands to the bed, next he secured her feet. She didn't resist, she had never resisted, not from the first night. It would only give him a reason to be rough.

She hated him for it, though, for leaving her in this humiliating position that eventually, sometime before morning, led to a need to stretch, to change position, to curl up into a little ball and cry like a baby.

"Dawn, you have to take your drugs, you need them."

Still refusing to look at him, she murmured. "I don't want anymore pills."

"Of course you do. They help you sleep, don't they?"

She turned her head to face him, reluctantly, accepting.

With one hand supporting her head slightly off the pillow, he gave her small sips of water to swallow them down.

"Think about what I said," he told her impeccably.

What did he say? She could not remember—something about life. Recollection came, vague at first, then more distinct. No, not about life, not exactly, it was something about not wanting to live.

As she looked into his intense dark eyes, she sensed that beneath the totally sincere hatred there must be another emotion. She refused to believe he would eventually take her life. She wanted to live, and clung to that hope. He hadn't threatened her with death for a while. Maybe mental and physical pain would satisfy whatever demon controlled him.

Left alone, she stared at the ceiling. John is right, she realized as the whimsical effect of his pills washed over her—what would I do without his magical dream-makers?

Dawn awoke in the night. She looked out into the darkness at a sky alight with stars. The stars held her mesmerized, wondering at how immense the universe is . . . how the earth is just a little part of a galaxy in an immense universe . . . *I am just a minuscule speck on this little part of a galaxy in this immense universe. Look at those stars—they go on and on and on . . . .*

Suddenly Dawn felt a terrifying sense of despair. She closed her eyes tight feeling like nothing—less than nothing, so small, so insignificant.

She opened her eyes. No, she couldn't believe that. It was exactly what he wanted. He would never have his satisfaction. She determined not to give in to such thoughts. There must be a purpose for her in this world—her life mattered.

How sweet it would be to curl up under the covers on the bed.

Dawn felt the pull of the drug-induced utopia taking her again. She began to drift far away from a dreary room and a musky, uncomfortable bed.

Thankful for the sleep—a cherished escape from the misery of lying with her arms and legs tied to the bedposts night after night, she fell languidly into darkness, welcoming the slow descent into a deep, soft void where sweet dreams flourished.

Dawn opened her eyes to sunlight, unwelcome, almost painful in its brilliance. John would be there in a few minutes, she knew, any moment the door would open, but seconds slipped by, minutes ticked away. He will be here soon, she thought deliriously.

He had to, and very *soon*, because he had not disturbed her in the night.

She felt the need, not so much a physical thing, yet, but the very thought of not having the drug created an undeniable dread within her soul, deep doubts of having any strength to go on. She needed the drug!

With a feeling close to terror, Dawn realized this would be his day, what he had been waiting for. How long had he been administering the narcotic? She floundered, at a loss, with no conception of time. How long would he make her wait?

The fear of what might happen made her want to scream for him to come and save her, but she would never give him the satisfaction.

Time passed in a nerve-racking haze. Apparently, he had determined to let her suffer. Dawn closed her eyes against the urge, determined to see it through without calling his name. It was what he wanted. He wanted her to call for him, and she wanted to.

Being tied to the bed increased the agony. She suffered in silence, choking back a sob, fighting the hysteria. She wanted to fold up in a little ball. Her body ached, her muscles tensed, she moaned, twisting her hands against the restraining ropes.

"You're hurting yourself." His superbly soft voice set her on edge.

Dawn stared at the ceiling refusing to look at him. When he wiped the perspiration from her face with a cool, damp cloth, she wondered why he would want to sooth her in the midst of torture.

"You want a fix, baby?" Gently, he turned her face to have eye contact. "Tell me . . . that's all you have to do."

Tears of anger and frustration filled her eyes. He was enjoying this, and it made her hate him.

"You're hurting yourself," he repeated. "Quit twisting your hands."

"What do you care?" she demanded, managing to subdue the tears. He would never see her cry! "This is what you wanted! To see me like this."

"There's a simple solution, Dawn," he said decisively. "Just say you need it. Tell me how bad you want it. Think about how it makes you feel, baby. Have you ever needed anything in your life?"

"Is that what this is about?" she said, confused by this new turn in his attack on her. "Is it about who I am?"

"Tell me you need to shoot-up," he said, implacably. "You need a fix. I want you to admit your dependence. I want to hear you say it."

Why not simply admit the truth? He had what she needed. She couldn't deny it, not to herself, certainly not to him, but she could not say the words.

Dawn shivered. "Have you ever seen anyone need it before?" she said with deep contempt. "You're a drug pusher, right? You must have seen the suffering effects of withdrawal . . ."

He smiled, actually smiled at her, and she realized to having admitted her need, not directly, but enough to cause her shame. She resolved to die today, die of withdrawal from the narcotic before ever telling him again that she needed a damn fix.

Oh, but she wanted it so bad! With this thought came more shame, a sudden urgency to urinate.

"I have to go to the bathroom," she whispered.

She felt degradation, revulsion, and humiliation. He obligingly untied her. Dawn sat up, and then slowly stood.

"Wait . . . give me your little hand."

She held out her hand. He turned it palm up. John placed a plastic bag in her grasp. "It's in there. What you need. Everything you need."

She stared in disbelief at the bag before raising her eyes to meet his uncompromising gaze. She moaned hopelessly.

He nodded; a wisp of a smile on his insufferably handsome face.

She escaped to the bathroom. Dawn stared at the clear plastic bag as she sat on the commode relieving herself.

She washed her hands. After drying them on a slightly soiled threadbare towel, she sat on the closed toilet seat for long minutes staring at the disgraceful contents of the bag.

Dawn took deep tortured breaths. It had to be done, it had to be now. She prepared the fix as she had seen John do, drew the liquid slowly into the needle and touched the tip of it to the inside of her arm.

Her hand shook.

"I can't do it," she cried.

She looked at the needle, at her bruised arm and the ugly thick band tied around it. Dawn took calming breaths, steadying her hand. Desperation overrode every other emotion.

As if someone else had control, she watched the needle penetrate her tender skin, the syringe slowly injecting the horrendous drug into her vein.

She stared at the reflection of a stranger in the mirror, raised a hand to push back a strand of hair that hung dull and limp, in need of washing. She gazed into eyes smudged with dark circles, large in a thin face.

Dawn turned away from the image. In some remote way, this person reminded her of a girl she once knew.

When she stepped out of the bathroom, John stood nearby leaning against the wall, his arms crossed casually. He had to have heard her desperate plea.

"Feeling better?" he said.

She knew better than to refuse to answer.

She searched his face for signs of mockery or contempt, for amusement at her expense, but found no trace of aversive emotions.

"Yes, I'm better. I'd like to take a bath."

"Okay," he agreed. "When you're done, I'll see you in your room."

Dawn sat in the water for a long time before using the soap and shampoo.

She towel-dried her hair, then combed it, feeling calm and warm, almost blissful, recognizing why she felt like this but accepting that it didn't matter.

She pulled on a clean white tee shirt that reached midway down her thigh, his words coming to mind. *I'll see you in your room.* He had never said those words to her before. She had an intuitive idea of what he meant.

"I will not lose myself," she said to her reflection. "I am Sommer Dawn Preston, and I'm special." She struggled to focus. "Someone told me."

It seemed an eternity since she had thought of her friend, the mischievous smile, the winking blue eyes, his teasing kisses.

Dawn paused at the door of her room, not surprised to find John waiting, but feeling somehow confused.

She looked at his lean, naked body without fear or revulsion.

He came to her, took hold of the hem of the tee shirt pulling it up over her head. He held her hand, led her to the bed, and then eased her down onto it.

John leaned over her. Their eyes locked as he slowly descended to claim her mouth in a sensual kiss that aroused her but also activated an incredible sadness.

Tears of despair filled her eyes, then, as his lips caressed her neck and he moved slowly down to explore her body with his enticing skill, she became aware of a deep longing, an intense, almost desperate need.

A stranger to herself, her whole being flooded with desire, compelled to respond, her body arched instinctively to meet his touch. A deep yearning overwhelmed her, consuming and unreal.

Dawn whispered his name, ran her fingers through his hair, drew his face to hers, pressing her mouth against his firm lips. She wanted to kiss him, to touch him, to taste him. She wanted nothing more than to please him and for him to satisfy this new sexual awakening.

She had never felt this pure carnal lust, freeing her of all inhibitions. She wanted him inside her, needed him to possess her. Dawn felt passion rising like a hot flame and cried out with spiraling delight, pleasurable waves of ecstasy surging over and through her yielding body, complete satisfaction. Still, as he moved away there remained a vague need of him.

When Dawn opened her eyes, he had dressed and lit a cigarette. He took a long drag. The smoke he exhaled swirled in a cloud, lingering in the air to mingle with smoke curling up from the tip.

For some odd reason she thought of demons—demons in the smoke. He offered the cigarette to her. She refused, but he patiently insisted.

"Are you satisfied, John?" She inhaled a gasping breath struggling for an ounce of self-worth. "You did what you promised you would."

When he turned his eyes on her, she shifted her gaze looking down at the smoke curling off the cigarette held between her fingers.

"Is that how you feel?" he asked impassively. "Do you feel like I did what I promised?"

"I'm addicted to heroin, you did that. You've possessed my body and for all I know, my soul, too. Yes, John." Dawn gazed at the smoke again, lost in the swirling, illusive images therein. "That's exactly how I feel."

When she looked back at him, his gaze locked her into riveting immobility. Unable to tear away, becoming lost in the depths of darkness, she had the sensation that he had not done what he intended at all, and she didn't want to know, she never wanted to know.

Dawn gave him the cigarette, it sickened her, but after she pulled on the tee shirt, she enjoyed sitting dispassionately enjoying the smoke show.

When he reached for the ropes, she grabbed his wrist. A disturbing thought occurred to her.

"Is that how they tied you when you were a little boy?"

John didn't say anything. He didn't have to say a word. Her eyes flooded with tears, his silent acknowledgement cutting through her emotions. Torn with grief, unable to separate the anguish she felt for herself from that of a lost child, she began to moan in unrelenting despair.

He took her in his arms. She balked at first, but he held her shaking body tighter as her sobs became deep and painful. Rocking her soothingly in his arms, murmuring and apologizing, John tried to ease her misery, but it didn't help. A damn had broken and an endless flow of tears spilled forth.

Eventually, the endless flow of tears did disperse. She took comfort in his embrace, beginning to relax. He loosened his hold as her troubled spirits quieted. Mixed emotions assailed her, deep feelings for the person in whose arms she rested. He smoothed her hair, still holding her as the drugs in her body ushered her into a welcomed, blissful peace.

John eased her onto the bed. She felt him clean her face with a cool cloth before she fell slowly into the wonderful, fluffy darkness.

When Dawn awoke alone in the room, she sat up in bed, stretching leisurely. With a sense of relief and assurance, she gingerly checked out the marks on her wrists where he had kept her tied for so many horrible nights.

Dawn turned, placing her feet on the floor, waiting for the dizziness to subside. She padded over to the door. When she tried the knob it opened, and she peered cautiously up and down the hall. Seeing no one, she stepped out hurrying down the stairs to Trixi's room.

It seemed imperative to talk to her right now. In her fogged mind, she could not even remember the last time, but Trixi's door wouldn't open.

She kept turning the doorknob uselessly, deeply disappointed.

Dawn cried out, shocked by the sudden grip of large hands that took hold of her from behind.

"Shut up, bitch." He slammed her face-first against the wall.

Dawn recognized the rasping voice and the smell of stale perspiration. Carl Howell turned her to face him.

Still stunned from her face slamming into the wall, Dawn tried to scream, but he pressed his large hand tight against her mouth. She struggled uselessly to avoid the brutal pressure as he skillfully molested her.

"You got it coming," he said with an ugly sneer. "It might as well be now. I'm gonna take you in the bedroom and fuck your brains out, bitch, and your little friend gets to watch the fun."

He slammed her against the wall again.

"You can relax and enjoy it, or I can hurt you, either way you want it."

Dawn made herself relax in his grasp. As he removed his hand slowly from her mouth, his hold slackened and she wrenched away. He caught her by the hair, dragging her back, his broad-carved face twisted with anger.

Panic welled in her throat choking off a scream as he drew his fist, she stared into eyes wild with rage and drugs. Dawn flinched helplessly in his grasp. A shudder passed over her body as Trixi's battered face flitted through her memory.

John grabbed Carl's fist and held it tight. His slight form deceivingly concealed his strength; he held the big man's wrist with minimum effort.

"Touch her again, I'll kill you," John said evenly.

The words hung in the air. John slowly released his hold on Carl's fist.

Dawn held her breath wondering what would come of this confrontation.

He had never threatened Carl before. Now Carl looked at John as slow seconds ticked by, seeming to weigh the odds of resistance. He finally released her, taking strands of entwined hair when he pulled his fingers away.

John's protective hand pressed her closer to him.

Carl's hands opened and closed back into fists. Dawn knew he wanted to make a move. A few more tense moments passed before he finally turned away. He was the bigger man, but ignorant and dependent, addicted to drugs.

"He's getting harder for you to handle," Dawn murmured as they walked toward the sofa. "Did you see the way he looked at you?"

"He's harmless."

She marveled at his delusion. How could he consider Carl harmless? "John, he scares me. I'm afraid of him."

"I'm the one you should be afraid of."

Dawn watched him withdraw, that inexplicable empty look came over his face, his eyes looked through her, his strong, slender hand gripped her throat with a tightening reflex. He wavered on the edge.

She waited anxiously, snatched from the illusion of hope—forced to accept the stark reality in which she existed—that John held her life literally in his hands.

He came back, slowly refocusing, gradually loosening the hold, leaning back on the sofa—his expression—like nothing had transpired. The terror passed, it seemed he had never been gone.

"Why did Carl think he could have his way with me?" she asked, terrified of the answer but needing to know.

John drew her close in the same protective fashion as before. "He wants to hurt you, but I promise, he'll never, *never* have you."

"Then why did he say that? Where did he get the idea that he had the right to take me?"

"That was before . . ." His voice faltered. He did not finish and she didn't ask. He didn't say anything for a while, lost in thought. Finally with his arm still affectionately around her, John said, "Don't leave your room again."

You don't have to tell me twice, she thought hazily. Of course she wouldn't leave her room again, not without John. That room would be her sanctuary.

Dawn lived in a drug-induced haze, enjoying the utopia his pills created. Heroin had become an imperative part of life. She could not imagine facing a day without it.

She called her mother regularly, talking to her once a week since arriving here. Happily, John had insisted, so Tina wouldn't get worried and call the police, at first with a threat, for some time now without any need of threats.

She had enough comprehension to know the drugs had her in a powerful grip causing her to simply not care. Dawn looked forward to the calls and had become adapt at making up all sorts of fun things she and Trixi were doing together.

She wouldn't even know what to do with freedom; the man, the drugs, the dependency, to be without them now seemed somehow disparaging.

Sure, she wanted to be free someday, wanted to see her mother again, but when that someday would be didn't really matter. Memories of her former life were comparable to remembering a dream.

She saw Trixi when they had meals. She hardly ever consumed more than a few bites, but John enjoyed Trixi's expertise in the kitchen as well as Carl when he had an appetite.

Trixi's face had healed, but she too, had lost a proportionate amount of weight. Dawn couldn't tell if she was on any sort of drugs. She had no idea what her friend was going through. They weren't given opportunity to talk. For the most part Carl kept Trixi isolated.

"What are you thinking, Dawn?"

"Many profound and complex wonders of the universe," she replied. "And sort of wondering what it would be like to be free."

He smiled. "Free? You want to be free?" he said casually caressing her thigh. "And I take such good care of you."

Dawn pulled her legs up to her chest, wrapping her arms around them.

She gazed steadily at him until he finally looked away.

John lit a cigarette, offered it to her, and she accepted it as unequivocally expected, taking a long drag, exhaling the smoke, wondering at what she had become.

"I'll let you go someday," he said evenly. "But when I do, I have to be prepared to never see you again. I don't want to think about it, right now, Dawn. I don't want to face it."

"Maybe I don't either."

Awareness happened gradually, John was shaking her, frantically shaking her. She resisted the disturbing nuisance of interrupted tranquility. Dawn moaned a feeble protest, realizing that she must have drifted off to sleep. It happened often, but he had never awakened her like this.

"Oh, Dawn." She heard the relief in his voice; saw it in his eyes as he gathered her in his arms.

"What's wrong?" she asked, bewildered.

She followed his gaze as he looked toward the nightstand. "You haven't used any of that H, have you?"

"No." But it's time.

"Carl is dead," he told her. "It must be contaminated. Somehow, you know, these things happen sometimes."

"No, I *don't* know." She grabbed his arms. "What do you mean? These things happen?"

He gently disengaged himself from her grasp.

"You can't be sure it's the heroin," she said desperately, following him into the bathroom where she watched helplessly as he flushed it down the toilet. "How could you do that?" She sat dazedly on the edge of the tub.

"I couldn't take a chance on your life. Come on."

"You had no right! Since when does my life matter? Why all of a sudden does my life mean so much to you?" she demanded following him back into the bedroom where she sank down on the bed.

Panic coursed through her as she felt the familiar urge. "I'm afraid. Oh, John, I'm afraid of this."

"It won't be so bad, Dawn. It will be bad, but you can handle it. You haven't been addicted that long."

She nailed him with a look of rage at his callous words before fear twisted her insides again.

"How can you know what I can endure? How can you know the extent of my addiction?" Her eyes met his despairingly.

"I know a little bit about these things."

It would be hard. She was on several hits a day, other drugs on top of it. It would be bad. It would be the worst experience she ever suffered or would ever suffer again. He had put the suggestion out there that it wouldn't be too severe, hoping that if she believed, it would strengthen her.

John sat beside her. "I know you're going to hate me," he said. "And I'm prepared for whatever it takes, but I want you to know straight up—"

"Don't say you would go through it for me." Her breath quickened as fear and helplessness assailed her. "Don't say it—because you've never been there."

"Dawn, if I could take it on myself, I would," he asserted compassion thick in his voice. "I can say it because I mean it—I would save you this suffering if I could."

She looked away, but something drew her gaze back to his. John's eyes had a softness she had never seen before.

"Then get it for me. You know where to go to get more," she said fluently, feeling hopeful. "You wanted me to acknowledge my need—you wanted me to say it. I need it, John, I do. I'm feeling sick—it hurts."

"I can't." He looked at her with uninhibited sympathy.

"Why not?" she demanded furiously not interested in his compassion or sympathy. "What's stopping you? Do you still have a sick urge to watch me suffer?"

"Dawn, don't." He reached out to her but she tore herself away.

"Don't touch me!"

Her eyes filled with tears that slid slowly down her face. She begged for his help, knowing he had the means to relieve her of the impending misery.

"I don't want to do this," she said desperately. "I've never been sick a day in my life."

She turned over facing the wall, wondering how to get through to him.

"I'll leave with you, John," she said quietly. "We can go where they'll never find you—I'll stay with you, baby. I can be so good to you—just please get me some drugs."

"It isn't you talking," he said softly. "It's your addiction."

Tears cascaded down her face, her throat tightened in frustration as she realized there would be no escaping the dreadful roller coaster ride.

No amount of money, no method of persuasion or extent of begging would convince John to get the drug soon to be more forcefully demanded by her body and mind.

Dawn waited, filled with terror of what would happen, not even knowing, just that it would be dreadful.

The hours dragged by, minute by minute as she suffered through a restless night. The sun's first rays penetrated the darkness. Dawn moaned as pain and realization surfaced.

"Are you satisfied now?" she said, assailed by her sick yearning. She began to shiver. "This how you wanted to see me isn't it! I hope you're happy now!" Dawn broke down, giving in to tears of anger and agony.

"You could get it for me," she accused. "You did this to me. This was your plan all along!" She turned away crying into her pillow.

He massaged her shoulders, his touch extremely gentle, but she couldn't stand to have hands on her.

"Stop it!"

"You want to be free," he told her. "You want to be free, Dawn, and you will be."

Every nerve in her body tensed. "You don't know what I want."

"You want to be free," he said adamantly.

"I don't want to be free! I'm not prepared to go through this, and you're not prepared to see me through it. Don't make me," she pleaded. Her throat ached with defeat as she realized, he was beyond reach, beyond reason. "It isn't fair."

Dawn paced the floor. John had nothing for her now, no magic pills, fluffy clouds or warm dreams. She wanted to kill him for it, but he had gotten rid of everything.

She slept for a while. She woke up in misery, pacing the floor, heat radiating from within her body, her clothes wet with sweat, then cold and shivering, she crawled back into bed, her body an unbearable ache.

Every time she woke up he was beside her. He gave her water, bites of chocolate, orange juice, too, but she couldn't accept much nourishment.

She flitted miserably in and out of sleep, climbing in and out of bed, going to the bathroom, wretched trips of misery where she suffered diarrhea and vomiting and sat crying, agonizing, yearning for relief.

With no comprehension of time, night became day, and day turned to darkness again and again as the symptoms intermittently ravaged her body. She felt like she had been sick forever and would never be well.

Unaware of the time frame or how many times she had been in here, she flushed the commode, then leaned over it as her body convulsed uselessly with painful, wrenching spasms and dry heaves.

Dawn rinsed her mouth, took a sip of water and her stomach twisted again. She sank to the floor pulling her legs to her chest, screaming for John.

He rushed in, gathered her in his arms, and carried her back to bed.

"You said it wouldn't be so bad," she whimpered. "I'm going through misery, and you said it wouldn't be so bad!"

The compassion in John's eyes served only to provoke her. Knowing that she would give love or money, grant his freedom or any favors for the drug she craved added fuel to the flame of hostility.

Filled with shame, anger and humiliation, Dawn pounded on his chest. He accepted the rain of blows until she exhausted herself.

He kept feeding her sweets and juice at intervals when she could accept it. Right now, she wanted nothing except to die, then fear of dying took over all reasoning, she curled up into a little ball of pain and cried.

Dawn slept again. She woke up feeling restless and miserable; he rocked her gently, calming and comforting, his voice tranquilizing. Trembling in his arms, she let him soothe her.

She slowly opened her eyes, feeling different, weak and helpless, but better. He fed her a bit of food, followed by small sips of juice. Her stomach gave a threatening twinge, and she held up a hand turning away.

"No more."

She leaned back, holding her stomach against the pain. When the ache eased up, Dawn took comfort in his arms.

"I need a bath," she whispered.

He assisted with her bath, washed her hair like she was a little girl, even made her smile when he put bubbles on her nose. Once she was safely out of the tub, he gave her privacy.

Dawn tried to avoid looking at herself in the mirror as she brushed her teeth. Dressed in one of his clean shirts, she made her way back to the bedroom where he helped her to bed.

"The worst is over," he promised.

Dawn opened her eyes to a bright new day. Sunlight filtered through the curtains in golden beams of shimmering light.

She left her room gliding down the marble staircase, on into the living room. A symphony of music filled the air as the drapes opened to reveal the fountain with glistening sprays of enchanted water shooting high into the air to sprinkle a million gleaming stars across the sky.

Dawn opened her eyes to the stark reality of a bare and grimy window in the dismal room of misery.

She responded with denial. "No," she moaned softly. "Please, no."

John came to her side, his arms impulsively embracing her.

She rested her head on his chest, felt the caress of his hands on her back, the stroke soothing her emotions.

"Does it hurt so badly?" he asked, tightening the embrace.

"I just . . . I dreamed I was home."

Chapter Thirty-Nine

John watched her sleeping. She had slept her first completely restful night in over a week. He had lost count of days as he attempted to help her through this overwhelming time of misery.

He had known it would be pure agony, but tried to play it down hoping if she didn't know how bad it would be, that it might give her more will to conquer the dependence.

He didn't know what he was thinking, really, except that he wanted to take it all back, to restore what he had stolen, the glowing look of youthful radiance and the innocence of never having touched drugs.

He couldn't give back what he had taken, of course, but he knew she would get past it eventually.

He had subjected her to abuse, subtle at times, often crude, and through it all, even during the darkest hours, living with the threat of death—she had been terrified—but John knew he would have had to kill her to extinguish the fire in her eyes.

In controlling her, he had lost control.

Dawn drew a deep breath, wondering if this could be another dream—she felt no pain. She opened her eyes to a new day.

"John?"

"I'm here."

"John, it doesn't hurt anymore," she whispered.

He held a glass to her lips and she took a long swallow of the cool, fresh water. Nothing had ever tasted so good.

She leaned back, taking another breath enjoying how truly wonderful it felt to be without pain. Dawn looked closely at the man responsible for the most horrendous experience of her life.

He had abducted her, addicted her to heroin. He had caused her suffering and shame, but somehow during the atrocious existence a bond had formed.

"I'm sorry for everything that I did to you."

"I know." She gave him an apologetic glance. "I used that against you, too. I couldn't stop myself. All I could think of was the drug, that you could get it for me, and you wouldn't."

"Don't apologize, Dawn. I wanted to help you in the end, but I did it to you. I meant to make you suffer, and once it started happening there was no control. When I wanted to take it back, I couldn't."

She noticed how tired he looked, his beard had started to grow and dark smudges around his eyes gave a haggard appearance. He couldn't have slept much taking care of her, being near every time she woke up.

"Dawn, I wish I could have let you go before your symptoms advanced. I should have gone to town and sent an ambulance. They could have done more for you at a hospital—they could have helped you."

"John, you did help me."

"What do I say to you?" he murmured. He took a shallow breath. "I had to see you through this, because there's something you need to know."

He bent his head slightly forward, the heart rending tenderness of his gaze filled her with wonder. She waited, giving him time to find words to express whatever emotions he might be feeling.

He looked toward the ceiling for an instant then back at her.

"I want you to know and understand that you were thoroughly drugged. I mean, not just with heroin, not just the pills." He sighed deeply. "You're not responsible for any feelings you had, physically or emotionally for me, okay? It wasn't you, it was—the drugs."

Her mind embraced the revelation.

He looked down, and then raised his eyes to meet hers again.

"I'll send an ambulance for you."

"You don't have to run, John."

He came over to stand beside the bed.

"You think I've changed, I'm still who I am, Dawn. I can never go back, only I didn't want you to ever have a doubt—" He reached a hand out to touch her face when—suddenly a force hurled him across the room.

A blast shattered the morning stillness. In the ensuing silence, she looked at John in dazed horror. Inexplicitly riveted, she stared, absorbing the shock. Half his head had been blown away, splattered against the wall.

Her heart beat furiously, the blood pounding in her temples as she gazed transfixed, unable to tear her eyes away from the appalling sight.

A bird singing outside the window distracted her and she turned her face aside feeling sickened. Dawn swallowed repeatedly, warding off the nausea, the room spun and grew hazy—she tried to take a deep breath, to regain control of her rapid, uneven breathing, but the air seemed cut off from her gasping and hungry lungs.

She came to being carried out of the house on a stretcher. The man at the foot of the stretcher, dressed in white, she recognized to be an ambulance attendant, next her eyes focused on Van walking beside her.

The attendants settled her inside the ambulance, and then started an IV drip. With Van seated nearby they sped away from the old mansion that had been her prison.

"Trixi?" Her voice, barely audible drew his attention.

Van leaned closer.

"Trixi—where is she?"

"On her way to the hospital," he said. "We're right behind her. The two of you can probably share a room."

"I want to go home," she whispered.

"I'm taking you to the hospital," he said, his voice rough with anxiety.

She gripped his hand. "I want to go home," she whimpered feeling panic and helplessness, emotions she never wanted to experience again.

She watched the resolve in his eyes dim in view of her desperation.

"All right, Dawn," he complied gently. "It's against my better judgment, but, I'll take you home."

She closed her eyes to see John's face—the tender expression—his eyes so fondly contemplative—reliving the sudden moment when he had been flung across the room by the violent force of a powerful bullet.

Remembering brought despair and intense shivering. Dawn felt the warmth of another blanket being tucked snuggly around her cold body.

"Wake up, Dawn, you're home."

She sat up with a tired sigh.

"They can take you in" he said referring to the two ambulance attendants.

"I won't have my mother see me carried in on a stretcher. I can walk," she said, feeling a bit indignant.

"Are you strong enough, little girl?"

She tried to smile at him but her lip quivered, and she dissolved into tears. He moved swiftly to her side, his arm around her shoulders.

"Are you sure you can do this?"

"I'm sure," she sniffed. "If they get this thing out of my arm and just give—give me a minute."

"Take as long as you need," he murmured rubbing her back soothingly.

An attendant removed the IV and secured a Band-Aid where the needle had been inserted.

Van gave her a handkerchief to clean her face. Dawn sighed wearily, but she felt calmer. "Okay, I'm ready."

He lifted her out of the ambulance, steadying her on the walk to the door where her mother stood waiting. Tina hugged her close. Dawn returned the warm embrace feeling deep contentment in the loving arms of the woman who had given her life.

"I think you should lie down," she suggested. "I'll make some tea."

Dawn felt herself reeling for an instant. She leaned against Van for support wondering at the sudden wooziness. With no allowance for protest, he swept her up in his arms, carrying her into the house.

"Where's your room?"

"Second floor, the third door on the right," she said feeling giddy.

Her gentle laugh rippled through the air, she hoped it was real laughter, not hysteria, but genuine laughter brought about by actual good feelings. She was home, no more misery, no more pain, no more fear; actual good feelings.

He placed her on the bed, positioning a pillow behind her back.

"Dawn?" Van sat on the edge of the bed.

She gazed into his understanding eyes, trying to control the overwhelming and mixed emotions that suddenly erupted.

"That's what I thought," he said as tears slid from her eyes.

She broke down completely, and he took her in his arms, holding her tenderly. "You don't know if you're comin' or goin' do you, sweetie."

She sighed despairingly. "I'm sorry. I don't know why that happened."

"You've been through hell—don't ever apologize for your emotions, okay? You'll feel better tomorrow," he promised. "Get plenty of rest today."

"I've had plenty of rest."

"You need more. Want me to tuck you in?"

Her head still against his chest, she nodded.

"Where are your gowns?"

"In the second drawer." Dawn indicated the chest-of-drawers to the left.

She removed the shirt, immediately pulling the sheet up to cover herself until Van came back to the bed with a lavender silk gown. She helped him slip the fresh gown over her head, feeling the silk smooth against her skin, inhaling the wonderfully fresh, faintly floral scent of her nightie.

He fluffed the pillow, and then repositioned it behind her back.

"Thanks." She leaned back against it contentedly.

"I'm going to leave, now. You do need more rest, whether you know it or not, you're completely exhausted. I'll be here tomorrow."

Van held her gaze for several crucial seconds. She could see the love in his eyes that he refused admit. Or is it, she wondered. In her state of mind, she might imagine love when the look may only be empathy.

"Only sweet dreams, now," he ordered softly before brushing a gentle kiss across her forehead.

Tina, waiting outside the door, came in as Van left. She set the tea down on the nightstand, and without a word, cuddled her close rocking her like a child. Dawn held tight to the sweet love of her mother.

"Mom, I have to tell you something." Dawn sighed painfully. She didn't even want her mother to know, but Tina would soon notice her arm. "Mom, he forced me to use heroin. I—I became addicted."

Tina's arms tightened around her. "Oh, my poor baby," she whispered, tears in her voice. "My sweet little girl."

"I—I'm not addicted any longer—I'll be okay."

"You will," she soothed, continuing to rock her. "I know you will."

The gentle rocking comforted her, Dawn drifted into peaceful sleep.

She opened her eyes lying quiet, not ready to move, wanting simply to absorb being enveloped in the comfort. She stretched leisurely breathing in the clean fresh scent of her bedroom.

She sat up finally. The day had passed and evening progressed. The little clock beside her bed read six-thirty.

Wondering suddenly about the month, Dawn hurried over to the wall calendar. February? It seemed time had stood still. He had taken her in February on the night of Valentines' Day, having no idea of the month and the day created an incredibly weird feeling.

She quickly flipped on the intercom. "Mom, are you there? I'm kind a curious about the month and day?"

"It's the second week of May, Dawn, May 14th."

May 14th. Three months—three months that seemed almost as illusive and surreal as a dream, and so much longer than three months!

"Honey, are you okay? Are you hungry? Could I get you something?"

"I'm all right, Mom," Dawn said assuredly, though she wasn't sure at all. She felt so disoriented. "I'll have some jelly toast, but I'll come down."

"Do you want tea or coffee?"

"I'll have tea, thanks."

She slipped into her pink silk robe that hung far too loosely on her slender form and the matching house slippers that seemed a size too large.

Dawn left her room hurrying down the marble stairs, on into the living room. The drapes were open to her grateful eyes. She happily viewed the fountain as it sprayed iridescent water high into the air to sprinkle down in a sparkling colorful cascade.

When she entered the kitchen, her mother gave her a tight hug.

"I missed you, Mom."

"I missed you, too, honey. Thank God for Van."

"John was going to let me go, Mom."

"Do you want to talk?"

"I will someday, just not—not yet."

She wanted to tell her mother everything eventually, but it all seemed too overwhelming right now.

Dawn sat at the counter, appreciative of her surroundings. She managed to finish a whole slice of toast with the cup of tea.

"Would you like some ice cream or sherbet?" Tina offered hopefully.

"Sorry, Mom," Dawn said with a tipsy smile. "Full tummy." She patted her stomach for emphasis.

Tina sighed dispiritedly. "You're so thin, honey."

Dawn could see the tears; hear the trembling in her mother's voice as she struggled not to break down. She knew Tina wanted to be strong for her.

She carried her cup and saucer to the counter by the sink pretending not to see. "I'm almost anorexically thin, Mom," Dawn said inserting feigned chirpiness, kissing her cheek before taking a glass from the cupboard.

"I'll eat more tomorrow. I promise!" She turned on the cold water.

"I know. One day at a time, right?"

"Yeah, Mom." Dawn forced herself not to look at her arm.

"If you wake up during the night—if you want something to eat—or just to talk, you come to my room. Okay?"

"I will. I'm going to take a shower. I'll be down after."

Careful not to spill her water, she gave Tina a hug. The familiar smell of her fragrant perfume blending with the fresh scent of soap and shampoo made her feel safe.

"I love you, Mom."

"I love you, kitten."

Surprisingly enough, Van was right. It wasn't long after her shower before exhaustion took her back to bed for the night. Relaxing against some pillows, she dialed Christi's number.

A warm, familiar voice answered. "Hello."

"Hello, Mike."

"Dawn—I've been thinking about you—a lot about you," he added.

"I appreciate that."

"I've missed you."

"Me, too."

"You want Christi, right?"

"Yeah."

"Listen, when you recover, we'll get together. Okay? For a drink—for dinner?"

"Yeah, I'd like that."

"Okay, I'll get Chris."

"Thanks." She thought about Mike's invitation. His voice had been husky, filled with compassion. A moment later Christi's clear, sweet voice came on the line.

"Dawn?"

"I thought I'd better call and let you know I'm okay."

"Are you okay?" she asked anxiously.

"Not yet, but I will be."

"Van called. He told us John had kidnapped you." Christi's voice trembled. "This is mind-boggling, you know. It just blew me away."

"We'll talk soon—so much to say."

"You sound tired."

"I'm pretty weak. I'm in bed right now, about ready to go to sleep."

"Thanks for calling—we've been worried, all of us."

"I love you guys."

"We love you, too."

"Soon as I'm strong enough, we'll get together, okay?"

"I'll be over to see you as soon as you're accepting visitors."

"You can come anytime, Chris."

"I'll see you soon, then." She paused. "Goodnight."

"Goodnight." Dawn turned off the lamp, snuggled under her sheet and closed her eyes with a contented sigh.

She awoke before daylight feeling well rested but lingered in bed enjoying the smooth, clean feel of the pastel sheets. To her amazement, she felt herself drifting back into light slumber. Dawn forced herself to snap out of it and sat up, swinging her legs determinedly over the edge of the bed.

Taking a leisurely walk around the circumference of her room, touching various objects so dear to her, helped her feel secure.

Gifts from her mother over the years, her Barbie Doll collection, a unique miniature Grandfather Clock, lovely porcelain dolls of various countries in authentic clothing. They looked realistic and beautiful.

She had dreamed of this so many times, it seemed imperative to make sure this time that it would not slip away, that she would not wake up in a damp, musky room with peeling wallpaper and no drapes on the windows.

She went into the bathroom, drew water in a glass, and applied toothpaste to her brush. What a pleasure, she thought emphatically, simply being able to brush my teeth in my own bathroom.

The feeling overwhelmed her, accompanied by faint dizziness. With sudden urgency, her lungs felt starved for air. Struggling with the frightening feeling of suffocating, she tried to take a deep breath, but again the passage of air stopped very short of filling her lungs. Her heart began to pound, and she held to the sink as increasing dizziness rocked her.

Finally, the room stood still again. Dawn drew in a deep breath, her lungs finally accepting.

She let her breath out on a sigh, studying her reflection, an incredibly thin and fragile image. The weight could be regained, but it seemed she had lost something and needed to find it but had no idea of where to begin looking.

Downstairs, in the kitchen, she brewed a cup of tea. Carrying it into the living room, she relaxed on the sofa. Desire rose unexpectedly within her, a fierce almost painful, empty feeling.

According to what she had ever heard, this was a mental issue. There could be psychological cravings for months. Something to look forward to, she thought ironically as the urge subsided, more to endure, but it, too, would pass. She determined that the psychosomatic would be no contest, time would free her eventually. Soon, she hoped, pushing off the sofa, the mental and emotional need for drugs was pretty severe, but at least it had passed quickly.

Dawn walked to the window. She opened the drapes, once again enjoying watching the fountain spray water high in the air to cascade down in its lovely, shimmering rainbow of colors.

She remembered last night, the desperation to get down here, to view the fountain, proof of reality.

As she thought back, the dream that had seemed so real at the time, did not seem real at all, but it had served to enhance the hopeless feeling of despair when she awakened in that desolate, dreary room.

After drinking her tea, she decided to take a shower, knowing that Tina would be up by the time she finished.

Dawn started to say something to her mother as she entered the kitchen, but the words got lost when she saw Van seated at the counter.

"When did you get here?" She sat on the stool next to him.

"Just a few minutes ago."

He took hold of her wrist, gently turning her arm to examine the damage.

"It's over," she said withdrawing her hand.

"Dawn . . ."

"I can't talk about it now."

"You will have to talk about it, though. You can't keep the hurt inside."

"Please, Van." She bit her lip. "Not now. Not yet."

"Coffee's ready," Tina said. "Are you hungry?"

"I don't feel hungry."

"You should eat something." Her mother looked anxious.

"Be nice to your mother. Let her fix you some toast," Van suggested.

Dawn grinned. "Okay, toast is good," she agreed.

"How about French toast?" Tina recommended. "Van?"

"I could never resist anything French," he smiled.

"Sounds wonderful," Dawn complied.

Van went over to the counter and poured them both a cup of coffee.

Tina whipped the eggs in a bowl, dipped the bread, and fried it in the electric skillet with the sausage along side. Seemed in nothing flat, she had their breakfast in front of them with butter and warm syrup.

He wondered what Dawn was thinking as she obediently nibbled the delicious toast. It seemed she was forcing herself to take even tiny bites.

Dawn, so beautiful, bubbly, and bright eyed, was a wisp of herself, but her exhausted eyes smiled at him. Van wished he could say the words she wanted to hear, that he was ready to settle down and make a home, but he could not be dissuaded from his purpose.

He could never let Dawn know how much he loved her, because he had to move on, his restless spirit wouldn't be stilled, not with so much that had to be done.

"Penny for your thoughts."

He grinned, giving her a secretive wink. "I'm thinking you look like a lost little waif who was finally found."

"Well, I sorta feel that way, too," she admitted, pushing aside one slice of the syrupy toast. "That will do for now."

"Okay, let's go out front," he suggested, standing. "It's almost time for me to head out."

They sat down on the patio chairs. She hugged her knees to her, staring out into the distance.

"How did you find me?"

"When I got back from a case I was working, I was catching up on Preston news and read about John escaping. I wish I'd found out sooner, Dawn."

Van held her hand gently pressing her fingers. "When I called Tina and heard your see the country story, I knew it was total fabrication."

He paused, watching a cloud cover the sun.

"Tina told me you called regularly, so I put a tracer on the phone."

"I wish you would have found me sooner, too," she whispered.

Dawn gazed with adoring eyes at the man she had fallen in love with so quickly and completely. "How is Trixi?"

"Trixi will be okay, but she's not in Preston. She was stable enough this morning to be transported to Texas by ambulance. Her folks wanted her there, to help her through it, you know, and to make sure she's okay."

Another flood of emotions abounded. "I'm sorry she had to get mixed up in this mess." She released her legs, stretching them out in front of her.

"It never should have happened. Dawn—"

"Did he have to die?" she asked abruptly. She cleared her throat gently, her voice had sounded choked with emotion.

Van looked at her, his expression of incredulity unguarded. "I couldn't take a chance on your life," he said after a long brittle silence. "I'm sorry, Dawn, I can't imagine you would care."

Yes, he was clearly surprised that she would care. She heard a rough edge to his usually smooth voice, noticeably disapproving of her sentiments, but he sighed, recovering his affability to an extent.

"He killed before, he would have again."

She thought about what Van said, and she didn't have the heart to oppose his words, but John had changed, he would not have killed again.

After a few quiet moments, he sighed. "I have to go now," he said softly. "I took time that I didn't have to be here. I'm supposed to be in Chicago."

"No need to explain." She tried to smile. "Go get the bad guys."

Dawn pushed herself to a standing position, lurching unsteadily as wave after wave of dizziness passed over her.

"Dawn!" He grabbed her in his arms to keep her from falling. "Okay, little girl, you had it your way, now you're going to the hospital."

"I think that might be a good idea," she said faintly.

Dr. Hamilton diagnosed her as suffering from dehydration, malnutrition and fatigue, not surprising, he said, considering what she had been through.

The suffocating feeling, pounding heartbeat and dizziness she suffered this morning had been an anxiety attack that hopefully would not happen again.

A needle in her arm slowly distributed, drip-by-drip, the fluids that her body needed. In a few days, if she began to eat a normal diet, once she began to regain some strength, she could go home and begin to rebuild her life.

The thought almost terrified her. The future seemed empty, she felt more alone than ever before, and it hurt to think about anything.

The feelings that assailed her were normal reactions, the counselor said when he had stopped by earlier today. Considering the experience she had been through, every lost and lonely emotion, the misery, the emptiness should come as no surprise.

Tears slowly found their way down her cheeks, overcome by a terrible sense of bitterness; she buried her face against the pillow to muffle the sounds of her normal reactions.

Chapter Forty

Dawn left the doctor's office, walking to her car in a bewildered daze. The possibility of pregnancy had been something she had refused to accept. When Dr. Hamilton insisted on a pregnancy test, it came back negative, as she had known it would. A false negative—how?

She hadn't had her cycle for three months, chalking it up to not eating or the drugs, or the trauma, anything except the option of being pregnant.

Now she put her forehead on her arms draped over the steering wheel and wept. Something had gone wrong with the test, because she was pregnant, very pregnant, *more than three months pregnant.*

Fumbling for the tissues in her glove box, she dabbed her eyes and blew her nose, then sat staring dully out the windshield.

In need of a sympathetic shoulder, Christi seemed the one to run to. A sympathetic shoulder? What she needed was someone to tell her it simply wasn't true.

Stunned beyond belief, Dawn still recognized the futility of sitting here doing nothing. Absently turning the ignition key, putting the car in gear, then pulling slowly away from the curb, she headed toward Fairview Boulevard.

Stopping at stop signs, keeping within the speed limit, even beneath the speed limit, didn't help her feelings, knowing the possible hazard of being on the road in this condition. Dawn thankfully parked her Impala at the curb in front of Christi's home, happy to have reached her destination.

She took a couple of deep breaths to calm herself before leaving the car.

Mike answered the door. “Hey, girl, long time no see.”

“You saw me last week,” she said hesitantly.

“That’s a long time for a lovelorn male pining his life away for you, doll! How about you, sweetie, how are you doin’?” He slipped his hand around the back of her neck, claiming a gentle, but sound kiss.

She felt herself yield slightly to his usual, playful advances.

“Mmmm, can we do that again sometime?” he suggested. “Like right about now?”

She gave him a light shove, laughingly caught up in his youthful gaiety. Why did she feel so old?

Then her eyes met his. She caught a subtle expression of understanding and the glimmer of a troubled look.

“I was on my way out,” he said softly. “Dawn—”

“Yes?”

“I’m here when you need me,” he murmured.

“Thanks, I appreciate that. I’m pretty sure the time will come.”

“Christi’s in the kitchen . . . Later, Dawn.”

“Later, Mike.”

She turned watching him walk away, then closing the door behind her, Dawn walked through the living room.

“Hello?” she called entering the dining area of the split-level home. “Mike let me in!”

“Dawn!” Coming out of the kitchen with a cheerful smile of greeting, Christi’s gladness turned quickly to concern. “Something’s wrong.”

Dawn opened her mouth but could not find the words. Christi put an arm around her as they walked into the kitchen.

“I’ll make coffee,” Christi said.

Dawn sat down on a cushioned stool at the counter. She took a deep breath. “Honestly, I could use a shot of bourbon.”

“I’ll do that then.”

It wasn’t long until Christi set a rock glass filled with ice and cola on the counter beside a shot glass of bourbon.

She had mixed herself a bourbon and coke. “I don’t do shots.”

“Me, either.” Dawn poured the liquor into the soda pop.

“Want to go into the living room?”

“No, this is fine.” Dawn took a little sip of her drink.

She had told Christi much of what happened, what she could remember of the time she spent prisoner to John. Now she had to tell her the rest, the severe consequences of the abduction.

Soft music emitted from the clock radio on the counter while seconds ticked by as she considered how unbelievable this pregnancy seemed.

Would saying it make it more real?

"I just came from Dr. Hart's office, Chris, I'm pregnant. I'm going to have John's baby." Even spoken out loud the words sounded fabricated and unnatural to her ears.

"What?" Christi's tone clearly relayed her incredulity. "I thought Dr. Hamilton ordered a pregnancy test and it was negative."

"He did but something messed up, maybe the lab, maybe something else. I don't know. I just know I'm pregnant. Oh, Christi what am I going to do?"

Christi was quiet for a time, looking contemplative and extremely sad.

"What are you thinking?" Dawn asked.

Christi took a swallow of her drink. "I know what I would do," she said, slowly with reservation. "But I can't tell you to do that."

"The embryo should have died," Dawn said dully. "Or I should have miscarried. It shouldn't have happened!"

"It shouldn't have," Christi agreed. "You've been through too much already." She leaned forward her voice filled with compassion. "I wish I could offer a solution, Dawn. But that isn't why you came here, is it."

"No, you're right, I didn't." Dawn sighed twirling the liquid in her glass. "I just needed to let you know, but—" She tipped her head. "I would consider any sound advice."

"I don't know how sound this advice is, I mean, I don't know about you, but it would work for me."

Christi leaned back on the stool giving her a deeply compassionate look. "What I was speaking of—" she said uncertainly. "And believe me I suggest this out of love for you. Have you considered abortion?"

"That was my first thought. I just—don't know."

"It's so hard to accept. I think I'd go crazy."

"I've considered that, you know?" Dawn took a breath, releasing it in a forlorn sigh. "Given the complications of my life, at times, I think a nice quiet breakdown would be a good choice."

"Seriously, I don't know how you've kept it together. Please, hold on."

"Hey, I was just kidding. I have a firm hold."

Dawn gave her an expedient glimpse.

"You're not okay—are you okay?"

"Well, pal, not super-duper, but I'll be all right, honest I will. It's just that this thing happened that shouldn't have." She smiled wryly. "And no matter how unfair we think it is, the fact remains, and I have to decide quickly what to do about it."

"How far along are you?"

Dawn pushed her drink aside. It made her feel nauseous.

"Going into my fourth month. It's um, almost a baby," Dawn glanced at her watch. "I'd better get home."

"But you just got here," Christi protested. "Couldn't you stay for supper? We're having stuffed pork chops. It's been so long—"

"I really do have to go." She offered an apologetic smile. "I don't know what I'm going to do, but I have a lot to think about."

"I understand." Christi stood as Dawn did. "Let me know what you decide, okay? And if you need to talk about it, I'm here." They walked toward the door. "And Mike, you know he's here for you, too."

"Yes, I know, I'll be in touch."

"Call me," Christi urged.

"I promise."

Dawn left Christi feeling calmer, but once home she went straight to her room. She collapsed onto the bed to stare at the cream colored ceiling contemplating the beginning of a new life that she did not want or need.

She wondered, sullenly, if she should have it removed.

Dr. Hart, although not pro-abortion, had told her he would perform the procedure. Arrive in the morning and be home in time for supper.

How convenient. It would hardly disrupt her day, much less her life.

What life, she thought. She ventured out once in awhile to go see Christi. Sometimes she accompanied Mike to a movie or dinner. I should have fallen in love with you, Mike, she thought morosely. It could have made life easier. How, though? She would have still been kidnapped and pregnant. Still in the same dilemma, *only she wouldn't be alone.*

Pregnant—the thought appalled her. Why? Why? Why! Regardless of it all, she remained thankful that John had told her about the drugs used to seduce her. Dawn realized also that there had been brain washing and mind control. She had been the victim of a strong, persuasive personality who made her a desperate and compliant victim and left her an emotional wreck.

She wanted to hate John, but he had been a victim, too.

Dawn shivered, turning over on her side. How could she tell Tina? Where would she find the words? For the first time she thought of another who would suffer as much as herself from this predicament. Having been a source of worry to her mother since she got out of the hospital, the news of this pregnancy would be the clincher.

An abortion would be the easiest answer. Tina would never have to know, and she would not have to go through the physical and emotional pain of having a baby to give away. No one would blame her, Christi had even suggested it, and her opinion meant a lot. But how could she sacrifice an innocent little life for her own convenience?

Dawn tossed restlessly as the feeling prevailed. She could not rationalize a way out of it.

The best solution to her problem was adoption, this choice rested well with her. There were always families who wanted newborn babies.

She decided to leave Preston, have the baby, sign adoption papers and then come home. She would never have to tell Tina about the pregnancy.

Dawn opened her eyes when she heard tapping on the door.

"Supper's ready."

She sat up rubbing her eyes. "Come in," she said.

"Were you sleeping?"

"Yes. I'm not hungry, Mom."

"I'll bring a tray for you," she said. "You should eat something."

"Okay, thanks."

Dawn reached for the phone. She adjusted the pillow behind her back, reclining against the headboard, and then dialed Christi, content that she had clarified her muddled thoughts.

She waited as a prolonged silence followed her disclosure to Christi that she intended to go away in secret and put the baby up for adoption.

"Dawn, are you—are you completely sure this is the path you want to take?" Christi asked hesitantly.

"I thought abortion at first," she admitted. "I just couldn't."

"You've thought it through very carefully?"

"I did—I can't keep it, but I can't—I just can't destroy it."

"Why aren't you telling your mother?" Christi said with a vague hint of disapproval in the normally accepting voice. "Did you think that through?"

"Yes, I did." Dawn felt emotionally distraught.

"Dawn, she's your *mother*."

Tears trickled slowly down her cheeks, but her voice remained steady.

"I can't tell her, Christi. It would be too much of a burden. With her deeply embedded feelings on the subject—oh, I know she would be a rock, and she would let me do what I feel is right, but I can't put her through this sorrow. It would hurt too much."

"What did she say about you leaving so suddenly?"

"I haven't told her yet. I dread it, I do. Not that she would try to stop me. She worries a lot, but she lets me make my own choices."

"Yeah—and how has *that* worked out—sorry, not funny?"

"In a way it was," Dawn said, but realized her eyes had filled with a whole new flood of tears. "On second thought, maybe not," she admitted.

"Tell her soon," Christi said with gentle urgency. "You don't want to wait until the last minute. And I hope you have made the right decision," she added after a pause. "I hate for you to go through it."

"I don't exactly look forward to it, either, but there's nothing else to do. Thought about it, came to a conclusion, stickin' to it." She wanted to say more, but words eluded her. It seemed that everything had been said for now.

"I'll be leaving soon, so I'll see you when I get back."

"I wish you could come over for a day before you go. We could have a barbecue—chicken, baked potato, corn on the cob?"

"I'd love to, but I'm just not up to it. I'm sorry," she faltered hating to turn down her friend, but she felt so dispirited.

"Don't be sorry, silly."

"As soon as I get back—"

"Call me."

"As soon as I get back, I will."

"You aren't going to call me until you get back?" Christi wailed.

"I don't know, maybe—but what could we talk about Christi? This will dominate my every waking moment for next few months, and I want to put it all behind me when it's over, so—it might be best just to wait."

"It might—I understand. Take care."

"I will, and I'll be fine."

"I'll be praying for you," Christi said. "I love you."

"I love you, too."

Dawn hung up and pressed the intercom. "Mom? Are you there? I'll be down for supper."

"Okay, kitten. Do you want tea?"

"Yes, that would be great, thanks."

She went to the bathroom. After rinsing her face and brushing her hair, Dawn dressed in comfortable lounging pajamas.

Christi was right, she had to tell Tina. She had to tell her tonight. Dawn dreaded telling her mother that she was leaving Preston, of being the source of more pain, but getting out of here within the week seemed imperative.

Since the decision and time had been determined, it would be wrong to keep it from Tina any longer.

Dawn walked slowly down the stairs, her hand caressing, rather than holding the banister. She loved this home; her heart would remain even though she was leaving.

Once she returned, Dawn determined, sighing with trepidation, she would never leave again, ever. She took a deep, calming breath before entering the kitchen to be greeted by her mother, who had finally begun to smile again. Now she was about to take that away, *again.*

It split her heart right down the center, but how could she tell her mother that she was pregnant? Even though Tina had always stressed that she could tell her anything, Tina had voiced on more than one occasion, her abhorrence of a mother letting her child go, giving a baby away as if it was no more than an unwanted item, which was exactly what this baby would be to her.

She could not fathom abortion, which Tina loathed even more, but this embryo or fetus or whatever it was at this stage was unwanted, unneeded, and a complete disruption of her life, but not for long.

She feared Tina could never understand or accept that point of view.

Dawn waited until after supper, determined not to ruin the evening meal, but of course, Tina knew something was up. When she broke the news that she had decided to get away for a while, it wasn't incredibly unpleasant.

On the morning she had scheduled to leave, after breakfast with her mother, Dawn lingered over a second cup of coffee. It was so hard to say goodbye again.

She had tossed restlessly last night, pondering the idea of telling Tina about the unwanted pregnancy, wondering if it was in her mother's best interest to keep it from her or if she was afraid to tell her, dreading her reaction. She didn't want this difficult decision to come between them.

The night had seemed endless. She woke up several times to stare through the darkness, hating that she had to withhold this painful secret, but knowing to tell her would be irrevocably devastating to them both.

Dawn had tried this past week to feel affirmative about leaving, to be convinced within her heart the validity of it. She needed to make this temporary move sound like a positive act whenever they discussed it, but a sense of inadequacy swept over her as she considered the many mistakes she had made in her life.

"I can understand that you need to assert some independence, but couldn't you take a place in town?" Tina sighed. "Dawn," she said hopefully. "The Broadway apartments are magnificent, and you would be close to home."

"I have to get away for awhile," she insisted. "This will be good for me, Mom. I know that when I get back home I'll have a better outlook on life. When you think about it, almost anything would have to be better than it is."

"You're holding up amazingly well, Dawn, considering what you've been through. Don't be so hard on yourself."

Tina walked with her to the car.

"Take care—call me—and come home soon."

"I will, just before you know it." Dawn hugged her mother.

"I love you, baby."

"I love you, Mom." She looked at Tina. *I'm pregnant, Mom, and I'm scared. I don't want to go. I don't want to be alone.*

Even so, she got into the car and drove away.

Dawn arrived in San Gabriel in mid-afternoon. She took a room at the Holiday Inn with intentions of finding an apartment as soon as possible.

She stretched out on the bed, her thoughts wandering back to a time when she believed in dreams coming true and wishes the heart made. That seemed like such a long time ago! She was irate at the trouble that had happened in her world to take away the happy ever after. She felt more desolate than angry, though, and sorry for herself, *because I'm allowed to feel sorry for myself!* Dawn thought of Trixi and the pity party joke, sighing regretfully.

Dawn turned on the television, turning off her dire thoughts for a while, before going out to supper and to buy an evening paper.

The food tasted bland, the romantic atmosphere depressing. Here she sat, alone in a room full of people. Smiling, laughing couples, putting their heads together in intimate conversation, sharing a secret smile, some of them slow dancing to the melody of a three-piece band.

Dawn gave up on eating. She bought a paper to check out the 'for rent' section with hopes of finding more homey living quarters. Settled in her room, she flitted over the rentals, pausing on the fifth one.

"For rent," she read aloud. "One bedroom with adjacent bath, sitting room and kitchen privileges, home cooked dinners served in family setting. Almost like staying at 'Grandma's house'. Grandma's house? Hmmm, I never had a grandma. This might be fun."

She circled it, deciding to check it out first thing tomorrow.

After a shower, she went to bed for a night of tossing and turning.

Dawn dragged out of bed as the first rays of sunlight touched the dark sky, she didn't want to be awake but her mind was racing.

Desperately in need of coffee, Dawn walked down the block in search of a restaurant. She found one easily enough, walking curiously into Darrel's Grill, the epitome of simplicity, with a jukebox and booths on one side, a counter on the other.

The place was packed with the breakfast crowd, folks on their way to work, or maybe coming off the nightshift.

Sausage, bacon and breakfast steaks sizzled on the grill, eggs were frying in large skillets, hash brown potatoes in another, next he was flipping French toast on a second grill. Wow! She watched the expertise of the counter and grill man as he worked quickly, dishing up various plates of food, admiring the grace and speed of two cute and efficient waitresses serving breakfasts and refilling coffee cups for the customers.

It kept her preoccupied until, one of them, Sherri, the nametag read, managed to grab a minute to take her order.

Since she had passed on supper last night, the smell of the food had awakened her appetite. Dawn decided to stay for breakfast and ordered steak and scrambled eggs with hash browns, coffee to drink, and coffee to go.

Breakfast was as delicious as it smelled, but she could only eat about half. Back in her room with the television a dubious diversion, the time ticked slowly by until a decent hour to make the call. She dialed the number and was cordially invited to come immediately for a viewing of the suite.

She drove to the huge, private home located just outside the city limits in a quiet neighborhood. A white picket fence circled a spacious yard.

Dawn opened the gate to walk up a quaint cobblestone path enjoying the scenery, plenty of shade trees in the huge yard, the sweet smell of blossoms in the air. A variety of plants along the perimeter of the porch and around the yard in attractive arrangements added bright bursts of color with the greenery.

She climbed the few steps that led to the open front porch with a roof and railing. A nostalgic porch swing hung from hooks to the left. On the right patio chairs around a large table suggested game playing and socializing.

Dawn opened a screen door to a comfortably cool area with lots of windows allowing plenty of light and a variety of green plants, some hanging, others on windowsills. She stepped inside onto durable dark green carpeting.

Two huge, leafy, potted plants sat on the floor in two corners of the spacious room furnished with a television, several medium sized patio tables and accompanying chairs.

Dawn listened to the quiet serenity of the area. It was exactly what she wanted. She pressed the doorbell. Soon an elderly woman with a halo of silvery hair made an appearance. She opened the door with a warm smile in greeting.

Dawn introduced herself, returning the friendly smile.

"Come in, Dawn," she said. "You can call me Goldie, everyone does."

"That's a pretty name."

"Thank you. My brother gave me the name, actually. My mother told me that when I was three and he was six, he said my hair looked like shining gold. He called me Goldie Lyn instead of Gwendolyn."

"That's darling," Dawn said, really touched by the sentimental story.

"Eventually, he shortened it to Goldie, and it stuck. Personally, I like it much better than Gwendolyn."

She laughed merrily, and Dawn smiled. "The name suits you."

The distinct, light fragrance of lilacs wafted back as she followed Goldie through the entrance hall and up carpeted stairs to the second floor.

The little woman walked straight with a firm, sure step. She stood no taller than five feet, small and sprightly.

Dawn entered the spacious room behind her, looking it over approvingly.

She could live with contemporary, not her preference, but it had a warm, comfortable quality, with shades of brown and beige in the main room, gold drapes and matching carpeting.

The room came complete with coffee and end tables, lamps, even pictures on the walls.

"This is really, very lovely," Dawn said noticing the dimmer switches, a nice touch. "It's so ready to move into!"

"My grandson renovated this apartment for himself and his bride." She led Dawn to the bedroom. "Then his job transferred him to San Francisco."

Dawn looked around the cozy bedroom, decorated in shades of blue. She walked over to the doorway of the adjacent bath.

"It's as perfect as can be," she enthused deciding that she would not have to look any further for a place to live.

She paid the eight hundred dollars for the first and last month's rent.

"Rent includes meals, Dawn," Goldie said as she wrote in her receipt book. "Supper is at six. Everyone is on their own for breakfast and lunch and responsible for their cleanup." She tore out the receipt.

"Nice to have you as a tenant, let me know if you need anything," she said, handing her the receipt, along with the keys for the front and back entrances.

"Actually, I do have a question," Dawn said as Goldie started to leave.

Feeling a little flustered but in need of advice, Dawn explained part of her situation to her new landlady. Goldie proved to be helpful and understanding, without question or qualms, she recommended a Dr. Anderson as a qualified and well-liked gynecologist in the area.

What a lovely person she is, Dawn thought, gently closing the door.

Dawn checked out of the motel right away, knowing she would be more comfortable once she had settled in the little apartment.

She didn't have any belongings with her, only clothes, which she promptly unpacked before going shopping for a few essentials.

After putting her purchases away, Dawn decided to relax for a few minutes, but fell into an immediate, deep sleep. She awoke to a persistent knock on the door.

"Yes, who is it?" she asked groggily.

"Supper is ready, child. It's after six."

"Oh, thank you, I'm not really hungry," she called.

"You need to eat! You're so thin," Goldie protested.

Dawn padded over to the door. She opened it peeking out.

"I'm afraid I fell asleep."

"I have fresh coffee, you know."

"Should I consider that a bribe?" Dawn asked with a smile.

"Absolutely!' she enthused. "Do freshen up and join us? We don't mind waiting a few minutes for your company."

Dawn felt warmed inside. Goldie made her feel like her presence might be considered a privilege. "Thank you, but I'll have a snack later."

"Nonsense, my dear. I'll have Patti bring a tray for you. You simply must eat something."

"Don't go to that trouble," Dawn objected.

"No trouble at all," she smiled. "But I'd prefer you to join us."

Dawn relented. "Okay, thanks Goldie. I'll be down, give me a minute."

The men stood upon her entering the room. Happily, the group gathered round the dining room table put her quickly at ease, beginning with Goldie introducing her to the other tenants.

A retired older gentleman, Mr. Cable, offered a wide, welcoming smile, a middle aged woman, Mrs. Sanders, local teacher and part-time librarian seemed an apprehensive type. A wrinkle frown between her pale blue eyes reflected a tense personality. Still, her reticent smile changed her appearance considerably, edgy but gracious.

Next Goldie introduced her to Fred and Judy Jarvis, a charming, young married couple, and a man in his mid-twenties, she presented as Paul Clayton.

Paul offered an attractive, friendly smile. "Pleased to meet you," he said warmly, his hazel eyes reflecting instant attraction.

"Thank you," Dawn murmured uneasily. She didn't want anyone being attracted to her, and she didn't want to feel any attraction, either, his natural appeal compounded her discomfort.

"And this is my granddaughter, Patti," Goldie finished with obvious affection. "She helps me run the place."

Dawn sat in the chair Patti indicated, eyeing a table spread, fit for anyone's Thanksgiving Day feast.

Dawn helped herself to small portions, a slice of baked chicken, peas and corn, and a small baked potato with sour cream. The generously sliced, homemade bread, tender inside with a crunchy crust, was delicious spread with rich creamery butter.

She found herself relaxing in the homey atmosphere.

They engaged in friendly conversation throughout the meal, bringing her into it, making her feel like she actually belonged.

Patti served cherry pie, topped with a scoop of vanilla ice cream for dessert. Dawn couldn't quite finish it. She complimented the cook, and then excused herself, retreating to her room to rest for a while.

About an hour later, she left out the back for a brisk half-hour walk. Upon returning, she did some gentle stretches. Dawn felt better after having overindulged, the walk and stretches helped tremendously.

She had been uncomfortably full, and so determined to use a bit more moderation when seated at Goldie's tempting table.

Eventually she wandered back downstairs and outside to relax in the swing on the front porch. She had not been there long before Paul came out carrying two tall, frosty glasses of iced tea offering one to her.

"Thank you," she said cordially.

"So, what brought you to San Gabriel?" he asked sitting next to her.

Maybe a purely sociable question, but Dawn had no desire for any sort of relationship, friendly or amorous. She wanted to discourage any advances.

"Paul—" She sighed wearily. "I left Preston because I'm pregnant and I didn't want my mother to find out. I'm putting it up for adoption, then I'm going back home." Dawn loathed being rude to him. He seemed like a genuinely nice person. "Excuse me, please, I'm tired, it's been a long day. I'll put the glass away when I'm finished."

He stood as she did, obviously puzzled by her abruptness. She caught the glimpse of confusion on his appealing face. *Please, leave me alone, I just want to be left alone, to be miserable and have my baby.*

Dawn sat down at a corner desk in her room feeling listless. She opened the checkbook to balance it out. She couldn't use her mother's insurance because the statements would be mailed to Woodland Drive.

After subtracting first and last month's rent, the balance was more than enough to pay the doctor and hospital. The amount automatically transferred to checking each month, would cover living expenses for the next few months without transferring extra from her savings.

She thought suddenly of the day she had to withdraw money from the bank for John. How had she managed to maintain her calm? Had the banker been as intolerable as she thought?

It was a vague memory, viewed through a hazy veil. Most of what she recalled about that day was fear for Trixi.

Dawn felt it coming on and had no choice but to accept the ache—the hunger, a craving for *something*. She had experienced this feeling before, and helpless in its grasp, didn't even attempt to elude it. She accepted the inexplicable emptiness gnawing at her as inescapable.

What had John given her to create the warm feelings of peace and tranquility? Was this a craving for heroin, cigarettes or the sedating pills? She felt a need that could not be named.

Dawn shuffled over to the bed absorbed by the sensation of the unwelcome void. Undressed and under her sheet, she waited miserably for sleep to take her. This episode seemed worse than any previous.

She awoke the next morning feeling calm and well rested having slept through the night. Last night's horrid experience seemed like a bad dream.

Upon entering the kitchen in search of coffee, Goldie offered blueberry pancakes and sausage with homemade maple syrup. Dawn protested to the difficulty.

"Nonsense," Goldie said dismissively. "The batter's already mixed, just have a cup of coffee and relax at the table."

"Everything does smell delicious," she relented. "But you don't have to think you need to take care of me," she smiled, gratefully.

"Nonsense," Goldie said, again. "You need care, child. Get your coffee and sit yourself down! I insist."

Dawn happily obliged. She ended up with a stack of blueberry pancakes, smothered in warm maple syrup with two sausages on the side. It was all yummy, very filling, but she enjoyed every bite.

Dawn insisted on doing the cleanup, pressing Goldie until she had to give in, but only to her assistance.

Later in the day, she made an appointment with Dr. Anderson.

Seated in his office she told him the whole sordid story, leaving nothing out about the abduction, the drugs she had been forced to consume the first two months of pregnancy, and her violent withdrawal.

He listened, looking concerned, nodding in understanding, giving her tissues when she cried. He assured her the hospital would be prepared and completely capable if there were any complications, also that there were many couples who would welcome a needy little one into their lives.

After her initial examination, he expressed concern of her low weight. She assured him that she would probably gain regularly, now, that she was staying with a lovely family.

The days passed uneventfully but at a nice pace. She felt at peace with her decision, had been informed by her doctor that a deserving couple had been chosen to be the adoptive parents.

Dawn made a habit of sitting on the front porch swing in the evenings and on Sunday afternoons. More often than not, Paul joined her. Talking to him came easy, he made her feel comfortable.

Almost without noticing, she began opening to him a bit, sharing a part of her life as he shared his with her, eventually feeling completely at ease in his company.

Then everything changed, Paul completely stunned her when he said, with no preliminaries, just a simple comment that he was falling in love with her.

"That's not fair! You can't blindside me like that!" Dawn felt agitated, maybe undue irritation, but it *was* unfair! "Anyway, don't be ridiculous," she told him. "I'm practically a stranger to you. I doubt you even know what love is," she challenged.

"Devotion and adoration," he said simply.

She stared speechless at the sincerity reflected in his warm hazel eyes.

"You don't even know me." Dawn averted her gaze, his eyes looked too earnest.

"Ever heard of love at first sight?"

"Devotion? Adoration? No." She tried to maintain her curtness, but she knew love at first sight far too well. "Don't say it," Dawn insisted. "Don't even think it."

"Okay, I won't mention love, but you won't know what I'm thinking," he said with a devious little grin that seemed to speak volumes on keeping secrets. Then he sobered.

"Can you tell me why you insist on punishing yourself?"

"You don't know so very much about me," she replied.

"I'd like to. You need someone, don't you? Everybody needs someone."

She looked helplessly at him. He had all the qualities any girl in her right mind would want, handsome, sincere and friendly, with a smile that made her feel like it was only for her. When he looked serious, as he did now, it was enough to make her want to reach out to him.

Before she could give into the urge, Dawn left him sitting, practically running into the house straight up to her room.

A few minutes later, she heard a light tap. When she reluctantly opened the door, she found him standing with his hands behind his back making a pitiful attempt to look contrite.

"What?"

"I didn't mean to upset you."

"It isn't you, Paul, it's everything." She opened the door wider. "Come in," she relented.

Dawn closed the door. She turned to face him with every intention of putting him in his place for the last time, when he took both her hands in his, gazing at her with warmth and simple caring.

"Paul, I don't want to hurt you. I won't be living here much longer."

"Then let's not waste any more time." His lips came down on hers, warm, eager, but so gentle. The kiss left her weak and confused.

"You don't understand—"

"I understand," he whispered. "Whatever happens—I'll understand."

She moved into his arms with a soft moan in protest against her own feelings. She felt undeniable desire as he held her against him.

"Now I feel like I'm taking advantage of you," he said when they parted.

"You're not."

"But you're vulnerable and easily—"

She slapped her hand over his mouth.

Meeting the tenderness of his eyes, Dawn made a decision, wrong or right, to take what happiness the day offered.

"Shut up and take advantage of me."

With a heartfelt smile, he scooped her up in his arms carrying her into the bedroom. Slowly undressing her, his touch more gentle than she had ever imagined a touch could be, his soft strokes left her impatient for more.

He rubbed his hand lightly over the length of her body, moving up to caress her breasts. She felt his warm breath on her skin, then his tongue doing thrilling swirls that left her weak and trembling.

She moaned, pressing closer.

"I won't break," she whispered.

Opening her eyes, she was met with a look of sheer lust in those usually placid eyes and then came the delight of more exuberant caresses.

They shared each other. If he gave her love, she gave what she could, feeling no shame for the yearning he evoked, only wonder.

"Do you feel guilty?" she asked, rising up on her elbow, gazing into his warm eyes.

"No, I don't feel guilty."

"Me either. I suggest we try again."

"Try to feel guilty?"

"Well, I feel like we should!"

"Sure, let's give it a go!"

He burst out laughing, and she joined happily in his merriment. When she laughed, it felt a little strange at first, then marvelous. It occurred to her how long it had been since laughter had been a part of her life

Chapter Forty-One

A month passed quickly by. Dawn felt relaxed with Paul, finally accepting the comfort of their camaraderie. Being away from home would have been a lonelier, more isolated time without him.

She could not grasp his reasoning, though, why he would choose to have a relationship with a pregnant woman who gave him no hope of a future, instead of someone who could offer the commitment he seemed to so desire.

"Why did you choose me, Paul?" Dawn said, feeling content with her head in his lap as he ran his fingers softly through her hair. "You could have any number of girls falling at your feet."

"I've never had a problem with girls falling at my feet," he replied laughingly. "And to answer your question, love is spontaneous, isn't it? A man can't necessarily choose the woman he falls in love with."

"Can a man at least choose the woman not to fall in love with, which happens to be me? And you said you wouldn't use that word anymore."

"No, a man cannot, and you started it," he reasoned, defensively.

"This conversation makes no sense," Dawn said happy to hear the phone ring as she tried to finagle a way out of it. "Wonder who that could be?" she thought aloud already figuring it was Tina.

With a relieved sigh, thankful to end the uncomfortable discussion, she hurried to answer the phone. Dawn felt a bit piqued at herself because he was right. She had breached the taboo area of discussion, giving him the perfect opportunity to speak of love again.

"Hello? Oh, hi, Mom."

"See you downstairs," he whispered leaving her to her conversation.

Dawn sat at the desk in the comfortable swivel chair prepared for the enviable subject of her birthday coming up in October. Her mom would want her to come home or she would want to visit.

Paul noticed Patti out on the porch, gently swaying on the swing.

"Hi, doll face," he said as he settled beside her.

"She's beautiful, isn't she," Patti said vaguely.

"Beautiful? Oh—Dawn. Yes, she is, and so are you." He tweaked her nose gently. "Why so melancholy?"

He had known her as a young teen, a lithe tomboy who could climb the tallest trees. He always thought of her as a cute little girl, with long, dark braids and a sprinkling of freckles on her doll-like face. Patti had outgrown the tomboy stage and the braids, but she would always be his little doll face.

"Do you love her?" she asked with a conversational air.

"You could say I do."

"You sound a little downhearted."

He sighed. "It's complicated, the feeling isn't mutual."

"Mmm, I know how you feel."

"*You?*"

Paul couldn't even mask his surprise that any red-blooded male would not return any love she had to offer. He considered her such a cutie. How could anyone resist?

"I'm very much in love with a man who doesn't even notice."

"I find that hard to believe."

"Believe it," she said wryly.

"He must be blind."

"In a way, yes, you could say that."

As Dawn came out, Patti said her good-byes. Paul wished he had more time to talk to her, but Dawn captured his attention.

"It was my mother," she said, in a voice he had never heard before.

"Dawn? Are you all right? Is your mother—?"

"Engaged—" Dawn sank onto the porch swing beside him. "I haven't even met the man!" she agonized. "I had no idea! And she's getting married—next spring. She wanted me to be the first to know she's getting married—in less than a year!"

Dawn buried her face in her hands for a dramatic moment.

"And how do you feel about that?" he said with a teasing glint. "I thought she must have told you she had a terminal disease or something."

"I'm shocked, is how I feel about it. I've had her to myself all these years, and now . . . we won't even have the same name anymore."

"I guess you haven't even considered that you might have a different name someday?" he suggested.

"No. I'm so selfish."

"I doubt that." He put his arm around her.

"Well, maybe not selfish. I do want what's best for her." Dawn leaned her head against Paul's shoulder. "Seriously, I have to be happy for her, right?"

She sat up. "My mother has been on her own for over twenty years. I wonder how she'll like having a man around the house."

"I don't know, is she as spoiled as you are?"

"Paul!" Dawn made an indignant sound, smacking him as he laughingly dodged and made a run for it. "You better run!" Instead of giving chase, she reclined on the swing with a smile. "You have to come back sometime."

* * *

"I have a question for you, Dawn."

Lying on the sofa with her head on his lap, she murmured a reply, feeling sleepy, but discontent. She had been uncomfortable all day.

"Don't answer right away," he ordered. "I want you to think about it."

She knew his intended question as soon as he told her to think about it.

"Please, don't do this, Paul."

"I want you to reconsider your decision—the adoption, I mean. I want you to marry me and keep your baby," he added quickly. "I love you, Dawn."

"But I don't love you." She sat up feeling nervous and unreasonably irritated. "I don't want to keep the baby, and I don't want to marry you."

After a long silence, she walked to the window to stare out at a dusky evening. Twilight time, not dark, but night was closing in with deepening shadows.

"I don't mean to be unkind," she said hopelessly.

He came up from behind, his arms surrounding her. He rocked her gently in his loving embrace.

"You've been good for me," she said softly, leaning her head against his arm. "I don't know what I would have done without you. You made me laugh again. But I can't lead you on, Paul. I don't have to think about it."

"Not even a maybe?"

She turned to look up at him feeling a sharp stab of guilt with more than one maybe in mind. Maybe she should have never confided in him, maybe she should have never let him kiss her, touch her, maybe this love affair had been a big mistake. Noting the look in his gentle eyes she decided not to vent her feelings, to keep the very many maybes to herself.

"I'm sorry, Paul, but I've been honest with you from the beginning."

"You have," he said agreeably. "I can see possibilities, though, sorry."

Dawn felt irritable and unhappy with herself. The time they shared had allowed him to spin a dream, to hope that she might—"Oh!" The pain, though not excruciating, was convincingly genuine.

"Are you all right?" he asked, his tone sharp with sudden concern.

"I just had a pain. Something's wrong." She made it across the room. "I've felt off all day," she said, uneasily lowering to the sofa.

"Yeah, I noticed," Paul agreed.

He settled beside her, hugging her comfortingly.

"I've had a few minor twinges, but this was different."

"It's too soon, isn't it?"

Dawn heard the worry in his voice, her fear intensifying.

"Yes, it's too soon," she agreed. "I'm only a little more than seven months, but that's not the worst of it, I haven't gained enough weight."

The baby would be very tiny. Would he be able to survive in this big cold world, such a teeny little baby? She moaned softly. "I think I'm in labor."

"I'll call Dr. Anderson."

"Okay," she whispered, reluctantly surrendering the comfort of his arms to huddle alone on the sofa.

Dawn tried to relax as he strode to the desk to make the call. While he was on the phone she rubbed her belly gently.

Dr. Anderson had scolded her good-naturedly, told her to gain as much weight as possible in the next two months; *the baby needed to grow.* She moaned miserably.

"Dr. Anderson said to get you to the hospital immediately," Paul told her coming over to the sofa. "Ready to stand up?" he asked holding his arms out.

"Yes, please."

He helped her to stand with ease. "There now, good to go," he said with a ready smile. "Good to go, right?"

Dawn felt tearful. "Paul, I'm scared. I didn't think it would be like this. I thought I had two more months."

"Shhh, it'll be all right," he murmured holding her.

"I'm not ready yet," she whispered. "And he isn't either."

"We'll get you to the hospital, soon. Everything is going to be okay," he promised. "Somehow, I just know everything is going to be okay, you'll see! I'll bring the car around front. Where's your overnight case?" he asked over his shoulder. "I'll take it as I go."

"In the closet."

He left through the back.

Dawn resisted the urge to walk through the apartment one last time.

Picking up her purse, she walked slowly to the door determined to leave without looking back. Feeling regretful sorrow, she took a deep, steadying breath before leaving, quietly closing the door behind her.

Dawn carefully descended the stairs, meeting Goldie at the bottom.

"Well, Goldie, this is it," she said perkily hoping to camouflage her doubts and fears. "I thought I'd have a couple more months with you, but this little fella decided different."

"I'll be thinking of you every minute." The little lady, who had been a grandmother figure since they met, hugged her close. "I know you and that baby will be just fine," she said encouragingly. "I wouldn't say it if I didn't mean it, I know you will."

In spite of her optimistic words, deep concern reflected in her crinkled blue eyes. Dawn gave this sweet, caring person a smile that she hoped would express confidence.

"Thank you, Goldie, for everything."

The car horn blared, summoning her. She said good-bye to Goldie, and to Patti who had just come in from the sitting room as she was leaving.

Paul looked at her anxiously as she settled in the car.

"You okay?"

"I'm all right."

"Are you sure?"

"Well, I don't feel like going to a party," she admitted. "And if I could avoid this, I guess I would."

Dawn gasped with a surprisingly sharp pain that became a low moan as the contraction held longer than the last traveling slowly across her abdomen.

"Since there's no avoiding it," he said with compassion. "Let's just get you there and get it over with."

They arrived at the hospital where emergency room attendants waited with a wheelchair to whisk her away from Paul and take her to a private cubicle to disrobe, put on a hospital gown and wait.

She reclined on the uncomfortable gurney. A nurse came in immediately, gave her a shot, along with sympathy and encouragement, then left her alone to berate herself for not getting in touch with her doctor at the first twinge of pain earlier in the day.

After awhile Dr. Anderson came in to examine her.

"Well, my dear, you are most certainly going to have this baby."

"Isn't it too soon?"

"Soon, yes, but not too soon. Try to relax."

He exited, and a few minutes later, the nurse returned.

"What happens now?" she asked feeling a huge degree of fear.

"It's upstairs for prepping, then Dr. Anderson will speak with you."

With the unpleasantness of 'prepping' over, Dawn didn't have long to wait before the doctor joined her to explain that nothing could be administered for pain.

"The shot you were given was an attempt to stop the contractions. I would have ordered bed rest, but there was no indication that you would go into early labor." He sounded almost apologetic.

"The heartbeat is no stronger than it was on your last visit, and since he isn't very strong, we need you to help with this delivery."

Dr. Anderson patted her hand and left.

Nothing for pain—it seemed unfeasible—help with the delivery? His words echoed dully within her mind as she wondered how she could survive childbirth without medication.

Dawn moaned in the throes of another contraction, trying to bring to focus that soon it would be over; the contractions were coming in rather quick succession. As time passed, though, it seemed too apparent that it would get worse before it got better.

The head nurse came in to check on her again.

"I'm having pains, why isn't he being born?"

"Your water hasn't broken dear, so I'm going to take care of that for you. Things should pick up after this," she said assuredly.

An indefinite amount of time and misery elapsed with nurses coming and going, keeping close scrutiny on her. Finally, when she didn't think she could stand it a moment longer two attendants wheeled her into the delivery room where an anesthesiologist and a team of nurses awaited.

Amid the haze of pain, her legs were fitted into stirrups. The contractions were coming steadily now. Dawn tried to follow the instructions given, how to breathe, when to push and when to breathe and wait.

She felt like screaming for medication but withheld the useless endeavor.

They commended her bravery, giving sympathy and encouragement at regular intervals, but she did not feel brave or encouraged. She felt tired, pain wracked and scared to death.

The contractions seemed to be ripping her apart. She could not imagine living through childbirth. This would end it all, despite their understanding and compassion. It didn't help. She was at death's door and knew it.

Dawn screamed. She didn't want to—she tried not to—but a scream tore from her throat as she tried desperately to listen to their coaching.

She prayed for it to be over. Then the pain receded for a moment; she became rational again, and could listen to the reassurance of those attending.

Dr. Anderson came in at last.

"It won't be long, Dawn."

Another wrenching pain caught her in its grip, she screamed again, crying, pushing and begging for it to be over—and within a matter of minutes, it was. After a last strong push, the anesthesiologist placed the gas mask over her face advising her to breathe deeply.

Before descending into darkness, Dawn wondered after going through all the agony why she could not witness her baby's birth.

She awoke briefly back in her room to see Paul sitting nearby. She gave him a sleepy smile. He stood, brushing a strand of hair back from her face. In that instant she saw how pale he looked, and worried, she noted. Why? Dawn drifted away again before actually contemplating the expression.

The next time she opened her eyes to a darkened room instantly noticing an odd sense of insignificance. She was glad that it was over, but the gladness of that stood alone without any accompanying satisfaction or contentment, she felt alone and lonely.

Tomorrow she would sign the adoption papers. Her baby would be given a home with parents who loved her, or him, whichever. *What does it matter?*

She slept again.

"Good morning, little sleepy-head."

Dawn opened her eyes to a nurse who stood by the bed, thermometer in hand. She stuck the thermometer into her mouth, held her wrist for a pulse check, and then affixed the wide band around her arm to take her blood pressure.

"You're vitals are good," the nurse told her, noting the chart before walking swiftly away to awaken other sleeping patients.

Alone again, Dawn made her way carefully to the bathroom. She voided, and then washed her hands and face. Weariness enveloped her as she viewed her pallid complexion under the stark lighting.

She turned away from the harsh mirror image.

Feeling uncomfortable and sore, Dawn sat in bed waiting for breakfast, wondering, now, why Paul had looked so concerned.

Her breakfast arrived, delivered by a bright and smiling Candy Striper who chatted happily about the weather as she set her up to eat.

She ate a portion of it before pushing the tray aside. Suddenly a vague inexplicable urge for a cigarette made her edgy, almost wishing for one—just one. In an instant, she realized the unhealthy aspects of such a thought.

Dawn dispelled it deliberately from her mind, realizing again the dangers that keep at a person even when the physical addiction is over.

She tried to relax, closed her eyes, and drifted into a half sleep thinking lazily, her baby, born November 2, 1970. Boy or girl? She would never know, but would the date be embedded in her memory forever? November—the beginning of the holiday season, a time of thanksgiving, and a time of rejoicing, a time of magic for children.

Could she live month-by-month, year-by-year without counting her baby's age, without wondering if he or she had everything a baby needs? If her baby was even *alive*? Dawn sat bolt upright, and grimaced in pain.

She leaned back and tried to calm her racing heart. Just at that crucial moment before her baby came into the world, they had put her to sleep.

The same girl who brought the tray came in to retrieve it.

"How is my baby doing?" she asked with every attempt to appear nonchalant.

"You'll have to ask a nurse." The young woman offered a sympathetic look. "Sorry, I'm uninformed about these things," she explained.

"Would you tell the nurse, I need to see her?"

"Sure," she smiled. "I'll make sure she gets the message immediately."

A few minutes later the nurse came in, her nametag read Faith Rose, the same nurse who had taken her vitals earlier. She was a large, simple woman, her face reflecting compassion for all. Dawn asked again about her baby.

"Preston?" She concentrated on the chart. "I'm sorry dear, I can't give you any information."

"Can you at least tell me if my baby is alive?" Dawn felt panic mounting. She hadn't heard her baby cry and then Paul's expression—she had to know!

"I can see you're upset," the nurse told her, concern reflected in deep blue eyes. "I'm not suppose to be discussing this with you, but it seems to me you certainly have the right to know he's alive. The tiniest baby," she added in wonder. "But perfect in every way."

Dawn held her empty arms to her chest. They would never hold her perfect little baby, but she would take a memory of him with her.

"I want to see him," she decided.

"It's against hospital policy for a mother putting a baby up for adoption to view the baby. We've found it's easier emotionally to avoid—"

Dawn interrupted her feeble explanation of why she couldn't see her son when that was all that mattered in the world. "I have to see my baby! I want to see my baby, and I want to see him now!"

Unable to understand the desperation she felt, or steady the tremor in her voice, the demand had a weak emphasis as she broke down into tears of sorrow and frustration.

Faith Rose put her arm around her. "You poor, dear child. You're practically a baby yourself."

"No, I'm not," Dawn sniffed. "I've just been—been through so much, and then the ordeal of childbirth, and not—not even knowing if he was alive."

"You referred to him as your baby," the nurse said noticeably alarmed. "He isn't your baby," she explained patiently. "You gave him away."

"I haven't signed anything," Dawn informed her with impulsive resolve. "I've decided to keep my baby."

"You had every intention of giving him away—" she said, concern written all over her expressive face. "This could be a passing emotional disturbance, ultimately leaving you with an unwanted baby—by then there may be maternal attachments making it more difficult to give him up . . . Would you speak with a resident counselor?" she offered hopefully. "He might help you understand what's causing the discontent, or the confusion, or at least help you make sure this is the right decision for you and your baby."

"Don't look so worried," Dawn smiled. "I'm not discontent or confused, not anymore." The tears abated quickly as a sense of strength came to her.

"I understand your concern—I'm sorry for the adoptive parents, but I know what I'm doing is right for me and my baby."

"Okay." She sighed uneasily. "Since you haven't signed any papers, there won't be any legal complications." Nurse Rose gave her an understanding, forgiving smile. "I'll arrange for you to be taken to see him."

As Dawn gazed through the protective glass into the incubator, at the tiniest life she had ever seen, that alone and lonely feeling swiftly dissolved.

"You're a part of me I can't let go," she whispered. "My precious baby boy, I'm sorry I didn't think I wanted you."

She longed to hold him close to her heart. As her eyes caressed the small, pink face it suddenly went all squinted, the cutest little thing she had ever seen. Then his mouth opened as a frail cry signaled his displeasure.

She felt a hand on her shoulder, the nursing assistant's comforting touch.

"Why does he have an IV?" she asked, hating that he needed it.

"That's to keep him hydrated and a little more nourishment while he's learning to take more formula. His tummy's still not quite ready to take in enough to sustain his little life. His doctor can explain it better."

Dawn read her nametag. "Is he hungry, Julie?"

"It's about that time, yes."

"He's breathing on his own, right? That means his lungs were formed—he's strong enough for that but he's being monitored. Is he in danger?"

"You've got a strong little fella, there. The monitoring is procedural."

Julie smiled. "He's breathing fine, and now I have to get you back to your room, young lady, so you can rest."

A tear slid silently down her face. "See you later, little guy," she promised, wrought with emotions, not ready to leave him yet.

"Have you decided on a name?" Julie asked pushing the wheelchair toward the exit of the nursery.

"No, I hadn't thought of it," Dawn admitted. "I didn't want to think of him as being real enough to give a name."

"Well, he's real enough, and 'little guy' is kinda cute, but you don't want to call him that forever."

"No." Dawn laughed, suddenly, feeling elated. "I have the perfect name!"

"How did you come up with a perfect name so quickly?" Back in her room, now, the nurse's aide helped her into bed.

"I'm naming him James Robert, after my dad. I'll call him Jamie."

"You're right. It's perfect—he looks like a Jamie. Now rest."

Dawn dozed on the verge of sleep when the door opened. She sat up, happy to see Paul. He placed a vase of roses on the bedside table.

"How are you today?"

"I'm fine."

"You look beautiful this morning."

"I'm a total mess!"

He tilted his head, as he looked her over.

"You look tired," he said agreeably, bending to kiss her forehead.

Paul settled in a chair near the bed.

"I've decided to keep him, Paul. I'm going to keep my baby."

He nodded. "I thought you might have a change of heart."

She was thankful for the approving tone, but then, she had known he would approve of her decision.

"I haven't felt such peace within myself for a long time," she confided.

"I thought I had come to terms, but I really hadn't."

Dawn leaned over inhaling the wonderful fragrance of pink, red and white roses. "Thank you, they're beautiful."

He scooted the chair closer to the bed. He held her hand, gazing into her eyes with love and unrequited devotion. Dawn felt miserable about that. They talked of little incidental things, but she could see the longing and the hurt in his expression even when he smiled.

It caused a repressive heaviness in her chest that shadowed her happiness. She would be going back to Preston, leaving Paul behind. She would never forget him, though.

He had given her laughter and strength, alleviated the loneliness of a desperate time, but she didn't love him, not the way a woman should love the man she marries. Paul was wonderful and deserving; he certainly deserved better than gratefulness.

Shortly after Paul left, Patti came into the room.

"Hi, Dawn. How are you?" She had a lovely vase of flowers from the vast array that grew on their property.

"A little tired, but happy," she replied smiling. "The flowers are lovely," she said appreciatively. "Thank you."

She placed the flowers on the dresser, walked back over to the bed, relaxing onto the chair Paul had vacated.

"I guess you and Paul will be getting married soon," she said sounding rather unhappy in the assumption.

Dawn had felt sluggish, she came instantly alert, startled by the suggestion. What had brought Patti to that conclusion?

"No." Dawn quickly dispelled Patti's reflection of her and Paul's relationship. "I'll be going back to Preston City as soon as possible."

The girl looked at her in surprise. "I don't understand."

"I don't either. What made you think we were going to wed?"

"You've been together all this time. It just seemed like the natural order of things. When he told me you decided to keep your baby—I took it for granted that you had accepted his proposal."

"No, Patti, nothing has changed except that I'm keeping my baby." Dawn looked at her confused. "Why would you think that?"

"Because I know he loves you, and you've been with him—" she faltered. "Have you been leading him on? Was he a passing fling?" The questions held no malice. She seemed to be trying to clarify her thoughts.

"That's how it must seem to you," Dawn said a warm flush of color on her face. "But I never led him on, and he was not just a passing fling."

She sighed, searching for words. "I was lonely, and he helped me through it. I think he was lonely, too. The two of you are good friends, aren't you?"

"More than friends, I hope," she answered softly. "I love Paul."

"Does he know how you feel?"

"No, I didn't even know myself until you came along," she confessed with a self-conscious grin. "We've been friends for years. He was always there for me. When you moved in to take first place in his life, it made me realize how much I need him."

"Patti, I didn't mean to—I would never have—I mean, if I had been aware of—of your feelings." Dawn stammered in bewilderment, trying to wrap her thoughts around this surprising information. She felt so sorry that she had interfered with a relationship they might have begun. "What I'm trying to say is—if I had known—"

"Don't apologize, Dawn, it isn't necessary."

"I think you should let him know how you feel," Dawn said, relieved.

"Oh, I will!" she said assuredly. Patti offered a reserved grin. "You opened my eyes, and even though it was a painful experience, I appreciate knowing what I want."

"He cares a great deal for you, Patti, and he deserves happiness. He's a good man—I know why you love him."

"I'll make him happy," she asserted. "I know I can."

"You will," Dawn affirmed. "I don't know how I missed the way you feel for him. I can see it now so clearly."

"You look tired," Patti said thoughtfully. "I'd better go."

"I won't be coming back to my apartment except to say goodbye." Dawn felt exhausted, physically and emotionally drained. "If you're not home well—I'll just say now that I hope the best for you and Paul."

"Thanks, Dawn. I hope the best for you, too."

She closed her eyes as Patti walked away.

A hospital volunteer woke her for lunch. She consumed everything on the tray and slept again. The next time she woke up, she wanted to see Jamie.

Having regained some strength, she requested to walk instead of being taken in the wheelchair. Happily Dr. Anderson okayed it. Being allowed to walk to and from the nursery, she could spend more time with her baby.

She arrived back in her room to a dinner tray on the bedside table. She enjoyed the food served here comparatively, but ignored the tray for now, it would keep. Dawn picked up the phone to call her mother.

Once she had Tina on the line, Dawn tried to explain her reasoning that had seemed completely sensible at the time, right up until she gave birth to her son. The words did not come easy as she tried to clarify intense emotions that she didn't quite understand herself.

Dawn could hear tears in Tina's voice, and a bewildered tone that clearly conveyed the disappointment she felt that Dawn had not confided in her.

Tina didn't lecture, but gracefully accepted her stumbling rationalization.

Thankful for her mother's unparalleled understanding, Dawn expressed her regret as best she could, but it didn't seem like enough.

In trying to spare her mother's feelings, she ended up hurting her worse. The person who loved her more than anyone could have helped her, as the nurse so aptly put it, work through any confusion.

Tina arrived in San Gabriel later that evening. They enjoyed a nice long visit. "I've rented an apartment right across the street," she told her. "I'll go pack up your belongings and arrange for your things to be moved in."

"I wonder how long before Jamie will be released to come home?"

"It could still be several weeks. He has to weigh in at five pounds, but more importantly, he has to be able to take the nourishment he needs on his own. Once he's consuming enough formula, I'm sure it won't be long."

"I know, and I understand, I just don't know why I can't have him transported to Preston."

"This is a good place for him until he's stronger. I'm anxious, too," Tina said, her blue eyes shining. "He's beautiful, Dawn." The time spent in the nursery had been deeply moving.

"He is beautiful," she agreed avidly. "But I wish we could come home."

"Jake and I will be here to spend Thanksgiving Day with you," Tina offered giving her a hopeful glimpse. "That's only a couple of weeks."

Dawn nodded, complying with a weak smile.

Her mother and Jake would be here for Thanksgiving. He hadn't been to her birthday dinner. She wondered how she would feel meeting the man who was taking her place in her mother's life.

"I think I'm still in shock finding out so suddenly that I'm a Grandma," Tina said quite happily interrupting her dire thoughts. "At least now, I know why you wore a tank dress to your birthday celebration!"

"It was festive," she replied grinning diffidently.

Her mother came to the hospital every day. She had taken a leave of absence and was able to stay until her release, to help her settle in the new apartment, but had to leave that same day.

Dawn fought the urge to cry, tears lingering just below the surface.

"Thanksgiving is not so far away," Tina reminded her, brightly.

"I want to be home for Thanksgiving," Dawn said, the tears welling in her eyes finally finding their way down her face.

Her mother smiled indulgently.

"We'll have a wonderful Thanksgiving celebration right here," she promised giving her a close hug. "Look what we have to be thankful for!"

"Do you think Jake will like me?" she asked uncertainly. "Do you think I'll like him?"

"You'll love him, and he'll put up with you," Tina said playfully.

Dawn laughed feeling more relaxed. She dried her eyes, at last realizing that being together was all that mattered.

In spite of the loneliness at her mother's departure, she had to smile. Tina had never been more radiant than when she spoke of Jake. He was beginning to seem very much acceptable in her mind.

Dawn returned the keys to Goldie, a sad interlude. She could have let her mother take care of it, but she wanted to convey her appreciation and say goodbye to the woman who had been so kind, understanding, and helpful.

Now she stood outside Paul's door, briefly delaying the last goodbye. With a wavering sigh, she tapped hesitantly.

"Come in."

She entered slowly. "Paul—" Dawn walked over to the sofa where he sat.

"You came to say goodbye," he said dispassionately. "I knew you would, but I don't want to." He grinned. His eyes were sad.

Dawn bit her lip gently, acquainted with the feeling, saying goodbye to someone you love while trying to keep your feelings in check so that person wouldn't know how completely you were falling apart inside.

"I couldn't just leave," she whispered.

"Come here," he said pulling her down on the sofa beside him. "If you ever need me—call me, understand? I'll be here."

"You have a life, Paul. You can't hold on." She gazed at this caring man feeling extreme guilt for what she had allowed to happen. "What we had is over, I'm sorry."

He entwined his fingers with hers. "I'm not sorry," he said quickly. "Please, don't be sorry. I'm happy for the time we had, it just wasn't enough, a lifetime, that's what I wanted."

He held her, the finality achingly evident.

Dawn took solace in knowing that Patti would soon pick up the pieces.

She struggled against impending tears as he kissed her one last time.

"Don't cry," he said tenderly. "Don't you dare cry."

He tweaked her nose gently to make her smile. "Now go on, get out of here. I want to remember your smile." He gently stroked her cheek. "I want to remember you like that."

Dawn resisted the urge to touch him again. Any further delay would only hurt. She glanced over from the door after she opened it. He stood with his hands clasped behind his back facing the window.

Chapter Forty-Two

The months passed amazingly fast as they were counted by her baby's progress. For nine months Dawn spent her time taking care of and deeply appreciating her son, content with life and extremely happy for her mother who was now Mrs. Jacob Robertson.

Instead of the spring wedding they had been considering, Tina and Jake waited to wed in the traditional month of June, on the first day of summer. It had been a lovely 'flower garden' ceremony.

Her mother had been exquisitely radiant in a lavender dream gown of flowing silk, satin, and lace, and the groom, Jacob Robertson, who preferred to be called 'Jake,' was overall, the proverbial tall, dark, handsome man, tanned and muscled from being a working supervisor in his company.

Talk about a perfect couple, yes, they were. The happy twosome left the following day for a honeymoon cruise to Hawaii.

When Jamie was nine months old, Dawn began doing volunteer work in the geriatric ward at Preston General two mornings a week, from eight 'til twelve, and at the battered women's shelter three mornings from eight 'til two, which still gave her plenty of time to spend with Jamie.

She enjoyed reading to the recovering elderly patients or simply visiting with them, and the Women's Shelter needed help in so many ways.

The women came from other areas, escaping abusive relationships, seeking a way to make it on their own. There were babies and children that needed to be cared for while their mothers either attended adult education classes, or job services classes preparing to seek employment when they were able to return to their own areas or be relocated if that was what they desired.

Some were only there for a few days if they had to flee their home to escape impending danger, deciding to return to possibly hazardous conditions with consistent hope that a miracle change would happen eventually.

Another three months flew by.

Christi, Billy and Mike threw her quite an extravagant party for her twenty-second birthday.

They celebrated Jamie's first birthday at the Women's Shelter where there were lots of kids to join in the celebration. Jamie curled up on the sofa and drifted off to sleep after opening his presents and eating cake and ice cream.

Jake carried him out to the car, and since Jamie had everything he needed at home, she donated his gifts except for a fuzzy, cuddly teddy bear from his grandma and Jake, that he had held onto from the moment he opened it, and snuggled up with in his arms when he fell asleep.

The holidays had been amazing. Thanksgiving Day meant more than it ever had before, followed by an enchanted Christmas season, watching Jamie's inquisitive brown eyes sparkling almost as bright as the lights on the tree when he saw the twinkling array of colors reflecting off the gaily-wrapped packages beneath.

Dawn smiled thinking about her baby, still small for his age but advancing very well, Dr. White assured her.

Now she sighed with mixed feelings of happiness and discontent, having finished feeding the six-month-old baby girl almost a full ounce of rice cereal. Sarah was so sweet. It was unbelievable that her mother had to leave because an abusive boyfriend had threatened the precious life. How could anyone—? Oh, she knew it happened, but it seemed so preposterous.

She placed the drowsy, contented baby in a crib with her bottle.

When she glanced at the large wall clock it came as no surprise that it was nearly two. Time always passed quickly here with much to be done, but it had been a little more hectic than usual with the children still excited over Christmas.

From the clock, her eyes focused on someone being escorted into the room. Her heart jumped before beginning a heavy pounding in her chest.

"Van."

Her eyes froze on his long lean form as she wondered, had she spoken his name aloud or had it only reverberated through her suddenly astounded mind?

"Can we talk?" he asked. "I mean, somewhere besides here."

Dawn felt mesmerized, impaled by his steady gaze, lost already in the depths of those magnetic brown eyes and that slow sexy smile. For a long moment, she could only stare at him speechlessly.

She felt a ripple of excitement and alarm. Why, she wondered hopelessly. He hadn't changed, if anything, he was more breathtakingly handsome than she remembered; his shoulders a little broader, his thick dark brown hair not quite as long.

Her eyes were drawn from his strong capable hands, to his firm, sensual lips. She knew that her feelings for him remained intact. With him standing in front of her she knew the love in her heart had simply lain dormant.

"Dawn?"

"Sure, I—just give me a minute." His presence upset her equilibrium, but she took a calming breath. "I'll be right there," she assured him with a smile.

He walked away, quietly closing the hallway door.

Dawn said her goodbyes. Thankfully the women present withheld any inquiries, just gave her pensively curious glances and encouraging smiles.

Van, seated in a chair in the vestibule, stood as she approached. His eyes held hers, his gaze warm and wonderful.

"You look amazing," he said affectionately. "There's so much I need to say to you. Can we get out of here? Maybe go to Lindsey's?"

"Sure, I'm finished for the day."

"Tina said it was almost quitting time." He squeezed her hand gently. "Why did it surprise me? It's so like you. Why not just donate money, Dawn?"

"I donate money, of course I do, but I like giving time, too."

"Of course, you do," he said magnanimously.

She tipped her head, giving him a self-effacing grin. "Who knows? Maybe someday I'll choose to be a simple, social butterfly," she suggested.

"You would be a spectacular social butterfly," he corrected admiringly.

Dawn gazed at him with adoration. Maybe he would never understand her, but that didn't bother her in the least.

They walked leisurely to Lindsey's bar, talking simplistic idle chitchat along the way, enjoying the typically lovely Preston weather.

Once they were seated in a booth in back of the cozy tavern, the waitress approached immediately. He ordered whiskey on ice. Dawn decided to have a glass of rosé.

Van lit a cigarette. He still hadn't kicked the destructive habit. Her urge for them had long diminished, but now she looked hungrily at the pack.

"I've missed you, Dawn. I can't begin to tell you how much."

Her thoughts were drawn quickly from the cigarettes to the man beside her. The scene seemed almost illusionary—she feared it might fade away.

"I finally admitted the obvious." He looked at her with love—with *love* in his eyes. "I don't want to live without you any longer—if you haven't met someone." His sigh held regret. "I lived with the bitterness, the hatred, the pain. I lived with it for years, but you changed all that for me. When I think of the wasted time—"

She could hardly believe the words her ears were hearing, but maybe there were happy endings after all! Maybe dreams did come true she thought as he covered her hand with his.

How long had she dreamed of this happening, yet known it never would? His gaze held hers, the love in his eyes she had never expected to see as he spoke the words she had never expected to hear.

"I took the promotion they offered. I'm going back to a desk job in three weeks. I want you to come with me. Will you come back with me?" His brown eyes searched hers as if he wondered what her answer would be.

"There's no one else in my life," she assured him. "I love you, Van. I want nothing more than to be with you."

"A simple 'yes' will do." He kissed her temple, caressed her fingers. "The 'I love you' part was really nice, though," he teased.

"It isn't—that simple."

"What's wrong?" he asked confused. "What could be wrong?"

What could be wrong? His fingers felt warm and strong as he held her hand, but he released her hand as seconds ticked by, took a sip of his drink, flicked ashes off the dammed cigarette, the tenderness of his gaze slipping away, being replaced by a look of subtle curiosity and wonder, but he waited.

"Van—"

"Tell me, Dawn," he said in a quiet, firm voice.

Dawn inhaled a trembling breath.

"I have a baby—" she murmured. "—while I was kidnapped—" Her voice broke, miserably, and then love for her son lent her strength. "I named him after my father, Van. Jamie is sweet and innocent—he's amazing."

She waited, hope a dim flicker in her heart, waited for his assurance of deep and abiding love, waited as despair drowned the hope, leaving her with a sense of emptiness and loss

She noted his clamped mouth and fixed eyes, changing in an implausible instant, his handsome face had become an image of contempt. When she touched his shoulder, he jumped as if he had been shocked.

"John or Carl, Dawn?" he said icily. "Or do you even know?"

She searched her suddenly useless mind for a defense, wondering how he could be so cruel. "You have no right!" she finally managed, gasping as he gripped her wrist.

"Answer me."

"You know without asking—"

The grip on her wrist tightened considerably.

"You convinced yourself that he didn't touch me," she said softly, agonizing over the startling fact that Van had been living in denial. "But you *knew*. You knew John Burton as well as anybody. You aren't so naïve."

He released her, his hands wrapping around the rock glass, gripping it so tight she thought it might shatter.

"Isn't he a constant reminder of your ordeal? Or was it as much of an ordeal as you professed?"

His words, loaded with unimaginable ridicule, left her speechless.

"How can you look at him without *remembering*?" he said with bitter emphasis. "Or maybe—was he a good lover, Dawn?"

Van grabbed her wrist in midair. She looked helplessly at her hand realizing with mild surprise that she had intended to slap him.

Dawn sat in stunned silence absorbing the emotional onslaught, the undue attack on her son, the shock of his lewd question—the sardonic look on his face—sent her temper soaring.

"His conception may have been a mockery of love, Van, but my baby does not in any way remind me—of the ordeal," she gritted.

"I knew you were nobody's innocent child," he goaded. "But you must have learned a few new tricks on how to please a man. We could have some fun." He gave her body a raking gaze. "I have a motel room nearby. Come on, baby," he drawled lazily, in a provocative voice that chilled her to the bone. "Don't play innocent."

"Van, how could you—" she said breathlessly. Dawn swallowed tears, almost losing the effort to control her emotions. "You know I was drugged, barely conscious of what was happening to me."

Trying to get a grip on her feelings a slow realization washed over her.

"You didn't have to kill him," she said, suddenly livid with quiet rage. "You wanted to see him dead. I remember what you told Dave Temple that night—that you would take care of Burton—well, it appears that you did."

The accusation hung in the air as her misgivings grew with his silence. The cold indifference in his eyes when they met hers seemed somehow worse than his anger.

Her throat ached with the need to scream her outrage, and still she wanted him to deny it, to call her a liar, tell her she didn't know what the hell she was talking about, anything except the damning silence.

"How could you think you had that right—? You had no right to be his executioner, Van."

"Miserable little slut." He threw his glass belligerently across the room.

Dawn saw it shatter on the hardwood floor. It seemed that all eyes turned in their direction before reverting quickly, obviously uncomfortable, and she thought, pitying her.

"Let me out of here," she choked, hardly able to speak as she determined to retain control for the next crucial moments, unwilling to give in to the relief of tears—to give him the satisfaction of seeing her cry.

He moved compliantly from the booth. Dawn fled the humiliation, finally letting the pain escape in a flood of tears. Clear of Lindsey's, she slowed her pace, fishing in her purse for Kleenex tissue.

Dawn took even breaths in an effort to compose herself, to repress a heartache that seemed unbearable. Her world had just collapsed around her, shattered at her feet like the glass on the floor in a little bar called Lindsey's.

She had not tried to surmise what his reaction might be concerning her son, but she had never expected such a public display of hostility and disgust.

Feeling bewildered and lost, Dawn turned in the direction of Fairview Boulevard. She needed to talk with Christi, needed the understanding and comfort of her friend. The moderate walk gave her time to settle her raging emotions, somewhat calmer she rang the doorbell.

"What happened?" Christi took in her tear stained face, the stricken look.

Dawn could tell Christi was bewildered by her shocking appearance. She wanted to tell her what happened, but discovered that her throat had tightened with grief. Dawn knew if she tried to speak the words would stumble all over each other and she would just be stammering in an effort to explain.

Her friend understood. Christi put her arms around her, the simple gesture evoking a fresh flood of tears.

"Come and lie down for a few minutes."

She led her over to the sofa, made her comfortable, and then left for a minute to return with a cool washcloth for her forehead.

Dawn's breath caught as she inhaled, almost snuffling like a baby who had cried far too long. This is ridiculous, she decided. She paused, taking some slow calming breaths.

"Better?"

"No, not really." Minutes had passed as her breathing evened out and her heart settled. Dawn sat up. "Well, yes, a little." She slowly shook her head, feeling incredulity. "Van's back in town," she said with a wry grin. "I think he proposed—" She inhaled a short breath. "And I'm pretty sure he said he loved me until—when I told him about Jamie, he changed."

Dawn shivered; Christi draped an afghan around her shoulders.

"It's okay," she soothed. "Take a minute."

"He said such awful things, such spiteful and malicious things."

"I'm sorry, Dawn." Compassion glimmered in her eyes. "Dawn."

Christi took a deep breath. She looked troubled but decisive. "Van confided something to me about John Burton. I didn't think there was reason for you to have to know, but now, you need to be told."

Feeling so confused and badgered she could still hardly speak, Dawn sighed resignedly. "What is it?" she said, weakly, not necessarily wanting but needing to know.

Christi leaned forward a little, her expression tender.

"When John was nineteen he went to New York City. No one knows even why he went, but while he was in New York, he met a kid who worshipped the ground he walked on." Christi sighed discontentedly. "You know John's personality—charismatic and influential."

Dawn began chewing her lip, getting the picture already.

"John turned him onto drugs. They hung around together for a while, but after a few months, he came back to Preston."

"What happened?"

Christi sighed again. "He overdosed on heroin."

Dawn ached with the awareness of knowing. Christi didn't have to tell her who the boy was that John turned onto drugs; Van's little brother, the would-be artist, the boy who drew demons.

"He blamed John," Christi said sensing that she understood. "Van turned his life's goal into getting the men responsible for corrupting the innocent. Maybe Denny would have taken a wrong path anyway, who knows, but John's influence was undeniable. I'm sorry." Christi looked at her anxiously. "Do you think if I had told you sooner it would have made a difference?"

Dawn shook her head. "No, I knew there was animosity. I just didn't know why and now I do."

When Dawn sniffed dejectedly, Christi gave her another tissue.

"I guess he kind of built it up in his mind that John never touched me. Crazy, huh?"

She cradled her head in trembling hands.

"It hurts so badly—he brought it all back! Why didn't he just stay away? Why did he have to come back and ruin things for me? I was happy."

"Happy? Dawn, you haven't accepted even a friendly dinner date for the past year."

Dawn shrugged helplessly.

"Can you honestly call that happy?"

She raised her head. "Yes, I call that happy," she insisted. "Lonely, maybe, but happy, and I've been busy, you know—" Her words faded, an inept excuse.

"If you made a conscious decision not to date, that would be different, but you've been subconsciously saving yourself for the illusive Van Morrison, and you know I'm right."

Dawn looked at her with dispirited eyes. "What are you saying?"

Christi looked a bit wistful. "You'll either have to get him or forget him before you'll be able to lead a normal life."

"All I ever wanted was to get married and live happily ever after. Isn't that naïve?"

"No, it can happen."

"It did for you, and I'm happy for you, but I must admit I envy what you have, Chris."

"Keep the faith, kiddo. You'll have it all someday."

She looked over to see Mike and Billy standing in the doorway.

"Thanks, Billy. I'll keep that in mind. Hi, Mike."

"Hey, girl." Mike crossed over to the stairs. "I'm gonna hit the shower," he said. "Join me, Dawn?"

"Another time."

"Don't play with my feelings, sweetie."

Dawn couldn't repress a smile. "Your brother's crazy-wonderful," she said watching his retreat. He had been filling out lately, gaining a little weight and muscle. The boy was maturing. After graduation he had chosen to go to work with Billy at Robinson Construction, Jake's company.

Dawn had been surprised because he had planned on going to college, but at least he was into adult education, taking some business courses, Christi had said, more studious than when he was in high school, which he had breezed through with little effort.

"I'm out back," Billy said, giving Christi a casual kiss as he passed by heading for the den that led to the patio.

Dawn glanced at her watch. "It's later than I thought, I'd better go."

"Won't you stay for dinner?" she invited. "We're barbequing."

"Tempting, but I need to get home."

"Dawn?"

She met Christi's concerned gaze.

"Are you sure there's no chance for the two of you? It seems like you've been in love with him forever."

"Chris, I have never felt such anger and been so completely torn apart at the same time." Now she felt empty and drained, her emotions spent.

"It still hurts like hell, but there's no doubt. If you had heard him, if you had seen his face—believe me, you wouldn't ask."

"I wish I could say something to help."

"You did, seriously. You opened my eyes to something I wasn't even aware of. Besides, talking to you always helps."

They hugged at the door.

"Try to hang tight." Christi shrugged with a cute grimace. "You deserve better."

"Sure."

"Van's bein' a jerk."

"I know," Dawn agreed with a faltering grin. "About the reason John went to New York? He went there to find his father—he wanted to kill him."

"Okay, I see." Christi shook her head sadly.

"I'll call you later."

"You better—and remember what I said."

"I will."

Dawn left Christi with a question answered that she had wondered about more than once. At last she fully understood Van's deep-rooted hatred.

Chapter Forty-Three

Van sensed their presence before he heard the shuffling feet and the muffled snickering. He turned, quickly scanning their faces, six young, tough looking punks. No personal recognition.

"Hi, guys," he said casually.

"Hey Morrison, got some coke, or maybe some H?"

"Come on fellas, let's not dredge up the old."

"How about this for somthin' new? It ain't right to treat a chick the way you did."

"You were at Lindsey's," he acknowledged.

"We'll teach ya better."

"How about, I agree with you, and we call it a day?" They began to circle. "You want to talk this over?" Van suggested. "I'm not here to cause anyone trouble."

"Fat chance, pig."

"Would a been better, you just stayed outta town."

"Cause we're gonna pound you down."

Van knew he had to act or they would have the first move advantage. He dropkicked the biggest one, sending him sprawling backward. A second charged at him without thought, which he dodged easily, grabbing the back of his shirt to send him smashing head-on into the brick building, then turned sending another one down for the count. Three down, three to go.

As he turned again, a chain caught him above the eye knocking him back. He caught it on the second swing, but then they grabbed him, seizing his arms from behind. His stunned effort to shake off the two holding him drew smirking laughter.

"Now you're goin' down."

"Care to even the odds a little, boys?"

Van recognized Billy's voice. Mike being with him evened the odds. Soon the three of them stood above the others in the alley. With Mike in the middle, they draped their arms around each other, laughing as they stepped over the sprawled moaning bodies.

"Should we notify the authorities?" Mike asked.

"Nah, they'll get over it. I just won't walk around Preston anymore this visit. My car's parked up the street," he said. "I think I need a drink."

"Sounds good to me," Billy agreed.

They headed out of the alley turning left toward Lindsey's. They sat at the bar in back of the crowded tavern.

"Christi tells me you were pretty rough on Dawn," Billy commented.

"Yeah, I guess I was."

"Don't you think she's been through enough?"

"Yeah, I know—"

He stared gloomily into the amber liquid of his whiskey, picked it up and drank the shot followed by a swallow of beer. Dawn Preston was a much too painful topic.

"Where'd you guys come from anyway?" he said.

"Mike had a feeling."

"Just a feeling? Just like that?"

"Just like that," Billy said with a slightly bemused glance.

"Lucky for me, anyway." Van touched his wound gingerly. "That was a senseless mistake letting the chain get me, could have cost me my vacation."

"Time spent at the Preston General couldn't exactly be considered vacation," Billy agreed.

"I should have been more prepared." He grinned wryly. "I appreciate it guys."

"Hey, I enjoyed it," Billy said with a grin. "You recognize those punks?"

"Never saw them before, never want to again."

"Sure you don't want to have 'em picked up?" Mike asked.

"Nah." Van felt uncomfortable. If they had not been defending Dawn in their own misguided way, he would have them taken in, at least for a night. "I don't think they'll be a problem."

Billy swallowed the rest of his drink.

"Take it easy, Van," he said. He threw some bills on the counter. "Give us a call before you take off, okay?"

"Sure thing, I'll stop by before I leave."

"Good. I'll let Chris know. She'll like that."

Mike turned slightly on the stool as Billy walked away.

"Something on your mind Mike?"

"What's up with you, Van?"

"What do you mean?" He looked at him warily.

"You know what I'm saying—why did you hurt her like that?"

"I don't want to talk about it." He didn't want to think about Dawn, much less discuss her. "There's someone I want to see. I was on my way there when I ran into my admirers."

He glanced at Mike. His expressive face appeared solemn with a touch of anger lighting his eyes. He and Dawn were good friends, after all.

"Are you trying to punish her for what happened with John? It wasn't her fault you know."

"I know, Mike, it wasn't her fault."

The jukebox began to play an upbeat tune.

He wondered why his words hadn't come out quite as smooth and agreeable as he had expected. He thought they would be calm, with pleasant implication, but his voice had sounded raw and unnatural.

He cleared his throat feeling self-conscious but defensive.

Logically, he knew it wasn't her fault, his first reaction had been way too harsh, but obviously, his feelings remained.

"You're gonna lose her, you know."

He noticed his hand clenching the glass. Consciously relaxing his fingers, he looked at Mike trying not to appear severe. "I already lost her. Something happened when she told me, something snapped inside me. I can't explain it."

"Damn right, you can't." Mike took out a cigarette. He tapped it on the bar a couple times before putting it back in the pack.

He motioned the barmaid to order another drink.

"No hard feelings?" Van said with an abstract glance. "I can understand your concern for Dawn, okay?"

"Can you?"

He didn't really care to think about it, but he did care about Mike. He did not want harsh or disruptive words with him. Another record began to play, strums of a hauntingly familiar melody.

Memories of the Basement flooded his mind. Memories of a gorgeous blond haired little girl being stalked by a psycho rapist, memories of a reckless young kid who just liked to have fun. Christi and Mike Temple. He felt the emotions like a kick in the gut.

"Listen, I'll see you before I leave Preston, okay? I have to split."

"Sure," Mike said pleasantly. "Later, Van."

Van climbed into the rental car he had left parked here earlier. He needed to see Nancy, to be with her, to feel the comfort she could give him. In her arms, he could forget what he did not want to remember.

Whatever it took, he had to forget.

It did not occur to him that Nancy might have moved until he knocked, and the door opened. He stood gazing into those clear brown eyes. Surprise registered first, then he saw what he wanted to see, emotion she couldn't disguise. He knew because he felt it, too, the same barely restrained passion.

"Come in." Her eyes lingered on the cut above his eye. "You've been hurt."

"It's nothing."

"It looks painful."

"I heal fast," he said casually dismissing the injury, closing the door behind them. Pulling her into his arms, he breathed in the light, clean scent of her and a lingering fragrance that stirred a memory, fueling desire.

She resisted for an instant before shifting her body to fit his.

"Why are you here, Van?" she questioned, her words muffled against his chest. "No word, not even a call. How can you just show up at my door?"

"I'm sorry. I didn't mean to be so negligent. Truthfully, baby I didn't even know I was gonna end up here tonight, but I need you," he whispered. "Baby, I need you."

He could hear the near desperation in his own voice.

"I want to love you," he said, his lips by her ear. "Let me."

"Love, Van?"

"Yes, love." He kissed her closed eyes, her face and her lips.

He felt her response and a piercing stab of guilt. "I have never lied to you, babe, and I won't. You know, I can't promise forever. I can only offer the time we have right here and now—right now you're everything to me, Nancy. I want to love you tonight."

"I think I'd like that."

She raised her face, the last of any resistance slipping away. She put her arms up around his neck. He brushed his lips against hers. They shared soft, teasing kisses. Her eager response fused an unbearable need. He moved his mouth over hers devouring its softness.

He closed his mind to the pain of today. It proved easier than anticipated, with Nancy so warmly receptive in his arms. His senses filled with the touch and taste of her, the sounds of her pleasure.

They made their way to the bedroom—dropping clothes along the way, falling naked on the bed. He wanted to take it fast and hard, but he stroked her rousingly, he kissed and tasted until her body squirmed impatiently beneath him—begging him to take her, only then did he succumb to the fierce passion pulsing through his body.

She had become quite a woman, the shy girl gone forever, lost somewhere in the past.

"You've changed, Nancy."

"Good or bad?"

"Sometimes bad is good," he replied.

"You haven't."

"I thought I had, but you may be right."

"Why did you come back, Van," she said again, her fingers playing idly with the hair on his chest.

"Does it matter?" He sat up, feeling some tension. "I'm on vacation."

"For how long? A week? Two weeks?"

"I don't know. Don't, Nancy." He kissed her to soften the dissuading words. "I don't want to hurt you. I didn't come back to open old wounds."

"It's not your fault if I bleed easily."

"Do you want me to stay away?"

After a moment of contemplative silence, she nestled contentedly against him. "We might as well enjoy the time we have," she whispered.

It occurred to him quite suddenly and unnervingly that it never entered his head, that she might be married or in a relationship. That could have been a surprise he wouldn't have appreciated.

Nancy sat up, pulling on a thigh-high, red silk robe. She favored him with a smile that could never hide the sadness in her eyes.

"Want to go out tomorrow night—I have to go now." He dressed quickly, and then sat on the bed.

"I'll spend the night with you," he added sliding his hand along her neck softly caressing. "I'll get here a little early so we can mess around before we leave, then we can mess around some more when we get back."

"Should we color you romantic?" she teased, winking her eye in a flirtatious, sexily inviting way that made him want to jump back in bed.

"I want to find you like this tomorrow." He ran his fingers lightly through her hair. Once more he almost changed his mind about leaving, the lingering kisses; her naked body beneath the robe.

"Mmm, and I was about to show you some reciprocation for the treat you gave me." She glanced at him seductively gliding the tip of her tongue over her upper lip, sexy as hell.

"I really have to go," he moaned kissing her again. "Hold that thought."

"Okay, love, it's on hold until tomorrow."

From the warmth of Nancy's apartment, he drove to the impersonal motel outside of town, his current living quarters for the next few weeks.

He sat in a chair smoking a cigarette, staring at the wall, occasionally pouring a shot from the bottle that sat on a nearby table, chasing the booze with a swig of beer.

A shudder passed over his body. He acknowledged that Dawn had no control over what happened, an innocent victim if there had ever been one. But knowing John had possessed her, that the two of them had been together, proved far worse than the thought of it.

There might have been a chance, but the constant reminder in the form of a child meant that he could never put it to rest.

He did respect and admire her courage. His words had been a thoughtless reaction that he wished he could take back. To experience what she had been through, and it had to have been hell—to keep and love a baby conceived in such misery took a special quality.

Van recalled her struggle for control, her obvious pride, her insistence that her baby in no way reminded her of the ordeal. How was it possible? How? He knew beyond any doubt that he did not have the courage that she possessed.

His hatred of John Burton could never be disguised. It would be reflected in his eyes every time he looked at her son.

* * *

Dawn tossed and turned, finally giving up on sleep.

She walked quietly to the nursery. Gazing down at her sleeping baby, placing her hand gently on his back, feeling his warmth; feeling him breathe. Dawn remembered vividly his fight for life. With a contented sigh, he turned onto his side.

Love for Jamie filled her heart, this love was incomparable. She finally understood a mother's love for her child.

She walked back to her room to sit in the window seat staring vacantly out at the foggy night as her heart broke.

The questions badgered her emotions. Why did Van come back to destroy the thread of happiness she had managed to grasp onto in this life? Why did he profess his love, then in the same instant snatch it away, leaving her disappointment beyond measure? How could love have been so fragile? And how could she live knowing he hated her with such passion?

She let the tears fall freely as she acknowledged, again, with a bitter dose of reality that it was over, positively, irrevocably finished. She closed her eyes reliving the pain of that final scene.

Where there had always been a vague chance that he would come back, an indefinite dream she clung to, a hope beyond hope, that lifeline had snapped.

It began to rain, large drops beating against the window. She stared dully at the rain cascading down the pane, contemplating the dark lonely nights she had waited.

A train whistle sounded somewhere far away. It resounded in her ears like a lost soul forever searching.

Van heard the lonesome whistle of a passing train in the distance.

As drops of rain began a crescendo on the windowpane, he experienced an eerie feeling of isolation, of being imprisoned in this lonely room.

He had built a future around Dawn, a life with her that could never be, and now he wondered if he would ever be happy again.

He took another slug from the bottle, followed by a swallow of beer.

Van struck his lighter gazing into the flame for a contemplative moment before he lit another cigarette, gloomily accepting that his life as an agent wasn't over yet.

Chapter Forty-Four

Thankful that she didn't work Saturdays, Dawn dragged out of bed after a sleepless night. She had barely managed to keep her emotions in check the evening before, escaping early to mourn by herself in the comfort of her bedroom.

"Good morning." Tina greeted her cheerfully as she entered the kitchen. "Look at Jamie. I think I need my camera," she added. "Now, where did I put it?"

While Tina retreated in search of the camera that Dawn knew wouldn't be far, she amused herself watching Jamie who sat secure in his highchair. Just learning to feed himself, he seemed to be enjoying the sensation of squishing oat cereal between his fingers and the feel of it in his hair.

"Good morning, baby boy," Dawn said with a wide smile. He rewarded her with a messy grin while smacking his sticky little hands together.

Tina returned. After she snapped a picture, Dawn dampened a washcloth, wiped Jamie's hands and face, gave him a clean spoon and a new beginning.

"Eat," she ordered.

He happily scooped up a spoonful of oats. When he got most of it in his mouth, she congratulated him.

"Very good!"

Dawn laughed as with another oatsy smile, Jamie proudly repeated the process. Then she sighed a bit discouragingly.

"Something's bothering you," her mother observed.

Dawn poured coffee to the brim in a cup she had already put milk into. She took a long, appreciative drink of warm caffeine.

"You look a bit haggard," Tina said with an inquisitive glance.

"Thanks, Ma," Dawn drawled with a wry grin.

"Still beautiful," her mother smiled.

"Well," she said on a sigh. "You know Van's back in town."

"I thought, maybe it had something to do with him."

Dawn sat on a stool at the counter. She looked at her son, then back at her mother. "He lost it when I told him about Jamie."

"I wondered why you were so quiet last evening."

"Yeah, thanks for understanding. I didn't really want to talk about it last night." Dawn took another swallow of coffee. "I spent a lot of time thinking—throughout a sleepless night." She tipped her head with a faint smile. "I might not look it, but I'm feeling some better."

"Given time, do you think he could accept what happened?" Tina wondered, compassion reflecting in her thoughtful blue eyes. "I know the circumstances of how you met weren't the best, but the two of you that summer were inseparable, considering his work and all—and he's been involved in your life since then—"

"I can't even consider it." She sighed forlornly, but most definitely resigned to the decision. "The things he said, the look in his eyes, such intense hatred of John, and he—it was a bad scene, Mom."

"You seem resolved to letting him go, now. You never were before."

"Absolutely resolved! I've loved a memory for too long."

Dawn stood to refill her cup. She *had* loved a memory; she had loved the man, far too long. In love with being in love, faithfully clinging to the hope of a dream.

She managed an afternoon nap when Jamie took his, so that evening Dawn felt more or less her usual self, preparing for her night out. It didn't take much effort, applying her make-up with customary expertise had become a basic routine.

She listlessly shuffled through the assortment of dresses in her walk-in closet, choosing a short, mint green cocktail dress with sleeves off the shoulder. Tastefully cut, it clung to her curves in an unpretentious and elegantly flattering fashion.

Dawn loved Mandy, her seamstress. Mandy designed all of her dresses, gowns, and swank, flirty blouses. Some of her creations had made it big time, worn by fashion models. She felt fortunate to still have her available.

Removing her pearls, she dropped them into her jewelry box, replacing them with emeralds. Dawn fastened a choker of the jewels around her neck. She pensively brushed her auburn hair.

It hung over her shoulders in soft, natural waves. Not a bad picture, Dawn thought solicitously, not bad at all, but make-up skills and precious gems could never disguise the sad eyes reflected in the mirror.

Saturday evening and time for her 'night out on the town', supper at the Cactus Flower, a drink in the lounge, not extremely exciting, but in her opinion, excitement could be considered highly overrated.

When Dawn stepped through the door of the supper club, her eyes inadvertently scanned the crowded dining room. She felt like falling through the floor or, at least, backing very quickly out of sight.

Van was there with a lovely young woman, but it was too late for retreat. He saw her in the same instant.

She considered retreat, anyway. Her resolve had sounded noble this morning, but right now sorrow felt like a huge, painful knot inside. Why subject herself to the agony of seeing him with another woman? On the up side, she thought, somewhat doubtfully, there could be a healing element in the painful experience.

Dawn took a calming breath. She glided gracefully to her table in the back, discovering it to be at a vantage point where she could inconspicuously study the slender brunette in his company.

Her adoration of Van was obvious. This girl was no stranger to him. The delicate beauty with exquisite taste, dressed in a sleek white evening gown, seemed completely at ease, and was clearly captivated by her escort.

"Are you ready to order, Dawn?"

The waitress drew her attention. Dawn glanced up. "Thank you, but I've decided I'm not hungry." She closed the menu, and then dismissed Maxine with a generous tip. "I'll have hors d'oeuvres later. For now, I think, I'd prefer something icily refreshing and very intoxicating."

Maxine thanked her, taking the menu, she moved on to another customer.

When Dawn walked by to cross over to the lounge, Van glanced up, his eyes sweeping over her in an achingly familiar way. The pain remained, but it helped her feelings to see a brief glimpse of longing as she passed.

When Jane stopped by her table, she ordered a Frozen Daiquiri, willing herself to relax, all the while wondering how she could survive being so near and yet so far from Van during the time he remained in Preston. Why was he even still here? He should have left by now.

Her eyes kept glimpsing the doorway where the two would enter in. Somehow she knew, without a single doubt in her mind, that after dinner, there would be drinks and dancing.

When they entered the room, his eyes connected with hers. He averted his gaze, but she could not look away, the struggle to ignore where they were being seated was a lost cause. The urge had too strong a pull.

A distance away, but effortlessly within sight, Dawn watched miserably, wondering why he had brought her here, how he could be so heartless.

When they danced and he held her close, moving effortlessly to the music, Dawn recalled all too well the feel of his warm embrace and every other tantalizing sensation of being in his arms.

Two drinks had always been a maximum, but she ordered a third. It went down easy as she soulfully watched the definitive couple. To an objective observer they could have been very much in love, but Dawn knew Van, and she knew it wasn't love.

The song ended, he bent his head close to hers conveying an intimate message. Dawn felt an edge of panic as she noticed he was walking toward her. He sat down on the other side of the small table.

"What are you doing?" he demanded, his tone coolly disapproving.

"Me?" She looked into his eyes feeling intense sorrow. "I'm suffering the pain of what could have been. How about you?"

He stared at her for many long seconds, his expression softening.

"Why, then?" He moved a strand of hair behind her ear, and she almost lost her fragile control. "You're hurting yourself, Dawn," he said in a dull, troubled voice. "Don't do this."

She bit her lip gazing deep into dark eyes that had always mesmerized. "Your date is waiting." She forced the words past the tightness in her throat. The last thing she wanted to do was send him back to her.

He left, walking decisively back to the one who sat watching and perhaps wondering, but Dawn wondered too, wondered about the identity of this girl, when and how he had met her, and why he had brought her out now when her feelings were raw and bleeding from the beating they had taken.

A handsome stranger asked for a dance. She politely refused. She sometimes accepted requests to dance, but not tonight.

Dawn ordered another drink. The ice froze her throat as she swallowed and then settled cold in her stomach. She looked around feeling some mild frustration, with the music, the laughter, a room full of noise and fun, she felt like the loneliest person on all the earth.

They danced again, stirring bittersweet memories. He kissed her, respectfully. This wasn't exactly a bar where you could make out like you couldn't afford a room. Dawn almost giggled, but a tear slid down her face as she finished her drink. She lifted the empty glass, giving a slight nod to her observant cocktail waitress.

Jane didn't disguise her look of concern when she served her another Frozen Daiquiri. Dawn started to take a drink, then set it back down very carefully. It was time to go. This had been a huge mistake.

She placed a fifty on the table under the glass and then stood slowly, heading toward the ladies' room first, concentrating to keep her walk straight.

Once outside, the night air did not clear her head. She felt miserable and drunk. Why did she let it happen? Purposely exposing herself to the pain, and then trying to drawn it out with booze. Her earlier rationalization made no sense at all. Seeing him with someone else held no healing elements, seeing him with someone else cut like a knife.

Dawn managed to get to the car without incident. She sat with her head on the steering wheel as the world spun crazily.

The door opened. "Move over."

She glanced up at Van. "What?"

"You're in no condition to drive." He stated the obvious in a coolly dispassionate tone, a simple observation that any idiot would know.

"Go back to your girlfriend. Leave me alone."

"Dawn, just—move over," he said, his voice lacking patience.

She slid to the other side of the car having no urge to provoke him but wondering why he would even care or consider it his business.

He took her place behind the wheel, started the car, and then maneuvered through the parking lot out onto the main road, gently accelerating.

He glanced toward her. "I thought your drinking was restricted there."

"Not anymore."

"Well, it should be. Why didn't you call a taxi?"

She couldn't think of an answer, he had asked too quickly. How fair is that? she thought. Now why didn't I call a taxi?

"That makes too much sense," she murmured. "Where are we going?" she asked, hoping her voice sounded clearer to him than it did to her own ears.

"I'm taking you home."

Of course, he was taking her home, where else would he take her? She felt thick for asking such a pointless question, but there was no way she would go home in this condition.

"I don't want to go home," she blurted. "Not like this."

"Where then?" he said with another quick glance.

"I'll spend the night with Christi."

The world still seemed to be spinning crazily. Dawn closed her eyes trying to stop the sensation, but her stomach lurched with a threatening queasy feeling, and she felt dizzier than ever.

Dawn opened her eyes again, turning to stare out the window. Not a good idea. Things were passing by too fast. She took a deep breath leaning her head back, then immediately sat up straight. Dawn gave up, anyway she went; she felt yucky. Keeping her eyes straight ahead seemed to work best.

When he parked in the driveway at Christi's house, she put a hand on his arm. "Van—"

"Don't, Dawn." He got out, walked around the car to open the passenger door and assist her. "Can you make it to the house all right?"

She shrugged his hand off her arm. "Yes, I'll be fine."

He turned, walking purposefully away from her. She watched as he paused to light a cigarette. With a dejected sigh, Dawn set her sights on the front door.

She staggered a bit, but concentrated on simply placing one foot in front of the other. Thankful that she had arrived at her destination without tripping over her own feet and falling flat on her face, Dawn leaned weakly against the doorframe knowing that she had no choice but to ring the doorbell.

She suffered intense remorse at her stupidity. How had it come to this, weaving with intoxication, having to disturb her friends after midnight? Dawn felt detestable, well, maybe not that bad, she amended, but she did feel extremely sorry and irritated at herself for this predicament.

Expecting Christi, she looked curiously at Mike when he opened the door. Handsome, she thought. What a handsome young man you are, my friend.

"Would you call my mother?" Dawn stepped inside and fell into his arms.

She opened her eyes to darkness, nausea and a splitting headache. She sat up slowly, turned on the bedside lamp, and then watched the room spin as the icky, nauseous sensation washed over her again. Dawn moaned with the rush of queasiness, holding her aching head to keep it from exploding, resisting the urge to dive back under the covers.

It would be great to escape these horrid feelings, but if she didn't get rid of them now, they would follow her into the morning sunlight.

Swinging her feet over the side of the bed, she sat quietly waiting for everything to settle.

She noticed her dress spread neatly on a chair, bringing to mind falling into Mike's arms.

Dispirited as she felt, her face flushed warmly with embarrassment. What must he think of her? Then she knew instinctively that he would understand. He would be more forgiving of her than she was of herself.

A housecoat lay across the bed. She put it on before going into the bathroom to splash cool water on her face. Dawn gargled and rinsed with mint mouthwash. It helped considerably.

She made her way to the kitchen for a cup of instant coffee, still a little bit drunk. Hung over and drunk was a horrible feeling.

Dawn sat at the table staring into her coffee realizing she had forgotten to add cream. Oh, well, black would probably serve the purpose better.

"How's the head?"

Dawn glanced over at Mike leaning casually against the doorframe.

"It hurts," she admitted ruefully. "Sorry if I disturbed you."

"You didn't." He went to the counter, turned the radio on low, and then sat across from her. "Did it help?"

"What?" she asked, feeling vaguely confused.

"Getting drunk. Did it help?"

"No, I'm miserable."

"He isn't worth it. He isn't worth the sorrow in your eyes."

"Oh, Mike, he was at the Cactus Flower with a girl!"

"That's no reason," he said with an edge of warning. "At least, I don't see the reasoning."

"Me either. It won't happen again." Dawn took a careful sip of coffee. She had thought she made it too strong, but it tasted okay.

She looked at Mike reflectively, remembering the crush she had on him, unbelievably, only a few years ago. Knowing he had put her to bed didn't concern her much. It wasn't nearly as hard to face him as she thought it would be.

"Mike, will you do me a favor?"

"Anything."

"Go out with me tomorrow night?"

He shook a cigarette out of the pack he had tossed on the table but didn't light it. "What's the point?" He tilted his head, looking at her uncertainly and quite solemnly, so unlike Mike.

Sitting at the quaint dining room table with a tasteful vase of flowers as a centerpiece, in the dimly lighted room with the radio playing softly, Dawn suddenly felt indecisive of her decision.

"I want to show Van that it doesn't matter," she said hesitantly.

"What doesn't matter?"

"Nothing. I want to show him that nothing matters."

"That's going to be a little difficult with your heart on your sleeve," he told her. "But I might be game. Might be," he emphasized.

"Are you playing hard to get, Mike Temple?" she said with a critical squint. "You said if I ever needed a friend you would be there."

"You remember that, huh?"

"Sure do—come on, Mike, I can trust you." She gave him her best pout.

He smiled slowly. "Trust me to what?"

"Why are you hedging? You said anything."

"I did say that," he nodded. The mischievous look she so loved alighted his sapphire eyes. "Let's make it for New Year's Eve," he suggested. "That way you'll have time to recuperate from this excessive night."

"Okay, agreed," she murmured feeling contrite. "I do need some recuperation time."

"Get some rest. It's going to be a fun night."

"I remember how you use to make me laugh," she said, noticing the melancholy quality in her voice as she looked at the boy turned young man.

"Yeah, I was quite the comedian in high school."

"You were always fun," she told him.

"Just for you."

"Mike, about tonight—"

He grinned. "You don't have to be embarrassed," he said, standing. Mike paused at the kitchen door. "You're welcome to fall into my arms any night of the week, sweetie, but Chris is the one who tucked you into bed."

Dawn smiled relaxed and happily relieved. She should have known Mike would never compromise their relationship.

Chapter Forty-Five

Dawn stepped into the silk silver pumps she had bought to wear with her glistening cocktail dress, a dress that Mandy designed specifically for her to wear for Van, but he hadn't shown up that year.

She twirled once in front of the full-length mirror, loving the shimmering sequins on the bodice and the way the snug fitting dress flared from the hips.

Her stylist had swept her long hair into a chic up-do, with silky tendrils framing her face. Usually she styled her own hair, but she decided to go for all-out pampering and her day at the spa included a visit to the salon.

Since she wanted her make-up a bit more dramatic tonight, instead of applying it herself, she let the make-up artist of the salon do the honors. Dawn could hardly believe the effect. She looked, to her surprise, like a cover girl model, and she felt dreamily sensual and flirtatious.

She fastened the vintage teardrop diamond on a white gold chain around her neck. It had belonged to the grandmother she never knew. Diamonds glimmered on dainty stylish dangling earrings, and she clipped on an elegant diamond bracelet. She had bought the earrings and bracelet to match the necklace and they did, to perfection.

Very sparkly, she thought somewhat cheerily. So what if a mournful look did linger in her eyes? Tonight there would be someone to hold her hand, someone to dance with; someone to care.

Mike gave a low whistle when she opened the door. Dawn could see genuine admiration in his warm blue eyes.

"Ah, Dawn, your beauty is what dreams are made of."

"Flattery, Mike?" she smiled.

"I could easily flatter you 'til days are no more, and mean every word of it." His glance swept her again. "You look amazing."

He handed her a dozen long-stemmed roses, held her face gently in his hands, barely brushing his lips over hers. "I hear you like roses."

"They're beautiful, Mike. Won't you have a seat, I'll be right back."

She took the roses to the kitchen to remove the wrapping from around the stems. What a lovely bouquet! Dawn snipped the ends off, then arranged the yellow and red roses amid dainty white baby's breath in a cut crystal vase.

Reentering the living room, she set them on a decorative table in the foyer. Mike came up behind her.

"They're not just beautiful, you know, they relay a message of love and friendship."

She turned quickly, her thoughts clouded with apprehension.

"Are you ready for the night?" he asked before she could imagine what to reply to his conveyance of the message of the roses.

"I hear it calling," she replied placidly.

"Good answer, but we could use some enthusiasm," he frowned.

Dawn discarded the uneasy feeling. "I hear you're a real good dancer!"

"Now that's more like it."

He held her arm, tenderly possessive as they left the house. She enjoyed the attentiveness tremendously and wondered why she had denied herself the pleasure of his company. As Christi said the other day, Mike had invited her to dinner more than once or twice before giving up.

They were seated, had ordered their meal and been served salad before Van arrived on the scene, escorting his former date. She noticed his eyes widen slightly when he saw her with Mike.

"Well," Mike commented. "Lover boy made it."

"And he's with her, of course," Dawn murmured. "Isn't she gorgeous?" She began pushing the lettuce around in her salad plate wondering where her head had been—thinking she could prove anything to Van by going out with her friend.

What was it she said? Show him it didn't matter? If anything this proved how much it did matter! When Dawn finally returned her attention to Mike, his usually bright eyes were dark with concern.

"Are you sure you want to subject yourself to this?"

"I don't, but I do . . . Does that make sense to you, Mike? Because I don't know what else to say."

"It makes perfect sense," he said approvingly. "And she couldn't hold a candle to you."

"You always know how to make me feel better."

"It's only true," he grinned.

She enjoyed Mike's teasing manner, and how he seemed always on the edge of laughter, so easygoing. Dawn found herself watching his mouth and tried to avoid being too obvious about the attraction she had always felt.

When Maxine brought their dinner, she couldn't help noticing his ease with the various utensils that could be daunting to some.

"I know my big fork from my little one, sweetie, and my round spoon from my oval—and what that particular knife is for."

"Of course you do! I didn't mean that you—wait a minute—" He seemed to have read her mind. She grinned. "You're incredible, Mike."

"And you're edible, Dawn . . . . Oh, come on, did I embarrass you, really? You're so easy!" His look was a subtly seductive gaze, a familiarity that she always considered a special compliment.

She smiled affectionately hoping it wasn't wrong to have these feelings.

"I can't help myself," he said. "When I'm with you, sweetie, it's just a part of me that won't quit."

"I've always enjoyed that little quirk in your character," she admitted.

"That's a quirk?" he asked looking bewildered. "I always thought it was a lovable trait. Anyway, I'm glad you enjoy it."

They finished their meal listening to the romantic background music with some light conversation. The silent moments were comfortable, too. Dawn reflected that she had always felt wonderful in the company of Mike Temple.

She wondered, vaguely, about the rumors that had circulated in school about his use of drugs. He had always, as now, appeared so alert, open and simply 'with it' that such speculation seemed absurd.

They crossed over to the adjoining lounge, taking seats at the reserved table. The cocktail waitress came to their table immediately.

"Shall I start a tab?" she asked Mike with a welcoming smile.

"No, Jane," Dawn said. "It's on the house."

"The usual, then?"

"No, thank you, I'll have a Shirley Temple to start."

"You can always have a Mike Temple," Mike offered with that habitual flirty little wink. "I'll have scotch and soda, please."

Dawn smiled at the private joke as Jane walked away.

"Mike, can I ask you something personal?"

"How personal?"

"I was wondering if you date."

"Yes, I date on occasion. I haven't been pining away for you all these many years, even though I inferred to that once."

"What I meant to ask is, if there might be someone special in your life."

"Oh, you want to know if there's someone special in *my* life."

"I don't want to cause you any trouble."

"There is someone, but there won't be a problem."

"Are you sure?" she said, unable to hide the uncertainties about being with him if there was indeed another girl. She felt a little bewildered. He was so flirty and playful, but, of course, he always had been.

"Are you sure?" Dawn realized she had repeated herself. "You're not just saying that to—" She lost her train of thought as Van and his lovely date passed by, being escorted to their table.

Dawn took a calming breath. It had only been a brief glance, but that glance had been riveting. Was he surprised Mike brought her to the lounge? Maybe he had expected Mike to take her home to sit out the evening alone.

"It's absurd, I know, but I feel like he's following me! How do I look?"

"You look sexy and shimmering—a sexy, shimmering delight."

"Do I look happy?"

He studied her intently, and then took her hand with both of his. "Are you ready to show Van it doesn't matter?"

Dawn smiled. "I'm ready."

"Now you look happy."

They joined the couples on the dance floor. He took her in his arms, holding her casually near.

Her body fit his, and he led so easily, it felt like they had been dancing together forever. They had shared only a few dances over the years. The New Year's Eve Party of 1968 came to mind now—their first dance. Maybe that's what made it the most memorable.

"You fit well in my arms, Dawn," he said softly.

"Seems I do," she replied.

"You practically float on the dance floor."

"You make it easy."

"It's like we were made to dance together."

Mike twirled her around once, breezily dipping her backward over his arm, he smiled down at her.

"Smooth move."

"Uh-huh, I knew you were up for it."

Securely on her feet again, he drew her intimately close.

The evening progressed as Dawn became better acquainted with this friend of many years, discovering, not surprisingly, how much they had in common. Once again it struck her that she had always felt effortlessly comfortable in Mike's company, along with a reticent wish that she had fallen in love with him instead of Van.

Falling silent, she wondered, nervously, why the wish had manifested itself so clearly in her consciousness. The wave of apprehension continued to wash over her, it wasn't the first time she'd had such reflections.

"Penny for your thoughts," Mike said with the sweetest grin.

Dawn regarded him with serious curiosity. "Do you know what I'm thinking?" she asked, recalling Christi telling her of his intuitiveness.

"Why would I pay for something if it's already in my possession?" he asked too sensibly. "That would just be a waste of a good penny."

"Then I'll keep my thoughts, thank you." Two details crystallized within her mind, Mike is a friend, and there is nothing wrong with a playful wish.

Satisfied with the success of their date, Dawn decided that asking Mike out had been an inspiration. Sometime later, taking a breather in the ladies' lounge, contemplating the simple pleasure she felt being with Mike, she noticed an unexpected look of contentment in her expression.

The contentment slipped away when she exited the lobby that led to the lounge. Van was sitting at a table impossible to avoid without going noticeably around. He stood at her approach.

"I want to talk to you." His gaze was steady, his implacable expression unnerving. The last thing she wanted to do was talk to him.

"No, thank you."

"Sit down, Dawn, please."

"So you can insult me again?" She started to walk.

He caught her hand. "Please, I won't keep you long." Van released her hand and then held a chair, which she reluctantly lowered herself onto.

"I have to ask what you're up to, Dawn," he said bluntly.

For a long moment she could only stare at him speechless. He didn't sound angry, but she still didn't want the confrontation.

She swallowed with difficulty and found her voice.

"What do you mean?"

"What are you trying to prove?" he said, sounding oddly discontent.

"What makes you think I'm trying to prove anything?"

"Then why come here?"

She bristled at his flash of irritation.

"Have you forgotten that I was born here? I was raised right here in Preston. You came to my town, and this is my preferred Lounge, and I was here first," she added defensively.

"Why Mike?" he demanded, an exasperated edge in his tone that she couldn't quite understand. She couldn't understand any of this.

"Why not Mike? The company I keep is no concern of yours."

He leaned forward. "Okay, play your little games."

"I am not playing games."

His dark eyes impaled her with a knowing look.

"You're using him to get to me."

"That is so unfair—and not true."

But it was true in a way.

"Think about it, lover."

Van stood abruptly. Striding determinedly away, he left her sitting.

Wishing she had taken a stand first, Dawn watched him stride quickly and purposefully back to the girl who had taken her place.

"Your eyes are bright with unshed tears," Mike said softly, when she joined him. "I thought you might be ready for that drink," he added.

His comment drew her attention to the Frozen Daiquiri.

"Thanks Mike." She took an appreciative sip. It seemed to cool the flush in her face and body. She took another deep swallow. "Thank you so much."

"You already thanked me."

"Not only for the drink, but you know that's a given." She tore her gaze away from his too sensuous mouth. "No, I meant thank you for knowing what I need when I need it."

"Hmmm, let me contemplate that for a moment."

"Just don't contemplate too much," she ordered recognizing that lazily seductive look.

"We can dance, then," he suggested with an infectious grin.

Dawn marveled at his many facets, to go from sexual innuendo to casual mode so confidently. She gave him a suspicious glimpse which he countered with an innocent, yet somehow beguiling expression.

"How do you do that?" she murmured offering her hand, which he took with grandeur.

He didn't say a word as he led her onto the dance floor where he swung her harmoniously into the circle of his arms.

As the evening progressed, they reminisced about high school. He confessed his trifling association with the Cobras.

"I figure Christi told you all that," he added. "I know she worried about me, but I didn't even own a switchblade!"

"She did confide her concerns," Dawn admitted. "I was, for some odd reason that eludes me right now, reassuring. I told her—" Dawn laughed softly. "I don't know why, but I thought you were level headed?"

"And I was—just a smidgen flighty, that's all. Couldn't I be both?" he suggested with that feigned bewildered look again.

"It seems contradictory, but for you, entirely possible."

She confided her regret, not just because of what her actions had led to, but the acknowledgement of how wrong it had been to go after John Burton.

The law was not hers to enforce, but she had been compelled. When she thought back, it seemed weird, an action she basically could not resist.

"I suffered a lot for that, and so did Trixi." She shook her head sadly. "I can't regret my son, though."

"And well you shouldn't," he said agreeably. "Now, let's celebrate! I survived my dangerous trifling and you, sweetheart, survived your daring compulsion. Come, my love. They're playing our song."

* * *

"Who is that girl," Nancy asked.

Van realized he had been neglecting Nancy as he watched Dawn on the dance floor. He could hardly keep his eyes off her as she and Mike danced. She had an ethereal quality in the flashing lights of the dance floor, mystical beauty, out of his reach.

"Van? Who is she?"

He turned his attention to Nancy. "She isn't important."

"She isn't? Tonight has given me the impression that she is," Nancy said, her voice unsteady. "Are you using me, Van? She was messed up the last time we were here, but she seems to have recovered."

"Nancy, would you please shut-up." Van wanted to take the words back the instant they were out of his mouth. He didn't mean shut-up. He just wanted her to stop talking about Dawn. "I didn't mean that."

Nancy snatched her purse, rushing away, moving swiftly toward the exit. He found her standing out front waiting for transportation.

"I'm sorry," he said. "I never used you."

She pulled away when he tried to take her in his arms

"If I did, then I didn't mean to. I never meant to hurt you."

"Take me home, Van—don't, just don't say anymore."

He pulled her coaxingly into his arms stroking her hair.

"It'll be all right, baby. Come on, it's almost midnight. I know a quiet place. We can bring in the new year together."

At last she relaxed. He didn't want to hurt her, he genuinely meant that. He felt incredibly sad knowing there was no way to say goodbye without hurting her again.

"They're gone," Mike said when they returned to their table. "It's no wonder. He couldn't take his eyes off you."

"Really? Are you serious?"

"Really serious," he replied.

"I wonder who she is."

"Does it matter? He hated seeing you with me. He's jealous and he's hurting. Were you aware of that?"

"No." Was it true? If so, she was glad. Mike was right, too, it didn't matter who she was. Dawn cast negative emotions aside. She felt at peace for the time being and accepted it happily.

At midnight shouts of "Happy New Year!" resounded. The band struck up 'Auld Lang Syne' amid cheers and whistles from the crowd.

As the words of the familiar melody drifted through her mind, they paused in their dance. He held both her hands, looking down at her with gentle understanding.

While she absorbed the undemanding awareness of his touch, his hands slipped up her arms bringing her close. Gazing up into his eyes, she felt lightheaded, and it had nothing to do with the drink.

"Happy New Year," he whispered.

His lips slowly descended to meet hers for a simple kiss that sent a sudden wild swirling into the pit of her stomach. Her heart beating wildly, she recalled 1968, how he had taken the privilege of kissing her with unexpected passion.

Even as she registered the shock of her eager response to the feel of his lips, she yearned for more than the one traditional kiss.

Raising his mouth from hers, he smiled softly. His arms encircled her, one hand in the small of her back drawing her closer, still. Molded against his body, her lips parted to his in a long, sweet kiss that knocked out all her defenses.

The band began a slow ballad, a song of lost love and new love.

As they started to dance, she instinctively pressed her lips against his neck. Panic rippled through her at the compliance of the impulsive gesture, she felt an immediate, almost irresistible urge to pull out of his arms, How could it have so quickly become dangerous, too emotionally tangled?

His hold loosened. Dawn relaxed a little, still her heart thumped nervously.

"You don't know what to feel, do you, Dawn?" His warm voice drew her from the complicated reverie. "There's just something about the midnight hour on New Year's Eve that turns me into a regular Casanova."

She caught the spark of humor in his eyes, that carefree mischievous look.

"Yeah, I know, half man, half party animal."

"Mmm, baby, talk like that, I'll be munching on your shoulder!"

She laughed with him, suddenly free of the anxiety that had been so overwhelming, so unexpected. Comforted by his easy cajoling, she enjoyed the rest of the post midnight celebration.

When Mike took her home, he turned off the ignition.

"So tell me, did you have a good time?" he asked turning slightly toward her. "Was it fun? Did I entertain you sufficiently to show so-and-so that it doesn't matter?"

"Yes, yes, and—how many yeses?"

"Good enough," he said.

She looked into his smiling eyes.

"Could we do it again?" He slipped his hand behind the back of her neck, caressingly. "How about tomorrow night?"

Dawn bit her lip, unable to completely disregard Van's accusation. The thought of using Mike for any selfish motive left her cold. She liked and respected him too much for that.

His teasing flirtations and unexpected kisses had always made her feel special. Why deny herself the pleasure of his company?

She would never abuse her and Mike's friendship. Van in his anger, had struck a low blow, creating doubts about her relationship with Mike. Dawn resolved not to let his words prove so influential to her way of thinking.

"I'll pick you up at six," he said, then with a questioning glimpse. "Is that okay for you?"

"It's good for me, but how did you know?"

"I can read your mind."

"Really?"

He sighed. "What if I could, Dawn?"

"It would be—a little awkward."

He leaned over, his mouth temptingly close for several seconds before he kissed her, his lips more persuasive than she cared to admit. The gentle touch of his mouth sent a wave of longing through her entire body. She struggled to suppress the feeling. She enjoyed his kisses and didn't want to think it was getting too emotionally risky.

"I can't exactly read your mind," he said upon releasing her from the mild, yet soul-searching kiss. "Relax, it was only a kiss goodnight."

"You know what I'm thinking right now?"

"Yeah, you don't believe me."

"So, you just said that to make me feel better."

"No, I would never do that," he said with a boyish grin.

"How did you know, then?"

He sighed wearily, as if barely indulgent of her whim.

"Would you stop it and tell me?" she asserted trying not to smile.

"Okay, Dawn. You were quiet for a long time. I could tell you were struggling. Then something in your expression—a little mix of serenity, resolve and happy—gave me a hint that we're on for tonight."

"I guess I'll buy that."

"Um . . . I have some oceanfront property in Arizona, Dawn."

She couldn't keep the smile off her face. "And you want me to buy that, too, I suppose?"

"Well—?" He shrugged casually.

Why did he have to be so unassumingly cute?

Mike got out, circling the car to open the door for her. "Get some rest," he advised. "Tomorrow's going to be better than tonight."

Dawn couldn't deny the happy she felt. Tonight had been wonderful, and the wonderful continued with the mouthwatering aroma of sizzling sausage awakening her appetite along with fond memories.

From twelve to eighteen, on New Year's Eve, after the midnight hour, several teens lingered to sprawl out and watch horror flicks until they fell asleep or until sunrise, whichever came first.

Those who had slept would wake up to head to the kitchen with the rest of them for a feast of eggs and crispy fried hash browns or the best French toast ever made, both dishes served with spicy sausage on the side.

She remembered the happiness as she helped her mother dish up breakfast to her friends round the table, no worries or cares, the privilege of youth.

Dark memories began to interfere. The New Year's Eve Party of '68, Ted was already gone—and then Carrie—there were no more New Year's Eve parties.

"How was your night?" Tina asked, thankfully ending her dreary thoughts.

"It was fun," she said. Dawn sat across from Jake. "How was yours?"

"It was magnificent! The celebration at the Déjà vu was exceptional," Tina enthused. "We got home just a while before you did."

Dawn kicked her shoes off. "Oh, that feels good," she said wiggling her toes. "Mike is nonstop on the dance floor. I love it, he's amazing, but I'm glad Carol's spending the night. I'm beat."

She had put an application in the paper for a babysitter. Carol Hanson, a studious girl, had impeccable references. She made herself available with minimal notice, and she was excellent with Jamie.

"I'll need Carol tomorrow, too," Dawn told them consciously toning down her enthusiasm. "We're going out again."

"He's a nice boy," Tina approved. "I've always liked Mike."

Her mother, never one to judge a person from the side of town they live on, had encouraged her and Christi's friendship, and Mike had been as welcome in their home as Paul or Jerry.

"Mike's fun," Dawn said agreeably. "He's a friend, someone I can trust, and someone I know won't let me down," she added, favorably. "I've always liked him, too, but don't get any wrong impressions. We're *just friends*."

Jake smiled at her, and she grinned self-consciously, wondering if her 'just friends' comment might have sounded a bit too expressive.

"The food's ready when you are," Tina called over.

"I've been ready," Dawn said pushing away from the table.

"You won't need Carol tomorrow," Tina said when Dawn came over to the counter. "We don't have plans. We'd love to spend some time with Jamie."

"Okay, great." She glanced at Jake. "Just don't spoil him too much."

Sitting across from her stepfather, she recalled how concerned she had been last year when she first learned that her mother planned to remarry. She soon discovered her worries were unfounded. He was one of the nicest people she had ever met.

He had eased into being a part of the small family with real warmth and affection. His characteristic kindness extended to Jamie as he conveyed patience and understanding when the baby was fussy or crying, as much as he enjoyed her son's laughter and antics.

Dawn peeked in on Jamie before she went to her room. He was sleeping peacefully, so sweet, so innocent and so beautiful. She placed her hand gently on his back feeling him breathe, recalling, again, his struggle for life.

Her heart swelled with love for her son. Anyone who couldn't accept her baby was not worthy of her love, and she didn't want to love that man.

Chapter Forty-Six

Dawn walked through her closet immediately picking out a blue, flowing cocktail dress that fell in layers of softness, midway down her thighs. Held in place by delicate spaghetti straps, the immodest cut exposed eye-catching cleavage, without sacrificing chic sophistication.

Dawn appreciated that the flirty cocktail dresses and gowns Mandy designed for her, were made interesting without giving the impression you were about to fall out of it. She had always valued elegance.

A blue sapphire oval and diamond pendant, on a white gold chain, adorned her neck, another heirloom inherited from her grandmother. Tina presented her with the lovely jewelry box and jewelry on her twenty-first birthday, left to her by her father's mother, mostly a variety of exquisite necklaces. Dawn had purchased matching attire for her wrists and ears for every vintage piece.

Sapphire drop earrings hung from her lobes, she fastened an elegant eternity bracelet on her right wrist, last of all Dawn clasped on the diamond wristwatch that Jake had given her for Christmas last year.

Her hair hung loose and flowing, her make-up more subtle, but her eyes were bright, now, with a light of anticipation.

"For you," Mike said handing over a bouquet of gorgeous red roses when she opened the door.

Before she could utter a word, he held her face in his hands, his lips touching hers in a gentle kiss that gave her a deliciously warm feeling of being in harmony with life, but the pleasurable emotion made her edgy.

He smiled sweetly after the edgy, apprehensive causing kiss, and said, "Your earrings are pretty. They match my eyes."

She grinned. The inane statement left her feeling completely at ease.

"I'll just put these in a vase." Dawn arranged the roses in a nine inch rose vase. She noticed there were six orange roses and six red, they made an interesting contrast.

She set the roses next to some other cut flowers in the living room.

"Mike, what do orange roses stand for?" she asked as they walked toward the car.

"Um—I think passion—maybe, they look good, don't they!"

He opened the car door. Dawn slid in, turning slightly so that she more or less faced him when he took the driver's seat.

"We don't have to go to the Cactus Flower," she said hesitantly.

He rested his hand on her thigh. "Cold feet?"

"Like ice," she admitted. "I don't know if I want to see him again."

"You know you don't want to."

"Maybe I should avoid seeing him, then," she hedged.

"Let him avoid you," he urged. "Come on, you'll have a good time."

Mike turned the key in the ignition.

"You're with a guy who is attentive to your needs, conscientious of your feelings." He shifted into gear, pressing gently on the gas pedal. "I keep you entertained with ready wit and boyish charm, but above all I'm modest, low profile and humble. How could you not have fun?" he demanded playfully, slowly rounding the corner, heading toward Sunset Drive.

Dawn laughed, her spirits lifted. "You are all that," she agreed. "Except for maybe the modest, low profile and humble, but I love you, Mike. You're the best friend a girl could have."

"Don't worry, sweetie, we'll show him it doesn't matter."

When he pulled into the parking lot, Dawn, deciding she wasn't hungry, suggested going to the lounge and eating later.

"Mmm, sounds good to me." His look made her blush *again.*

"You and your double meanings!" She smacked him on the arm.

"You have a dirty mind," he said casually. "Get it outta the gutter, baby."

"In no way am I admitting to that claim," she said laughingly.

He smiled faintly. "I'll never forget how you look tonight, Dawn. Did you know blue is my favorite color?"

Dawn looked thoughtful. "I don't think so."

"I thought you were trying to impress me."

"Do I look impressive?"

"You did know my favorite color is blue."

She smiled secretively at the guy you can't keep secrets from.

"Well, you look good in a suit and tie, and I don't think I've ever told you that before."

"Yeah, babe, that compliment's way late." He opened the car door. "So let's go dancing."

A pianist in back lent a relaxed atmosphere making it difficult to imagine this as the same nightspot that had been pulsating the night before. Dawn appreciated the tranquility as they placed their drink orders.

"Mike, can I ask you a question?"

"Lay it on me." He leaned back a little, looking at her intently.

"Do you use, Mike?" she asked straightforwardly.

"Oh, you walked right into that one," he said shifting in his seat.

"What? Maybe you did then but you don't now," she said uncertainly. "I hope not, anyway. I wonder because, I heard things about you in school."

"Uh, yeah? What things?"

"I always attributed it to gossip and never gave it much thought."

"I'm glad you didn't give it much thought, because anybody can say anything, you know, and I don't use women."

His gaze dropped unhurriedly from her eyes to her shoulders to her breasts. "I believe women should be treated with the utmost respect."

"You know what I mean," she said giving him a reserved look.

"Oh, you were talking about drugs—I never did, never wanted to—I didn't even have the urge to experiment." He leaned forward a bit looking at her with solemn blue eyes. "I like to keep my senses."

"I knew there was nothing to it, but I wanted to hear you say it."

"I had a problem with alcohol once."

"How did you know you had a problem with alcohol?"

"Chris clued me in that I was becoming a teenage alcoholic, so I quit for a while. Then after a time, I decided that I didn't want to quit drinking, so I modified it." He grinned engagingly. "Don't want *those* kinds of problems!" He held out his hand. "Care to dance?"

"I would love to."

The evening passed amid dancing, laughter, and savory hors d'oeuvres at about ten.

"It's almost eleven," Dawn said. "He won't be here tonight."

"Apparently not, but we won't miss him, will we! Let's go for a ride."

Mike seemed unusually quiet once they left the club, different somehow, different in a way that left her feeling at odds. After limited conversation and a brief cruise, he turned in the direction of Woodland Drive.

It seemed strange that he would take her home so soon.

Dawn knew she had no logical reason, as a friend, to monopolize his time. Still, she gave definition to the troubled stirring of emotions—*jealousy* and e*nvy*—petty feelings that she should not be experiencing. He had a life, and every right to be with anyone he chose.

He parked in the driveway at the front steps.

Leaning toward her, they kissed, but he didn't pull away this time. Mike moved his hand to the back of her neck, running his fingers through her hair.

Dawn closed her eyes accepting the warmth of his lips on hers, teasing with deliciously tempting little kisses, accepting the first intimate sensation of his touch when his hand moved under her dress gliding smoothly up her thigh, accepting his caress, light and tantalizing, urging her closer.

She moaned softly, burying her hands in the thickness of his hair. His mouth finally settled on hers in a long, sweet kiss. It was what she wanted—but no! Everything was getting all mixed up in her head.

She wanted to remain friends, always, and this is not what friends do! The thought had a determined ring, but not quite enough finality to pull her out of his arms.

Dawn gave herself to the kiss as logic and reason gallantly battled the excitement she could not seem to bridle. She had hoped to suppress her deeply passionate nature, but it wasn't happening.

I should have known better! She berated herself fiercely for allowing him to sweep her away with his sexy mouth and experienced touch.

When he released her, she put space between them trying to ignore the way her lips felt—still warm and moist from his kiss, the way her body ached for his caress and the tears that burned behind her eyes.

Mike traced his thumb slowly down the edge of her face, then gently across her lips. "You moved away from me awfully fast. Did I scare you?"

He slipped the strap of her dress over one shoulder. "Sexy," he whispered, his lips touching her shoulder.

"You didn't want to bring me home and leave me?" she said uncertainly.

"No, I want to go somewhere and have fun with you. Want to?" His eyes sparkled. "Or does that scare you, too?"

She nodded. It scared her to death.

"It's intriguing, though, isn't it?"

She gazed into compelling blue eyes. It sounded fascinating.

Dawn looked back out the window, felt his hand on her shoulder, and turned to him again, unable to say a word.

He stroked her face, the affectionate gesture causing an ache in her throat.

A love song began to play on the radio, a song from the sixties, the past—the not too distant past. Memories overwhelmed her, a surge of pain rippled through her, but she didn't cry a single tear. With effort, she brought her attention back to the present, and he considerately changed the radio station.

He pulled into the parking lot of the only rental place near. The little, insignificant 'no tell motel' outside of town.

"You don't mind coming to a motel, I hope. Living with a sister and brother-in-law has some disadvantages—Dawn?"

After a quiet moment he placed a warm hand on her shoulder.

"It's not wrong," he said quietly. He put his hand under her chin urging her to look into his eyes. "I'll show you how right it can be."

He went to register, leaving her alone with potentially troubling thoughts. Dawn didn't have to wonder why her thoughts were so discontent; she knew it was because too much had happened over too short a time—too much pain and she was afraid this would lead to more.

"Number nine," he said when he got back. He leaned over kissing her quickly. "Lucky number nine."

Mike held her hand as they walked toward the door. Once inside, he took her in his arms. Dawn felt the dress slip over her shoulders and glide to the floor in a fluffy heap at their feet. Then he lifted and placed her on the bed.

She opened her eyes, thankful for the dim lighting. He was beside her, their naked bodies temptingly close, the heady fragrance of his rich, musky scent, seemed more potent since he disrobed.

Dawn wanted to move closer, to breathe him deeply into her. She wanted to, but something held her back.

"You have no reason to feel shy," he said, drawing her away from the contemplative reflections. "Are you with me, Dawn?"

"I am—I mean; I am a little shy. We've been friends for so long."

"It seems like I've waited forever for this," he murmured. His arms circled her in a warm embrace. "You're my fantasy, Dawn."

"Fantasies are fun," she whispered.

"And thrilling," he added.

They kissed. They talked. He brushed away another tear.

"Your wish is my desire," he said, his mouth against her burning skin creating incredible sensations. "Your desire is my pleasure."

"You're a sweet talker, Jon Michael."

He rose above her to gaze deep into her eyes.

"I can take you higher than you've ever been."

"Then do it," she replied softly, receptively.

She couldn't believe the challenging tone, and Mike, well, he didn't need any more encouragement. She denied reservations pushing all doubts to the farthest reaches of her mind as he ran his fingers gently through her hair.

Dawn yielded to the searing need which had been building for months. An illusion of love, a sweet, wonderful dream of his kisses and caresses, murmured words of affection carrying her away to his fantasy world, fiery and delightful sensations rising higher.

His lips caressed her mouth, neck and shoulders. He took the time to explore every sensitive inch—attentive to her senses, arousing surges of pleasure from places she had not even thought of as being erotic—until she felt delirious with yearning.

The two became one in sweet, reckless abandon. Mike proved his promise, his lips, his touch, his body—ignited a flame more than ready to blaze. Dawn buried her face against his skin muffling her cry of pleasure, reveling the feeling as delicious spasms took over her body.

Still in his arms and breathless from the loving, she came back to earth with a bleak, painful realization.

"What's wrong?" He reached for the pack of cigarettes on the nightstand.

"Mike, I didn't want this to happen," she protested.

"Yes you did."

She sat up to look at him in the semi-darkness.

His lighter blazed for an instant before he snapped it shut without ever touching the flame to the tip. He tossed cigarette and lighter into the nightstand drawer.

"What we did was incredible," he said earnestly. "And I won't apologize. You're, sexy, innocent, wild and wonderful, and I might add, incredibly delicious." He grinned as a warm flush engulfed her.

"It's going to ruin everything," she blurted anxiously.

"No, it won't."

"We had something special, something a man and woman usually cannot share, a friendship without complications, Mike, and that means a lot to me, you know. Now I've probably spoiled it."

He sighed. "No, you haven't."

She shivered miserably. "I didn't intend this. I wanted us to be able to go places and do things together—and enjoy each other. How could I let this happen?"

He answered the question with his lips pressed against hers, answer enough. "I enjoyed you," he whispered.

He pulled slightly away inquisitive blue eyes searching for an answer. "Do you trust me?"

"You know, I do."

He captured her fingers tenderly in his grasp. "Sommer—" His expression stilled and grew serious, his eyes gentle and contemplative. "I promise you, this night won't make a difference in the part of our relationship that means so much to you. Do you believe me?"

She shrugged, wanting to accept the assurance, needing to be convinced.

"Was I wrong to lose control?" His lips touched her shoulder. "Maybe—but I'll never be sorry. This doesn't mean it isn't possible to be friends."

He ran his fingers softly through her hair.

"We have tonight," he urged kissing her once, then again more deeply. "There is no right or wrong now—only the moment."

Slowly his hands moved downward, his touch igniting a need that she could not deny. He had always been more than wonderful, more than delightful, but his passion—his passion could not be denied.

"Let go," he whispered. "Give yourself to me, just for tonight."

She let herself go. He had her will, and he knew more about enjoyment than she had ever anticipated. The pleasure of his love engulfed her. The erotic sensations overcame the doubt that had invaded her consciousness.

Once again she wondered, after the loving, why she had ended up in her friend's arms tonight. She sighed in pleasant exhaustion, snuggling against him, their legs entwined. Dawn fell asleep in his arms.

He woke her sometime later with sensual kisses and the exquisite pleasure of his hands on her body with a gently teasing touch, taking his time, creating within her once again an unquestionable yearning. Like a blazing flame, she burned high and hot, yielding eagerly to his need and to hers.

Her arms traveled slowly up and around his neck, she returned his kisses fervently, feeling a flood of affection.

As they made love for a third time she felt like he had taken her somewhere out of the ordinary, another place, another time, maybe even another world.

"Mike—" Panic touched her as she spiraled back to earth, back to reality.

"Don't say a word," he whispered. "No disillusions, no regrets—that's my promise. Remember what I said, I'll always be your friend."

She gathered her clothes to go freshen up, taking the anxiety right along with her. She had gone too long with a veiled emptiness, unaware, until Van came back to destroy the semblance of peace she had managed to blind herself into believing was hers.

Dawn struggled with her conscience, fears, and uncertainties. She didn't want to regret what she let happen, but it was difficult to discard uneasy feelings—the affection she experienced still frightened her, the feeling much more than sexual desire.

Of course it's more, she rationalized, an endearing friendship—and she wanted that friendship—she didn't want anything to jeopardize it.

Mike gave her a whimsical smile when she entered the room. She knew reflexively that everything would be all right, simply accepted it because she had his assurance.

As they stepped outside, she saw Van a few doors down just opening the door to #16. He glanced in their direction looking at her for several timeless seconds before disappearing inside, the door closing with a firm finality.

Mike slipped an arm around her waist. Dawn leaned against him as her legs went suddenly weak. Upon entering the car, he turned on the radio and she wrestled with her emotions to the tunes of "Love Me Tender", "Chantilly Lace", "Be Bop a Lula", and others on the drive back to town.

Mike's station—the fifties slot.

Once home, he turned off the ignition but set the key so the radio still played. He reached over, idly caressing a stand of hair, before placing it meticulously behind her ear.

"So, how do you feel?"

"About?"

"Getting caught," he whispered. "Never mind . . . I'd like to take you out again—dinner, and drinks—slow dancing." He looked at her expectantly.

"I can almost promise not to seduce you."

Recalling the smoldering passion that had thrilled her, the ecstasy of being held against his strong body, Dawn felt numb with indecision.

He paused with a halfhearted sigh. "Okay, I promise."

"Give me a call me tomorrow," she suggested. "I'm beyond thinking."

He gave her hand an affectionate squeeze before getting out. When he opened the door for her, and she climbed out, he held her hands, bending toward her with a playful smile.

"Can't call you tomorrow," he said blithely, touching his forehead to hers, eye-to-eye, face-to-face. "It's already morning."

He stood straight again.

"I'll call you this afternoon—late this afternoon," he suggested.

Dawn agreed. She knew she would go out with him tonight, they had things to discuss.

When Mike quietly let himself into the house, he found Christi sitting in the living room, awaiting his arrival.

"I'm a big boy now," he commented. "No need for concern—"

She trailed after him into the kitchen. "For your information, my concern is for someone else, now. How was your date?"

"I hope that's a different book," he said, noticing the paperback.

"Don't try to change the subject."

"Fantastic. Just super. My date was superb."

"You look like the cat that ate the canary, entirely too satisfied. Mike, did you? You didn't—did you?"

"No, I didn't eat the canary."

"Mike?" She leveled her eyes on him with that no nonsense look.

"Okay, I did eat the canary, so to speak."

"You took advantage of my best friend."

"No—well, yeah, I guess I did, but she wanted me to."

"How can you say that?"

"Because." He took a Pepsi out of the refrigerator, and then settled onto a cushioned stool at the counter gazing expectantly at his inquisitive sister.

"Don't you think she's vulnerable right now?"

"I know she is. Chris, she's my friend, too . . . And I think that's her main concern . . . She ever mention someone named Paul?" he asked distractedly. "It's not Jenson."

"Do you think she tells me every little thing?" Christi asked innocently.

"You girls are best friends. Doesn't she confide in you?"

"Eventually, sometimes it takes a while."

"Yeah, but if she did, and she told you not to say anything about whoever he is, you wouldn't, cause that's just who you are."

"Well, of course I wouldn't."

"I think it must have been a short term relationship—whoever he is—he's been out of her life for a long time now, and I know who he is now," he said, slapping his palm down on the counter. "She did tell you," he grinned.

"I thought I was past that."

"Seriously? You'll never get past that—and seriously, don't worry about Dawn."

"Seriously?"

"I said it, right? Now, I'm taking her out again tonight, so I need some rest." He dropped a kiss on her blonde hair. "Goodnight."

Christi grinned to herself as Mike left the kitchen. Happiness filled her—could it really happen, her brother and her best friend? She remembered when Dawn presented her with diamond earrings on her sixteenth birthday. She had been at a loss to what she might get her friend. Dawn had replied, "How about a kiss from that handsome brother of yours?"

Dawn had liked him, even then, but it hadn't been possible—that was high school. Now there were all sorts of possibilities.

Chapter Forty-Seven

Sitting at a small table in the lounge at the Cactus Flower, Dawn idly picked the cherry from her whisky sour. She could not put what happened last night out of her mind and doubted if Mike could either.

It couldn't be erased like it never happened, regardless of what he said. They had known each other intimately. It made a difference.

Mike took her hand gently drawing it to his mouth, nimbly removing the cherry from her fingers with his teeth.

"Mmm, yummy! You're a thousand miles away," he commented.

She looked at him—wondering—maybe for him it was possible.

"Sorry, Mike. I was just thinking."

"You're drinking a whiskey sour, I have to wonder, but okay, what are you thinking about?" He gave her his undivided attention.

"You say some off the wall stuff, Mike," she said reflectively.

"Not so, you usually drink a frozen daiquiri, the difference between a whiskey sour and frozen daiquiri is immense. The difference scares me."

"I see," she nodded.

What she saw was the definite glint in his eyes. Noticing the amusement, she laughed in spite of everything. Perhaps all was not lost.

"I'm serious," he insisted. "You can tell me what you're thinking."

"You don't know?"

"No, what I said is true. I can't exactly read your mind."

"I am greatly relieved, but I'm leery—that look was devilish."

He smiled agreeably. "Yeah, well, most of my looks are." Mike covered her hand with his. "I'll never lie to you, Sommer, but I do have an idea of what you're going through. You need to live for today. I know, we'll never forget," he added hastily. "But there's enough going on right here and now."

He made it sound so easy.

"No, we'll never forget," she agreed musingly, experiencing a strange loneliness. "Everything has been wrong for so long."

"But it's getting better," he said encouragingly.

"Is it? I don't know, Mike."

"You've been afraid for a long time." Mike tipped his head slightly, his expression tender. "It's no fun, is it?"

"No." She shifted uncomfortably. "No, it isn't."

"You're feeling some heavy-duty pressure, Dawn, and I don't want that. There's no reason for it, you know? We enjoy each other's company, always have, right?"

"Always." Ever since they met, she enjoyed being around him.

"Let's take it from there." His hand still warmly blanketed hers. "We're young, the night is ours, time enough later for profound contemplation."

She lowered her eyes, stirring the drink with a swizzle stick, wondering how to cope with these different feelings, so much to consider. Everything seemed to be happening so quickly. One night they were friends, the next they were lovers and now they were—what?

Unsure of the whole emotional entanglement, mostly unsure of herself, Dawn thought maybe she needed a respite, following up immediately with the perspective that maybe she had become paralyzed by fear as she had long ago advised her mother not to be.

"Dawn?"

She glanced up, smiling a bit self-consciously. Mike had come over to her side of the table without her even noticing. She needed rid of this preoccupation of dreary thoughts, at least for tonight.

"They're playing our song," he said with a cockily presumptuous grin.

"Anybody ever tell you you're ornery?"

"Yeah, someone told me that once. Only I think she phrased it as being a hellion."

He led her onto the dance floor, holding her close enough that she felt secure and protected in his arms as their bodies swayed easily to the music.

"I appreciate what you've done for me," she said.

"The pleasure is entirely mine."

"Seriously, I don't know what I would have done without you."

The simple truth brought on more unwelcome contemplations. *What would I do without you now?* Dawn couldn't avoid the awareness of the other person in his life. *How long can you be here for me?*

There was no answer to the mindless questions, no answer at all, except the arms that held her, and the wonder of her erratic imagination, making Mike a part of her future.

Dawn rested her head on his chest breathing in the tantalizing scent of him, carried away by the masculine fragrance, giving in to the simple joy of not worrying about anything, just taking a breath, needing to feel the relaxing sensation of freedom that had unexpectedly developed.

The song ended, another began. They remained on the dance floor.

Dawn tried to weigh the structure of events, wanting to be friends with Mike, and still recalling the passionate night of love.

"Remember that I won't ask more of you than you're able to give."

She gazed up at him in wonder noticing the natural amusement in his vivid blue eyes, eyes that glowed with love of life, mischief and just plain happiness.

Mike's understanding amazed her, but what if she asked more of him than he was able to give? As she tried to smother the worrisome question, Dawn realized that Van was cutting in on their dance.

Stepping aside, Mike pleasantly conceded. She watched him walk toward their table before Van drew her attention.

She felt tense at first, puzzled and more than a little nervous. Then her body relaxed to the familiarity of his embrace, the impassioned memory of what they had shared, as he led her in the dance.

When the song ended, he kept her close, like he didn't want to let her go.

When he did release her, his hand rested on her shoulder, as if he wanted to take her in his arms again. Another melody, an achingly familiar love song began, but she took a step back putting distance between them.

"Van, we can't," she said softly.

His hand dropped away from her shoulder.

"I have a table in back. Can we talk?"

Remembering their last encounter, she felt in every way defenseless against any possible verbal attack he might offer. The instinctive reaction evaporated immediately, a simple instance of being overly cautious with her tender emotions.

She wondered about his intentions, though, as he held a chair for her, then sat down on the other side of the small table for two. He leaned forward, sincerity reflected in his warm brown eyes and solemn expression.

"First of all, I have to know if you can ever forgive me for the things I said that day. I don't even know if I deserve your forgiveness, Dawn. I was way over the top."

His eyes regarded her with gentle contemplation, his voice deep with emotion. A knot rose in her throat. She took a sip of water.

"I can forgive you," she finally managed.

"And what I said about you and Mike?"

"Yes."

"I'm leaving tonight, Dawn," he said quietly.

She felt a moment's squeezing hurt, then a deep feeling of peace.

She looked at him intently, the casual handsomeness of his face, the tough, lean physique radiating erotic masculinity, he'd always had that alluring sensuality.

Her heart thumped uneasily as she struggled with mixed sentiments.

"Maybe I'm wrong for feeling the way I do, but I had to see you again."

Dawn heard what he said, but it took a few seconds for the words to sink in. Since he had told her he was leaving and taken her hand in his, she had been absorbed in abstract reflections.

"I'll be in touch." The soft brushing of his fingers against her cheek brought on a rush of memories. "Is that all right?"

She nodded, unable to trust her voice.

He slipped his hand to the back of her neck, leaning forward. When he kissed her, a kiss that meant goodbye again, she waited, expecting the rush of misery, that overall aching emptiness of his leaving, for the tears to gather that would fall after he'd gone, but it didn't happen.

Those feelings belonged to another now, as Van had been hers for the short duration of his time here.

Dawn watched him walk away wondering if he felt any regret for what might have been. It was enough to part as friends. He had said he would be in touch, had expressed regret for having hurt her so deeply. It was enough.

She walked back to where Mike sat waiting, immediately noticing his relaxed demeanor. He always seemed to have it all together. Now he raised his eyes to meet hers as she stopped at the table.

"Can we go for a ride?" he suggested.

Dawn readily agreed, some fresh air would go nicely right about now.

Mike drove a distance out of town before he pulled over, parking in front of a heavily wooded area.

The distance between them in the small car seemed insurmountable.

She became too conscious of the hushed stillness.

Dawn wished he would say something, but he just stared out the window. He seemed to be far away in thought. Where are you, Mike? Dawn turned resolutely away from gazing at his arresting profile to stare pensively into the darkness.

The silence stretched on until she couldn't deal with the distance between them. Filled with indecision, she longed for the familiarity they had shared.

"You lied to me," she said briskly.

"Yes, I did." He nodded a couple of times looking contritely thoughtful.

Dawn blinked in surprise. "Can you tell me why?"

He took a pack of cigarettes out of his shirt pocket, shook one out, and then opened the car door.

"Let's walk," he suggested.

He discarded the unlighted cigarette. They strolled side by side along a well-worn path through the woods. She wanted to reach for his hand, to feel his touch, but something kept her from reaching out to him.

Dawn remembered the easy friendship they had shared. Dawn felt lost without it. She didn't know what to say. Her mind had told her to resist, but her body refused. Her mind told her to listen to reason, but her feelings for him had nothing to do with reason.

A wave of apprehension swept through her as she thought of that other someone in his life, someone important to him.

Torn by conflicting emotions, her thoughts kept reverting to last night, burning with the memory. It seemed improbable, no it seemed *impossible.* She could not fit a picture of Mike, so understanding, so caring, in the frame of the man who had made love to her with someone else in his life.

"Remember the night, I asked if there was someone special in your life?"

"I remember."

Dawn looked at his handsome profile as they continued walking all the while wondering about the girl who shared his affections. A burning ache grew in her throat. "Do you love her?"

"More than she will ever know."

"Then how could you make love to me the way you did?" she demanded.

Once again she ached to reach out and touch him. Her feelings for him were so tangled she didn't know which way to turn. She accepted the blame, after all, she had instigated the relationship, but he was at fault, too, and now she felt defeated and disenchanted.

"You're the one who said no emotional involvement," he reminded her.

It was a saddening and deflating statement, why had she said that?

"You didn't want to ruin a perfectly good friendship, remember?"

"I don't want to." Dawn sighed in deep frustration. What did she want? And if she knew what she wanted, could she even have it?

Is it time to let him go, she wondered, time to move on? Her whole being recoiled at both thoughts, it seemed so unfair.

"We felt a physical attraction," he said simply.

"To put it mildly."

"I'm not sorry for what we did—I could never be sorry. It was what we needed at the time, Dawn. When I said it wouldn't happen again, I meant it."

"How could you have meant that? And you said it wouldn't change anything, and everything's changed, and how could you have meant that!"

Mike stopped walking. "What are you saying?"

"I'm saying—I'm saying that it wasn't strictly physical with me. I meant it to be. I didn't want to—"

"Fall in love?"

"But something happened, and I don't understand it. I'm over Van, Mike," she said without hesitation. "I'm not sure what I'm feeling, but it's something like I've never felt before."

"I know," he said quietly. "And I know what you're feeling."

"You know a lot, don't you," she murmured.

"Yeah, but that's easy." He turned her to face him. "You've been special to me for a long time, Dawn."

"I'm the special someone?"

"Always have been, and always will be."

"It happened so fast."

"Your words, not mine."

"I mean, less than a week ago, I didn't even realize." She looked at him speculatively. "Why didn't you tell me?"

"You weren't ready." He traced the curve of her face gently with his thumb. "I had to wait for you to let go of the past. I had to be sure."

"But once you did know—once you were sure—"

"Sweetie, I couldn't *tell* you that you were over Van."

Dawn wondered suddenly if he had planned everything, but he couldn't have. He couldn't have known she would ask him to take her out, but once she did . . . She had trusted him and he had blatantly stolen her heart right out of Van's pocket.

He had wined her, and dined her—"Was it your plan to seduce me?"

"No, Dawn, never. I admit that I was the last person in the world you could trust—only because I love you." Mike ran his fingers through her hair.

"I did not have calculated sex with you, Dawn, it was spontaneous pleasure."

"Truly?"

He grinned sexily. "Absolutely, but we're not going to have spontaneous sex again until we're married."

She looked at him surprised, then suspicious, and then questioning.

"Oh really?"

He sighed. "You might talk me into it, if you ask nice."

"You're very witty, Mike," she said smiling with pleasure.

"I have something to show you," he said, draping an arm around her shoulder as they resumed walking.

When they stepped into the clearing of a small meadow, she gazed up at the night sky. "Did you plan the full moon and all those stars, Mike? Is this your magic?"

"I'm glad you recognize the magic," he said appreciatively. "I thought it was just me. I come out here sometimes to think, just to get away."

Captivated by the fairy-tale excellence, the dreamlike quality of the forest that surrounded them, Dawn stood silent, completely taken by the serene pleasure, a rustling in the underbrush, an owl in the distance, the woodsy fragrance on the breeze.

It was too perfect, she knew, but it should be perfect in every way imaginable—because it would be a night to remember forever, a moment in time that must never be taken for granted.

"How did you do it?" she whispered, not wanting to disturb the enchantment. "I didn't think the hurt would ever go away."

"Oh, little kiss here." He touched the edge of her mouth. "Little kiss there." He moved his hands up her arms pulling her a bit closer.

She looked into his eyes recalling the first kiss, being swept off her feet by a dauntless sixteen-year-old boy in a dingy Southside apartment and the many successive innocent and not so innocent kisses over time, the engaging flirtations, the secretive winks, so completely unpredictable—fun-loving and jubilant.

Dawn realized in that timeless instant that she did love Mike. He left nothing to be desired. A lover and a friend, she knew life with him would be filled with affection and laughter.

"If you love me," he whispered his mouth so close they were almost touching. "Why won't you say it?"

"I'm afraid to—"

"Admit it?" His lips finally brushed against hers, she sighed longingly.

He framed her face in his hands; his lips came coaxingly down, taking her mouth in a sweet and sensual kiss. Dawn returned his kiss, giving herself freely to the fiery delight of awakening love.

Raising his mouth from hers, he gazed into her eyes. "You don't have to be afraid anymore," he promised. "I won't hurt you Dawn, and I won't let you hurt me."

"Then this must be where happily ever after begins."

He put his arms around her. Dawn relaxed her head on his chest, the warmth of his arms exactly what she needed.

"Happily ever after is a wonderful concept."

His arms tightened, drawing her into a closer embrace as a cloud drifted slowly across the moon.

The End

CPSIA information can be obtained at www.ICGtesting.com
Printed in the USA
BVOW030440111212

307773BV00003B/6/P

9 781479 737413